# LEGEND OF SILENE

## By WILLIAM L. CASSELMAN

*Edited by: Susan Smith*

LEGEND OF SILENE
By William Casselman
©2017 By William Casselman
Edited by Susan Smith

Cover design by Cheryl Eaton –
Conclusions Unlimited Web and Graphic Design
www.conclusionsunlimited.com
Production design by Robert Jacobson

Published by:
Alaska Dreams Publishing
www.alaskadp.com

1ST Print Edition April 2018
PRINT ISBN numbers:
ISBN-13: 978-0-9903454-5-9
ISBN 10: 0-9903454-5-9

E-Book versions available.
Please visit http://www.alaskadp.com for links.

**TABLE OF CONTENTS**

# DEDICATION

To my wife Mona and to my mother, Vivian Lee Welch. She left us at 91-years old and now she dances with the angels. My mother loved to tell my brother and I stories of heroic figures, of bold and stalwart knights and the princesses they rescued; to the great authors who have inspired me over the years to keep on writing, even after the 100th rejection slip arrived in the mail and to my publisher, Robert Jacobson of Alaska Dream Publishing, for giving me the opportunity to put my ideas into print. I would also like to thank Susan Smith, my editor, for her dedicated work in my writing projects.

# ACKNOWLEDGMENTS

I want to acknowledge my Lord Jesus Christ and the 37-years I have followed Him, and all those times this relationship has carried me over the rougher spots in life. I know for a fact He has saved my life 5-times, and this involved life-and-death in my 20-years of work as a police officer. I also believe it is my Lord who gives me my ideas on what I write and quite possibly even how to write the stories.

This is why I write Christian-fiction. I've wondered how our lives might have been different if we'd walked down a different hallway, path or attended a different school. I may not have decided to join the armed forces or entered police work, but this is the way I was directed.

The many choices we have made every single day that in some cases could've changed our directions. I've witnessed so many miracles in the lives of my marriage and in the lives of my children, now to include grandchildren and great-grandchildren. Who knew, I'd ever get this old? Only the Lord.

I've also thanked him abundantly for forgiving me when I fall on my face and sinned. He is always there to pick me up, wipe the dust off His child and point me in the right direction. He is also there to listen to my complaints, but more importantly, my prayers. For without the Lord, this story and the other novels I've had published would not exist. For though I have always been a good storyteller, it was a real struggle to become a writer. The use of the American language has always been a difficult chore for me to handle, especially in the written form.

I also wish to acknowledge my children; born by blood, marriage, fostering and those accepted into our inner family, for all the support they have given me over the years. Even if it was simply keeping their children quiet near Grandpa's writing desk. They've had to endure long hours of listening to my stories, keeping their patience over these years. Here in Alaska, Appa is the Native language for grandfather, and this is what they all call me. Akka is the word for Grandmother. Now hundreds of people call my wife Mona and I by these Native names and we feel blessed by it. The Native people of Alaska are extraordinary people.

I wish to acknowledge the Norman Olson family in Dillingham. When Norman heard Mona, who was still in the Air

Force and was coming to visit me in Dillingham, he moved his whole family out of their home and let us use their home. This provided us with privacy I wouldn't have enjoyed since I lived with three other police officers. Later, Norman saved my life, when he warned me of an ambush having been set up for me and the officer riding with me. We would have been killed. We soon afterward being warned spotted the 8-people with high powered rifles stepping out of the bushes they were hidden in. We came that close.

I would like to add, Mike Kimbrel, Frank P. DeMario and Charles "Chuck" Dudley. These three men were my best buddies during my tours in Vietnam and Thailand. Following Thailand, Chuck and I were stationed together at Edwards Air Force Base, California. I'm back in recent contact with Mike and this means a lot to me, war buddies are as close as brothers.

# INTRODUCTION:

SILENE, LIBYA, NORTH AFRICA
1197 A.D

**H**er name was Asalah, which in Muslim meant Purity. She was a daughter to Omrah, a seasoned soldier in the Army of Silene. Said to be a bright and considerate young lady, she was three months past her 15th birthday and coming of age for marriage. Her dark brown eyes with long black lashes were known to turn many a young man's head and with long shiny black hair like her mother's, her father was already struggling with concern over too many prospective suitors. But now he needn't worry, her future had been taken from his hands. This very morning Asalah was going to die.

Thick ropes and metal manacles secured the young maiden to the massive sacrificial stone, gruesomely stained with the blood of previous victims. Too weak to stand, fearfully she slumped in the wet sand and knelt at its base. Her throat was raw from hours of screaming and her brown eyes reddened from a long night of weeping.

Once more she drew from deep within herself, finding an inner strength she hadn't known she was capable of and struggled to her feet. Again, she fought against her bindings, chewing the leather knots and causing her to bleed from new injuries.

In the distance, the blue-green waters of the lake began to stir, boiling up to produce an ominous white froth. Ripples widened out and built until three-foot waves crested and crashed down upon Asalah's bare feet.

Slowly, almost cautiously, either some level of intelligence or only animal instinct, the top of the creature's monstrous head broke the surface. The terrified maiden became deathly still. Her eyes grew wide with fright, while she stared into the cold glassy ink-spot eyes of the beast. These eyes were almost lifeless in nature and each one the size of a knight's shield. Then, as its full head became visible and the greenish lake water cascaded from its huge gaping mouth and her petite body trembled at the sight of the dragon's glistening yellowish teeth; some the size and sharpness of a soldier's scimitar blade and the front fangs nearing the size of a fighting man's spear.

Sending forth even larger waves, which crashed upon shore, striking Asalah in the chest, caused her to fear drowning. The dragon rose to its full height, a towering 50-feet. Swerving it head from right to left, observing the beach for possible predators and upon seeing none, it returned to look down upon its sacrifice with hungry anticipation.

Its amphibious head began to rock back and forth, seemingly working in tandem with its four large flippers, propelling itself into the shallow waters, drawing closer to its helpless prey. Covered entirely in a thick bluish-green hide, which shone in daylight hours and glistened in the moonlight, its massive body was longer than a Libyan warship and nearly as wide. The beast was also scarred from its many battles with the soldiers of Silene. Its age was unknown, but since the time of recorded history many brave Muslim knights had given their lives attempting to slay this dragon or its parents. Through word of mouth and stories remembered, the first two great beasts had suddenly appeared in the great lake and years afterward, a young dragon was seen swimming through the waters. No one could remember how long the parents had lived, or how they had perished, but first one and then the other vanished and the people believed their bones now rested upon the floors of the great lake. Decades and then centuries had passed since the beasts appeared, ships were sunk, crews lost and not a single body found and still this last dragon remained to terrorize the people of Silene.

As the township's only recourse, a lottery began by royal decree. By lot, a maiden or virgin slave, either captured in raids or purchased in the market, was chosen and sacrificed to this dragon in the vain hope the kingdom would survive. All the townspeople hoped and prayed to Allah for a miracle, that the dragon be slain before their daughter might be chosen. But the dragon continued to bring desolation upon the land surrounding the lake, causing the townspeople of long ago to construct a great barrier wall to protect Silene.

However, a prophecy came forth in only a whisper at first, born from a time when Silene was a Christian kingdom and the sword of Islam had not yet blazed through North Africa. Of how a stranger would come out of the desert, mounted upon a gallant steed and armed with a lance named Ascalon, who would do battle against the beast and free Silene from its curse. Centuries passed but only a few still remembered the words of the prophecy and the poor Kingdom of Silene remained cursed in the desert lands of Libya.

King Ramie, Grand Ruler of Silene, his beautiful queens long dead, had only three adult unmarried daughters remaining to rule beside him. Standing upon the battlement, he mourned grievously, as another maiden was devoured by the dragon. He knew, in another two-weeks, another girl would be chosen. There was little or nothing he could do to stop the event. His townspeople wanted to leave, to escape, but the Caliph of Libya, feared they would bring the curse with them. He kept armed patrols on the road to Tripoli and in the surrounding desert to prevent this. Crossing elsewhere, meant crossing the border to Egypt; which could lead to either death or enslavement at the hands of the Egyptians, or worse, the Berbers. All that was left was the great desert to the south and a painful death for lack of water. So, the townspeople remained in their homes and prayed for the birth of sons and if they did have daughters, that they might be found unsuitable for the lottery.

Standing beside the king was Brother Samuel, a defrocked Irish priest and a man with a secret past. A close advisor to King Ramie, he looked away from the gruesome sight and whispered a prayer for Asalah's soul. Sun up and sun down he had prayed to his Christian God, pleading for a miracle to save this Muslim kingdom and bring forth salvation to these people he had come to call family. He didn't know it, but his prayers were about to be answered, for the Lord was indeed working in His strange and mysterious ways to answer Brother Samuel's prayer and thus, "The Legend of Silene" was born.

# 1 – THE OLD STORYTELLER

TRIPOLI, LIBYA, NORTH AFRICA
PRESENT DAY

The North African mid-summer sun, Libya's seemingly colorless flat desert countryside and a sweltering breeze blowing in off the southern Mediterranean Sea did little to help Tripoli's tourist trade. There were also the ever-present black flies to consider, which came in all sizes and appeared to prefer the scantily clad sun worshipping foreigners over the well-covered locals. The crowds were small today, as most tourists decided to stay on board their luxurious cruise ship and enjoy the air conditioning or a relaxing pool side retreat with the offered iced drinks, constant servers at their beck and call and those eight buffet meals served daily.

Yet even in this intense summer heat there were local children, who cared less about the heat than their parents. They made a daily trek to the fountain for an afternoon of splashing in the cooling waters and frolicking with their friends. Stone masons who had lived three thousand years ago, left their startling artwork in the form of this fountain; which had become a weathered white stone centerpiece for an already ancient courtyard. Standing 15-feet high and supported by the ancient warriors of Greek mythology; the fountain was thought to have been ordered by Alexander the Great. Drawing from a deep well, its shimmering waters flowed into a circular pool. Here shimmered women gossiped and washed the day's laundry, while at their feet bathing children giggled and splashed one another, while several youths attempted escaping the vengeful grasp of a soused older sibling. Surrounding the fountain, spanning out like a wagon wheel, was a small bazaar of colorful booths. These portable stores were capable of being broken down and packed up in less than an hour, bustled with hurried tourists; men and women from far off lands who looked for bargains, while they haggled over prices with proprietors. They all fought helplessly to dodge the noonday flies, while two-uniformed police officers; one armed with an automatic weapon slung over his shoulder, kept a watchful eye out for terrorists or the occasional thief. Here, a purse or satchel could vanish quickly and worse, a Muslim suicidal bomber could strike against the infidel.

The shops, partially shaded by both ancient and modern buildings, were a mixture of Arabian, Greek and European architecture, most in dire need of repair. For here in Libya, the hot desert sun and blistering sandstorms took a toll on these structures.

Casually, a lone, elderly man walked by one such dilapidated structure, a French bank built in the early 1900's. He made his way slowly through a mixed throng of foreigners and city dwellers. Upon recognizing the old man, joyful children began surrounding him. He lingered a bit, as his custom was to share a greeting or two with the young ones and then, he moved along at a slow carefree pace as the children followed.

The aged Sunni, Master Storyteller Hareeme Jafaee, seemed unaffected by the afternoon heat or the many flying insects buzzing about, as he approached the fountain where two women quickly made a place for him. Out of respect, the younger woman provided a soft cushion for his comfort and a cool drink of water from a wooden ladle. At 87-years old, Hareeme Jafaee stood well over six-feet in height, with long slender legs and arms. Under his deeply tanned skin from a lifetime in the desert he had the white skin of a Caucasoid Berber. His shoulder-length hair was gray-white in color, tied back in a single ponytail by a long leather string of dark brownish color. On his long narrowing jaw, he maintained a tidy beard. Though his bright blue eyes radiated with youth, the deep wrinkles surrounding them marked his age well. He also bore a single two-inch long knife scar on his right temple and another scalp scar on the opposite side from a well-aimed clay kitchen pot from one of his late wife's angry outbursts. She was well-known for her fiery temper and he missed her greatly.

Unlike his late Egyptian wife, Hareeme was the descendant of Berber pirates who once sailed the deep blue waters of the Mediterranean, and the infamous desert raiders of the Sahara. From his studies as a young man he had learned how his Saracen ancestors had at one time given their lives over to the Christian faith, only later to accept Islam in the 11th century when the great Muslim armies swept across the desert sands of North Africa.

For many years, as a young dockworker, he plied his sweat and muscles to the coastal trade waters of Tripoli and listened in the coffee shops as the various storytellers', entertained listeners with tales of great courage, mystery and suspense. Their stories were a rich mixture of Muslim and Christian prophets, Greek and Roman heroes of ancient times and the pirates and raiders who plied their trade throughout the Middle East. He found that he had an aptitude for the art of storytelling and gradually, the young dockworker became a Master at his craft and left the manual labors behind him.

Settling himself by the fountain, he waited, while people gathered about him and prepared to hear today's tale. First, he removed his turban and placed it upside down on a parchment of rug laid out before him. A worker was worthy of his pay and he lived on what few coins he made by telling his stories. Parents shushed their noisy children, while curious tourists stood in whatever protective shade was offered, unaware of what was transpiring before them, but noticing all the attention being given to this old man.

He waited patiently for his audience to settle, as he gazed upon the soft white clouds racing above like a herd of wild stallions in flight, driven on by the hot winds in the higher elevations over the Mediterranean Sea. But after a suitable silence, he turned to the young ones about his feet and asked a question.

"What tale do you desire of me today, my children? Be it of pirates who pillaged these coasts in ancient times or the great Alexander's march on our lands of long ago?

"Maybe you would like to hear a story of the elusive Ali Baba and his vast riches, or the beautiful princess who was rescued from slavers by her handsome prince?"

"We'd like a new story!" A young boy shouted out from the fountain, the gentle waters lapping at his knees, who then quickly ducked as his mother reached over to swat him for his rudeness.

"Storyteller," a pretty, young girl said politely, "We have Americans here today...Could you tell us a story of them?"

He thought for a moment in silence and then replied, "Yes, today I will tell you a new story, one of great courage, of how three gallant American warriors came to our country. Men who did battle in a far-off land, who mysteriously soon found themselves in our desert. These were men of different families and of different color, who journeyed far and through a strange and great magic, pierced even the barrier of time and distance to save a beautiful princess from a most hideous monster." Jafaee looked down into the wide eyes of a small boy, his face filled with a look of anticipation and wonder.

Outside the immediate group of listeners, he could hear the voice of an interpreter relating his statements to a tourist group and then he continued, "Of these three warriors, all destined to become great knights, one would stand out alone through his bravery and unyielding love for his beautiful princess, and would always be remembered as our history recorded his great feats in battle to save her."

Reaching down with his right hand, Jafaee caressed the smiling face of a girl toddler, taking a brief-moment to scan the faces of those nearest him.

"It was long-long ago, in a time when great heroes were needed. When strong hearted men, rode gallant warhorses with only a lance and shield in hand, looked-into the fiery eyes of a dragon and charging bravely into the fray."

"Dragon?" A young boy asked in an almost piercing shriek of a voice.

"Yes, my young one, a dragon," He said and smiled back at the boy. "A creature so foul as to devour whole villages, sink ships of war and no knight or army of knights had been able to defeat it." Jafaee glanced around the crowd of listeners and waited for the interpreter to catch up.

"Until, a mighty miracle occurred. And having said so, now begins my tale of the Legend of Silene." He hesitated, watching the young and old eyes grow wide with anticipation.

"Listen well, my children and let me take you first to a faraway land, one which had seen more than 400-years of barbaric war and now, the Americans had come..."

## OUTSIDE EASTERN BORDER OF THE A SHAU VALLEY
## SOUTH VIETAM
## 0550 APRIL 25, 1968

Upon the grassy, hard-packed dirt landing pads of Fire Base Alpha-One, thirty-four UH-1 Huey Helicopters and six Huey gunships, were being prepped for today's early morning mission. Droopy-eyed pilots, still under the effects of an 0400-hour wake-up call, stomaching lukewarm powdered eggs and burned bacon, now held paper cups filled with steaming hot coffee, while they attended briefings in two separate open-sided tents. Two were needed due to the number of helicopters involved in today's operation and here, they received mission landing coordinates, today's radio frequencies, weather updates and additional flight info for the Op.

Outside the tents, their various crew chiefs, having been up much of the night preparing their birds for today's mission, made sure each bird was topped off with fuel. Meanwhile, blurry-eyed door gunners lugged about 1,000-round canisters of ammo for their M-60 machine guns and made sure their weapons were ready for action. The more experienced door gunners, having learned their lessons at other's expense, were also busy laying extra flak-vests down upon their jump seats for added protection from a hard to explain, if not lethal, Purple Heart.

Over 400-U.S. Army troops belonging to Alpha, Bravo and Delta Companies, 187th Infantry Regiment of the 101st Airborne Division, The Screaming Eagles, were scheduled to fly out this morning and be delivered deep within the infamous A Shau Valley. While the helicopters were readied, these troopers were sitting on the ground or standing about under a series of stretched green canvas canopies, dimly lit by dozens of standing lights. They were finishing off a morning breakfast of powdered eggs—scrambled, canned ham slices-barely cooked and thick peanut butter on cold, limp toast. Still, it was a bit more protein than what the pilots were getting, but for these ground troops, this would be their last hot meal for several days to come. During that time, they'd live on C-rations, salt tablets and malaria pills, and only the tepid water they carried in their canteens.

A thick layer of smoke rose above the men, as smokers finished off their last cigarette before flight time. They wouldn't be smoking again until the new base camp was secured, and this always caused the two and three pack-a-day guys some pre-mission jitters, knowing how quickly withdrawal would set in and the tremors would start.

Facing intolerable heat, a question of unknown enemy strength facing them, and an unforgiving jungle filled with snakes, it was their assignment to penetrate deep into the A Shau Valley to locate and destroy the headquarters of the 29th North Vietnamese Army Regiment. There was also the dark tales of the A Shau to take account of; which were most often spread about by senior NCOs who wanted to frighten the new troops. How whole armies from long ago had completely disappeared in the A Shau Valley and how their lost spirits continued to haunt the jungle, fighting to find their way back to the real world.

This so-called legend had more than a few green troops a bit rattled, much to the delight of some seasoned vets, who looked for anything to break-up their own pre-operation heebie-jeebies. While off in the distance they could all hear the heavy artillery from two-nearby firebases already pounding the jungle floor with 105mm and 155mm fire support before the helicopters would even launch. The soldier's briefings had also advised them of how U.S. Air Force F-4 Phantoms from Udorn Royal Thai Air Force Base in Thailand and Marine F-4 Phantoms from Bien Hua Air Base, north of Saigon, would provide the needed air cover for the operation. It all sounded so safe.

Corporal G.W. Sanders was a young man from Southern California and newly appointed to the position of assistant squad leader for 3rd squad, 2nd Platoon, D Company. He stood sweating under a green canvas canopy, having finished his savorless meal, he was plagued by buzzing insects drawn to the overhead hanging lights and the smell of morning chow and human sweat. He wore faded green jungle fatigues, recently washed by his momma-son and they were already showing white salt stains to his armpits. He also wore well-broken in and scuffed up combat boots, having saved a second shined up pair for main camp inspections. Inside his duty boots, he wore a single pair of thin black socks, but he kept another eight-pair in his well-used rucksack. He'd learned from the veterans how valuable clean socks were and scrounged up the additional pairs after his second week in-country.

His green canvas rucksack, which rested at his feet, was a retread from a friend, who had gone home after finishing off his 12-months. A well-used E-tool was strapped to the side of it, along with a newly issued machete. His M-16 rifle, with a loaded but un-chambered 30-round magazine, was slung over his left shoulder. Strapped around his narrow hips was a green web belt, which held his two canteens, one bayonet with an extremely sharp double-sided blade, six full ammo pouches and a single first aid pouch with one medium-size compress combat bandage and six-band-aids. He learned early on to carry the band-aids for foot blisters and nasty bug bites. He also carried a tube of dry foot powder in his rucksack, having already suffered one bad case of trench foot in an earlier operation.

His green canvas combat suspenders, which helped handle the weight of his heavy canteen belt, were tightly draped over his shoulders. These suspenders also held the weight of three fragmentation grenades and a KA-BAR Knife hanging upside down for easy grab. On his head, he wore a steel helmet, which was slightly cantered to one side and draped over with a green-leaf camouflage cover he'd borrowed from a Marine grunt.

On this cover, he used a black ballpoint pen to maintain a counting of his remaining days in sunny Vietnam, the names of the men in his squad and their blood types. He also kept this same list of names in a small note pad, kept in his left front shirt pocket with a pair of well-used and chewed upon #2 pencils.

Nervous and fighting down a case of the pre-flight jitters, GW looked through the crowd of soldiers and was amazed by how many young men had picked up the habit of smoking cigarettes since coming to Vietnam. A habit he had stayed away from. He soon spotted his newly appointed platoon leader; a greener then grass shave-tail 2nd lieutenant with only two weeks in country. GW noticed his lieutenant was speaking with a narrow-faced South Vietnamese Army captain, who wore the black and white QC (Quan Canh-Military Police) helmet and matching armband.

GW was startled when his platoon leader suddenly pointed straight at him, with the South Vietnamese captain nodding his head in acknowledgement and then the captain also raised a hand and pointed in GW's direction for confirmation. GW's first response was to look around him, to see whom the lieutenant was pointing at, but there was no one standing immediately close by and he realized he was the center of their attention. Wondering what it was all about, GW then took notice of a much smaller and poorly attired older Vietnamese man standing beside the QC captain. At first thought, GW thought the man had to be close to 100-years old.

Apprehensive and standing alert, GW watched as both the QC officer and the old man headed his way and wondered what kind of trouble he was in now? If he should make himself scarce real fast or wait to see what this was all about? But realizing there wasn't anywhere to go, he was after all stuck in a remote fire base in South Vietnam, he decided to hold his ground and see what was up?

He thought over what prior action of his could possibly have brought him into the QC's attention, but nothing came to mind. But, the old man accompanying the officer began to hold his attention and GW wasn't sure why or how, but somehow, he felt he'd seen him somewhere before.

From the get-go, GW was busy and hadn't spent any time in Saigon or Danang, nor had he befriended any of the South Vietnamese women, so he knew it had nothing to do with this old dude claiming him for a future son-in-law. Yet, as the old guy drew closer, GW continued to believe he'd seen him somewhere and this bothered him. He had a good memory and didn't like puzzles, and then it came to him. He'd seen this man in a dream, maybe more than once, but even that was hazy and now he felt somewhat bewildered by his sudden appearance. Especially, here and now, what's goin' on?

The old codger limped along on spindly and deeply scared up legs, favoring his left foot some and leaning on a wooden staff. He was dressed in soiled cut-off green shorts, and a faded green short-sleeved shirt that appeared to be a uniform of some type from long ago. GW tried to estimate the old man's age, but here in South Vietnam, with such harsh living conditions in the boonies, draining the very lifeblood from a person, it was hard to really tell a local's age once they hit the senior citizen stage. Black hair turned silvery gray, wrinkles covered a face like a city road map, blackened teeth fell out from chewing too much beetle-nut and blindness came to far too many of them.

GW watched as the old guy walked slightly humped over; as if carrying a 90lb field pack on his back. Seeing the codger smile as he passed by the soldiers, GW's expression turned to one of disgust when he saw the old man's loss of all his front teeth. He also bore several facial scars and, on his arms, were what appeared to be numerous burn scars and several undistinguishable tattoos. His long black and gray hair was quite oily and loosely braided with several strands of multi-colored beads of both green jade and wood. On his feet, which showed evidence of arthritis, he wore the ever-typical Vietnamese Ho Chi Minh' sandals; hand tooled leather from cast-off military goods and soled with old tire rubber.

Tied to the old gentleman's wooden staff, which was longer than the old man's height by several inches, was a soiled green canvas bag. It swayed back and forth in rhythm to his feeble steps.

"Excuse me, Corporal, is your name Sanders?" The South Vietnamese QC captain asked in perfect English. He approached GW from the side, but when GW turned to acknowledge him, the captain saw GW's nametag; which confirmed his identity.

The QC captain was dressed in starched green fatigues, with his boots displaying a fresh shine and he bloused them US and French airborne style, as was the custom. The captain wore a black leather belt with a matching holster holding a Colt 1911 .45 caliber pistol. The belt also held a single leather ammo pouch holding two-loaded magazines.

"Yes, Sir!" GW replied hurriedly, as he snapped to attention and rendered a quick hand salute.

The QC captain returned the salute in a leisurely manner and then stood with his hands on his hips, as he addressed GW. "You may stand at ease, Corporal," he ordered. Then in a lower voice, he said, "Your lieutenant said I could have a few moments with you, if you do not mind?"

"Yes, sir," GW replied. He was glad the captain spoke English because his Vietnamese was extremely limited. He could get his laundry done, but it always came back with too much rice starch or order a Vietnamese to stop in their tracks and he could order up a beer. But that was about it.

"We have a few minutes before formation, Captain," GW added. He then asked, "What can I do for you, Captain?" GW smiled down at the old man, whose full height only came to a couple inches above GW's elbow.

Standing six-foot, four-inches, having a thick barrel-chest and muscular build, GW wore his brown hair cut Airborne short. Deeply tanned, he inherited piercing, almost cobalt blue eyes from his mother, which attracted many a flirtatious young lady while in high school. This also got him into trouble numerous times with the girl's boyfriends and he had learned the art of fisticuffs early on. From his father's side of the family he gained his height, thick bones and a sudden temper; giving him a tendency to jump too fast into a fight until his height and build caught up with him and fewer people wanted to cause him trouble.

From his four years of high school football, he'd gained his muscle, but for the wrestling team he struggled every season to hold his weight to a 215-pound range. Now after humping a 70-pound field pack through the sweltering jungle for five months, he'd become quite a bit leaner and estimated his weight to be well below 200-pounds. His only unattractive marking was a one-inch scar on his lower right jaw, earned in a scuffle from his teenage gang days in Pomona, California. It was the school's sports program that drew him away from the youth gangs, and just in time. Several members of his old gang were now serving serious time in prison or they were dead.

Preferring to go by "GW", his close friends liked to call him "Colonel" in jest, referring to Colonel Sanders' Kentucky Fried Chicken. Recently he'd been awarded a Bronze Star for Valor, which also came with his corporal stripe and his new position as assistant squad leader. The man he had replaced was still in the hospital.

"Corporal, this is Tas Ninh, a Montegnard holy man, who showed up at the front gate late last night. Your MP's turned him over to us." The officer gestured to the old man, "Except for him speaking out your last name, they couldn't understand his mountain language; a Jade dialect I happen to be familiar with." The captain then smiled back at the old man and said a few words to him in Jade, and then turned back to GW.

"He has traveled for more than a week to find you, Corporal; quite a task for a man of his age. His mountain village is more than 110 kilometers from here and most of it is all uphill. Have you ever seen him before?" The captain stood to the side so GW could see the old man clearly.

"No, Captain," GW said. He shook his head from side-to-side. Yet in the back of his mind he still felt some bizarre familiarity with this man. "I think this is the first Montegnard I've ever met."

"Your Green Beret works with them," The Captain said. He then continued, "It's a good thing I speak Jade. The Montegnard people have seven dialects that I know of." The captain then rattled off several words in the Jade language, while GW waited.

Several other young soldiers, all armed to the teeth and freshly fed, had taken-root around GW to observe the interplay between him and the two visitors. Until the order was given to form up, there was little more to do, and it helped with the case of jitters many of the men were dealing with. Most of the men were on their first combat mission and new troops often suffered from nervous shakes and any distraction was considered a blessing. They'd already written out their wills, spent times with a pastor and gone over the operational directives, but they still had this miserable waiting period and the old guy was sort of interesting.

The Captain turned to GW. "Remember, Corporal, I am only the messenger interpreting for him and not the one who might be considered crazy." He shook his head, glanced at the old man again and then continued, "It seems this holy man has had dreams of you...Fourteen-days of dreams and that's how he knew your name. He was to leave his village and travel here, to arrive by this morning and present you with three gifts."

"Fourteen-days ago?" GW said in disbelief. "Captain, fourteen-days ago, only the top brass knew about today's mission and we were still at Camp Eagle."

"You got me there, Corporal, but like I said...I'm only the interpreter."

Looking from the Vietnamese Captain to GW, the old man nodded his head a couple times and then offered his staff to the captain to hold. He then used both of his aged and arthritic hands to untie the soiled canvas bag. Opening it, he removed two items: a smaller hand-stitched leather bag and a well-worn brown cloth wrapped around something about the length of a ruler, almost triangular in-shape. He then spoke in his native tongue for several minutes and once finished, he waited for the captain to translate.

"Corporal, my family raised me to respect the mountain ways because I have a family member on my mother's side that was rescued by Montegnard people and another relative who broke with traditional ways of the Vietnamese people and married into them.

"You will understand...The Vietnamese people in general think of the Montegnards as your people used to think of the American Indian, but I am sorry it goes both ways...They strongly dislike the flatlanders as they often call us.

"I found out early on that I had an aptitude for their language, but only two or three of their dialects. But this one..." Captain looked down at the holy man and sighed, "Well, his story sounds pretty strange."

"What did he say, Captain?" GW smiled down at the holy man again and waited as the old gentleman grinned back, exposing the large gap from his missing teeth and the few remaining teeth covered over in the blackened stains of beetle nut juice. GW knew the Mountain people and their Vietnamese neighbors often used the beetle nut juice to kill the pain of toothache, but it also caused the rotting of teeth and was quite addictive as a natural narcotic.

GW waited for the captain's answer and continued to smile as he looked down into the old man's twinkling dark brown eyes, which were surrounded by deep wrinkles of age and the scars that came from a life of hardship in the mountains.

"He says he knows you are headed for a big battle, where your courage will be tested many times in a strange far-off land

and he was to come here and give you these things this morning, as you will need them for the ordeal ahead. He also says to tell you that there will be three of you for the journey that awaits you and to be brave, everything will be revealed in time and a great reward is to come."

The holy man lifted-up the smaller leather bag and presented it to GW, who cautiously opened it and examined the contents. A strange odor shot up at him and he cringed. "This is dried meat," GW said. He pulled out a piece and took a closer sniff. "Is this beef?"

The QC officer took a whiff of the meat and told GW it was water buffalo.

GW then pulled out a handmade wooden cross nearly seven-inches in length, which hung on a necklace made from what he was told to be elephant hair.

The holy man spoke a few more words and the captain translated, "He says you and two others will need this meat, made especially for you. The cross, from a faith he does not follow, he says is for you to wear later. He was told in his dreams to make it for you and even though he does not understand why, he complied." The Captain glanced back at the old man and then returned his gaze to Corporal Sanders.

GW studied his two gifts with a look of befuddlement and remained silent, trying to figure this out. The holy man then knelt to pick up the third and larger item; one wrapped in a soiled cloth. Removing the top layer of fabric, he exposed a thick foot-long piece of flattened and highly sharpened black flint rock. It went from a five-inch wide base to a pointy end. Fingering the edge with amazement, GW felt that it was extremely sharp, probably sharper than his bayonet--and he kept a fine edge to his bayonet.

He'd heard how flint knives could cut through just about anything, but this was unlike any flint knife he'd seen before. It looked more like a giant arrowhead.

"He says this he also made for you, taking him several days to hammer out the blade edges for the use ahead. He was also directed in his dreams to name this piece..." The captain spoke to the holy man again and then replied, "you're to call it Ascalon."

GW stared at the flint piece for a moment and then asked, "Ascalon...Does that mean something?"

The captain asked the same question of the old man, who only replied with a few words of Jade. Each time, GW heard the same word; "Ascalon" and the captain said that there was no translation in Montegnard or Vietnamese.

"I really don't understand any of this, sir." GW glanced around and saw how several of his comrades were nodding their heads in wonder.

"Corporal, I've experienced some strange things in my life, but I'd never shame a holy man, especially one who 14-days ago, knew you'd be here this morning. He's come a long way and made you some nice gifts. Besides, buffalo meat will come in handy where you're going."

"Okay, Captain." GW agreed. He knelt-down to place the gifts within his already bulging rucksack. "Would you tell the old gentleman thank you and that..." GW stood up, glancing around. The old man had mysteriously vanished, lost among the thick crowd of troops.

The Captain grinned and then said, "Corporal, these mountain holy men are a strange people."

"Yes, sir, it seems so." GW stood up, saluted the captain, and thanked him.

"Good luck, Corporal," the QC captain said. He returned GW's salute and then turned to walk away, just as orders began to be shouted out for the troops to form up.

"Third Squad, you guys get over here!" Sgt. Backer, a burly Texan man with a loud booming voice ordered. He pointed to where he wanted his people.

"First Squad, get in line!" Sgt. Sommers yelled. A thin NCO from Salem, Oregon, he had a startling, high, shrieking voice and began waving his right arm in a circle for attention and then pointing to the spot he wanted them.

In a much lower tone of voice, Sgt. Williams shouted out an order to a troublesome PFC, "Pick up your trash, Sidmore! This isn't your trailer court back home and your mommas not here to clean up after you."

Second Lieutenant Richie, another 90-day wonder from Los Angeles with a BA in History, yelled to his men in a nervous voice, "Second Platoon, form up. Get it movin', people!" This was his first combat mission and the veterans could hear the tremor in his voice.

The war in Vietnam was hard on young officers; too many 2nd lieutenants with little training were falling before the enemy within their first 60-days of combat. But more were being mass-produced back home through 90-day Officer Training Schools.

Upon completion, most of them were handed their graduate certificate, a pair of 2nd lieutenant's gold bars and orders for South Vietnam.

Soon all the men were lined up in a semi-loose formation for their last equipment check before boarding the Huey's. A half-dozen of the birds were slotted to make two-trips, but that second trip was mostly reserved for headquarters staff, additional medical personnel, a supply of extra ammo, stretchers and body bags. Field medics would fly out with their assigned platoons, to be immediately ready for the first casualties.

GW felt the glare of Sgt. Riley, his squad leader and knew he was supposed to be doing something. Only right then did he remember to ensure his squad had everyone in it and then report that fact back to his squad leader. Sgt. Riley was a man of small stature and almost no sense of humor. He was on his second tour of duty in Vietnam and this was his fifth major operation and the death of nine young men assigned to him wore heavily upon his Airborne warrior spirit. With two Purple Hearts, he had no room for humor and really disliked having to break in a new assistant squad leader, his third in five months. Two were killed in action and one was severely wounded.

"All accounted for, Sgt. Riley," GW said in quick time.

"Right," Riley replied in a tone of disgust. "All right, get 'em loaded, Corporal."

The crew chief for GW's Huey was an unusually tall character for an army aircrew member. Standing at least six-foot, seven-inches and string bean thin, he stood by the side of the bird like a perched flamingo with one foot on the Huey's skid. He watched with a keen eye, while the soldiers climbed on board his aircraft. "No trash on my bird. No gum wrappers, cigarette packs or butts. No puke either. It all goes outside. Let the jungle have it, I gotta clean this bird and if you want a round trip ticket you'd better keep this one clean!"

Once strapped in, the crew chief then remembered to order the men to ensure their rifles were on safe, "I don't want some nervous fool putting a hole in our engine and knocking us out of the sky, I ain't no infantry puke and don't plan on humpin' through some dang jungle."

GW visually checked his men's weapons, ensuring they were all on safe and nodded to the crew chief, who then spoke into a helmet microphone to the two-pilots in front. "We're all set back here."

Within minutes, the birds began lifting off and GW felt that initial rush as they left the earth. He smiled and wiped nervous sweat from his forehead with the back of his right hand. He loved flying in Hueys, especially at treetop level and felt it was better than any carnival ride. He even considered looking-into a transfer, becoming a door gunner, but then he learned the survivor rate for door gunners was pretty low.

The guy pulling door gunner duty to his right looked quite capable, if not a wee bit wacky with a steel-plated Marine Corps flak jacket on him and two Army flak jackets under him. The man grinned back at him, nodded once and then returned to peer out over his M-60 to the jungle below like a hawk in search of prey. He also smacked his gum like a 13-year old cheerleader.

I'd be an alcoholic within a month, GW thought.

Once in-flight formation, GW focused on the mission ahead and what was expected of him in his new position as assistant squad leader. He'd been in combat before, but he was deeply concerned about going into the A Shau Valley.

Everyone, including the new guys, seemed to know the stories of the A Shau Valley. How it was a cursed and bloody land, where victims piled up amongst the knotted undergrowth of the jungle floor. Of how the valley was overshadowed in myth and legend from centuries of nightmarish tales and said to be a land where massive predatory creatures of a prehistoric nature were supposedly seen, capable of gobbling up men in a single bite. There was also supposed to be ghosts of the dead, supernatural beings who simply appeared suddenly in ghoulish detail and dragged soldiers downward into the earth, right in front of their terrified comrades.

Tales of an unsolved mystery were whispered in the ranks, of how a large force of armed men had entered the A Shau Valley nearly 400-years earlier and only to disappear completely. Legend had it that their ghosts haunted the valley. It was stories like this that made a lot of the men onboard these helicopters feel a bit edgy and it didn't help that some of the seasoned veterans added their own slant to the tales of supernatural to frighten the new men; especially new officers.

## A SHAU VALLEY
## 0745 HRS/SAME MORNING

For most of two hours, heavy artillery had bombarded four separate landing zones, attempting to confuse the North Vietnamese on where the Americans would make their actual landing. It was proven to be a poor strategy, one that seldom worked and wasted a lot of expensive shells, because the North Vietnamese or Viet Cong spotters covered the entire region and runners would deliver the news to the nearest radio when the Screaming Eagles had eventually landed.

Finally, at the appropriate moment, the order was given to bring the troops in. The Regimental Commander, a full colonel with years of experience from serving in Europe and preparing for a Russian invasion, flew in the command ship at a safe height of 2,000-feet and he observed the operation begin. With an excited grin on his face, he grabbed his executive officer by the arm and said, as the first helicopters swept in and touched down, "Piece of cake." He then said into the bird's microphone for his pilots to hear and adding, "We'll have 'em located and on the run by nightfall."

The lead pilot glanced over at his co-pilot and shook his head. The co-pilot, who was on his 12th such major operation, only nodded his head in understanding. They both knew this colonel was about to gain an education in jungle fighting and it was the poor ground pounders down below who were going to pay the price.

"Lock an' load, boys!" Sgt. Riley ordered loudly. He watched as the men took their rifles off safe and pushed the rifle's selector to semi-auto. "Point 'em out the doors!" Riley ordered, complying with the crew chief's beady glare.

Everyone was nervous now, ready for a hot landing zone and it was mostly half-scared teenagers who jumped from the first birds and assumed their positions for immediate combat. They took up defensive positions right away, following their training and ready to fight for the ground they stood upon. They lay on their stomachs, rifles posited towards the tree line. Only there was no shooting and as the birds lifted off, these men were met by an eerie wall of silence from the surrounding woods and no enemy in sight.

Unable to hear anything as the dry grassy plain was blown hard from rotating helicopter blades, GW landed hard upon his stomach and lay prone in his firing position. With a heavy rucksack on his back and for added insult, a squad mate's boot in his face, he shoved it aside and waited for Riley's orders. He pushed his helmet up for better visual range and cautiously scanned the nearby tree line over the sight of his M-16.

His trigger finger felt as if it was swelled up, a feeling he remembered from previous actions and his hand trembled slightly with adrenaline surging through him. He waited to be fired upon, even for a NVA or Viet Cong to come shooting up out of a spider hole, but still no sound of gunfire rose-up to meet them. Only the bugs attacked, which feared no man or animal, as they buzzed and crawled about in various sizes, shapes and colors.

Within moments of landing, platoon leaders organized the squads into larger defense positions to surround the landing zone for arriving Hueys to off load their wary passengers and fly away. Once all the birds had departed, the valley was left in an unnatural quietness. No sounds of animals moving about and no birds. The only noise beyond what the Americans made were the sounds various bugs gave off with their different sounding taunts to fellow insects and calls of alarm when these human giants crushed their homes or swatted them out of hand.

This strange silence made everyone uncomfortable, from veteran to new guy. Some would prefer the sound of gunfire to this absence of the natural. For the seasoned men, this lack of nature usually meant the enemy was close by, near enough to observe them, but not yet prepared to do battle. However, this would soon change. In the coming hours, the 29th North Vietnamese command structure would rally its forces from outlining areas. From deep within nearby mountains they prepared to meet the invading Americans in force and drive them from this valley.

**THAT FIRST EVENING IN THE A SHAU VALLEY:**

It was hot—sweltering hot. The dense jungle growth surrounding the make-shift helipads quickly became an open-air steam bath. GW, who was manning a defensive position in a thick stand of undergrowth, had already emptied his first canteen. He felt dry mouthed. The wet heat drained him all too quickly, making him feel like dried fruit. He was relieved when the sun had set, and darkness fell upon the valley. After the first hour or two the water tasted bitter and it had grown quite warm. Oh, what I'd do for a Coke with lots of ice.

His day-old uniform was drenched in sweat and the old green towel he kept around his neck to wipe his sweaty face was already dry. He also knew he was perspiring more water out of his body than he was putting in, but he must conserve his limited water supply. Salt tablets helped some, but they also created a memorable taste, but Vietnam seemed to suck the very juices out of a man and dehydration was a constant medical problem. If it wasn't the sweat, it was the mosquitoes draining their blood and no one on an outer defensive position wanted to give away his position by swatting a mosquito or verbally complaining about it.

GW was due to check his men's positions for a third time since darkness fell, when the enemy began probing the perimeter defenses with sporadic gunfire. He knew from prior firefights an enemy AK-47's had a distinct sound and discipline along the line was hard to maintain. As night closed in, the airborne troops could almost feel the eyes of the enemy glaring back at them through the pitch darkness. Meanwhile, various types of flying creatures launched their own offensive on the men's faces to add further insult.

A spattering of gunfire from jittery trigger fingers kept everyone alert, while squad leaders and their assistants remained busy quieting down their people's nerves with a hard knock to the tops of their helmets. Giving them a stern warning of how they were giving their positions away to the enemy with illuminated tracer fire. Every fifth round was a tracer, which could help a shooter direct his own night fire but could also identify the shooter's placement.

Having been out here before, GW knew the humidity seemed to be worse under cover of darkness and dampened his sweaty towel with a few precious drops of water from his canteen to wash his eyes out. Then as he sat behind a large deadfall for cover, he watched as the heavy weapons platoon fire off 81mm mortar flares. These were the evening's first flares ordered up by Alpha Company's commander, whose troops manned the southern perimeter positions. In response to those flares, the enemy's first barrage of mortar fire struck the US encampment at approximately 2000 hours. Seven lethal rounds of high explosive struck well within the perimeter and killed or wounded nine soldiers. Calls went out for medics and before long a squad of men was carrying stretchers of wounded men into the first-aid area. For the dead, black body bags were removed from stiff-sided cardboard boxes and lifeless soldiers were placed inside them for later removal.

GW could hear the distressing sounds of wounded men and remembered his earlier firefights, where he'd lost two friends over a span of two-weeks. Now more men were falling in a war so far away from home. Here, in the A Shau Valley, lying in holes or on poncho liners behind logs, they wondered if they might survive, the brave young men struggled to remain stone-faced. With clenched teeth and watery eyes, they fought to remain silent as medics cut away their uniforms and began to probe their wounds even before the morphine could do its job. While others screamed in pain, or called out for a loved one, one or two begged for God's forgiveness for one sin or another, to ensure a clean soul when the final darkness might come to claim them. A Catholic chaplain, a young captain from a Spokane, Washington fellowship, moved among the men to deliver Last Rites or to pray for a wounded man's quick healing.

The Chaplain stopped and knelt beside one sergeant; a new arrival with an arm blown off from mortar fire. He could be overheard, pleading to God in a raspy voice for a miraculous healing as his blood seeped into the ground. Nearby, another youth of only 18 years old from Maine gently pulled on the medic's shirtsleeve and simply asked him to stop the pain with a plea, "Please..."

A 2nd lieutenant from Boston struggled to stay awake in fear he would never wake up again, his legs shredded from shrapnel. While a soldier from Seattle, bleeding from three AK-47 wounds to the upper body pushed the medic aside and implored a buddy to end it for him here and now. But for most of them once the morphine hits, sweetness entered their veins and transformed their nightmares into a euphoric state of peace. Even worse was the mounting pile of filled body bags; dead men waiting for that last flight home to be buried by their loved ones. An American flag would be draped over their coffins, an honor guard would be present, and a few kind words said over them to hopefully cushion the blow for their parents or a wife.

The Regimental Commander was back at the fire base and had realized he didn't have to be concerned with locating the 29th North Vietnamese Army; they'd been found and appeared to have surrounded his encampment with superior forces. This was not going to be the cakewalk he had hoped for.

With the arrival of an early dawn the first of many medivac helicopters began arriving to make hot pick-ups; full stretchers were literary thrown on board as the bird hovered dangerously and taking enemy fire. Door gunners raked the tree lines with M-60 machinegun fire, without ever seeing an enemy soldier to aim at.

The Regimental Commander, a man whose thick calloused palms continued to sweat profusely, tried to wring them dry. He was airborne again and had requested a flight of Marine F-4 Phantoms to provide air support for the medivac helicopters. He then watched from 2,000 feet above the encampment as aircraft arrived on scene. He slammed his fist against his knee and once more grinned, as these huge Phantoms bathed the surrounding hillsides in a blast of napalm hell. He waved a clenched fist in triumph, watching flames burst upward to a height of more than 100-feet, consuming everything in reddish, orange and yellowing liquid-fire. But the enemy had its traffic controllers too, who issued warnings through various sources on how the American fighters were en route. The 29th NVA went underground into a vast network of tunnels dating back to the days when the Viet Minh first fought the Japanese and then the French. By the time the ground had cooled some, the NVA poured out of their mountainous refuge to return to their positions to once again harass the 101st positions with intense mortar shelling, rocket propelled grenades and gunfire. By the end of the second day, American casualties had mounted well over the acceptable range and they still hadn't been able to leave the valley floor. One overly burdened doctor and his five-medic staff stayed steadily busy with shrapnel and bullet wounds, while enemy mortars continued to pound the encampment.

Decisions had to be made quickly from higher headquarters, whether this operation was becoming too costly a price to pay. Newsmen, who watched the helicopters return with the severely wounded and dying, began reporting the numbers of killed and wounded to the American public back home. These men of the press stood beside the wounded, notebook and pencil in hand or a hand-held tape recorder and listened to a tale of a failing operation.

The fateful decision to withdraw came down from high command in Saigon at 0540 hours; the order for their withdrawal from the A Shau Valley by 1500 hours.

## SECOND DAY IN THE A SHAU VALLEY
## 1437 HOURS

GW's squad was hit pretty hard. He'd lost three men to serious shrapnel wounds from mortar fire only an hour earlier and was reduced to five-men now. Sgt. Riley had taken an AK-47 round in the shoulder and was in the aid tent, leaving a nervous GW in charge as acting squad leader. And through it all, so far, he had not had a clear shot at the enemy and his uniform was soiled with a mixture of Sgt. Riley's blood and white streaks of salt stain. His face was covered with a dozen or so insect bites, dried blood splatters from other wounded and filthy grime from the valley floor. He was beginning to wonder if enlisting in the Army was such a great idea, especially when he looked in the frightened eyes of the men he was now in charge of. I could've borrowed some money and gone to college, be chasing girls across the campus or playing football in front of 10,000--screaming fans. But no, I'm sitting here 6,000 miles from home waiting to get my butt shot off. Oh, I'm such a clever boy. Listened to some smooth-talking recruiter on how I can use the GI Bill to go to school without having to borrow any money. Right now, I'd like to have that recruiter right here beside me...GW's train of thought was broken when 1st Lieutenant Joseph T. Radkins appeared in front of him. Radkins knelt-down behind a fallen tree to avoid enemy fire and grabbed GW by the right shoulder to get and hold his attention. Radkins' blue-gray eyes were almost bulging with tension, as a heavy sweat dripped from his brow. GW couldn't help but notice how Radkins was literally shaking with nervous energy, or most likely fear. He got close to GW's right ear and shouted out orders for GW to follow him, "Your squad is to join up with me, Corporal. You'll be with what's left of my 1st platoon."

GW nodded his understanding and waited for Radkins to let go of him. Once he did, GW went to his men and directed them to follow him, "Grab everything you've got, I don't think we're coming back here any time soon."

Once Lt. Radkins had all four of his undermanned squads together in one location, he briefed them on what was upcoming, "Order for retreat has gone out, helicopters are in the air and it's now our duty to defend the LZ. We're to hold the line, while the airlift takes place," 1st Lt. Radkins' said in a high pitched nervous voice, making GW think of Audie Murphy in the movie about his life story.

"What about my platoon, Sir?" GW asked. He was not relishing the idea of being placed under the command of a frightened officer, especially one given the dangerous task of pulling a rear-guard action.

"Your lieutenant is wounded. Your squad leader is down, and your company commander volunteered you for this duty. Tough, but that's the way it is. Understand, Corporal?"

"Yes, Sir," GW replied. He didn't know what else to say, his CO had given his squad the short straw and they were stuck with it.

"We will move to the aid tent and hold our position there until everyone else is out. Five birds will stand-by for us and we'll jump aboard for a quick snatch and grab job." Radkins then reached out and pointed his right index finger at GW, "Your squad has the northern position, which means you will be last to board. But the gunships will be providing cover fire. You understand, Corporal?" The explosions and rifle fire were making it hard to be heard and the pungent odor of sulfur was causing GW's eyes to water.

"Yes, Sir!" GW yelled back. He didn't think this was such a great idea, but as a new corporal he didn't have a lot of say in the matter and put his life and that of his men into Lt. Radkins' sweaty hands.

"You'll wait for my order to pull back. If I'm down, my platoon sergeant will give you the word. You got that?" Lt. Radkins waited for GW's nod of understanding and then moved on to the next squad leader.

With a deep heart-filled sigh, GW turned to his remaining squad members and ordered them to gear-up, "We're last squad in line, so make sure you got plenty of ammo and grenades 'cause we ain't comin' back here," GW ordered. He then glanced around to get his bearings and to see where the lieutenant was moving the rest of this newly formed platoon. If his count was right, there was just enough men to make up three squads and they'd been handed an assignment a fully manned rifle company would have a hard time handling.

"Stay low!" GW ordered and then in a low crouch, he followed the last man in the squad toward the aide tent's position. He didn't want to lose anyone along the way and decided on the rear-guard position. Meanwhile, enemy bullets zinged by overhead and struck the deadfall he'd made a home behind earlier. Then he heard an explosion right behind him, the concussion wave forcing him to the ground and debris raining down upon him. He knew a mortar landed pretty close to where he was only moments before and it sent a cold chill through his body. But he had to keep moving or his small squad would get pinned down and possibly overrun.

Overhead, a flight of three A1E Sky Raiders aircraft was on scene to provide air cover for the battalion's withdrawal. The Sky Raider was a high-valued prop driven World War II aircraft that could provide excellent ground support with its slow air speeds and heavy armament.

But it didn't take long before the Raiders had run low on fuel and ammo, and they were ordered off. They were supposed to be replaced by a flight of six-Cobra helicopter gunships coming in from a nearby firebase, but through a tragic mistake they were diverted elsewhere. Before they could be diverted back, Lt. Radkins' command was being overrun by more than a hundred North Vietnamese and the US survivors were making a mad dash into the jungle.

Two of the helicopters used for the airlift had taken heavy fire and were ordered away and without protective air cover, the other three-birds retreated to a higher elevation to avoid being hit by enemy fire. Seeing his command fall apart below him, the Regimental Commander ordered the three birds to return and the pilots reluctantly agreed. Sadly though, it was too late to stave off a massacre.

Seeing the American's strength on the ground reduced to less than a platoon of soldiers and no air cover overhead, the 29th NVA launched a massive ground assault with over 300-troops. They came in from three sides, pouring out of the tree line like hungry wolves pouncing upon wounded prey. When Lt. Radkins saw what he was facing, he quickly positioned his men into a tight "V" position, with the LZ behind them. He ordered in artillery fire from the nearest fire base, but it was too late. The enemy was already running across the landing zone like crazed men and right at his defenseless rear flank. Dozens of them had fallen under the fierce, but short-lived artillery barrage, for now they were too close to Lt. Radkins' command. He had no other option but to order his men to retreat deeper into the dark netherworld of the A Shau Valley. Unfortunately, the enemy was ready for this with another deadly trap in the waiting.

Within moments, 1st Lt. Radkins, who once had dreams of becoming a general officer someday, had taken three bullet hits from an AK-47. He now lay motionless upon the jungle floor, his lifeless eyes staring into the dense tree canopy above. His dying radioman lay only a few feet away, his last thoughts on how hard it was going to be on his mother when she was notified of his death. He then closed his eyes for the last time as an enemy soldier knelt beside him and began stripping him of his equipment and valuables.

Unable to see very well in the thick undergrowth of the jungle floor, US soldiers ran in panic, as they attempted to escape the on-coming enemy. Only a very few soldiers made any attempt to stop and return fire. Three of the men, terrified beyond understanding, dropped to their knees, tossed their weapons aside and plead for mercy. Their eyes filled with tears of fear, the three of them only 18-years old had lifted their arms up in surrender. But an order was given from deep inside the mountain fortress, no prisoners were to be taken today--the Americans were to be executed where they were found and stripped of all their equipment. So, these terrified young men died with horrified expressions on their faces—gunned down by 18 and 19-year olds from the City of Hanoi. Much like their victims, they too were terrified by war, but today they were driven on by a strong desire to avenge their fallen comrades.

Surprisingly, GW found himself out in front when the NVA threw the next ambush. The US soldiers were being herded along a dried stream bed and for some strange reason the enemy machine gunner had allowed him through, before he pounced upon the few survivors with animal-like viciousness. Struggling to keep his nerve, his eyes darting all about for the enemy, GW didn't think there was anything else to do but run deeper into the shadowy darkness of the A Shau Valley. It was either flee or die a gruesome death at the hands of the NVA. He had briefly seen what had happened to those who tried to surrender, and it wasn't pretty.

Leaving the jungle, he slung his rifle over his shoulder and began a hazardous climb up the rocky sides of an embankment on all fours. He ended up tearing the knees of his right pants leg and scraping some of the hide off his right kneecap. But within seconds his path was blocked by rock outcroppings and he was forced to drop back down to the thick foliage of the narrowing valley floor and continue his flight from the approaching NVA.

Not one to give up, he went back up another rocky hillside further down a natural trail formed by rain fall and mudslides. As he climbed, the crumbling earth slid through his bleeding fingers and his mind raced far beyond rational thought. He only knew that to stop meant a painful death, so he continued to scale the rocks and when he couldn't go any further he'd drop back down into the jungle, continuing on. But first he'd listen for the enemy to see how close they were and then he'd sprint through the bushes, jumping from rock to rock along the steep embankment with his rifle now out in front of him and his rucksack straps burning into his shoulders.

In his panic, he thought of dropping the rucksack, which was nearly empty now, but rational thought stepped in and he realized he might need what he still carried. So, he plowed on ahead and it was moments later when he realized he had picked up two other Americans in tow.

For some reason, he couldn't currently fathom, he slowed down and allowed the two men to catch up. Then without wasting breath by talking, the two men simply waived GW on and followed in his footsteps as they jumped over deadfalls, climbed hillsides and splashed through a series of small streams.

Worn out by a mixture of fear and exhaustion, their muscles tight and burning, and their minds filled with the pictures of the death behind them, the three of them had no other choice but to stop for a quick breather. GW dropped behind a large fallen tree, its sides covered in growth, which concealed him from the enemy and the other two fell-down beside him. Exhausted, they had collapsed like three cast-off dolls, but within moments they were discovered and were suddenly locked in an intense firefight with an enemy squad.

Lobbing three grenades to cover their hasty retreat further up the valley, they ran into the shadows of a deep ravine and feared they had reached a box canyon. Then to make matters worse, GW tripped over the undergrowth and bloodied his face when he slammed into the base of a large tree. He fell backward into heavy brush but maintained a tight grasp of his rifle. A few more steps and one of the other men, a Black youth, repeated GW's act of gracefulness when his foot caught a thick ground vine and the third man had to help both of his weary comrades to their feet.

Unfortunately, there was no time for first aid, so they used the sleeves of their sweaty uniform shirts to wipe the blood away and then kept on running. Several times they shot at nothing but shadows amongst the growing blackness surrounding them. Fear was now driving them. Not the enemy. They had no idea where they were running to and if anyone was even out there to help them. They had no radio, not even a flare or a smoke grenade to mark their location.

"Stop shooting!" GW ordered. "We're giving our position away."

"Right," one of the others, another corporal, replied half-heartedly.

The ravine continued along and whenever one of them fell from lack of strength, another man would stop to give him a hard jerk by the fallen man's rucksack strap and help him up. No words were spoken between them now, not even a whisper; in fear the enemy might locate them by the sounds of their voice.

Bleeding from many minor wounds, caused by rock cuts, tangled undergrowth and the occasional tree, GW and the two Americans continued at a slower pace to catch their wind. Heavy sweat from the torturous humidity and constant and near overwhelming fear was taking a heavy toll on their bodies. Enemy fire was a constant reminder the enemy was right behind them and they were wary of another enemy trap. But the three soldiers had no other options except to push on into an unknown territory.

Nightfall soon blanketed the valley in a thick humid cloak of black paint. They couldn't see beyond a few inches, causing them to stay in physical touch of the next man or risk becoming lost in the heavy undergrowth, or possibly running right into an enemy patrol. They knew there were wild animals out here and one of these predators was tigers. GW had seen one off in the distance on a previous operation and believed this animal was the largest cat he had ever seen and wasn't too sure his M-16 could stop such a critter.

Still, GW remained out in front, swatting pestering insects, while probing the wall of darkness with his bayonet tipped rifle. When he next turned his head toward the right, he heard a strange sound; a quiet whine-like sound and before he could even gather a guess what it was, he immediately ran right smack into a rocky embankment. A protruding rock contributed to a third blow to his poor injured nose and he was knocked backward toward the ground and into the legs of the man behind him.

Without an exchange of words, GW was helped to his feet by a strong right arm and for a long moment, the three of them stood together silently while GW tasted blood from his bleeding nose--again. He decided the strange sound was tree branches sliding across the cliff face in a light breeze. Either that or a jungle demon was tormenting them. The three of them decided they liked the tree branch idea better.

His hands locked on his rifle, arms trembling, he forced himself to slow his rate of breathing down by slowly inhaling and exhaling quietly. Once under control, he whispered ever so quietly to the other two, "I think we should use this rocky ridge to our right as a guide. Keep it on our immediate right. That way this side is covered." The other two men agreed with quiet grunts of approval and after a brief rest and a single gulp of warm water from their canteens, the three of them quietly moved off with GW continuing out in front.

Within moments, GW, whose face was swelling from insect bites and run-ins with various objects, realized he was inching his way along a narrowing ledge of rock. He used his left foot to probe the edge and through his heightened sense of fear, imagined a steep drop off to his left. A false move could result in sure death and because of the darkness he had no idea how deep the abyss might be--a drop of a foot or a death plunge of 100-feet or more?

"Lean to the right, there's a drop off to our left," GW whispered back. He then began moving along in dire hope the edge would hold them and lead to where they could stop and rest. They were slowly climbing and shooting below had stopped. They hadn't heard a sound from the valley for some time and GW hoped the enemy had returned to the landing zone to plunder the encampment of anything they could carry away. The enemy knew with the rising sun the US would use their artillery to blow the area into oblivion.

Within a few moments of creeping along the rock ledge, rifle slung over his left shoulder so he had his hands free, GW stepped over thick growth of tree roots and suddenly fell forward into a deep, dark hole. Unable to stop his cry of alarm, he let out a scream when he landed hard upon his right hip. Thankfully, his rucksack absorbed most of the impact and he immediately felt ridiculous when he realized he'd only fallen into a depression of only four-feet. Bruised up a bit, but nothing broken, he regained his feet and promptly warned the others not to move.

Shouldering his rifle again, he cautiously felt around with his hands and soon found an aged growth of vines and tree roots that had partially covered over the hole he'd fallen into and it was big enough for all three men. He had found the hiding place he'd been searching for.

"Come on down, but be careful," GW said in a whisper. He lifted his hand up for the next man to grab and be guided down into the hole.

Once settled into the hole, the three men wearily dropped their rucksacks and set back for a well-needed rest and a couple gulps of warm water. GW used this opportunity to wash his bloody and sweaty face off with his filthy neck towel and winced from the pain it caused his face.

Sitting there in the darkness, fighting off the mosquitoes, GW finally learned who his two fellow survivors were: Corporal Paul Grant and PFC Richard Hughes, both members of 1st Squad of Lt. Radkins' ill-fated 2nd platoon of D Company.

It was PFC Hughes who soon discovered the hole they were sitting in was an entrance into a cave of sizable proportions. While moving around for a more comfortable position, the earth behind him gave way and he fell backwards into the cave.

Hughes asked for his rucksack and GW handed it to him. From it, Hughes pulled out his flashlight and turned it on. First making sure the beam of light couldn't be seen from outside by shielding it with his hands, a quick search revealed the cave to be the size of a single-size car garage. The ceiling was several feet over their heads and covered in tree roots and a rocky outcropping. They took a chance and after removing the other flashlights from GW's and Grant's rucksacks, and cautiously illuminated the cave. But only away from the opening in fear the enemy might see the light from down below.

All three agreed this was a place they could defend, unless the enemy shot an RPG in through the opening. But then Corporal Grant, who walked off to explore, soon discovered another cave attached to the first by a short natural shaft. This second cave was larger than this one and easier to defend if the enemy attacked. So, they picked up their packs and cautiously ventured deeper inside the mountain.

Grant didn't like caves. "Don't like bats," he complained. "They get in your hair and take root."

"It's a choice of bats or NVA," GW reminded him. "I'm going a bit farther in. If you want to stay here you're more than welcome too," GW said and continued moving along. He used the flashlight, keeping the beam directed at his feet as he inched along and occasionally shot it toward the ceiling, fearful of what unknown threat that may lie ahead. He also didn't want to run head first into a low hanging rock.

"No. I'm coming," Grant replied reluctantly.

Once deep inside the mountain and growing quite exhausted again from their flight and the traumatic memories of what they left behind, the three men agreed to stop for a lengthy rest and some badly needed sleep. The cave's floor was hard rock, with the occasional stalagmite or stalactite, and some crumbling rock debris coming off near sheer walls. Several times they felt moisture on the walls, but they never saw any actual streamlets or puddles.

Making their way to the back of the cave they found no evidence the enemy had ever used this cave and no sign any of the jungle critters had used it either and this struck GW as unusual. Back home, he knew all sorts of animals took refuge in caves and wondered why it wasn't the same here? But he was happy to see most of the insects had stayed outside, nearly all his exposed flesh was now covered in bites.

GW remained hopeful the natural cover at the entrance would keep their hiding place a secret, at least long enough for them to get a few hours' sleep and possibly find an alternate exit point—preferably one far away from the enemy. As ranking man; GW's promotion to corporal coming just four days before Grant, he set up the guard duty shifts with him taking the first three-hour watch, while the other two men slept. Then Corporal Grant would follow, leaving PFC Hughes to take the early dawn watch. They didn't need a fire, not with the temperature in the cave being in the mid-70's and the flames' glare could give their position away. But before going to sleep, a food, ammo and water check was accomplished and some degree of first aid for bites, scratches and cuts. Instead of blisters, GW's band-aids were used on his face and his compress battle dressing was wrapped around his knee.

Water check revealed each man was down to one full canteen of water in his rucksack and a partially filled one on his belt. Food wouldn't be a problem for a day or two, they still had some C-rations left, but ammo was going to be a major problem. They had no salt tablets left for they relied on the platoon medic to carry extra tablets and the last medic had been gunned down while trying to help a wounded soldier. PFC Hughes had a long laceration to his left leg; now covered with his battle dressing, and both of his arms and legs had minor abrasions from running through the jungle. Corporal Grant had sustained abrasions to both knees and elbows, along with a grazing wound to his face from an enemy bullet, which came all too close after it had ricocheted off the hillside and burned him with rock fragments. Both men also suffered from a multitude of bites, stretching their limited supply of first aid ointment to cover them with.

Thankfully, the cave was several degrees cooler than outside and they had nearly stopped sweating. Still, GW insisted they open their C-rations and use what small bit of salt they had to keep them from dehydration. "We'll use half of a packet of salt now and save the next half for tomorrow," GW suggested.

"You got any ideas on how we're going to get out of this mess, Corporal?" PFC Hughes asked GW. The young Black PFC was busily dousing some water on some arm scratches on his left wrist and back of his hand.

"Hey, take it easy with the water!" GW ordered and then calmed himself down a bit before he answered Hughes' question, "Now? No, but after some sleep maybe we can figure this out."

"Yeah, I feel like my eyelids are about to weld shut. We can talk later," Grant said. He sprawled out on the cave floor, took his helmet off and laid a heavily soiled green towel over his face, in fear of those bats he kept talking about. He had positioned his rucksack under his head and held his rifle over his stomach and said a weary, "Good night."

"You want me to stay up with you, Corporal?" Hughes asked. He wasn't sure if he could go to sleep for fear he'd keep seeing the faces of his dead comrades. For a city boy on his first combat operation, the last few hours were quite traumatic on him.

"You've got six hours of sleep coming," GW said. "Knock off the talk and get some shut-eye." Hughes nodded his head in response, which could barely be seen from the illumination of a single flashlight pointed upward at the ceiling. He then moved off a few feet to find a flat surface to lie down upon. But he kept his helmet on, bracing his head up against the side of the cave with his rucksack and held his rifle closely beside him. Though Hughes wasn't sure he could sleep, he was unconscious within minutes and even snoring lightly.

Today might have been the worst day in his young life, but his dreams were of fishing with his dad. The nightmares would come soon enough, but right now he was a boy in a small fishing boat struggling with a sea perch in San Francisco Bay, looking in the smiling face of his father, as the huge fish was brought to the surface. They fished whenever the opportunity presented itself; which those days became less and less in number, as they both grew older. While the others slept, GW, his helmet still on, held his rifle upright and leaned the right side of his dirty face up against the side of his M-16. He turned the flashlight off to conserve the batteries, but kept it attached to his combat suspenders for ready use. Assuming his deep thinker role, he began looking back on his life and particularly the tragic events of the last two days. He wondered if he would ever see home again or his father. His mother had died three years earlier and he had no brothers or sisters to comfort his old man when the government's official notification came of his death. If they never made it out of this cave their remains might never be found, and he would be reported as Missing-In-Action and presumed dead. But knowing his father, the old man would spend the rest of his life waiting for GW to come walking through the front door.

He tried not to think of his ex-sweetheart; his former high school love, who had been kind enough to send him a Dear John letter two months and five days after he arrived in South Vietnam. "I just want to be able to date again, it's nothing serious. I'm sure when you come home we can resume our relationship," she had written. He read it over several times, having a hard time understanding who this girl was who had written him and what happened to his girlfriend--the love of his life and almost his fiancé? Then a week later he got a letter from a high school buddy attending college with her, which told him of how she was hanging out with the anti-war crowd—one jerk in particular—and it did look serious.

Struggling to stay awake, his thoughts jumped from her to that weird holy man who visited him before they left on this disastrous mission. With it so dark, he used his hands to locate his rucksack and open it. Through feel, he pulled out the strange gifts and wondered why he, a kid from Southern California, was chosen to receive such strange offerings? So, why me? What makes me so special? And just who was that old dude?

As a near overwhelming odor of meat struck his senses, he was very tempted to eat a piece of the dried buffalo meat. But after some inner debate, he decided he could wait until they'd used up their cans of C-rations. The only good side of C-rations was as they used the cans up; their rucksacks would grow lighter. The meat's, dried out, should last for a while, as-long-as, I keep it covered. But I'll keep it secret for now—keep it for emergencies. But he felt the wooden cross in his hand, cut out from a single piece of wood. There was a single hole at the top, which held the length of coiled elephant hair. He thought about it for some time, not having before given much thought into this whole Christian thing. His mother had been a believer, but his dad was one of those Easter and Christmas believers. His dad had always said Saturdays were for household chores and Sundays were for relaxing and watching football on television.

Yet, as he held the cross in his hands he could almost feel a sense of warmth emanating from it. Not knowing why, GW removed his helmet and draped the cross over his head. It hung down to his chest, about the same length from where his dog tags hung.

GW then examined his ammo again. He still had the magazine of ammo in his M-16, with 12-rounds left in it, and two loaded magazines in his pouch. He was out of grenades and knew this limited supply of ammo was barely enough for even the briefest of firefights.

Corporal Grant had reported only one loaded magazine in his pouch and six rounds left in his rifle's magazine. He also had one fragmentation grenade. While PFC Hughes had apparently left his rifle on full automatic in all the excitement and used up nearly all his ammo with exception of six-rounds still in his rifle's magazine and no grenades left. GW took eight-rounds out of his full magazine and presented them to a very grateful young PFC. He also ordered him to keep his rifle on semi-auto fire, for there would be no other gifts of bullets. "That's all you get, make 'em last," GW told him.

They all carried sharpened bayonets, but Grant and GW also had KA-BAR knives with an eight-inch blade taped to the left side of their combat suspenders with black electrician's tape. These knives would come in handy when the ammo gave out and they were down to hand-to-hand combat. With his eyelids gaining poundage with every passing moment, GW placed his rucksack against the side of the cave and rested his back against it as thoughts of home and his turncoat ex-girlfriend returned to haunt him. He wondered what his dad was doing at this moment, how he had taken it when GW wrote and told him about the Dear John letter? You never did like her, Dad. Must've seen something, I couldn't.

He had asked himself over and over how he could've been so wrong about his girlfriend? He was ready to pick out a diamond ring and pop the question during his R&R in Hawaii with her, but he hadn't told her about that trip either. How stupid I was! Man, I'm glad I didn't waste any more money on her. Part of him was glad he found out who she was before they got married. If she couldn't handle three months waiting for him, she'd never last out the duration of a marriage. He pictured her face in his mind, seeing all that blonde curly hair cascading down her shoulders and those deep blue eyes that seemed to swallow him up and let out a deep heart-filled sigh. Then suddenly, his anger erupted, and he struck the cave floor with the butt of his rifle in frustration and hurt. Then as if on cue, he suddenly felt a growing movement in the hard rock all below him. A deep rumbling sound began, growing with intensity and seemed to reverberate off the rock walls like the insides of a stereo speaker. He thought the very earth was releasing a moan of pain and it was becoming deafening. At that same moment, a hot wind blew up from deep within the mountain and he picked up a pungent odor of sulfur that began to burn his eyes. It was growing hard to breathe and his throat grew painful with each breath. He pulled his shower towel from around his neck and began breathing through it and started yelling for the other two men to wake up. But everything was happening so fast and he barely had time to scream out a warning before his world suddenly turned topsy-turvy.

His right hand was white in color from tightly clutching his rifle, when he struggled to rise, but the earth danced about him and sent him bouncing off the rocks like a small rubber ball. In those first terrifying moments, he initially thought the enemy was using mortars or even artillery against them, but as the rumbling sound increased, GW soon realized he was experiencing an earthquake growing to a momentous scale. For the briefest of moments, he began to suspect the mountain they were in was a dormant volcano and these caves were its lava tubes, but then his mind became lost in confusion as everything continued to spin. Softball and then basketball-size rocks gave way from the cave ceiling and rained down upon the two sleepers. He yelled out a warning, but his voice went unheard, as the cave's rumbling sounds grew louder to match with the increasing violence of the ground quakes. Rocks of all sizes fell and bounced about, causing rock dust to fill the cavern, which made it even harder to breathe and visibility in the darkness was reduced to zero. He couldn't even see the hand in front of his face.

Unable to stand, GW attempted to use his rucksack as a shield to fend off blows to his head from falling rocks. Only his helmet had saved him from being knocked out from the huge rocks, but one rock felt like a large man's uppercut to his jaw. Then he was knocked to the ground. Shock waves grew with even more intensity and while being lifted from the floor and slammed up against the cave wall, he was finally knocked unconscious and slid to the cave floor into a mangled heap.

Unseen by these unconscious Americans, the unthinkable began to occur; the cave began spinning in an unnatural bizarre-like whirling motion, which caused the men and their equipment to be tossed about. Much like GI Joe dolls in a gyrating blender. Faster and faster they spun until a ten-foot long crack suddenly formed in a rock wall closest to where the Americans lay pinned to the floor. Expanding to several feet wide, they were then sucked through the opening, much like an astronaut sucked into space through a blown air lock. The opening was now wide enough to reveal a cosmic-like vortex of spiraling rainbow colors. All three unconscious soldiers fell into this spiraling and miraculous tunnel of time, either feet first or face first they went. Here, distance had little meaning, for in this strange void of time, myth and legend had formed a corridor of existence in a briefest moment of reality. Outside the cave entrance a great landslide of rock, debris and mud poured down the mountainside, leaving no evidence these three Americans had ever been there.

# 2 – BIZARRE AWAKENINGS IN A FAR-OFF PLACE

SILENE, LIBYA, NORTH AFRICA
INSIDE THE CASTLE
1178 A.D.

Brother Samuel's loud bellowing voice could be heard throughout the ancient stone castle, echoing down the long stone passageways to let everyone within 100-yards know he was once again in search of his wayward pupil. "Princess Lennia!" He shouted. "You'll not escape me, again, young lady." Princess Lennia, who was long overdue for today's studies, would often play hooky whenever the upcoming subject turned to math. Today, she was hiding out in the stables, grooming one of her favorite horses and ignoring Brother Samuel's loud outbursts, as they carried outside through the castle's large upper portals.

Admittedly, Brother Samuel was a big man and overweight by good 70-pounds and he was nearly bald with just a tuff of white hair over each ear that thinly joined in the back of his head. A joyful man to be sure, he also bore a thick white beard of some length, with bushy, unruly gray-white eyebrows over his dark blue eyes. Though some of the men were into plucking their eyebrows, Brother Samuel thought the practice to be extremely vain, if not painful.

He was approaching his 75th birthday and struggled with arthritis, lately. He was beginning to feel weighed down all too often with lengthy bouts of depression and a soured stomach. And to add to his many burdens, Brother Samuel was quite the oddity here in Silene. For Brother Samuel was not only a Caucasian, he was also a Christian monk in a world of dark skinned Muslim Saracens.

Today and as always, he was attired in an ankle length brown robe—one sorely in need of washing, as he stormed about the castle in search of his delinquent pupil. Strangely enough for a lone

Christian in the center of Islam, he carried with him a limited authority of the King; a position with the royal family, which gave him the privilege of running to ground his youngest student and chastising her with a harsh word or two.

One by one, he checked out each of her favorite hiding places in hopes of finding her before her father learned of her disappearance and punished one of his daughter's handmaidens for letting her disappear. On more than one occasion a young girl had taken several lashes of a whip because Princess Lennia had decided to go off riding, when she should have been at her studies.

Princess Lennia, third daughter to King Ramie—Grand and Exalted Ruler of the Northern Desert Lands of the Sahara, Lord and Protector of the Silene Kingdom and fourth in line for Royal Caliph of all Libya, was also her father's favorite and lately his most bothersome child with her all too often mischievous antics. She was delivered by his third wife; a beautiful prize who had come to him from the Berbers as a token sign of friendship. For the Berbers often sailed by Silene's shoreline and were sometimes in need of safe harbor when winter storms broke upon the coast, or when an Egyptian fleet or an English ship was too close for comfort. Petite in stature and as beautiful and wild as a dark evening summer storm approaching the coastline, Princess Lennia's long black hair was held together in a single braid by three golden rings; given to her by her mother on her sixth birthday. Each ring was engraved with the writings of the Berbers and it was even rumored the gold had come from the treasures of the Great Alexander. Unlike her sisters, whose eyes were of a dark brown color, Princess Lennia's eyes were of radiant blue, a trait passed down to her from her Berber heritage. Her skin was soft and of a light golden-brown color. She preferred to dress in gowns of shimmering white and to these she added lightweight veils of golden and silver fabric intertwined—to entice, but not to reveal her hidden beauty.

Indeed, King Ramie loved all his daughters equally and had hoped to one day marry all of them off to rich princes or at least wealthy tradesmen, but unfortunately, Silene was a poor kingdom. A once grand city of ancient times, its great harbors filled with ships laden with the rich cargos of the East, it was now plagued by disease and pestilence, not to mention the presence of a foul hellish creature of gigantic size. A beast which had long held Silene hostage in a curse that kept proper suitors away and even worse, re-routed the land trade routes from Egypt to Tripoli away from Silene and deeper into Libya.

The coming of the creature and its parents was passed down through the ages by word of mouth and only recently, by the occasional written word. It spoke of how Silene's great lake had once been part of a wide natural harbor, which spread into the southern waters of the Mediterranean Sea. This waterway had not only allowed ship captains of ancient times to safely bring their vessels off a stormy sea to unload their goods at Silene's busy docks, but also a safe refuge from raiders during long voyages. But somewhere in times of long ago, a great cataclysm caused the earth to rise-up and form a narrow stretch of landmass, separating the ocean and the harbor. This event had formed a large saltwater lake near Silene. It was in this lake that two of these great sea creatures had suddenly appeared and became trapped, never again to return to their ocean home. From that day on, the people of Silene lived in utter terror as the dragons—as they came to be called—preyed upon the locals for their nourishment.

As time passed, only one great dragon remained, a baby, which had grown to be even larger than the others. All alone, it had become vicious and struck out against the people of Silene at any opportunity, as if blaming them for its parent's deaths. No one knew how long these creatures could live, but this final dragon had been occupying this lake for over 100-years.

The people prayed to their various gods for deliverance from this evil and when this didn't work, they then pleaded to the various kings and caliphs for help. But all to no avail. Bounty was offered and many a great knight went forth, only to end their valiant quest in a violent death.

Silene sent its armies of men-at-arms against this creature, but all failed as they fell before the dragon's monstrous strength. Its thick leathery hide deflected arrow, spear and lance, and a gaping mouth filled with sharp teeth terrified even the bravest of men and sent their horses into flight. Volunteers would man boats of war, armed with every weapon available, only to be sunk and the crew members never seen again.

Now not a single boat would venture out upon the lake, for the others that had tried, even staying close to the shorelines, were tossed about the beaches as shipwrecks, their hulls crushed, and their crews now marked as missing and presumed dead. Fear of being sucked down and devoured by this heinousness and foul monstrosity curtailed any use of the lake and Silene's fishing trade was moved west to the newer docks built closer to Tripoli. Sadly, all taxes for the use of these docks went to the Grand Caliph in Tripoli and leaving none for the King of Silene.

Years ago, Brother Samuel stumbled upon Greek records in the castle's library that spoke of such monsters having lived in the great ocean to the north and how they traveled in great numbers to prey upon smaller sea creatures. These ancient scrolls spoke of how the largest of these animals could rise out of the waters with necks reaching to the tops of a ship's main mast; their blackened mouths filled with sharp teeth the length of a two-handed sword and two large glistening eyes that reportedly could turn a man into stone. These simple records spoke of how a single creature could sink a boat in mere moments and devour the terrified crew. The dragon had four great flippers, two on each side in the place of legs, which were longer then the tallest of men. These fins allowed it to swim faster than the fastest fish or boat and drag itself up from the waters to sun bathe upon the beaches and feed upon its captured prey.

When hungry, it made short work out of a small herd of 20-sacrificial sheep or a single virgin tied by heavy chain to a large sacrificial rock now deeply stained a crimson color from a hundred years of blood; all to temper the creature's anger and protect the kingdom. This sacrificial offering was a practice Brother Samuel utterly detested and he had tried to stop for many years, but without success as these twice a month meals continued; an abomination to be sure, but one that seemed to keep the creature from coming ashore to destroy the City of Silene. This sacrifice and the lottery that was conducted to select the next victim was one of the duties carried out by the Royal Family of Silene. Truly a duty the King wished he could stop, but he saw no way to of ending this hideous practice.

There was of course a prophecy, but here in the ancient lands there was always a prophecy. North Africa was a land of fulfilled and unfulfilled prophecies dating back to the times of Joseph and the saving of Egypt during its seven years of severe drought. This prophecy told of how a brave knight would suddenly appear from the east to save a beautiful princess and slay the dragon, which would free the people of Silene of the curse. But the king had seen so many prophecies unfulfilled and he put little faith into this one.

## THE ROYAL FAMILY OF SILENE

Every day following afternoon prayers, Princess Lennia was scheduled to meet with Brother Samuel in the king's library for her lessons on language, geography, math and religious studies. Although a devout Muslim, King Ramie was concerned with the gradual return of Christianity to parts of Northern Africa and had ordered his youngest daughter to learn these Christian ways from Brother Samuel, so she may advise her father in the years ahead. For as in long ago, Christians were pounding at the doors of Libya and other parts of North Africa in their drive east toward Jerusalem, and King Ramie wanted to prepare for the future. Two great crusades had come to the Holy Land and there was talk of a third one coming east. With great ships passing by the shores of Libya on their journey east, King Ramie knew crusaders would soon contact his people and he wanted to be prepared for these knights, who reportedly carried great shields of white marked with a large red cross to honor their Lord. He had also heard of atrocities, but none witnessed by his people and he was concerned such rumors might be started by religious fanatics hoping to maintain a wide division between the faiths.

King Ramie was rapidly approaching his 68th birthday and knew his years upon this earth were coming to a-close. He feared for his people since he had no male heir to pass on his royal title. Unless his daughters married, civil war could very well tear his country apart as various tribal chieftains would rise-up and fight for control of his small kingdom. For though somewhat of a roly-poly character of medium height, with balding black hair and a long flowing beard tipped with gray, the king was sincerely loved by most of his people. Truly, there were those who had lost their daughters to the lottery who often turned their backs when one of the royal family members rode by, but he ordered no action to be taken for these signs of disrespect. For the King truly understood their grief and bitterness. But the king worked hard to make life as easy as possible for his kingdom and sincerely wished he could stay alive long enough to see one of his daughters wed.

He had inherited his throne at the young age of 12-years old. His father died at the age of 54-years when he fell from a horse during a hunt and from his father's freak accident, King Ramie became afraid of horses and seldom left the castle. Unless by wagon or atop a well-trained camel. King Ramie was also a bit of a superstitious fellow but struggled with his inner demons to remain open-minded enough to ideas that could make his kingdom more prosperous. For his wealth was limited and with the mysterious death of his third wife, he was now left with only his three daughters; two of whom were not nearly as beautiful or gentle spirited as his beloved Princess Lennia.

The king's second daughter was Princess Lannia, an unattractive 19-year old, who was quite the tomboy. She was dark chocolate in color like her Nubian mother and of a muscular build from her many hours of hard riding and swinging a sword. She wore her black hair cut short like a man, rarely wore a veil, and always carried a golden and jeweled short sword at her side. Away from the castle and riding with a loyal company of warriors, she wore a breastplate of bronze armor over her royal blue silken garments. She enjoyed hunting the desert wildlife and had taken down a lioness with a spear at the age of 16-years old. The king had also heard rumors that she had gone so far as to take a female lover, the daughter of a camel herder, and this infuriated the king to the point of demanding her arrest. But then he canceled that order, knowing such a charge would quickly bring her death. A cleric from Tripoli had heard of her sinful activities and arrived in Silene to seek her death for such behavior, but the king wouldn't listen to him and ordered his daughter into the deepest part of the Sahara Desert for a time. Being fourth in line for Caliph, he wasn't too concerned with gaining the title and rarely took notice of over-zealous clerics who wanted his daughter's head.

Princess Lannia's mother had been the king's favorite concubine, one soon elevated to the position, if not title, of wife after Princess Lannia's birth. Sadly, soon afterward the woman died suddenly from suspected food poisoning. As Princess Lannia grew she learned to greatly dislike the royal court's intrigue and politics, and often rode out into the Great Sahara with a company of loyal cavalry assigned the task of protecting Silene's and Libya's southern border from possible invasion. The King felt this best, but he did love his second daughter and deeply missed her.

Oldest of the daughters was 23-year old Princess Lonnia, who was also the tallest of the three girls and sadly, the least attractive due to a tragic accident. At the young age of 15-years old she suffered a fall, down one of the stone stairwells and sustained a fractured jaw, broken nose and a crack to the left eye socket. She healed, but the bones never mended quite right, which left her with the knowledge she would never be able to use beauty to gain a suitable suitor. All too soon she became the victim of many a nasty joke, mostly from the boys her own age and their girlfriends. From this she learned to hate, a hate born from hurt and then revenge. She avoided all attempts of warmth from her father, or her youngest sister. Grief and a hardened heart of stone drove her to study the cloaked arts of alchemy, treachery, lies and deceit-- weapons to strike out against her adversaries. Jokes between friends eventually turned to fear, as she learned how to pit one friend against another to gain what she wanted and later, the useful concoction of various potions and poisons gave her a suitable outcome. These she was taught by an ancient crone, a slave woman from Egypt, who, when the princess turned 19, was later found dead outside the castle walls. The slave's neck was clearly broken, and some believed it to be a result of the fall, but there were others in the castle who believed Princess Lonnia had done away with the slave woman during one of her bouts of rage. An extremely jealous woman, Princess Lonnia greatly resented the king's affection for her stepmothers and the arrival of her youngest sister. She gave no thought to Princess Lannia, who would rather play soldier and seemed to prefer women lovers, and truthfully, the middle sister frightened Princess Lonnia and she was happy to have her absent for long periods of time.

There was also quite a bit of talk that it was she, Princess Lonnia, who poisoned the king's second wife; infuriated over a Nubian concubine being lifted-up to the position of beloved wife. Princess Lonnia's own mother had fallen overboard during rough seas while hugging the shorelines of the great Mediterranean Sea en route to Tripoli and drowned. This sad event happened when Princess Lonnia was only two-years old, which caused the princess to fear the ocean and its hidden mysteries. While making any crossings to seek out the dark treasures of Greece and elsewhere, she would remain in her cabin and never come out to look upon the waters for fear some strange force would pull her overboard and into a watery grave.

Most of Princess Lonnia's day was spent lounging about the royal chambers, reviewing court documents and being waited on hand and foot by a team of handmaidens. These were handpicked young ladies she often mistreated, and they had come to fear her. Or she'd work alone in her private laboratory on some new concoction or experiment. When she turned 18-years of age, another task befell her; she requested and was given supervision of the kingdom's infamous lottery. The man, a loyal advisor of an elderly age who had carried out these duties, was found dead in his bed. Thought to be simply his age, unbeknownst to the king, Princess Lonnia had done away with the man with one of her special poisons placed in his pillows. She wanted this lottery to be hers, a way of seeking vengeance on those people who had scorned and ridiculed her over the years.

Here in Silene, every two weeks a young virgin was chosen by a special drawing for sacrifice. The names of young girls, ages 13 through 21, unmarried and virgin, were placed in a wooden chest. From here, Princess Lonnia would supposedly pull out a name of the next victim in the presence of her handmaidens. Immediately afterward, the chosen one would be removed from her family under the close watch of Royal Guardsmen and quickly taken to the castle for an audience with the king. Afterward, she would have a time to pray, to prepare herself for the terrible fate awaiting her. In the event the young lady chose to refuse this honor, the law decreed the entire family could be put to the sword on the spot or taken to the dungeon and never to be seen again.

In return for their loss of their daughter, the family was provided with a small bag of ten-gold pieces and the knowledge their loss of a loved one had saved the City of Silene for another two weeks. Unfortunately, the City of Silene was beginning to run low on virgins and King Ramie was gravely concerned. Four-years prior, a similar problem arose and the Silene Royal Guard, under the command of Captain Rynarr, had conducted a series of raids into Western Egypt. They brought back with them more than 50-young ladies. Those had all been sacrificed and once again they had to pick young girls from their own city. Unfortunately, the border with Egypt was closed, now patrolled by Egyptian cavalry and they were refused access to the west by the ruling Royal Caliph of Tripoli. All though he understood the plight of Silene, the Caliph didn't want to risk open war between his kingdoms. But as in years past, he had ordered dozens of young female slaves be transported by caravan to Silene, until the people of Tripoli grew weary of this and requested the Caliph cease such offerings.

There was a belief amongst the people of Tripoli who felt the Kingdom of Silene should be abandoned, the cursed people enslaved, and the castle left to crumble under the desert sun and the harsh ocean winds. But the Caliph had remained steadfast in his support of King Ramie, yet his patience was waning and now he had this troublesome Imam to deal with.

In past years, several families had taken their pleas before Brother Samuel to intercede, but without success on his part to overturn a longstanding royal decree. Although a monk of the Christian faith, he had come to be respected for his great knowledge and his love for the local people. But Brother Samuel could not save them, though he tried every time an intended sacrificial victim appeared before the king. He would make his case before the king, who would sit upon his throne and simply lower his eyes in shame. But from her royal seat beside him, a black-hearted Princess Lonnia would honor her assigned office and hold her father to accountability by noble decree that set the lottery in place long ago and could not be revoked. Only the death of the dragon by any means could remove the curse and stop the lottery.

So once again another terrified victim was delivered to the lakeshore, secured by chain to the huge blood-stained rock to await her horrid death. A man with a mission, Brother Samuel had attempted several times to slay the dragon himself with his various inventions, but none of his newly devised weapons could pierce the thick bluish hide of the dragon. Worse, in the process dozens of volunteers had lost their lives in the attempts. Also, whenever the dragon felt endangered, it would simply slide back into the great lake and vanish beneath the waters.

Finally, in fear of losing too many combat troops or the loyalty of his frightened men, King Ramie ordered Brother Samuel to cease further attempts at killing the monster. This caused Brother Samuel to take refuge in the depths of the castle in deep despair, until Princess Lennia located him and coaxed him out. She loved the old man and in time could bring him out of his depression, but he would continue to debate with King Ramie and Princess Lonnia over these sacrifices. At least now he had an older Princess Lennia fighting in his corner and a king who was losing patience with the ever-growing darkness of his oldest girl.

## BROTHER SAMUEL

Forty-two-years ago, a very water-logged Brother Samuel was found lying unconscious along the shallow tidewaters on Silene's vast ocean shoreline. He was strangely attired; all dressed in tan colored garments of a strange weave, secured in the middle by a narrow belt and wearing strange footwear never seen before. Once awakened, he spoke in a foreign tongue that baffled his rescuers and began to behave in a crazy fashion as he struggled with the very people who had saved him. Twice, he made attempts to return to the ocean and injured himself in the process by tripping over large rocks and banging his head. When mounted-knights arrived, he lost all reason and finally made the mistake of assaulting a king's warrior. Placed in chains, he was drug behind a warrior's horse for a long painstaking trip to the castle dungeon.

Here in this dark and foul-smelling hell, fighting off large rats, daily torture and bouts of dysentery, he surprised everyone by surviving three long years. While doing so, he slowly learned the local language from fellow prisoners. This included a Greek sailor who taught Brother Samuel to speak and even write the Greek language.

Eventually, two burly guardsmen dragged him before numerous members of the royal court for examination and much later he was brought before the king's two chief royal advisors. During these encounters, his extraordinary intelligence in engineering became known. Soon after, he appeared before the king. While in the dungeon, Brother Samuel had taken notice of the ancient Roman and Greek style plumbing; stone aqueducts carried water from a large water tank on the castle's upper level to transport refuse and drinking water throughout the castle's water closets and kitchen, and down into the lower levels. Here, slaves had taken the solid refuse and would turn it into fertilizer for the farm lands and liquids were carried along a narrow pipeline into the sea. But the aqueducts had fallen apart, and no one refilled the great tank on the castle's roof. Brother Samuel had shown the jailers and then members of the court how the ancient indoor plumbing of the castle could be repaired and once more provide services to the castle again. He then shared this plan with the king and a work party of 150-slaves was given to him and repairs began shortly afterward. Twice daily a detail of men and slaves went to the nearest fountain and filled the many barrels needed to fill the newly constructed water tanks on the roof and the occupants of the castle were quite grateful to Brother Samuel. He was removed from the dungeon and over time, he and was allowed-to tell his story of how he had come to their shores. He spoke of how he was a man brought up in Ireland, a peaceful country west of Britain, and raised in the Christian faith. When showing a startling intelligence for one so young, an elderly priest took him from his mother at the young age of six-years old and trained up in the ways of the church. He became a monk at the young age of 16-years old and was later sent to the Holy Land with the Pope's first crusade. But, he was ordered to return to Britain when the Second Crusade was unable to secure Jerusalem from the Muslims. He also added how his superiors found him to be in disfavor with the church and recommended him to be defrocked by the Pope for his despicable and blasphemous acts in helping the Muslim people.

In his story, he told of how he had befriended many Muslims during his journey to the Holy Land and while traveling, he attempted to study some of the Muslim practices to educate himself further in their ways to draw him closer to the people. During these travels, he found many of these people to be in dire need, some of them tortured by Christian knights, and offered them aide. Often, these were innocent men, women and children. Such action on his part would not be tolerated by the Christian clerics and he was sent home in shame. But while sailing through the Mediterranean Sea and off the shores of Libya, pirates attacked his ship and as a prisoner, he was later thrown overboard to drown. While in a private meeting, he told the king that for his many acts and good deeds he had shown the Muslim people, God's mercy and grace had allowed him to survive the watery grave and he had washed up on the shores of Silene.

Taking an instant liking to this man and seeing his high level of intelligence from his statements and drawings for plans of the castle's plumbing, he allowed Brother Samuel to move about the castle freely to offer advice. A much older King Ramie would later designate him a royal teacher for his daughters and provide room for him in the upper levels of the castle. Over the years though, the Muslim king and the Christian monk had become close friends and played many a game of chess to test their wits against one another. Brother Samuel's later inventions had accomplished much to benefit King Ramie's kingdom and the king was extremely grateful.

But a wary Brother Samuel carried a dark secret behind those joyous and intelligent eyes. Had the king ever learned the truth about who Brother Samuel actually was; how he had arrived in Silene, King Ramie would've had no choice but to have him executed as a devilish fiend from Hell. Brother Samuel had kept this bizarre secret to himself for a long time--that is until three strangely attired foreigners had showed up in Silene.

## INSIDE THE CAVE-WAS IT STILL 1968?

Benefited by their newly issued flak-vests and Korean War era steel helmets, Corporal Paul Grant and PFC Hughes survived the avalanche of rocks and debris and gradually, but painfully, regained consciousness. Both men were startled to find themselves so bruised and battered, coughing up mouthfuls of cave dust and wiping the grit and grime from their bloodshot eyes. Their initial actions were to pull out canteens and clean out their mouths and once able to breathe freely, they crawled about on all fours for several moments in the dark until they located one of their flashlights on the cave floor. Grant's flashlight lens ended up broken, shattered by a large rock. But Hughes' flashlight worked, and they used his light to find the rest of their equipment scattered about the cavern floor. Grant made sure to remove his flashlight batteries before helping Hughes with the search and then promptly slammed the flashlight against the cave wall in his frustration. He hated having to rely on anyone, especially this young PFC. But he wasn't going to take Hughes' flashlight away from him, even though he out ranked the man. Grant believed it was his own fault for not taking better care of his own equipment and besides, he believed they'd be outside the cave soon.

"Wonder where Corporal Sanders is?" Hughes asked. He aimed the flashlight beam around the cave but couldn't spot GW.

"Don't know, but he's got to be around here somewhere..." Grant then hesitated.

"What?" Hughes asked loudly, his voice displaying his frustration over the events of the last few days, the recent disaster and now being in this dreadful cave.

"Look at my rifle!" Grant exclaimed. He was knelt-down, now holding his M-16 up to show a twisted rifle barrel and broken stock. This was a first for him, he'd never seen a rifle barrow twisted like this before and couldn't understand what could have caused it. There were no rocks on top of his rifle and yet it was utterly-destroyed.

Hughes hadn't even thought of his rifle and now aimed his light about the cave in search of his and soon located his rifle lying on the cave floor. He was stunned to see how similar damage was done to his own M-16; the barrel mouth was smashed together, as if done by a powerful vice, the handgrip busted off and the stock completely shattered.

"Damn Mickey Mouse toys!" Grant shouted. "They're useless!" His loud voice resounded off the walls of the cave and echoed down a small narrowing shaft.

"Let's find Sanders," Hughes suggested. "He's got to be here somewhere." Using the flashlight, Hughes cautiously moved about the cave until he finally located GW's body lying in a far-off corner of the cavern. He was alive, but unconscious and his legs were covered in a pile of dirt and rock. GW was also bleeding from the mouth and his right ear, which at first caused Hughes to believe GW, had suffered some internal injuries.

"Found him!" Hughes yelled out. Sidestepping several larger boulders and leaping over smaller ones, Hughes reached GW's side and began cleaning the debris away.

Grant, first yelling at Hughes, "Hey give me some light, or I'm liable to break my neck in here," hustled over and they both began uncovering him.

"He's coming around!" Hughes said excitedly. He tossed another armful of rock to the side and discovered GW's M-16 underneath GW's right leg. The weapon had a shattered stock and a bent barrel, which now resembled a boomerang and Hughes was totally confused. He briefly wondered how much force it would take to cause such damage to the barrel and it was under GW?

"Looks like whatever happened to our rifles got his too." Hughes held up the broken M-16 for Grant to see.

"You're a big college boy, you got any idea what happened here?" Grant asked.

Hughes didn't respond verbally but shook his head and propped up a semi-conscious GW. He then handed the flashlight to Grant, pulled out his canteen and poured a few drops of water on his towel. He then commenced to wash off GW's face. While doing so and looked to Grant, "Your guess is as good as mine, Corporal, but maybe Corporal Sanders knows something. He was awake when all this apparently happened."

With audible grunt of pain, GW collapsed unconscious again and almost an hour later, slowly opened his eyes wide, surprised to find his head cradled in Grant's lap. He moistened his dry lips some with his tongue and then whispered a raspy, "You're alive?"

"Looks like it," Grant replied. He then helped GW up into a sitting position before handing him a canteen to wash the cave dust out. "Only a sip now, I'm not sure how long this water has got to last us."

"Thanks," GW replied. He washed out his mouth and spit the dirt out. He then cautiously blew his nose; somewhat afraid he might cause his head to explode in the process. He had a real-bad headache.

"What do you remember, Corporal?" Hughes asked. He'd torn open his last first aid packet, a simple kit he kept in his rucksack and began cleaning some of GW's many cuts and abrasions. He'd already taken care of the worst ones, stopping the bleeding and now he could finish the job.

"You're certainly not going to win any beauty contests for a while, but I didn't find anything major and I suspect you'll get along without any stitches," Hughes said.

GW looked about the room, while Hughes worked, which was now illuminated somewhat by Hughes' flashlight pointed to the ceiling. It was braced between two rocks, providing a dim, but suitable light for them to see by. But Grant kept checking over his shoulders, just knowing he was about to be attacked by a 20-pound killer bat. The cave room, clearly larger than the one they first camped in, was similar in size to a two-car garage.

Hughes told GW of the man-sized tunnel leading deeper into the mountain, "We haven't checked it out yet...We were waiting for you to come around."

"You guys fell asleep...A bit later the mother of all earthquakes hit...Don't remember much after that. Except my head and stomach feels like I've been spun around on some weird fair ride, I'm all queasy-like inside. I've had motion sickness before and I feel the same way...But, I can't explain how...I'm totally lost."

"Yah, now that you mention it, I woke up feeling dizzy," Grant said. Hughes also agreed with them, "Me too. Like a change in air pressure and one heck of a wild roller coaster ride."

"Quake must've given us a wild ride...Guess we're lucky to be alive," GW said. Then slowly, he stood up, using Hughes' shoulder for support and feeling like an old man as every part of his body cried out in complaint.

"Well, we've got no rifles, one grenade and our knives," Grant said. He displayed GW's rifle to him, which stunned the young corporal.

"My sixteen...it looks as if Superman got a hold of it and started to make a pretzel." He then asked Grant, "Do the other flashlights still work?"

"Mine is busted, but I'll check yours...once we find it." Grant dug around in dirt and after a few minutes of searching he found GW's olive-green GI issue flashlight near a large boulder by the entrance to the first cave shaft and he turned it on. It worked, and the extra illumination seemed to calm the three men.

"Mine was busted up, but I took the batteries out," Grant said. "Plus, I've got an extra set in my rucksack."

"Okay then," GW said. "Next item on the agenda is to eat something and then we'll reconnoiter, see where this OTHER tunnel goes." He then pointed to Grant, "Dust has settled, so after you eat, you check the entrance to the first cave and see if it's still open." GW pointed to Hughes, "We'll move off in the other direction for 20 to 30 feet or so." He gave his flashlight to Grant. "We'll meet back here in ten minutes."

For a few moments, they consumed a small bit of food. Concerned this would be their only food for a while, they wanted to stretch it out. They shared a can of pork slices and each took a single gulp of water to wash it down. Finished, they tossed the can aside and stood up. GW then pointed Hughes off toward the tunnel's entrance. "You're on point and I'll be right behind you, but this may be a short trip."

As the three soldiers checked out their surroundings, all of them felt a strange uneasiness from all the rock surrounding them. There were no other sounds, no breeze and only their steps upon rock debris and their few nervous whispers.

As they moved out, GW thought over what he'd learned of his two new comrades. Prior to this mission, he'd only seen them in passing and had never spoken with either of them. But he liked what he saw in their eyes and what he'd seen in their actions over the last few hours. They hadn't panicked, standing their ground when they needed to, and best of all, took his orders without giving him any lip.

At 22-years old, Grant hailed from a speck of dirt 32-miles outside West San Antonio, Texas. His mother was of mixed blood; Hispanic/White Mountain Apache and his father of a, Irish/Navajo bloodline, who could trace his roots back to early Texas Territory days. Grant's great-grandfather was a Texas Ranger, who fought the Comanche and was killed defending his homestead from northern carpetbaggers following the Civil War. Grant was of medium height, an inch under six-feet, with a broad hairy chest and a short thick neck. From years of hard work and a high school weight room, he had developed a strong muscular build and by his own admission he could dead lift 450-pounds and bench press 380-pounds; which was a school record, he told GW. From his father's Irish lineage, he inherited a square jaw with a dimple in the middle, but he also bore a rather flat nose his mother's people had passed down to him. In 1967, he graduated from high school, where in his senior year he made All-League Second Team as an offensive guard for the school's football team. Since the age of four-years old he had worked on his parent's small horse ranch, gaining some horse and cow savvy, but had grown weary of the dust and the stink of horses. So, he decided it was time to stretch his wings and see the world at the government's coin by joining the army. He knew it was only a matter of time before the draft board requested his presence and decided to make it his choice, not Uncle Sam's. Not that it mattered much. He still ended up in Vietnam. Grant dreamed of seeing Europe as his recruiter had promised; but instead, he saw the dirt of boot camp, the long hikes of Advanced Infantry School and five harrowing drops from Parachute School at Fort Benning, Georgia before receiving orders for Southeast Asia. After a 22-hour long plane ride to Vietnam, the heat and humidity sort of reminded him of home. During his R&R and not wanting to return home on leave, he lied to his parents and spent a short vacation on the beaches of Hawaii.

PFC Richard C. Hughes was the oldest of the three men, but he had waited until late in 1967 to enlist in the US Army. A city-bred 23-year old Afro-American male from the streets of San Francisco, California, he tipped the scales at 179-pounds and stretched out to a lean five-foot, ten-inches. His face was long, and his chin came to a point, but it was his eyes that were the most noticeable; they were dark gray steel in color and seemed to give the appearance of being larger than normal. GW thought he resembled one of those pouting, made-up medieval court-jesters when he was sad, which was most of the time since they came together after the attack. Like the other two fellows, Hughes had played some football in high school, but barely made the junior varsity in the tight-end position. But for him, it was the academics he favored over sports. This resulted in him receiving a two-year scholarship to a local junior college. A limited scholarship, he had to work part-time and full-time in the summers to cover the cost of books and tutoring in a couple subjects he had troubles with. But after walking the city streets for days and sitting through several interviews, he finally landed a job with the city's museum as a tour guide. His knowledge of dinosaurs, a hobby since he was old enough to pick a 25-cent dinosaur toy up, got him a job in the museum's Natural History wing. With hopes of earning a second scholarship, Hughes studied hard at first, but his book learning suffered drastically when he fell hopelessly in love with an older woman; a staff member at the museum. Losing his scholarship and unable to continue in school, he came up with Plan B and proposed turning their relationship to the next step, only to learn she was already married and was only out for a thrill ride with him.

Brokenhearted, he fled the museum in tears and walked through the business area of San Francisco all night. Next morning, he found himself standing before an army recruiting station where a smart-looking highly decorated Army Recruiting sergeant was more than prepared to lend a sympathetic ear and offer up some career advice. Sure, Europe sounded like a great place to go. "Very educational and within six months, you'll be looking at a soft tour in Germany or maybe England," the recruiter guaranteed. But like so many others before him, he was soon on a slow plane to Vietnam's scenic wilderness.

As the other two proceeded cautiously deeper into the cave, Grant retraced their steps to where the cave entrance should have been and there he came up against a wall of solid rock. It appeared as if the cave entrance had never existed and nothing looked at all familiar. Rattled a bit by his discovery, he brought the sad news back to the other two, who were waiting for him. "We're sealed in, but it's like there was never an entrance there," Grant advised them. He then asked, "How about that way?"

"What do you mean, it's like there was no entrance there?" GW asked.

"It's like this cave here, nothing looks familiar. The room is bigger and none of the trash we tossed about as we came through is still there."

"Must've been the earthquake," Hughes suggested.

"Got to be," GW replied. He then told Grant how the tunnel continued-on. "Hiked 'bout 20-yards in and it kept going, but we needed to wait here for you."

"From what you've said, seems like our only choice is to head deeper into the mountain. Hopefully we'll find a way out in that direction," Hughes said. He then pointed the flashlight down through the narrow tunnel and added, "Not even a bat in sight."

With Hughes leading off, GW in the middle and Grant pulling tail-end Charlie, they proceeded on. For the next four-hours they stepped over rocks, avoided stalactites and stalagmites of all sizes and shapes, until GW brought them to a halt. Pulling his rucksack off his shoulders, he suggested they eat something to keep their strength up.

"Think we can build a fire?" Hughes asked. He had his rucksack off and retrieved a can of beef slices from it. Like most soldiers, he had his own P-38 can opener and made quick work of opening his dinner, "This stuff would taste a whole lot better warmed up."

"Only if you can find something to burn," GW answered.

"You'd better wait. I haven't felt any breeze and a fire might burn up some of our oxygen," Grant said. Opening his rucksack, he stirred it around as he looked for something of interest and then added, "We'd better make that chow stretch too, may be here for a long time. I sincerely doubt the Seventh Cavalry is coming to dig us out." Grant then plopped down on the cave floor and sat cross-legged with his rucksack braced behind him against a boulder and GW's flashlight pointed toward the ceiling. A bright beam hit the ceiling and it expanded outward to give off a dim light shining off the cave walls.

"You guys see any bats?" Grant asked. He pulled out a tin of crackers, hard enough to break a tooth and a second tin of peanut butter. The soldiers often joked about using these C-ration crackers for trap-shooting and debated, whether a shotgun pellet would even put a dent into one.

"Not yet," Hughes replied and then grinned at GW. "How do you feel about giant cave worms?"

Grant shot Hughes a snarled expression and a raised eyebrow, but it was lost in the dim light. "Funny guy...But we'd better use only one flashlight at a time, got to go easy with the batteries."

"Good idea...Turn yours...I mean mine off and we'll take a short rest before moving off again," GW said.

"How many extra batteries have we got?" Hughes asked. He then tipped up his can and licked up the juices as they dribbled out.

GW dug into his rucksack and pulled out an extra pair of socks. "Nope, I got no batteries. This is like only the second time I've even used a flashlight out in the field and I keep my extra batteries in my foot locker." He then took off his boots, shook the dirt out and changed his socks. One thing he'd learned in the boonies was to change his socks often to prevent trench foot and was happy he carried extra socks with him whenever he went into the field.

"I'm still hungry," Grant said. Giving in to temptation, he then dug into his rucksack for his prized can of beanie-weenies. He'd been saving this can and decided now was as good a time as ever for a treat. They all knew that beanie-weenies was one of the few C ration dinners safe enough to consume, most of the others caused digestion problems, diarrhea or simply tasted foul.

GW recalled how soldiers would sit around the camp and talk about their ideas for revenge against the people who made these C-Rations. No one ever really knew just how much Uncle Sam paid for these canned meals, which came in individual boxes to provide a full meal for each troop. But, they came to realize how Uncle Sam hated to throw anything away because the soldiers were finding cans dated back to World War II. They didn't even use grenades that old, but the government had no problem feeding the soldiers such old meals. GW glanced around at his new friends and then looked down the tunnel, wondering how far it went and if there was another way out and then decided it was time to reveal his secret. "Listen, I've got some dried water buffalo meat in my rucksack. But, I think we should use up the canned food first 'cause they're heavier and we may need the meat later...In the event we have to dig out- extra protein." He pulled his E-tool off his rucksack and stretched it out for use. He would carry it out in front of him, prepared to use it as a weapon if he needed one.

"Where in the hell did you get water buffalo meat?" Grant asked. He watched GW with the shovel, while he sloppily spooned cold beans into his mouth.

"You won't believe it..." GW went on to explain what had happened the morning they left the firebase and how the Holy Man had mysteriously appeared with his three gifts. Both men listened without saying a word, as they finished off their brief lunch and washed it down with a small mouthful of stale warm water.

"Weird," was all that Grant could say, before he wiped his mouth with the back of his sleeve and tossed the can aside. But he kept his plastic spoon and placed it in his upper left shirt pocket.

"I've heard about these mountain holy men," Hughes said. He then sniffed his neck towel, was revolted by it and then shrugged as he draped it around his neck. He knew he might need it if his eyes were filled with cave dust again. He then pulled his filthy rucksack back over his shoulders and leaned back against the cave wall. "They're similar-to American Indian shamans or what you probably know as medicine men. Though I think most of it all sounds like voodoo to me," Hughes said. The handcrafted leather bag got his attention and he asked, "You think the meat might be poison?"

Suspicious, Grant's eyes grew cold and that one eyebrow he liked to use to heighten his expressions rose. "I've heard that some of those Montegnard people aren't all that crazy about us."

"Look, I had a couple bites before that last attack and I'm still here and no GI's...okay?" GW replied.

"Well, holy man or not, we've got to check out the rest of this cave and see where it goes. These walls are beginning to close in and I'm in need of some fresh air." Grant slung his rucksack over his shoulders and grabbed up his shovel, which he extended to full length. "I'll take point."

"Should we leave the ammo?" Hughes asked.

"Just extra weight," Grant said. "Our rifles are no good anymore and I doubt we'll find any weapons down here...Unless it's an AK-47 with a NVA holding it."

GW had tossed out anything he wouldn't need from his rucksack and was carrying it slung over his left shoulder. He only hoped that if they encountered any cave beasties, his shovel was equal to the task. He didn't admit it, but he didn't like bats either and he wished Hughes hadn't said anything about giant cave worms.

Hughes let out a deep audible sigh and stood up. After he slipped his rucksack over his shoulders, he followed the others down the long dark cavern with his own shovel ready for action. Being last in line, he was always turning around to make sure nothing was sneaking up behind him. He'd flash his light off and on, but there was absolutely no sound except for what they made as they proceeded deeper into the mountain. For more than an hour they traveled through the perilous passageway, ducking under low ceilings and climbing over large boulders that blocked their path. It was decided between them that they would take a ten-minute break every hour and drink a mouthful of water during their fourth break in hopes of stretching out their meager water supply. GW had told them about the odor of sulfur and hot wind before the great quake, which now seemed strange because the temperature gradually turned cooler as they traveled through the stone corridor. Occasionally, they came upon dried roots sticking out from the ceiling and these they broke off and carried them along in their packs for fire tinder. Later, these were used for small fires that helped them keep warm and cooked their remaining C-ration meals. Hughes also grabbed up several handfuls of dried-out undergrowth they discovered on the cave floor, shoving these into his rucksack for possible torches. They all knew the batteries would only last so long and they were beginning to think they'd be using torches all too soon. As they made their way, each man taking his turn at point or rear-guard, but it was more the utter silence in this strange dark underworld, than the surrounding darkness, that kept the men on edge. They heard no insects or any animal life, no sound of running water and this unsettled them, wearing on their nerves. By the end of the first long day, the stress was already draining away their life's energy.

Banking to the right and then the left, the narrow passage continued. Hughes said it was like the tunnel was made by one of his giant cave worms on acid and he got a thump to the chest from Grant in response. "Told you, no more worm jokes...got it?"

"Sure...sure, sorry. I was only trying to ease things up," Hughes said.

"Oh, I'm eased up," Grant said in response. "But this place is really closing in on me."

At one point the passageway opened into a massive room the size of a school auditorium, with stone balconies scattered about and several deep bottomless-like holes. Hughes dropped a rock down one and they never did hear it strike bottom. They quickly backed away from it. The roof displayed hundreds of stalagmites of various lengths, some even reaching the cave floor. They were soon in a near impassible maze of stalactites. Here, they needed their shovels, which they swung like pickaxes to clear a path through the stone forest. They broke these rock formations off, using their towels to wrap around their mouths and noses, and this laboring chore wore them out. Breaks became more frequent, while their canteens became lighter. Still, this seemingly endless passageway allowed the three soldiers to amble on in hopes of finding a way out. GW said he believed this stone corridor to be an ancient lava tube for a long extinct volcano. Hughes agreed with him, but he'd already had that idea and the others didn't remember how he eventually mentioned it that first day. GW and Hughes knew nothing of South Vietnam's geological plates or if there were any extinct volcanoes in Vietnam, but it helped them pass the time. GW recalled a book he once read in high school; Journey to the Center of the Earth by Jules Verne. This was also a story Hughes knew, who helped GW tell the story's basics to Grant during a break.

"Well, I don't mind telling you all I wouldn't mind finding those jewels or those giant mushrooms, but all those monsters are another story," Grant said.

"I don't think those monsters would even fit in here, besides there is nothing for them to eat in here if they did," GW replied.

"There's us!" Grant exclaimed.

"It's only a work of fiction," Hughes added. With a hand over his face he struggled to stifle a laugh at his friend's expense.

"Isn't this Verne-dude the guy who wrote 20,000 Leagues Under the Sea?" Grant asked.

"Right, Walt Disney made that movie out of it with Kirk Douglas and James Mason," GW said as he stepped over a large boulder. He didn't know what kind of rock this was, but he wondered if there was any gold or silver down here?

"Okay, so this guy wrote all about submarines long before they had any. So, maybe he knows something about monsters too," Grant said. He then added, "Course, I sure don't expect to find any giant squids or other sea monsters down here."

"You have a real imagination, buddy," Hughes stated in a matter-of fact way, and then laughed. He couldn't help it, the stress of the last couple of days had worn him out and his only response was to break into loud laughter.

"What are you laughing at?" GW asked in a tone mixed with contempt and disbelief.

"No offense, Corporal," Hughes said. "But this whole situation…with us. Everything! I mean we're down here spelunking in this cave in some South Vietnam mountain and no one even knows if we're alive or dead. I can't help it."

"Well quit making so much noise," GW ordered. "No telling what's up ahead of us and I'd rather not give them or it too much of a warning." GW shook his head and reached back to slap Hughes on the shoulder in a friendly way and got him moving again.

They tended to agree with each other at the next rest stop, in how they were traveling along a level plain. At no time did the three men feel they were traveling on a downward slant into the earth or climbing uphill. Grant had voiced the opinion that their route was possibly taking them through the width of a mountain range, which bordered the A Shau Valley. He was hopeful the passageway would lead them to an exit far away from the enemy. Hughes nodded his head in agreement and GW simply, who hoped they were both right, let out a soft sigh and muttered, "Well probably end up in Laos."

Using their watches to go by, they would stop as close to midnight as possible when they found themselves in a clearing with enough room to take an eight-hour rest. Seeing no reason to post a guard as they hadn't found any sign of the enemy or meet up with any nightmarish-like cave creatures, they built small fires from the dried roots they found and promptly fell asleep together with their thin poncho liners to cover them. As an added precaution, Grant set up trip wire at each end of the tunnel. He had no trip flares but figured who or what they tripped would make enough noise to wake them up. After so many long hours of travel through the perilous passageways and bypassing many dangerous obstacles, GW was bone tired and his snoring grew loud from weariness and echoed throughout the cavern. If there had been any cave creatures, Grant thought GW's strange monstrous sounds would have chased them off as it resounded off the cave walls. He thought the noise was reminiscent to the howl of an Irish Banshee he'd heard in a movie.

For three days, they made their way, stopping more often now and a few times their tempers lashed out at each other in verbal dispute. More than once, one of them exploded and struck the rock walls with his shovel in a fit of frustration. This was partially caused by fear of the unknown and growing fatigue, and now they were down to the simple torches Hughes had put together with tinder and dried roots.

During the middle of their fourth day, they had a silent lunch of dried buffalo meat and they each thought ahead to yet, another long, 12-hours of brutal travel.

GW broke the eerie silence, "Either of you got any idea why our rifles were bent up and nothing else? I mean our shovels are fine and we have our knives."

"Nope," Grant replied between bites.

"Not me," Hughes added. His voice was raspy from a dry throat.

"Okay," GW said. He then returned his attention to his dinner, or was it breakfast?

They'd lost track of what day it was and whether it was evening or daytime. Their watches only gave them the minutes and hours, and along the way they had forgotten what day it might be.

Yesterday, an imaginative Hughes made the announcement he'd named their subterranean kingdom Moria, "It's in reference to J.R. Tolkien's book, 'Lord of the Rings', one of my favorites."

"Okay by me," Grant said. His throat was dry too, they only had a few pitiful drops of water left and we're rationing it to a sip every eight hours, along with a bite or two of buffalo meat.

They hoped to make both the meat and the water last as long as possible and GW realized if not for the meat to keep them going, they might have easily given up and simply plopped down on their backsides to starve to death. Whenever he thought of that, he recalled the little old man and wondered what importance those other two items might be? Still, they continued, each man wondering when the passageway might end, around the next corner to where a sudden bottomless drop-off awaited them, or would they come upon a solid wall blocking their way?

His hands beginning to grow raw from all the rock, GW stopped and dropped his rucksack. He had an idea. Retrieving a pair of dirty sock, he pulled them over his hands to make them mittens and offer some form of protection from all the sharp stony edges. Seeing what he was doing, the other two men followed suit. At times their grips on their flashlights and shovels became slippery, but it was better than all the skin abrasions they had received along the passageway.

"Good idea, Corporal," Hughes said. "Too bad we didn't have any of those gloves the helicopter pilots have. The door gunners wear them too."

"We ever get out of here, I'm going to get a pair and keep them in my rucksack...If, in the event I ever find myself back in some dang cave again," Grant said. He struck the cave wall with his shovel in anger. "I really hate this place!"

They continued for another couple hundred yards, but as the time approached 12 o'clock on their watches, with canteens now empty, their mouths dry and the supply of buffalo meat gone, the passageway suddenly widened out to a room the size of a basketball court. Within moments they soon realized the room ended abruptly. There were no passageways leading off in any other direction but the one they came through. Dejected, the three weary men stood silently before a sheer rock wall with their hopes crushed.

"Well, this has really been fun," Grant said. Dry-mouthed, his voice was raspy and not knowing what else to do, he dropped to his knees and stared at the filthy socks on his hands. His face and arms were grimy with sweat and cave dust, his t-shirt now the color of the cave floor and his hair moist in sweat and dust. He was carrying a shovel filled with burning tinder, having used up the last of the torches and only a couple handfuls of tinder left to light their way.

Pulling off his rucksack, GW simply dropped it to the ground and leaned up against a chest high sized-boulder. With closed eyes, he slowly shook his head in defeat and was surprised he had enough moisture left in his body to produce a tear. Then, without saying a word, he took off his helmet and threw it hard up against the wall of rock, and watched it bounce off in the extremely dim torchlight. Their eyes had grown accustomed to the dim light, but very soon they would be in utter darkness and this frightened all three of them. Being blind could mean falling into a hole and having talked about it earlier, they all had the same idea that starving to death would be preferable to dropping down some bottomless pit.

"Well..." Grant hesitated and then made a stupid suggestion of, "We could knock each other over the head or maybe slit each other's wrists."

"You're an idiot!" GW said in a raised voice. "I didn't come this far to have my bones rot in some stinkin' cave."

"So, you got a better idea?" Grant waved around the room and yelled, "Looks like to me we're stuck here in some strange Hell...We're out of water and we're out of food...And beginnin' to wish I'd stayed behind and just gone down fighting with our buddies."

"No!" Hughes yelled. "It can't end here." He got between Grant and GW, glared at both, and in a plea-like voice, said, "We've come too far. We've survived so much...it simply can't end here." Hughes then looked up, listening as the echoes of his outburst carried back through the tunnel. In his anger, he tossed his shovel aside and began pounding against the opposing wall with his fists. "No! No! No-o-o!" He shouted over and over until GW grabbed him by the shoulders and hugged him close to his chest.

"We're not dead, yet." GW said in a whisper as a weary Hughes burst into tears.

As the tinder's faint illumination begin to dim further, Grant hurriedly laid another handful of dried plants on and blew on the embers before darkness could enclose them all.

"Wait a minute!" GW yelled. He'd noticed something in the upper wall, a small light or was it his imagination? "I think there's some kind of light shining up above. Let the fire die and you'll see it too." GW pointed to a spot on the rock wall and waited for Grant to extinguish the torch.

"Mister, ah sure hope you're right," Hughes said as he rubbed his tired eyes with grimy palms.

Grant cautiously withdrew some of the unlit material from the blade of his shovel and as the remaining embers cooled, the men watched with rising hopes as the cave brightened with barely enough light for them to see some difference in the darkness. It was not much light, not enough to write a letter or read a book by, but enough for them to know there was daylight streaming through a small crack or hole the size of a silver dollar. GW estimated the opening to be close to 15 or 16 feet above them and began to look around for something to use in the place of a step-ladder.

The opening gave these men a surge of renewed hope and not waiting for the others, GW climbed up on one large boulder, which lay snug up against the wall and then jumped to another rocky outcropping sticking out from the face. After nearly losing his balance while standing on one foot, he made another leap, which landed him on a single rock sticking out nearly a foot and closer to where he was within an outstretched hand of the hole.

Ignoring the applause and shouts from below, he felt around the rock face and discovered the top of the wall wasn't solid rock but quite possibly fill dirt from a previous avalanche. "There's dirt up here!" He shouted down to his friends. "I think we might have an easier time digging through if Grant's grenade has enough firepower to enlarge the hole."

"Too bad we left all our ammo behind, with the added gun powder we would've had a bigger bang," Hughes said.

"You want to go back for it?" Grant asked sarcastically.

"No!" Hughes replied bitterly.

"Sorry," Grant apologized. "I guess we're all on edge, so let's back it down a notch." He then knelt over to dig into his rucksack for his lone fragmentation grenade.

"Any idea what's on the other side?" Hughes asked.

GW glared down at him, how am I supposed to know what's on the other side, but then remembered Hughes was on the fragile edge of sanity and gave it his best shot, "Probably more jungle, hopefully less North Vietnamese, but it's gotta be better than this place."

"Yeah, we've got to have water soon or we'll die," Grant said. He began to carefully climb the boulder with the grenade clipped to his combat suspenders. He would then hand it off to GW with a cautious lob. There wasn't enough room on the outcropping for two men to stand, but he would ensure the pin was still in place before he tossed it up to GW.

By this time, the men had already taken their fatigue shirts off, but wore their suspenders over their soiled t-shirts. The suspenders were connected to their canteen belts, which now held empty canteens, empty pouches and their bayonets. No one wanted to get rid of a canteen, in the event they came across an underground stream--which they had not.

"Bring a shovel up with you. I'll dig it out some before placing the grenade. But you two had better find a safe place." GW warned them. "Rock splinters, shrapnel and dirt are gonna be flying everywhere."

"You've got three-seconds, so make like Flash an' get out of there fast," Grant reminded GW.

After handing off the shovel and then the grenade, Grant and Hughes began moving deeper back into the darkened passageway. Without light, now that GW was blocking what little illumination they had as he worked with the shovel they scraped their legs against the rocks. Hughes tripped over GW's rucksack, but caught himself before smacking into a good size boulder with his face. But neither of them seemed to care about minor injuries, all their thoughts were on escaping this nightmare and nothing else seemed to matter.

Ever cautious with the grenade now snapped to his suspenders, GW used the shovel, locked into position of a pickaxe, to dig out a small depression in the wall for a foothold big enough for his size 13 double E boots to fit into. This allowed him to climb up closer to the hole and dig out a space around the hole large enough to place the grenade. He then stopped for moment, confused somewhat when he suddenly realized he was picking up a strange odor coming through the hole and he knew it wasn't possible. "Hey, I can swear I smell the ocean!" GW shouted to his friends.

"Ocean?" Grant questioned. "You're crazy! We're too far away from any ocean."

GW had to agree with him. However, this smell was from a salt-water source of some kind and it didn't make any sense to him. They landed in the A Shau Valley, which meant they were at least 200-miles or more from the Gulf of Tonkin, and in the last six days, if it was only six days, he knew they sure hadn't hiked no 200-miles; not that it didn't feel like they had since his whole body was one big bruise. Besides, by his estimation, they'd been walking northwest, not east or south which was in the opposite direction from the nearest ocean.

Ignoring the scent of salt air for the moment, he finished his work and tossed his shovel to the cave floor, hoping to keep it clear from the blast range. He knew he would need it again. A quick glance about the room, helped by more light, he got into the room with his digging, he soon spotted a large squared-off boulder close by. A rock big enough to cover him and hopefully close enough he could reach in the three to five seconds the grenade's safety provided before detonation. He sincerely hoped this grenade was not a dud, nor that it detonated too early. Government issue...Anything was possible! It's always the lowest bidder for these government contracts. Just makes a guy feel all fuzzy inside in how the government looks out for his fighting men.

"Say a prayer, cross your fingers or whatever you guys do for luck," GW shouted and then added, "Here we go!"

Holding the grenade with his left hand, he yanked out the pin with his right and then GW slipped the grenade into the depression. He then dropped two feet to the near-by rock, took another short jump and then nearly a ten-foot drop to the floor below. He used an airborne roll from parachute training and jumped to his feet. He raced for the chosen boulder and was barely behind it when the grenade exploded, showering the cavern with rock debris, thick clouds dirt and dust.

"Did it work?" Grant shouted out, as he poked his head out from behind Hughes.

"I can't see anything, yet. We'll have to wait for the dust to settle," GW replied. Leaning against the boulder, he cautiously stepped out and waved a cloud of dust away from his face. "But it seems to be lighter in here though."

In a few moments, they saw how the hole had enlarged quite a bit, now nearly two-foot by two-foot in size and enough of the dirt wall gone to show them their escape tunnel was going to be better than four feet long and they had a lot of digging ahead of them. Beautiful rays of sunlight filled the cave now, making it easy for the three men to see by and giving them an additional burst of hope for freedom.

"Hey, I can smell the ocean!" Grant yelled with enthusiasm. He approached the wall and looked up at the opening. "That's a big hole."

"Smells like the West Coast," Hughes added excitedly. He wore a big smile on his face, going nearly ear-to-ear.

All three men were covered in a thin layer of cave dust, most from the previous days of traversing the passageway and now an additional layer from the blast. But they didn't care, nor did they mind the added long hours of labor, which provided even more grime on their uniforms. With the added light, GW first thought they resembled hard rock miners. But then his mind went into work mode and they went to work clearing the debris away.

"Can anyone explain this ocean smell to me?" Hughes asked. "I mean, we're way too far away from the Gulf to smell it. Maybe it's a salt river of some sort?"

"Can't explain it and don't want to," Grant replied. "I'm not goin' to kick a good horse. All I know is that there is fresh air and we're getting' out of this cave real soon."

After wiping away some debris from his shoulders, GW was the first to climb up to the hole they made with the grenade. Then with hours of digging through packed dirt and pulling the rocks toward him to drop back into the cave, he stood with the top half of his body in the hole and for a moment, he smelled the fresh air and relished in the gentle breeze. "You guys are not gonna believe this, but I can see the water out there and it's no river." GW said in wonder. "It's a radiant blue-green in color with at least five-foot curls breaking on a white sandy beach and I can't see anything on the other size."

"Then dig, man...Dig!" Grant yelled as he picked up his own shovel and began climbing atop the boulder GW was standing on to relieve him.

"Look, there ain't enough room up here for both of us," GW warned him.

A sweaty Grant grabbed a hold of GW's shoulder to keep from falling and said, "I'll dig for now and then Hughes can relieve me. Okay?"

Grant stared at a blank faced GW for a moment and then GW sighed and replied, "Okay, sure, but dig fast."

Below them, Hughes, who had nothing to do for the moment, sat down for a breather and watched as Grant attacked the hole with a wild abandon. "We're too far away from any ocean, guys," Hughes said.

GW dropped to the cave floor and stepped up in front of him. "It doesn't make any sense, but we're getting out of here and that's all that matters." GW sat down for a moment and in a tired voice, he said, "Grant knows that an' I know that, but whatever ocean it is, the water is right there out in front of us and pretty soon I'm gonna be swimming in those waves." GW said with a restored eagerness to his voice. "I'm thirsty, I'm hungry and I'm real tired of this stinkin' cave."

After several minutes of digging, shoveling dirt all over GW and Hughes, Grant stopped suddenly and said, "Wait, I think I can squeeze through now." He then dropped his shovel down to GW. "Here...catch!"

While waiting, Hughes stared at his filthy hands in the sunlight and grimaced, "I'm really gonna need a shower."

"Man, after six days in this hole we all stink," GW said.

Up in the hole, Grant was about to poke his head into the hole and make his way through the narrow tunnel they had dug. A moment passed, both Hughes and GW waiting in silence below and then Grant shouted out, "I'm through! And you guys are not gonna believe this view."

GW was next, but he needed to do some additional shoveling before he could wiggle his thick muscular body through the hole. He then stopped at the end of their short excavation to take in the sight before him: An endless body of sparkling dark blue-green water that went to the horizon, under a cloudless sky of light crystal blue. GW thought the sandy shoreline was made up of seemingly untouched white sand, which seemed to run from one end of his view to the other end. There was not a single structure in sight, no tire tracks and better yet, there was no jungle. Not even a single tree and this amazed him.

"I...I don't get it. Where are we?" Grant asked as he looked up at GW. Grant had made what appeared to be a ten-foot drop and was kneeling in the sand. He had a handful of the white sand in his right palm, "It's pretty warm. Kind of reminds me of the sand in Hawaii."

First through the tunnel, unable to turn around and nothing to hold on to, Grant had to drop headfirst, to land in the soft sand on his left side. He attempted an Airborne roll but didn't gauge the distance right. But the sand cushioned his fall, though it still hurt his left shoulder. But he didn't seem to care. He was outside that cursed cave with and there wasn't any North Vietnamese Army nearby and no endless jungle growth to strangle him. The ocean breeze was warm, but quite a bit fresher then the cave he left behind, and he took in a deep lungful to ensure he was cleaning out all the nasty stuff he'd been breathing in for the last few days.

"Hey, it's my turn!" GW yelled. Looking out at the ocean, GW shook his head in amazement and then his attention came back to earth, when he remembered he was in-charge of this small party. They still had a couple chores to do yet before any partying began. GW yelled back at Hughes, "Hughes gather up the equipment and start shoving it through. Then you can drop it down to me."

Hughes picked everything up and after climbing up the cave wall twice, he had everything in the hole and began shoving it through. It didn't take long and after a good once-over to make sure they had not left anything behind, Hughes was ready to crawl through. GW piled up the three rucksacks, shovels and helmets on the sand. Then first then watched as Hughes dropped to the sand, which was quite soft and cushioned their fall. What made it even more enjoyable was how the warm sea air enclosed all around them in a soothing embrace and it reminded Hughes of home. Hughes had followed the gear with a perfect somersault move and then an airborne roll, before he leapt to his feet with arms outstretched like a circus trapeze artist who had completed his act. "You'll notice perfection in every move."

"You guys are a couple of clowns," Grant said. "Come on, let's get moving. We still need fresh water and some food."

GW stretched the kinks out and walked over to pick up his equipment. Now stripped to bare chests, they each tied their helmet and shovel to their rucksack and strapped on their web belt with empty canteens. Last of all, they slid the rucksack straps over their shoulders.

Hughes wanted to run toward the waves to wash his body off and Grant was ready to agree with him, but GW stopped them, "Look, we don't know where we are and who might be around here. I don't want to go off like some beach-surfer dudes and end up with our backsides in a sling because we got careless. So, let's stay close to this cliff and see what's around the bend. Okay?"

"You're right...Almost forgotten we were still at war," Grant said in response.

They had kept their flak-vests but carried them in the bottom of their rucksacks. Boots were heavily scuffed up from the cave floor and their fatigue pants were mostly in shreds around the knees and they'd need some patches for their backsides. Shirts and soiled underwear from heavy sweat, and several pairs of socks, which nearly stood on their own, were all in need of a good wash. They were also wadded up inside their rucksacks; shoved in on top of their flak-vests. Their towels were at least as filthy, or more so than the three of them were, but the men had them draped around their necks still. They'd grown used to the foul odor emanating from them.

"Hughes, you take point and we'll follow in a moment," GW ordered. "But stay close to the cliff face for concealment and don't be in any hurry. There's no telling what is ahead of us. Don't know about you guys, but I feel like any minute we're going to find Dorothy and her little dog, Toto, hanging around behind some rock."

PFC Hughes, wearing a child-like smile on his face, simply responded with a single nod of his head.

"Just don't get too far ahead," GW ordered a second time and Hughes nodded his head again. Then without a word, he turned to proceed at a cautious pace.

GW and Grant took a moment to examine the cliff face beside them. The rock was clearly weathered from battering storms, but it was also apparent from the rock that a landslide had occurred sometime in the past, which covered over the opening to their cavern. The hole they had dug out was a good 60 to 70 feet below the top of the cliff, but only 12 to 15 feet from the cave's ceiling inside. There were no trees or natural growth to be seen anywhere, on the beach or above the face of the cliff. Except for the beautiful shoreline, the coast was barren of life. Not knowing if it was low or high tide, the ocean was only 40 to 50 feet from the base of the cliff and it appeared to GW, the beach went on for miles to what he believed to be his west and he'd have to look around the bend to see what lay in that direction. At one point the rocky ridge came to within only a couple yards of the ocean surf and it got GW to thinking about digging for clams. The sun was straight up, so both GW and Grant figure it was noon or a bit after. Though they were all extremely elated to be out of that cave, they were bewildered as to where they might be and how they got there.

"You got any ideas where we are?" Grant asked.

"Not a one," GW replied. "But at least we're outside."

"Amen to that!"

Hughes surprised them a moment later when he returned on the run with a rather strange and excited expression on his face. GW also noticed Hughes' pants legs were dripping in water. Hughes came to a sudden stop right in front of GW and pointed off toward the direction he had come with his left arm raised. But now he was out of breath from running so hard through the deep sand, he had to catch his breath before he could tell them what he had discovered.

"You go swimming?" Grant asked him. "Don't you remember the Corporal here telling us to stay out of the surf?"

After some hesitation and looking first at Grant with a look of frustration and then GW, he tried to clear his mind before responding. With his hands raised up in a universal signal of telling them to wait a moment, Hughes let out a deep lungful of air and replied, "There's a fresh water stream up ahead...It empties into the ocean." Hughes then knelt to catch his breath, before he continued, while Grant and GW stood waiting impatiently for the PFC to get on with it.

"So, go on already," Grant said, "What's got you all excited?"

"But that's not the weirdest part, Corporal," Hughes said to GW. He shook his head, struggling to find the words as he again pointed off behind him and in a trembling voice, he said, "Way off in the distance, around this bluff, there's some kind of huge castle and what looks to be a village...A real castle! Like from Cinderella and Disneyland."

"What are you talking about?" GW asked. But not bothering to wait for an answer, he grabbed up his rucksack, helmet and shovel and walked past Hughes. He followed the man's footprints in the sand, with Grant and then Hughes following up behind.

Clearing the rocky cliff face and then the bend of large boulders that made up what GW referred to as the bluff, he came to an abrupt halt. Through a shimmering haze brought on by the hot desert air and cooler ocean air currents, he could truly see an ancient castle off in the distance.

"I don't believe this..." GW said and then when he heard the other two coming up behind him, he turned to face them and said, with his arms stretched out wide, "Where are we?"

"You both see the castle, right?" Hughes asked. "I'm not seeing things?"

"No, man, we see the castle...We just don't want to believe we see it," Grant said.

Off in the distance, about three miles away, stood a massive stone castle of medieval design or of what Hughes would later describe as Middle Eastern and Greek meets European style, construction. For in fact, the castle originally built on a smaller scale by the armies of Alexander the Great as a defense against local tribesmen, was added on by Roman builders, followed by North Africans stone masons, with an Eastern European influence. The five-wall or near pentagon shaped Castle stood atop a huge natural stone base, which gave the top floors of the multi-level structure a clear view of the surrounding countryside and the ocean. The three of them could make out numerous strange flowing multi-colored flags waving from assorted castle towers. GW, who had excellent vision, said he could make out smaller buildings surrounding the much larger structure that appeared to be several stables.

A castle! GW thought, a real King Arthur castle and I'm seeing it. We're seeing it! He looked at the two men, "All three of us are apparently seeing the same thing, so it's not a mirage. You are seeing it too, right?" He asked Grant, who couldn't respond. Grant simply stood there with his eyes wide, his mouth partially hanging open and he pointed toward the castle.

"Yup, it's there all right...But where is here?" Grant asked.

GW looked out over the ocean, feeling relaxed as he watched the white surf break on the beach. Somehow, we've come out of the A Shau Valley, only to find ourselves next to a strange, but spectacular ocean. An ocean richer in color then any I've ever seen...and a fairy tale castle where none should be. Where no ocean should be...and where's the jungle? GW wondered in silence and then asked, "Where's our base? If this is the ocean and we somehow walked further than we thought, which in its self is impossible, there should be some US military presence around here somewhere. We'd at least have an R&R Center here and I don't see any helicopters buzzing about or the contrails of any zooming airmen flying their precious fighters across the skies."

"Do you think we're dead?" Grant asked. "Maybe this is some sort of heavenly paradise and that castle is part of Heaven?"

Must have been the meat...most likely were still stuck inside that mountain, suffering from a lack of oxygen, food poisoning and probably dehydration." Hughes suggested. "...And this is all one big illusion."

GW decided he'd tackle the castle later. Right now, he needed fresh water. His throat felt like sandpaper and he was concerned it was about to close-up on him. So, he walked toward the streambed, which lay before him and he slowly knelt in the cooling water. He could feel it's refreshing coolness surge up through his ankles, then his calves and eventually work its way up to his stomach. It felt so good. His whole body seemed to soak it up like a sponge and he promptly plopped down in the stream and laid back to let the waters rush over him.

The streambed was only ankle deep, but a good 20-feet in width. GW slowly took in several gulping mouthfuls of the water and once satisfied he wasn't going to die from thirst, he began to bathe himself. Soon afterward, he even took his rucksack into the water and emptied out the filthy contents into the water. He washed everything thoroughly and laid the items out on the sand to dry under the hot sun. After washing out the rucksack itself, he pulled out a plastic bag which held his soap and razor. He began running the water through his hair, soaping it down and decided the shaving could wait for now. He nearly slurped up a quart of water before he remembered his two buddies and turned to see if the others were joining him in the pleasurable affair.

"Are you seeing this in color, real color?" GW asked them. "Can you feel the sea air and smell its freshness? Can you taste this clear water and hear those seagulls overhead? Is this all real, or what?"

"What's your point?" Grant asked, as he sucked up a double handful of water.

GW didn't answer, but not wanting to waste the moment, he began to fill his canteens. He didn't want to take the chance this would all vanish before him. Not even bothering to think it out, that if the stream did disappear the water in his canteens would also most likely vanish.

"Look, I can touch the sand, taste the water and my nose still hurts from when I first hit that rock wall, nearly a week ago. This isn't some dream, that isn't a mirage over there and this water tastes oh-so sweet." He scooped up another handful of water and drank it down, as his canteens continued to fill. The pain of a dried throat quickly began to lessen.

All their pants and boots were soaked by now, not that they cared and now Grant and Hughes were busy refilling their canteens too. They still had to do their laundry because while GW was doing his wash, Grant and Hughes got into a water fight.

At that moment and for no reason he could think of, GW took the notion to reach into his rucksack and retrieve his Montegnard wooden cross and drop it over his head. It simply felt like the thing to do and this simple action would end up saving their lives.

Grant saw a small silvery fish jump nearby and then without further hesitation, rolled over on his back and laughed out loud as the water washed over him, cooling his weary muscles and filling his mouth with a taste like golden honey. Sitting up, he studied the castle behind them and then looked to GW, "Okay, I buy it that we're here, but tell me how did we get here and just like you said earlier, where is here?"

GW didn't answer right away. He studied the creek and followed it for some distance with his eyes until it vanished into a set of low hills. There were no mountains within visual range but accept for the bluff behind them. There were a lot of low hills off in the distance, which seemed to surround the castle. But between the castle and the nearby hills, there were several miles of desert-like flatlands. He couldn't see any farms, but the castle could be blocking them from view. He then turned to Grant, "You got me, bud, but for now I say we rest up, maybe catch a fish or two and if not, we look for something else to eat," GW replied.

"Maybe we can knock one of those gulls down, or find their nests and collect some eggs," Grant said. He then began looking around for a rock to throw. Right now, he was sure wishing he still had his M-16, he could take down a lot of sea gulls with a burst of automatic fire.

"Guys, I think we'd better wait on the food," Hughes said. His voice had taken on a tone of caution and he was pointing again toward the castle. "Looks like we've attracted the attention of the local welcome wagon and they really don't look all that friendly to me."

"No! This is too much...Are those knights?" Grant asked in astonishment. He stood there in the water, his eye wide with amazement and observed riders on horseback coming toward them. Still sitting in the shallow streambed, GW turned at the waist to see a group of splendid looking mounted men coming their way. As they grew closer, he counted eleven men in all, appearing to be dark-skinned males, who were wearing dark blue turbans with silvery colored veils covering their faces. They had on dark blue long-sleeved tunics with blossoming black riding pants. Each man was mounted upon what GW knew from history class to be termed black warhorses. The gallant looking steeds were covered in cloth trappings of shimmering dark blue and bordered in golden and silvery striping. They came forward at an easy trot, displaying a well-disciplined column of two files of five riders, with one splendid looking horseman out in front. Wearing silvery gauntlets, their left hand carried a large circular shield made of a shiny metal with an obscure coat of arms painted on them, and they maintained a tight grasp upon the reins of their highly aggressive looking mount. In their right hand, they held a long wooden lance of some eight feet in length, tipped by a long metal shaft, which ended in a very lethal looking arrowhead-shaped metallic point. Where the rider held the lance, a metal covering protruded outward to protect the rider's hand during battle.

GW remembered seeing such weapons in several of the medieval movies he'd seen as a kid. His favorite was Knights of the Round Table, but these knights were no Hollywood stunt-men. Or for that matter, they were not even Englishmen. By their manner and horsemanship, GW saw these men to be the real thing and probably quite capable of handling any given situation.

"They look just like some kind of Arabian knight!" Grant shouted excitedly as he began to back up out of the creek bed and move toward the rocky bluff. "Where the heck are we?" He said in a frightened voice and looked toward GW.

"Oh, this just keeps getting better and better," GW muttered. Shaking off the water and wiping his face, he jumped up from the stream, grabbed up a shovel for defense and his KA-BAR.

Grant jerked his KA-BAR knife from its suspender sheath and only then did Hughes remember to draw his bayonets from off his canteen belts. The three of them now stood side by side with a shovel in one hand and a blade in the other.

"Well, there went your idea this was some sort of heavenly paradise," GW said and then he stopped as the knights began to spread out into a single row with the leader out in front. GW remained in the center of his two friends and he continued, saying, "...because these dudes sure ain't no angels, partner and they don't look too particularly happy to see us." GW then ordered the men to quickly put on their flak-vests and their helmets.

"How can you tell, Corporal?" Hughes asked. "Their veils are hiding their faces."

GW took up a defensive posture between Grant and Hughes. "Because PFC Hughes, the very professional looking officer out in front has the beady eyes of cold killer...so, no one makes a move. Let's see what they want. Maybe it's only a big misunderstanding...or, we've stumbled into their sacred spring and we're really in for it."

"And to think we climbed all the way through that dang mountain for this!" Grant exclaimed.

"Must've been the grenade, the blast caught someone's attention," GW said. He remained motionless on the opposite side of the stream bed and watched as the horsemen approached at a slow walk.

Going by only the limited amount of bare flesh being shown, a dark brownish color and their hair black, GW suspected these people to be from Northern Africa, possibly India or one of the other Western or Central Asian countries...but as to how they found themselves so far from Vietnam was only adding to the dilemma they had found themselves in.

Hughes, studying the horsemen closely, was reminded of some of the paintings he had seen in the museum. Racking his mind to recall, he suddenly realized these men and

their uniforms matched with the 12th to 14th century period of the Middle East.

"Corporal, I've seen these kinds of uniforms before and you'll probably think I've really lost my mind, but these are Muslim knights...the kind of people who fought King Richard in the crusades. I've seen their paintings in the museum I used to work in, but they existed in the 12th through the 14th centuries."

"Yeah, maybe it's some sort of reenactment ceremony, like they do for the Civil War and the Yankees get to clobber the Rebels again," Grant suggested.

"Both of you shut-up!" GW ordered. "I don't know what this is, where we are or who they are, but they've got us outnumbered and those pig-stickers they carry can do us a lot of serious harm...So be quiet."

The next few moments passed in silence, as the three terrified Americans stood ready to defend themselves with only shovels and knives. With their helmets and flak-vests still on, and wearing combat green pants, GW couldn't help but wonder what a curious sight they might be for these approaching knights?

A tight grasp around his bayonet with his right hand, GW reached up and lifted his Montegnard cross up. He studied it, having felt a strange warm sensation from it when the knights first appeared. Thinking it was first the sun, he now held it up and following a mental nudge, away from his body for the knights to be able to see it.

"What's that for?" Grant asked. "You hoping for a miracle, or making your peace with God?"

"I don't think they're vampires, Corporal." Hughes said. "Though I'm beginning to believe anything here might be possible."

"That Holy Man gave me this cross," GW said in a low voice. "The meat saved us, maybe this cross will help too." He then gazed upon the mounted knights in wonderment, struggling with belief, for the sight before him were indeed actually these splendid looking horsemen.

The eleven horsemen were now within 25-feet of them and had slowed down to a slower walk, as they approached their side of the creek bed. Then a curt sounding order in a strange foreign tongue was given by the lead knight, to whom the ten knights responded by crossing the streambed and quickly forming a wide circle around the three Americans.

The cliff stood several yards behind them, and they now had steel tipped lances pointed at their faces, blocking their escape. Still, GW and his two comrades stood their ground with knives and shovels in hand, while the knights held fast to their position. GW thought they were awaiting further orders from the leader; a man whose authority was apparent by the way the other horsemen watched him. The leader then tapped his silvery metal spurs into the sides of his beautiful black steed and entered the water, as the horsemen gave him room to approach the strangers.

"Oh, what I'd do for an M-16 right now," Grant wished in a whisper of a voice.

"Do not make the first move," GW ordered. He kept his gaze locked upon the leader, debating with himself what move he would make if the man attacked.

"I can probably pull one guy off his horse, but you two have to handle the other ten," Grant said. His use of humor to break the tension flopped and he could now feel the sweat now pouring down his chest.

"Do not move, Grant, let's see what they do next." GW again ordered. He then added, "No more jokes either."

Over the next moment, an eerie tense-filled silence prevailed between the Americans and the strange horsemen, as both parties visually inspected one another. Finally, the lead horsemen, his cold dark brown eyes scrutinizing each of the three men, jabbed his silver spurs into the side of his horse again, which responded by darting forward and moving right toward GW. But before the horse could stomp GW, who had backed up and readied his shovel for defense; preparing to make a wide one-handed baseball bat-like swing. Then suddenly, the knight reined his horse in to stop only a couple feet from GW. He also took notice how the other two men didn't shy away but were ready to come to the defense of their friend.

Frightened, but refusing to show it, or at least hoping they didn't see his whole-body trembling, GW glared back at the horseman. He could feel the horse's warm foul breath on him, but he held fast as the leader slowly moved his lance point down and came to within mere inches of GW's chest.

Having dropped the cross from his grasp, prepared to do battle, GW's first thought was to knock the lance aside with his shovel, but some strange inner voice whispered in his head that he should stand and wait. So, he held his heart in his throat and surprisingly, rather than attack, the knight used the sharp point of his lance to lift the wooden-cross up a few inches from GW's chest. After an extremely long harrowing minute in GW's young life, as opposing forces held his thread-like life in balance, the mounted man pulled his lance away and the wooden-cross dropped back to bounce in beat to the 130-thump-a-minute heart rate GW felt pounding in his chest. With his left hand, gloved in ornate black leather and a silvery wristlet, the lead knight leaned his lance against his horse and lifted his hand to his face to pull aside his silken veil. This revealed a dark olive complexion and a narrowing face, covered by a well-trimmed black moustache and a well-trimmed beard that came to a fine oiled point. He wore small double hoop earrings of both gold and silver in both ears, which reminded GW of the drawings and paintings he had seen in school of Saracen knights from the Middle Ages. He knew Hughes was right, but nothing for the moment made any sense to him and he remained mute.

This knight was not a big man, for his chest armor hung loosely about him and GW guessed him to be less than six-feet in height. However, his arms appeared strong and his mount was a beautiful sight to behold; all black, in the 16 to18 hand range, an extremely long flowing black mane and tail; well-groomed and with muscles clearly defined. The creature's eyes of piercing black glared down upon GW. When the lead knight finally spoke, it was in a strange language GW and his friends were unable to understand. Then the knight turned to Hughes and in an abrasive voice, spoke again, which caused Hughes to step back in alarm. But the Americans could only shake their heads in response. Hughes knew he was being yelled at, maybe even cursed, but he had no idea the words being spoken or even what language it was in.

GW hoped the man understood that he wasn't saying no to a possible question, but he simply didn't understand the man's language. Then GW remembered the cross and held it up as he pointed at his chest, "Christian. I am a Christian."

Grant gave GW a hard look, "You think that's smart? These people look as if they might eat Christians for lunch."

"He looked as though he knew what the cross was, so I'm going with it. You got a better idea, I'm listening and you might notice--so are they."

The knight responded by also shaking his head in response to show he didn't understand GW's words and then pointed his lance toward Hughes and again said another string of words to him. But Hughes could only reply with a negative shake of his head, which seemed to confuse the knight or worse, irritate him.

"I get the idea they've seen people of your skin color before, Hughes. But us lily-white dudes seem to confuse them some," Grant said

The knight then issued a sharp-tongued order to his men, which caused the other knights to respond by lifting their lances into a non-threatening posture.

"See. The cross worked...at least for now," GW said with relief.

The leader issued forth another set of orders and the formation of horsemen opened their circle up. Then with the lead knight moving out across the stream bed at a slow walk, he headed off in the direction of the castle. When the Americans didn't move, the nearest horseman moved forward to give them a hard shove into the streambed with the front right flank of his horse. One knight then lowered his lance and made a gesture with the point and aiming off toward the castle.

"I'd say it looks like we've been invited to come along," GW said. He then grabbed up his rucksack, pulled it over his left shoulder and gestured with his shovel toward the castle. "So, fetch your packs and move out before they start using those pig-stickers to prod us along."

"I'm surprised they didn't take our weapons," Grant said in amazement. But he did sheath his knife to ensure they knew he wasn't a threat, not that they would. Each of the knights was also armed with a very large scimitar and a dagger.

"Look at the size of those swords they carry, they probably don't feel very threatened by our little blades," GW replied.

"Back home one of those scimitars would bring you a thousand or better from any collector," Hughes said. He continued to praise the beauty of their weapons, while Grant continued to eye the Arabians.

"You think maybe we can ask for a ride?" Hughes suggested after he picked up his rucksack. He slid it over his right shoulder and belted on his canteen belt in a rush, while he walked.

"I wouldn't bet on it," GW answered back over his shoulder. "It seems they want us to walk."

"These guys probably think we're dumb infantry pukes...wonder if they'd understand we're 101st Airborne...Screaming Eagles?" Grant asked his buddies.

"You go right ahead, Grant," GW suggested. But Grant simply shook his head in response.

With knights now on both sides of him and having spent his life on a ranch, Grant kept checking out the horses; eyeing their length of stride, muscular structure and he suspected several centuries of careful breeding had gone into these handsome warhorses.

Grant recalled reading of a black Arabian breed, but these mounts were the first ones he had ever seen. He thought he had heard they had died out in the latter part of the 19th century, but now believed he was apparently misinformed.

"We're in for a fast walk, guys and over soft sand, so cut the gab and let's keep up," GW said. He quickly attached his shovel to his rucksack, but kept it extended as before for a quick grab if needed. He also adjusted his canteen belt and suspenders for the rough hike ahead. Sand was tough to hike through, especially at the pace being set by the horseman out in front.

Another order was shouted out and four of the knights split off from the group and retraced the stranger's footprints through the soft sand, which led back to where they had blown the hole in the wall.

"I'd sure like to know what these guys think when they find our subway exit from Moria," Hughes muttered. Heck, this experience is beginning to size up into a great screenplay, but that's if we ever get back to the USA to write the screenplay?

After ten minutes or so of hiking across the desert sand, GW was growing winded from hiking through the often-deep sand and attempting to keep up with the mounted warriors. He glanced back over his shoulder to the other two and said in a low voice, "I've got a real weird feeling, guys, a sixth sense maybe, but before too long we'll know what's happening here." GW then added, "Not that we may like the answer. Something strange has happened to us and there's got to be an explanation and maybe that castle up ahead will provide the answers."

"Any of you guys watch The Twilight Zone?" Grant asked. "My old man loved the show. Maybe next week he'll see the episode we're starring in right now."

GW shook his head in response and then looked to the leader of the knights, who stood tall in his leather stirrups. It seemed to GW, and he wasn't sure why he felt this, that the knight seemed to be showing some concern for a large lake up ahead or maybe it was a harbor. He couldn't help but notice how the leader kept looking toward the lake and then he noticed all the men were too, that is until they veered off to the right to give the lake a wide berth. But even then, they continued to glance back over their left shoulders. This made GW wonder if they were they expecting danger from the direction of the lake. Having gone by this end of it, GW could see it was in fact a very large lake and there was a length of sand separating it from the ocean. Still, he didn't know if there was a channel from the ocean into the lake at the other end.

But this strange behavior by the knights caused him to stop briefly to study the lake off in the distance, but then a knight used his horse to again prod GW onward. Still, for a moment in time and while studying the waters, he felt a strange feeling of fear run up his spine. A tingling sensation he'd often heard described as if someone had stepped on one's grave. This feeling of apprehension caused him to stare off toward the lake until his vision was eventually blocked by an utterly gigantic wall of carved stone blocks.

# 3 - A BIZARRE ENCOUNTER IN WONDERLAND

THE GRAND CASTLE
KINGDOM OF SILENE
THE DUNGEON

In the wide openness of North Africa, the Castle of Silene lay approximately two-miles directly south of the southern shores of the massive Mediterranean Sea. The main two-story fortification was first constructed upon a rocky knoll in the time of Alexander the Great's famous march to Egypt and other parts of North Africa. Unlike other fortifications of the period, the Castle of Silene was indeed an unusual sight for the Sahara Desert. Normally, a castle of such size in this part of the world would be constructed with one side up against a hillside or mountain to make use of the natural elements as part of the defense. In doing so, this would reduce the amount of openness that must be protected against. However, Alexander the Great, a young man whose armies had conquered most of the known word, feared no one and his generals felt this fortification should have a clear view of all the surrounding areas.

The Castle of Silene castle was assembled by slave labor, who painstakingly and with severe loss of life, moved massive stone blocks into Libya from various rock quarries located deep within Egypt. Later, with the influence from Eastern Europe, the Castle of Silene was enlarged to its current size and now resembled many of the great castles found in Europe and Britain.

Yet, for a person who traveled the known world, one could easily see the two major differences in the Castle of Silene from other European fortifications; an 80-foot tall Muslim prayer tower and a rather large mosque with a dome roof in the center of the city. A second, but smaller mosque was located on the first floor of the castle's main structure. Massive in size, the stone structure overlooked 50,000 acres of farm and pasture land, and a large lake shaped much like an American football. The lake was nearly a mile-wide and over six miles in length. With only the great emptiness of the Sahara Desert to the south, east and west, and the blue-green waters of the Mediterranean Sea to the north, the Castle of Silene and its surrounding homes and shops resembled a large island situated upon a calm sea of white sand.

Prior to the great cataclysm that separated the waters the Castle of Silene was initially built as a supply point for the Greek army traveling in all directions. It later became a strong point of defense for the northern shoes of Libya against sea-going raiding pirates and invading armies from surrounding countries. Slave labor had worked for many decades to complete the castle's new additions and its great exterior walls, which surround the castle in an elongated pentagon shape. Inside the battlements, the main castle stood five-stories high and had two-levels below ground. Besides the prayer tower and the defensive towers along the battlements, there were 25-assorted towers of different heights and sizes to provide the utmost in luxury for visiting dignitaries, the king's high-ranking court officers and the king's family. A newer tower was built for Brother Samuel; who was often seen admiring the stars at night. Two hundred yards directly north of the castle stood a single stone wall, which was 30-feet high, over ten feet thick at the top and nearly 18-feet thick at the base. Upon completion, the wall, which took several years to complete, was nearly one-mile in length and manned at all-times by dedicated Silene foot soldiers. An elaborate alarm system of antelope horns and large gongs was set up to announce the sighting of invaders or any other threat to the kingdom. The wall was also constructed in a gradual curve which presented an illusion of sorts to a sea-going invading army, causing them to suspect the seemingly impregnable wall also encircled the castle.

On the five corners of the castle's great exterior wall, which stood between 30 and 40-feet in height, were strategically planned defensive battlements that were manned at all-times by army bowmen; both longbow and the newer crossbows. Over the great main gate, which faced to the west, were two small roofed-over towers, separated by a 20-foot distance and manned by members of the elite Royal Guard, who were armed with both bow and spear. These spearmen were on hand to thwart any attempts by horsemen or foot soldiers that might try to bring down the gate with a battering ram or set fire to it with vials of oil and torch. Leading away from the castle's main gate was a hard packed, well-traveled dirt road; double in width of a large horse drawn wagon and it wrapped around the exterior walls. From this roadway, similar, but smaller roads made their way throughout the town like the wooden spokes of a huge wagon wheel. Homes were built close to the castle, but the civilian stables were positioned on the town's outer perimeter, which opened out to the king's pastures. The remaining land, with exception of the acreage between the great wall and the lake, was used for an assortment of farms and all this was well protected by the king's mounted guard.

There was also a single dirt lane, well-marked by the occasional thick wooden post and sign, which led a traveler onto the great ocean. But the road stayed at least a half-mile from the lake all the time. From this lane, a connecting roadway led to the City of Tripoli. A well-mounted man would take at least three days of hard riding to cover the distance between Silene and Tripoli. An equal distance stood between Silene and the nearest border with Egypt, the route only used by camel trains and sheepherders. These people would pay handsomely in taxes to cross the border and all too often the greedy Egyptian guards would still simply seize whatever property a traveler carried unless a bit of gold exchanged hands for the guard's personal taxation program.

Inside the Castle of Silene the exterior walls of the castle keep were often more than one-foot thick. These outer walls were showing their age and constant ware against the hot summer winds, coastal sea storms, Saharan sandstorms and salt rich sea air. There was always a lack of funds for repairs and either one part or another of the castle was left to stand in disrepair, the elements struck the fortification like an incurable disease. Not that it mattered, for Silene no longer had the slave labor it needed to make the needed repairs and bring the great stone blocks from Egypt.

The first floor of the castle keep held the great kitchens, servant quarters and main hall. The smaller mosque was located here, used by the people of the castle. The second floor held the quarters of the army officers, the king's main library and various classrooms, and the armory. The third floor was used for visiting dignitaries and their families, also additional open rooms for various uses and the king's personal kitchen. From the open-air balconies hung huge multi-colored flags to designate the individual or family who occupied the interior rooms. Here, on these flags of various sizes, displayed a knight's coat-of-arms, or a court official's family-crest. On the rare event a foreign dignitary was visiting, their country's flag would be displayed, for all to see from the grounds below.

The fourth floor was used for the king's main meeting hall, Brother Samuel's quarters, his rather large laboratory and a two-room classroom. The top floor was used only for the royal family, their personal chambers and King Ramie's dining room. There was also the King's game room, where he played his many games of chess with Brother Samuel. The Game Room's wall was richly decorated with silks from the Far East and several pieces of armor were on display from other lands. There were also furs of all sizes, mostly animals the king's daughter had killed, and this included several lions.

The castle yards held five large stables for both horses and camels. Nearby were six long troop barracks for the King's men-at-arms and two smaller barracks for the elite members of the King's Royal Guard. There were various outdoor kitchens, where large blackened clay stoves were always cooking for men and slaves. The area also maintained watering facilities for the troops and the animals. South of the castle were two large training yards for the men to practice their arts of war; one for mounted troops and the other for the foot soldiers. But outside the city to the east, the cavalry trained in larger formations and the occasional mock-battle was fought. This is also where grudge fights were settled, almost always to the death.

There were dozens of window openings, or portals, of various sizes in the castle's exterior walls and some of these displayed a smaller flag or banner for the occupant. From the castle's towers waved lengthy ribbons of royal blue, these fluttered with the wind or hung limp on those calm days. But to the alert observer, several of the flags and banners were in tatters; evidence of the poor state of wealth Silene was presently in.

From below ground level the castle dropped down two levels; the first level for food storage in the cooler temperatures underground and stables for those animals awaiting slaughter. The very bottom level though held the ancient Dungeon of Silene, where prisoners were held in dreadfully filthy cells until the King's various tormentors could torture them slowly with the infamous rack, branding iron and even deadlier tools of the day. Upon orders, they would also end the prisoners' lives quickly with the bloodstained blade of a large axe.

Currently, the Town of Silene consisted of some 232-homes of various sizes and value. There were 34 multi-purpose retail shops for food and wares, and two public stables in disrepair. Near the castle were also three extremely poor inns and a large Mosque. Most homes were built from sand and stone by using remnants of the harbor docks or ship wrecks. Wood timbers were brought in from the old sea docks destroyed in the great earthquake, which is believed to be what caused the forming of the lake. Some of the building materials were brought overland on wagons from the rapidly dwindling cedar forests near the City of Tripoli. Still, the transient open-air shops were quite colorful, as summer winds blew the shop's brightly colored fabrics about. Most of these shops came to Silene from Tripoli, their wares lashed on camelback or in aged wagons pulled by sluggish oxen. These shops spent most of the year in the cities like Tripoli but came to Silene for festival and now encircled Silene's two large fresh-water fountains. It was these fountains and the nearby stream that provided drinking water for both city and castle. From these fountains the people carried their daily supply of water to their homes or shops, using large clay pots carried in carts or smaller clay pots carried on the shoulder or atop the head of a slave woman, a child or in a poorer family-the wife.

Twice a week a small convoy of carts, pulled by eight oxen and under the protection of the Royal Guards, left the castle grounds, making the short trip to one of the fountains, spending the day filling massive clay pots for the great tank on the roof top of the castle keep and a second tank, where water was stored for the great kitchen. Each cart was driven by an experienced man and assisted by three able helpers who would fill the water jars.

The great wall to the north of the castle took over 14 years to build by very frightened slaves. As they worked, their wary eyes always kept a close watch on the lake in fear of the frightful dragon that lived there. First it was mounted troops who guarded the slaves, but later, as the wall was completed, guards would walk the wall. These foot soldiers maintained a constant vigilance on the slaves, as well keeping an eye on the lake before them. They were always prepared to sound the alarm if the foul dragon, unhappy with its sacrificial gifts of sheep or maidens, was once again on the prowl. As a secondary concern, they watched for human invaders. But it was the dragon they really feared, for no man had been able to stand against it and its savagery had forced the hardest of men to turn away as the dragon fed.

# THE AMERICANS FIND A HOME IN THE DUNGEON

With the afternoon heat beating down on them unmercifully, the three Americans were quite curious over what had happened to them. It was a weary and frustrated threesome who finally reached the outskirts of the city. The knights rode through a large herd of more than 300-sheep and it was GW, who first spotted the herd of camels off in the distance and called out.

"Do you guys see those camels over there?" GW pointed in the direction where more than two-dozen of the animals were standing or lying about. The sheep was one thing, but camels meant they were a very long way from Vietnam and now they were more confused than ever.

"Those are desert camels!" Hughes said. And though extremely troubled about all the strange happenings, as were the other two men, he was still a history nut and was really enjoying this whole Arabian Nights thing.

"Are there more than one kind?" GW asked. He then turned back around, able to duck under a kick from a nearby horseman for not moving along fast enough.

Hughes kept walking as he talked, nearly stumbling when he came upon a deep spot in the sand and screamed out in terror when he sunk up to mid-calf. Then he stopped sinking and felt foolish, especially after several of the knights laughed at him.

Hughes climbed out with Grant's help, wiped the sand off and continued on talking as if nothing had happened, "One hump and two hump camels for North Africa and most of your Middle Eastern countries, but there is also the Siberian camel. The Siberian Camel doesn't have a hump...I think. But, what you got here is the desert variety camel, which means...Well, I'm not exactly sure what that means."

"What it means, dude; is that somehow, we three stalwart young men have hiked all the way across Asia in six or seven days," Grant said.

GW was about to put his two-cents in when the foul odor of the city struck his sense of smell, "Oh, man, this place wreaks!" Silene had everything from open sewer water, rotten and decaying garbage piled about and the ever-present stench of animal feces. He even observed several men and some boys urinating in the open, while overly-thin dogs fought over a bone nearby.

Hughes pointed to two women up ahead. Their hair was in disarray and they were being led about by a rope around their wrists by a very disgusting looking character riding on a very tired looking ox. The man, who appeared to be in his mid-50's, had wrinkled dark-skin and his hair and beard was graying. He wore soiled tan colored clothes and brown leather sandals. He occasionally gave the women a good yank on the rope to make sure they kept up and slapped the head of the ox with a long, thin piece of palm branch.

For a moment, the sights and smells about him, GW tossed the idea around in his head that he had died, and this was truly the gateway into Hell.

Here on the outskirts of the rustic looking city, the Americans were stopped, and soldiers suddenly appeared on foot to strip them of their weapons and packs. They were then tied up with their hands tightly behind them. Loops of rope were wrapped around their necks, which Grant started to object to and kicked one of the soldiers. The man pulled a short sword and was about to seek revenge, when the lead knight yelled out a harsh command and the man, his head now bowed, quickly put his dagger away.

GW saw this and ordered Grant and Hughes not to resist, especially since there were now several lances pointed in their faces. "Keep calm, guys. They don't want us dead...not yet anyway."

Once the party continued and the Americans came into view of the population, everyone in town came outside to observe them. Within moments, spectators became overly enthusiastic and began throwing things at them; rotten food, small rocks and apparently, whatever they could get their hands on.

For the next hour or more, after having endured being paraded throughout the City of Silene, the men, who were now covered in rotten debris and bleeding from several minor wounds to face and body, found themselves standing before a great wooden gate of towering size. GW thought it had to be at least 20-feet high, supported by lengths of a blackened metal and the two sides were each nearly 15-feet in width. He saw how the gate was also topped with a Roman-style arch of stone and at the top of the arch was displayed a shield-like crest, which matched with the shields carried by the knights around them; a blue horse raised up on its back two legs. Had GW or the other two men been archeologists, they would've noticed numerous engravings in the gate's stone support columns from both Greek and Roman civilizations. One engraving was even the Roman Eagle, which signified members of a Roman Legion had once been quartered here.

Sore and injured from their maltreatment and utterly dumbfounded by their experience, along with being stared and laughed at by people taunting them, GW now felt a far greater foreboding facing them on the other side of the gate. He also took notice how when the huge gate was opened by nearly a dozen soldiers, the townspeople quickly vanished.

The Americans were not aware that they were under the escort of Captain Sid Rynarr of the King's Royal Guard; a man who had protected them from those overly enthusiastic crowds people. He couldn't stop things from being thrown and he wasn't about to use force to disperse the crowds, but Captain Rynarr did use his horse to protect GW from an elderly, but dangerous woman with a wooden club. Rynarr was fully aware the people were tired, poor and angry and he also knew the old woman had lost her son to Egyptian raiders several years earlier. In her grief, he believed she probably thought these strangers to be Egyptian by their bizarre clothing and sought vengeance.

"Do you get the sense that we're not welcome here?" GW asked. He attempted to lean up against the castle wall, with a large piece of rotten food matter hanging from his chest and then jumped back. He quickly learned this stone had hotspots, which radiated with the sun's afternoon reflected heat.

Shaking his head in wonder at the foolish stranger in strange apparel and upset the gate had not opened as he came in to view, Captain Rynarr was not happy. He had to use his lance to pound its metal point hard against the wood, wondering where his men were who were supposed to be manning the gate towers. He had done this once and with growing agitation, was beginning to knock a second time when the massive gates slowly begin to creak open.

With only a look of scorn for the frightened men manning the gate, Captain Rynarr led his prisoners inside the compound. With a loud order the Americans could not understand, most of the horsemen proceeded toward the nearest stable, leaving three horsemen to assist Captain Rynarr with the strangers. The mounted men didn't trust the foot soldiers with the chore, a rivalry born from the first armies of Biblical times.

Turning around before the gates could close, GW took a final glance at the town, If, I didn't know better, I'd say we jus' bounced back to the Middle-ages or came upon someone's movie set.

There was no electricity to be seen; no wires or power poles. There was no running water, except at the large stone fountain they walked by, and the streets were a mixture of sun dried hard packed dirt and desert sand. Men and women were dressed simply, poorly, and the fashions and armor all matched with circa 10th to 14th century.

Where's the Vietnamese? These people are Arabs, or at least Arab looking. Where the heck are we? That question continued to bounce about his mind, where...where...where? What the heck is this place...and when? How...How did we get here? He was tired, but he couldn't help but remember how fearful the knights had looked as they rode near that body of water and their strange behavior surprised him, for they were such a hardened-looking company of men. Were they afraid of something in the lake...maybe some kind of taboo? They behaved like well-disciplined cavalry troopers by the ocean when they took us captive, but clearly behaved differently when we approached that lake. This whole thing just doesn't make any sense, none of it. If anything, I'd say the heat got to us, but we've only been in the sun a few minutes before we sighted the knights...and the ocean, what's with the ocean? It shouldn't be there...we shouldn't be here! I'm locked into some kind-of bizarre nightmare and I've taken these two guys along for the ride. GW's head was throbbing, and he was tired of thinking about the how's and why's. He was bleeding from several small wounds, plummeted with rotten garbage and rocks, sweating up a storm from the desert's heat combined with the ocean's high humidity, and he was just bone tired from the whole experience. Since that very first day, when the North Vietnamese attacked, his life was one of stress and he'd gladly pass it all off as one big nightmare and wake up back at Camp Eagle, with the sergeant screaming in his ear. "Get up, you lunkhead! Your workday begins at 5 a.m., and we've got a new op to get ready for."

Instead, GW was inside the walls of an ancient castle, with several military men-at-arms, rushing toward him. They were all attired in dark brown tunics, dust covered black pants, metallic armor of a silvery-like finish for their chests and back, and brown colored turbans and no veil. They carried sheath-less curved scimitars, nearly three feet long, which appeared out of the shadows to take physical control of the Americans.

The three prisoners were then roughly handled, while herded across a large inner courtyard and through a darkened archway. Here, they were rudely shoved down a narrowing passageway and with his arms tied behind him Grant even fell flat on his face. Two soldiers pulled him to his feet and he came up kicking, until a third soldier stepped forward and struck Grant to the side of his head with the hilt of his scimitar. Rendered unconscious, his head bleeding, the two soldiers were now forced to drag Grant along the dimly lit corridor. Illuminated only by torchlight, GW and Hughes were reminded of their unpleasant cave experience.

Hughes, who didn't like the way Grant was mistreated, shouted out his dislike for these soldiers and ended being slammed up against the stone walls several times for his attitude. GW was surprised how Hughes got several kicks in against the guards, disabling two of them, but he ceased his actions when the point of a blade was placed under his chin. When all was said-and-done, Hughes was also now bleeding from a couple head wounds. GW, was mostly left alone unless he tried to stop walking and then he was kicked in the back or dragged forward by the loop of rope around his neck. GW tried to order Grant to cease resisting, but to no avail and now he hoped both Hughes and Grant would survive this ordeal. After a long length of a stone and mortar hallway, they were taken down two flights of huge stone stairs, each stone being four feet long and three feet wide, with a thickness of over a foot. GW had to wonder how they got suck large blocks of stone into such a narrowed stairwell. He also noticed the cooler air temperatures as they descended.

"What, no elevators?" GW asked in an attempt at bravado. For a reply, he was then cuffed by a foul looking brute for his speaking out.

When they reached the dungeon, the three men—Grant was now conscious--were even more confused by what lay before them. They no longer offered any further resistance and had followed their guards without speaking a word until they reached what GW knew could only be an ancient dungeon. The foul smell was nearly overwhelming his senses and from the museum display of torture devices and crude jail cells, GW knew he didn't want to stay here too long. And GW decided five minutes was too long for this joint. The Dungeon smelled of rot, human waste and smoke. The main room was filled with diabolical machines of pain inflicting torture. Tools here were used to stretch a person, to burn and remove a limb with the swing of a massive axe blade. Dark chains of various sizes were draped along blood stained walls and attached to large rings nailed into the stone. Some if the chains ended in large sinister hooks, which hung from the ceiling. To one side of the room were several open-air barred cells. It was here that GW, Grant and Hughes were untied, but then violently thrown into a single cell and the door clanged shut behind them. The sound alone, resounding off the dungeon walls, told GW, 'Abandon all hope, ye who enter here'.

They took turns examining each other, cleaning off the garbage and as far as GW knew, Grant didn't appear he have sustained a concussion. They were still able to keep track of time because surprisingly, they still had their watches on their wrists. No one had bothered to remove them, and GW thought this was probably because the watchbands were made of simple leather and not a bright shiny metal and these people apparently didn't know what a watch was. GW hadn't seen a watch or a clock since they arrived in the city and not a single piece of modern machinery and he mentioned this to the others, "Guys, I haven't seen anything that says we're still in the 20th century, but I don't see how that's possible." GW then looked to Grant for a response.

"You got me, fella. I still ain't figured how we got here and who are these dang people are?"

Hughes, rubbing the back of his head, looked to his buddies, "Will, they're Muslims and I know this because of the prayer tower we were marched by. The weapons they have are of museum quality and probably from the 10th to maybe the 11th century, but I could be off by a couple hundred years either way. Oddly enough, their shields are of a Greek design."

"And you know this how?" GW asked.

"That museum I worked at, we had several Greek designs on display from the periods surrounding the times of the crusades," Hughes replied.

"Okay, professor, what else have you noticed?" Grant asked.

"Well, they speak some kind of Middle East dialect, but one I've never heard of and we had a lot of people visit the museum from the Middle East. Their accent is quite strange, but it was easy to see that guy in charge was some kind-of officer. Those guys at the gate feared for their lives when he glared at them for making him wait."

"Did you guys notice the colors of that ocean out there?" GW asked.

"Nope! Scenery ain't much my thing, Corporal," Grant answered. There was an edge of anger to his tone of voice. "Is you one of those nature lovers, Corporal?"

GW shot him an icy glare, he was more than ready to stand up to him, "Don't get too cocky, Grant. We'd better stick together here and settle our differences later."

Grant thought about it for a moment and then nodded his head, "Okay, sorry about that. Too much to take in here and I still think I'm gonna wake up back in my bunk and this was all a bad dream...drank too much of the Vietnamese beer."

"Let's get some rest, I think we're gonna be needing it." GW suggested and the other two agreed with him.

During that long hot afternoon and into evening they were pretty much left alone, only checked on by a single jail guard who maintained his distance. Unlike the other guards, they'd seen earlier outside the dungeon, this jailer was a subterranean creature with stooped over shoulders and dressed in a shabby black cloth robe with several burn holes in it. He wore a small dagger hanging from a thin twine around his narrow waist and carried a leather whip over his shoulder. His greasy black hair was in disarray and his long beard was equally unkempt. Three of his upper front teeth were missing and the rest appeared to be rotten with decay. One eye was glazed over and all together he was really a frightening looking character and he only spoke to them in angry sounding grunts.

"I've seen this clown before," Grant said. "It was in some Saturday night drive-in horror movie and his name was Igor."

Not getting any room service from their new friend, they thankfully still had their canteen belts on, which gave each man two canteens worth of fresh tasting stream water. This would be enough for several days if they rationed it, for they would come to learn that the air down here in the dungeon, though quite cool at night, could turn sweltering hot and humid, especially when the dungeon master had his fires burning. The man liked to keep the fires stoked when he had prisoners, never knowing for sure when a court officer might want a prisoner tortured or possibly executed. He also enjoyed waving red-hot branding irons around to frighten the Americans, with his guttural laughter added in for special effects. GW saw how their good-hearted jailer looked with envy at their clothes and boots and was sure their garments might be the man's payment for his dastardly duties.

The floors of the dungeon were filthy with thick layers of oily grime and the cell floor was covered in old bits of straw, coated in splotches of what looked to be a lot of dried blood. It was hard to tell by torchlight, but with all the scurrying noises about the room, they knew there were rats about, noisily excited by the arrival of fresh prey and seemingly to be in great numbers.

"Think they'll feed us?" Hughes asked.

"Look around, you sure you want to eat anything they have to offer?" Grant replied, and GW silently nodded his head in agreement.

For the rest of that day and the entire night they remained alone, the exception being the bizarre looking jailer, who would look in on them every two to three hours. He would rarely say anything, but simply pop his head through the door, sneer at them, laugh, and then be gone until the next visit.

"Do you get the idea that clown is sizing us up for all these fancy toys?" Grant asked.

"If he gets close enough, I'll get that dagger off him," Hughes said in a confident tone.

Grant then looked to GW and asked, "So, Corporal, you got any brainy ideas yet? Have we walked into a loony bin, or are we the loonies?" He leaned against the cell bars and tried to get drowsy for his turn to nap. They took turns sleeping on a rotating shift; one asleep for four hours and the other two awake to ensure the rats stayed at bay.

"All I have is questions...Lots and lots of questions." He kicked one of the lower cell bars in frustration, "None of this makes any sense!"

"Maybe the NVA caught us in the cave, we were all unconscious from that cave-in and they drugged us with some new mind drugs. You know the CIA was accused of doing that last year with some of those Berkley hippies?" Hughes said. But he didn't believe it. He knew one person having a psychotic event could be explained, but not three people sharing in the exact same episode, unless of course that I've imagined the other two of you and you're all part of this crazy fantasy.

"No, it doesn't work. Too many factors here to be one of us having a single mental breakdown. But, this whole thing is too farfetched to be normal, something has happened to us...but why us?" Hughes took a turn at kicking the cell bars and then retrieved his canteen for a sip and washing a handful of water over his face.

"Maybe it's only me having this nightmare and I've created the other two of you." Grant said as he looked at both GW and Hughes with wide crazy looking eyes.

"I already thought of that and that's when I said it doesn't work," Hughes said.

GW wasn't so sure, so he walked up to Grant and punched him hard on the left arm, "Did that hurt?"

"Yeah," Grant said curtly. "But I could still be dreaming it all, including the pain in my arm. Thanks a lot...Now I'll never get to sleep."

"You could also go crazy by trying to figure all this out as only a dream," Hughes said. "Have any of you ever experienced anything like this in your dreams? I haven't." He then added, "No, this is all real, all too real. But the big questions are how and why?"

"Like I said before, too many questions and too few answers," GW said. "But you'd better get some sleep, Grant. We've got to keep alert, wait for a chance to escape."

"Sleep!" Grant exclaimed. "Look down at this floor? I'd probably wake up with rats chewing on me or something worse trying to climb in my ear." Grant glared at Hughes, "You and those dang cave worms!"

"You made your point, but Hughes managed it and you really need to rest," GW said. Then he kicked the floor straw around and upon inspecting closer, pulling a few of the more soiled ones out and casting them outside the cell, he made a bed for Grant with the least offending bedding material he could find. GW then looked at Hughes, "You take this watch for our friendly jailer and I'll watch for rats. If it's big enough, I'll wrestle for best two out of three and we'll have it for breakfast."

"Funny...yuk!" Grant said. With a revolting look on his face, he glanced about the cell floor to see if any of the straw was moving about. He then tossed his flak-vest down on top of it and plopped down on top of it. He wasn't about to lay out flat, but he leaned against the bars and kept his legs crossed in order-to keep all of him on top of the flak vest.

They'd lost their rucksacks, shovels and knives, but they'd been allowed to keep their pants, boots, canteens with belt, and their flak-vests. The vests had confused the locales, wondering why these strangers would wear such heavy tunics and they found the material quite strange. It did not appear to them as any form of armor, so Captain Rynarr allowed them to keep it.

Hughes again washed his eyes out with fresh water because the foul fumes in the room were making them water and the jailer's two fires were transforming the dungeon into a giant cook stove. GW then took a couple sips to fight off dehydration and while keeping to his feet, he leaned against the grimy cell bars and released a deep depressive sigh. While standing there, he watched over his two friends and continued to check his watch every few minutes. He was also wishing he was home in San Francisco, fishing with his dad and bringing in a whopper for dinner. But the thought of a smoked perch made his stomach rumble and he focused on another memory. As time slowly passed by, the smoke from the dungeon's fires burning at their eyes and listening to Grant's snores, every few moments both GW and Hughes would wash their faces down with a few droplets of tepid water from their canteens. With each precious drop used, they both wondered if their captors would replenish their supply.

"Try to imagine we're in some Turkish bath," Hughes suggested.

"Do they smell this bad?" GW asked.

"I have no idea," Hughes replied. "According–to my dad, all the bath houses in Frisco are hangouts for hippies, dopers and homosexuals. He thought one was as bad as the other, but at least he said most of the queers bathed."

"I take it your dad was not of the liberal persuasion?"

"No. He was of the 'God will strike down these perverted souls', persuasion." Hughes replied and then wiped his eyes with the sweaty palms of his hands. The salt burned, but the pain seemed to help him stay alert.

"What did your old man think about you joining up and coming to Vietnam?" GW asked in a whisper, hoping not to wake up Grant with their conversation. He had noticed how grumpy his new friend was lately and figured it was due to a lack of sleep, and of course their current situation. I'm surprised the guy isn't having a raving nightmare right now. But he's sleepin' like he's got no worries...lucky dude.

"My old man, he's a pretty–good guy actually thought all young men should serve their country to maintain our freedom. Though he really didn't understand our presence in Nam, or what we hoped to accomplish here. Now I wonder if I'll ever see him again."

"Yeah, I wonder about that too." GW broke off the conversation and plopped down onto his flak vest on the floor. His legs were tired and crossed them to massage his left calf. "Man, if

I wanted to walk so much I'd have joined the infantry...My feet hurt."

Hughes grinned in response. Being airborne they did a lot of foot work and he hadn't jumped out of plane since leaving the states. They rode helicopters everywhere, then hiked out a few miles, got picked back up and flown back to Camp Eagle. This was his first major operation, but the hike they had made to the cave and traveling through the underground corridors was the most walking he'd accomplished since leaving Advanced Infantry Training, before leaving for Jump School.

Hughes maintained his watch on the door, his hands loosely grasping the cell bars and he was no longer concerned with their filth. Looking out over the various torture tools, he wondered, which of those do I get? What can I tell them? I don't speak the language...Maybe we should stage a jail break...I could handle Igor all right but using a scimitar and a spear wasn't part of my basic training, and I sure don't like horses.

A few moments later, the demonic looking jailer opened the door to look in and this time he laughed with a vile sounding chuckle at his prisoners before he once again vanished.

Hughes glanced down at GW, "I do not take that as a good sign, Corporal."

"You're probably right." He looked over at the nearest fire pit, where three branding irons were in the coals and burning red hot in color. "If they try to use one of those on me...or you guys, someone's gonna die."

It was late afternoon of the second day of incarceration when they received their first real visitor; Captain Rynarr, who was attired in his royal blue tunic and plume black trousers. He wore no armor, nor a veil, but was wearing his silvery gauntlets and a very fanciful jeweled hilted scimitar on his left side. There was also an equally adorned sheath-less short sword and sheath on a second-wide silvery belt with the weapon to his right. When Captain Rynarr entered the dungeon, he brought a long shimmering blue scarf up to his face, attempting to block the putrid fumes from reaching his nose and took a quick glance about the room. Even with the scarf covering his face, GW had no trouble recognizing the look of disdain upon his face and felt an unexplained surge of hope awaken in him. There was something about this man that GW was drawn to and he knew it had something to do with the cross GW wore about his neck. Captain

Rynarr shook his head in disgust and with a shrug of his shoulders, he walked over to where the branding irons were now smoldering and kicked them off the fire pit. The irons landed on the floor and nearly set fire to some old straw, but the jailer rushed by Captain Rynarr and stomped down on the debris to keep a fire from catching. Shaking his head in disgust, Captain Rynarr continued to look about the darkened room. He detested the nauseating odors emanating from the dungeon floor and he issued forth a curt order that sent the jailer quickly away. Captain Rynarr then slammed the dungeon's door on the jailer's retreating backside so he could be left alone with the strangers.

Approaching the cell, Captain Rynarr gestured to GW with his right hand, the one holding the scarf, to come forward. He also displayed a small silver dagger in his left hand, which appeared as if by magic, to show GW he had further protection if it was warranted. Using the bars on the far wall to help himself up, GW wiped the oily grime off his hand and on to his pants and told the other two men to relax. He moved toward the remarkably well-dressed knight. There was no hint of a friendly expression upon the knight's face, as he inspected GW with a hard glare. Only a foot from the bars and not wanting to get any closer, GW waited to see what the knight wanted. He didn't have to wait long. Captain Rynarr gestured with an open right hand, palm up and used his dagger to gesture at the wooden cross hanging from GW's neck.

"Seems our host wants to see my cross again, either of you got any ideas?"

"I say, you might as well let him have it," Grant said. "By the time these fellows get through with us, you probably won't have a neck to hang it on."

"You might have a point there," GW agreed. Cautiously, keeping both eyes on Captain Rynarr, he lifted the cross over his head and slowly presented it to Captain Rynarr. Once in his hand, Captain Rynarr backed away from the cell, casually nodded his head twice and then turned to leave the dungeon.

"Probably wanted it for a trophy, he'll drape it over your helmet and tell all his friends how he killed another Christian in a great valiant battle," Grant said mockingly. Then with a sneer, he added, "Officers, they're all–alike."

"This is all too much...It's impossible! There is no way we can be in some desert country, much less thrown back in time to...whatever year this is," Hughes shouted out. Then he slammed his fist up against the nearest steel bar and cringed from the pain it caused.

"Calm down, Hughes," GW ordered. "It won't do you or us any good to lose our heads. We all have questions and there are no answers. We 're stuck in a cave for six days and suddenly, we appear halfway around the world." GW threw his hands up in the air in frustration and his face displayed an expression of bewilderment.

"Maybe, maybe there's someone here who knows…" Hughes was saying, but then he stopped suddenly, when he heard the dungeon door creak open.

"Is that good old American, I hear?" A deep sounding voice bellowed out the question, as the dungeon door swung open wide and an older, very overweight man dressed in priest-like garb entered the room. Behind him, Captain Rynarr came through the door and immediately closed it behind him to keep the all-too-helpful jailer from entering.

"You…you speak English!" GW exclaimed, his eyes wide with hope. Grant was now on his feet, standing beside GW and staring at the elderly man before them.

Brother Samuel couldn't help but smile. Except for himself and his young pupil, Princess Lennia, who was still having trouble with pronouncing some of Brother Samuel's strange language, he hadn't spoken his native tongue with anyone else for over 40 years. There were times he was concerned he might even forget how too and made the decision to teach English to the Princess to help him from not forgetting. Brother Samuel knew the English knights would be forthcoming, traveling through Libya and he wanted to be ready to receive them. He had high hopes that his presence here could possibly prevent some of the atrocities recorded in history.

"I wasn't trying to ease drop, gentlemen, but sounds carry quite well down here. I have always suspected the stone work allowed for previous kings to hear their enemy's tortured cries, without actually being present to view the ghastly scene," Brother Samuel said. He walked closer to the cell, cringing from the foul smells and sighing with revulsion at seeing the tools of torture about him. He then gazed upon the strangers silently for a moment and then knowing he was being rude to these young men with his silence, he put his right hand out and said, "Welcome to the City of Silene, home to his royal highness, King Ramie, Lord Protector for the northern lands of Libya."

"Libya?" GW asked in astonishment. "This is Libya? We're in Libya, as in Libya, North Africa?" His hand automatically reached out to shake Brother Samuels, but then he pulled it back, as he heard the name of the country he was in. There was something completely wrong here and the confusion only added to the stress he was feeling, and the act of shaking hands with a complete-stranger standing on the other side of his cell felt all too weird.

"Where's Libya?" Grant asked. Geography was not one of his best subjects in high school and his question seemed to relax the moment.

"North Africa, Grant. Didn't you hear me when I asked him?" GW rebuked him and then stated matter of fact-like, "We've nearly come clean across the world, or through it," GW said. His shot Grant an angry glare and then turned to Brother Samuel.

GW then asked the question that had been bugging him since they climbed out of that hole and spotted the castle. "Okay, I can almost buy that since we're here and it's apparently not some nightmare the three of us are sharing. Can't explain it, but with so much desert sand and the blue ocean out there, I know we've left Southeast Asia. But now, let's have the cherry on the sundae to make this nightmarish experience complete, what year is this? I mean this castle, these people...I feel like we've traveled back in time to the days of King Arthur and you're Friar Tuck."

Brother Samuel was forced to stifle a laugh, "Friar Tuck...I like that." He grinned at Captain Rynarr, who didn't understand any of this.

"I was wondering when you might get to that question and I hope you're ready for the answer." Brother Samuel looked in the young faces of the three men and then calmly replied, "This is the year 1178 A.D."

He let that sink in as the Americans stared back at him with their mouths open and then they glanced at each other. Doubt quickly turned to bewilderment and then they realized he might just be telling the truth. All three walked away from the bars, depression dogging their heels as they wondered if they'd ever see their loved ones ever again?

Grant leaned against the far wall, ignoring the grime and seemed to be studying a multi-legged insect crawl up one stone and then the next. Hughes, he simply dropped down to the floor on his knees and seemed oblivious to the old straw bedding that reeked with the odor of human feces. And GW, he began pacing the small cell like an expectant father in a hospital waiting room, with his arms behind him, while he thought over what had happened to them.

"I know that hit you men pretty hard, believe me. This also happened to me, in fact I too learned of it in this very dungeon. But, there was no one who spoke English then and I was imprisoned here for three-years, standing up to their torture, while I learned their language and proved my worth to them, so that I would be released." He then turned to look at Captain Rynarr, patted him on his left shoulder with a friendly hand and then looked back to the three bewildered prisoners before him. They all wore an expression of loss, but his face was one of anticipation, hoping they might be able to provide information he'd waited so long to hear.

"Now gentlemen, I have so many questions to ask of you and I can't tell you how happy I am to be able to converse in our native tongue once again. It's been so very long since I've held a good old conversation with men such as your selves."

GW looked back at the old man and right then he spotted the wooden cross the man wore around his neck. He first thought it was his but noticed there were some differences; his cross hung from elephant hair, while Brother Samuel's hung from a thin braided twine. The simple design of the cross was the same, only the type of wood was different. "Are you a priest?"

"I am now, but before I tell you about me, please share with me something about yourselves. From your field packs and equipment, I know you to be American soldiers, am I right? Maybe Marines?"

"Marines?" Grant said in disgust.

"Quiet, Corporal Grant!" GW ordered. He then replied with his full name, date of birth and service number, "You will understand, sir, that as prisoners we may only give our name, rank and service number."

Brother Samuel stared at him for a moment and his eyes grew concerned, as he thought this over. "Geneva Convention, right?" Brother Samuel turned to speak to Captain Rynarr, who nodded his head once in response and then left the room without glancing back.

"I apologize," Brother Samuel said. "I'd like to open the cell door, but for the moment this is impossible. However, I hope to be able to remedy that very soon. In the meantime, I guess I'd make you more at ease if I identify myself and tell you of my own story," Brother Samuel said in an almost whisper of a voice. "Strange to speak of it now, as I've kept it hidden for so long that it feels like a previous lifetime. You'll understand, for around here you can be killed if you tried to explain what had happened to me and now, to what has happened to you three."

Slightly bent over from back strain, Brother Samuel ambled over to a far wall and retrieved a wooden stool. This was going to take some time and standing wasn't easy on his old arthritic bones.

"It was November 8, 1942. I was a naval liaison officer aboard the HMS Hartland--a British destroyer, operating off the Port of Oran. Not too far from here actually...We were supporting an operation preparing to land a sizable body of British, Australian and American troops in our battle against the French forces then occupying the land. Instead, we wandered right into an ambush and the entire beachhead opened up on us with shore batteries." His eyes became watery, as he recalled that night in his mind, replaying the scenes of death and destruction.

"Those Brit's, they were a good bunch of boys, but they sure liked their tea. I couldn't stand the stuff myself, preferred my coffee black and hot as a witch's cauldron." He glanced around the room and stretched his arms out wide. "Getting old isn't what it's cracked up to be, my friends. Teeth fall out, hairline recedes, vision goes and...you probably don't want to hear all about my woes right now. GW shook his head in response and turned to sit back on his flak vest, while both Grant and Hughes were still on their feet and listening to every word.

"So, I was acting as liaison officer to the British Navy and charging up some outside stairs for my assigned battle station, when next thing I knew, I was blown off the deck from an explosion. I flew through the air and landed in the water. I still remember floating around for some time, owing my life to a water-logged life belt I usually kept under my bunk. That night for some reason, I remembered to put it on." Brother Samuel smiled at the three men and then continued, "But, I still swallowed a lot of seawater, while the waves washed over me, and the current seemed to be carrying me away. Before long, I couldn't see my ship anymore. It was dark, smoky and the battle was waging. No one seemed to be hearing my calls for help and I lost sight of all the ship's lights in all the smoke from the battle. Then the strangest thing happened, the water began to bubble all about me, like it was boiling, but strangely, it wasn't hot.

"Some strange colors suddenly appeared beneath me, like a swirling rainbow and they rose up to encircle me. Next thing I know I was caught in some kind of spiraling whirlpool and it sucked me down. I fought to get out, knew I was going to drown. Thought it was some kind of rip tide or a whirl pool, but the current was too strong and then I lost consciousness." Brother Samuel stopped, expecting to see looks of disbelief on their faces, but when he didn't, he continued with his story.

"I awakened to find myself being dragged out of the water by several dark brown skinned men. Poor guys, they probably saved my life and I vomited up about a gallon or two of seawater on them, when we reached the beach.

"Thinking they could be allied to the French, I tried speaking a few words of French I knew, but they didn't understand me. I even spoke some of the local dialect I picked up for this operation, but they simply shook their heads and continued to pound on my back to get all the water out of me, until I finally got them to stop. I had to push them away and I guess they thought I was fighting with them.

"Then this strangely dressed soldier showed up and began screaming at me in this weird gibberish of his, while waiving this weird, but very lethal looking shaped sword around in my face. I know now it was a scimitar but having never seen one before or knowing what he was saying, I was fearful for my life. All I could think to do was respond with my best haymaker." He grinned and then gestured back toward the door.

"That was Captain Rynarr who just left us, head of the Royal Guard and it was his father I knocked down and believe me, after that brief exchange, it took some time before his old man and I became friends. It embarrassed him greatly to be knocked cold by an unarmed man, especially a strange white man. It didn't look good for the King's Captain to be abused in such a way. But time heals all wounds and now you could say I'm like Captain Rynarr's Dutch uncle."

"Were you the first white man they'd seen?" Grant asked.

"No, but the only other white men around here are Berbers; rough-necks...gangsters you might say and often identified as pirates. Silene was not on the best terms with the Berbers back then.

"I also learned later they first thought I was most likely a Berber chieftain and Captain Rynarr senior was already anticipating a glorious execution for me."

"Excuse me, sir, but what was your rank in the navy?" Hughes asked, still somewhat skeptical over the whole idea of these weird lights and time travel thing.

Brother Samuel reached into a large pocket in his robe and removed an old black leather wallet. From it, he carefully withdrew his old military officer's ID card and a California driver's license. He smiled, while he glanced over them before handing them through the bars to Hughes.

GW was back on his feet and he took the wallet and ID from Hughes, he then handed them to Grant. All three of them noticed the dates on the two ID's, which lined up with Brother Samuel's story."

Brother Samuel then removed a beaded metal necklace from the same pocket, from which dangled his military dog tags and a class ring.

"Annapolis, Class of '37," he said proudly. "I was...and I guess I can still say I am a Lieutenant Commander in the United States Navy, but I haven't been paid for over 42 years. Just think of the back pay if I ever got back." He saw their eyes grow wide as the three of them again viewed his ID cards and dog tags.

"I had more hair back then, but no beard, as you can see." He stood up from his stool to stretch his back, "From your things I gathered you three are members of the US military. From your earlier response to my question of you being Marines, I'd have to venture to say you're soldiers."

"Yes, sir," GW said. Then assuming the position of attention, which caused him to wince a bit from all the bruises and sore muscles he called the other two to attention and saluted.

"Commander Samuels, my apologies for earlier statements I made," GW said. He then went on to introduce himself, Corporal Grant, and PFC Hughes. "Sir, we're members of the 101st Airborne Division, previously stationed at Camp Eagle, South Vietnam. During an operation into the A Shau Valley, our unit was attacked by North Vietnamese regulars on April 25th, 1968."

"1968, you say. That's 26-years from when I disappeared." Brother Samuel shook his head in wonder and then asked, "Then the war is still going on?"

GW looked to his friends in puzzlement and then he understood what Brother Samuel was asking about and he broke into a grin. "Sorry, sir, we were fighting a different war. Your war...World War Two, ended in 1945 with the defeat of Germany, Italy and Japan." GW then began giving Brother Samuel a brief rundown of the history of the United States between 1942 and 1968. Of how President Roosevelt had died in office, handing the reins over to Vice-President Truman, who then dropped two atomic bombs on Japan and of how Adolph Hitler committed suicide moments before the Russians could take him prisoner.

GW saw the smile widen on Brother Samuel's face when he heard of the end of World War II and General Eisenhower election to President. GW then spoke of the Korean conflict of the early 1950's, what he remembered of it from history class and rattled off the names of the next presidents to follow Eisenhower, and then the beginnings of the Vietnam War. When he had finished, Brother Samuel remained silent, his smile gone and a startled look on his face from hearing of the continual warfare across the world.

"Wow...looks like we have a war for every decade. I'd hoped mankind would get along after World War Two." Brother Samuel stood up and ambled about in front of the bars, then he remembered to ask another question, "And what of the bums?"

"Bums, sir?" GW asked in confusion.

"Dodgers, man...Brooklyn Dodgers! What happened to them?"

"They moved to Los Angeles, sir. Last I heard they were doing okay, but I'm not a baseball fan."

"They moved to LA? My old hometown was Brooklyn, but I got transferred to the West Coast before they shipped me overseas and now I hear the Dodgers go and get moved to Los Angeles..." Brother Samuel shook his head and laughed heartedly.

"Sir, can you get us some chow?" Grant asked. He liked baseball with the best of them, but his stomach was his top priority right now.

"Right," Brother Samuel replied. "It will not be what you're used to, my young friends, but our food here will fill you up...and you're lucky, the food they served me down here, what little it was, gave me the runs." He grinned and then walked to the cell to offer his hand again to each man, after he had retrieved his things, "Welcome aboard, shipmates. First thing to do is to get you fed, some much better quarters, and tomorrow you'll begin your language classes."

"You've got enough pull to break us out of here, sir?" Grant asked.

"You'll still be under guard, Corporal Grant, at least for the time being. However, I will advise Captain Rynarr that you're my people, lost at sea like myself, and you were trying to find a way back home to Britain."

"Britain, sir?" Hughes asked.

"Oh yeah, I'd better fill you in on my story...the one I use here." Brother Samuel then went on to explain the whole monk thing.

Afterward, Hughes asked him, "What about me, sir? Not a lot of Blacks in Britain in the 12th Century, they hadn't begun the slave trade yet."

"Not to worry, young man, you are now a Nubian." Brother Samuel reached in the cell and patted Hughes on the shoulder. "There are a lot of black Moors in North Africa, which is what Captain Rynarr first thought you were and it confused him that you couldn't understand him. But to play it safe, we will say you are from the land of Sudan...a Sudanese. You were simply accompanying your friends here as a...." Brother Samuel had to think for a moment and then said, "...as an official escort from your native court. No one will really care, that is until you learn their language, court protocols and customs. Muslim laws are pretty strict, and death is often the result for violating one protocol or another."

Captain Rynarr opened the door and looked to Brother Samuel, to see if he was finished. Brother Samuel waved to him with a friendly gesture and said a few words in the local dialect. Captain Rynarr then entered and stepped forward until he stood beside Brother Samuel. He gestured to the three Americans and asked Brother Samuel several questions concerning them. Once finished, he awaited Brother Samuel's reply.

Instead of replying to Captain Rynarr, Brother Samuel spoke to GW, "My dear Captain would like to know if either of you are indeed warriors? His question concerns the upcoming festival and he desires to know if you can ride well enough to participate in Silene's upcoming festivities? I will tell you this invitation is a sign of respect, due to our friendship and you should consider accepting his offer." Brother Samuel then quickly asked, "Can either of you ride a horse by any chance?"

"Sir, would you please advise the dear Captain that we appreciated his earlier treatment of us, mainly letting us live and that in fact we are all warriors. We look forward to this...festival," GW said. With respect in his eyes, he looked to his captor.

Grant stepped forward and clutched the bars with his hands and said to Brother Samuel, "Yes, sir. I can ride. I was born to a saddle on a Texas ranch and I'd give my eye teeth for a chance at one of those black Arabians."

Brother Samuel smiled and then advised Captain Rynarr of their answers. He then turned to face GW and continued to speak in his English tongue. "In my excitement, I forgot to give you my real name. I am or should say used to be, Sam Albright. I truly am Catholic, and I left behind a beautiful young wife and one baby son. With all this time shifting business I imagine him to be a few years older than you men." Brother Samuel lowered his eyes as his heart continued to grieve over the loss of his family so long ago.

Then remembering his new friends, Brother Samuel looked in GW's eyes, "Here they all refer to me as Brother Samuel, a defrocked Catholic priest from faraway Ireland."

"Sir, you really don't sound very Irish," GW said. He also wore a bit of a smirk on his face as he said it.

"To these people, I am about as Irish as they're ever going to see."

"Thank you, sir, for coming here," GW said in a grateful tone. "For the first time in the last seven days, I think we might just survive."

Hughes stepped forward, a twinkle to his eyes and he asked, "By the way, sir, where might be the nearest rib joint...an A&W, or maybe a McDonalds hamburger joint? In the event we do get released."

Brother Samuel burst out laughing, which surprised Captain Rynarr, who backed away from the old man. "Sorry, gentlemen, but I've never heard of McDonalds, but if you take a hard left at the main gate and make a right at the next stop sign...Oh, I can see you three are going to be a lot of fun." He made his way to the door, still laughing, and he let Captain Rynarr leave the room first and then, before stepping through the doorway, he asked, "You mentioned you were not an avid baseball fan, what other professional sports are going on now?"

GW was the first to answer, "Me personally, Sir? I like football and sometimes basketball. My team is the LA Rams."

"Professional football? They were trying to make it work before the war began, but most of the men went off to fight."

"Big money in football, sir. Television did a lot for the game and all the other pro-sports."

"Television?" Brother Samuel looked back with a question on his face.

"Oh boy, we have a lot to catch you up on, sir," Hughes said with a grin.

Brother Samuel quietly nodded his head in response and then remembered a final warning, "Learn the customs fast, men and seriously, make sure you leave the womenfolk alone. Over here they'll cut your head off for simply looking at the wrong lady. They may appear to be ignorant barbarians, but in this time their customs and tradition make up the center of their culture. You understand what I'm saying, gentlemen?"

All three men came to attention and responded with, "Airborne, sir!"

Brother Samuel shook his head in puzzlement and then asked, "And please explain to me what that means?"

GW grinned and then said, "Means-can do, sir. We understand."

"Good." Brother Samuel replied and then smiled, "Oh, that's right, you're the trusting souls who jump out of perfectly good airplanes. I've heard about you. But dear God, why couldn't I have been sent some crusty salt-water sailors?" He left, and the three Americans relaxed, probably for the first time since they found the fresh water streambed near the cliff.

Within the hour, a very displeased jail guard returned with a servant, who carried a large wooden platter of chow for the men. Snarling at his prisoners, he begrudgingly opened the cell door, so the servant could hand the food to them. But Igor showed his contempt for them by swiping a roasted half-chicken for himself and a clay mug of darkish water.

Still, the three men had plenty of greasy roasted chicken, a half-cooked leg of mutton, some strange half-cooked veggies and a platter of very tasty homemade bread to fill their stomachs.

There were also some dates, which none of the men sampled. A few hours later, Brother Samuel returned with six men-at-arms, each carrying a bright metal oval shield with the castle's blue dancing horse coat-of-arms painted on it and a large golden-colored scimitar in hand. One of the Silene soldiers was shorter than the rest and the size of the scimitar looked like a two-handed affair, yet the man carried it proudly, if not a bit awkwardly.

GW, Grant and Hughes picked up their vests, making sure to wipe the bottoms off before putting them on and then they were cautiously escorted along the stone corridors and up the wide stairwells, from the dungeon to an upper level, three-floors up. Here they where they were placed into a single windowless room, which held three wooden beds with, intertwined ropes in place of springs. There was single large brown rug upon the stone floor and several clothes that the men thought to be what the Libyans used for blankets. They were also surprised to find their rucksacks in the room, which still held most of their stuff. Only their shovels and knives were missing and that they could understand, prisoners were not allowed to have weapons in their possession.

"Did you notice that look of remorse on the jailer when we left?" Grant asked the other two men

"He's just a lonely, misunderstood man in a low paying job with little chance of promotion. I've got an uncle like that, but not nearly as ugly," Hughes said jokingly. This got a laugh from the others.

GW and Grant promptly washed off their feet from a bucket of water provided for them and changed into clean socks, while Hughes pulled on a clean, but extremely wrinkled white t-shirt he'd saved. Outside the locked wooden door were two guards armed with shield and lance. They were members of the Royal Guard, who were rarely used for such duty and Brother Samuel saw this as a sign of Captain Rynarr's respect for Brother Samuel's friends.

After a long night of restful sleep, for they were all extremely tired, they were awakened when one of the guards, the larger of the two and quite sinister in appearance, opened the thick wooden door and allowed for a timid looking male slave to enter. He was carrying another large platter of food and the three men knew breakfast had arrived.

"Guess we better learn to like greasy chicken, mutton, warm water and homemade bread with weevils in it," Grant said. The tray held the same items they had had the night before, but it was sure better than nothing at all.

"Tell you what, I'll take this over C-rations anytime," Hughes said.

"What about the tin of pound cake?" Grant asked.

"Well, that's about the only good thing about C-rations...and beanie-weenies."

GW nodded his head in agreement and then prepared an old-fashioned poor boy sandwich, surprising the manservant by his strange method. This was the first sandwich he'd ever seen, and he smiled as the others repeated the process.

"Think they have any Mayo?" Grant asked between bites.

"And mustard," Hughes added in wishful thinking.

It was a couple hours later when the door opened again, giving off a loud creaking noise when Brother Samuel entered. There was no way anyone was going to sneak in on them, not with that creaky door. Not that the guards would allow it. Those were some serious looking troops, who looked as if they chewed on steel for lunch and made many a maiden shrivel with their harsh stares. Brother Samuel was wearing his customary robe and felt a bit strange when the three soldiers jumped to their feet and assumed the position of attention.

"All right, enough of that, from this point forward you men do not have to behave as if I am your superior officer...unless I order it so," he added. "I thought about it last night and being that we have no means of escape from this time zone and a priest normally doesn't have personal bodyguards, we must act as if we are old friends from sunny Ireland." He pointed at Grant and GW, "You two are my clan members and presently soldiers of fortune and you, Mr. Hughes...you were sent to bring these two back to the Sudan to work as mercenaries, when it was learned you two had no problems in working with Muslims."

"We understand, sir," GW said. "But it's a bit hard to break with military custom once we realized you were an officer."

"Yes, I understand, but we must now deal with the cards dealt to us. We are here and here we will stay...Or, until another bizarre event occurs, and we're somehow returned to where we belong. But I've been here for 42 years, gentlemen. You had better adjust yourselves to this time-period...Unless one of you have a time machine in one of those packs?"

"Brother Samuel, just why were you defrocked from the priesthood?" Hughes asked. "In case we're asked about...uh, once we know their language."

Brother Samuel grinned in response to the question. He glanced at the two guards, knowing they could not understand a word he was saying and replied, "I needed to come up with some excuse to why I was leaving the Holy Land and have a possible in with these people. If you remember your history...um, how'd you all do at high school?"

"I graduated and worked in a museum, but my specialty was dinosaurs," Hughes said.

"I graduated too, but history was not one of my best subjects," Grant said.

"And how about you, Mr. Sanders," Brother Samuel asked, gesturing to GW.

"My thing was sports, girls and fishing...but I got my diploma. Thought about junior college, but we couldn't afford the books."

"All right," Brother Samuel said. He wondered for a brief-moment if his own son had made it in to college or if he was in this Vietnam war these young men spoke of? "Well, this was the time of the second Crusade, which failed and the coming of the third Crusade led by King Richard of England. Many of these men, which history knew to be the Knights Templar, wore the cross of Jesus Christ on their tunics and shields. They supposedly owed their allegiance to the Pope and not to King Richard and were an unruly lot. They raped the land and people for profit and their own sinful urges. Knowing this tidbit of history and desiring to survive amongst these Muslims, I created a story about my past. How I was being sent home for giving aide to the Muslim people. I knew quite a few of these desert people from North Africa to Syria were badly mistreated and Christianity has suffered for it ever since. By the time of the fourth Crusade, Muslim people across the Middle East were openly killing any Christian they could lay their hands on for revenge. We had left the Holy Land strung with the defiled bodies of Muslim women and murdered children, so I have worked very hard to show that not all Christians are sons of the devil."

"How do you do that?" Grant asked.

"By teaching simple logic in the king's court and helping the people with some minor inventions, such as restoring the Roman waterworks system in the castle to bring clean water back into the city from an underground river. I have the fountains running again and the castle has an ample supply of fresh water from the large tank overhead, which sends water down through a thousand or more feet of clay pipes.

"I have also halted the torture of men who've not had the chance to defend themselves in front of the King's ministers." Brother Samuel, weary from his hike up and down the castle stairs, plopped down on GW's rope bed. "Oh, what'd I give for a good feather mattress?"

"They have chickens, sir, can't you use the feathers?" Hughes asked.

"The armors save most of the feathers for arrows, plus there is the stench. Not quite up to factory standards you understand, Mr. Hughes."

"Yes, sir," Hughes said with a grin upon his face. He then looked at his rope bed and appreciated the simple workmanship. He didn't mind the rope bed too much, once he got his flak-vest spread out to shield the upper part of his body from the stiff abrasive ropes. From his experience in the museum, he had learned how most people in the past lined their rope beds with various animal furs, but they had found no furs in their new quarters and made do with their vests and whatever they had that worked in their rucksacks.

"I've been teaching basic studies to the king's daughters and to his youngest girl, a course in English. Six years ago, I became First Advisor to King Ramie, a high honor and possibly the only Christian in the world to hold such a post in a Muslim country," he said with a note of pride.

"What about this king, does he know about us?" Grant asked.

"Certainly, you do not keep secrets from his royal highness if you want to keep your head. But as I said, he knows you are my fellow countrymen and Mr. Hughes a Sudanese with ties to the high court there. This protects him from becoming a slave here, and yes, they do practice slavery here and believe me it's not based on color of your skin."

"What of this upcoming festival we heard you speaking of, sir…I mean Brother Samuel?" GW asked.

Before he could answer, Brother Samuel grabbed the clay bottle of water and took a large gulp. "Nasty stuff, but you'll get used to it…Ah, what I'd give for some ice tea." He then glared at the three men for a moment, "You three sure upturned my apple cart."

"Sir?" GW asked, not sure of Brother Samuel's meaning.

"Oh bother, it's only an old man's whining ways. I'd become used to my discomforts but seeing you three has brought my old complaints back to the surface. It's not your fault."

"How do you ever get used to weevils in your bread?" Grant asked, holding a chunk of bread in the air and flicking a large blackish weevil to the floor, where Hughes stepped on it.

Brother Samuel shook his head, smiled and then answered, "Learn to think of them as a protein source, Mr. Grant. But in another month, we will have fresh fruit and dates. Hopefully, the herdsmen will also bring in some lamb from the healthier herds to the west and fresh fish from the fishing fleets to the northeast. Dates we have, but they're down to the bottom of the storage pots and I won't eat them myself."

"The festival, sir?" GW asked again. He was curious about the event.

"Oh right, Mr. Sanders. Sorry. You have-to understand how exciting it is for me to have fellow countrymen here. The Liberian language can be quite boring once you master it...No good ol' American slang. But a lot of people here speak your basic Arabian too and some of the other African dialects.

"Anyway, as to the festival...They actually hold a lot of festivals here, but once a year they hold this big shindig...funny, that's a word I haven't used in 45 years...shindig!" Brother Samuel smiled again, suddenly recalling a celebration with his wife's family before he shipped out and then after a moment of silence, his smile dropped, and he returned to the present, "Lots of games and rows of colorful booths selling food and fruity drinks. No liquor here, my friends, remember these are Muslims and they do not partake of alcoholic beverages. However, they do make a nice drink made with honey.

"Then comes the major reason for the festival; soldiers of the king and any outsiders desiring to participate in various events of war-craft skills, do so before the Royal Family. These events include swordsmanship, use of the lance, shield and spear, of course horsemanship and archery. Then will come their version of an English joust and it will often involve several or more riders at a time. Non-lethal you understand, no points on the lances, but a knight could still get a few ribs busted from the blunt end of a sturdy lance or a shoulder dislocated if thrown from a horse."

"Is there some special reason behind the festival, the king's birthday or anniversary of his coronation, or is it much like our town fairs?" Hughes asked. He liked Brother Samuel, who reminded him of his former boss—Mr. Whitney Johnson, the museum curator. Mr. Johnson was good natured, had stood about five-foot, nine-inch in height, bent over at the shoulders from arthritis of the spine and a good 40-pounds overweight. Brother Samuel looked down at the stone floor, "No, you might say the actual reason behind the festival has a more sinister connotation behind its occurrence."

"Sinister?" Grant asked, noticing the immediate change in Brother Samuel's demeanor.

Brother Samuel looked to the three men, holding his eyes on each man for a long silent moment before he finally replied, "Yes, gentlemen, I said sinister. Sadly, the soldiers of the king's army must compete in the festival and those chosen for their prowess with weapons and display of courage are assigned next year's duty for protecting Silene from...from," Brother Samuel felt a hesitation, a feeling of sounding like a crazy superstitious old man to someone who had never seen the beast in the lake. He slowly stood to his feet and listened as his knees creaked, "You might as well know right now, the City of Silene has its own dragon; a fearsome beast that lives in the lake to the north." Brother Samuel saw the dumbfounded look on their faces, recognizing it as probably the same expression he wore when he first learned of the dragon.

"Yes, I know. Sounds like something from Grimm's Fairy Tales. But believe me, gentlemen, this creature is very real and twice a month an innocent virgin is chosen by lottery to be sacrificed—actually, she is fed to the dragon. It's the duty of the soldiers chosen for a year of duty to guard the wall that separates the township from the lake and enforce the lottery. They claim the chosen victim from her home, escort her to the castle for an appearance before the king and then guard over her until she is taken to the chosen spot...where she will meet a horrific death. There is a large rock on the western shoreline, which is covered over in human blood from over a century of sacrifice.

"Here, she is bound by heavy chain and abandoned to await her fate. Between such...meals, the guards deliver to the lake small herds of sheep to keep the beast happy and the city safe. In the event the dragon is not satisfied and ventures toward the city, the men guarding the wall are prepared to give alarm and if need be, to sacrifice themselves to protect their king and the Kingdom of Silene."

"Have you seen this...dragon you speak of?" Hughes asked. He was trying hard not to smile. But the frightful look to Brother Samuel's eyes was of a man clearly tortured over what he has observed. Hughes knew this was no laughing matter, but the idea of a dragon still made him shake his head.

"I know, sounds like the delusions of an old man, but yes, I've seen the beast hundreds of times over the long years and believe me, though I do not believe in dragons, I have come to believe this beast is some kind of aquatic dinosaur. I think this horrid creature, or its parents were caught up in time, much as we were." Brother Samuel looked at the three men, who remained silent.

Brother Samuel raised his hands in a gesture of significance to the point he was trying to make, "Listen, ancient writings tell of a great cataclysm here, one that created a narrow land mass between two bodies of water, which I suspect formed our lake. Its salt water, not fresh water and this could possibly account for the beast's existence. If the animal or animals, as the writings specify more than one creature, were then trapped by the event and left to live in this salt-water lake, people here would believe them to be dragons. No one in this time knew anything about dinosaurs. However, I believe there is only one creature now and he must be very old, but who knows how long a dinosaur can live?"

"So, this beast is confined to the lake and surrounding shorelines?" Hughes asked.

"Yes, he or she is unable to leave the shoreline and cover the distance to the sea and there is only one recorded incident of the dragon ever attacking the castle and this was why the wall was constructed. I suspect it may have been our current dragon's parent, since it happened so very long ago and at a time when the Greeks inhabited this location."

"And does he have feet or fins, short necked or long necked?" Hughes asked in all seriousness.

"You sound as if you do know something about dinosaurs, Mr. Hughes."

"I've studied them as a hobby while growing up and worked two summers in the Natural History wing of our museum in San

Francisco." Hughes sounded excited. The chance to see an actual living dinosaur would be fantastic, unbelievable even.

"The beast's skin has a bluish-green coloring to it and is extremely thick; none of our weapons have been able to pierce it. And the beast is quite large, and very formidable. It has four fins, each twice the size of a large war horse and a long neck that when fully extended...I believe it reaches a height of some 50 feet or better. It also has an ugly reptilian head; quite lizard-like in appearance and about the size of a two-axle wagon. But that a mouth, it's nightmarish in appearance and filled with horrid teeth, each the size of a razor-sharp scimitar."

"Have you seen it on land?" Hughes asked, now even more excited.

"Yes, but never far from water. It seems to use it fins much like a seal and pulls itself forward. But the distance to the ocean from the lake is too great for it, so it remains confined to the lake."

"Why hasn't anyone killed it?" Grant asked. "Surely there are enough men here to mount an attack."

"Yes, Mr. Grant, we have plenty of troops, but arrows cannot pierce its thick hide, nor do swords or even lances. We have tried, gentlemen, but after losing so many men in our attempts, the king ordered a halt to any further attempts. Not that the men complained, they'd grown quite frightened of the beast from prior tales and witnessing their own fruitless attempts.

Knights were devoured in plain sight, horses ripped limb from limb and in some case the men were simply crushed, as the beast plowed over them in its return to the water. In the past, boats were used to attack the dragon, and all were sunk, and every man lost.

"Even those chosen to spend a year on guard duty fear for their very lives, expecting the dragon to once more attack the city and they'd be the first line of defense against an undefeatable creature. Most of them believe the dragon was sent from the very pits of hell to destroy them. At least that's how they believe, that the Dragon of Silene is a curse from the devil. I realize the dumb brute is trapped and will live out it existence here. We've seen no other monsters, so I do not believe there are any young ones about and when this one dies, the kingdom will be released from its supposed curse."

"Have you tried to explain how this creature is a dinosaur, that maybe they could dig a canal that would allow the creature access to the ocean?" GW asked.

"Mr. Sanders, give me some credit. I've spent all my years here trying to explain the dragon's existence and invented several different weapons, attempting to destroy the creature, but to no avail. I have no way of creating gunpowder and the poisons I've concocted have had no effect. The men fear the beast too much to attempt digging a canal as you suggest and now I spend my time trying to stop this accursed lottery. But the king's hands are tied as the lottery began by a king's decree long ago and he cannot stop it...nor would the townspeople allow him. For though they are the ones who give up their daughters to this accursed lottery, these people fear the dragon even more."

"I've been thinking," Hughes said, nodding his head as he spoke, "and I believe this dragon of yours sounds like a Plesiosaur or Plesiosaurus. They traveled in great packs, or pods, hunting much like the Orcas; or killer whale as they are commonly known. But I'd need to see it before I'm sure. The one you describe is much larger than any remains ever found for such a creature. But being an ocean critter, I guess most of the bones can only be found in the bottom of the sea. The ones earlier discovered were found in dead seas and the animals may have retreated to the larger bodies of water as the waterways shrank with time...Only a thought."

"Oh, you'll see it, Mr. Hughes. You can't stay here too long before making a sighting," Brother Samuel said. "You'll also see the old wreckage of the fishing and sailing vessels that once sailed upon the lake and attempted to slay the beast, now they line the shores for miles as a constant reminder to the creature's viciousness."

"Not even an army of knights can kill this...creature of yours?" Grant asked. He still didn't quite believe in the existence of the dinosaur, but he was also having trouble with his current situation and was beginning to wonder if his whole world had gone tipsy.

"No, Mr. Grant," Brother Samuel said. His voice was filled with sadness, memories of past failures and the men who had died because-of his failures caused him great grief.

"Our warhorses are fearful, our men-at-arms afraid, no one even attempts to do battle with the foul thing anymore and I for one do not blame them. For this thing is like a manifestation of evil itself."

"I'm amazed, sir. If evil, where is your faith?" GW said with his voice filled with a note of sarcasm and then felt ashamed for saying it.

"Do not belittle my faith, Corporal. You have only been here a few days and I have lived here these 40-odd years. I've watched many a brave man fall before this vile thing and many a young woman sacrificed out of fear." Brother Samuel turned toward the door to leave and then looked over his shoulder to say in a heated tone, "Captain Rynarr's father died in one such attempt. He was trying to save his only daughter who was chosen for lottery. Captain Rynarr lost both-of-them that day and I still grieve over my fallen friend."

GW felt like a foolish child and he apologized, "I am sorry, sir. You're right of course, but maybe between the four of us we can think of a way to destroy this dragon."

Brother Samuel turned to look hard at GW and then said, "You are young and from a modern time. So yes, maybe we can. But first, you must learn their language and it will be a difficult task for you have little time before the festival. Tonight, we will begin, right now I must attend to my other pupil and she is probably off on her latest attempt to conceal herself from me. She has a strong dislike for math, but a keen mind."

"When will we have a chance to meet this princess?" GW asked. He liked the idea of meeting a real princess, one who actually lived in the Middle-Ages. "Kind of like a story from the Arabian Nights."

"Unfortunately, Mr. Sanders, it will be months, maybe years before such a meeting can take place. She is protected by a loyal army and loved by her entire kingdom. Strangers, especially foreigners of such lower class, should not expect to be brought before the royal court...at least not until they've displayed some act of great courage, or completed a task worthy of an appearance before the king."

"So, I shouldn't hold my breath you mean."

"Do not get your hopes up," Brother Samuel said and then he grinned. "You have much to learn, young man." He patted GW on the shoulder and left the room.

Hughes walked over to GW and put a hand on his other shoulder, "This isn't some fairy tale, Corporal. No kissing the frog or defeating the nasty troll under the bridge. We'll be lucky to get out of this room and share a cup of wine with a beautiful farm wench."

"No wine, Hughes, they're Muslim remember?" Grant said.

"Aw, that's right. I'm Baptist myself...Well, partly Baptist, but maybe the beautiful wench part will still apply." Hughes walked toward the door and knocked, in hopes of getting the guard to answer. But the door didn't open, and Hughes returned to his bunk in silence.

"We're not in Kansas anymore, Toto," Grant reminded him. He then laid his head back and thought over the last few days.

"Who am I, Grant...the Tin Woodsman, Scarecrow or the Cowardly Lion?" GW asked.

"You're ranking man, you choose," Grant replied in a weary whisper.

"I'll pick Glenda the Good Witch," GW replied. "She at least had a bubble to fly around in. Maybe it could jump forward eight centuries."

"We should get some more sleep. You're all beginning to sound a bit strange," Hughes suggested.

"Strange? Hughes, might I remind you how we've jumped back in time, traveled half way around the world to a fairy-tale castle and met a mad monk who used to be a naval officer from World War II. Not to mention a dinosaur that people sacrifice young virgins to and you say we sound a bit strange." GW jumped up from his bunk. "I'm going off my rocker, this is like some mad dream and I'm going to wake up stuck in that damn cave with the NVA waiting to ambush me, as soon as I stick my head out...Strange? Hughes, you have no idea." GW plopped back down on his bunk, rolled over on his right side and tried to get to sleep. A nap right now might clear his mind for he was still weary from all those days in the cave and the startling realization he was back in the 12th century was extremely draining.

"Sure glad I quit smoking two months ago," Grant said. "I'd be climbing the walls by now if I hadn't."

"I never smoked, Corporal, but I'm looking for a spot on that proverbial wall right now," Hughes said. "Besides that, has anyone figured out what these people use for toilet paper?"

"Get some sleep, Hughes. I'll let you know later." GW then closed his eyes, Toilet paper? Right, we've used up all our C-ration

TP. Better check with Brother Samuel on that. And language, I was never good with languages. Flunked Spanish twice and he wants me to learn Arabic? Boy, my old man would be laughing his head off if he knew what was happening to his boy.

# 4 – A HORSE IS A HORSE, OF COURSE–OF COURSE!

CASTLE OF SILENE
IN BROTHER SAMUEL'S CLASSROOM

Brother Samuel's classroom and bedroom were of a small affair; two rooms in size, with eight-foot tall stone walls to a wood ceiling, supported by 14-inch beams. A wooden floor was covered over by two-large dark brown woven rugs and the outer walls of these fourth level quarters were made of stone blocks nearly a foot thick. Because of his standing in the king's court, he was provided with quarters having six, five-foot tall and two-foot wide window-like openings for ample air flow. His rooms faced the southwest, giving him a partial view of the lake and further on, the ocean. There was also a small balcony and when he ventured out on to it, this allowed Brother Samuel a good view of the training yards below. Though he was up high enough to keep most of the bugs out, he was still able to smell the offensive odors from the stables below. The positioning of his quarters allowed Brother Samuel direct sunlight during the long summer days and besides the increased heat, it did provide the appropriate illumination he needed for his extensive studies.

Two large Egyptian tapestries of a mosaic design hung from opposing sidewalls, covering the aged stone and each of these hand-woven pieces was indeed quite colorful and involved months of workmanship by gifted weavers.

For his convenience, Brother Samuel had his one-room classroom located adjacent his quarters. He often studied late into the night and often bleary-eyed he was known to stumble into his bed for a few hours of sleep before returning to his library of books. Most of these soft leather-bound books, held together by thin strips of lamb skin, he had written himself. Others were gathered from his visits to Italy, Greece and from friends who had visited the Holy Land.

His own bed was constructed of heavy wood and stout rope to handle his hefty frame, but it was also thickly laden with furs given to him by the king as gifts and he slept quite well in the winter months. But in the hot summers, he often slept on his extra wool robes for padding and left the furs on the floor. More than a few times he simply laid one of his robes down upon the stone floor of his balcony and slept under the summer stars and relished in the occasional ocean breeze. His few books, for he had less than fifty volumes of his own and twenty-one books from various writers, stood on a roughly built wooden shelve. Books were few in this age and for other than his own, the rest came from other authors, which he had borrowed, bought and traded for over the last three decades. He occasionally added to these books or made changes with his own knowledge of local geography and history, of math and current events of the day. But his editing was restricted to when the precious parchment became available. He sincerely missed having a decent paper writing pad or a chalk board for instructing his pupils.

Today, Brother Samuel, his brow deeply furrowed with concern, looked down upon his single pupil; Princess Lennia, with a stern glare to his eyes. She was seated at his heavy wooden school table and he awaited her answer to his last question.

"Come, come, Princess," he said impatiently, "We have gone over this several times. From the Atlantic Ocean, what island lies at the entrance to the great Mediterranean Sea?"

She looked up at him from her high-backed cushioned chair, lined with stretched camel hide and padded with sheep wool, smiled back at him and batted her wide blue eyes, which often seemed to radiate with a sparkle of mischievousness. Her blue eyes had come from her mother, who was of Berber descent. But her smile quickly vanished, seeing the look in his eyes and she asked, "Why do I care about islands so far away? We have no large seafaring ships, Brother Samuel. Our fishing fleet, small that it is, never journeys very far from our shores. Besides, I now wish to hear about these strange men Captain Rynarr brought in."

"That will be enough about my countrymen, young lady!" Brother Samuel said in a raised voice, using his English to make a point. Besides the king and her sisters, Brother Samuel was the only other person in the world who would dare to speak so harshly to her. This was a favor granted to him by the king himself, knowing how strong willed his daughters were and, also knowing his good friend, Brother Samuel, would never abuse such a boon.

He turned away from the princess and walked over to a large wooden table, built strong from Teak wood brought from the east and could hold a thousand pounds easily. At-the-moment, the only thing on the table were a few rolls of parchment and a strange ball shaped stone; about the size of an NBA basketball. Once the rough shape was delivered to him upon his request, after he found it near the natural rock base of the castle's foundation, he had labored for weeks to fashion a globe of the earth. He used a stone chisel to outline the continents. Brother Samuel only used this teaching tool with Princess Lennia and knowing it to be a blasphemous item for the current time-period and that it could well seal his doom if discovered, he trusted only her to keep his secret. He kept it hidden from curious eyes and the many spies of devilish Princess Lonnia by simply leaving it out in the open. No one knew what it was, for everyone else still felt the earth was flat. To even suggest it as being round could get one burned at the stake for practicing sorcery and being a heretic.

All morning, her questions focused on the three Americans and Brother Samuel had grown weary of it. He felt like a protective father, knowing he must keep her from them. Not only for her sake, but also for fear it could cost them their lives because the cultural barrier between royalty and these simple men from Ireland and a Nubian from Sudan was far too great to risk such an encounter.

Only last night he had fought a brief battle of wills with Princess Lonnia over the strangers and this was held in the King's presence. She strongly desired to have them executed or at least enslaved and sold in Tripoli, as a-way to strike back at Brother Samuel. The two of them kept a running feud going, tiring the king and making a lot of the people in the castle jumpy. But Brother Samuel had won out, by explaining to the King how two of them were of his family clan in Ireland and to kill them could bring down a curse upon the people of Silene. Both Brother Samuel and the King knew foreigners would be passing through his lands, especially with so many people traveling to the Holy Land, and he didn't need Irish clan members causing him any trouble with blood feuds. Brother Samuel didn't like to use superstition as a weapon, but he was fighting for these young men's lives. He knew how the king was mildly superstitious and these Americans, with their sudden appearance and strange attire, troubled him greatly. Their equipment and clothes had truly puzzled Captain Rynarr, especially the green colored helmets the men had worn and their inner shells to protect the head from the heavier outer surface. Captain Rynarr had never seen anything like these metal helmets before and had one of his personal guards attempt to slice into one with the stroke of his scimitar. This resulted in only a scratch and a dent from where the blade made contact and bounced off, which, when reported to the king, caused some degree of concern. These foreigners to the north had armor far superior to their own shields and breast armor.

Brother Samuel did not say anything about the helmets. But he did advise the king that to enslave or execute the Nubian, who represented a royal court in Sudan, could most likely bring forth hostile action from the Sudanese in response to such an act, and possibly even a war. But it was the king's own weariness of his oldest daughter's arrogant attitude, her loud disrespectful outbursts in his court and his knowledge of her sinister desires to seek out the dark powers of alchemy, which swayed him in to allow the strangers to live.

King Ramie placed them in Brother Samuel's hands and closed the affair by dismissing them both with a wave of his hand and returning to his bedchambers for some well-needed quiet time. Whenever he was forced to deal with his oldest daughter, the episodes always ended with him suffering from terrible headaches and a bout of indigestion. Brother Samuel had advised him these attacks of discomfort were brought on by physical stress, but this was a medical condition the king could not understand and would not be diagnosed for centuries to come. Grief he could understand and was thankful for the seclusion of his inner chamber, left darkened at all-times with heavy woven rug-like curtains pulled closed against the sunlight. This offered him some small degree of relief.

For the immediate future, the Americans were to be kept under guard and as expected, Brother Samuel was ordered to teach them the local language, Libyan customs and traditions of Silene.

Once the meeting had ended, Princess Lonnia, whose eyes were aflame with anger, leapt from her throne and stormed out of the royal court. But not before stopping in the stone arched doorway to assume her best lordly stance and direct a hard glare of superiority toward Brother Samuel. She then surprised him by exposing her teeth in an animalistic ferocious way and released a deep animal-like growl. But she wasn't done yet, for she then offered up this threat, "One day you will lose to me, old man and on that day, I will have your fat head on a spear for all to see."

Brother Samuel watched her vanish from the halls of the royal court and knew all too well how serious her threat to be. He only hoped the kingdom's youngest princess would be ready for the throne before that day, as he knew Princess Lonnia would surely bring hellfire down upon the Kingdom of Silene, if she was allowed-to rule. He must do everything possible to prevent such a thing from happening, even if that meant taking harsh steps to end Princess Lonnia's life. There were simply too many people at risk in the event Princess Lonnia became queen and he sincerely hoped the Lord would understand his actions.

"Why does it anger you so, my teacher?" Princess Lennia asked. "These are your people I speak of and I would like to know more of them." Princess Lennia then followed Brother Samuel to the table with the stone globe upon it and pointed right at the small island etched out upon the entrance to the Mediterranean Sea. "This you have called the Island of Gibraltar, but I find that a very unusual name."

"Yes, you have the name right and for the life of me I cannot remember where the name came from." His eyes softened toward her and he looked upon her with admiration. He loved her like a favorite daughter and it was hard for him to stay upset with her. In some ways, though admittedly several years younger, the princess reminded him of his lovely wife when they had first met so very long ago. He was thinking back to that moment when Princess Lennia broke his concentration, "You have taught me to be curious, Old Man, to learn things and these countrymen of yours make me curious.

"Unlike yourself, these men, including the Nubian, appear to be warriors. This was told to me by my hand maidens and I trust their assessment."

"Well, your handmaiden gossips too much." He walked to the nearest window and looked down upon the training yard. "And at one time I too was a young warrior...before I became a priest." Below him a dozen soldiers were training with swords and shields, locked in mock-combat.

After a moment of silence, he turned to face her and asked of her quietly, "What would you have me tell you that your handmaidens do not know already?"

"You say two of these men are of your Christian faith and I have heard one wears the cross of your Lord, but why do they dress in such strange green garments, and wear such strange shoes?"

Brother Samuel laughed, his belly jiggling, as this was not one of the questions he expected from his pupil. He returned to the globe to once again show her where Ireland was, "Our home is made up of mostly green forests and tall green grass. So, they wear green to camouflage themselves to hide from their enemies." He had spoken in English to use the word camouflage and awaited her response.

"Camo...camoflag, what is this word?" She asked, with a look of bewilderment to her eyes.

"Camouflage. Now please say it again several times...camouflage."

"Camoflag...camoflagg," upset she tried it again, "camouflage."

"Yes, now spell it out for me."

It took some time with a well-used piece of parchment, but Princess Lennia finally had it spelled right after her seventh attempt and she received a broad smile from Brother Samuel for getting it right.

"When I first arrived in Silene I was wearing similar garments, for my priestly frock was lost at sea."

"What is this camouflage you have now taught me to say and spell?"

"As I said, my young princess, it is clothing in which matches in color with the colors of trees, bushes and grass, to hide from your enemies. It is also an action in which one uses bits of grass and tree limbs to hide oneself, your cart or wagon and even your home from an enemy. This art of camouflage works very well in Ireland and other countries I have visited."

"Will it work here?"

Brother Samuel smiled at his young pupil, "You have palms, but no real trees or bushes. But possibly, I believe by digging a hole in the sand and covering yourself over with a cloth of a sandy color, you could remain motionless until your enemy approached and then jump up to surprise him." He remembered how the American Indians had used such a way to fight against the US Calvary in the southwest.

"This will give you time to impale him with a short spear or use a scimitar to cut him down." He had also read in several intelligence dispatches how the Japanese were using such holes quite effectively against the Marines in the Pacific islands.

"You should tell my father of this. For we have many enemies, and this is a good...trick," she struggled briefly to remember the word trick, "...to use against the enemy."

For the last year, the teacher and pupil used a combination of English and the local Libyan dialect to converse. Whenever someone else was around, like a handmaiden or Princess Lonnia, they would use English to talk between them and this infuriated the oldest princess greatly. They also spoke in Greek, as Brother Samuel had learned the language from several fellow Greek prisoners. Whenever there was a prisoner from another land, Brother Samuel would visit the dungeon to evaluate him. When the prisoner was found to be a good fellow and having some degree of intelligence, the King allowed Brother Samuel to bring him under-guard to the classroom. Here, Brother Samuel could learn his language and gain valuable intelligence. Most often afterward, the prisoner was given his freedom and allowed to join one of the caravans headed out of Libya. Others, the unruly ones, were enslaved and forced to work in the stables or sold. There was no Geneva Convention in the 12th Century.

Princess Lannia, the middle sister, was so unlike her two sisters; she disliked being confined in the castle and preferred the open air, hunting with her troops and even fighting whenever she had the opportunity. She had mastered the sword, lance and spear, and feared no man or beast. The exception being the accursed dragon, which she and her men avoided by a great distance, whenever coming or leaving the castle.

When she was in the castle, she worked in the armory and cared little for the goings on between Brother Samuel and Princess Lennia. As a pupil, she had little interest for schooling and tired quickly of Brother Samuel's lessons.

But it was Princess Lonnia who worried Brother Samuel the most, for she had been a highly intelligent pupil and apparently too smart, as it turned out. He had caught her several times going through his pile of parchments and books, and as result, he had stopped short of teaching her geography outside of the Mediterranean Sea. It wasn't long before they reached an impasse, which soon turned into a deep dislike for one another. Princess Lonnia quit attending classes, upsetting her father and without the king knowing it, she had later gone out and found herself an aged Egyptian shaman to train her in the dark arts.

King Ramie felt it was a blood-line thing, for her mother was also interested in the darker things of life, but not in the zeal of their daughter.

The people of this shaman's Egyptian community lived along the Upper Nile River. He had offended his people for causing great distrust between neighbors and there was a price on his head in Egypt for speaking out against the reigning Pharaoh of that time. When Princess Lonnia discovered his secret whereabouts, she found him quite hungry, but still incredibly arrogant and boastful of his great talents in alchemy and some of the ancient arts of black magic. A bag of gold was his price and she paid it freely, which he in turn used to pay his debts and she added to this amount with the gold needed to bribe their way out of the country. During such travels, she rarely went as a Libyan princess, but by her bearing, people knew she was of at least a higher court office. Unfortunately for this aged shaman, she was already planning his demise as she placed the gold in his hands.

From knowledge that he passed on to her, she had attempted to poison Brother Samuel three times, but the holy man had always outwitted her. An assassin was out of the question, he had Captain Rynarr protecting him and no accredited killer was willing to take on the job and tangle with the good Captain and his Royal Guards. Added to her grief was the fact Brother Samuel had made many attempts to kill the dragon and had grown to be a favored figure among the townspeople. Even when he spoke out against the lottery, one of the few who could and still live, they loved him, for they knew he was only doing it out of concern for the People of Silene. Still, Princess Lonnia continued to plot Brother Samuel's death and that of her own little sister; Princess Lennia. She resented the relationship the young princess had with their father and just about everyone else in the castle. If her plans were to work out, she had to have Princess Lennia out of the way, along with the bothersome Brother Samuel.

"This armor they wear is so very strange and they came to our shores without any real weapons in their possession...only those small daggers and...I think they called them shovels...though they do not look anything like the shovels you have built for my father."

She looked about the room for a moment and then returned her admiring favorite uncle gaze to her old friend. "I've been told the metal of these strange helmets and even these shovels are extremely strong, and their daggers are very superior to our own." Princess Lennia said.

"Their spears and bows were washed overboard, my Princess, but they have quick minds and can fashion new weapons if needed. I have been told that some of the knives my countrymen carry, were made from the flaming rocks that fell from the sky." He was hoping she would buy the story of the meteor being used, for the night sky has been filled with many a falling star of late. Then he thought of something else to explain the skills of his countrymen.

Brother Samuel had remembered reading of how the Army's new airborne troops were reportedly instructed in hand-to-hand fighting techniques. When he was in California, the Rangers were being put together for training in England as a combat unit, much the same as the Marine Raiders were being readied for warfare in the Pacific.

"In Ireland, we are taught from childhood how to fight with our hands for those times when we have lost our weapons."

"Truly, this is so? Then you must show me this fighting, what is it called?"

As usual, Brother Samuel had talked himself into an area he wasn't prepared to answer, for he hadn't had the time to talk further with his three new friends and he needed something to tell her something for the moment. He grinded his teeth for a moment, but keeping his headed turned away from his pupil, for he truly resented all the years that had passed by and the resulting forgetfulness of his mind. He then turned toward her with a smile on his face and replied, "It is called wrestling, my Princess." He knew nearly every high school kid was taught some form of wrestling, even if it was schoolyard tussles over who got to date the prettiest girl in class or some bully wanting another kid's lunch money.

Right then, a flash of memory had him recall just such an event in his own 5th grade year. A rather large 6th grade bully had been stealing lunch money from the younger boys and he had finally targeted a young Samuel. When it was all over, the 6th grader was on his way to the nurse's office for a bloody lip and nose, and Sam had become a playground hero. Though both boys ended up spending the afternoon after school and later, they had become best friends and went off to Annapolis together- the older boy one year ahead of him. During his first year, Samuel was tortured by nearly every other second year cadet, but not by his good friend. Sadly, his best friend was assigned as an officer aboard the Arizona and he had perished in the attack on Pearl Harbor.

"Wrestling!" She exclaimed. "I know of this wrestling you speak of. Is their wrestling different from ours, the type taught by the ancient Greeks? Even the Turks use this wrestling and are quite good at it."

"In some ways, yes...it is the same, but now we should return to our studies."

"Can you have them demonstrate this art of wrestling for the king?"

Brother Samuel shook his head in frustration, not for the Princess, but for himself.

"Possibly, my Princess, I will ask it of them. But right now, they must learn the language of your people."

"I could help!" she said with a burst of enthusiasm.

"No. You are a Princess of Silene. You will not meet with other men who are not presented to your father in court, and only then under a proper chaperon. These men have a long way to go before they are ready to be presented to your father, much like I was long ago. Remember, I have told you how it took me three years of sitting in that dungeon before I was able to be released and another seven years before I was first allowed to sit in court."

"But I am bored, Brother Samuel. These strangers will help me learn of other people's ways. Do you not agree with this...logic?"

"No, I do not. Now let us return to your studies. We will now talk about the Holy Land and the debates between Muslims and Christians over ownership for the City of Jerusalem."

Princess Lennia's expression was a display of one perturbed and she returned to her chair by the table, crossed her legs and arms and glared at Brother Samuel with very unhappy eyes.

"Princess, you must learn of these things if you are to govern your people justly. Many wars will be fought for Jerusalem and some of your people will participate in these wars, as the Muslim world rises-up to defend the city. You should know why this may or may not be needed, and to not just go blindly off to a far-off land to make war that will cost you many lives." Brother Samuel then thought back, remembering how many troops simply went to war in 1941 and so many of them never knowing the true reason behind the war in Europe. Japan was easier for everyone, they quickly realized the need for war and it centered on the sneak attack upon Pearl Harbor.

Yet, he seemed to recall how many sailors in San Diego had asked him, "Why should we be fighting the Germans in Europe?" A lot of these same men were of German or Italian heritage and they were troubled by possibly fighting family members.

In response, all he could do was try to explain what he knew of Hitler's drive to control all of Europe and Mussolini's dictatorship of Italy. From what these men from the future had told him, America would eventually come to know how truly evil Adolph Hitler was by the end of the war in 1945. The numbers of executed Jews, Polish and Gypsy's shocked him into a stunned silence. Outside the millions of men and women who had died in combat, the number of Jews, Gypsy, Polish, Russian and Germany's political prisoners executed by the Nazi war machine and the Russian Army exceeded more than 15 million people.

"But, Brother Samuel, I will never reign over Silene. I am third daughter and we have no brothers. The crown will pass down to my oldest sister's husband...when she gets married."

"Princess Lonnia...married? I have serious doubts she will become a queen, not unless she takes the throne by force and I say this with no disrespect," for he knew Princess Lennia sincerely loved her older sister, "...but she is not a likely prospect for a wife. She grows older and her old injury has sadly marred her looks. The throne is also one of the poorest in all of Libya because of our foul creature.

"No, the throne will pass down to one who loves her people above herself. This will be you and this is also why you must learn everything I can teach you. So, you will be a wise and gracious Queen."

"You have so much faith in me, Brother Samuel. I wish you could be 40-years younger and I'd make you my King." She looked at him with loving eyes, the unhappy glare now gone. For besides her father, Brother Samuel was next in line to hold her heart.

"You flatter me, my Princess, but I will not allow you to talk me out of your studies. So, let us speak of the Holy Land and the troubles there."

"You are a strong willed old man...but my dearest friend. We will speak of the Holy Land and I will learn."

## THE AMERICANS

GW and Hughes leapt to their feet when the wooden door creaked open, but Grant was still napping. With little else to do, they were catching up on their sleep between meals. While awake, they spoke of their homes and families, sports and most importantly--girls. Then to pass the time they told stories they had learned while growing up and it was Grant who had the most interesting tales; he spoke of Texas and its many legends. Hughes liked the laughable tales of Pecos Bill and especially the one of him lassoing the whirlwind. GW preferred hearing the more serious stories of the Texas Rangers and of Davy Crockett's last stand at the Alamo.

With a broad smile on his face, Brother Samuel entered the room and greeted each of his new friends, before he took a seat on the foot of GW's bed. GW winced when he heard the bed creak loudly under the old man's weight.

"Welcome to our happy abode, sir," Hughes said. He then presented a modest, yet proper, bow at the hip.

They were happy to see Brother Samuel, but even happier to see he was soon being followed by a large servant fellow, who carried a large oval-shaped wooden tray. A top the tray were four clay goblets and a large pitcher of drink on it. Feeling somewhat claustrophobic, GW asked the servant to keep the door open and once he had the guard's permission, he did so. But the two guards quickly moved in to stand in the doorway, desiring to keep a keen eye on their prisoners; for to lose a prisoner in the castle meant a painful execution by dismemberment.

Having been awakened by Brother Samuel's arrival, Grant wiped his eyes and swung his bare feet to the floor. He was glad to see their new friend and soon asked, "When can we get out of here, sir?"

"Yes, sir," Hughes said, speaking between gulps from his cup. "...these stone block walls tend to remind us of that cave we spent way too much time in."

Brother Samuel nodded his head in understanding, "Gentlemen, I have good news for you, I have received permission for you to take a walk with me in the afternoon...Under guard of course."

"Today?" GW asked in anticipation.

"Yes, today." Brother Samuel stopped talking abruptly when he heard Captain Rynarr's voice in the passageway, ordering the guards to stand back to allow him to enter the room.

Brother Samuel greeted his friend and then offered him a drink from his own goblet, which the captain declined with a casual shake of his head. He then gestured to the three men and spoke to Brother Samuel for some time, while the Americans waited in anticipation for the translation.

When Captain Rynarr was finished, Brother Samuel replied with a couple words, after which Captain Rynarr left the room and the guards returned to their positions in the doorway.

"Some further good news, gentlemen," Brother Samuel said. "Captain Rynarr has granted you a tour of the Royal Guard's stable. He requests for each of you to select a horse from their available stock, as he would like to observe your riding skills."

"What then?" GW asked, with a look of curiosity on his face.

"If you can ride well enough, you will be able to have your own horse and I will say they have some very fine horses here."

"Do you ride, sir?" Grant asked.

"Not any more, young man. Too fat, too much arthritis and last time I rode I was sore for three days and could barely walk-- much to the dear captain's amusement."

Grant looked to his friends, "I can ride anything they've got, but what about you guys?"

Hughes shook his head and sighed, "Last time I rode a horse it was a wooden one on a carrousel, and I was nine-years old." He smiled at his own inability and then suggested, "Maybe they have a camel?"

"I am sorry, Mr. Hughes," Brother Samuel apologized. "What few camels the king has are used for transporting goods to Tripoli and back."

GW smiled, envisioning Hughes and Grant atop a pair of camels, remembering a Bob Hope and Bing Crosby movie when the two famous comedians rode across the desert in Road to Morocco. He knew it was actually-on a soundstage, but the effect of an open desert was there.

Brother Samuel broke GW's daydreaming by asking him about his own ability to ride a horse.

"I've done some riding, sir, but mostly during Boy Scout summer camp. But in high school I had this girl friend, she owned three horses and we did some riding...mostly to get far enough away from her parent's house so we could fool around a bit." GW said and then grinned, as he recalled the young lady.

"Pretty gal, but one of her horses got the best of me though, stopped dead in his tracks while we rode through an orange grove. I was thrown over his head and right into a tree and you know what? I could swear that horse was laughing at me as I hung upside down in that orange tree."

Brother Samuel laughed, "Well, I guess we will see what we will see. I'm not sure what the good captain has in mind, but eventually you all must learn how to ride, use their weapons and become citizens of Silene."

"You don't think they'd just let us leave?" Grant asked, but he wasn't sure where they would go even if they could and that was the first question Brother Samuel asked.

"Where would you go, Corporal? Here at least you are protected by my relationship with the captain and the king. Anywhere else, you'd be taken prisoner and assuredly slain as an infidel. And if you were to make it to Europe, what then? Do you speak German, Italian or French?"

"What's an infidel, sir?" Grant asked.

"Over here an infidel is an unbeliever...one who is not Muslim," Brother Samuel explained.

"Oh," Grant replied. Then he frowned. He looked over at the guards and the scimitars they carried. "They got any swords in a smaller-size?"

"You make a good point, sir," GW said. He ignored Grant's question about a sword and said, "I guess we'd better get used to becoming citizens and using their equipment."

"Fine," Brother Samuel said. "Now finish your drinks and let us take a walk." Brother Samuel set his goblet down and turned to address the guards. Both were quite ready to leave their boring standing post and felt quite obliged to escort the prisoners through the castle and out into the courtyard. Additional guards would be waiting for them in the courtyard in the event the infidels tried to escape.

One of the two guards, Hirim Mushad, was a large bearded fellow, who GW thought the man could have played offensive tackle for the Chicago Bears. He wore a metal chest plate, which was dented somewhat from apparent weapon impact points. This covered over his tunic of deep blue, which then covered a heavy shirt of mail. His large muscular arms were exposed at the forearm, which bore many scars; some from burns and others that appeared to be from knives or sword cuts. Mushad seemed to be a thoughtful man, who rarely smiled, and his intelligent dark brown eyes seemed to be always moving to take in everything around him. He had survived 18-acts of personal combat, while rising in the ranks of the Royal Guard and had participated in five wars in battling Egyptian raiders. To date he had sustained nine wounds of valor in his service to King Ramie. Once this was all explained to GW, all the young man could think was, I've never known anyone with nine Purple Hearts...wow!

Mushad scrutinized the Americans, wanting to ensure they held no item that could be used as a weapon. His partner, Rachid Raymon, was less caring and would gladly spear the prisoners, or even better, hack them down with his scimitar. Then once he had proved himself, the good Captain might then return him to his prior duty of guarding Princess Lannia. He had been sent to the castle for upsetting the Princess during a hunt, mainly by taking a kill she had intended for herself.

Raymon was half-Libyan and half-Berber, which accounted for his light skin. He was also much smaller in height compared to Mushad, but nearly as wide at the shoulders. Though his arms were empty of battle scars, his face bore a five-inch long knife scar from a brawl with several of the Caliph's soldiers in Tripoli over the issue of a certain Sudanese dancing woman. Unlike Mushad, he was a simple man, who loved to soldier and had no desire to rise in rank. In fact, since returning to the castle he had learned to have a great animosity for Hirim Mushad's arrogance and utmost desire to seek promotion.

During guard duty, Mushad had come to appreciate GW's subtle ways, for he handled himself well and thought much of the welfare for the two men with him. He saw how this GW also offered great respect for Brother Samuel and Mushad sincerely liked the old man and his fondness for the young princess.

Still, the young Nubian troubled him some. Mushad found it strange that the two other men treated him as an equal and though of the same Muslim faith, he greatly disliked the black Moors. But this was the first time he had met a Sudanese and found himself curious of him and the apparent friendship between the three men. He wondered if there were any Black Moors in this Ireland but hadn't asked Brother Samuel of this.

The other stranger, the one who liked to laugh a lot and ask so many questions, also had the keen eyes of warrior. He had seen how Grant had admired their weapons and Mushad knew it to be folly to give them any chance of escape or to cause harm to Brother Samuel, even if Brother Samuel said they were of his people. Mushad knew a lot of his relatives who wouldn't think twice before slicing the throat of another family member if the price was right or an offense was given.

Hirim had been with Captain Rynarr when they took the three Americans prisoner. He saw how they had a desire to fight but had the intelligence to know they should wait for a better time and this thoughtful action he respected in a warrior. Unlike his fellow guard, a man he thought barely capable of holding his shield upright, Hirim was looking forward to proving himself as a superior soldier and thus, gaining a higher rank in the Royal Guard. His wish was to someday replace Captain Rynarr, when the man was too old to carry out his duties and another Captain of the Royal Guard was needed to defend the king's throne.

## IN THE COURTYARD

PFC Hughes was notably nervous over the idea of climbing up on a horse, as he somewhat reluctantly followed the others into the stable to view the horse stock--though he was glad to be outside and hoped for a chance to see the dragon.

Brother Samuel had observed Hughes' nervousness and remembered his suggestion about the camels, "Mr. Hughes, the king's camels are currently outside the castle walls, preparing for a caravan to the shoreline to receive a load of fish for the castle pantry. If you'd like, I could ask Captain Rynarr if he would authorize a ride for you upon their return."

The thought of riding a camel caused Hughes to smile, "Thank you, Brother Samuel, but I'll hold off on that for now. We'd better see how I do with the horses first."

Grant shook his head, chuckled and said, "My man, just remember, horses don't eat meat. Oh, they may stomp you, kick you around a bit, bite you and even roll-over on top of you, but they won't eat you."

"Thanks," Hughes replied. He shot a hard glance at Grant for his caring words of wisdom.

The stable before them was constructed of aged wood beams and sideboards graying from the ocean's storms from the north and blowing sands from the south. This one stable alone held stalls for 100-horses and there were several large water troughs in view. Behind the stable was a very large corral, where some ten-young horses were ambling about.

A dozen or so stable workers would carry buckets of water to the individual horse troughs once a day, brought from a huge storage tank, which was refilled once a week from the great fountains. Additional large water troughs were scattered about the courtyard and corral and a few of them, which had taller sidewalls to them, were designated for camels. The Americans were to learn that camels and horses didn't like to share the same water trough, and it apparently had something to do with the different animal's odor. Though out in the open desert, they would share the same oasis pond out of need.

Currently, most of the stalls were empty and Brother Samuel advised his friends that he'd been informed earlier how that the king's cavalry was out on various patrols. "They maintain a constant vigilance for fear of invasion from the east. These are troubled times with the Egyptian people. They find no problem with raiding Libya and Silene's caravans have become a major attraction for them. They steal our sheep, our horses and when possible, our women. In the last year, we have had seven farms attacked, which left us with nine people dead and two of the farms burned to the ground."

"Why doesn't your king declare war and attack Egypt?" Grant asked.

"Our good king is only one leader in Libya. The Great Caliph who rules over Libya resides in Tripoli and he knows his country can ill-afford an open war with Egypt. Their armies out number ours by better than 5 to 1, and we have no chariots to speak of. But Egypt; still, they remain a major power in North Africa. Not quite what they were in ancient times, but still a capable foe.

"We also caused enough trouble several years ago, when we raided into Egypt in response to their attacks and the Caliph was so upset, he nearly replaced our beloved king. But cooler heads prevailed and now we fight a defensive battle."

"It's your ball game, sir," Grant said. He then shrugged his shoulders in dismay and added, "We're the new kids on the block and I guess we've got us a lot of stuff to learn."

"Yes, you do, Mr. Grant and now, how about we examine some horse flesh."

Grant nodded his response and they were escorted to a set of stalls near the castle-side of the stable, where they observed only five horses. Brother Samuel, not too happy with the shape of the horses, withheld comment and advised the guards to stand back as his friends looked the horses over. He then reminded Mushad that the courtyard gate was closed and there would be no possibility of escape, if these young men even chose to attempt escape on horseback. Brother Samuel then translated his words to the three Americans, pointing upward to the various bowmen manning the towers.

"Be careful, gentlemen, some of these men would like nothing better than killing you for simply the sport of it."

"No problem, sir," GW said. "It's just nice to be out in the open again and smell the salt air."

"That's not what I'm smelling," Hughes said.

"Yes, it brings back memories...the smell of a ranch," Grant said.

"I think Hughes is right. This stable reeks of horsecrap," GW said.

"Right, that's what a horse ranch smell of...one of the reasons I left. I got real tired of shoveling it every day!" Grant exclaimed.

"I doubt you will have-to shovel it here, Mr. Grant...unless, that is, you fall into disfavor with our king."

"Any chance we can get a look at that dragon?" Hughes asked.

Brother Samuel was dismayed by Hughes' enthusiasm, "Later, Mr. Hughes. Right now, you are to inspect the horses."

"Yes, sir," Hughes replied. He almost rendered a salute but stopped himself.

"Sir, I wanted to ask you about our rucksacks," GW said.

"What about them?"

"Inside mine was a certain object and it's not there now."

"You mean that strange flint knife of some great size?"

"Yes, sir, that's the one."

"Not to worry, Mr. Sanders. I have it in my classroom and will return it when Captain Rynarr allows you to have weapons. I must say, I found it to be extremely sharp." Brother Samuel lifted-up his right index finger to display a recent laceration.

"It means a great deal to me, sir. When we have a chance, I'll fill you in on how it was given to me."

"I look forward to it, Mr. Sanders," Brother Samuel replied and then watched, as Grant was first to approach the horses.

Grant, who was quite knowledgeable of horses, knew these animals to be of poor quality and not exactly the beautiful black Arabians he had expected. By the frown on Brother Samuel's face, Grant knew how he even saw how old these five nags were. These five were retired cavalry stock and now used for pulling manure carts from the stables.

Brother Samuel wasn't sure what Captain Rynarr was pulling, but from his friendship with the man, he decided this might be simply an initial test to see if the strangers knew their horses. People who climbed out of a hole in the mountainside might not be the best judge of horseflesh.

Captain Rynarr had not told Brother Samuel or the king how his men had back tracked the three strangers to the hole in the mountain. Nor how two of his men had used ropes tied to climbing hooks to secure a hold on the bluff and make entry into the mountain. They reported finding no evidence the three strangers had come from a shipwreck and stopped retracing their steps deep inside a darkened cave when they were no longer able to see through the darkness. This report greatly confused Captain Rynarr, but he withheld saying anything for he was very fond of Brother Samuel, and he wondered why this holy man was claiming these two men as family. He was even more confused by the Nubian, who though labeled a Sudanese court officer, spoke no Arabic.

No, for now he would wait and watch and try to discover just who these three strangers were and why Brother Samuel was covering for them. Before Grant could voice his objection to the condition of the horses, Captain Rynarr approached and spoke to Brother Samuel. Who then learned he was right. Captain Rynarr was indeed testing these three men as to their knowledge of horses. Even Hirim Mushad, who observed the horses and their poor condition, was beginning to wonder the intent of his captain, until he heard Rynarr speak to Brother Samuel.

Leaning against a thick wooden stable pole for support, Brother Samuel spoke to the three Americans, "Captain Rynarr is asking what you think of these horses and if you would choose one for a demonstration of your riding skill?" He then gave Grant and GW a quick wink to say, play along.

"Captain Rynarr isn't expecting Mr. Hughes to ride, for he is a member of a foreign court and will not likely be asked to compete in the festival. But he was curious if Mr. Hughes could select a proper mount or possibly demonstrate his inability to do so and, in the process, show how foolish the Sudanese were in the area-of horses."

While Hughes gave Captain Rynarr a guarded look, Grant nodded in reply and walked over to peruse through the stalls and examine the five mares more closely. Running his hands over their backs, he could tell these horses was either approaching their 12th or possibly 14th birthday, or maybe even older. They had all been ridden hard, and all the horses' underbellies were covered with the scars of sharp metal spurs.

Grant hated most spurs, especially the Mexican five-point spur, which punished a good horse. The ancient single triple point spur literally stabbed the animal. He personally used a rounded spur, but only when he seriously needed one; as with a horse that refused to respond to physical commands provided by knee pressure, use of the reins and the occasional boot heels to the flank. He had noticed earlier on that Captain Rynarr wore spurs with what appeared to be numerous small points, much like his own rounded spurs back in Texas. In the fourth stall, he noticed a degree of intelligence in the eyes of one white and gray mare. A horse that had clearly seen battle and had carried her rider through many a fight and survived the torture a warhorse experienced. This mare was the one he selected to ride. Being a stranger to the mare, he cautiously removed her from the stall, while whispering to her in a gentle tone and running his hands over the mare's forehead and along its neck. He scratched her ears and petted her nose, but always talking to her as he used his voice to gentle the horse down and accept him as a partner. Captain Rynarr saw this and shook his head in admiration for a man who knew how to speak to a strange horse.

Declining what they called a saddle; basically, a rounded piece of leather over a thick wool blanket, which decision surprised Captain Rynarr, Grant led the horse out into the courtyard and without another word he suddenly leapt upon its back. He grabbed a handful of gray mane and proceeded to kick the horse forward with the heels of his combat boots impacting the horse's belly.

He thought about a more cautious approach but remembered this was a horse bred for battle and knew he needed to demonstrate his mastership of the animal for Captain Rynarr and Brother Samuel.

Memories of better days sparkled in the mare's eyes. She was no longer a beast of burden, pulling along a foul-smelling wagon to the whip of an angry stable hand. No, she was being ridden by one who knew how to ride and once more she felt the wind in her face as the blood of life surged through her veins. She charged forward in response to Grant's commands and tasted the hot air of the desert through her flared nostrils.

For the moment, he forgot about his predicament, about being stuck in the 12th century and held prisoner of a Muslim king. He forgot his reasons for wanting to leave the ranch and join the army. He even forgot the day of battle and the long days and nights in that nightmarish cave. No, now he was atop a horse and nothing else mattered as he rode into the wind and felt the renewed strength of the mare grow with each stride.

With a loud shout of joy, he ran the mare in a large circle, showing his complete control over the old warhorse: a horse that remembered better days and demonstrated this by responding to Grant's physical leadings. After five circles around the courtyard, throwing in several figure-eights and a leap over the tongue of a feed wagon, Grant brought the horse to a dead stop right in front of Captain Rynarr. The senior knight surprised everyone by his refusal to move an inch, as the horse rushed toward him and his eyes gleamed with appreciation for the display he had just witnessed. Winded a bit from the run, the mare looked down upon Captain Rynarr and raised her head high, breathed deeply in and out through her flared nostrils and pounded her forward and back hooves into the hot sand.

In response, Captain Rynarr gave the mare a pet on her nose, while Grant slid off her. Captain Rynarr then stepped up and slapped Grant on the shoulders, a sign of respect for a fellow horseman. He then spoke to Brother Samuel, who interpreted the captain's words for everyone to hear, "He says you are a very fine rider, one who clearly knows the mind of a horse and can bring out its best. He thought this one to be useless now, a puller of carts, but now he knows it was the prior owner who appears to be useless. He has decided that this mare will be used for the training of future knights, she is too valuable to be pulling a cart and he thanks you for demonstrating this."

Grant looked from Brother Samuel to Captain Rynarr and simply nodded his head in response but remembering to smile to show his understanding and appreciation for the compliments.

Captain Rynarr then pointed to GW and followed his gesture by waving his hand over the remaining four horses and Brother Samuel said, "You may pick one, but choose wisely, my young friend."

Shaking his head in wonder at the events surrounding him, and shrugging his shoulders back to stand erect, GW walked purposely to the stalls to look the four remaining horses over. To him they all looked pretty–sorry, knowing that Grant had selected the only good one in the bunch. Lifting–up his head to see if Grant could offer up any advice, GW suddenly laid eyes on a black speckled white Arabian tied up to an outside rail adjacent the castle wall. For him it was love at first sight, the horse was everything GW had imagined a warhorse to be and he felt strangely drawn to it. The steed was strong and quite tall at the shoulder. GW was to later learn the horse stood a good 18 hands. He had a long flowing white–blonde tail that almost touched the ground, to match his equally long uncut mane. The stallion had large clear eyes, with pupils the color and sparkle of black jade and he seemed to be glaring right back at him with surprising intensity. Mostly white through the stomach and neck, with some black speckling to the legs and nose, the horse displayed a starburst of black speckling on the rump and a darker shading to almost black about the back legs. For GW, this was the horse he wanted, he dreamed of from all those days of playing cowboys and Indians with the neighborhood kids.

"Brother Samuel, would you please advise the dear Captain that although I appreciate his offer of these fine mares, I would choose that beautiful stallion over there." GW pointed to the horse and Brother Samuel followed with his eyes to see what GW was pointing at.

By this time, Grant had returned his horse to the stall and was in the process of giving her some water and rubbing her down with a handful of hay. At GW's suggestion, he looked up to appraise the horse himself and commented, "He might be a bit too much for you, GW. There is fire in those eyes and amazing strength in his legs. You might end up in that orange tree again, or worse, smacked like a fly against a stone wall."

Looking the horse over from a distance, Brother Samuel had to agree with Grant, for the horse was a beautiful specimen and he wondered if GW would be able to handle such a strong animal. Captain Rynarr turned to where GW was pointing and saw the horse the young stranger wished to ride. He had to smile, for he knew this animal and had known his previous owner; a man who had suffered a fall and would no longer be able to ride, which resulted in no one wanting the horse, believing it was cursed. Speaking to Brother Samuel, he explained the horse's history and cautioned this young stranger's choice and again he gestured to the four horses before them.

Brother Samuel took GW aside so they could speak alone, "This horse you wish to ride injured its last owner and now everyone is afraid to ride it. Captain Rynarr is preparing to have it taken to Tripoli for the stud market. He feels this horse could injure you and since you are a friend of mine, a clansman, he feels you should demonstrate your ability with one of these four, here." Brother Samuel looked to the old plugs in the stalls, "You only have to show you can stay on a horse, further training will come in time. You've already demonstrated some knowledge of horse flesh by refusing these, so please ride one of them to make Captain Rynarr happy."

GW listened to Brother Samuel and then looked to Captain Rynarr, "No, sir, I still choose that horse over there. But, I ask, if I am able to ride the horse four-times around the courtyard..." GW hesitated. "...then the horse becomes mine and I will pay for him when I am able to earn some money...whatever they use for money here."

Letting out a deep sigh, Brother Samuel then interpreted GW's words for Captain Rynarr. Who after a moment of thought nodded his head in agreement and GW stepped forward and offered his hand to seal the deal. Unsure of what this stranger was doing, Brother Samuel quickly stepped up to advise Captain Rynarr of what the gesture meant and how it was used in Ireland to close a deal or a sign of friendship, or a greeting. He then demonstrated the proper response by shaking GW's hand, adding a smile to show the gesture was friendly and not a move to disable an opponent. He explained that the right hand was used as most everyone carried their weapon in that hand and this was to show there was no ill will intended by this handshaking.

Nodding his head in understanding, Captain Rynarr brought up his right hand and cautiously shook GW's hand. Feeling the strength in GW's grip, he responded in kind and now shook his hand with mild enthusiasm, until GW broke the grip and began to walk toward the horse he had chosen.

Meanwhile, as this was all going on, an extremely nervous Hughes was pacing the stalls in fear Captain Rynarr might still ask him to ride one of these monstrous animals. Hughes' fear was not going unnoticed, Jar Hafe, a low-ranking member of the king's regular army, stood by and began to chuckle. He then pointed at Hughes with a taunting gesture, a signal of utter distaste that almost always brought on a fight.

Hafe was quite large for a Libyan, nearly as tall and wide as Mushad and almost as muscular in the legs as Raymon. Full bearded and greatly overweight, his rude actions and foul mouth had given him the reputation of an ill-mannered oaf and was greatly disliked by Hirim Mushad. It was Hafe's poor behavior that kept him from joining the Royal Guard, but he cared little of this. What Hafe enjoyed was a good fight, any kind of brawl and he hoped with enough encouragement this Nubian might comply, and he could kill the dark skin.

"This Black is frightened like a small child, his sweat drips to the ground like rain in the winter and soon his yellow water will run down his legs," Hafe said. He sneered at Hughes and continued to point at him in a taunting fashion.

"Stand aside, Hafe," Mushad ordered. He was moving to stand between Hafe and Hughes.

"You lower yourself to protect this coward...this babe who quakes at the sight of these aged mares...ones no longer worthy of feeding and only good enough to pull these foul carts." He pointed to the refuse wagons and then with a taunting finger, pointed back at Hughes, "I say feed this Black to the dragon, we do not need his cowardly kind in the presence of brave soldiers." Hafe stepped by Mushad and shoved Hughes hard from the back, knocking him to the ground.

Mushad responded in turn by using his large oval shield to knock Hafe sideward, where his feet got intertwined with a rope and he fell to the ground with his right hand, landing in a pile of horse manure. With his right hand to be fouled in such a manner, it was the utmost insult to endure and he was not about to let this pass unpunished.

With a loud growl, Hafe jumped to his feet and shook his hand to remove the foul debris. He rushed to a wooden troth and quickly washed the debris away and then glared at Mushad with violence in his eyes and even though weaponless, he prepared to charge him. But he stopped, frozen like a statue, when Captain Rynarr moved in between them with a silver dagger in his hand aimed at Hafe's mid–section.

"Enough! You have insulted this man. You, gutless toad! In doing so you have brought insult to me and for this you will be punished." Captain Rynarr pointed to two Royal Guardsmen, "Take him, remove this vileness from my sight. Later, I will decide his punishment."

Struggling with his guards, Hafe shouted back, "But, my Captain, that man is not worthy to be in your great presence. I will gladly take any punishment you decree for any insult I made against you, but please, Captain, not for insulting this…Moor of dark skin."

Hughes pulled himself up from the sand and observed the interaction between the men with interest. He then walked over to Brother Samuel and asked for an interpretation of their words. After hearing the exchange, he asked Brother Samuel to interpret for him and then he went up to stand before Captain Rynarr.

"Please ask Captain Rynarr if I may respond to this man's brutish actions and his words. It is true I do not like horses, only because I've never been around any. But I do take affront to this slime laying his filthy hands on me. So, I challenge him, right now, to a hand–to–hand fight with no weapons. This will be a private duel with only his great abundances of fat and small brain against my so–called repulsive Blackness."

Brother Samuel studied Hughes for a moment and then asked, "Are you sure of this?"

"Yes, sir," Hughes said. "Please translate my words."

Once translated, Captain Rynarr looked upon Hughes, studying his physique and then glared at Hafe with disgust. The oaf had Hughes out muscled and greatly outweighed, but Captain Rynarr understood a sense of upholding one's honor. He also wanted to know how this Nubian fought, hearing from Brother Samuel that all three strangers were skillful in the art of wrestling. Captain Rynarr had wrestled against both Turks and Greeks, learning much and losing most of his matches, but he had never been defeated with a sword.

Originally taught by the Greeks and then the Romans, the people of the Middle East had used wrestling to strengthen them and learn an opponent's weakness. Captain Rynarr had seen Hafe wrestle others, usually in a drunken brawl and he was seldom defeated. Only Mushad had bested him in the King's matches and this had caused a strong dislike between the two men. Captain Rynarr knew that one day Mushad would have to kill Hafe, if only in self-defense. He knew Hafe was of the type to strike from behind, just as he struck out against this Nubian.

In the center of the courtyard, GW waited to see what was going to transpire before he approached the horse he admired. He didn't know it, but from the royal balcony, Princess Lennia was watching all that was taking place and was for some unexplainable reason, drawn to this one rather large man out in the center of the courtyard and she continued to watch him.

Brother Samuel listened as Captain Rynarr issued his decision and then translated for the three Americans. "You may fight Hafe, without weapons and he will see how you defend yourself against such a large man. Prepare yourself. Mr. Hughes."

"Hey, Hughes, you sure you want to rumble with this big dude?" Grant asked with concern for his friend.

Hughes only grinned back in response and then walked to the center of the courtyard; between the stable and the castle wall, and where the sand was the hottest from such openness. Here, he stripped his t-shirt off and began to stretch out his muscles with stretching exercises. But he wasn't given much time as Hafe quickly approached. The big man had an evil glint to his eyes, a sneer on his face and his huge fatty hands out in front to grab Hughes by the throat right off. There was no starting bell, no time clock and Hughes realized he was probably in a fight for his life as Hafe grew near with his massive catcher-mitt sized hands of his. Unfortunately, Hafe never had the chance to use those big mitts of his. Hughes quickly stepped in, grabbed Hafe by the right wrist, reversed Hafe's momentum with a wrist curl, forced his arm up high and then reversed motion, which promptly threw Hafe into a forward summersault. Hafe landed hard, unsure what had happened to him, but he spat out a mouthful of sand and stood to his feet. He then growled out some obscenity and charged Hughes like an enraged beast.

Once again, Hughes used Hafe's own momentum, grabbed him by the collar of his tunic, placed his right foot in Hafe's fat stomach and rolled backward, throwing Hafe over his head and into a second face full of hot sand. This brought applause and shouts of support from GW and Grant. Even Brother Samuel was clapping his hands. Mushad stood off to the side, observing every move Hughes made and his respect for the man improved greatly with each move this Nubian made.

Hafe was slower in getting up this time, but he wasn't done. Wiping the sand off his face and sneering at his opponent, he again charged and like before, Hughes used Hafe's own strength and speed to throw him about the courtyard.

Captain Rynarr was stunned. He had never seen this kind of wrestling before and stood there with his mouth a gape as Hughes, the much lighter man, tossed Hafe about with wrist rolls, over the back throws and even a hand chop to the back of the neck, which finally laid the oafish Hafe to rest. The big man was still breathing, but he was clearly out for the count.

Captain Rynarr ordered two of his men to load Hafe into a cart, "Take him to the dungeon. Tell the jailer, thirty-days of bread and water."

GW walked up to Hughes, patted him on the shoulder and simply asked, "Judo and Karate-right?"

"Right, but a bit more of Judo though," Hughes replied. "My father enrolled me in a YMCA Judo class when I was six-years old. He wanted me to be able to defend myself. I hold a Third-Degree Black Belt and was preparing to test for my First-Degree Black Belt in Karate when I enlisted."

"I know they taught us Judo at training school, but nothing like what I saw today. Remind me not to get you mad," Grant said as he approached and shook Hughes' hand.

"You never used that stuff against the NVA," GW said.

"Judo has little effect against an AK-47, Corporal."

GW laughed, "Yeah, you're right...Good match though. I think you taught that oaf a lesson he won't forget."

"I doubt it," Hughes replied. "He's the type who never learns until someone kills him."

Brother Samuel came forward, "You amazed me, Mr. Hughes. I have seen this Judo demonstrated before by a Japanese liaison officer before the war, and you make it look so easy."

"Thank you, sir. Normally I wouldn't have challenged such a man, but I felt he needed a demonstration. Maybe next time he sees a Black man he will think twice before insulting him...or at least he will be wary."

"I overheard you also know this...Karate, what is this?" Brother Samuel asked.

"Karate is simply another Japanese form of martial art, sir. But Karate is considered a very aggressive act, while Judo is mostly a defensive form. Once the war was over, a lot of Japanese...experts set up businesses in America. They taught this form of hand-to-hand fighting to anyone willing to pay the price for lessons. I took Karate up because several of my friends at the YMCA did, and I found it quite invigorating...but a bit hard on the hands at first. Let me demonstrate." Hughes walked over to the stable and picked up a board approximately three-inches thick. It was some four-feet long and he asked both GW and Grant to hold it securely for him between them.

As Captain Rynarr, Brother Samuel and several others observed, Hughes approached the board and after some thought, assumed the proper position and then came down hard with a chop of his right hand—breaking the board in half. To follow this up, he pointed to a supporting fence post for part of the stable and again, after some thought as into proper placement, dashed forward several steps, went into the air and with a flying kick, he snapped the support post in half with his right foot. Captain Rynarr was speechless, as well as everyone else.

Finally, Brother Samuel came forward and said, "You really interest me, Mr. Hughes. I've never met an enlisted man quite like you before."

"I can understand why, sir. In your time, most Black sailors worked in the ship kitchens, the laundry and graves registration. Now...or in our time, things had improved some. We're finally able to carry guns, fight alongside the white man and we can also become officers. This was all brought about by the Civil Rights movement of the 1950's, but we're not done yet." Hughes smiled when he said it, but he felt a heart-filled tug to his heart. He waited dearly for the day that Black men and women were truly considered the equal of whites.

"Yes, you're quite right. I grew up in a multi-racial neighborhood, played stickball with a lot of colored and Puerto Rican kids. We all rooted for the Bums back then. But after Annapolis, I was sent to the West Coast and saw my fair share of racism in Los Angeles. It sickened me how they were treated in the service. When a ship went down, no matter what color you were, black, brown or white, you drowned."

Before anyone else could speak, Captain Rynarr approached and offered a cautious hand in greeting to Hughes. After seeing what Hughes could do, he hesitated before clasping hands in this new fashion. Captain Rynarr then spoke and afterward, he waited for Brother Samuel to translate—a tiresome thing.

"He wants you to teach what you know to his Royal Guard and in return, he will teach you how to ride, use the lance, the scimitar and the shield."

"I'd be more than happy too," Hughes said, with a big smile on his face.

After seeing what Hughes had accomplished with Hafe, Mushad walked up to Hughes and after resting his shield against his leg, he also offered up his hand in friendship. An unusual custom for him, Mushad seemed to understand its meaning and wanted Hughes to understand that he could count him, Hirim Mushad, as a friend and fellow fighting man.

"Okay," GW Said for everyone's benefit, "I'd like to ride my horse now."

"Be very gentle with him, GW," Grant warned him. "Talk to him quietly as you approach and in an even tone. Then walk him around the courtyard before you try to mount him. Pet his neck and forward flanks but avoid his other parts for now."

GW nodded his head in response, but he kept his eyes on the stallion. The horse was beautiful to the eye and though tied to the railing, he stomped his feet much like a Tennessee Walker would in a race, while he waited, calculating, as this strange man dared to approach him. He was called by a Libyan name, but GW wasn't told what it was, and nor did he care, for he would name him in a language he understood.

This stallion had been a warhorse for four years and already gone through three owners. One had died valiantly in battle, another had died less gallantly; sick from a strange desert malady and the third, a brutal man, who lashed out at him with a leather quirk, had simply fallen off him during a patrol and was injured. The many scars on his flanks displayed his courage in battle and now, he waited to be taken to the market for trade or sale.

As GW came closer, the stallion pounded his great hooves against the sand to warn this stranger off, but GW still grew closer. Only the rope that tied him to the railing prevented him from raising his head to frighten off this man who smelled funny. He looked this stranger over, for his skin color, odor and hair were far different from the others.

"My friend, you be very still now," GW said in an even tone, slightly above a whisper. "I've chosen you, my..." GW grew silent as he cautiously stepped forward to grab the rope that secured the horse to the railing. "Yes, I will call you Valiant, for you appear to be royal in your blood lines and I will treat you as one knighted."

His words, though in an unknown tongue, were calming and Valiant did not find his strange odor offending. Above all, Valiant sensed no fear in this stranger and it was surprising. He had sensed the sweat of fear on everyone who came near him, until now.

"I will not hurt you, Valiant," GW whispered. He slowly lifted-up his right hand to pet his muscular neck and then gently brushed his nose. "I will not use spurs to scar your sides and I will feed you well, my Valiant," GW whispered again. He then untied the rope slowly and cautiously began to walk him, remembering to stay on his right side, the side he would mount from.

He'd never ridden without a saddle and wasn't sure if he could now, half expecting to simply slide right off Valiant and embarrass himself before the others.

"I want you, Valiant. You and I will be partners...friends," GW said to his horse. "I foresee many adventures before us, Valiant, but first we must make this first ride to show the dear Captain that you are indeed mine." GW continued to walk him as the others watched, but he ignored them all and centered all his attention on Valiant.

High above, Princess Lennia watched this strange large man act so gently toward this warhorse, behaving so un-warrior like with this simple animal. She watched as GW walked this giant of a horse, admittedly a fine-looking animal, around the courtyard. Never had she seen a man treat a horse in such a way, creating a bond of sorts between animal and man, and this intrigued her greatly.

"Well, I guess the time has come," GW said with a note of hesitation to his voice. He looked at Valiant's back and wondered if he could jump on without looking like a complete fool. No saddle meant no stirrups, nothing but only his own strength to get himself on board or this could end up being a very short ride. GW gently rubbed Valiant's backside, stroking his neck and continuing to speak gentle words to keep him calm.

"It's show time, Valiant," GW said with a deep sigh of apprehension. "It is time to see if I've made a wise choice, or a foolhardy one." GW looked him in the eyes and then with a tight grip of mane and rope tie-down, wrapped around his neck, he pulled himself aboard with a short jump and surprisingly, found himself straddling Valiant's wide and muscular back. When he didn't buck him off, GW used his knees and a tight grip on his mane and to the rope to urge him forward and surprisingly, he responded. In fact, and to almost everyone's surprise, including his own, he rode Valiant cautiously around the courtyard four times and then dismounted him in front of the others.

Petting Valiant's nose and caressing his neck, GW knew that a strange bond was being formed between him and this gallant steed. Something he would never have suspected to happen, especially not in the 12th century. Proudly, he led him to a stall, while the others waited and then stepped forward to congratulate him on his achievement.

"Mr. Sanders, I do believe you have made a conquest," Brother Samuel said in admiration.

"He is one beautiful horse, GW," Grant said and Hughes, wearing a big grin, silently nodded his head in agreement.

"I heard you call him, Valiant," Grant said. "Why that name? Sounds kind of corny."

"My dad used to read me stories of Prince Valiant and I really liked the movie. I just thought it fit when I was looking at him."

Captain Rynarr then stepped up and petted the horse's nose lightly. He then said something to Brother Samuel, gesturing to GW and then the horse.

"What'd he say?" GW asked.

"Occasionally, a man and horse become one. When this happens, a great warrior is given birth and he sees this in you two. A cursed horse is no longer cursed, but no other man may ride him." Brother Samuel looked at Captain Rynarr for confirmation and then looked back to GW, "He gives him to you, a gift, but I suspect it is a gift with a price. Someday he will call upon you to repay the debt in some way." Brother Samuel pulled GW away from the stall, "Remember, Mr. Sanders, as much as I am fond of this man and respect him, he is still Libyan, a man who loves his country and his religion above all else. No matter how long I've been here, I still have trouble comprehending them and their ways. They simply do not think as we do. Please remember that, Mr. Sanders."

"Yes, sir...I will."

"Well, my boys, you have certainly provided some entertainment today. I suspect your guards will be removed soon, but Hirim Mushad seems to have taken a liking to you all. I imagine he'll probably hang around on his own when he's not on duty," Brother Samuel said. He was then silent for a moment as he considered something. He looked to the three Americans and said quietly, "Maybe he will become your teacher, for he is a fine swordsman and surely gifted in the lance and bow. Any chance any of you took up fencing or archery?"

They all shook their heads in response.

"Guess we can't have everything," Brother Samuel said with a big chuckle escaping from him.

"When can we see the dragon?" Hughes asked.

Brother Samuel shrugged his shoulders and shook his head, "You remind me of my pupil, Mr. Hughes. But soon, you'll see the creature, as I'm sure the beast is nearby. The next sacrifice is only three days off and our ever-delightful Princess Lonnia is probably quite busy with choosing the next victim."

GW winced when he heard about the sacrifice being so near. He had hoped to find a way to assist Brother Samuel in ending this tragedy. Not knowing what else to say, he nodded his head in understanding and went off to get a bucket of water for Valiant.

Subdued by Brother Samuel's announcement of the sacrifice, Grant and Hughes both walked over to the stall to examine GW's new horse and seeing how such a horse was given to his friend, Grant was hoping to visit the Silene herd soon. If Captain Rynarr kept his word, and Grant saw no reason why he wouldn't, he could be choosing a black Arabian for his very own. He only wished there was some way he could transport a pair of Black Arabians back to his parent's horse ranch in Texas. Man, would the old man flip to see a pair of blacks like these...he'd probably give half of his herd for a pair like the ones the guards ride...maybe his whole ranch.

Thinking about his parents and Texas got him homesick and he meandered off a bit until one of the other courtyard guards shouted at him and gestured for him to return to the others.

"Yeah, I'm comin'," Grant said. As he got closer to Hughes and GW, he whispered, "Man, I feel like the Connecticut Yankee in King Arthur's Court. You guys ever read it?"

"I did," Hughes replied. "But why are you whispering? They can't understand us."

"I don't know. Just humor me...how about you, GW?"

"Yeah, I read it too," GW agreed. "Saw the movie once, Bing Crosby was pretty cool in it and Rhonda Fleming, she is gorgeous!"

"At least he was in England," Grant pointed out. "I had enough of the desert growing up in Texas."

"Could be worse, Mr. Grant, you could have ended up on an island inhabited by head hunters or cannibals, or possibly the frozen wastelands of the Antarctic."

"Brother Samuel, you're beginning to sound more like a priest then a navy commander."

"Why thank you, Mr. Grant," Brother Samuel said graciously. "Now if we're all done here, and Mr. Sanders is finished tucking his horse in for the night, let's head back. I know it's got to be dinnertime because my stomach is growling."

"We can hear it too, sir," GW said. "In fact, I think that lady up there heard it also." GW pointed to the balcony from where Princess Lennia was watching.

Brother Samuel looked up and upon spotting Princess Lennia, that growling in his stomach was quickly overpowered by fear. He then looked to his three charges, "You never saw her, you will never see her and if you do, you will never speak to her. Understand?"

"Who is she?" GW asked.

Brother Samuel glared at the three Americans and stood at what he remembered to be a military stance of attention, "At this moment, gentlemen, you three are being addressed by a superior officer. Do you understand what I have said?"

Stunned by his statement and stern tone, the three men assumed the position of attention and replied in unison, "Yes, sir!"

Brother Samuel studied the three men for a moment and then broke the silence, "I am sorry to have to do this, gentlemen, especially after what I said earlier about putting aside military rank, but for you three, that girl...that lady is a death sentence and a very painful death at that. So, please remember that."

Brother Samuel looked to the sand below his feet briefly and then walked away, leaving Mushad and Hafe to escort the troubled Americans to their room. There was nothing else he could or wanted to say currently. A great day was shattered for him by a simple observance of a beautiful woman in an overlooking balcony. A cultural thing he had learned to accept and now must teach to his three young friends. This brief exchange brought back memories of all the mistakes he had made years ago and how close he came to death several times for violating one tradition or another. The responsibility for the lives of these three men bore down on him heavily and it made him wonder, who'd be coming through this bizarre time barrier next and when?

# 5 – THE WICKED WITCH

Princess Lonnia's interest in alchemy and the dark arts of ancient Egypt continued growing, as she feverishly sought out ways to corrupt her nemesis Brother Samuel, or kill him if corruption failed. But all her fiendish plans over a period of several years had proved fruitless. Poisoning his food failed, but she began suspecting he had been forewarned as the poisoned food was left untouched. She first believed it was one of the kitchen servants, a group of slothful louts, who might have warned him of her dire plot and being a suspicious one, two of them felt her violent wrath with a leather lash and no longer able to perform their duties, they were later sold in Tripoli for a mere pittance as cripples.

If it had not been for Brother Samuel's intervention, there might have been others maimed or even killed, and his interfering actions only added fuel to the fiery hatred she held for him.

Unable to dig out the culprit, she ceased her attempts to poison his food, but attempted other means and went so far as to leave poisonous fluids in his bed—but to no avail and all this sent her into periodic rages. But in truth, it was one of her own handmaidens; a slightly humpbacked and very unattractive girl, who had lost her beautiful older sister to the dragon several years prior and sought her revenge against the Dark Princess.

The handmaiden, while returning a fur cloak to the princess's closet, had overheard Princess Lonnia coming through a hidden doorway from a secret room below the princess's bed chamber. Not wanting to be discovered and bearing knowledge of this secret entrance, she remained hidden and waited as Princess Lonnia secured the door and returned the thickly woven tapestry to cover its presence from being seen. Princess Lonnia was not alone though. She had her aged shaman with her and was gloating over all the pretty victims she had led to their deaths through the

161

way she had rigged the lottery. She even mentioned the handmaiden's sister by name and that of others, who had at some point rejected Princess Lonnia's friendship in her younger days.

Her shaman, who limped from a crippled right leg, moved about the room and ambled behind Princess Lonnia, as the two of them held a leisurely conversation about future plans. Because she was much too afraid to move from concealment, she came to learn of how her sister and so many others had gone to their deaths. Not chosen by lot as required by law but doomed to their hideous fate by an evil Princess, whose own sickened jealousy toward anything beautiful assured a grisly death for Silene's fair maidens.

Princess Lonnia had also learned through a careless tongue how Captain Rynarr's most trusted men conducted daily searches of Brother Samuel's quarters for the presence of hidden assassins, or any deadly insects or venomous snake left lying about by a vengeful princess. But even with all these safeguards, Princess Lonnia never stopped conspiring to kill the good monk. She had left poison on the ropes of his bed and even gone so far as to saturate his robes and furs, but he still lived. Now, her quest for vengeance would also include these three strangers Captain Rynarr had picked up on the beach. If only because two of them happened to be his clansmen and she sincerely hated the Nubian race, because she was shamed once by a Nubian prince.

So, whenever the handmaiden learned of another attempt on Brother Samuel's life, she would send world to him through a trusted knight and not once, had she accepted payment for her assistance.

Currently, Princess Lonnia had other things on her mind. She was in her hidden laboratory in search of a new potion; one powerful enough to turn her hideous troll–like appearance into a thing of beauty. She persisted in her attempt to become the envy of every woman, and desirous of every man, but to this time, her potions had only made her ill. Her secret laboratory was a small windowless room concealed under the northwest battlement. She had massive tapestries of Moroccan design to cover each of the four stone walls and on the stone floor, an ancient floor rug of straw from Isfahan. This hidden room was a safe refuge for her and here, with a wisp of candle smoke lingering around her, she was entertained by the images of strange faceless shadows dancing gracefully about the room to a silent rhythm of their own making. Such shadows gave Princess Lonnia a strange peacefulness of the mind, while she studied a large weathered Grecian text in search of yet another ancient concoction.

Princess Lonnia's eyes were of a dark brown, nearly to the point of ebony, and they sparkled by candlelight. One darkly painted eyebrow rose with a murderous anticipation, as she turned the ever-so brittle pages and took great effort to understand the aged words from a much older world. But it wasn't only the search for beauty that stimulated her, for she was also contemplating the upcoming lottery. Once again and as her official duty directed, she would be the one to choose the next sacrificial victim and this brought her great delight.

An evil smile began to form, as her vision fell upon the next few lines of a long dead language. Yet, once again her smile slowly vanished, replaced by an angry scowl, when she realized the pages revealed nothing she might be able to use. She then turned from her book with disgust and paced across the floor with her noticeable limp. She wore a shaman's thick robe of a reddish hue color, bordered by fine golden threads. The same cloak was once owned by her former teacher; a vile man trained for decades in the black arts of the Egyptians and secrets of the ancient Babylonians. He had suddenly and mysteriously disappeared one night and only the princess knew where his body lay--yet another victim to one of her treacherous potions. Horror stricken, like all his former victims, and utterly confused by her act of disloyalty, he tried to call out, but fell unconscious. Poison in a single date fruit had paralyzed him and with the help of her one trusted handmaiden, she entombed him alive in the north wall of her laboratory. Afterward, she hung the heavy tapestry over the tomb to cover over her sloppy brickwork. Ironically, the design of the tapestry displayed a tranquil moon lit scene over the shores of the Nile River and the great pyramids from where the shaman had once lived. She thought it a fitting covering for the old man who had opened her mind to the powers of black magic. Even now, she imagined hearing the scratching of the old man attempting to escape his tomb, but so much time had passed that she knew he was surely long dead by now--if only by starvation or lack of water.

Two of her laboratory walls were lined by dark wooden bookshelves, which were piled high with priceless manuscripts kept in leather bound tubes. These shelves also held various tools for the practice of witchery and alchemy, items she had acquired from her numerous trips to Egypt, Baghdad, Damascus and one lengthy voyage to Athens that had left her seasick for days.

She collected secrets, concoctions and potions from her fellow sorcerers, renegade Muslim clerics, and dejected Grecian scholars, and from ancient libraries and many an estate foreclosed upon by the Libyan kingdom. With these weapons of dark warfare at hand she planned to seize the throne of Silene and eventually, all of Libya would fall at her feet. But Princess Lonnia didn't plan to stop there, for she, in her growing madness and thirst for power, had envisioned her becoming the next Queen Cleopatra. She saw herself sitting upon a golden throne, decorated in an abundance of precious stones and ruling over all of Africa. No, nothing was going to stop her and certainly not some old monk and his loyal Captain of the Royal Guards.

Clad in a simple dark one-piece garment of smoke blue silk and a loose veil of matching color worn over her face, she walked barefooted across the thick Egyptian straw rugs and went to stand before a small wooden floor chest of Grecian design. This same antiquated chest, encrusted with a display of fine silver, showed some of the Grecian gods she held in reverence and it was in this chest that held the names of those eligible young women selected for the lottery. She knew each of the names and how the name slips had grown fewer in number with the passing of every month.

They had quickly used up the slave girls taken from past raids into Egypt, for far too many of them were found unsuitable for sacrifice; either not virgins at the time of the raid or deflowered during the long journey back from Egypt by what she referred to as slovenly soldiers. Some of the slaves taken in raid or bought in the markets, upon hearing tales of their eventual fate from drunken guards, had committed suicide before reaching Silene. Others scarred from rough treatment by previous owners or disease were found to be simply too unattractive and by lottery standards, each victim must be viewed upon as attractive and thus worthy of sacrifice. Because of this, most of the women in town prayed to Allah they would give birth to sons or if daughters were born, they would be of poor looks or crippled in some way.

So, as afternoon prayers approached, she must again choose a name from the chest and this gave her a feeling of unmitigated power. She glared into the eye-sockets of a bleached white skull of a horned ram and thanked the dark gods she served for this gift. For she relished in this selection process, which should be done by chance, but out of spite she periodically selected names of the more beautiful girls in the kingdom. This was her revenge against great Allah for her misfortune of being cursed with such ugliness; a result of a single accident. This was her way of striking back at the all those who used her misfortune to become the target of almost every joker in the kingdom. This was also the one time she had sole control over the proud Captain Rynarr and his Royal Guard. She was able-to send him and his knights out to secure the chosen victim, a task she knew he utterly detested and this only made it even more enjoyable for her.

Since the young age of 13, when misfortune befell her, and she plunged off the steps, Princess Lonnia sought revenge; to bring death against those who secretly mocked her and spurned her friendship in youth. She would go so far as to choose those sisters of Silene's handsome young men. Men who had snubbed her time after time and thus hardened her heart into a piece of dark ash.

There were no mirrors in Princess Lonnia's laboratory or bedchamber, or even the castle's royal family passageways. She detested her appearance and didn't care to be reminded of it. Her fall and lack of medical expertise left her with a misshapen nose, cheeks now reminiscent of pig jowls, two upper front teeth missing, and a mouth scarred badly from upper left lip to jaw-line. Her left eye drooped a bit from the socket fracture and on her neck, she bore a messy looking knife scar from her own attempt at suicide when she was 17 years old. A court doctor sealed the wound with a blazing iron, while the king's personal guards held the screaming girl in place.

Princess Lonnia seldom made a public appearance and even then, she was heavily veiled in dark colored silk, with only her dark piercing brown eyes, heavily made up, showing above the veil. This did offer her some dignity, but in her hatred for Allah she never wore it in her private rooms.

Her handmaidens were slaves she had purchased cheaply in the slave market, quite ugly themselves and equally disfigured from birth defect, or from violent abuse by past owners. She had beaten them with whips and terrified them into total obedience with threats of death and maiming. Three of them lived in utter fear of the princess, only the one who heard the princess boast of her sister's death held some degree of courage. Disfigured yes, but this brave young maiden, who maintained a pretense of fear, only waited for the day she could strike and destroy Princess Lonnia to avenge her sister.

Admiring the chest, a true antiquity from a time before Alexander the Great ruled the world Princess Lonnia carefully opened it and withdrew the parchment slip. She already knew the name of the girl she had earlier selected for tomorrow's sacrifice but needed the special heavy palm-sized parchment slip of a yellowish color for Captain Rynarr to authenticate and then carry out his assigned duties.

A girl of only 14-years and oldest daughter of a local sheep herdsman, Princess Lonnia had selected her for a trivial offense the girl's older brother had made against her sometime in the past. So far back she couldn't remember what the offense was and why she hadn't simply had him slain on the spot. Not that it mattered now, her revenge would be sweet as she imagined the girl, crying out for her parents, was seized from her home by Royal Guardsman and brought to the castle for a brief audience before the king.

As required by the infamous and long-standing Court Decree, the King of Silene would bring the intended sacrificial offering, the virgin, before the throne to explain why this action was to be carried out and how honored she should feel for offering up their life in the protection of her king, her family and neighbors. In most cases the intended victim was terrified beyond understanding and would thrash about hysterically, while restrained by guards.

Then escorted, or in some cases carried, from the court, the victim was then examined to ensure suitability and afterward, allowed a private time to pray before Allah in a small windowless room. Upon the appointed time, she was then gagged and chained to a horse drawn cat and transported in the early morning hours to the sacrificial site; a large rock where bloodstained chains from a thousand sacrifices awaited her. Once secured to the rock, five guardsmen would sound ceremonial antelope horns to let the dragon and everyone else know his feast had arrived. The guards would then remove her gag and retreat from the site rapidly, leaving the hysterical girl to her horrid fate.

If a family attempted to interfere with the Royal Guardsmen, they could be summarily slain on the spot, removed to the dungeon for torture, or later sentenced to a lengthy stay in a Tripoli prison. In the event the dragon killed the would-be-rescuers, no further action would be carried out against the family. This was the case of the elder Captain Rynarr, who had attempted to free his daughter and fell before the creature.

With parchment slip in hand, Princess Lonnia left her hidden room and locked the thick wooden door behind her with two bulky padlocks. With the keys hanging from her neck, she then walked up a darkened narrow passageway and pushed aside a large tapestry to enter a much smaller room, this one illuminated by a single tall candle. This room was her closet, which held her storage; twelve large chests for winter furs, her childhood clothing and various gifts from her father, which she refused to have lying around her bedchamber.

Leaving this room, she proceeded up another circular flight of 12-stone stairs, until she reached a closed door. This was kept locked from either side she was on and only she had the keys. Unlocking the massive door, she ignored its creaking sound and then closed it behind her. She then secured it from her side with a heavy metal hasp and an aged lock. She always lived in fear that someone would discover her secret rooms. This resulted in her carrying metal keys on a necklace about her neck. This often caused a metallic jingling sound, but being the Black or Dark Princess, as she was often referred to as, no one would comment on her strangeness.

A large thick curtain of wool weave, dyed to a dark blue hue, covered the secret door and only she and her most trusted handmaiden knew where this doorway went. And for extra assuredness, Princess Lonnia had this handmaiden's tongue cut out over two-years ago; which ensured her silence.

Before summoning her four handmaidens with a loud clapping of her hands, she took in a deep breath and reveled in the rich aroma of frankincense that permeated the air. This aroma helped her to relax somewhat and only then was the handmaidens were summoned.

In total silence, these frightened women nervously shuffled about, dressing their princess in fine dark brown colored silk garments. They adorned her with fine gold and silvery jewelry and finished with a soft shimmering robe of the royal family's dark blue color. She also wore a long veil of smoke-blue silk that reached up to the bottoms of her eyes. Its fine jeweled border matched with the headdress she wore and cascaded down below her waist. She slid her feet into modest leather sandals; each adorned with a single red ruby. Satisfied with her clothing, she clapped her hands only once to release her four servants and they quickly returned to their room down the hall from Princess Lonnia's bedchamber. Like wisps of smoke, they seemed to guide across the room in silence until Princess Lonnia was left alone in her room.

The Dark Princess then walked out of her bedchambers, each other step displaying a slight limp, for she still felt the pain from her long ago fall; both physically and in her misguided spirit. Her limp was a continual reminder for what had befallen her, and life's pain fed the fire of hate she held for all those around her. It took her several moments to reach the royal court from her room and while walking through the well-lit passageways and with an air of indifference, she snubbed the half-hearted greetings of her father's petty underlings and guardsmen. Upon entering the massive ornate throne room, she limped to her high backed ornate throne and seated herself with a bold display of open disdainfulness, flaunting her blue blood before her father's people with a look of scorn. She then provided to her father a single nod of her head, concealing her ugly sneer behind a silken veil.

The throne room was massive in size and from here the king held court and welcomed visiting dignitaries, which had become a rare event. The room was illuminated during the day with 15-huge window openings, but during the evening several dozen torch stands were lit. Numerous tall candles were also placed as needed because the king was uncomfortable with dark corners, wary of a hidden assassin.

The south end of the decorative room could hold several dozen standing people, while they waited to see the king. The opposite or north end of the room set the four thrones of the royal family on a raised platform made of stone. From the walls hung great and ancient tapestries of all colors and from many faraway lands. There were numerous metal and wooden shields of several designs and color strewn about, and various flags displaying an honored individual family's coats-of-arms. Massive straw mats were placed beneath matching sets of Moroccan rugs to cover the cold stone floors.

Surrounding the thrones as a backdrop were thick woven curtains of King Ramie's colors; dark blue and silver hues. Four handpicked Royal Guardsmen in full battle armor stood guard over the royal family. With spear and shield in hand they would gladly give their lives to protect their king and his youngest daughter, but they were not quite sure if they would do the same for Princess Lonnia.

Princess Lonnia's throne, quite elegant in style and a foot taller than her sister's, was a gift from her father on her 13th birthday. It was constructed of fine dark cedar wood from Alexandria, with softened cushions of dark blue purchased in Tripoli and decorated with jewels from her family's treasure chest.

In the absence of a queen and as protocol decreed, her throne was positioned to the king's immediate right.

Though so close to her father's throne, she would often ignore her father's conversation, as she did tonight, as he spoke with a minor dignitary. She loudly summoned a court officer and upon his arrival, she then immediately issued an order in a raised voice to have the Royal Guard lieutenant of the Court summon forth Captain Rynarr.

In a rapid response, he appeared before her, knelt-down before her and awaited her words. Satisfied with his timely arrival, she ordered him to stand and then in a loud voice, "I want Captain Rynarr here this evening, Lieutenant and preferably within the hour." She had purposely said this loudly enough for all the court to here.

"Now no excuses, Lieutenant...Find him now, or you'll face 30-days of bread and water...or," she said with a sinister leer, "...maybe 30-lashes."

Used to her threats, from imprisonment and torture to dismemberment, the Lieutenant simply replied in a soft and courteous voice, "Yes, my princess." He then bowed with military precision and turned on his heels to leave the courtroom in suitable haste, but not running fearfully as Princess Lonnia had sincerely hoped.

"My dear daughter, I wish you would remember that man is an officer in our Royal Guard and not some house servant to be kowtowed for your amusement," King Ramie said in a strained whisper. Out of proper decorum he attempted to restrain his temper before the court officers in attendance. Though a King, he felt as a father he should critique his daughter's conduct while alone with them and not in a full court, but a simple word or two in a low whisper were clearly suitable for her rude actions.

"He still serves the throne; Dear Father and I demand strict obedience from all those who serve us...even one of our most prestigious Royal Guard officers."

"A man loyal to the throne will better serve the kingdom then one who hates his master," King Ramie reminded her.

"You are too easy, my Father, but this is your kingdom," Princess Lonnia replied and then looked away. For the present at least, but that will soon change, dear father. She did not wish her father to see the look in her eyes, for it was one of contempt and loathing.

Captain Rynarr knew all too well of today's date and was expecting the summons to appear before the king. But at this very moment he was locked in an intense duel of wits with Brother Samuel. They were playing a game of chess and because of this it took the anxious lieutenant a few moments longer to locate him in Brother Samuel's quarters.

Having been discovered, Captain Rynarr released a deep sigh and looked in the kindly eyes of his old friend and stood to his feet. "I must bow to my royal summons, my good Christian friend."

"You simply do not want to face another defeat, my good Muslim Captain," Brother Samuel said in a friendly response.

"Truly, you would have once again defeated me for I see no way out of the trap you laid so skillfully for me." Captain Rynarr then bowed, presenting the Arabic gesture of blessing with the right-hand fingertip touch of the upper chest, the mouth and the forehead. This gesture was used for both a greeting and for saying goodbye. He then turned and led the young lieutenant out of the room. The lieutenant, who was accompanied by a castle guard of four men-at-arms, carried a lit torch through the stone passageway to light the way for his captain.

Already knowing all too well what this summons meant, Captain Rynarr sought out one of the castle's knight-in-training; a young man of only 13 years, and ordered he go to the stables immediately. "Locate my detail of ten Royal Guardsmen and advise them to prepare themselves for tonight's duty."

This was not a task the Royal Guardsmen took personal enjoyment in, but they carried out their orders. Captain Rynarr's early notification gave them time to ready themselves, by ensuring their mounts are saddled. More importantly, this allowed them a moment to enter the castle's mosque and offer up a prayer to Allah for mercy upon their souls, for the task ahead of them this night was a dreadful one. Captain Rynarr believed this sacrificial duty to be a distasteful chore and especially one for true warriors of Allah to carry out. Having to remove a young girl from her home weighed heavily upon his heart and he so wished it was otherwise.

Nearly an hour after the lieutenant was sent out to find him, Captain Rynarr, dressed in his Royal Guardsmen tunic, but without a weapon in view, made his appearance before the court. Bypassing everyone else in the large room, he proceeded forward and knelt on his right knee before the King. He kept his face veiled, as allowed, to hide his own displeasure for Princess Lonnia's presence at the right side of his king. He knew all too well how the Black Princess wanted her father dead, but the good king was unwilling to listen to such warnings and ordered Rynarr to cease such accusations in his presence.

Princess Lennia and Princess Lannia were not present tonight. Princess Lannia was on patrol to the south of Silene and Princess Lennia was studying in her quarters. Brother Samuel had requested of the king that his youngest daughter not be present for these barbaric ceremonies and the king allowed it. He too wished to spare his youngest girl from observing such practices as this lottery selection.

"You sent for me, my liege?" Captain Rynarr asked of the king. Then with a hand gesture from King Ramie, he stood to his feet.

"No, it was my daughter, the Princess Lonnia, who sent for you." King Ramie again gestured with his right hand, but this time toward his daughter and then continued with his conversation with a visiting minor dignitary over new trade routes being planned by the Caliph. Though his thoughts were not entirely on the business at hand, he attempted to listen to the exchange between his captain and his oldest daughter.

Captain Rynarr clenched his bare hands into fists and then looked to Princess Lonnia. He then lowered his eyes and simply waited, as Princess Lonnia remained silent and looked down upon him with her best cold icy glare. She knew the deep contempt Captain Rynarr held for her and why he had not rushed to appear before her to demonstrate this feeling of ill-favor.

Angry, she again recalled how she had lowered herself to once want this vile toad as her suitor, be he kept his distance like all the others and this incensed her to the point of attempting to hire an assassin to kill him. But all feared Captain Rynarr's sword and his contingent of loyal Royal Guardsmen. So, she used moments like this to remind him of his place here in the court, to intimidate the good captain before the others and he returned her anger by simply tolerating her silly child-like behavior in silence.

A good five-minute period of silence passed between them, as she left him standing before her. Then she slowly stood to her feet and calmly walked around her throne and that of her father's, glaring down at the captain. Those in attendance were sadly used to her poor conduct and remained silent as to not risk her anger. But once satisfied the proper amount of time had transpired and ignoring the tiresome expression on her father's face, she broke the silence with a curt, "Take it!"

She threw the small yellowing parchment to the floor and shouted, "Carry out your duties as required or face the executioner's axe."

"Thank you, your highness. As always, your command will be obeyed." Captain Rynarr picked up the piece of parchment with the girl's name on it and bowed before the king. He then abruptly turned and marched out of the throne room, without another glance toward the princess.

King Ramie, his face flushed with anger, sent the embarrassed dignitary away with the wave of his hand and turned to glare at his oldest daughter. In a whisper, but stern tone, he said, "If I ever see you treat my Captain of the Guard in such a discourteous way, I will...I will..." He couldn't finish, unable to come up with a suitable punishment for his eldest child. But Princess Lonnia interrupted him, "What, my father? How will you punish me for teaching our officers proper respect? They are to obey our orders without question and be fearful of ever looking upon us with contempt in their eyes, as your dear Captain Rynarr looks upon me."

"You go too far, daughter!" King Ramie exclaimed in anger, startling the others in court, which brought complete silence to the large room. A dozen or more people either brave, or possibly simply curious, raised their eyes to observe King Ramie stand up from the throne, scowl at his daughter and then leave the court in a huff. Such actions were becoming more often as Princess Lonnia's disrespectful attitude toward her father worsened and nearly everyone wondered where this battle of the wills would lead.

With one daughter carrying on quite sinfully with another woman and acting as if she was a man-at-arms, and another daughter behaving in such a disrespectful way toward the King, the officers of the court were fearful such things could reach the ears of the great Caliph in Tripoli. He was the only man powerful enough to act against King Ramie.

With Captain Rynarr and her father now gone, Princess Lonnia lingered behind her father's throne and ran her hands over the expensive woodwork and thought of the day this would be hers. Flames seemed to radiate from her eyes as she clenched the arms of his chair and for the moment, she totally ignored the people in the throne room and quietly spoke a curse of death over her father. She then spoke a second and third curse, aimed at Captain Rynarr and Brother Samuel. She wanted both dead and even day-dreamed of driving an ornate dagger into each of their hearts.

For even with the king's death, she knew Captain Rynarr wouldn't follow her orders and would most likely give his allegiance to her youngest sister. Brother Samuel would immediately suspect her of killing her father and probably sway the Royal Court to follow Captain Rynarr. Too many of the members of court were afraid of her, far too many for her to simply assume the throne and though she had several dozen soldiers in the regular army under her control with bribes, blackmail and threats, she'd not been able to gain the support of a single Royal Guardsmen. Such was a necessity for her plan to be carried out, or the deaths of the dear captain and his friend, Brother Samuel. With a swirl of her silken floor length cape, she straightened her shoulders, gave a hard shrug to demonstrate her arrogance and left the room to everyone's relief. Some of those present could almost see an aura of darkness surrounding her, following her like a storm cloud, as she disappeared through the archway. These who were loyal to their king and could see her strong desire to someday seize control of the kingdom, began to pray for his protection from the dark arts of the Black Princess.

Moments later, Princess Lonnia, still angry from the exchange between her and her father, was back inside her laboratory. She now looked upon a thick book of ancient chants, one she had paid very dearly for. The hefty price was far more then she wanted to pay, and, so far it had gained her nothing but the death of her former teacher, through a potion which brought on complete paralysis. With only his mind awake, his death would be slow and tortuous.

As she carefully turned the brittle pages, each filled with the archaic words written in a dead language no longer used in the 12th century, she looked for something that would empower her with a mighty weapon to use against Brother Samuel. The departed shaman had taught her how to read the words of a civilization that had perished so long ago, but so far nothing had worked. She was beginning to wonder if that wooden amulet; that simple cross the monk wore around his neck, protected him from her curses and poisons? She knew about this prophet Jesus he followed, for the Koran spoke of him, but she never believed this poor man from

Nazareth could truly have passed along the powers to thwart her dark spells with only a chunk of carved wood. No, she felt there was something else protecting Brother Samuel and she was determined to find out what it was.

For several long hours, she studied this text and others like it, but nothing stood out to her and she finally put her books away. There were still words or symbols she did not understand and now wished she had waited on killing the old shaman.

But she had grown hungry and knew the king's personal kitchen would always have something ready in the event the king had one of his sudden hunger spells. So, locking up her rooms, she slowly climbed the stairs, favoring her crippled leg and entered her bedchamber. There she changed clothes once again with the able assistance of her obedient and fearful handmaidens and then headed downstairs for an evening meal.

## THE ROYAL DINING ROOM

An ornate room of great tapestries and massive woven rugs, King Ramie set in a tall-backed carved wooden chair, which weighed close to 200-pounds. At the top of the chair was a beautiful carving of his crown, and the back of the chair was the continued carving of the kingdom's shield. The chair was done by a highly skilled artist from a century ago and only the reigning king may sit in it.

King Ramie sat at the head of the huge wooden table more than 16-feet long and the planks making up the table top were of rich cedar. The table was covered in a cloth of dark blue, with a set of silver dishes and three lit candle stands upon it to illuminate the eating area. He smiled as his youngest daughter; Princess Lennia, when she graciously entered the room and seated herself at his left hand. But then his smile transformed into a frown, upon Princess Lonnia's arrival and her expression of disdain. She seated herself at his right. It appeared all three of them needed sustenance this night and though somewhat unusual, the king felt somewhat comforted to have two of his three daughters present.

Prayers had finished, and King Ramie had quite the appetite. As he decreed, Brother Samuel set at his left, beside Princess Lennia, as he was the King's closest advisor. Captain Rynarr, when present, sat to the left of Princess Lonnia, which often led to some spirited conversations between the two and on more than once occasion ruined the meal.

After some light-hearted discussion with Brother Samuel, he looked to his daughters and waited to see if they had anything to say. King Ramie had decreed long ago that all those present at his table could speak as equals, unless of course the king decided a subject should be closed before things got out of hand.

King Ramie laid a leg of lamb down on his silvery plate and addressed Princess Lonnia in a condescending tone, "My dear daughter, I am surprised to see you here tonight. Lately, you have taken your meals in your quarters...as if to shun us."

"I only felt in need of your company, my Father," Princess Lonnia replied in false pleasantness and the king simply smiled back in the same mocking way.

The dinner party then remained silent, while a dozen servants entered the room and delivered the meal for the princesses; platters of fresh white fish from the Mediterranean Sea and plates piled high with grilled Antelope steaks obtained from Princess Lannia's recent hunt near Tripoli. There was also freshly made loaves of bread from the castle's kitchen, still quite warm to the touch. Added to this was a bowl of mixed fruit and a sour juice made from dates, which brought a smile to Brother Samuel's face. This was about the closest he would find to a fermented drink in Libya.

"My friend," the king asked as he raised a wooden goblet to his face, "What of these strangers...these clan members of yours...how do they fare?"

"Thank you for asking, my liege. Captain Rynarr," Brother Samuel gestured to the captain's empty chair with his right hand, "...has tested them to observe their skills as warriors. I believe he has found two of them to be adequate horsemen, but strangely untrained in lance and sword. However, he has also discovered the Nubian to be quite superior in hand-to-hand fighting skills and the man has graciously agreed to train our soldiers in these skills. I watched as he disabled a larger man than himself with one blow of his hand and could also break a three-inch board with the side of his hand. Then he demonstrated for us a most unusual flying kick, in which he broke through a four-inch corral support pole. It was an incredible thing to observe, your majesty."

"I can see by your tone that you were very impressed by your clan members." Princess Lennia said.

"Yes, my Princess, I was."

"If Captain Rynarr is agreeable as you say, indeed, have this Nubian train our men and please provide an instructor for these other two...clansmen," The King said to Brother Samuel. But then added, "I am surprised, Brother Samuel, these clansmen of yours would be inexperienced with the lance and sword." King Ramie then wiped some fruit juice from the side of his face with the sleeve of his tunic.

Brother Samuel had tried to introduce the use of napkins at the dinner table, but no one wanted to use one. It was simply easier to use one's sleeve or in a woman's case, the end of her veil scarf. "My King, had you given them a staff or maybe a large club, they would demonstrate their talents; for these are the weapons of Ireland, unless of course they are in the service of the English King. But I believe most Irishmen would rather die than serve an Englander."

"Did you not serve an English king when you traveled to the Holy Land?" Princess Lonnia asked. She had her dinner knife pointed at Brother Samuel, which was a rude gesture of accusation.

"No, my Princess, I served my Lord. But it was the Pope who sent me to the Holy Land. I was ordered to accompany the knights and men-at-arms to provide spiritual enlightenment and to hear their confessions. I was to also bless them and perform Last Rites over them before they departed this world...or as in most cases, over their dead bodies."

"Yet, it was this same Pope, you say, that ordered you home?" Princess Lonnia asked in a sarcastic tone.

"I have told my story many times, my Princess, but yes, it was this same Pope who ordered me home and removed me from my religious order. For in his eyes, I, a lowly monk, was a blasphemer, for offering aide to the Muslim women and children—Innocent victims of a terrible war between Muslims and Christians."

"But Brother Samuel, as a Christian, especially a religious teacher, shouldn't you have shunned the Muslims and obeyed the order of your Pope—a man looked upon as your Christ on earth?"

Brother Samuel, who was wishing he could finish his meal, rose up to Princess Lonnia's challenge and placed his slab of antelope meat back down on the plate and turned to face her with a small grin on his face, "My dear Princess, had you remained in my classroom, I would have instructed you in the ways of Jesus Christ, a great prophet recognized by your own faith. For in his teachings, all people are the children of God. In his eyes, religious sects or ethnic backgrounds should not separate the people of this earth. This is what I taught, as I was taught long ago by my teachers."

King Ramie interrupted them before things got to loud and soured his stomach, "I know from ancient writings of how the people of this kingdom were once followers of this Jesus, before the Word of Allah spread across the sands like a raging fire. I have heard how the teachings of this Prophet Jesus have spread across the northern lands too, which has already twice brought great armies to secure Jerusalem. But each time they have failed before reaching there."

He had a look of grave concern on his face as he continued on, "Many will die in these futile attempts, Brother Samuel, many warriors from both armies. Is this what your Jesus Christ would want?"

"No," Brother Samuel answered. "Jesus Christ spoke of peace and brotherly love. He did not teach of war, of killing your neighbor or enslaving women and children."

"As usual, my good friend in this we do agree. But I have heard of another army readying themselves for a third such venture, but now is not the time to discuss such things." King Ramie gestured to Brother Samuel's dinner plate. "Finish your dinner, my friend, for it is hard to sleep on an empty...or even a sour stomach."

Brother Samuel smiled at the king and then turned to look at Princess Lonnia, whose cold eyes were glaring back at him. He raised his eyebrows and nodded his head, You, keep trying, lady, but your father is too smart for your little ploys. He is concerned for his kingdom and what a holy war could mean for his people and you have no idea of what is coming. War after war after war will shake this land for 200 years, and then again in a future time this land will be bathed in the blood of its people. All here will see starvation and ruin to follow and all you're interested in is playing power games. I do feel some pity for you, but you have given your life over to a darkness I do not understand, and it is this that will destroy you.

Princess Lonnia lifted her eyes to boldly glare at her father, but then calmed down and returned to her meal. She agreed there was still some time, though not too much. For in the near-future, her father and this fat Christian holy man sitting at this table would be gone and she would be the one sitting at the head of this table.

## IN THE TOWN OF SILENE

While the royal family was at a late meal, Captain Rynarr and ten of his most trusted guardsmen, the same men who had taken GW, Grant and Hughes prisoner, departed the castle grounds on horseback for a casual ride into the City of Silene. Townspeople with young teenage daughters knew what was happening by their late evening appearance and rushed their daughters into their homes, praying fervently to their Allah that the guardsmen would pass them by.

At an easy gait, Captain Rynarr felt a wave of pity for the fearful expressions on the townspeople's faces, as he led his men outside the city and headed south. Here lay the homes and farms of the kingdom's herdsmen. Within moments, a cry was shouted out in warning, as the guardsmen worked their way through the great herds of sheep.

Captain Rynarr knew where he was headed. He had known this particular herdsman all his life and saw him to be loyal to the king. He also knew the young lady chosen for sacrifice, having seen her as a little girl and then a young lady chasing the sheep about, as his guardsmen rode about the kingdom. This was not a task he enjoyed, knowing this herdsman and his family would now look upon the king and his soldiers with hatefulness for what was about to transpire in their lives.

Surprisingly, seeing the guardsmen approach their simple wood frame hut, built generations ago from salvaged dock lumber, hand fabricated ropes and dried wood brought from the hills to the east, the young lady chosen for tomorrow's sacrifice stood bravely in the open doorway. She knew why they were coming and even with fear in her eyes, she nodded her head in understanding, when Captain Rynarr dismounted his horse and approached.

Captain Rynarr was greatly impressed with this young woman's conduct but was ever watchful for how the herdsman and his family might act. But they all remained silent, though their eyes radiated with bitterness for having one of their own chosen for such a grisly fate. There was hate in their eyes to be sure, not so much for the guardsmen, men they knew who had a sad duty to carry out, but for the whole horrifying idea of losing their daughter to this curse upon their land.

The bag of gold dropped at the feet of the father, as Captain Rynarr reached out for the youth's hand. She responded in kind, to be led away from her family home and followed him to his horse. No words were exchanged with the father, who fought off the tears. He watched his daughter leave his side for the very last time. But the mother and younger sister, they both cried out and two of the dismounted guardsmen blocked their path without giving harm, when they tried to reach out to the chosen girl.

Out of respect for her courage, Captain Rynarr decided that she would ride to the castle behind him, rather than be carried by another of his guardsmen. With a last look at the father, Captain Rynarr nodded his head once and then turned his warhorse to the right and headed back through the sheep flocks. The two dismounted guardsmen remained at the house for a moment, to ensure there would be no problem; then, they rode to catch up with the detail. Though rare, there had been problems in the past and more than one guardsman had been killed or injured while carrying out this sickening duty.

Unable to speak to this brave lady, while they rode, for he was far too ashamed of his task, Captain Rynarr rode on with his outriders behind him. No one spoke during the brief journey back to the castle, for all had grown weary of this gruesome task.

Riding through the city, Captain Rynarr could feel the eyes of the people burning into him and as a usual practice, he would avoid entering the city for the next three or four days after the sacrifice. Before, with his father and the captains before them, anger would spread right after the event and blood was shed by some outspoken townspeople. One of two would get their courage up and attack those Royal Guardsmen who had carried out the loathsome chore.

Riding inside the castle grounds, the huge gate closed behind them and under dim torchlight, Captain Rynarr dismounted his warhorse and gently lowered the quiet young lady to the ground. She weighed less than 100-pounds and wore a simple gray dress, no shoes and her shiny black hair was worn in a loose ponytail. One knee was scraped up from a spill while herding some unruly sheep, but her skin was of a soft olive complexion. She was a beauty to be sure, if not a bit filthy from her work day, and Captain Rynarr knew if she had not been chosen for sacrifice many a young man would have fought over her attention in the years to follow.

"You are a brave one," Captain Rynarr said to her. But she remained silent, biting down on her lower lip to stifle off a tear and looked about the castle grounds through frightened eyes.

Captain Rynarr grasped her shoulders, looked in her eyes, "Listen to me now and continue to honor your family with your courage. From here you will be taken inside the castle to be prepared for an audience before the king and a physical examination. I pray you maintain this courage, for rare it is for one so young and it shows great honor to your father."

"Captain," She said in a trembling voice. She looked up into his dark eyes and felt the tears flowing down her cheeks, "I do want to honor my father, but I am so scared."

"It is no fault to be frightened, little one, but to stand without the need of restraint speaks well of your upbringing." Captain Rynarr had great respect for the herdsmen, who fought the summer drought and winter storms to maintain their flocks. Two of his favorite warriors had come from such families and he saw this same inner strength in this girl.

Two castle guards suddenly appeared at her side, backed by a man carrying a large flaming torch. The guards started to grasp her thin arms tightly when Captain Rynarr stopped them, "Hold there," he ordered. "She can walk without your clumsy assistance."

"Yes, sir," the senior of the two replied. They quickly stepped away and left the girl standing.

Trembling, she nodded her thanks to Captain Rynarr and slowly walked toward the castle keep's entryway. Not once in her young life had she been inside the castle grounds and now, she would be readied to appear before the king himself. As she disappeared into the darkness of the castle keep she thought of her parents and her four younger brothers and baby sister. For the first time in her life, she wished she'd been born a boy.

Captain Rynarr met with Brother Samuel near a private entrance to the throne room, both men somber for the ordeal that lay ahead. Every two weeks they weathered this event, relying on each other's strength to see it through. Twenty-four maidens a year had brought an utterly depressive and haunting spell upon the kingdom and everyone was beginning to ask the same question that weighed heavily upon King Ramie's mind, "What will we do when there are no suitable maidens for sacrifice?"

A hardened warrior of more than 25-campaigns and border skirmishes against Libya's enemies, Captain Rynarr was not a fearful man, but this duty to the King in escorting young ladies to their doom was tearing him up inside. It only worsened when he had to remove such a brave girl, one he knew, from her parents. Five times a day he prayed for Silene's curse to be lifted and the foul dragon destroyed, but Allah had not seen fit to answer his and all the other's prayers.

The number of marriages in the kingdom was down by more than 50-percent, mainly because of the lack of young ladies and this has also brought down the number of children being born. Slowly, the population of the kingdom was dropping and there was little King Ramie could do about it. The Caliph would not allow the people of Silene to move elsewhere and now, the Caliph's soldiers patrolled the road to Tripoli to ensure this decree was enforced. To move to Egypt meant death and the desert to the south held little hope of being crossed. No, it appeared to the king that his kingdom was going to slowly wither and eventually die, because of this strange curse held over them.

Within the hour, several royally attired court ladies escorted the young girl, now prettied up in expensive finery, before the king for presentation. Once again, she stood without the requirement of chains or manacles, surprising even the hardened Princess Lonnia, while the court officer read out loud the lottery's royal decree for all to witness.

All court officers and senior ranking soldiers from both the army and Royal Guards were ordered to be present for the official reading, unless official duties had them elsewhere. This the king demanded of them, so all may share in this morose burden.

Then came the king's questioning of the five court ladies accompanying the young woman to ensure the girl was indeed a virgin and without disease followed the reading. Three questions were asked and all three were answered favorably to show she was indeed suitable for sacrifice. King Ramie then turned his attention to the young lady, who was now on her knees in homage before her liege, "Do you have any questions, my dear?"

Biting her tongue for fear of screaming, her eyes watering up, she could only shake her head while keeping her eyes lowered. But before the king could order her removal to a private room for prayers, Captain Rynarr surprised everyone by breaking with protocol and stepping forward to address the king. He almost couldn't believe it himself, when his mouth opened, and he heard himself pleading loudly for this young woman's life.

At first stunned by Captain Rynarr's outburst, for this was the first time he had ever done such a thing, Brother Samuel suddenly stepped up to echo the cry for mercy, "Show mercy upon this young one, my liege."

Others then joined in, raising their voices to join in this sudden cry for the girl's life and even Princess Lennia rose up from her throne to address her father, "Truly, father, this is a brave girl and one this kingdom so gravely needs. Let her live, my king and choose another."

Seeing that her father was being swayed, Princess Lonnia quickly shot to her feet and shouted out, "Sire, this lottery be of a royal decree, unchallengeable and none may be freed from it!"

King Ramie knew this to be true, but then he thought of something and ordered the court to be silent.

"What my eldest daughter says is true, but it also says in that same decree the selected one for sacrifice may be replaced if both king and the intended victim agree. Then a new victim would be chosen the same day." King Ramie ignored the icy glare in his oldest daughter's eyes and stepped down from his throne to approach the girl. With a gentle hand to the bottom of her chin, he lifted her head up and looked deeply into her tearful eyes.

"Tell me, young one, would you have another chosen in your place?"

Her voice weak, she looked in his kind, but troubled eyes and whispered, "No, my king. I would not wish this on another, for I could not live if it were to be so."

King Ramie nodded his head in understanding, "I can see now why my Captain has offered to plead in your behalf. Your parents will be proud of you, for I will send my Captain to tell them of your courage and statement." He ordered the guards forward and they gently lifted her to her feet and slowly, with respect for her demonstration and they escorted the young girl from the throne room.

The king then tuned to face Princess Lonnia, "I tasked you with this duty because I know your heart to be cold and you would be untroubled to carry out this vile chore. Yet, I wish I could see some sympathy in your eyes for such a brave young woman. A girl that I wish you could be like." King Ramie then shook his head in disgust and walked out of the throne room without a word to anyone else.

Embarrassed by her father's outburst and gentle treatment of the intended victim, Princess Lonnia, who was still on her feet, swept her long flowing robe behind her and stomped out of the room like the spoiled child she was. This left only Princess Lennia in appearance and the whole proceeding had greatly disturbed her. She saw the bravery displayed by the young woman and Captain Rynarr's attempt to save her. With such a display of emotion about her, she once again couldn't understand why Allah had not stepped in to destroy this vile beast and end the deaths of so many young women. For the first time, she really felt a strong feeling of doubt in Allah and this weighed heavily on her heart.

Seeing Brother Samuel accompany a much-saddened Captain Rynarr from the throne room, Princess Lennia returned to Brother Samuel's classroom. From his windows and by the stable's torchlight, she was able-to observe the three strangers stand beside a water troth and converse, but she was unable to hear their words.

One of them, the one she had learned was called simply GW, a strange name she could only speak truly in Brother Samuel's Irish, had gained her curiosity. His name came from her mouth sounding like, "Gee-double-U", and she found him to be quite a large man and extremely handsome. But she was a distance away and would like a closer look to be sure of her appraisal. She also observed how well he had ridden that accursed stallion and this greatly impressed her. She had always thought the steed to be a majestic animal, having watched it several times in the training yard and was saddened to learn it was on its way to Tripoli for trade or sale. Now it seemed the stallion would stay, and this made her happy.

Knowing Brother Samuel would be returning soon, she left the window edge and by candlelight, made her way back to her bedchamber. Her heart was heavy tonight. She knew a very courageous girl was in the prayer chamber, awaiting a terrible fate and before first light Captain Rynarr would be escorting her to the great wall. There, she would be held until an hour after sunrise and then taken by a small company of fearful guardsmen to the ghastly rock of sacrifice.

Not so long ago three guardsmen, moving to slow to escape, were caught by the great dragon and devoured. Only then did the beast turn on the terrified sacrificial victim. This horrific memory of the dragon's great size rising from the waters in an unimaginable burst of great speed to strike out at the guardsmen remained in the minds of the escort detail. Since then they had changed their way of doing things and now only one man truly risked his life and this man's life was drawn by lot between the detail of guardsmen.

Princess Lonnia had no such cares for this young maiden, in fact she wished she could simply tear the girl's heart out for all the embarrassment she had caused her before the king and others of the court. Still, in a few hours the girl would be torn from the chains and ropes and this picture in her mind of shed blood and gore began to cheer her up some.

With a sinister smile, she turned the fragile pages of an ancient Arabian text in hopes of finding a suitable plague she could curse the Royal Guardsmen and their beloved commander with. Last year she had contaminated the guardsmen drinking supply with what she liked to term as a witches' brew and several men had fallen seriously ill, but then Brother Samuel had stepped in with a remedy and she was furious. For a whole afternoon and into the evening the handmaidens to the Dark Princess was forced to listen to her shrieks, curses and breaking things, with the occasional whipping thrown in.

## THE ROYAL GUARDSMAN'S STABLES

Looking out over the night sky, GW was in awe of the magnificent view of the heavens above. He couldn't remember ever seeing so many stars and how this young moon of an old world, though only half-full, shined ever so brightly. The spectacular sight led him to recall how God had said to Abraham, how he would multiply his children to equal the number of stars in the heavens. He could not remember the exact words, but he knew it had something to do with this prophesy and now he understood it. For each star he could see, he knew there had to be thousands or maybe even millions of stars he could not see with his naked eye.

He'd come to the stables to check on Valiant one last time for the evening, making sure his new friend had plenty of water. He brushed him down once more, making sure is long tail and main were untangled. Satisfied, he returned to the fire where his friends waited.

Though the daylight hours of the desert were well over 90-degrees and often hotter, the darkness brought with it some chilly evenings. The sand became cold to the touch, forcing the men to use either woven blankets or furs to sit upon as they gathered around small fires throughout the courtyard to tell stories, listen to words read from the Koran and share a joke in the company of friends.

Paul Grant and Richard Hughes were sitting cross-legged on thick wool blankets of a natural bland color, attempting to converse with Hirim Mushid in hand gestures and mispronounced Libyan words. A small fire burned brightly between them, illuminating their faces and casting off strange shadows to the castle grounds behind them.

They were finding the language barrier a tough one to crack, causing GW to wonder how Brother Samuel ever conquered it. Richard was having the most luck though, getting a word here and there and giving Hirim several belly-laughs in the process with the mispronouncing. The old warrior, crusty to the bone, had grown to like these three strangers and was giving up a lot of his spare time to help them with swordsmanship and the proper carrying of a lance while on horseback.

However, Richard was nearly a total loss as a mounted knight. Though he might be able to disable the toughest of the king's warriors on the ground with his martial art skills, horses completely terrified him. So, Captain Rynarr decided to keep Richard's feet planted firmly on the ground and was having him learn the deadly art of archery, along with the proper use of the scimitar. If he chose not to return to Sudan, which would involve some dangerous travel if he did, he would not be able to become a knight of the Royal Guardsmen without the required horsemanship. But he could eventually become an officer of the army and in charge of the battlements, supervising the archers and a company of foot soldiers.

Leaving Valiant's stall, GW saw Brother Samuel's windows illuminated with the faint glow of candlelight and was surprised to see a silhouetted and smallish figure looking out over the courtyard. He sensed there were eyes resting on him but felt no alarm. From the distance between the stable and the castle, GW wasn't sure who this was, but it sure wasn't Brother Samuel and he decided he would ask the good monk tomorrow on who had access to his room in the evening. He wrestled with the thought he might be impertinent in asking such a question, but GW was also concerned about spies and the safety of his friends.

"What's the matter?" Richard asked.

"Nothing," GW replied. "I was just thinking this could be a real groovy scene if it wasn't so weird." He didn't want to alarm his friends by the shadow in the window. If he had to guess, he thought the figure to be that of a woman or a possibly a boy, and most likely nothing to be concerned about.

"This whole layout is too bizarre to take in," Paul Grant said. He waved his right hand about and added, "We got to live it day by day, and hope to God we'll wake up someday back in our bunks in dear ol' Vietnam and coming off a bad drunk." He stirred a stick in the fire and thought of his folks back home.

"You think we'll ever get this lingo down?" Richard asked.

Paul pointed his burning stick at Richard, "Not just the lingo, old buddy, but it's this whole Muslim law jibe." He then pointed his stick at the castle keep, "Man, it's gonna be a long time before we even get a chance to ask one of these lovely maidens out for a roll in the straw."

"Around here, a roll in the straw could prove fatal, lover boy," GW warned.

"I dig you, man, but if I'm going to go I want it to be for a good cause," Paul replied with a grin.

"You guys ever wonder about the possibility we could become our own descendants—our great-great-great something grandfathers?" Richard asked.

"Man, don't start with that…I'm having trouble just getting my mind around the present, I sure don't want to think about the future," Paul said.

GW turned from thoughts of girls to thinking of their recent experiences and the snatch and grab of Brother Samuel from World War II, which kept gnawing at him. He couldn't help but wonder if anyone else had been jerked out of time, tossed on their heads and planted in some far-off land. He wondered if this is what might've caused the UFO scare of the 1950's or even if the UFO greenies were the ones who created this time travel thing in the first place? Maybe they like playing with us, see how we react to different situations. GW shook his head to clear his thoughts. I'm really cracking up, not only do we got some dragon, but next thing you know I'll be looking for a flying carpet and some friendly genie in a lamp.

"GW, your eyeballs are beginning to spin, you sure you're feeling all right?" Paul asked.

GW broke into a grin, "I'm fine...just so much to think about. I'm asking myself why this happened to us, and maybe who else might've been grabbed, in the last couple thousand years or so?"

"Yeah, I wonder about that all the time," Paul added in. "Don't talk about it much, can't see any reason for dwelling on it. Not like we can do anything about it."

"Why not?" Richard asked. He looked at his friend across the fire and said, "Maybe some of our great inventors were actually from the future...Like, Leonardo Da Vinci or Galileo. Maybe they came from the future and got stuck in their past, made the best of it and civilization moved on with their help."

GW shook his head in frustration and asked, "Either of you some great inventor, a painter or explorer? I know I'm sure not some guy who can improve this world...I even have trouble changing the spark plugs in my dad's truck. I don't paint, don't invent and can't see what I could do to make this place better by my returning to the past and especially here in Libya." GW stood to his feet and said, "Look, this is Libya and for the life of my I can't recall anything coming out of Libya to better the world. Do you?"

The other two shook their heads and Richard muttered, "Just a thought I had."

"Look, we're here now," Paul said. He then pointed his burning stick downward to make his point. "Brother Samuel's here and has been for over 40-years. So, unless one of you has got a time machine in your back pocket, we ain't going back."

"But we should talk about it, even if it's only to keep me from going crazy," Richard said. Right before he threw another piece of kindling on the fire and sending an explosion of sparks into the night sky. "Who knows, maybe because of us being here history is changed."

"Hey, easy with that stuff, man," Paul said in a loud voice, as he backed up from the fire.

"They may be used to it, but it still stinks!"

Several days ago, the three of them were startled to learn the strange kindling they used for evening fires was dried sheep or camel poop, mixed with straw. Oh, they had all read about buffalo chips from Zane Grey's western novels, but they never thought of how bad sheep and especially camel chips, smelled or that they would be using them to keep warm by.

GW ignored the stench, "I can't help but wonder how many people were hit with this...whatever it was that grabbed us." GW then looked at both of his friends. "We were all knocked out, but Brother Samuel described bubbling water, weird colors and a whirlpool that sucked him down. Yet, we were in a cave...no water, no bubbles and none of us saw any colors."

"We were knocked out, remember? Paul said. But then he fell silent. Science bored him, and he would rather talk about girls and horses.

"You still look like you've got something else on your mind," GW said to Richard.

"Yeah, I do," Richard answered in low voice. "I am troubled about one thing. Something with enough physical force to bend the barrels of our weapons, make them unusable, but not cripple or kills us...it simply doesn't make sense. Our bones should be broken...snapped like twigs and we should be dead!" Richard exclaimed.

This outburst unsettled Mushid, who wondered what the strangers were talking about and why the one called Hughes was getting upset? He recognized the troubled expressions on their faces but couldn't understand a word they spoke between them. He tried to learn, but their words were too difficult for him to understand.

"Manifest destiny...That's it!" Richard suddenly blurted out. He jumped to his feet and raised his arms skyward in triumph. This action caused Mushid to leap up in response, with his scimitar in hand and thinking intruders were upon them.

Seeing Mushid's reaction to Richard's outburst and movements, GW cautiously kept his arms out wide, with open palms outstretched toward Mushid and he attempted to calm the big warrior down. "Mushid, it's only Richard getting excited. Calm down...put your sword away, please." GW pointed at the scimitar, displaying a big smile in hopes of calming Mushid and then he turned to give Richard a hard look. "Sit down, Richard...you've alarmed our well-armed friend here."

"Sorry," Richard said. He smiled at Mushid, nodded his head several times and returned to his blanket.

"What's this manifest destiny crap?" Paul asked, struggling to keep from laughing in the event an enraged Mushid decided to start swinging that lethal looking sword of his around and chasing Richard across the courtyard.

"This was all meant to happen," Richard whispered. He waited for Mushid to sit back down upon a blanket of foul smelling camel fur he used and then relaxed.

"Meant to happen?" Paul asked, now totally confused.

"Yes, meant to happen," Richard replied. "We were saved from that ambush, driven into that cave and sent back in time for a purpose. But we couldn't bring our automatic weapons with us. That would change the balance or better put, change the course of world history. Remember, as far as I know the Chinese haven't even discovered gunpowder yet, much less the world having a working M-16 back in the 12th Century."

"What about Brother Samuel?" GW asked.

"Same thing, he was needed back here for some particular purpose and it might be as easy as saving our lives for what lies ahead for us," Richard said. A big smile on his face, he looked up at the stars with a whimsical glint to his eyes.

"You're saying this is a God thing?" GW asked, ensuring to smile in hopes of relaxing Mushid, who still appeared to be somewhat cautious looking and maintained a tight grasp on his scimitar.

"God...or possibly something else," Richard replied.

"Don't tell me you're talking about little green men, are you?" GW asked in disbelief, though he'd been thinking the very same thing only moments earlier.

"Listen, smart guy, UFO activity has not been proven or disproved. All I'm saying is that we have some options here."

"Come on, UFO's." Paul challenged. "I'd rather go with the God idea, makes more sense. But I might point out to you gentlemen, these people are Muslims and their Allah is not our Christian God."

"God is God, everyone is His and when Allah started out he was the God of Abraham." GW said curtly, hoping to shy away from the UFO topic. If little green men were responsible for this, he didn't want to dwell on what they might be doing back in the future. No, he'd go with the God angle, but he still wondered why him and why these two guys? Brother Samuel, he could accept, he'd become a missionary to the Muslim people and was openly accepted by the Muslim king—a very unusual thing to have accomplished. All GW had to offer these people was the shirt on his back, some high school science knowledge for which he obtained a 'C', and some surprising skill with a very large horse.

His lance work wasn't too great yet and swinging a scimitar from horseback nearly dislocated his right arm when he went through the drills. Still, everything that's happened since the morning they left the firebase for the A Shau Valley and his earlier meeting with that old Montegnard shaman added some weight to this whole God thing.

GW wasn't a hard-core Christian by any bets, not like his Dad. He only attended church services on Christmas and Easter, or when he couldn't escape his Dad's insistent glare. The days of Vacation Bible School were long ago and very few of his friends were churchgoers. Still, he believed, but more in the Big God sense: Ruler of the Universe-Creator of Mankind, but probably too busy for little old me-type God.

After some thought about the subject, GW turned to Richard and said, "Yeah, God may have caused this to happen, but I still ask you—why us? We're not missionaries. I mean I barely attend church, much less see myself deliver a stirring Bible message to the growing masses...and Muslims. Let me remind you, PFC Hughes, these are people who didn't cotton to the whole Christian idea, especially after what happened during the crusades. A thousand years later and you can still set them off when you mention Christian."

"Yes, I know," Richard said. "I've read about what those so-called Christians did to the Muslims in their gallant crusades...All in the name of Jesus Christ." Richard then added, "I'm a Christian, proud of my family's heritage and I know...I can sincerely say, my Lord wept for what was supposedly all done in His name...a sin that to our day in 1968 continued to form a massive unbreakable wall between Christians and Muslims."

Paul listened to both men and decided to put his two cents in, "That cross you were given, GW, that wooden one you wore, it did help us out and probably saved our lives that day out by the stream."

GW nodded his headed in agreement. "Okay, we have decided that for now, God is responsible for sending us back in time...maybe. Maybe this is that manifest destiny you're talking about, but I'd feel a lot more comfortable knowing why us?" He then slowly stood to his feet and grabbed up his blanket.

"I'm calling it a night, guys. Haven't had this much to think about since my high school finals...which I barely passed I might add." GW reached over and patted Mushid on his shoulder and then made gestures with his hands to show the three of them were headed for bed.

Grunting in agreement, Mushid rose and began kicking dirt on the fire. It was foolish to leave an open flame so near the stables. He reminded his new pupils of this by pointing from the fire to the horse stalls to explain why he was putting the fire out. More than once one of the Americans had walked off leaving an open fire unattended and he had scolded them with a slap across the shoulder and pointing at the fire.

Richard smiled, "I suspect Smokey the Bear is letting us know about fire safety again. But it might be easier to teach him proper English then for us to learn Libyan." To which, Paul and GW nodded their heads in agreement before they headed for the castle keep entrance and a night of sleep. For all three, they hoped for some dreams of home.

# 6 – THREE KNIGHTS IN BOOT CAMP

With dawn an hour away, GW was already up and back in the courtyard working with Valiant. A small area of the courtyard was illuminated by torchlight, giving him just enough light to train in the use of the lance and shield, without a bunch of people watching, laughing themselves silly for his ineptness and offering up words of advice he couldn't understand.

Once mounted, he held strapped securely to his left arm a battered and discolored circular metal practice shield. He hoped to gain a feel for its weight, but it felt clumsy and he kept rubbing the top of his leg with it. In his right hand, he struggled to hold the lance locked in place, inside his right arm and held securely by his wrist, while he prepared to attack a man-sized target of straw. The straw man was tied to a tall wooden pole, buried halfway into the ground. The target was also at a height similar in height to an enemy mounted soldier. But as-of-yet, GW hadn't hit the heart-sized mark on the dummy and most of the time the practice point of his lance dropped to within inches of the ground before he was even within attack range. Twice he dropped the weapon to the sand and GW sensed Valiant was even getting discouraged with him. To make matters worse, the practice dummy had even unseated him, when the lance became stuck in the dirt at the foot of the pole and he was hurled from his saddle. The weight and feel of the lance caused a lot of pain to his right wrist and with each miss and mishap, he had gained the gratitude of several arriving onlookers, mostly stable hands, which belly laughed and pounded each other on the back with boisterous gayety at GW's expense. While GW was able-to remain mounted most of the time this early morning, Paul Grant was not faring as well. He had only arrived a short time ago and was on the ground, armed with an aged scimitar and a well-scarred and dented shield, working feverishly on his swordplay through several physically demanding exercises.

Mushid looked on from the side wall of the castle keep, a goblet of date juice and a hunk of warm bread in hand for breakfast. He had wondered how anyone could be so clumsy with a scimitar. With Grant's muscular build, Mushad thought the stranger would have had no trouble in mastering the sword, but apparently by seeing what he was witnessing—He was wrong. With a sigh, he tossed his goblet aside and took up his training shield. With a wooden training sword in hand he moved into challenge Paul. In two moves he had knocked Paul off his feet with a hard blow to the shield. Paul sat there, stunned by the mighty blow and his whole shield arm was tingling.

Paul had always heard these camel-riders were a bunch of wimps, but he knew better now after going one-on-one with his teacher for a whole ten seconds. Mushid once again gestured with his wooden sword for Paul to stand up and prepare to defend himself.

"Give me a minute, will yuh? I think you broke my arm," Paul complained. But he rose-up, released a weary sigh and painstakingly brought his shield up to protect himself.

Then with speed Paul thought was impossible, Mushid delivered light blows to Paul's shield and various parts of his exposed body. As an apprentice, Paul was not allowed to wear armor yet and within minutes, he was already bruised throughout most of his body by a toy sword and he suspected he now sported three bumps to his skull from blows delivered with the flat side of Mushid's supposedly non-lethal training tool.

Finally, Paul had had enough of this and lost control of his temper. He rushed Mushid, swinging his play scimitar like a man battling a pesky mosquito with a fly swatter. In response, Mushid blocked one blow away with a sharp crack to Paul's elbow, forcing him to drop his wooden scimitar and then drove his wooden sword between Paul's legs to trip him up. Paul cried out in pain as he fell flat-faced to the warming sand. There Paul maintained his prone position for a moment longer and then cautiously lifted his head to observe Mushid standing to one side of him, shaking his head slowly in disapproval. Paul also saw how several stable hands and they too appeared to agree with Mushid; shaking their heads in bewilderment for Paul's poor swordplay. Then much to his surprise, they egged him on with hand gestures to rise-up and fight again.

Paul was much too sore to give his instructor a good old-fashioned knuckle sandwich, but he did slowly and painfully rise to his feet to face him again. He wasn't about to let this dude get the best of him, not while he was conscious at least.

Outside the courtyard and nearer to the castle keep's main entrance, Richard Hughes was already sweating profusely under this early morning heat. He was instructing ten-men in hand-to-hand fighting, while wishing he had both slept-in longer and stopped by the kitchen for some breakfast. His stomach was growling, but now he would have to wait for lunch.

After morning prayers, he began the session with stretching exercises, which he had to teach to each man individually because they found the exercises quite foolish at first. But Richard was patient and with Captain Rynarr's authority behind him, he made sure they completed the exercises by tossing one over-sized ruffian on his ear to prove his position as instructor. After that, they observed every move Richard made.

Richard preferred these early morning training sessions, having learned how fast the desert temperatures rose with the rising of the sun. Captain Rynarr also stressed, using Brother Samuel as an interpreter, how most attacks occurred at the hour of dawn and he wanted his men to always be prepared for this eventuality.

A dozen torch poles illuminated the training area Richard used, as the night's sky turned gray with the coming of dawn. He had ample room and would select a victim, to demonstrate the next exercise on him. This area also gave the ten men some practice room for sparring with one another. Thankfully, as they moved into the actual throws, the warm sand cushioned most of the judo moves and the ten men survived their new taskmaster's hourly drills.

Once these ten men were given the very basic of instructions and Hughes was satisfied with their progress, another ten-man group would be selected for beginner training. He would then have two-man groups going and soon, the whole training yard would be filled with guardsmen tossing each other about and slamming one another to the ground like archery practice dummies. Judo was not an easy skill to master, but even the initial moves were new to these soldiers. As to the Karate, it would wait until the men learned to harden their hands in a way they had never done before. He set up buckets of sand and the men began driving their stiff fingers into the sand to toughen up the skin. A lot of the men complained about pain, but Richard would show them his hands and why it was needed, by breaking a board held between two skeptics.

Captain Rynarr had ordered Hughes to train a fighting force of 100-men. He now planned to use these men as the vanguard for Silene's newly formed force of dismounted troops. Richard thought dismounted guardsmen as too long a title and instead referred to them simply as grunts; a U.S. Army term for infantrymen. Unfortunately, the word didn't translate well into Libyan, but the word grunt caught on and even Captain Rynarr was calling them grunts before the end of the third day. It was during this early morning hour of training that the three Americans first heard the strange horn-like sounds off in the distance. Suddenly, all laughter stopped from the courtyard and even Mushid, who was teasing Paul with the point of his wooden sword, suddenly stopped his action to stare off to the north with a grim look on his face.

Hearing the strange sound of the horns, GW pulled his shield from his left arm and strapped it to a leather thong on his saddle. He then removed the hot and heavy GI helmet from his head after bringing Valiant to a halt, so he could dismount. He was extremely sore from practice and carefully climbed off the tall horse. He leaned his lance up against Valiant's side and listened to the strange sounding horn.

GW looked about the courtyard and couldn't help but notice the abrupt change in the mood of the Royal Guardsmen and even the stable workers, while off in the distance the horns played a ghastly unmelodious tune.

Then with his lance and shield in hand, GW walked Valiant to the closest water trough. While the horse drank, he took his lance, shield and helmet to Valiant's stall. The lance was placed up against the stall roof, held in place by three wooden pegs. He put his helmet on a railing post and his shield hung on a peg beneath it. He then approached Paul, who was also curious as to what was going on with the horns.

The guardsmen who trained with Richard promptly left their teacher standing alone in the courtyard to scale the north wall, using the huge stone stairs nearest them to gain access to the battlements. From there, first one man and then another began pointing northward, while others climbed to the various battlement positions to observe the happenings to the north.

Curious, the three Americans came together in the middle of the southwest courtyard and stood there wondering what was going on to cause such strange behavior by the troops. Mushid was standing behind them, wanting to go to the wall but knowing his duty was to remain with his three trainees.

"You got any idea what's happening here?" GW asked his friends.

"Hey, maybe it's the dragon," Richard said excitedly.

Before they could say anything more, Brother Samuel came from the castle keep and hurriedly approached them. It was clear to see how upset the old man was by the look of grief on his face. Brother Samuel stopped abruptly before them, his aged eyes displaying the anger he felt within him. Without speaking, he looked to the north and then, turning to his friends, he clutched his hands tightly together in front of him and remained mute as he shook his head from side to side.

Concerned for his new friend, Richard was the first to speak, "Brother Samuel, what's wrong?" Hughes asked and then pointed to the north castle wall.

"Everyone seems to be upset." Paul added. He turned to face Mushid, "Even the big guy here seems peeved about something."

Mushid looked at Paul, seeming to understand that his student in arms was talking about him. But it didn't make him uncomfortable, he had come to understand the language barrier and what was transpiring to the north had probably confused the three newcomers.

"Commander?" GW said, hoping that by using Brother Samuel's navy rank he might break out of this strange behavior.

It did. Brother Samuel looked hard at GW and then he nodded his head in understanding, "I am sorry, my friends, for my silence. But this is the day of sacrifice and the young woman chosen to face the dragon is truly one who should've been spared such a fate...as they all should've been." Brother Samuel's voice was grumbling. His hands were clenched into tight fists and his brow deeply furrowed, when he suddenly locked eyes with GW.

His voice low, Brother Samuel continued, "Today, another fair maiden of Silene is to be sacrificed and I couldn't help her. Even the king wanted to save her, but an ancient royal decree prevents him from doing so."

"You mean," Richard stammered, "...you mean some girl is being fed to that dinosaur out there?"

196

"Yes, Mr. Hughes," Brother Samuel replied softly. "As I told you before, twice a month a new maiden is taken to the lake, secured by chains and rope and the dragon..." He looked at Richard, "...the dinosaur is summoned by the blaring of antelope horns."

"I thought you were joking about the sacrificial offering!" Richard exclaimed in wide eye astonishment.

Brother Samuel looked upon Richard with a hard glare, but his eyes turned sad and he placed an aged hand upon the man's wide shoulder, "No, my young friend. This is no joke and yes, this dinosaur exists, and it continues to feed upon the young women of this kingdom as it, or its parents have for centuries."

GW looked to the walls lined with soldiers and guardsmen and saw how no one seemed to be speaking. All eyes were locked on the lakeshore to the north. Though he knew from being on the wall earlier that the great wall to the north prevented all but those high atop the corner battlements to see the lakeshore. He then remembered from what Brother Samuel said how the guardsmen who secured the girl to the rock would hastily retreat on horseback behind that large wall, while seemingly everyone in Silene waited for the dragon to arrive and accept its next victim.

What GW couldn't understand was how the townsfolk and soldiers stood idly by in fear, while the dragon devoured the victim and might decide to continue coming toward the city for further tribute.

GW didn't know that outside the castle's lower north wall, a full company of soldiers stood ready to repel the beast if it ventured toward the city. They were also armed with newer weapons created by Brother Samuel; a catapult for rock and fire, and large cross-bow type spear throwing devices that could hurl a 20-foot long spear more than 300-feet. Though these weapons had been invented long ago by the Greeks and used by the Romans, King Ramie had never seen one before and was impressed by their construction. But even though the huge spear had knocked the dragon backwards on two occasions, it hadn't been able to pierce the creature's thick hide. And the catapult couldn't be aimed rapidly enough to strike the moving creature, though on one occasion it had sent out a large boulder, which rolled after impact with the ground and appeared to have smashed the dragon's left fin. The great beast released a great roar, frightening the onlookers, but still claimed its victim.

Also, behind the great wall to the north stood a force of 30-men mounted on warhorses that were prepared to reinforce the Royal Guardsmen in the sacrifice detail if the dragon made a move toward them. They would attempt to confuse the beast, as the guardsmen made their escape.

The great beast had never broken through the defensive force, either because it was too far from water or the huge wall had deterred it from going after the town and castle. But it had attacked the great north wall in the past and devoured several men-at-arms who fought from the battlements. Grabbing them with its massive teeth and while horrified onlookers observed, swallowed them whole down its long throat.

Fire seemed to help somewhat in deterring the beast away from the wall, but it always escaped by returning to its watery home. As an additional backup, Captain Rynarr kept a second force of 30-Royal Guardsmen on the northwest edge of the township and if needed and when a great gong mounted in the castle's prayer tower was sounded, they would enter the battle. A force of 64-mounted soldiers from the army was kept inside the castle's main gate, a last resort to protect the castle. All these fighting men from the regular army and the royal Guardsmen were in place for the day of sacrifice. Civilians were also prepared with torches and wagons of straw to ignite with fire, in the event they were needed to save their township. Plus, as a final stopgap, smaller catapults designed by Brother Samuel were positioned on the northwest and northeast battlements and these could hurl flaming baskets of straw and oil at the dragon if it got that close.

These various fighting elements and weapons were created over time as the citizens of Silene fought for their lives against the hellish creature, as it laid siege to their community and gobbled up the occupants.

With horns blown to summon the beast, Captain Rynarr ordered his men back behind the great wall, while he remained on foot beside the young maiden. This was extremely unusual for him to do this and he surprised his men by his actions. He stood there staring off toward the lake and again ordered them to withdraw and seeing the cold look to his eyes, they obeyed.

Captain Rynarr held the leather reins of his warhorse coiled around his left hand, while he wrestled with his duty to the kingdom, and his weariness of delivering yet another victim to this fowl creature.

In his early years of knighthood, he had participated in three separate attacks against the dragon and all had failed. He'd seen one of his horses devoured and all too many men dismembered. He'd watched as his father gave up his life to save Rynarr's sister, but all in vain, as they both died a horrid death. His own life was saved when three of his men held him back from making a reckless and fruitless attack to avenge his family that day. Mushid had been one of these men and he had taken the beating his future captain gave to him for interfering.

Nothing had worked; no weapon and no poison. The beast continued to live on. Its thick bluish hide showing the scars of such violent attempts and each year 24-girls gave up their lives in sacrifice to feed its horrendous appetite. Over the years, the dragon shredded the knight's armor with its teeth and their beautiful black Arabian horses tossed aside, as if they weighed nothing. Water attacks were attempted; leaving the shorelines of the lake littered with the broken shells of many a boat and so many crewmen missing.

Now, all he could do is simply watch the lake and wait in dread for the dragon to surface. He would then bid his sad farewells to such a brave young lady. But still, he wanted to relieve her of such a fate, to gently end her life with a simple stroke of his short sword upon her tender neck. However, such an action was against royal decree...But who would know?

Captain Rynarr looked to the surface of the water and still seeing no movement, turned to his charge and studied her youthful face. He was saddened by the dark, blood coated chains, which now held her fast to the rock. There were also decaying bones lying about and even a couple of skulls. Manacles were used to secure her ankles and wrists, giving her only a small amount of leeway to swing her arms or move her feet.

Damaged links and manacles left scattered about the shoreline afterward would be replaced the next day by frightened castle blacksmiths, who, though guarded by a detail of knights, were ready to give flight at the first ripple in the water. But after a sacrifice of young maiden or a small flock of sheep, the dragon was known to return to the far side of the lake and here it was suspected the foul creature had some kind-of underwater lair.

She stared back at Captain Rynarr with tear filled eyes, her mouth clenched tight. He knew the screaming would begin when the dragon burst from its watery home and made its approach. Even he, a battle-scarred warrior, quaked in his boots upon seeing the creature up-close. This was one of the reasons why he maintained a tight grasp of his horse's reins, otherwise his mount would surely give flight upon the creature appearance.

"Listen, girl—for such courage as you have displayed, I am willing to take a chance, to end this quickly for you. No one would know if I was to show mercy and use my dagger. There would be pain, but only briefly and you would sleep."

She looked in his eyes and saw the inner pain this great knight was in, but she was fearful for her family. "What of my parents, of our home if someone was to see?"

"Once again, you demonstrate such care for others. How I would have liked to see you grow, to be a great lady for your family and a bearer of good and strong sons for our kingdom," Captain Rynarr said. With a glance over his shoulder, he looked to the waters.

"You must decide now, but I promise you nothing will happen to your family. No one will know, for I will act when the dragon first appears, and all eyes will be upon it."

The horns blew again and off in the distance the waters of the lake began to churn and white foam formed upon the surface. In the distance, an audible gasp could be heard coming from the great wall. This gasp seemed to signal the army, who now knew the dragon was coming in answer to its summons. No further blast on a horn would be necessary.

"I ask one thing, young one...please forgive me," Captain Rynarr said. He grasped the hilt of his dagger, deciding to use it over his short sword.

It was right then that the dragon's hideous head breached the surface and slowly, it rose to a towering height of 30-feet or more above the churning white waters.

Seeing this, the girl's bravery shattered, and she let loose with a frightening scream, causing Captain Rynarr to turn and lay his eyes upon the nightmarish creature. His horse, terrified by the dragon, raised herself up and fought to tear the reins from the Captain's grasp. If not for the metal mail of his gauntlet, the reins might have stripped the skin from his hand. But Captain Rynarr held her firm and with both hands wrestled her back down.

Slowly and maybe cautiously, the slithery-looking dragon began its approach to the shore. With its huge and almost lifeless eyes, it looked to the great wall to the south and even further toward the city. Its thick hide glistened with water being shed and its huge eyes began to sparkle in the morning sunlight. It began to rock its head back and forth, a motion needed to propel itself forward with its massive fins onto the shoreline.

"I have no time left, you must decide now!" Captain Rynarr said in an excited voice.

Eyes wide, her face shaking and body trembling wildly against her restraints, as if in a fit, she suddenly stopped and glared hard at Captain Rynarr and shouted, "Do it now!" Only then did she remember to add, "Ah forgive you, but ah'll not forgive the princess...Curse her cold black heart! May she feel the weight of these chains herself someday!" But none could hear her curse except for the Captain.

Captain Rynarr couldn't wait any longer. He quickly moved beside her to block the view from the great wall and sliced her throat with one quick movement. Her head dropped, as shed blood fell upon her chest and her eyes slowly closed. Then, upon seeing how close the dragon was, only a couple hundred yards away and nearing the breakwater, he couldn't wait any longer and sheathed his dagger. He then had to fight to control his frightened mare so he could mount and flee to the south. Once a top his horse, he needn't bother with spurs, for the horse released a burst a speed like never-before.

The three Americans accompanied Brother Samuel to the castle's north wall and made their way to the northwest battlement. They stood beside one of three catapults and watched as Captain Rynarr left the large boulder on the lake's shoreline and rode hard to reach the great north wall and safety.

From atop this battlement they could see over the top of the great wall and they laid their eyes upon the beast for the first time. They were speechless, unable to believe their eyes as the creature clumsily ambled forward on its floppy stomach toward the victim.

Richard was the first to speak, his voice cracking with excitement, as he pointed to the north and exclaimed, "That thing's bigger than any Plesiosaurus on record, maybe twice as big!"

"Take it easy, man," GW said to him. "Remember, that thing you're so excited about is about to eat that young girl and no one around here is happy about it."

Richard stared at GW and then looked to Brother Samuel, who was glaring back at him, "Yes...I am sorry. I forgot all about the girl."

Brother Samuel nodded his head in understanding, remembering how he felt when he saw the creature for the first time. He then looked back to the north and began to pray for the victim and her family.

GW was confused by Brother Samuel's almost peaceful actions. He watched him quietly pray, while grasping his wooden cross. Meanwhile, several of the Muslims around them also prayed to Allah, as the dragon left the waters and approached the rock.

No one was close enough to hear her screams and almost always the victim feinted and no longer moved when the creature drew near. Because of this, no one was surprised by this girl's lack of movement when the dragon dropped down to seize her still body.

Thankfully, almost all were too far away to see the grisly scene be carried out as the victim was ripped from her chains and devoured by the beast. Only the guards upon the great wall could see this and most of them turned away. With such an event occurring every two weeks, even the hardiest of souls had lost their appetite for observing the creature feed.

It was over quickly, far too quickly in Princess Lonnia opinion. She stood upon the roof of the castle keep, from where she enjoyed the show and now looked forward to selecting her next victim.

Meanwhile, the army stood ready, waiting to see if the dragon would return to the waters or move toward the city. Those soldiers with the duty stood upon the battlements of the great north wall, antelope horns in hand to give the alarm if the dragon made a move to the south. A cleric in the prayer tower stood beside the huge gong, ready to sound alarm if the horns began to sound repeatedly.

But not this morning, the creature seemed satisfied with its offering and didn't even hesitate to use its great flippers and turn around to return to the breakwater. Within a moment, it returned to the deep waters of the lake and only the top of its head could be seen before it vanished in the distance.

As with the first gasp of sighting the dragon, a sigh of relief could be heard throughout the city. They would later mourn the young lady, but for now the citizens of Silene were relieved to be alive and their city not under another attack from a creature surely born in Hell itself.

"Now you know what this town endures, my young friends," Brother Samuel said in seriousness. With his right hand, he made the sign of the cross in the air and then directed the three young men to proceed in front of him down the stairs and out into the courtyard. Before they walked out into the sun light, Brother Samuel said in a low voice, "Every two weeks this tragic event occurs and soon...soon, we may not have the maidens needed for this dreadful duty."

"What then, Brother Samuel?" GW asked. They cleared the archway and were now standing outside and in the near stifling heat of the day.

"First, let us drop the Brother Samuel bit. Between us, I like the name Sam much better, okay? No one else around here will know the difference anyway."

"Thanks, Sam," Paul was the first to reply. "My first name's Paul, you already know GW and Mr. Judo himself is named Richard."

Sam looked out across the courtyard for a moment, thinking of the years he had lived here and the ghastly number of young girls who had gone to their death before this horrifying sea creature. He had spent thousands of hours on his knees, asking God to intercede on behalf of these people, but he'd received no answer, nor any miracle, which would put a stop to this on-going tragedy. It left him with a sense of doubt in his own personal faith in God and like his dear Princess Lennia, it weighed heavily upon his heart. He then turned to look at his three new friends.

"I think the city should be abandoned, Paul," Sam said. "...in answer to your question. The citizens would probably flee to Tripoli, if the Caliph would allow it, and I...I would probably stay right here and fight that foul abomination until God struck it dead or I too fell before it."

The three newcomers remained silent, as Sam led them toward the stables.

## ROYAL GUARDSMEN STABLES

More than an hour passed before Captain Rynarr entered the castle courtyard. He slowly dismounted and almost reluctantly handed the reins of his warhorse over to a silent stable hand.

"Brush him down well, feed him and give him water after he cools down."

"Yes, Captain."

Rynarr observed the hand-to-hand training Richard was again conducting and noticed the lack of drive the men were showing under the hot sun. But he understood, he wasn't feeling too well himself and decided he needn't reprimand his men. He then walked over to where Paul was knelt on the ground, exhausted, as Mushid once more tapped him on the top of the head with his training sword.

"Yeah, I know," Paul said. "I stepped off with my right foot when I should've used my left. But give me a moment, my head is ringing." Paul knew Mushid did not understand him, but the larger knight knew his pupil was winded and walked over to a nearby water barrel for a drink.

Shaking his head in disbelief, he gulped down a ladle of murky water and wondered if these Irishmen would ever master the scimitar. Captain Rynarr left him and wandered past the stables to see how GW was doing with his training.

Here, a look of astonishment came upon his face, as he watched man and horse work as one. This was as it should be, but it was far too early in their training program and this surprised Captain Rynarr.

A transition had occurred following this morning's sacrifice; GW and Valiant now rode together, forming a deadly weapon through an aggressive steed and a deadly lance. GW seemed to have no problem holding the heavy training lance and he had just pierced the red heart outline of the practice dummy. He then startled an already amazed Captain Rynarr when GW suddenly brought Valiant to a sudden stop with a jerk of the reins and applying a force of pressure from his knees and against Valiant's sides. While a speechless Captain Rynarr observed, his mouth hanging open behind his veil, GW tossed his lance aside to the ground and wheeled Valiant around on her skidding hindquarters—as if he had popped a wheelie on a BMX bicycle and flipped it around on its rear tire. This was a surprising move with a horse and unseen before in Silene. GW behaved like a man who had ridden horses for years instead of days and this Valiant was performing far beyond its previous training.

GW then pulled his practice wooden scimitar from beneath his left leg and while holding the reins in his shield hand, he once again charged the dummy. With a controlled burst of speed, GW raced up to the dummy and whacked its straw head off with a directed slashing sword movement that caused the stable hands in the area to shout and wave their arms with approval. They all knew it was not easy to cut the dummy's head off with a wooden sword and yet, this stranger had accomplished the feat with so little training.

Seeing Captain Rynarr standing nearby, GW slowed Valiant down to a canter and dropped his training sword to the ground. He then dismounted where Captain Rynarr was standing and fondly patted Valiant's neck and stroked his mane.

A short bedraggled stable hand appeared suddenly at GW's side and took Valiant's reins in hand to walk the horse around the training yard to cool him down before giving him water and taking him back to the stall. All of 16 years old, the stable hand, an orphan, was one of the few people GW allowed to walk and feed Valiant. The horse seemed to have taken a liking to the young lad and didn't bite him like he did the others who came too close.

"You ride very well," Captain Rynarr said. He wished GW could understand him, but he couldn't. But when the good captain lowered his veil, GW recognized the smile on his face and bowed slightly in return, as he had seen others do.

Frustrated by the inability to speak together, Captain Rynarr sent another stable hand running to locate and bring back Brother Samuel. While waiting, he gestured for GW to follow him over to a shady spot and ordered an elderly servant man to bring forth water and fruit from the castle's kitchen.

Meanwhile, Paul, who was exhausted and sore from his practice session with Mushid, dragged his weary body over to join GW and Captain Rynarr. Mushid, clearly a bit upset that his student had taken upon himself to leave without Mushid's approval, soon followed. Two servants suddenly appeared to gather up the training equipment and return it to the storage area inside the stables.

The servants of the castle were divided into three main groups: stable workers, those men keeping the castle grounds clean and tasks performed outside the castle keep, and those who were assigned chores inside the castle. There was also a higher ranking of servants for those who served the individual court officers and the royal family. Handmaidens assisted the women and squire-like young men served the knights, army officers and other court officers not serving in either of the military units. There was also the kitchen staff and blacksmiths; those rough looking characters who worked outside the castle on the wooden carts and shoed the horses. Inside the castle, there were the armorers who created and maintained the various weapons for the castle's personnel. A highly trained armorer was worth his weight in gold.

Individual dignitaries visiting Silene also brought with them their own servants, who were often housed within the castle in servant's quarters, unless the dignitary wished otherwise and wanted them close by. Outside the castle grounds were the fishermen, farmers and herdsmen for camel, horse and sheep, and hunters, whose job was to keep a steady supply of meat, vegetables and fruit on hand for the king's tables.

In the culture of Libya, a man or woman could be sold into slavery for unpaid debts. A wife and/or a child could be used in trade to barter for land or animals. Most all laws came with a punishment of death or dismemberment. Some servants were prisoners of war and still, there were others who were born into a certain servant trade; following their parents' various trades and these people lived and worked in the castle or upon the grounds, as their parents before them. Some servants were paid, while others only received a place to live, food to eat and the protection of the king.

To run smoothly, the castle and grounds, and great herds, needed a minimum of 500-servants. At present, King Ramie owned only 273 servants. He had few funds to increase his staff and morale was very low amongst the people.

One step above servant-hood was the basic men-at-arms soldier; either dismounted or mounted. Next in line came the corporals and sergeants, who earned their rank through loyal service and acts of heroism. Above these were the elite Royal Guardsmen; dismounted and mounted--but having not been knighted. The dismounted guardsmen were assigned to castle duty and the protection of the king and his family, guarding the castle's court and manning the castle's main gate. They were also assigned the duty of protecting any visiting foreign dignitaries. Mounted guardsmen patrolled the frontier, maintained a presence outside the city, patrolled the road to Tripoli and handled tasks as assigned by the guardsmen officers.

The Army of Silene had its own officers, equal in standing in rank, but not held in such respect as those officers knighted by the king and in leadership roles among the ranks of the Royal Guardsmen. Above all of them though, there was Captain Rynarr, who rarely saw a day off and had not ventured outside the borders of Libya since assuming command of Silene's military. He had also never been married.

Supervising the lottery detail, a task he chose to take upon himself, Captain Rynarr personally selected the Royal Guardsmen who would to stand guard over for the royal family. Other officers in the regular army under him were left to supervise castle defenses, changing of the guards and duty schedules, and supervising the men manning the great wall to the north. In the event of war, these men would lead the various units, but still under Captain Rynarr's command, who reported directly to the king.

Though not of nobility, Captain Rynarr had earned his spot beside the king much like his father had; from bravery as a soldier and a good leader of men. An officer in the regular army and later, knighted as a Royal Guardsmen officer, he rose to become the captain when the previous senior officer fell before a raider's arrow. Still, there were times he wished he could return to the simpler ways of a Royal Guardsmen lieutenant. He had grown weary of command, the horrid lottery and his constant battle of wits with the sinister Black Princess.

Relaxing somewhat, Captain Rynarr shared a clay bottle of cool well water and some slices of a mango-type fruit with GW and Paul. Yet, he was relieved to see Brother Samuel leave the castle keep and come in their direction. This was partly because the language barrier being a major handicap and he enjoyed the old man's company. After his father's death, Brother Samuel had become like a father-figure to him and he truly appreciated his advice. Out of loyal friendship for the older man, Captain Rynarr stood to his feet and with a slight bow to his two new friends he walked over to meet Brother Samuel.

A bit out of breath, Sam looked to his old friend and said, "Your servant said it was important, yet I arrive to find you relaxing in the shade with my countrymen." Sam stopped to give a courteous Muslim blessing for his old and dear friend. "How may I be of service, my friend? "It is very frustrating, old man..." He often referred to Brother Samuel in this way, but only as a personal sign of respect and when no one else could overhear them. "I need to be able to converse with these new men and find this lack of ability very frustrating...This one you call GW s great promise as a knight. Though he must earn this title of course, but I have never seen anyone take to a horse so well in so little time. It was as if the horse and man were one."

"Yes, I understand," Sam replied. "Richard is taking to our language quickly, as if a second tongue, but young Paul and GW need much more class work," Sam said. He lifted his arms to show his own frustration with this problem. "However, you have ordered their military training to take up most of their time and this reduces the amount of time they can spend on learning our language. I have also heard how Paul remains slow with the scimitar, or should I say clumsy?"

"Yes, and he troubles me," Captain Rynarr replied. "These men are your friends; your clansmen and I wish to honor you by training them, so the king can knight them in due time. But this Paul might do better working with the catapults. He is indeed strong and can ride well enough, but a knight must be able to use our most trusted weapons–the lance and scimitar."

Sam frowned in response and then said, "Maybe you could let me have him as my personal assistant for a time. He will learn our language quickly and possibly succeed me as court advisor for when I pass on to my reward." He continued before Captain Rynarr could again voice his ideas of what he thought was a Christian reward; this usually pertained to hellfire and Brother Samuel did not feel like getting into a debate, currently. "Meanwhile, GW can continue on with his knight training."

Captain Rynarr thought about it for a moment and finally agreed with a nod of his head and a single stroke of his beard. "Come, we will tell them now."

So, it was done. Paul was handed off to Sam and he wearily followed him inside the castle keep, clearly relieved to be out of the hot sun and in the cooler passageways of the castle keep. While outside, Mushid was given complete control over GW's training, who was also given the task of instructing GW in the Libyan language. Every phase of his training was now to be taught in the local dialect and often, Mushid would none-too gently tap GW on the shoulder when GW repeated a word wrongly. By the end of the first day, GW was seriously bruised on both shoulders and upper arms, but he was learning the language and it reminded him all too much of Army boot camp.

## BROTHER SAMUEL'S LIBRARY

"Sam, I do appreciate you doing this, but, I'm not too good with languages. I stumbled about with Vietnamese, while everyone else was learning what they needed to get by with," Paul said. Entering the room, Paul was very impressed with Sam's library.

"What words were those, Paul?"

"You know...how to order a beer, get your laundry done and find a babe," Paul said. He stopped when he saw the look of confusion on Sam's face.

"Come-on, Sam, the Navy hasn't changed that much in 35-years."

"Aw you forget, Paul, I was an officer and a gentleman, far above such things as finding a babe. Besides, you might recall I was married and it's been a long time since I ordered a beer...though I do miss the taste of a cold brew."

"Forgot about your wife, sorry," Paul said in a low voice. He then sat down on a wooden stool, placed before the table Sam used to study on. Sam had started using a tall stool years before due to his back pain growing worse. He often was forced to lie down when the back pain hit the Ice pick jabbed in the spine range.

"Since we're now alone, I want to share something with you." Sam gave Paul a hard look, "Occasionally, you will see a young lady in this room and she is quite beautiful. I ask, no make that an order, that you not speak to her at any time...until I have granted you permission. Understand?"

"Sure." But then Paul remembered the order part and added, "Yes, sir."

"Good. Now we can go back to Sam and Paul."

"Can you tell me who she is at least?" Paul asked.

"She is my pupil, that's all you need to know right now."

"Okay, whatever."

"This is serious, Paul. Remember what I said to you in the courtyard the afternoon GW spotted a young woman watching you all from the window above? How it could bring you a painful death to become involved or even in the company of such a woman?"

"Yeah, I remember," Paul replied. Reaching out, he fingered a stack of thick parchment on the table top and wondered what this strange stuff was and where all the paper might be.

"Same goes for this young lady. Her father would disembowel you and then dismember you by pulling you apart by a horse for each arm and leg."

"I said I understood, Sam. You don't have to give me nightmares."

"Paul, though I am an older man now, I do seem to remember being a young man once and if nightmares can save your life, I'll be happy to provide a list of the torture techniques used by that creepy character in the dungeon."

"Can we change the subject, please? That dude was really weird...We called him Igor."

Sam chuckled and then walked over to secure a rolled parchment from a near shelf, "What do you think about these time travel events?" Sam asked, as he unrolled one of the parchments to examine its contents and wait upon Paul's answer.

"Sam, you've got to tell me what this stuff is? I know it sure ain't paper." Paul had a look of puzzlement upon his face, while he fingered the parchment before him.

"No, it is not paper," Sam agreed. "This is what will be known as parchment, which comes from the skins of sheep or goats."

"Sheep skin?" Paul said in disbelief. He shied away from the parchment on the table and wiped his fingers on his pants. He never did cotton to watching some of his dad's ranch hands skin out a steer. They only kept a small herd on the ranch, mostly for feeding the family and the hands, and the 4th of July barbecue they hosted for the neighbors.

"I actually prefer the sheep over the camel skin and we have an immense supply of it here in the kingdom. Mostly from the old ones, their wool is no longer suitable for the weavers. But all in all, we should be grateful, for Northern Africa was a region primarily inhabited by goats and it was the armies of Alexander the Great who brought the sheep from Greece to clothe and feed them with, as they marched."

"So, you skin them, clean and dry them like a cow hide and then use them for writing paper."

"That's correct," Sam said. "The American Indian used deer a buffalo skin to keep a record of their lives. This is similar."

"I doubt you'd ever get one of those into a typewriter."

"Not to worry, we've got several hundred years or more before that happens." Sam pointed to the globe on the table, "Now back to time travel, you were about to say something about what you thought."

Paul studied the globe briefly, "Well, I've given it a lot of thought and we've talked about it some, but this science stuff was another bad subject for me," Paul said. A frown formed on his face and then it changed to a smile, "Tell you the truth, Sam, if it wasn't for sports and my dad's brother being on the school board, I'd never had made it through high school. Still can't figure out why I'm having such trouble with that sword and shield stuff. I could rope a running horse when I was 10-years old, but ol' Mushid's liable to beat me to death if I can't get it figured out."

"You certainly look strong enough, Paul, but I'll teach you some moves that might help you. I was on the fencing team at the academy. Not Olympic material, but I did all right and we defeated Army in my senior year."

Paul bent his arm and studied his right elbow, "Must be my elbow. Hurt it three times playing football and it never came back 100 percent. After a few swings with that blasted sword I feel like it's on fire. Some Doc at Boot Camp called it 'tennis elbow', but I never played tennis in school and thought he was crazy."

Sam grinned, "It's a condition common with tennis players, but also comes from other sport maladies like football and baseball," Sam said. "We'll work on it, but right now I want to talk about time travel and show you why I brought it up." Sam walked over to a large wooden chest below one of the windows, opened it with a loud creaking noise and brought out a piece of flat wood.

"Doesn't anyone oil anything around here? Everything creaks, like some monster movie and I keep looking for an oil can."

"You get used to it after a while, Paul. Oil is for burning and can be hard to come by so no one wants to waste it on something as simple as a creaking joint."

"But I thought this was the land of oil?"

"There is oil and I'm sure someday there will be oil wells all over this desert, but right now it is extremely hard to get to. Our oil mostly comes from fish, and it takes a lot of work to get enough fish oil to satisfy the needs of a castle this size."

Paul shook his head in wonder and then studied the piece of wood Sam held. He thought it might be a piece of ship wood or dock planking and estimated it to be just over two-feet long, better than six-inches wide and about an inch or more in thickness. Both ends showed violent breakage and blackened burn damage. Paul thought from its weathered look it was probably quite old.

Sam placed the piece of wood in Paul's hands. "I found this piece of wood 26-years ago, during one of my many travels along the Egyptian sea coast, when I could get around better on horseback and the border with Egypt was still open to us.

"It was deep inside an old shipwreck and I estimated it to be maybe 400 or 500 years old from its Grecian design, or much older. I'm not sure, but I believe some of the broken urns were clearly Greek in design because they carried the characters of ancient Greek gods no longer held in such esteem by the current Greek populace."

"Okay, you've got me," Paul said. Shifting it about, he looked the wood over. "What's so important about it?"

"Turn it over, Paul."

Paul did what he was told and was astonished by his find, "This is English!" Paul exclaimed.

"Right, now what's it say?"

Paul was simply stunned, but he quickly recovered and read the writing out loud, "Isaac Montgomery, 1986—LA, CA."

The writing was deeply carved into the wood by an unknown instrument and blackened with what Sam thought to be probably ash. "1986?" Paul asked. Then carefully, he handed the piece back to Sam, who wrapped it up and placed it back inside his trunk.

"Clearly proof the same time travel event which trapped us has happened before and at least, by my estimation, clearly hundreds of years before my trip and later in time than yours...according-to our Mr. Montgomery's 1986 episode.

"We can't say exactly, for we are not sure how old he was when he came back in time, or when he carved those words." Sam talked as he walked about the room. "Why didn't he put down any other information?" Paul asked.

"We'll never know. He may not have known his current year and it's very possible he was a galley slave and did not have an opportunity to provide further information.

"He may have showed up one day, was enslaved as a stranger the next day and died in a shipwreck a few weeks later. Or, he could have survived the shipwreck to become a wealthy tradesman or even an officer in the Egyptian military. There is simply no way of knowing how his life ended, Paul. Only that he did appear long ago and took a moment to record those few words on a plank of wood."

"I hope he made it."

"So do I, Paul," Sam replied whole-heartedly. "Now, I want you to look at my globe here."

"Your globe...it looks like a round rock with lines chiseled in."

"Well, if you cannot tell what this is, I shouldn't have to worry about one of Princess Lonnia's spies discovering its true purpose." He pointed to the various lines he had spent many hours on, "This is the Northern Hemisphere, my young sir and I use this for some of the lessons I teach...but it will work for this demonstration as well." Sam rolled the heavy globe toward him and keeping it in front of him, he moved it around the table in a small circle.

"You're teaching them the earth is round?" Paul asked.

"Only one person," Sam replied harshly. "But, we'll discuss that later. I want you to listen to my theory and watch my demonstration...or I will drop this on your foot."

Sam continued to roll it slowly in a circle, widening it out some to prevent him from growing dizzy. "This is the earth orbiting the sun...we'll use that that piece of stone, as the sun." Sam rolled the globe toward the stone, which was about six-inches square.

"Try to ignore the disparity in sizes for my demonstration."

"What's disparity mean?" Paul asked.

"Never mind...We will cover English after you've learned Libyan." He then reminded Paul to focus on the stone globe, "I believe as the earth circles the sun it passes by or through a portal...a time portal of sorts." Sam made a small circle with his right finger and thumb and placed it beside the globe.

"There might be some sort of time portal in the universe, a naturally occurring phenomenon, and maybe more than one. Say a sort of invisible room in space...or something similar...like room-sized bubbles or even larger." Sam leaned against the table for support as he faced Paul.

"While the Earth circulates the sun, these small rooms...or portals...Maybe a vortex is better than portal, comes in contact at a given location on the surface of the planet."

"Where'd you hear the word vortex?" Paul asked.

"Advanced Engineering at the academy or maybe it was H.G. Wells, now be quiet and listen. You can ask questions when I'm finished." Paul nodded his head in agreement.

"When a man meets one of these vortexes, he is transferred back into time. "Sam raised his hands and pointed his index fingers upward, and then spun them around in a tight circle.

"Possibly this vortex has no control on where it sends someone; history or future, or possibly there is a higher source...maybe even God is involved in who is selected and where in time they end up. And again, it may be totally random, and we ended up here all by chance."

"Sure sounds screwy to me, Sam."

"From what you've all told me, you were facing almost certain death, much like I was and very possibly God intervened. You've been transported back in time to accomplish something important, maybe we both were. You mentioned how your weapons were destroyed, the steel barrels bent and yet none of you suffered a broken bone."

"Okay. You have a point there...Then if you're right and God is behind this, what did this Montgomery accomplish?"

"I don't know, but maybe it was to accomplish an act never recorded in written history. The complete world history of the last 3,000 years would never fit in one library, not to mention a single history book. However, I do have faith in God and my being here has affected the lives of many people and remember, Paul, it also saved your lives."

Paul thought about it for a moment before he replied, and Sam waited patiently, "Okay, I can buy this vortex thing, that something brought us here and apparently, this Isaac guy too...I can even buy this whole Earth orbit bit, but God doing it...you lose me there, Sam."

Sam smiled, "At least you're honest." Sam rolled the globe back to its proper place on his table. "This vortex event makes me wonder how many other men...or women, have been transported back into the past and what they might have accomplished with their knowledge from their own time." Sam walked about the room in silence and then burst out with, "Maybe it was this Isaac who knew that if you took tin and mixed it with copper you could produce bronze, and the bronze-age came to be. Or he might've manufactured the first medicines for his time, or he was on hand to guide the wise men to Bethlehem." Sam shook his head. "We'll never know, Paul, but I do hope he accomplished something to better mankind."

"You think creating bronze weapons helped mankind, Sam?"

"Weapons are also hunting tools, Paul. A young man and a strong wooden shaft tipped by a bronze spear head can also be a good defensive weapon for when a raiding tribe outnumbers his family by ten-to-one odds."

"Man, you sound a lot like Richard. He brought that time travel stuff up the other night. Called it something…" Paul thought about it for a moment, "Oh yeah, he called it 'manifest destiny'. Said how some of our greatest inventors might've been from the future, people brought back to the past and what they already knew, and how to make it work. Like you, redesigning the old Roman waterways in the castle with your engineering training from Annapolis and those weapons you built to attack that dragon with."

"Which none have worked so far," Sam said in aggravation. "Oh, I've hurt it, but we certainly haven't stopped it."

"Well, now you've got us here Sam, maybe we can come up with something?" Paul walked over to lean on the window ledge and looked down upon the training yard. He quickly spotted GW attacking yet another standing dummy with his lance.

"Man, he is really getting good."

"Who?" Sam asked, while he walked over to join him at the window ledge.

"GW," Paul said. "He is one naturally born horseman. That guy can turn that horse of his and make a hard reverse with little effort…makes me look like some dude out for a weekend ride with my sweetie."

Sam stood there and observed as GW brought Valiant into a sudden, but sliding stop, the horse's, rear-end dropped on the ground and both horse and rider wheeled a hard-left turn to explode back in the opposite direction with an awesome display of strength, agility and a burst of speed.

"I didn't know a horse could do that." Sam said in awe.

"Oh, they can but I've only seen it when two stallions are duking it out. Not when a rider was on him."

"It was like the horse knew exactly what GW wanted a second before GW knew it himself," Sam said in appreciation. Then something caught his eye. Off to the left, there were the young unblemished hands of a girl resting on the window ledge further down the castle's wall. He couldn't see her face, but from the rings she wore, Sam knew the young girl to be Princess Lennia and a deep pain in his chest told him trouble was brewing.

He pulled Paul away before he could notice the girl in the window, "I was in Egypt once...oh, about 15-years ago, and gathering what I could find in relationship to Biblical records and searching old shipwrecks on their beaches, when I spotted two full-blooded German shepherds running along the shoreline. As far as I know, these were very uncommon canines for this location and time-period, made me wonder if they too had been caught up in some time...bubble. They looked happy and an Egyptian lad was running with them."

"What happened to them?"

"I don't know, but I have wondered if one was a female and other a male, could they have some kind of effect on the world of dogs and their previously known countries of origin?"

Captain Rynarr was extremely appreciative of GW's skill. Though he had seen the young man ride with his own eyes, he had a hard time believing this GW was new to this. Still, he trusted Brother Samuel exceedingly and from watching Grant and Hughes' lack of skill with the weapons of a knight, he gave GW the benefit of doubt. But he still had to wonder, how could this GW become such a fine horseman in such little time? And the horse, this Valiant as GW named him, was nearly sold off as a cursed animal. Valiant was now looked upon as a prized stallion and GW had already turned down several good offers for purchase of the horse.

Captain Rynarr stood there with hands at his waist and watched as the horse negotiated such sudden and nearly impossible turns, and without losing his rider. He knew right then, this was a move that must be taught to his knights. A maneuver that could bring victory to many of his men, turning on their opponents before the enemy knight was ready to return to combat. Not in a joust of course, for there were rules, but in real war there were no such noble gestures offered. It was kill or be killed.

For his reward, today, GW only earned increased training under a hot unmerciful sun and more grueling language lessons. Now, nearly everyone he encountered was instructing him the language. They pointed to something and told him what it was in Libyan and demanded of him to repeat it several times before he was allowed-to move along. He learned how Captain Rynarr had issued orders for GW to learn the local language quickly and it seemed everyone was becoming involved in his education plan.

A result, within a few days, a weary young and bruised man, who suffered a pounding headache, had learned a basic usage of the Libyan language, and he had the soldiers, slaves and visiting town locals to thank for it. Soon, GW and the others were allowed– to leave the castle grounds for short time periods, but only if accompanied by either Sam or Mushid. This rule was mainly enforced to protect the three strangers from any harm from the locals. There were several people who hated the white skinned Berbers for past atrocities, or any strangers who were found walking amongst the townspeople unescorted.

In this way, it was not long before the people of Silene had come to know the three Americans and befriended them as a way of showing respect to Brother Samuel.

# 7 – A PLOT FORMS

P rincess Lonnia carried deep within her crippled body a sincere hatred for everything that lived in the kingdom. She had come to secretly like the title given to her as the Black Princess, though she severely punished anyone who would make the mistake of uttering that name within her earshot. In the dreadful accident that injured her body so grievously, something had happened to her mind to turn her into the sorceress she had strived so hard to become. She wanted to control everyone around her and used everything from the ancient arts of black magic as a weapon against the superstitious lot, simple bribes for the greedy and blackmail or threats of death to those who stood in her way. She was a formidable force and only the king, her father, stood in her way of claiming the throne.

She was once again at work in her lab. Her gleaming long black mane of hair was hanging in loose tangles about her face and the aged shaman's robe was draped loosely over her bare shoulders. Suddenly, she released a cry of anguish, frustrated, and she angrily shoved a book of spells off her tabletop. She had bought the ancient book three years prior from an old witch in the darker region of older Damascus, remembering a foul decaying odor about the vile woman reminiscent of being at death's door. She had promised her the parchments within the aged and fragile book were written by a long ago dead civilization and would bring her great magical powers. But first she had to pay a sizeable price in silver coin before she uttered the magical words to release the book's authority over to her. But after months of laboring over the text and scribbling out hundreds of translations, she eventually discovered the various brittle parchments within the leather-hide bound book contained only concoctions and herbs she had already learned about; simple worthless spells and simple sleeping potions. She had been conned by an old biddy.

The Black Princess glared at the wall where the old shaman was entombed and remembered the promises the old geezer had made to her in her thirst for true black magic and archaic forms of sorcery. Where tales were told of how a spell or potion could turn a man into a beast of burden or better yet, change her blocks of melted bronze into bricks of gold.

During the last ten years, she had collected numerous poisons and sleep agents from afar, but her two main enemies were too quick-witted for her and the assassins she sought out feared the two men she wanted most dead. Captain Rynarr's reputation with a sword and the men who rode with him had become legendary and he protected the good Brother Samuel with his life.

She needed better light to see by and lit a second and a third candle. All three were in a bronze candle stand placed in the middle of her table, centered to provide maximum illumination if needed. The light also cast bizarre shadows on the walls and ceiling, where they seemed to dance to a silent tune and as she gazed upon these shadow creatures parading about her, she began to relax. Often, her facial pain from the long-ago accident, was extreme and she had learned to medicate herself in such times. Her old shaman had taught her how to grind up various flower petals from a poppy; which grew to the Far East, into a fine white powdery substance. This powder, mixed with either a date drink or inhaled in small amounts, would ease her pain—and it did.

She limped about the room, slightly disoriented from medicating herself and while favoring her injured leg, released an audible sigh of surrender. She leaned against the table and bent over to pick up the old book off the floor and plopped it back down on her tabletop. After several moments of deep and somewhat hallucinogenic thought, she decided the room had become much too confining and smoky. She dropped her robe and left the lab but struggled with her balance while climbing the stairs. Once back in her quarters, she quickly changed into a simple lightweight red robe, tied her hair back with brown leather straps, and walked over to where several heavy dark blue wool drapes covered her windows.

Pulling a section of drape aside, she was at first stunned by the bright sunlight that burned into her eyes like flaming arrows and brought her hands up to protect her eyes. Once recovered, she looked outside from her room to observe the castle's training yard below. She often watched the men train; it stirred her night dreams where a secret lover would cherish her, and her deformed body was now beautiful like no other.

As she regained some of her mental capabilities with the drug's high wearing down, she was surprised to see many of her father's Royal Guardsmen standing about the stables and this perturbed her. She felt the king's men should always be busy doing something, even if that meant endless drilling. But, apparently, these men felt otherwise as they lingered about in conversation, but a few sat in the shade of the stable and watched a single knight work out on horseback. Only then did she spot the ever-loyal Captain Rynarr standing among these knights and her eyes were certainly not of lust when she glared down upon him. If she had been good at archery and in her present mental shape, she would've fired arrow after arrow down upon the faithful captain to pin him to the earth like a camel hide staked out for cleaning. But alas, her only weapons were her knowledge of ancient black arts, her library of archaic writings and her strong desire to see him dead.

From her lips, she whispered yet another curse and sent it his way with a wave of her hands. But nothing happened. Captain Rynarr seemingly remained unaffected by her black magic and this angered her even further, causing her to slam her fists down against the window ledge. Wincing from pain, she then jerked back the drape hard and turned to look about the room for any item she could rip or break in frustration, but as she closed the drape Princess Lonnia suddenly recalled one of the strangers on horseback. She opened the drape wide and ignoring the bright sun, saw that this rider was indeed one of Brother Samuel's clansmen. Who else would have such white arms in Silene?

At first, she was enraged, but then this changed to admiration as she noted his ability with the horse. She remembered having heard of her handmaiden's gossip about this man who could ride so well and his two friends. Because they were clansman of Brother Samuel, they had now become her sworn enemy too. Her handmaidens were summoned, all of them quite afraid when seeing the rough shape their princess was in. All too often she would simply begin beating them for no reason and later, she would never remember having done it.

She gestured them toward the window and pointed to the white man on the horse. One of the young girls, who walked with a crippled right leg caused by her former master's use of club upon her during a drunken episode, spoke of how this one below in the yard was called GW. Princess Lonnia recalled the silly name and thought it bore no real meaning. She also knew he was not yet a true knight but was in training and possibly to become one of Captain Rynarr's illustrious Royal Guardsmen.

There was a sudden sparkle to her eyes as she watched GW do battle with the various dummies in the training yard and honestly, she was truly impressed with his abilities and that of his mount. All the time hoping they would both tumble in the sand and break each other's neck.

Her crooked mouth began to form a hideous grin while she observed GW and an idea began to give form in her devious mind. She was beginning to see a way; a plot was forming to strike back at Brother Samuel. One, that if her dark gods blessed her with insight and planning, could very well spell the end of the good monk and bring her ever closer to the Throne of Silene and the end of Islam in Libya.

Releasing the heavy drape and now lost in deep concentration, she began to wander about the room and finally, dropped onto her soft bed of silks. Here she lay, while her handmaidens stood to the side and waited while she ran a lengthy silken cloth of blue hue between her fingers and she hashed out her plan. She didn't think it a difficult idea to carry out, the only problem lie in how best to present it to her father. To introduce it in such a way that not even the troublesome Brother Samuel couldn't interfere with it being carried out.

First, she would do away with one infidel--this GW infidel. Then the others would soon follow. By then she hoped to have found her magical weapon to use against Brother Samuel, Captain Rynarr and members of the Royal Guardsmen—and possibly a way to control the dragon and force it to bid her will.

Staring at the high ceiling above her bed, still in a somewhat hallucinogenic euphoria, her thoughts dwelt on an idea for a new concoction powerful enough to control the hellish beast and destroy her enemies. She had read how the ancient gods had controlled the flying serpents or fire breathing dragons and saw no reason why she could not learn of such a way to accomplish this too. All she needed was the right spell, the right potion and no one on earth could defeat the forces of hell she had in her power.

Smiling, her face extremely moist, she brought her hands together to clap loudly twice, a signal to summon her maidens. She had forgotten they were already present. Once they stepped forward, very nervous in their actions, she at first berated them for taking too long and then ordered them to prepare her bath. She would not admit it to them, but her injured leg was quite sore again and she needed to soak it. This would also allow her a relaxing time to contemplate her plans for the demise of this handsome young knight-to-be and hopefully both of his friends.

## IN THE CASTLE TRAINING YARD

Sweating profusely from an extremely rigorous work out, GW slowly dismounted Valiant's back to ease the pain somewhat and once his feet were planted firmly on the ground, he reached up to pet Valiant's nose. The stable boy appeared at his side and he handed the reins over without a word. There were muscles in his body he hadn't used for a very long time and he was beginning to understand what saddle sores truly were. Man's legs are not built to go around a big horse, I'm gonna be bowlegged within a month. No wonder cowboys always walk so funny-like. My lower back burns like the dickens, I've got shooting pains down both legs and I feel like I've spent the last three hours on a runaway pogo stick. Even my arms hurt from carrying that dang lance.

He turned to glance back at Valiant as the big horse was led away, "I love you, guy, but times like this I sure do miss having a 1966 Mustang under my butt." He then addressed the stable hand, "Groom her well, youngster and a double feeding." He wasn't sure the stable hand understood him, but he also knew the young man knew his job.

GW then walked over to the water troth and after he dipped a wooden bucket into the water, he promptly raised it up and poured all the water over his head. While he relished the cool down, an equally weary Richard Hughes wandered over to join him in a drink of water and a few slices of fruit a servant had prepared for them.

For nearly two hours Richard drilled his men in hand-to-hand combat, teaching them to use Judo throws and various Karate kicks and hand blows against their sparring partners. Once their teacher left to join GW, all ten-men took advantage of the reprieve and sought out a shady spot against the castle's keep. Within minutes an older servant delivered two water buckets to them and a wooden platter of melon fruit and dates.

Mushid, who was of course used to the heat, rested earlier while observing GW and Richard train. Now he held a handful of juicy grapes to munch on and shook his head, while Richard and

GW took their breaks. He knew they should take their water breaks more often under this hot desert sun but thought they should learn this on their own. Experience was a great teacher--even if it meant dehydrating Richard's ten students.

Mushid smiled as his two young friends, who with great thirst gulped down the water and jokingly wrestled over the last few slices of fruit. Mushid then turned to the old servant who brought water to Richard's ten-students and with a loud shout, ordered him to rush to the kitchen and bring back a platter of cold roast mutton or chicken.

"How goes it?" GW asked Richard after nearly drowning himself.

"I'm beat, Corporal, sir." Richard replied mockingly. "This heat is murder."

"Are those guys learning anything?" GW asked as he took another handful of water to wash over his face.

"Some." Richard said and then took another large gulp of water before continuing, "Oh, they won't win any tournament medals, but they'll give the other guy a bruised back side and maybe a broken neck."

"Well, you're making Captain Rynarr happy. At least I think so, hard to tell with that man." GW said as he dropped the bucket back into the water troth, dipped it full and poured a nearly full bucket over a surprised Richard.

"Thanks!" Richard exclaimed as he shook his head to clear out his ears.

"You looked like you needed it." GW said with a grin. "I know you might not sun burn like me, but you can sure dehydrate as fast as I can."

"It's depressing to think we'll never feel air conditioning again." Richard said before he used his old GI towel to wipe the leftover water from his hair and face. Since overly strict officers or loud-mouthed NCOs no longer surrounded them, Richard, GW and Paul started growing their hair out and beards.

"I saw the captain looking at you too with what might have been admiration while you rode down those dummies. Have-to admit I was impressed myself. You and Valiant seemed to have bonded, it's like you're one...It's a bit weird actually." Richard said. While he wiped his arms off, Richard studied GW's face for a moment and then asked, "You sure you only rode horses with that girlfriend you spoke of?"

"I also said summer camp. But look, I've got less hours on the back of a horse then you have growing that ever-so manly beard of yours." GW said. He then reached down to draw up a handful of troth water to shower in Richard's face in jest.

"I believe you, but you ride a whole lot better than most of the guys around here."

"Don't know how to explain it, man, but it's as if I can read Valiant's mind or he can read mine. It didn't happen right away, but something happened to us right after that girl was sacrificed. We sort of...we sort of clicked. Don't know how to explain it any better."

"Well like you said, we're stuck smack in the middle of a bizarre fairy tale and anything is possible."

"Like we said before, buddy, this is more like an episode of Twilight Zone."

"Right, fairy tales are for kids." Richard then gestured with his right thumb back over his shoulder, pointing to the north. "I'm only happy that's not some T-Rex over there. At least our dinosaur friend is confined to the shorelines. An adult T-Rex would make have made short work out of this place."

"You sure know a lot about dinosaurs for a lowly private."

Richard grinned, "Brain power, my dear Corporal and Black brain power I might add."

"So, you're saying knowing about dinosaurs is a Black thing?" GW asked.

"You didn't know that Afro-Americans are considered the foremost dino-doc's in the country? We're far more intelligent than whites." Richard said with a smirk on his face. He wrapped his now wet GI towel around the back of his neck and enjoyed the relief it gave him.

"I can buy that. You guys simply used global slavery as a free ride to see the world and do your dino-doc research along the way?"

"Now you got it!" Richard exclaimed with a raised clinched fist. "Let the white man pay the bills and we can dig up the bones and pick the cotton on the side."

"Are you seriously believing your own rap here, brother?"

Richard shook his head, "Not really, I've never been one of the cool guys. I'd rather spend my time in a good library or museum, or maybe a good Judo workout under a warm sun...But not quite this hot." Richard felt the temperature was well into the triple digits and was hoping a nice sea breeze might blow in to cool things down.

"I think we've both been in the sun too long." GW said in a serious tone. "C'mon, let's go inside for a while."

"Yeah, I can't believe I'm joking about slavery. My old man would clobber me big time if he heard me talking like this." He looked about the courtyard and then said, "This place must have a couple hundred slaves and we're standing here joking about it."

Richard then gestured toward Mushid, "I'll tell him what we're doing. Besides, I'd rather eat my mutton inside and without all the flies."

GW nodded his head in agreement. He then took a moment to observe the various servants working the stables and around the courtyard, wondering what kind of life they had here in Silene and what they had to look forward too. GW shook his head, watching as two young boys struggled to push manure cart away from the stables. The horse was much too old and too weak to handle the chore and GW thought the two kids were far too young for such duties. He wanted to help, but his inner voice stopped him. To interfere with local ways could lead him and his friends, right back into the dungeon.

Maybe someday we can change things here...and maybe that's why we're here. GW ran to catch up with Richard, "You know, we came here as prisoners, complete strangers to these people and as infidels, and now we have a better life than most everyone here. It don't make sense."

"I can't believe were actually using the word infidel in our conversation," Richard said, kicking the sand with his boot. "Sam had to explain to me what that word entailed...And it leads me to believe I am right about manifest destiny."

"You talkin' about that Manifest Destiny thing again? So, tell me what's it got to do with the word infidel?"

"There's got to be a reason for us being brought back here, GW and it sure isn't to stand here doing nothing while some should've been extinct dinosaur chows down on beautiful girls."

"Well, have you had any interviews with God lately?" GW asked, as they walked along. "Maybe you've had a vision of some kind or some dream? Look, I know I'm not too up on my scriptures, but I know the Bible speaks of God talking to people through dreams and vision. Not too many got spoken to directly, like we're talking here."

"Hey, GW, only dreams I've had are of a thick steak smothered in onions and I sure miss my Pepsi-Cola, I could drink a six-pack of that every day."

"I know, but I'm a Coca-Cola man myself." GW said with a depressive shrug of his shoulders and a deep sigh. "Last night I dreamed of a juicy Papa Burger, French fries covered in ketchup and an extra side of thick cut tomatoes."

"Oh, knock it off!" Richard complained and then approached Mushid to tell him what they were doing. His newly acquired skill with the local dialect allowed him to nearly speak fluently with the locals, but he still had some problems with pronouncing a few of the words and their unusual usage of verbs.

## ROYAL GUARDSMEN DINING ROOM FOR OFFICERS

As a favor to Brother Samuel, Captain Rynarr had granted the three strangers permission to use the officer's dining room inside the castle keep. Here, there were lots of windows, which allowed for the cooling sea breeze to pass through the room, and big enough for five large wooden tables to be placed without crowding. Ten simple high-backed wooden chairs surrounded each table, four each to the sides and one chair at each end for the senior officers to sit. GW found it was much cooler here in the late afternoon than sitting outside pestered by flies. Richard though, he soaked in the artistry of the room and loved to gaze upon dozens of multi-colored shields of various designs, and the assorted weapons, which hung from the wall. According to Mushid, some of these shields were of Greek, Roman and even Persian design, and were taken from the enemy from as far back as the time of Alexander the Great. The weapons, some Greek and Roman, consisted of spears of various lengths, swords of different design and length, and several deadly hand maces mixed in with deadly looking battleaxes. In one corner of the room and on wooden frames, stood the bronze body armor of a long ago dead Greek warrior, and the opposite corner stood the leather armor of an Egyptian soldier.

When GW entered the room his first thought was of how this was what a warrior's dining room should look like and wondered if the officer's clubs back in his time were similar, with war trophies all hanging about? Weapons seized in battle from enemy officers and flags or banners belonging to the various Army units serving on base or gifts from visiting fellow officers. Being a member of the famous 101st Screaming Eagles, he imagined a lot of German and Italian war trophies from World War II and possibly Korea and suspected there would be a good share of paraphernalia from the war in Vietnam.

A lowly enlisted man and a brand-new corporal as it was, he'd never been to an officer club or even an NCO club, but had hoped to one-day chow down heartedly during one of the famous NCO club steak and beer nights he'd heard about. But not now!

Richard, his thoughts on home, sat in silence for a moment, while watching a servant make his way through the room to bring him and GW a wooden platter piled high with last night's roast chicken. He'd learned the kitchen staff kept it cool by placing the cooked meat in one of the sub-levels, but it needed be used up the next day. In this desert heat, Richard knew the meat wouldn't last long and two days seemed to be about the longest they could safely keep it.

GW was about to take a bite from a skinny chicken breast when he heard Richard exclaim, "Man, I'm homesick!"

GW simply shook his head in response, "You got that right!"

"You think we'll ever get home, GW?"

"I want to hope, but Sam's been here a long time." GW was beginning to lose his appetite as his thoughts fell to home and family.

"At least I'm here with you and Paul. I'm not sure how I would've handled this otherwise." Richard raised his water goblet and toasted, "Airborne!"

To which, GW raised his goblet and echoed the toast and added the traditional, "All the way!"

The two men finished off the rest of their meal in silence and washed it down with goblets of warm water, which came with a mild after taste of melon. They then waved thanks to the servants and were in the process of leaving the dining room when several other junior officers blocked the doorway as they entered the room.

Most of the Royal Guardsmen officers and men had either seen or at least heard of the strangers; Richard's strange fighting ability and GW near magical skill with a once cursed horse. They also knew of the stranger's relationship with their captain, who they all respected and feared, and Brother Samuel, who they considered as friend. So, upon seeing the two strangers, they, as most junior officers would do to a senior officer, attempted to respectfully glide past the two men without saying anything.

But GW wanted to give a greeting and was about to, when right then came the afternoon call to prayer. A cleric, his hands clasped in front of his mouth to boost the strength of his voice, stood upon the castle's prayer towel and called out for all to hear that it was time for afternoon prayer.

All Muslims participated in the five daily prayers and as often with most religions, they conducted additional prayers as needed to bless their food or in need of a time for guidance, or healing.

Almost immediately, a middle-aged cleric a-top the town's prayer tower began to repeat this call and all the people of Silene were either beginning their prayers or hurrying off in search of their prayer rug to conduct their prayers upon. As required, they would aim the front of the prayer rug in the direction where Mecca lay and offer up their prayers to Allah.

GW was fascinated by this total devotion, but as it was, GW, Richard, Paul and Sam were the only non-Muslims in the kingdom and not wanting to stand out as heretics and possibly offend someone GW and Richard decided to head for Sam's room to see what the other two infidels were doing to pass the time?

## PRINCESS LENNIA

A very troubled Princess Lennia quickly backed away from the window's edge, not wanting to be seen by Brother Samuel as she observed GW train with the stallion named Valiant. She had learned of the horse's name through her handmaidens and had watched GW's near miraculous riding skills from her window.

She found herself being drawn to this strange young man and couldn't understand why she was feeling this way. True, he was quite handsome and his skills with a horse and lance had improved greatly from his first day not so very long ago. She felt her heart race whenever she saw him, and she nearly always smiled under her veil when a word about him was spoken around her. Yet, she knew him to be an infidel and this confused her greatly, but then Brother Samuel was also an infidel and her father loved him as a brother. The whole true believer versus the infidel in the articles of faith of Islam had never bothered her much before, with the exception being Brother Samuel. Now, once again, she was greatly troubled and was not sure how to proceed.

Until now, she had felt no sexual attraction to any man in the castle. Her only love for a man presented itself in her parental feelings for her father and her grandfather-like characterization of Brother Samuel. True enough, at one time she thought she could grow to like Captain Rynarr or one of his key officers, but only a simple brotherly-like friendship developed between all of them and to the best of her knowledge, her father hadn't received any suitors in search of her hand in marriage. Not that she even desired this type of marriage arrangement. She truly wished to learn more about this one-true love Brother Samuel spoke of during her schooling; of this Romeo and Juliet, who made her heart race and then turn to grief as she learned of how they had died for their forbidden love.

Princess Lennia learned through Brother Samuel of how Christians believed in a one-flesh bond between husband and wife, how they were equal in the sight of God and the man was to love his wife as much as this Jesus loved his people. But this one wife at a time confused her greatly, as she knew of many wealthy men who kept dozens of wives. Yet, her father, though a king, maintained a monogamous relationship with his wives.

She didn't realize Sam was walking on dangerous ground by instructing her in such things, but Princess Lennia gave her word that no topic they spoke of in class would ever be repeated unless he gave her permission to speak of it.

Princess Lennia recalled there were some suitors of minor standing who came to the castle when Princess Lonnia was of marrying age, but they were all driven away by her appearance, erratic behavior and unbecoming shameful outbursts.

Later, Princess Lannia became old enough and several men had come from afar to seek after her hand, but they too left the castle quickly when looking upon her manly appearance and hearing tales of her sexual persuasion.

Of the less appealing suitors, these were repeatedly refused an audience with either King Ramie or his daughters, and this included a young Egyptian prince hoping to enlarge his properties to include the Kingdom of Silene and add yet another princess to his collection of wives.

Thankfully, King Ramie was a man who desired his daughters be married to a man of some wealth and one who would lead a monogamous lifestyle, as he had done. Though he knew it next to impossible, he felt the oldest daughter should be married first, or at least the second oldest. But that apparently was not to be, and King Ramie looked to his youngest and most beautiful daughter for the grandchildren he desired and a male heir for the Kingdom of Silene.

Still, as King Ramie confided in Brother Samuel, he wanted his most favorite daughter to marry for true love, but as the months passed by, he wondered if this would ever happen. Either because of the accursed dragon or the poor financial condition of Silene, not a single suitable suitor has approached the main gate of Silene to seek the King's audience for Princess Lennia's hand in marriage.

Princess Lennia tried to speak to Brother Samuel about these new men from Ireland, but he refused to discuss them with her and of course this only added to her curiosity to learn more about them. She had her handmaidens busy with clandestine operations behind Brother' Samuel's back and even attempted a discussion with her oldest sister concerning GW, but Princess Lonnia was in a foul mood and only expressed her desire to have them hung up by their thumbs in some slave market.

When Princess Lennia approached the window ledge again, she glanced to each side to see who might also, be observing the training and seeing no one, she looked down upon the stable stalls and saw how GW was dismounted. He was petting his Valiant in an unusual gentle way for a man as he hand-fed him. Such compassion for a horse would normally be considered unbecoming of a Saracen. Though, thinking about it, she did recall observing Captain Rynarr care for his own mount in such a fashion. Which made her wonder why the other knights thought only of their mounts as simply dumb animals, and not a friend?

From her observation point above the stables she noticed a look of approval on Captain Rynarr's face as he observed GW's training and from the scene below, she also believed a friendship was building between these strangers and the large knight called Mushid.

She decided right then that there was something very special about these three men and, particularly, the one called GW. She wanted to know more and quickly, for her curiosity was aflame. The Princess Lennia would inform her handmaidens to seek out their castle informers and learn whatever knowledge they could of this GW, and in doing so, she had no idea the trouble she was about to cause for this young man from Southern California.

## BROTHER SAMUEL'S LIBRARY

It was late afternoon and radiant beams of sunlight filled the room with a yellowish glow, casting a large shadowy figure of a man bent over the table against the far wall. Deep in thought, his worried brow was covered in sweat; his tan cheeks moist, he wore a damp U.S. Army towel wrapped around his head like a turban to keep him cooled off. Paul, laboriously studying a large table-sized parchment, was helping make some minor adjustments on a highly-detailed diagram for one of Brother Samuel's new weapon systems he hoped to one-day use against the dragon.

Paul thought the wooden monster sort of resembled a siege tower, combined with catapult on top and arrow firing devices on each side. He seemed to remember seeing such a thing in an old movie about the medieval period, which led him to wonder if Sam would be credited in history as the one who invented it. Another war machine invented by the mad monk of Libya!

While studying the diagram; working hard to make a change here and there for Sam's later viewing, Paul didn't hear GW and Richard walk in from the passageway. He was startled when both men greeted him in the strange Libyan dialect. He fought to shield the parchment from spying eyes.

"Oh, it's you two clowns." Paul said with relief in his voice.

Hearing the voices, Sam walked in from his bedroom doorway, bidding them both welcome, "My, my, you do well with the Libyan language. It took me much longer to master their tongue, but I admit the dungeon atmosphere was pretty depressing and here, in only a few days, you have the freedom of the castle."

"Great teacher, we both thank you." GW said mockingly as he bowed at the waist.

Paul raised his hands up midway, palms pointed inward, and said, "Hey, look what Sam's found." Paul then left the table to dash across the room to Sam's chest. Without asking permission, he opened the chest with a loud creak and retrieved the wood plank. "He found it in some shipwreck in Egypt."

With a raised eyebrow showing his concern for Paul's ill manners, Sam approached Paul and said, "Paul, I'd appreciate it if you would ask first before rifling through my private property. We have little privacy here as it is, alright?"

"Oh, I'm sorry, Sam. I was just so excited to show it to them."

"I know." Sam replied good-heartedly, then watched as Richard and GW viewed the engravings and grinned as he saw their eyes grow wide in wonder.

"It's happened before, and you have further proof of it." Richard said with exhilaration.

"Yes, but even in my excitement upon making the discovery, this piece of evidence only made me wonder of how more many times this event has occurred and too whom?" Sam replied.

GW returned the plank to Sam, who handed it over to Paul, "Please return that to its proper place."

"Sure, Sam." Paul replied quietly and then added, "I'm sorry I got it out without asking, you probably wanted to surprise these two like you did me and I ruined it for you."

"It was a small thing, Paul." Sam said as he placed a kind hand upon Paul's shoulder.

"You should have seen me at the academy during my plebe year, I made so many mistakes I nearly lost 35-pounds from my nervous stomach, penalty details and extra push-ups and assorted chores I did for all the upperclassmen. But I made it to my second year and then discovered how much fun it was to torture the plebes."

"But why torture them? Why not help them, like a big brother?" Richard asked.

"Ah, the voice of a true protector," Sam charged in a serious tone and with a raised finger pointed upward, he shouted, "Out to defend the underdog and strike terror into the hearts of all oppressors." Sam then he smiled and with a gentler voice, said, "I'm not really making fun of you, Richard, for I truly felt the same way as a plebe. But then I came to learn exactly what it meant to be a naval officer." Sam walked over and sat on his stool, his legs were bothering him today and he needed to rest them again.

"I came to learn why the plebe year was so tough on us and I hope it still is." Sam said, and he recognized the confused look on Richard's face, his expression was much the same as his during his first grueling year in the academy.

"I'm not sure if all the military academies operate the same way, but they probably do and most base their ways on a proud tradition for cranking out fine young officers. Now you must realize they have only four years to provide their men with a specialized college education and on top of that, you're grilled over with all the naval regulations, traditions and basically how to keep a young ensign from sinking one of Uncle Sam's battleships and causing the death of hundreds of sailors.

"To get this all done in such a finite amount of time, they rely on the upper classmen to challenge the plebes in any way possible, to see if these first-year men have got what it takes to cut muster. Some of them cannot handle the pressure and they leave the academy and these are the ones we want out.

"Can you imagine an officer on the bridge of a ship who can't make a decision during battle or maybe a typhoon?

"We're hit hard and from all angles, but when we become upperclassmen, we also hit just as hard to ensure the plebes beneath us can take it and become naval officers the academy can be proud of. Understand?"

"Yes, sir," Richard said, but he wasn't sure if he did. He would have to think on it more.

"Too bad the drill instructors at boot camp don't take the time to explain why they had to stand on our backs during push-ups, kicked us in the rear whenever they thought we need a good swift kick, or slammed trash can lids on our heads to make sure we had a good night's sleep, and always felt 0455 hours was a nice time to wake up." Paul said.

Beside him, both GW and Richard nodded their heads in agreement. Neither man would ever forget what their drill instructors did, and how odd it felt after boot camp ended. They learned to respect these men who devoted their lives to making every day a vision of Hell.

"I'm talking about officers, gentlemen, not lowly enlisted men, especially those who like to jump out of perfectly good airplanes. I mean you people actually risk your lives on something Chinese worms puke out and then you have someone you don't even know, probably an underpaid civilian with a drinking problem, some slob who lost his wife to a good looking naval officer, pack your chute for you."

"Airborne, sir...all the way!" GW exclaimed with pride.

"And I thought the British were crazy." Sam said, holding his hands up in surrender.

With little other entertainment to offer, the four men remained in Brother Samuel's library for some time; discussing the possibilities of who else this time travel event might have caught up and what events in history they may have affected. Sam explained to GW and Richard his theory on the time bubble and of course Richard repeated his ideas on how some of the great inventors may have been involved; ripped out of their own time and transported back to history to possibly affect time's key events.

"Can you imagine coming back here, in this time-period, and try explaining to some shipbuilder how a boat made of only bronze could float?" Sam asked.

"I got news for you, Sam, I still don't understand how all those steel ships or cement barges stay afloat and I've seen them. We had one of those cement floats in a lake nearby my home and I always expected it to sink—but it never did." Paul said.

"We'll have shipbuilding 101 at some future date, gentlemen." Sam said, but he then switched the topic back to time travel. He had a theory this time event might also transport someone into the future and wondered how a victim of such an occurrence would be treated?

"Depending of course on how far forward in time, but if our jump is any scale to gauge, most likely he'd be considered intellectually backwards and sent off to school for the mentally challenged." Richard said.

But after more than an hour of discussion, their stomachs began to grumble, and the topic of time travel gave way to their appetites. They left the library, heading for the dining room for a late dinner.

"Let me guess, roast mutton or roast chicken?" Paul said as they walked down the torch lit passageway.

"You could be right, but we may be lucky and find a meal of barely warm sea bass if the fleet is in." Sam said.

"Have you ever taught them how to fry anything, Sam?" GW asked.

"Yes, but our supply of olive oil ran out a couple years ago and with the borders closed it might be sometime before we get more. Tripoli wants too much for their olive oil. They order it from the Middle East and have the funds to pay for it. And the castle staff use what fish oil we glean from what we catch in the nets for the lamps." Sam said as he walked in front of his friends. With his wide girth, it wasn't comfortable for someone to walk beside him in the narrow passageways.

"Maybe we can give the cooks a few ideas, show them how to bake the meat the way my momma did and hopefully explain to them the need for them to keep their long hair tied back so it doesn't end up in our food." Paul said. "I've found a few strands of greasy hair and it doesn't help my appetite any."

"You are welcome to try, youngster, but be wary of the head cooks as they might take offense and at a bare minimum urinate in your melon juice or sneeze on your meat." He said and then saw the looks of unbelief in their eyes.

"I'm very serious, my young friends. These people really do not like advice of any kind, the kitchen is their little kingdom to hold court in and they hold all outsiders in contempt and hate foreigners most of all. I'm lucky I haven't been poisoned."

Sam didn't think it worth mentioning to them right then of how Princess Lonnia had indeed attempted to poison him on several occasions, not suspecting they were in any danger from this evil woman. But he would soon learn otherwise.

## THE ROYAL COURT

For more than an hour a somber Princess Lonnia behaved unusually, holding her silence as her father held court. She remained mute while the king handled many kingly protocols for an upcoming visitation from a trio of Tripoli court administrators. He also discussed trivial matters with his own court officers over taxation issues and then listened to a senior knight from the regular army complain about his upcoming escort duty to Tripoli. He felt a less senior knight should be forced to take the duty and felt Captain Rynarr had saddled him with the task due to a previous offense the knight had made concerning the Royal Guardsmen's lack of respect for his men in general. Offering a kind ear as the senior knight complained, the king finally shut him off with a wave of his hand, "Your complaint concerns me, but not the way you had hoped for."

King Ramie's expression turned to one of scorn as he glared down upon this senior knight, "I feel a man of your years in my service and experience should have known not drag out a favor from one of my court advisors to obtain this audience with me over such a trivial matter. Such complaints should only come before the throne when all other avenues have been used.

"So, have you taken this complaint to Captain Rynarr, advise him how you feel and why?"

"No, Sire."

"Now you force me to make a decision." King Ramie stood from his throne, "You will ride escort for the party, but as second-in-command. An officer of lesser rank will be in charge and you will take all your orders from him. I will also allow Captain Rynarr to select such officer.

"Further, I direct Captain Rynarr to assign you to every escort duty you may be available for over the next year and in each case, you will be second-in-command. I feel in this way you will learn some humbleness, at least I assuredly hope so." He waved his hand over the knight, "Depart and the court advisor who brought you in before me may depart also. I do not wish to see his face for a month."

Princess Lonnia looked upon her father with eyes of disbelief. It had been a very long time since the king had addressed a knight in such a way and she wondered if the old man was regaining some back bone. She also enjoyed seeing the look utter defeat in the senior knight's face as he stumbled backwards from the throne room, his arm being yanked on by the ousted court officer.

Today was a rare event for the Black Princess, as she forced herself to behave in a reserved way, while she waited for the perfect opportunity to address her father. Patience was not one of her virtues and several times she had to bite her lip to keep from interrupting. Most often she would simply and rudely interrupt her father, no matter who he was talking to, and have her say, to get the matter on her mind over with. Her bad behavior had become the norm, and few had come to expect better from her when she was in attendance. In the eyes of the court officers, she behaved unlike any Muslim daughter would be allowed too, especially the daughter of a king. Such bad conduct toward a king could often bring on long term confinement or in some cases, even death.

Finally, believing she had waited enough time, Princess Lonnia gestured to her father to get his attention and whispered, "Father, might I speak to you?"

This strange behavior of hers, in displaying proper court manners surprised King Ramie, who wasn't even used to his eldest daughter's attendance for the more boring day-to-day court matters.

Though knowing her to be there, he hadn't said anything for fear he might break the spell and she would embarrass him as she had done dozens of times. She once even went so far as to depart the throne room without asking his permission during a visitation of a minor Caliph from Western Libya. Her rudeness did not escape the young Caliph, who asked for her to be punished immediately for such behavior. To this request, Princess Lonnia returned to the front of the throne room, asked the required permission to depart from the king's presence in a mocking tone and then laughed in the Caliph's face before she limped away. This left the young man stunned and to make matters worse, he no longer held any respect for the King of Silene—a man who apparently could not control his daughter. It was on that night King Ramie came very close to having Princess Lonnia beheaded, but while storming about his bedchambers in anger, he remembered a promise he made to his long dead wife so longer ago; to always love and protect their daughter and it was a promise he made before Allah.

"What is it you desire, my daughter?" King Ramie asked with some degree of hesitation. For far too long they had exchanged heated words and he deeply concerned she might push him too hard and as king, and not her father, he would be forced to respond to her disrespectful conduct. But her response surprised him.

"My father, I wish to travel." She said. "I desire to cross the lower Sahara and seek out some rare herbs I need for my work."

"Daughter, you know this is a very dangerous area? Our troops have made contact with many Egyptian raiding parties. Cannot your sister, Princess Lannia, perhaps find or trade for these rare herbs?"

"No, my father," She replied in a soft voice only her father could hear.

"Only I can choose the right plants and while considering my journey, I have received insight from Allah on how this could also be a time for many of our young knights in-training to journey forth as my escort and prove themselves if a battle is indeed necessary."

This made King Ramie pause to think, for Captain Rynarr had made this suggestion himself only two days prior. 'I would like to send out a small party, my liege, of young knights-in-training and under proper supervision who could then prove themselves in battle with the Egyptian raiding parties who dare to enter our kingdom.'

King Ramie knew several years had passed since the last campaign and for a man to become a Knight of Silene he must wage combat against an enemy of the kingdom.

"Father, I am not suggesting a party of such size that might come to the attention of the Egyptian army. I need simply a small party of perhaps ten Royal Guardsmen and regular mounted soldiers of your army who desire to prove themselves for knighthood."

"I will think on it, my daughter and bring the idea up to Captain Rynarr later this evening. If he agrees, I will let him select the force who will escort you."

"Thank you, my father, but I might suggest you allow one or two of these...Irishmen, I believe they are called, to come along. As I come to understand, the one called GW is in training right now and is said to be quite the horsemen."

"I will bring this suggestion up also, my daughter. But how long do you feel such a journey may take—for you know the festival approaches?"

"Only the passing of a moon, my dear father," She was saying. A 14-day moon cycle would be required for the journey and this would give them ample time to return before the festival began.

"What of your other duties?" King Ramie asked, and she knew him to mean the lottery.

"This will always be a problem for me, my father, since the lottery comes every two weeks and it takes quite some time to travel across our vast desert. However, with your permission, I will make the required selection before we leave and seal the name in a pouch. This same pouch I will give to Captain Rynarr to keep until the appointed time. He will then open it and collect the next victim.

"Selecting a new victim, every two weeks is creating a serious problem. We must send a delegation to Tripoli to appear before the Great Caliph and request he allow us permission to purchase at least 100 slave girls. But this time, all will be examined by our best people before sale to ensure we do not end up with a similar lot we claimed in Egypt."

"That would be expensive, my father, but I do agree we are running out of suitable young maidens for the dragon. If his hunger is not satisfied, he will turn on the city and only the great Allah knows what might happen then."

"You know I have appealed to the Caliph himself for assistance, but he only sends me advisors who explain this is

Silene's burden to endure and he will not interfere with Allah's will."

Princess Lonnia smiled, secretly doubting if the great Allah even cared about Silene's burden. Besides, she had designs on the dragon herself and it didn't involve killing it. With such a creature doing her bidding, she would have a great weapon to use against the coastal communities of North Africa and then all the Mediterranean Sea.

"Permission to leave your presence, my father," She asked.

Still uneasy by her unusual politeness, he nodded his head and smiled. This behavior of hers had bewildered him, but then a court advisor took that moment to step forward with a desire to again address the taxation issue and King Ramie forgot about his daughter strange behavior.

Princess Lonnia rose from her throne, accomplished a simple curtsy, which was hard on her leg, and she then slowly walked out of the throne room with most everyone in attendance watching her with stunned expressions on their faces.

## KING RAMIE'S PRIVATE CHAMBER

Both Captain Rynarr and Brother Samuel were attending the king, as this was a private time for them to discuss the day's court events and any military matters the king should be brought up to date on. It was during the latter part of this meeting King Ramie mentioned his daughter's request for a small party to escort her into the southern Sahara Desert in search of rare herbs.

"She also echoed your suggestion of how it might be a good time for some of your young apprentice knights—to earn their knighthoods if they make-contact with any Egyptian raiding parties."

"Couldn't Princess Lannia find these rare herbs of hers, my King?" Captain Rynarr asked. He knew Princess Lannia was currently operating in the southern part of the kingdom but was also out of contact with the king for the moment. It would require a small party to go out in search of her to pass along orders from the throne and Rynarr did this only when something out of the ordinary had popped up. By keeping the princess out in the field, she was not an embarrassment to the king by her blasphemous conduct. But she was also an effective weapon against the raiders and her knights had accounted for many victories. What riches the kingdom had were mostly brought in by Princess Lannia's command; seized from caravans illegally trespassing Libya and raiding parties who fell before her lance.

"I asked her that very same question and she replied only she could pick out the right plants."

"My king, I find it strange for Princess Lonnia to request this journey. I know how hard it is for her to ride, even by camel. This will mean taking a horse cart and we all know how uncomfortable that is for desert travel." Sam said as he looked down upon a chessboard and thought over his next move. He and the king were playing a game, which had last for three nights and Sam was thinking he was within three moves of having the king in checkmate.

"I agree, but these herbs must be of some importance or she wouldn't be requesting to make the journey." King Ramie replied as he kept a close eye on his chess opponent's moves.

"But what of the lottery, Sire, who will perform her duties in making the selection?" Sam asked.

"She has planned for this too by making the selection ahead of time and giving the name to our dear Captain in a sealed pouch. He will then open it upon the appointed time and in this way the laws of the lottery will not be broken." King Ramie said as he gave Sam a hard look and then moved his rook into position in hopes of claiming Sam's bishop in his next move. As he saw it, Sam was now forced into a decision of losing his bishop or finding his king in check.

Captain Rynarr cared little of the on-going game. He was more concerned with why Princess Lonnia would endure the discomfort of such a long and possibly perilous journey into the southern desert region. He was also in a quandary in why she went so far as to mention this unusual concern for the young men seeking knighthood. This was not like her and this request of hers made him mighty uncomfortable. He had been burned more than once over the years when Princess Lonnia's behavior became one of sweet and innocent, only to transform herself back to her true self, when her lies or scheme became known.

King Ramie tapped his right foot while he awaited Sam's next move and then tossed in a distraction to clutter his opponent's thoughts, "My dear daughter also suggested one of your young clansman, the one you call GW, participate in this journey. She had heard he was also in training to become a knight." King Ramie's ploy worked as Sam became distracted and moved his bishop from possible capture and thus opened-up an opportunity for him to place Sam's king in check. So, he moved his rook into place and smiled, "Check, my dear friend."

With the suggestion of GW going along, Sam was surprised, and he completely dropped the game from his mind. He was deeply concerned for his young friend's life, suddenly realizing how Princess Lonnia might be setting this whole journey up to have GW killed. In doing so, she would have her vengeance for losing face before her father in the earlier issue of the three stranger's lives.

Sam ignored the chess move and was about to address the king, when Captain Rynarr spoke up, "Sire, with the life of our dear Princess in possible jeopardy, I request I be able to lead this party and as my place as Captain of the Royal Guardsmen, choose the young men I feel best able to protect her. I will choose five men from the Royal Guardsmen and five men from the regular mounted troops." Rynarr glanced over at Sam and then back to the king, who continued to monitor the chess board with great interest, "We will also take 20 men-at-arms, two wagons, plus the cart for the princess, and if attacked or we come upon an enemy force trespassing upon our land, these men who display their valor in my presence will certainly win their knighthood," Rynarr remembered to add, "With your agreement of course, Sire. But as to this GW, I will leave that decision, with your permission, to Brother Samuel. For this man is his clansman and he may not feel this GW is ready for such a test."

Sam laid his goblet of date juice down, stood up and stepped away from the chess game for a moment. He wanted to think and pray over this problem, a behavior both the king and Captain Rynarr had grown used to and respected him for. For they knew a man to make rash decisions was often a fool.

Sam walked over to the window ledge and observed a splinter of a moon rising above the dark desert floor. He gazed upon an unlimited number of stars sparkling in the dark sky and briefly wondered whether, or not man was alone in this great vast universe?

With his eyes now closed tightly he took this matter before the Lord and thoughtfully asked for His help. He truly believed GW's life would be endangered if he traveled with this party, knowing the treachery of the Black Princess. But, he also knew to refuse such a request could bring a cast of shame over GW's head before the king, one he may never be able to lose.

As he prayed, he felt strange sensation as if a weight lifted from his chest and for a moment thought he might have heard a soft whisper of a voice in his head. Usually the answers to his prayers took far longer and more often than not, the answer was a silent "No", but he never stopped praying and asking.

Somewhat startled by what he felt, he slowly turned to face his two friends and with their eyes upon him, said, "My King, I feel my young clansman is quite ready to prove his worth. With the Captain's permission, I will notify him of this journey so that he may prepare."

King Ramie studied his friend's eyes, this Christian religion often confused him, and he couldn't help but wonder how close his dear friend and advisor walked with his Christian God—especially receiving a word in such little time? He knew his daughter was receiving Christian teachings, for this was his request so he may better know the people coming from the northern isle of Britain. But he also saw a strange sense of joy and inner peace in Brother Samuel face, something he never saw in the faces of his own clerics and this tended to concern him. He would ask his daughter on this, maybe she could explain this satisfaction he saw in Brother Samuel. But until then, he must respond to his oldest daughter's request.

"Then it appears my daughter's request will be granted and you," King Ramie casually pointed to Captain Rynarr with a chess piece in hand, "will pick your men for a 14-day journey to the south."

"What of the lottery, Sire?" Captain Rynarr asked.

"Select one of your trusted lieutenants to handle the task and send him to me so that I may talk with him." King Ramie then gestured to the chess game, "My old friend, do we continue now, or do you wish more time to think of your escape? But I believe your attempts will prove futile."

"A moment, my Liege," Sam said as he studied the board with renewed interest.

The board was quite large, constructed of dyed cedar of light and dark squares, and the pieces were of hand carved teak wood from the Far East. The set's king piece stood nearly 8-inches in height and the lighter stained side was carved in a Grecian style, while the opposing darker King made in a Roman likeness. The chess set was an extraordinary gift from a visiting dignitary of Damascus and had become one of the king's favorite past times.

A grin broke out on Sam's face as he spotted an escape, one that had apparently escaped the king. He reached down and from a grouping of pawns he moved his only remaining castle across the board and captured the king's rook.

Palming the rook, he looked the King Ramie and said, "Your move, Sire."

King Ramie's face flushed over, frustrated with having made such a stupid mistake—a mistake of a beginner. He'd lost sight of his strategy because of his daughter's journey and was now in jeopardy of losing the game.

"We will continue this game tomorrow. It appears I am too flustered over my daughter's plans to keep an eye on my game. Is this acceptable, my friend?"

"Of course, Sire." Sam said and then added, "I might remind you, my Liege, that you have defeated me more than half of the times we have played, and I feel your failure to notice my castle's placement was only due to this strange journey."

"You needn't worry about my pride or my knowing how many times you have let me win. You are truly a master of this game and by playing you I have learned much." He placed a hand of friendship on Sam's shoulder, "But now, my friend, I will say goodnight, for I am tired, and tomorrow is a long day. We must equip my daughter's party and see them off. For us old men, we will stay behind and enjoy the comforts of our station."

"Well put, Sire." Captain Rynarr said. "As I ride in the hot sun, I will be thinking of you two resting in the shade and wish I was with you."

"Protect my daughter, Captain." King Ramie ordered in a serious tone. "I know of your dislike for her and she would probably enjoy watching your beheading, but she is my daughter and a Princess of Silene."

Captain Rynarr stood upright and placed his right fist over his heart, "Sire, I am sworn to protect the royal family with my life. You need not worry. For anything to happen to Princess Lonnia, I would already be dead and all my men lying at her feet."

"Thank you, Captain. I should've known you would always choose duty over your own feelings. I only wish…" King Ramie didn't finish, remembering as king he must withhold his true feelings from even his most trusted friends. But before leaving for his bedchamber, he smiled to both men and offered a single nod of his head in friendship.

Sam looked down upon the chessboard and smiled, remembering all the games he played in his youth and the day he proudly became a member of high standing in the Naval Academy Chess Club.

He then looked at Captain Rynarr and placing a hand on his shoulder, he said, "Watch over my clansman, my friend, for I truly believe the Black Princess wishes him harm."

"You have my word." Captain Rynarr said as he again placed his hand over his heart.

## THE AMERICAN'S ROOM

Paul was lying on his bed. His head braced against the stone wall, as he attempted to make sense of a weathered parchment Sam had given him to figure out. On it was imprinted in dark ink various symbols, none of which Sam could understand and thought Paul should give it a try.

"Maybe fresh eyes might see what I have overlooked."

Paul took the parchment from Sam's hands, "Where did you get it?"

"Long ago a great sandstorm revealed the remains of an ancient caravan. Among the items brought back to the castle was this rolled parchment. I knew it to be ancient, but beyond that I have been unable to decipher."

So, with his homework assignment in hand, Paul returned to his room to examine the parchment closely and hopefully come up with an answer. But all he saw before him were strange writings and various unidentifiable symbols.

Richard was sitting on the floor, his back braced against his bed as he sewed up a new rip in his pants. He hoped his pants would survive another month or so, but the workouts, sweat and heavy humidity were taking a tow on their uniforms. They'd each broken most if not all, of their bootlaces and were now using leather strips they'd cut off from old sheep hides. None of them appreciated the uniforms the Guardsmen wore; thinking them to look quite silly—girly-like, and they hoped their uniforms would last for as long as they were in Silene. But, they knew it was only a matter of time before they'd be wearing the clown suits and were glad no one they knew back home would be around to see them.

For GW, this free time allowed him to stretch out and rest his weary muscles. He'd painfully become a cowboy and had the saddle sores to prove it. Sam had lanced several boils and treated blisters on GW's backside, but his skin was now toughening up and he could mount Valiant without releasing a painful sigh.

He had no western saddle to sit on, only a round piece of rough sheep hide over a section of thick woven blanket clothe. Paul had helped him make what could pass for as stirrups; wide leather strips in loop and attached to the strange saddle by a leather belt, and after seeing how well this new saddle worked for GW, several of the knights and other mounted men were now using this stirrup invention too. This made them both wonder if the saddle stirrups of modern day had been invented here in 12th century Libya by time travelers from the future. That is until Richard popped their balloon when he made it clear stirrups had been used quite earlier in history.

"Hey, have you guys seen any of these symbols before?" Paul asked as he held up the parchment for them to see.

GW studied the various symbols, but shook his head, "All Greek to me."

"You know, that old saying actually works here." Richard said and then pointed to a symbol in the lower corner of the parchment. "Where'd Sam find this?"

"An old caravan was uncovered by a sandstorm." Paul said.

"Well, I'm not sure about the rest of those symbols, but that one," Richard pointed at the lower symbol, "...looks like something I saw in my museum back home. I remember it was on a banner or maybe a flag."

"So, what is it?" GW asked.

"The curator said it was ancient Israeli, probably from the time of Solomon."

Right then they heard a loud knock on their door, it opened wide and Sam walked in. They no longer had a guard, although Mushid was often in their room, but he came as a friend.

"Rough day?" Sam asked them.

"I have complete sympathy for those cowboys who spent months taking cows across the western frontier." GW said.

"And I," Richard added, "feel as if I've been thrown, chopped and kicked by an army of ninjas." He displayed the rip he was sewing.

"What's a ninja?" Sam asked.

Richard grinned, "An ancient oriental assassin, trained in all sorts of deadly skills. Not someone you would like to come up against in a dark alley."

"Sam, Richard here thinks this one symbol might be old Jewish." Paul pointed to the symbol.

"Really...Jewish, you think." Sam set down on Paul's bed and looked the parchment over.

"We had all kinds of displays in the museum where I worked, but I remember seeing this symbol on an old flag or banner. My supervisor, the curator, said it was believed to be from the time of King Solomon."

"Well, we are in the right part of the world. I seem to recall how King Solomon had diamond mines in Africa, or so the legend says." Sam said, as he studied the symbol.

"Oh, I remember that movie," GW said with excitement, "it was King Solomon's Mines with Stewart Granger."

"You'll have to tell me about that some time." Sam said and then he changed the subject and addressed GW, "You are going on a trip, young man."

"A trip...me?" GW asked in quick response, with a wide-eyed look of surprise on his face.

"Yes, my boy. Princess Lonnia is taking a journey to the southern desert for 14-days, or as they say here the passing of one moon, and she has requested an escort. She has also requested you by name to be part of that escort."

"Okay, why me?" GW was suddenly suspicious.

"She is saying she wants to gather special herbs and use this as an opportunity for the young trainees to gain their knighthood. Here, a Muslim must prove himself in combat to be knighted."

"So, I ask again, why me?"

"She has seen you train and feels you too could become a knight, if you prove yourself worthy on the field of valor."

GW released a sigh, "Do I have to go?"

"I have given this some thought and feel you must. If you decline you will be painted with a shadow of cowardice and may never gain any standing in this kingdom."

GW looked to both of his friends, who both strangely remained mute for the moment. Then Paul put his hands out, palms up in a gesture of surrender, "Looks like you got no choice here, man. You can go, see some flat desert country and catch some rays, maybe get in a brawl, or stay here and dig a nice hole to crawl into."

"Okay, I'll go." GW said with a deep frown on his face.

"Good." Sam said and then added, "Now let me tell you about Princess Lonnia and why she probably wants you on this journey." Sam looked upon GW with an expression of concern; one like the expression GW recalled on his father's face when GW boarded the plane for Vietnam.

"I suspect the Princess, whom we often refer to as the Black Princess behind her back, wants to kill you."

"What?" GW shot up from the bed and somewhat dazed by Sam's statement, looked at the three men in his room. "Why does she want to kill me? I don't even know her."

Sam looked upon GW with deep resolve, "Because of me." Sam said in a calming voice.

"You? What did you do to her...besides calling her the Black Princess, and why is she Black?"

Sam gestured for GW to sit down, "Okay, I guess now is the time for me to bring you up to date on court intrigue. Better to have you prepared for what may lie ahead."

# 8 – A PERILOUS JOURNEY

With an early sunrise upon them, Princess Lonnia's armed escort was hurriedly preparing for today's travel. Men and knight rushed about the stables to ready their mounts, while servants and blacksmiths ensured the wagons ready for travel and securely loaded for the long journey across the perilous desert sands. While other soldiers slept in, except for those due to relieve the night shifts, other servants feverishly worked to fill the wooden and skin-lined water barrels to the brim. They made sure to cover them over with tanned skins and wooden lids to keep the bugs out and then had the burly court yard laborers secure each one to the side of the wagons with long thick strands of rope. The ropes also had two other uses; to protect the bulging wood plank sides from breaking from under such a heavy load and in the event a wagon got stuck in the sand, other horses would use the long strands of rope to pull the sinking wagon out. Some of the rope would be used for picket lines to tie the horses to at night, used to prevent them from running off in a sudden sand storm or to prevent them from easy prey to a desert raider.

Heaping food baskets were packaged the night before and in such a way as to protect them from direct sunlight and not risk spoiling over an extended time in the desert. Extra weapons were stashed securely, but for quick access if needed. Heavy sacks of feed for the horses were checked a second and third time by the senior stable hand, before they were stored in the second wagon, along with the heavy cook pots, nearly a cord of dry firewood for cook fires and any other needed supplies for this journey.

The men glanced over their shoulders while they worked and looked toward the castle keep's main archway, expecting the arrival of Captain Rynarr any moment. He was due to appear and as always, he would observe their preparations and then once satisfied with the wagons, he'd quickly issue the order to move out in his distinct authoritative voice. Some had learned from harsh experience that Captain Rynarr would leave behind any man not found ready to go, and for the apprentice knights brought along on this long journey, who dreamed of knighthood and glory, such a mishap would prove disastrous to their career.

Except today, things would be somewhat different, for with Princess Lonnia coming along the senior Muslim cleric would be coming outside with King Ramie to offer up a blessing over this mini-caravan.

A strong sea breeze suddenly blew in from the north and for a few brief moments, man and beast delighted in the cooler temperatures these northern winds offered up. As an added plus, the foul odors of the stables and what they contained were swept away to the south. The men, weary from working under 90 plus degree temperatures, relished in this brief moment and stopped what they were doing to simply stand there with uplifted arms and take in a deep lungful of air. For that brief-moment, they welcomed the cooler sea winds, as it washed over them.

Near the stables stood two-wooden sided single axle carts; each constructed in scrounged up wooden planking and covered over in a dark tan woolen fabric to keep the sun out. The rough insides of these carts were softened by tanned camel-leather to protect the goods and keep bags from tearing open. Well-used to be sure, their wheels were no longer rimmed in metal and were now padded in leather belts to protect them from heavy wear against the hot sand the caravan would journey through. At best these wagon carts may have another year or two before being turned into manure haulers for local stable work. But for now, they were determined to be suitable to carry all the additional supplies needed for this journey.

The second cart, the newer of the two and which was only built the year before, was rushed to the stables when it was made known the Princess desired a separate wagon for her sleeping furs, blankets for padding against bumps and her extra clothing. Though, most of her extra clothing was already placed aboard one of the heavier wagons earlier in the morning. These items were stored in three extremely heavy leather and wood trunks, held together by bands of bronze. She also had her own supply of food items, for her and a single handmaiden to eat. But the very thin handmaiden was doubtful she would get much of the food, for the Princess was always nibbling on something.

Stable hands were busy hooking up a beautiful matching set of black mares to the ornate cart to be used by Princess Lonnia and her handmaiden. Three pairs of draft horses of a grayish color were hooked to the other three wagons and the other smaller cart.

Princess Lonnia's single handmaiden was only 17-years old and though not too excited about leaving the safety and routines of castle life, she was kept busy loading the princess's belongings with great care. To tear a royal garment or misplace a single item of jewelry could bring about a quick and harsh punishment from her foul tempered mistress. She had felt the sting of her whip numerous times and her back, though hidden by her clothing, was heavily scarred from abuse. She also had a bad feeling this trip would bring on even further mistreatment if she wasn't extremely careful.

While the one of the double axel wagons would carry the long lances and the heavier battle axes and maces, each of the horsemen in the company would still carry both a scimitar, shield and either a short sword or dagger. Unlike the longer bladed weapons, their daggers were double-edged and straight. They also wore an armored shirt of chain mail under their tunic; color designated in brown for Silene's regular army and dark blue for Royal Guardsmen. This uniform included a matching colored turban with a shiny bronze metal cap and veil. Upon each horse were draped trappings of either brown or blue, corresponding with the man's unit. For this journey a small arm's length ribbon of royal blue hung from the horse's reins to signify this to be an escort for a member of Silene's royal family. One of the guardsmen would also carry the flag representing the royal family; two horses standing in royal blue color upon a white flag and having the king's golden crown between them, while a mounted soldier would be assigned the duty of carrying the flag representing The Kingdom of Silene.

The horsemen and foot soldiers were also expected to carry with them a day's supply of water and food for them and their horse; a safeguard in the event they became separated from the company in a sandstorm or in battle.

GW, who had no uniform issue, now wore the blue uniform of the Royal Guardsmen; a surprising gift from Captain Rynarr, who also provided a drape of royal blue for Valiant. From a cursed retired warhorse, Valiant had been transformed to a gallant steed in shimmering costume and he even outshined the Black Arabians. GW was extremely humbled by Captain Rynarr's gift and he again thanked him for the gift to Valiant too. Brother Samuel had advised

GW the night before of how the captain had made a gift of Valiant to him for his long bone-weary hours in training. Now GW no longer had to fret about how he could repay Captain Rynarr for Valiant's purchase price.

The scimitar GW carried was a loan from his friend, Mushid and a weapon of fine quality. It had once belonged to Mushid's older brother, a man who had died in a campaign against a band of Moroccan pirates several years earlier. GW heard the story of how Mushid slew the man who had killed his brother and reclaimed the blade.

"Kind of improves the value of the sword when you hear the whole story, doesn't it?" Richard asked GW, who only nodded in return as he ran his hand along the blade and admired the ornate silvery handle.

GW, who was quite moved by Mushid gesture, accepted it with a display of gratitude, by lifting the fine blade to the sky and waving it about as he listened to it swoosh cleanly through the air and watched the sun shine off its blade.

GW was also armed with his US Army issue bayonet, preferring it to a dagger and his KA-BAR knife, which he kept strapped to the outside of his right GI Boot. He wasn't wearing his combat suspenders and thought his boot was a good place for the knife, especially since he was now mounted. But he continued to wear his fatigue pants under the blue tunic. He felt naked when he tried wearing the men's loose fitting plumed pants and received a raised eyebrow for it from Sam, shaking his head in dismay for GW's apparent lack of appreciation for Captain Rynarr's gift of clothing.

"C'mon, Sam, I feel like I'm gonna slide right off the horse," GW pleaded. "This is my first ride out and I don't want to look silly by falling off Valiant every hundred yards."

"By the look of your pants, it is only a matter of time before you're forced to wear the local pants or risk a real-bad rash from riding naked." Sam then walked off for his attention was needed elsewhere.

Mushid had also presented GW with one of his older lances, which was now stored in the second cart with the others. The white lance, which was slightly over 10-foot long and bore a hand guard of simple metallic-design, had seen little use and Mushid prayed for Allah to bless it for his new friend. He was able-to identify it by Mushid's family markings; a small blue horse with an arrow facing upwards between its two raised hooves.

Princess Lonnia, who rested upon a thick pile of furs in the comfort of her cart and fanned by her handmaiden, was still clearly upset when she had learned Captain Rynarr would lead her party. She startled her handmaiden when she actually released an animal-like sounding growl, when she spotted the Captain in the main archway with her father. But then she got control of her temper and she allowed her mind to fill with dark visions of the dear captain lying dead alongside this GW character's lifeless body. Both, she hoped, would be killed in a gruesome manner, as befit the hatred she bore both-of them. But in truth she had never even spoken to this GW person, but he was Brother Samuel's clansman and a kinsmen's blood was still blood she sought to see spelled.

Thinking of the near future, she began to pat a small black pouch of gold she wore on a leather belt about her waist. Next to it, she wore a long Greek-styled dragon-shaped handled dagger of fine silver in a matching sheath. A large ruby was inlaid as the eye of the flying serpent and she had purchased the finely made dagger in Baghdad four years earlier, preferring it to the simpler and less expensive looking Silene dagger.

Her driver, a stuttering middle-aged and gnomish-like gray haired man, was visibly trembling, while he sat perched upon the cart's seat. His thoughts filled with dread when he took the reins from the stable hand for the two horses now hooked up. Clearly shook up by being in such close-proximity with the rumored Black Princess, he had forgotten to thank the young stable hand for his assistance. He wished to Allah he could trade places with the other driver, his younger brother and disabled servant, who had only one eye and was missing his right ear from a stay in the dungeon long ago for failing to pay his taxes.

Once the carts were moved into line with the wagons, Captain Rynarr casually walked through the courtyard and inspected the rest of his company. In line behind the two carts and three wagons were five large sour-faced camels from the king's herd. Each camel carried a large and heavy load, additional supplies needed for the 37-men and two-women company. Captain Rynarr, who knew something about the beasts, noticed that two of the camels were several years older than the other three animals. He disliked the older beasts, often known to be quite contrary when riled and either liked to bite or spit at anyone standing nearby. As a young lad, he had lost a chunk of shoulder to such a beast and had never forgotten it.

He gave the three-young camel handlers a stern look. He'd only recently discovered the youngest herder was just 18-years old, and this was only his second trek across the open desert. Shabbily dressed and lightly armed, Captain Rynarr shook his head in wonder and made a mental note to learn who had assigned these animals to such young herders for this trip. He then checked the animal's heavy loads and then moved on along the line.

Until the company received the order to leave, the herders allowed the camels to remain kneeled and while they waited, they took one final word of advice from their fathers for the journey ahead.

Twenty stout-looking men-at-arms stood about in loose formation, whispering to one another of their various views on being assigned this idiotic detail. A long hot trek across the southern desert in search of herbs for Princess Lonnia was not their idea of a good time. To add to their woes, they would have to keep up with mounted men and wagons. Added to their misfortune, they were being forced to walk behind five foul smelling camels, which would all too often leave behind clumps of manure for them to watch out for.

The men were also unhappy to be on any detail involving Princess Lonnia, knowing her temper to lash out at anyone, at any time and for any reason. There were far too many rumors circulating through castle concerning her being a witch, the mysterious disappearance of her strange shaman and several other deaths unaccounted for. All in all, the foot soldiers, who were basically a suspicious lot, felt a dark cloud surrounded this trip and it left them feeling quite jumpy.

Each foot soldier wore the army's brown tunic and was armed with a seven-foot long spear, a long rectangular-shaped silvery shield, which bore King Ramie's coat of arms for his regular army: crossed scimitars in blue below a Greek styled horse head of the same color. The men also carried a shorter version of the scimitar on one hip and a dagger on their other side for close in fighting. Rather than a leather belt, as worn by the mounted soldiers, the foot soldier wore a thick cloth scarf about his waist and a canvas pack upon his back. Among other items a foot soldier would carry, the man would also have his woven prayer-rug for his five-times a-day, holy prayers to Allah.

Hand-picked by Captain Rynarr for this journey, these men-at-arms, all of good physical shape, wore short beards and were in their mid-to-late 20's. In direct leadership for this small company of men-at-arms was a 27-year old lieutenant, who reported directly to Captain Rynarr and would be also mounted. But at the-moment, he walked along with the captain for a moment, learning from the older officer, as the men waited for the order to move out.

Captain Rynarr dismissed the lieutenant and mounted his horse, so he could visually inspect the ten guardsmen who would provide escort for the princess's cart. He had personally chosen each man for the detail, based on seniority as a knight-in-training, their prior experience and training. He only added GW to the detail upon royal request, though he knew it was King Ramie's wish as a favor to Brother Samuel. Although, Captain Rynarr was extremely interested to see how well this Irishman would conduct himself under battle conditions? That is, if their party was attacked by desert raiders, which was doubtful because of the size of their party.

In response to Mushid's many requests to come along, Captain Rynarr finally relented and consented to allow the huge knight to join him. In truth, with such novices in the company, Captain Rynarr could use the older knight's expertise if they should encounter an enemy force. He also knew Mushid was supervising GW's training and this would allow the two of them more lance time, possibly even a joust or two for entertainment, as the party moved south. This new move GW displayed with his warhorse could prove extremely valuable in a time of war and he wished to see more of it.

Captain Rynarr had heard of this great chivalry the knights from the isle of Britain and of Northern Europe were said to practice, but he suspected in war the gloves came off and it became a no-holds barred winner take all situation, and chivalry was all but forgotten. He also believed that in time, he and his men could very well be facing some of these English knights, especially if the Kingdom of Silene is ordered by the Caliph to send their knights to Jerusalem to combat the invading European armies.

Due to Princess Lonnia's royal presence in the company, protocol directed King Ramie and one of his senior clerics to be present to see them off. Prayers were to be offered to send the company of troops off with Allah's blessings. But both king and cleric were overdue, and it was causing Princess Lonnia to become quite irritated and in her frustration, she used her good foot to kick her driver in the back. She then yelled, "Go to the kitchen, oaf, and bring me some fresh fruit. If you linger, little man, your head will be posted on the main gate as a warning to others who fail to heed me!"

Witnessing the heated exchange, Captain Rynarr rode over to the cart, bowed slightly and asked, "My Princess is there something I may do for you?" This sudden interruption allowed the driver to escape further abuse and scamper off to run the errand.

"No, Captain Rynarr," She said in a low tone. But then her voice grew louder to finish with an exclamation of, "I want to depart...Now!"

Ignoring her outburst, Captain Rynarr glanced away from her to observe one end of the company to the other to keep from replying in heated words. With the release of a sigh, he looked to her and tactfully said in a calm voice, "I apologize, my princess, but we wait upon your father, the King."

Her mood simmering, she only nodded her head once in response and then violently backhanded her handmaiden across the face, "You brought me out here too early, you stupid..." Princess Lonnia's outrageous display was interrupted by the arrival of her father and his cleric; an elderly man whose thick graying beard covered his chest. The cleric's white robe, though dragging across the sand, had woven into it a thin line of royal blue about the arm cuff; this was to signify his station as senior cleric to the king.

Long ago, Silene was home to a prominent Imam, but the man left because of the dragon, its violent curse upon the township and the dreadful lottery. Now only a senior Cleric handled the Muslim religious practices for the Royal Family and supervised the minor clerics under him.

Seeing her father, Princess Lonnia relaxed somewhat and waited quietly for the driver to return with her fruit. She also totally ignored her whimpering servant, while she arranged her furs to ensure her comfort and then rested back against a large pillow.

Captain Rynarr, spotting the king's arrival and thankful to leave the princess's cart, dismounted his horse and knelt on one knee before King Ramie. Behind the Captain, all his horsemen dismounted and dropped to both knees in the warm sand. Then with bowed heads before him, all except GW, who remained standing by Valiant and bowed at the waist, the cleric offered up a prayer for their safe travel.

Normally an infidel would be slain on the spot for not kneeling in the presence of the king or for such a Muslim blessing, but all had learned to understand of how the three infidels had gained the same exemption as Brother Samuel from such things; so, GW was ignored. Though there were some murmurs in the ranks from guardsmen and soldiers alike, who were unhappy with this disrespectful arrangement.

With an aged hand, the cleric waved out toward the company and quietly, he continued to offer up a rather lengthy prayer as the sun continued to bake down upon the men and animals. With the king beginning to release several loud sighs, the cleric's voice grew louder with the passing of minutes and finally grew into almost a shout, when he called out Allah's name. Everyone within hearing range, except for GW and Brother Samuel, began responding in kind until "Allah" could be heard throughout the castle yard and up through the multi-level keep. This unsettled GW, but he only clutched Valiant's reins tighter to keep his horse from rising up on his hindquarters in all the excitement of the moment. "I guess you're not of the Muslim faith either," GW whispered to his mount.

King Ramie slowly walked over to the royal cart to have a few quiet words with his daughter, which allowed the handmaiden time to wash her tearful face off from a water bucket a servant provided. It was Captain Rynarr who had sent the servant over with the bucket, for he seriously detested the way Princess Lonnia treated her young handmaidens.

After his brief meeting, King Ramie walked back over to where Captain Rynarr now stood at the head of his column and spoke with him, "Be safe, my friend, and keep a close eye on my oldest daughter."

He then added in a whisper of a voice, "Even I, for one who loves her, suspects there is something more to this journey then the simple gathering of herbs. Be on your guard."

"Yes, sire," Captain Rynarr said. He then saluted his liege with a quick right fist placed over his heart and then gave the horsemen in his detail the order to mount up. Once mounted himself, he swung his horse around and loudly issued the order for the company to move out.

Looking back over his shoulder at the king, Captain Rynarr observed his liege raise a hand to wave at him and watching this, GW, who rode toward the rear of the last wagon, was moved by this display of emotion between these two men and he reached down to pat Valiant on his neck. "Strange relationship between a king and a captain...but what do I know? I'm out of time, out of place and I'm riding off into this blasted furnace of a desert with a bunch of Muslims."

While looking ahead toward the open gate, Captain Rynarr thought over what King Ramie had said to him about Princess Lonnia and he decided it would be a good idea to keep the princess and her handmaiden away from the drinking water and food supply. Death by poison was not an end he wished for himself or his men. He would have the lieutenant issue what food and water supplies her royal highness would need outside of what she had brought for herself. He would also place one of his Royal Guardsmen on watch over the water and supplies during the night. He didn't want to take any chance of being poisoned while on this supposedly safe herb-gathering trek into the desert.

Knowing the princess and her dark ways, he suspected she would think nothing of poisoning them all and blaming it on her handmaiden, which might be why she brought along such a young girl to assist her.

Once clear of the main gate, Mushid sent two of his most senior guardsmen out as scouts. They would ride out ahead of the company until they reached the open desert plains to the south. The plains offered miles of vast openness, with only a near endless series of rolling desert hills going off in every direction and soon enough, they would need to add flankers and a rear guard.

The rest of the horsemen followed in double-file, with Mushid staying out in front, giving Captain Rynarr the freedom to move about. Mushid set a leisurely pace, which allowed the foot soldiers to keep up, as they trudged through the ankle-deep white sand and muttered their complaints amongst them.

The wagons and carts followed the lines of horsemen, both guardsmen and regular army mounted, with the princess in the front cart. Then the five camels followed in single-file, with their masters on foot. Last of all, were the 20 men-at-arms and their lieutenant, who rode a gray speckled Arabian mare beside them.

Once well away from the castle, Mushid assigned two army horsemen to ride back 100-yards or so for the duty as rearguard.

One guardsman rode off to the far right and an army horseman rode to the far left, as flankers. Captain Rynarr then made a decision to ride at the head of the main column and ordered Mushid, "You will stay with the princess as her personal guard. If anything was to happen to her…"

"I will offer up my life to save her," Mushid replied. Though his face displayed a soured expression of what he thought about this, Mushid then responded with an obedient, "At your orders, Captain." He jerked his horse around and rode back to the royal cart.

Captain Rynarr thought of assigning another man, but with exception of the army lieutenant, Mushid was the only man available who could carry out the task. Any of the other riders were sure to be too afraid of the Black Princess to effectively carry out their responsibilities and this included keeping an eye out for the Princess's misbehavior.

Proceeding south, the company traveled an estimated 10-miles that first day, when Captain Rynarr gave the order to halt and set up camp. When Princess Lonnia noticed what was happening, she immediately sent Mushid forward to summon Captain Rynarr to her.

When Captain Rynarr road up to her cart, Princess Lonnia complained in strongly heated words, "We still have time before the sun sets, Captain, I say we should go on."

Her shimmering veil covered most of her face, but not her piercing eyes, which clearly radiated the contempt she held Captain Rynarr in. This hard look of hers didn't escape him and nor did it intimidate him.

From long experience of having to deal with the princess, he kept his voice even and calming, as he replied, "Princess Lonnia, our men-at-arms are weary of hiking through the soft sand. Ten miles is quite a distance for armored infantry and making camp now will be easier to accomplish in the remaining daylight. This is better than to have overly-tired troops attempting to do so in the dark." Captain Rynarr then patted the side of his mount, "Our horses need food and water, and this is a good place to spend the night. The area is wide open, the low hills are at a distance and with the three-quarter moon tonight this will prevent an enemy from sneaking up on our camp."

"Alright," Princess Lonnia said in reply. She then turned away from the Captain to address her handmaiden, ordering her to refill their water bottles. Their cart carried a 20-gallon water container, which Captain Rynarr would ensure was always full. But from her disdainful attitude, Captain Rynarr understood he was apparently dismissed and he rode off.

Dismounted, he walked his beautiful black horse around the busy encampment for several moments before removing the horse's trappings and securely tying off his mount to a ground rope; a picket line, tied between the wheels of two wagons. One of his trusted novice knights would water the captain's mount, now that his steed was cooled down, for at the moment Captain Rynarr wanted to conduct a thorough inspection of the surrounding hills and he would do this by foot. His backside was sore from the long hours in the saddle and a good stretch of the legs would loosen things up. But first he stopped by one of the wagons and secured a bow and a quiver of arrows, in the event he spotted a bird, or possibly an enemy in the distance. Out here in the vast Sahara Desert, one was not sure what one would find, and all strangers were treated as enemy until proven otherwise.

Cook fires were going before too long, foot soldiers were massaging their sore feet and horsemen were busy watering and feeding their mounts. Two-soldiers, picked by their lieutenant, were given tonight's duty as camp cooks. He divided the other camp chores between the remainder of his men; both mounted and a foot. Though not knighted as yet, the mounted men would soon be shouldering the camp chores equally with the infantry, by order of Captain Rynarr, which brought some delight to the small weary troop of men-at-arms. Only Captain Rynarr, his lieutenant and Mushid would escape this drudgery. Even GW was about to find himself pulling his share of the load, not that he minded much. He'd rather keep busy and was really trying to form some friendships among the men. But as if yet, only Mushid and Captain Rynarr would have anything to do with him.

Princess Lonnia's handmaiden prepared their evening meal from the goods they carried in a wooden trunk, which was lashed to the back of the cart. The wagon drivers and camel herders kept to themselves and shared a single fire to cook on. This also kept the military and civilians separated, which prevented quarrels from breaking out and a lesson Captain Rynarr's father had taught him long ago. Part of the problem was how badly the herdsmen often smelled, causing them to be the blunt of many jokes. As for the wagon and cart drivers, they were simply servants or slaves and not to be considered as equal to the military. Although from long experience, Captain Rynarr had seen many a slave or servant stand against an enemy force, while a knight would ride off and this sickened him. He had ordered the death of several knights who had behaved cowardly and seen to the freeing of many slaves who had behaved bravely upon the field of battle.

Before dusk came upon them and the desert turned cool, Mushid had set up four guard positions 20-feet out from the camp. These would be changed often to keep the men alert. But this would also mean Mushid and the young lieutenant would only get part of a night's sleep, as they maintained a lookout over the guards. There were also two guards pulling duty on the wagons, carts and horses and either Mushid or Captain Rynarr staying close to Princess Lonnia's tent.

If someone was to enter the camp and either harm or kidnap Princess Lonnia, all three senior men could never return home; honor would decree they take their own lives for failing to guard their princess.

GW had seen Princess Lonnia limp around her cart, belittling her driver and shoving her handmaiden about, but he still didn't understand this detail and why Sam warned him about this strange crippled woman in the dark garments. He saw the looks of dread on the driver's face, when he left the cart to join the cook fire, lingering about with the others, until he was summoned back by royal command for failing to do something or that she needed something else. He'd observed the fear in the eyes of the handmaiden and similar expressions on some of the men who wore the guardsmen's royal blue and nearly all the men-at-arms and mounted troops who wore the green tunics. He didn't understand it, but for some reason most of these warriors seemed to fear this princess.

The only monarchy GW knew anything about was the English Queen and if her he knew little. But this princess, she didn't behave in any way he thought a princess should. GW had observed the men offer up a quick word of prayer when they saw her as they quickly turned away in hopes they were not seen. With exception of Captain Rynarr, Mushid, her driver and handmaiden, all the others gave her cart and tent a wide berth unless standing guard.

When GW attempted to speak to Mushid about Princess Lonnia and how the others behaved, the big man responded with a shake of his head and look of disapproval.

Deep lines appeared across his forehead as his bushy eyebrows came together, before he turned his back on GW to walk away from a very confused American. "What'd I say?"

So, GW, who didn't know what else to do, avoided the royal cart and tent and made sure not to have any eye contact with her royal highness. Not that he need worry, Princess Lonnia only left her cart once or twice an evening to stretch out her bad leg or move into her tent. The rest of the time she stayed inside her cart and made life miserable for her elderly driver and young handmaiden.

Princess Lonnia had a plan and she initially put it into play once her father had granted her permission for this trip. She took her second most trusted handmaiden aside and sent her into town under the pretense she was shopping for silk, but she was actually searching out an Egyptian spy; a man who often masqueraded as a traveling rug and wares seller from Western North Africa. The handmaiden, 20-years old and an orphan, was to identify the man by his cover identity; Mousad el-Hamin. She was deliver into his hands a written message. Princess Lonnia knew the handmaiden could not read, so she was not concerned with giving such an important message to her.

His description and the location of his trade booth were provided. The message, written in Egyptian and sealed in a small pouch with five gold coins, identified her and how she was under armed escort into the southern desert region. She also provided the number of men in the company; mounted and infantry, and how she, eldest daughter to King Ramie, was not to be harmed. But she wanted to caravan attacked and all others were to be killed. She promised a significant payment to the spy and a small fortune to the brigands who would carry out the attack. But she would only have on her half of the gold, hidden in a small chest, and the remainder of the promised loot would not be paid until after she was safely returned to Silene. She was smart enough to know she risked being held for ransom but believed her father would plead to the Great Caliph for the asking price and he would pay it. Such was actually a standard practice among royal families and while waiting for ransom the prisoner was usually treated quite well. But she didn't want to be away from the castle for all the time a ransoming might take up. No, this way, she would get what she wanted with the death of Captain Rynarr and this GW fellow and return to her future kingdom in time to enact the second phase of her diabolical plan.

The spy would leave Silene immediately and ride southeast until he contacted with one of the Egyptian raiding parties known to be operating in Libya. Though thought by most to be only brigands working the desert, Princess Lonnia had known for some time these raiders were in fact Egyptian soldiers. This was a way for the Egyptian troops to gain battlefield experience and in doing so they tested Libya's resolve in defending their eastern border. The raiders were also able to map trade routes to bring an army across the desert, knowing where the water holes were, in the event war did break out. With so many major sandstorms, known routes could be buried under 20-feet of sand within a couple of days and large pockets of quicksand could be awaiting an unwary traveler. Legends had told of whole armies vanishing in the desert and a good commander wanted to be sure where he was sending his men to fight. The massive Sahara was never to be taken for granted.

Princess Lonnia had known about the spy for some time, a light skinned older man who could pass for a Berber or a Greek, though in fact his heritage was Roman. He had done various tasks in the past for the dead shaman, but this would be her first contact with him. But she knew he worked for gold and asked very few questions.

Princess Lonnia also ordered the spy to kill her handmaiden in order-to protect his identity, for she saw her loyal servant as simply a tool in her war against her father, Captain Rynarr and Brother Samuel. If her plan succeeded, the good captain and this GW person would be killed outright in the attack or they would be put to death by her father for allowing the king's daughter to be seized by brigands. There was also the chance they would commit ritual suicide in shame, but in any case, the thought of them dead brought a smile of sheer wickedness to her face as she made her plans.

One of her first concerns was if the loyal, but not too smart handmaiden, found the spy? Princess Lonnia wouldn't know for sure if she reached the spy and he in fact did kill the girl and locate the brigands she needed. For all she knew, the stupid girl could wander off and be attacked by some of her father's barbaric soldiers and used as they saw fit. Or the girl might have taken this chance to escape the Black Princess's torturous ways and steal the bit of gold she carried.

Princess Lonnia's other concern was her second sister, she didn't know the whereabouts of Princess Lannia and this could end her plans all too quickly if a large force of fierce Royal Guardsmen rode in like avenging angels to break up the attack. But her concerns about her handmaiden were proven groundless. She found the spy, who though wary of the girl, read the princess's note in the back of his booth and after some thought, pocketed the initial payment of five gold pieces. He then quickly grabbed the girl by the arms, silenced her with a hand over her mouth and killed her with a quick snapping of her neck. He, with the help of two loyal Sudanese slaves, rolled her up in a used Moroccan rug and draped her over the back of a camel. The girl's body was then taken out into the desert and she, still in a woven rug of dark blue hues and many lines of red thread, was buried in a shallow hole of sand.

The spy, who had his own sources inside the castle through bribes, sent a verbal message to one such source, who delivered a sealed message, also written in Egyptian, to one of Princess Lonnia's handmaidens. In less than 24-hours, Princess Lonnia had her answer in her hands and it cost the spy only one silver coin to a former Egyptian slave, who now worked in the castle kitchen. The note advised the princess of how an attempt would be made to contact one of the raiding bands operating to the far south, but there was no guarantee he could find him. She would have to take a chance and hope the plan could be carried out. She knew it was only a chance, but she saw no other way to kill this clansman of Brother Samuel and now she had Captain Rynarr to eliminate and she was hopeful.

Once breakfast and morning prayers were accomplished, the Company slowly moved out and within an hour found themselves under an unmerciful blazing sun. They trudged along through ankle deep sand, as they crossed the crests of one dune after another to avoid the really deep sand pits in between. They had left the hard-packed plains and would have several miles to go before they could escape these tiresome sand dunes.

The Dark Princess had once before journeyed south, under a much larger escort until she came upon a large oasis and here she had found the ruins of an ancient civilization and plants she had never seen before. It was the ruse of finding this location again that she had used with her father. Captain Rynarr had been along on this lengthy journey and this was one of the reasons why he had insisted on the extra supplies and the addition of the foot soldiers.

GW' backside cried out in pain and he made the decision to dismount and walk Valiant up a long stretch of sand dune, which surprised Captain Rynarr, who had not given that order.

Seeing him afoot and not waiting for word from Captain Rynarr, Mushid rode forward to where GW was and asked him why he walking beside his horse? Though GW was improving with his Libyan language and understood the question, he wasn't sure if he could word the answer right. So, he pointed to his behind, massaged his right-side butt cheek twice and added an expression of pain to get his point across. In response, Mushid laughed out loud and rode back to advise Captain Rynarr of GW reason to dismount. GW didn't have to turn around to hear Captain Rynarr's laughter, Yeah, the jokes on me, but my butt really hurts! And I've got at least 14-days of this to look forward too. GW looked to the sky and whispered, "God, what'd I do to deserve this? I'd give anything for a Honda dirt bike right now." He then looked in Valiant's black glossy eyes, "No offense, boy, but I am not a cowboy yet."

Three hours later, the company made camp overlooking a massive stretch of white plain and GW was relieved they were leaving the loose sand behind. Then he learned it was now his turn to act as camp cook. "Well, so much for the hot shower and 40-winks."

GW surprised the man he was assigned to work with when he made up a runny sauce from spices, added water and crushed fruit to provide the men a spicy barbecue sauce for a batch of wild birds the men had shot down earlier in the day. Outside of Rynarr and Mushid, who had traveled to Tripoli and experienced all sorts of cooking, no one else could remember having such a tasty meal and several of the men slapped GW on the back in appreciation.

GW had grown weary of mutton and was beginning to wonder how camel might taste. "They look like large dear…well, sort of. Maybe they taste like venison…or most likely horse!"

Captain Rynarr insisted GW provide the ingredients of his strange sauce to the castle kitchen staff. Mushid also hoped the sauce would help make the dried out roasted mutton and chicken more appetizing as the barbecue sauce brought on a tangy sweetness to the meat and he liked it. GW didn't bother to mention that if the cooks and cook staff bothered to wash their hands the food would taste a lot better. Wonder if I could find the stuff to make Mayo?

Princess Lonnia, who wasn't known to offer up any form of praise and not even knowing GW was even the cook, had sent her handmaiden back to the fire twice for the well-seasoned bird meat. When she had learned there was wild bird to consume, she had advised Mushid of her desire for some.

"Yes, my Princess. It will be done." Mushid walked away, biting his lip in contempt. He knew she carried her own food and there were additional supplies for her in the other wagon as needed. Now she was taking food from the hungry men who served her, but he also knew this was her right as a member of the royal family and he could not question her.

But whenever, the handmaiden came within reach of the cook fire, Captain Rynarr kept the girl under close eye to ensure she had not added anything to the men's food.

## THE RAID

After six long days of hard travel, the tiresome journey, which was leading far deeper into the Sahara than Captain Rynarr was first told, was becoming a point of contention among the foot soldiers. Even Princess Lonnia was growing quite grumpy. She had become even worse with her foul mouthing and physically abusive with her driver and servant. Her daily long confinement in the cart's uncomfortable, and small living space had tested her limited patience and she was nearing the point of ordering Captain Rynarr to turn around and return to Silene. The cart was exceedingly hot and there was little if no air circulation under the heavy tarp. She could either suffocate inside the cart or pull the tarp down and risk shriveling under the grueling sun.

Mushid, who rode close to the cart for the princess's protection, heard the physical abuse the girl suffered and could do nothing. He was forced by duty to ignore it and this weighed heavily upon his conscious. He truly loved his king, but this Black Princess made him wonder how Allah would allow such a woman to live. He had seen the shame his king suffered at her expense and saw how she lashed out against his beloved captain and Brother Samuel with her temper and cutting words. He knew if it be any other woman, she would have suffered a terrible fate long before this.

Restless and angry, Princess Lonnia had expected an attack in the evening of the third day, but none came. As the fourth day past by she wondered if the spy had become lost in the desert before locating the Egyptian raiders? Unsure, she had erupted into a fit of temper and verbally lashed out at everyone within ear shot. She followed this up by assaulting her handmaiden again; kicking her and throwing her bodily out of the moving cart.

The handmaiden, shaken from the attack and whimpering from her injuries, showed the bruises from earlier assaults about her face and body she limped behind the cart wheel. The driver stopped the cart and the girl dashed out to flee across the sand and seek protection aboard the nearest wagon. She hid behind the driver and begged the timid man to safeguard her.

The man, who was troubled by her cries and the tears that poured from her blackened eyes, could only stare back at the girl and with a gentle smile. He began to pet her hair in an attempt to comfort her, while he sat there with the leather reins of his wagon grasped loosely in one hand and brought the caravan to an abrupt halt. He was then caught unaware when three men-at-arms came up and violently dragged the screaming girl out of the cart.

Only the sudden intervention and diplomatic words of Captain Rynarr prevented the frightened handmaiden from being whipped by Princess Lonnia's order. He had reminded the princess how this handmaiden was her only servant and how she would probably never survive 30-lashes, or worse. "You'll be unattended until our return, my Princess and only the driver to speak with as of your needs as we travel."

Princess Lonnia glared at Captain Rynarr with a look of ice and then looked upon her frightened driver with utter contempt in her eyes, before she sighed deeply and relented, "You speak with wisdom, Captain Rynarr." She gestured to the servant girl with a wave of her hand and then said to Rynarr, "For now I will spare this vile worm of impudence and we will move on."

It took several moments, but Captain Rynarr was finally able to talk the handmaiden into returning to the cart, where she promptly begged the princess's forgiveness and nervously prepared a small platter of sliced fruit for her mistress in hopes of calming her.

Captain Rynarr could only wonder how much longer this young girl would live, knowing it was only a matter of time before Princess Lonnia had her punished with the whip or even killed by the sword to satisfy her bouts of anger. He hoped they wouldn't have to travel much longer before reaching their destination and Princess Lonnia could gather her precious herbs.

Remembering his last journey out this way, he thought they would've reached the oasis by now, but the great Sahara had a mystery about it and many locations known only a year before could be buried beneath a mountain of sand now. The winds had uncovered many ruins from past civilizations, only to cover them again with a single storm. Many a known watering hole had disappeared, and he knew they only carried enough water for 16-days of desert travel. So, out of safety concerns for his men and Princess Lonnia, he would allow the caravan to go for two-more days and would then order a return to Silene even if the Princess objected. Her safety and the concern of her father, far outweighed her orders or temper tantrums.

Moments after sunrise of the seventh day, a large force of mounted Egyptian raiders suddenly appeared to the southeast, the bright glare of the new morning sun hiding their approach. Had they been an hour earlier or even attacking under a moonlit night, they would've caught the encampment by surprise. But with the gradual rising of the sun and still at some distance away, an alert soldier on guard duty saw their scouts silhouetted before the rising sun and shouted out the first of many warning cries.

Captain Rynarr had stopped his company at the scene of some extremely old ruins, mostly crumbled to the ground now, but a pillar or two still stood to identify them of a Grecian style. Here an old well, surrounded by stones carried over from the ruins, had served the people of Libya for hundreds of years, but was now dry. There were several summers the well was found to be dry and the bones of those unlucky travelers could still be seen spread about. Other times, water was brought up and many a caravan had owed their lives to this finicky well. For Captain Rynarr and his people, they had found the bottom of the well to be only dry sand.

It was at these ruins where Captain Rynarr and his small company of men would have to fight off a large force of mounted men to protect their princess. Captain Rynarr had never known of such a large raiding party to be operating in the southern Sahara, otherwise he would have brought additional men along. Normally, Egyptian raiders numbered less than two-dozen mounted men, so there were fewer to spread the spoils about. But the force facing him now was three-times that or more.

Awakened by the alarm, Princess Lonnia rose from her sleeping furs and dug around in the cart, as she sought out her small gold chest. Finding it, she quickly felt for the gold pieces, money she hoped would satisfy the raiders, or if kidnapped for ransom, or to use in trade for not being raped by a leader's slovenly underlings. As for her contemptible handmaiden, she could care less what happened to her and even thought to use her as part of the price to protect herself.

Having the weight of the gold in her hand and her face veiled, she glanced outside her covered cart to watch, a smile on her face, as her men prepared for the oncoming attack. She still couldn't see the enemy force yet, but from off in the distance she could hear their strange sounding battle yells and knew by the sound, it could only be coming from a great force of men. She then pulled her head back inside and gazed upon her sleeping servant girl, with an evil smile upon her face as she thought about what might happen to her disloyal servant. She was glad now that Captain Rynarr had interfered, knowing this pitiful girl would receive far much more pain than what her soldiers would've inflicted.

The girl was suddenly awakened by the noise outside, wiped sleep away from her opening eyes, cringing from her bruised cheeks and was startled to see her princess glaring down upon her. The handmaiden was alarmed, even more so when Princess Lonnia said, "You need not worry, child. I will take care of you." Princess Lonnia said this in a calming tone and petted the girl's head in a motherly fashion. Then suddenly, she changed her mind about using the girl as a token gift to these Egyptians and drove her ceremonial dagger into the young girl's chest with all her strength.

There was no cry, it was too sudden and Princess Lonnia kept her other hand over the girl's mouth. Then after ensuring the girl was dead, Princess Lonnia wiped her dagger off on the inside of the girl's skirt. She then whispered a prayer to some dark Egyptian deity and once finished, she thought nothing more of the girl after covering her over with a pile of dirty clothing.

The driver was off with the horses and camels, so he didn't witness any of this and now with the alarm given. Drivers and herders would stay with the animals to protect them from being driven off. Armed with only their staffs, short swords and daggers, they would do their duty unto death and the courageous young herders, if not a bit too boastful to cover their childish fears, hoped they could get a few licks in before it was all over.

GW was awakened early and as usual with a backache. He never enjoyed sleeping on the ground and waking up with sand in his blanket and inside his tunic and pants, even his nose, only seemed to worsen the whole camping experience. He was in the midst of saddling Valiant when he heard the first shout of alarm and the many echoes to follow, as word quickly spread through the small encampment. One very excited soldier, who stood nearby for guarding over the staked-out warhorses, suddenly ran up to GW and shouted out the call to arms in his right ear, while excitedly pointing to the southeast.

Wincing from a jab of pain caused by the loud shout, GW turned to where the man pointed and spotted a great line of horsemen charging across the desert, riding through heat waves made visible from the sunrise. Not sensing the true danger yet, he thought the horsemen looked magnificent in their mounted charge over the low sand dunes.

The bright morning sun reflected off their bronze armor and swords they swung about over their heads to intimidate the enemy, which only added to the spectacular effect unveiling before him. GW could only stand there dumbfounded and watch. Here he was, a city boy of the 20th century, actually standing here deep within the Sahara Desert and observing a 12th century cavalry charge. This is unbelievable! Almost like that Cleopatra film, but I'm really, here for the real thing.

Fascinated, he could now see how each rider carried an oval-shaped bronze shield in their right or left hand, and either a short sword with a wide blade or a lengthy spear in the other hand. They also wore a spike-like headdress, which reminded him of the headpieces he'd seen in such movies as The Crusades. Though not taking the time to make an actual count, GW estimated a minimum of 100-raiders were attacking, and for a brief moment, he stood there wondering if they might have chariots like the ones he saw in the movie Ben-Hur.

Unable to move, he stared in awe at the raiders with child-like admiration, but the spell was abruptly broken when Valiant, the more experienced of the two, turned and nipped his rider on the hip, whinnied and paced the sand excitedly with his right forward hoof.

GW yelped in pain and glared back at Valiant in anger, but then realized where and who he was and whispered a grateful, "Thanks, buddy. Forgot where I was for a moment."

Once hurriedly finished with saddling Valiant and now mounted, GW looked to the raiders and even in his limited knowledge of 12th century warfare, saw there was no bowman among them. He immediately shouted this fact out to Captain Rynarr, who was also mounted, but the captain only had time to nod his head in response. They both knew the enemy's absence of bows would be to Silene's advantage.

GW glared at the oncoming horsemen and sincerely wished he had an 81mm mortar on hand, or at least an M-60 machine gun to dwindle down the odds a bit. He then turned and made a fast dash for the wagon carrying his war lance. There the wagon's three drivers were hastily handing out weapons to the mounted troops and men-at-arms. Once that was done, the wagon drivers prepared other weapons, and only afterward would they run to where their draft horses and camels were to offer up some form of defense.

Captain Rynarr issued orders to the company in loud, but strangely calm and authoritative voice, while the lieutenant's voice was excited and he sounded a bit befuddled. But the men-at-arms knew their job well and they responded to the emergency with well-practiced order.

GW heard his name called out and with lance and shield in hand, he pulled on Valiant's reins to fall into formation with the other horsemen. The weight of the lance felt strangely light in his hand, his gauntlets felt like he'd worn them forever and he knew it was due to his excitement and the adrenalin surging through his veins.

Meanwhile, the young lieutenant, with scimitar waving, moved about to place his men-at-arms into position immediately in front of Princess Lonnia's cart. Bows had been issued and two of the wagon drivers quickly stuck three arrows in the sand in front of each man. Once this was done, the remaining arrows were placed in the sand in a lengthy row behind the line of bowmen. They would fire the first three arrows on command and then fall back behind the row of arrows to fire at will. GW saw that they were the mortars of today and knew he wouldn't want to fall victim to one of those lethal looking arrows. The points were 4-inches long, made of bronze and were jagged so they couldn't be pulled out easily.

Captain Rynarr shouted for the lieutenant to release the first arrows, in response, the young officer, seeing his men were ready, ordered the men to let go with the first volley.

As GW watched nervously, the Egyptians drew ever closer, and their numbers and ferocity grew far more frightening with each second. The order was given, and the first flight of arrows was launched into the heavens. Captain Rynarr ordered the second volley away and GW watched with astonishment as the men-at-arms remained calm and fired off their second arrows, which rose up in pursuit of the first flight of arrows. Ever higher they rose into the sun and then, they began their descent from the clear blue sky like diving birds hungry for prey.

Unable to escape death from above, several Egyptian horsemen were struck down by the first flight of arrows. Horse or rider, or both, tumbled across the sand. Then a third volley was fired, and the men stepped back behind the row of standing arrows and rearmed themselves. Once the arrows were used up or if they ran out of time, the men would drop their bows and pick up spears to slay the enemy with. When the battle became close combat, the men-at-arms would then arm themselves with scimitars, short swords and daggers.

The second volley of slender wooden rods pierced the enemy's ranks and stopped several more of the horsemen with mortal or disabling wounds. Three of the horses stumbled and threw their riders to the desert floor, where two of the men were crushed beneath the hooves of other horses. Several of the horses were spinning about with arrow shafts sticking out of their backsides or necks, and they refused to obey the commands of their riders. One horse stopped short, an arrow in its neck, throwing its rider right over its head and sent tumbling across the sand. Only to stand-up, dizzy and be struck down by an arrow.

The third volley over shot most of the Egyptian riders and only two men tumbled from their mounts with arrows in them and the one man on foot. One would die there in the sand, while the others, only lightly wounded, rose to press in on foot. One of the horses in the lead was killed immediately, falling to its side and crushing the left leg of its rider, who lay pinned beneath his dead mount.

Further arrows were fired, toppling several more of the enemy, but then it was time for close combat and the bows were quickly dropped and spears, and shields lifted to defend their princess. They may fear her and dislike her, but she was of the royal family and they were sworn to protect her with their lives.

Twenty soldiers, each man sweating from nerves and the morning heat, began to mutter their prayers to Allah, as they surrounded the royal cart in a tight circle. But what they didn't know was how this traitorous woman secretly wanted the Egyptians to kill every one of them, especially Captain Rynarr and this infidel known under a strange sounding name of GW. Since the name could not be interpreted in Libyan or Arabic, most of the people in the castle pronounced it as Ge-e-e Du-u-bah-h Uo-o-o. It took some doing, but GW had finally gotten those close to him to pronounce it correctly, though they were confused when he said his name had no meaning. In the Muslim world, all names had a meaning and these three strangers confounded them.

Seven of the men-at-arms formed a line with their lieutenant, who was dismounted, to break the point of the charge before the horsemen could reach the cart. For this they would use their long spears to unseat the rider.

An experienced warrior, Mushid actually-felt invigorated with the call to battle. Mounted, he took up his lance, nervously handed to him by a frantic wagon driver and raised the point straight up to allow the morning breeze to catch hold of the Royal Guardsmen's blue banner and wave it proudly. An exact copy to the artwork on the guardsmen's shield, it bore the king's coat-of-arms and was attached to the lance directly below the eight-inch metal point of the lance.

Once all the weapons were issued and arrows made ready, Mushid then ordered the drivers to standby with the camel herders, "If we fall before those sand fleas, you must protect the princess with your lives!" He then quickly took up position beside the princess's cart, to block an enemy lance from reaching his royal mistress.

Captain Rynarr, looking majestic in his royal blue splendor and ready for combat in all his finery, shouted out his orders to the mounted troops. He then accompanied them and now used only rapid hand gestures because it was too hard to hear anything now with the enemy's shouts so close. As planned, he would take the five-brown tunic horsemen to the far right of the encampment, while the Royal Guardsmen would move out to the far left. Then upon his signal, they would close on the enemy's charge in what they termed as a scorpion move. The men-at-arms would be the deadly tail of the scorpion, using their spears to impale either rider or horse, while the horsemen would be the pincers. Sadly, he knew in this instance there wasn't enough men for the pincer move to perform as planned against such a large enemy force, but Captain Rynarr had no choice but to carry out the move with what he had.

Due to the accuracy of the bowman, the Egyptian raiders were reduced by 11-killed and 12-wounded. Several horses lay wounded in the sand with arrow shafts sticking out of their necks or backsides and already the desert vultures were circling the scene. Another three horses stood about the bodies of their fallen masters, one with an arrow sticking out of its rear flank and the pinned man now lay motionless.

GW spotted several rider-less warhorses continuing with the charge, as they were trained, but they were no longer much of a threat unless a soldier wasn't quick enough to avoid the horse and was trampled on. Their trappings flopped about as they rushed forward, their eyes wide with fear for they no longer felt the weight of their master. Still, their mere presence added to the intimidating effect of the charging raiders.

As he awaited his next order, GW struggled with the events transpiring around him; only a month ago he was dropped by helicopter into the jungle, armed with a deadly automatic weapon to fight in a major battle against the North Vietnamese Army. Now he was carrying a wooden lance, mounted upon a great warhorse and facing a 12th century enemy in the Sahara Desert. Surprising himself, his face an expression of worry, he looked to the heavens and prayed, "I'm having a real hard time keeping a grip on this, God and could use a little help here."

GW then glanced up the length of his lance and felt the weight of his shield bare down on him, knowing it to be only one-step above a training shield and would never stop a spear point head-on. He felt so inadequate for the battle ahead. But he carried it high as Mushid had taught him and prayed to God he could help stop this Egyptian horde.

He had never sworn an oath to protect this princess, but he had his own life to consider and the life of his new friends, and he tightened his grasp about his lance and let out a very deep sigh and shrugged his shoulders as Valiant stepped out for war.

By GW's estimation the raiders were still some 100-yards out or less but were rapidly closing the distance and they looked really fierce in their wild splendor. Their horses were of a mixed lot in color and size, but every one of them was coming on like a raging locomotive and this again caused GW to wonder if he was truly up to this? He gazed down upon his bayonet, reassured this wasn't a dream. He really was a man from the 20th century, stuck here in the 12 Century and simply not some 12th century knight who was going crazy. Or am I?

Captain Rynarr had his lance held high and there was a strange gleam to his dark brown eyes, as he issued the order to move forward. Court politics baffled him, the games they played to compliment the king and this intrigue they talked about only angered him. But combat, one man pitted against another, this he understood all too well and found out a long time ago he thrived for battle and he hated raiders.

These horsemen who had no allegiance to any country, had entered his kingdom to steal, rape and kill, and for this they would die. Their numbers didn't cause him to fear, for he had faced greater numbers in the past. No, but what did bother him was to discover, from their formations and weaponry, they were in fact Egyptian soldiers disguised as raiders. He had suspected something from the size of the enemy but watching them charge he recognized similar tactics from prior encounters with the Egyptians. With the lack of experience of the men riding beside him, he knew this could prove fatal. Yet, he also knew after this battle the survivors would know the sounds of combat, the face of death in the men they killed and most likely the shedding of their own blood from the wounds they received. The survivors would also know what courage truly was and be proud of their actions this day.

Yes, battle was indeed something he could understand, that and the feeling of a good scimitar in his hand and a brave foe facing him. He relished in the surging of his blood, the heightened sense of real life, as his heart raced to the point of exploding and he waited for that one particular-moment when all time stood perfectly still; foe-versus foe a second before first contact, as it always did in true combat.

Valiant rode well across the hard-packed sand and GW sensed his gallant warhorse felt the same rush of excitement, as they moved into position. The more experienced of the two, GW hoped Valiant would keep GW from fleeing in the face of the enemy, which he was contemplating at this very moment. His hands were trembling, sweat poured over his face in streams and the shield strap from his hands felt clammy. Under his shirt of mail, his chest was already drenched and wasn't able to even feel his legs anymore. But he continued to look forward, facing into the enemy, who were now directly under the rising sun. All he could see were their outlines, but he could sure hear their shouts and shrieks.

This was the effect the Egyptians planned for, to have the blazing brightness of the desert sun behind them to blind the Libyans, and it was working to some degree. But Captain Rynarr, an experienced desert fighter, knew their intent and this was why he had his two forces ride out wide in the pincer movement before closing in on the enemy, allowing them to avoid looking directly into the sun when they turned to face the charging enemy's lances. GW thoughts suddenly jumped to that orange tree, the one he was thrown into as he felt each of Valiant's hooves strike the sand. He felt his legs again, as the vibrations rise up through Valiant's muscles and they moved forward at a cantor. Each horseman held his lance pointed to the sky and GW gripped his gloved hand tightly around the lance's leather-bound hand piece. His other hand was clenched in a fist, the double-leather straps of the shield were held in place by his damp palm and forearm, while his scimitar blade, without a sheath and held only by his belt, bounced off his left leg with Valiant's stride.

When they came to an abrupt halt along a sandy knoll, GW saw Captain Rynarr and his five-horsemen move into position across the desert floor. They were at least 100-yards or more apart and this move of Captain Rynarr's caused the raiders to separate into three elements to engage the Libyans. The larger group would attack the center, to do battle with the men-at-arms, while the remaining two groups would attack Captain Rynarr's force and the Royal Guardsmen.

Though he knew they were facing at least 3 to1 odds, GW never heard the order to charge. Suddenly, Valiant moved out in a rapidly increasing charge beside the other beautiful Black Arabians. The horses shined with sweat, their eyes wide with expectation and their heads lunging forward to increase speed. Startled by Valiant's lunge, all GW could do was lock his legs tightly and grip the reins to hold on.

Captain Rynarr was in the lead of his five-man force, his lance now lowered to impale his target. Each of his men had committed themselves, lowering their lances and rushing forward to strike the enemy line. There would be no cowards today upon this desert battlefield and it made Captain Rynarr proud.

For GW things seemed to be moving in slow motion, the desert around him had suddenly become a world of unreality, surreal and almost blurred in movement. He could feel his heart race; about to launch out of his chest and he felt droplets of sweat slide down his cheeks from behind this stupid veil they insisted he wear. He also felt Valiant's every movement, every breath, as the gallant steed charged forward like a beast possessed. Yet, all about him he sensed a strange sphere of unworldly silence closing in on him and suddenly, he couldn't breathe and thought he was about to drop his lance.

But then, right when he felt he was about to pass out, something took hold of him, right arm grew hot and surged with adrenalin. His lance became as light as a feather and the shield arm relaxed, as he lifted it high to cover his chest and face.

He couldn't explain it later to his friends, but GW suddenly felt like he could lick a hundred men and not having much experience in actual jousting, he knew to now lower his lance into place like an experienced knight and prepared to impale an onrushing Egyptian. They came together like two steam locomotives, the sound of GW and the Egyptian slamming shields, armor against armor, was astounding. Their two enraged warhorses collided with one another and a scream escaped a dying man's lips as GW's lance pierced the chest of the opposing rider.

GW didn't stop to celebrate his victory. He didn't have time. The dying rider slid from his horse, a piece of lance protruding from his body and GW swung Valiant around as he had so many times in training to give him time to pull his scimitar from his belt. Then with an explosive swing, he sliced right through the man's shield and knocked a second man from his mount.

Off to GW's left, Captain Rynarr had rushed in to impale his opponent with his lance and was using a bloodied battleaxe to fight off two raiders. Seeing how his captain was in trouble, GW fought his way through the Egyptians and rode to his captain's side. He slammed Valiant into one Egyptian, knocking both horse and rider to the ground. He then used his scimitar to wound another man with a mighty slash of his blade. This allowed Captain Rynarr to slay the other one with a downward blow of his axe.

While GW was locked in personal combat with a single mounted Egyptian, sword against sword, Captain Rynarr quickly checked the number of his surviving troops and sadly realized he had lost three of his riders with his initial charge when they broke through the raider's force. He was now facing eleven of the enemy with only two young riders and this inexperienced GW. As to how GW got all the way across the field of battle to help him, Captain Rynarr would ask later. For now, he had a battle to wage and win to protect his princess.

GW's force of guardsmen was down by one man and battling a force of 13-mounted men. But not a man to dwell on superior numbers, Captain Rynarr let out a warrior's yell to praise Allah and waded in with a swinging axe. The other two riders followed to cover his back and gave a good account of themselves, as the Egyptian raiders began to fall back from under their courageous attack. While the mounted units fought on, the raider's main force rushed the encampment and nearly overwhelmed the defenders. But the men-at-arms stood ready to repel them with long spears braced in the sand, held down by the weight of the men and their lethal points facing the enemy. This spear point was the first weapon the raiders fell upon. Horses were impaled, knocking the men-at-arms down and crushing one man beneath another rider's wounded animal. Several of the raiders fell upon the spear points, but then it was hand-to-hand, and it looked as if Silene's brave soldiers were fighting a futile action against an overwhelming force.

Seeing the fight going badly, the three young herdsmen left their animals to the driver's care and ran to the soldier's aide. Picking up better weapons from the various scattered bodies, the herdsmen gave a good account of themselves. One of the herders, a young boy of 21-years old, grabbed up a bow and several arrows and then climbed onto the seat of the supply wagon. From there he delivered a stunning blow against the enemy force, killing three men, before he was struck down by an Egyptian spear.

Watching all this from her cart, the Princess was enraged to see how well her company was doing against the larger enemy force. Her faced flushed with anger, she began cursing her men and spouting off prayers to the Egyptian gods she followed in hopes they would suddenly appear to slay these men of Silene. But the battle continued as these men-at-arms fought so bravely and died without a whimper to protect their evil and unworthy princess.

It wasn't long before Captain Rynarr and his blue tunic horsemen and one surviving mounted soldier joined in the battle around the wagons carts. The clash of steel and cries and shouts of men could be heard across the desert, as Libyan and Egyptian fought for their lives and blood seeped into a dry desert.

Mushid impaled one Egyptian, driving his lance through the man's shield and sending him toppling off his horse. He then whipped out his scimitar and with a boisterous yell, began slashing out at the enemy. Some of the enemy backed away, afraid to enter combat with this fiendish lunatic with a sword.

The older herdsman boy, hiding under the second supply wagon, waited for the right moment and sprang up to drive his recently acquired sword into the left thigh of a mounted Egyptian. As the man screamed out in pain, Mushid moved in to finish the job with a slashing movement across the man's throat. Saluting the herdsman boy, Mushid returned to the battle, while the boy jumped on the back of an Egyptian rider and drove his dagger deep into the man's side. He then shoved the man off the horse and used it to collide with another enemy horseman.

Without a command, Valiant rose up on his back legs and kicked out with his front hooves to strike a startled Egyptian, sending him tumbling off his horse. This move of Valiant also nearly dropped GW onto his backside, but he was able-to hold on with a handful of Valiant's mane. "Nice move, boy, but next time give me some warning!"

Gleaming swords and heavy battle axes clashed with metal tipped lances and spears, many a dented shield was strewn about the plain, and dozens of both horse and men lay dead, or wounded from both sides. But before the sun reached mid-morning height in the sky, the fight was finally over.

Then followed a thankless task, the severely wounded of both sides were put out of their misery by the victors, for it was better to die quickly then to suffer a slow death in this desert heat.

Prisoners were roped together by hand and waist. The lesser wounded men from both sides, the ones who couldn't ride, were placed in the second wagon. They were shoved together like sardines in a can because Princess Lonnia wouldn't allow a single one in her second cart. Horses carrying the Egyptians survivors who could ride were without reins and roped together in line with the camels. Two soldiers were assigned to guard the prisoners in the wagon, forced to walk behind their wagon and listen to their moans. Guardsmen accompanied the mounted prisoners, who were warned they'd be put to death if they caused any problems. GW couldn't remember much about the battle or the weird silence that seemed to separate him from reality. It was gone now, and he couldn't remember when his hearing had returned. Nor could he remember how many men he had either wounded or killed, or even recall the faces of the enemy. He knew that some had cried out when they fell before him and his warhorse, Valiant, but it was all as if a dream... or a nightmare.

Though he wasn't wounded, his arms felt as if he'd been carrying one hundred-pound weights in each hand and he was surprised to see the hand-held side of his broken lance lie on the field of valor. But he still maintained a tight grasp on his bloodstained scimitar and his well-dented shield, a display he had taken many blows, now hung loosely from a leather strap tied to his saddle.

Valiant bore several light wounds, but from the snorts coming out of his nose and the steady gaze of his dark eyes, GW knew Valiant was okay and probably ready for another fight. But GW was bone tired and he seemed to recall a similar weariness from when he and his two friends ran from the North Vietnamese. Yet, staying in saddle, Valiant carried him about the field, while the surviving six men-at-arms secured the enemy's weapons and wearily carried them back to the third wagon. With the wounded filling the second wagon, they tied some of the weapons to the sides and discarded the damaged ones.

There wasn't much talking in the wagon, as both raider and Libyan glared at one another with hatred. One was going back to Silene as a prisoner and the other a blooded veteran. But both hoped they would survive the long trek back. The time it took to return to Silene, the heat and lack of any medical help would cause several of these men to perish and be buried along the way.

The drivers, who stayed with the camels and carthorses, were glad to be alive and back with their carts. Even the driver, who drove Princess Lonnia's cart, was relieved to be hitching up his horses again. But when summoned by the princess, his relief returned to one of grief.

"Do something with this," Princess Lonnia ordered. She startled the driver when she removed a silken covering and exposed the body of her dead handmaiden.

Though the driver knew the princess had murdered the girl and unable to say anything, he carefully pulled the young girl's body out of the cart and with one of the other drivers to help, they carried her to where the other bodies were piled.

Mushid, observing the young girl's body and seeing the uncomfortable look on the driver's face, dismounted to examine the body. He quickly found the killing wound to the girl's chest and was certain it wasn't caused by a raider's sword for the wound was too small. Yet, he too knew nothing could be done since the battle was fought around the princess's cart. But Mushid did tell Captain Rynarr of the killing and what he suspected.

"We will bury all of them, the girl too," Captain Rynarr ordered. His eyes were cold as he looked back over at the royal cart, but he remembered his promise to the king and reminded Mushid of his duty to King Ramie.

"Yes, Sir," Mushid replied. But he looked away, so his captain would not see his expression of anger.

"She is the princess, Mushid, and we have no evidence to bring to the king. You and I know what happened and someday Allah will judge her," Captain Rynarr said.

"Yes, Sir," Mushid repeated.

"We bury our dead and then make camp off to the north, so we will no longer have to see the blood that was shed upon this sandy plain."

Mushid though wounded twice but still riding, left a slightly wounded Captain Rynarr's side and ordered two of his surviving horsemen to follow. Both men bore wounds from the battle but were able-to ride and roundup the few Egyptian horses that still ambled about and remain near their dead owners.

Captain Rynarr dismounted and examined a serious wound to his horse's right flank. Including himself, Mushid and GW, three others of the blue tunic horsemen had survived and in Captain Rynarr's opinion this was truly miraculous.

Upon returning to Silene, he would request the surviving horsemen receive their well-earned knighthood. He wasn't sure what to do about GW though. The man had saved the captain's life, probably more than once and had slain at least ten of the enemy force, which was an extraordinary feat. But he wasn't a Muslim and had not observed the other traditions and rights for becoming a knight. No, Captain Rynarr decided he would have to take this matter of GW and the other two new comers up with King Ramie, which would probably involve a debate with the senior clerics. Right now though, he needed to lay his dead to rest in their blankets or sleeping furs and only then, would he deal with the princess. She wasn't going to be very happy about the company returning to Silene, having not gathered her precious herbs, but another trip would be planned and this time he'd bring along a much better prepared fighting force.

Once the survivors took care of the dead, using the healthy prisoners for labor, they moved several miles to the north. Captain Rynarr, his muscles sore and his brow furrowed with worry, lay on his back and looked up to observe the blanket of twinkling stars. In this brief moment of quietness, he had time to think and he began to wonder how those Egyptian soldiers had found them in this immense Sahara Desert. He knew chance encounters were possible and this was the reason why he had brought along his company of men, but rather than wait in ambush further along the trail, where the desert met with a series of rolling hills, they attacked now and directed their main force against the encampment. This was their mistake, allowing Captain Rynarr's horsemen to separate into two elements and attack the enemy from each side. A good commander would have used his main force against the cavalry first and then the infantry, but they attacked as if they knew a valuable prize awaited them in those wagons and carts. This gave Captain Rynarr the advantage and it cost the Egyptians their victory.

Mushid had also noticed how the raiders were not carrying any food or water with them when they attacked but had left their supplies at their encampment to the south. Mushid and a weary GW had back-tracked them to a small oasis to the southeast. This could only mean the raiders had left their encampment to wage a planned battle. Either enemy scouts had discovered Captain Rynarr's company, or this was no chance encounter and that really bothered Captain Rynarr.

"Sir, these Egyptians knew we were coming." Mushid said. His voice was in a low whisper, when he returned to the encampment and knelt beside his captain. "Only an alert guard saved us from defeat and it cost him his life."

"He did his duty and is now with Allah," a tired Captain Rynarr replied.

Mushid glanced over to the royal cart, "Captain, these were no raiders like the ones we have encountered before. These men were Egyptian soldiers and they wanted the princess, for their main force attacked the encampment to seize her and carry her off." Mushid then pointed to the royal cart, "They probably wanted to ransom her and if not for the courageous herders, they might have taken her."

"You would never have allowed that to happen, my friend."

Mushid shook his head, "Captain, I was nearly overwhelmed when the Egyptians burst through the line. That one young boy killed three men with his bow and stabbed two others before they killed him...such a brave lad. He would've made a good soldier."

"Yes, he was a brave lad and I will ask the king to reward the father of that dead boy and appoint the oldest boy, who also did well, to the army. He fought quite well for one without any training."

"But, Captain, what I'm trying to get at...I think someone informed the Egyptians she was out here, and it makes me wonder, why did she insist on inexperienced troops? Why bring along GW, he was the most inexperienced of all?"

Captain Rynarr gave him a stern look, "We will speak no more of this, Mushid." He then turned away and Mushid realized he had been dismissed.

Disturbed by all these questions and his captain's actions when he brought up his concern about the princess, Mushid decided he needed a quiet walk out into the desert and take his concerns to Allah. He had bandaged his wounds earlier, but they were bleeding through his wrappings and would need to take care of it before an infection took hold.

Restless and disturbed by Mushid's suspicions, Captain Rynarr had his own questions about Princess Lonnia desire for this journey and this attack by such an overwhelming force of Egyptian soldiers posing as raiders. Only through Allah's mercy and grace had they been able to defeat the enemy. But he had lost too many good men today, including the young lieutenant, and taking the survivors back to Silene was a bitter victory. With so many unanswered questions concerning the attack, he did not look forward to bringing this matter before the king and speaking of his suspicions concerning the king's daughter.

Glancing over to the wagon where the horse's feed was kept, he watched as GW tenderly fed his horse. He had watched in wonder as GW had been almost-loving to his mount, like parent and child, as he treated Valiant's many minor wounds from the battle. He found them to be such an unusual team of man and horse, unlike any he had seen before. Yet, here this novice had defeated ten Egyptians and even saved the life of his captain. For a brief moment, a thought suddenly filled his mind as he recalled an old prophesy; of a strange knight who was said to be the savior of Silene. But he tossed it aside. This man was an infidel. Still, I must also inform Brother Samuel how well his clansman fought today, for GW truly distinguished himself as a gallant warrior. Strangely unlike any other man I've ever fought beside, as if his talents were directed from heaven and he, an infidel? Yes, truly a shame the king's sword may never touch him in honor.

# 9 – A NEW DANGER LOOMS

Princess Lennia, dressed in a shimmering white gown, black plumed pants, with a jeweled headpiece and an open veil, was sitting cross-legged upon on a fur rug on the floor of the classroom. She was looking much like the tomboy Sam remembered, instead of a royal princess. They were in the middle of an English language lesson and Sam seemed to be distracted. He had said nothing when she played hooky from her earlier math lesson to go riding. Now, they were in the midst-of discussing what a noun was and she was troubled by Sam's strange mood. But their classroom time ended when a young male servant arrived at the door with dire news concerning Princess Lonnia's trek to the south.

"Sir, the king has sent me here to..." Somewhat shy, the young man stood nervously in Princess Lennia's presence, her veil down and he stumbled through his first words.

He took in a deep breath, let it out and looked only at Brother Samuel, "Pardon me, Brother Samuel, but I've been sent here to advise you...Princess Lonnia escort detail was attacked by Egyptian raiders. Captain Rynarr sent one of his Royal Guardsmen on ahead to notify the King and report on Princess Lonnia's safety."

Sam, who had a large parchment in his hands, placed it on his table top and addressed the lad in a calm voice, "Do you have a number of those injured in the attack and when should we expect them here?" Sam had learned from long years of experience of working with the servants and slaves how he could bring out more information from them if he talked to them in a calming tone; treating them as an equal, for this was as he saw them. Unfortunately, most of the Silene's upper level of society, the prudes, which was how Sam thought of them, the exception being most of the Royal Family and Captain Rynarr, believed those beneath them as hardly worth speaking to. Sadly, beatings were common punishment in the castle, even though they were all Muslims and occasionally, a servant was ordered to the dungeon for some attitude adjustment.

In Sam's case, normally the servants would speak openly with him and even sit in his presence but having the princess present in the room made the man uneasy, especially since her face was open and she made no move to lift her veil. She thought the whole veil thing was ridiculous and disliked having her face all sweaty.

The boy replied to Sam's question, "Yes, sir," his eyes then wandered from Sam to the lovely Princess Lennia and then back to Sam. "The King wishes you to prepare for the wounded. The Captain's report is that there are many who are in need of you."

Sam nodded his head in understanding and waved the boy away. "Thank you, Marcus." The boy was a former Greek prisoner who was made a slave and purchased at Tripoli's slave market. Once it was discovered Marcus had several years of education from a reputable school in Athens, he was released from servitude in the kitchen and put to work for the royal family in a semi-secretarial type role and occasionally a castle runner.

Sam was concerned for the lives of the wounded men in the company due to the hot summer temperatures and what the heat could do to an unclean wound. He turned to his pupil and requested she rejoin her father.

"I need to gather up my medical supplies and you should be with your father for when Princess Lonnia returns. He will be concerned for your older sister and you are capable of soothing his fatherly worries."

"Why?" she asked. "My oldest sister has little love for my father or I, and I sincerely doubt she will even care if our father is there to welcome her back." Princess Lennia pointed to the outside, "She will care nothing for these injured men and will be in one of her foul moods for having to return early from her trip into the desert. I imagine she will simply stomp off to seclude herself in her quarters.

"Can I not help with those who are wounded?" Princess Lennia asked.

Sam shook his head, "My dear, it is not fitting for a princess to have her hands covered in the blood of her subjects. Furthermore, those same men would be made very uncomfortable by your presence."

"Oh, all right. But I'd rather be with you." Princess Lennia turned away and walked to the door, but then abruptly stopped and turned to face Sam. She had an expression on her face which displayed some degree of uneasiness, as she asked her next question, "Wasn't GW...uh-h, wasn't your clansman in this escort?"

Sam, who was already looking for his medic bag under the classroom table, froze in place when he heard his pupil mention GW's name. He then stood up straight, ignoring the ache in his back and looked at her as a disgruntled father might look when he just caught his daughter kissing a boy on the front steps of his house.

"GW?" Sam asked. "You seem to know his name and now you apparently feel some concern in regard to his safety. Is there something I should know, my princess?"

"Brother Samuel, I am only inquiring as to...well, if you think your clansman might be one of the wounded?"

His eyes softened somewhat, and he approached her, "My princess, though I sincerely appreciate your concern, you must understand...you endanger my clansman's life with your attention to him. He is not of your faith, nor your high status and not of your kingdom. If your father saw this same look on your face I just witnessed, GW would soon be facing a headman's axe and possibly the same fate for his two friends."

"Why?" She asked. "Why, dear friend may I not have at least the illusion of knowing a handsome young man?"

She walked across the length of the room and then turned to face her teacher, "I hear the handmaidens gossiping of their many lovers and their exciting dreams for a future with one of them, but I am allowed none of this?" She held her hands out wide, palms up, in a gesture to say life is so unfair.

"Now you say I cannot even have the feelings a young girl has at my age for it might endanger a young man's life. This isn't fair!" Princess Lennia turned in anger and ran through the doorway and down the darkened stone passageway. The delicate sound of her steps echoed through the hallway until Sam could no longer hear her.

"No, it's not fair, my princess...but it is the life you have, my dear," Sam whispered. He then sighed deeply and returned to seeking out what supplies he would need to treat the wounded men. His major concern for the moment would be the number of men in need of his service and exactly how bad they were injured. One of the things he had learned in this 12th-century was how the tools of warfare were far more-ghastly in the rendering of human flesh than a modern-day bullet.

His limited medical training came from his days long ago in the naval military academy and later, on board ship working with British doctors after their ship took a single torpedo from a German U-boat. The ship hospital was simply overwhelmed by the number of injured soldiers and sailors on board, and they needed all the extra hands they could find to help.

Over 40-years of experience here in Silene had given him the ability and knowledge to extract arrows from tissue and bone, to sew up sword and spear cuts, and even deliver a baby or two. But the baby part only came after King Ramie offered him a special provision to do so, over the heated complaints of his Muslim clerics. He was still an infidel and should have not been allowed to even touch a Muslim woman, but Sam shot holes in their complaints when he delivered a baby boy after both clerics and midwives thought the child was dead. This same boy was now approaching his 22nd-birthday and carrying the unusual Muslim name of Samuel. Now even midwives sought out his knowledge and expertise with difficult births.

However, more benefiting for Silene was how he taught the midwives and a few of the local witchdoctors, as Sam jokingly referred to them, correct hygiene procedures to prevent germs from spreading long before such basic principles were in usage among western civilization.

Paul, in obedience with Sam's wishes, remained clear of the study during the hours the young princess was in attendance. Ground rules were strictly enforced, but Sam couldn't help but notice how she often lingered about the study, in hopes she might encounter one of these strange young men.

Up until now, Sam thought it was simply a curiosity of hers for these three friends of his, but apparently her concern centered on one particular-newcomer—GW and this really worried him.

When word eventually reached Paul and Richard's ears of the attack in the desert, both men left their current duties and went directly to Sam's study, missing the young princess by only moments. Thankfully, she was hurriedly on her way to the upper levels of the castle keep and they didn't pass each other in the stairwells or passageways below.

Sam was lugging around what he referred to as his black bag, which was in fact a set of huge saddlebags made of fur-covered camel hide. He filled these two bags with semi-sterile bandages; boiled and left to dry in the hot sun and of various lengths and dimensions. He also had clean water in clay bottles, which had also been sterilized through boiling and his handmade medical instruments; finely sharpened scalpels, a long-handled pliers-like device for pulling steel arrowhead out of the body and personally forged tweezers- his 14th set since given a free pass to the blacksmith's forge. There were also rolls of heavy and lightweight horsehair twine that were made for him for stitching purposes and thick blanket weight bandages to bind broken ribs with.

He had left his study in a hurry, shouldering his heavy saddlebags, when he encountered Paul and Richard in the adjacent passageway.

"We heard the troop was attacked," Paul said. Handing his torch to Richard, Paul relieved Sam of the heavy bags. Large sections of inner passageways were quite dark unless torches were in use; covering stonewalls in centuries of black soot and leaving a pungent odor to linger. Sam had tried to build a circulation system, designing large wind powered fans set up on the roof to draw out the smoke, but he ran afoul of the clerics. These superstitious old men suspected Brother Samuel's idea was witchcraft and attempting to keep peace and save his advisor from being executed as a heretic, the king placed the project on hold.

Sam was dressed in his dark brown monk's robe, but over it he wore a large leather apron made from a camel's underbelly. This was to keep the bloodstains off his robes. He talked with Paul and Richard as they walked through the narrow passageways, while also remembering to acknowledge any of the locals he might encounter along the way with a nod, a single word in greeting or a quick wave.

"The king's messenger said there was wounded, but he didn't know how many," Sam said over his shoulder, "I'm on my way down to the courtyard now. We'll set up a field hospital there and I'll need your help.

"You've both had basic first aid, right?" Sam asked, while he rushed down through an intersection of passageways.

"What about GW?" Richard asked, ignoring Sam's question. "Did you hear if he was among those wounded… or killed?"

"No word on casualties by name; except for Captain Rynarr being alive, since he sent the messenger ahead of the escort." Sam stopped and turned to look at both men, "I asked you if you've both had first aid in the service. Now did you or did you not have the training?"

"Sure, we both did," Paul replied. "They gave us basic first aid in Boot Camp."

"Then you have more training then any of these so-called witchdoctors they have here." Sam resumed his march down one passageway and then another, huffing and puffing like an ancient steam engine, as he began to descend the stone stairs.

When he reached the bottom of the stairs, he turned and with a flushed face from exertion, he faced Richard, "I once read how the Greeks, rumored to be the Master of Medicine, passed along their medical knowledge to the people of the Muslim world after Alexander the Great raided in to Northern Africa. The Romans had done much the same thing, but as far as I can see the doctors here were apparently out building sand castles when the training was offered. They kill more people then they heal and germs—they have no idea how much infection they cause simply because they won't wash their hands before treating a wound." Sam shook his head in frustration.

"The very idea of boiling their instruments is beyond them," Sam said. "As you can tell by my complaints this is a real sore spot for me and I've yet to convince the doctors I'm right and they're wrong. I'm simply an infidel, which is their only response when I've attempted to debate the subject of medicine. Germs could not be seen with the naked eye, so they refuse to believe in such things. I'd give anything for a simple high schooler's microscope!"

By the time they reached the courtyard, dozens of servants were already busy setting up several canvas open-sided canopies to shelter the wounded from the hot sun. Food and lukewarm juices from the kitchen and fresh water from the nearest fountain were being set up in the shady side of the castle keep. Additional men-at-arms were ordered from the barracks to assist with prisoners, while stable hands were on hand to take control of the horses. Everyone knew the small company was on a forced march home and the men and horses would be exhausted. A senior stable hand was ordered to make sure the troths were full of water for the thirsty animals and an ample supply of hay was brought over from the storage barn.

Paul noticed the main gate was standing wide open and saw how dozens of townspeople were already standing around the entry, while others lined the main street to welcome home the soldiers. Richard, who was worried about GW and their mutual friend Mushid, left Paul at Sam's side to climb a wooden ladder to the top of the southern wall. Once atop a battlement, he looked hard out across the desert for any sign of the returning troop. A nice set of binoculars would sure come in handy right about now.

Richard heard one of the guards to his right shout out his spotting of the escort detail; they were already at the town's southern edge. The soldier, who held a spear in his right hand, was waving it in the air above him in excitement. He turned to Richard and said, "They will be here in a matter of moments and will be coming through the main gate."

"Thanks!" Richard replied. Of the three men, Richard had quickly taken to the language and was now quite fluent in it, though he was still struggling with their form of writing.

Paul came to the foot of the ladder and yelled up to Richard, "Sam wants you down here!"

"I'm coming," Richard shouted back. But before he reached the ladder to climb down, the escort detail was now in full view coming down the main road to the castle and their low numbers worried him.

Sam had one of the blacksmiths set up a small fire pit nearby to sanitize Sam's scalpels, knives and an assortment of fish-hooks he created for stitching the wounds. He found that horse tail hair made a pretty good stitching material and was long enough for most wounds. With no fermented beverages of wheat or grape allowed in the kingdom, under Muslim Law, Sam had no way to anesthetize the wounded. In a few cases he thought about simply knocking them out but knew the chance of skull fractures outweighed taking the chance. He only prayed the more serious wounded were already unconscious. Otherwise, he could only give them leather straps to bite down on and asked several strong soldiers to hold them in place while he did what needed to be done.

He had tried gaining the king's permission to gain access to some of the natural opiates he had known were growing in China and Afghanistan, but once again those same clerics and local witchdoctors prevented him from doing so. Sam only wished he could get one of these clerics or a witchdoctor under his knife and see how long they lasted before crying out for some kind-of pain reliever.

With both Paul and Richard standing before him, Sam gave them a rundown on how he worked things, "We operate on the more serious ones first; arrow, lance and sword wounds. Then we treat broken bones, lacerations, minor cuts and bruises.

"But first we make sure they are breathing and then stop the bleeding." Sam knelt under a canopy with his bulky saddlebags and began to lay out his supplies and equipment. "You have your knives, so put them on the fire and then go wash your hands thoroughly." He then tossed them each a large palm-sized bar of goat milk soap, one of his more greatly admired gifts to the women of Silene.

"What about GW?" Paul asked in a worried tone.

Sam looked up, his expression quite stern, "Paul, we will know about our friend when the company arrives. But the wounded are our primary concern, do you agree?"

Paul stared back at Sam with cold eyes, but he softened and nodded his head, "Yeah, you're right. I'm just worried about the guy."

"So am I, Paul, but now you should be doing what I told you to do."

"Yes, sir," Paul said, and Richard quickly echoed it.

King Ramie, who was extremely upset to hear of the attack, left his courtroom politics to his many advisors and proceeded to the nearest window ledge. Realizing he was on the wrong side of the castle keep, to see anything to the south, he rushed out of the Royal Court and began descending the many stairwells. Two court guardsmen, responsible for the king's safety, rushed to follow him down. Their armor and weapons clattered loudly in the stairwells and the king looked over his shoulder to give his bodyguards a stern look for making such a racket.

Upon reaching the bottom floor, he burst through a double-wide wooden door and walked outside to stand upon a large stone viewing platform to wait for Captain Rynarr and his daughter. It was from this same platform the king would address the citizens of Silene on numerous occasions. The two Royal Guardsmen quickly took up position directly behind him and began observing the immediate area for possible threats to their king.

After several long moments of marching back and forth across the platform, making the guards extremely nervous, King

Ramie saw the two advance riders for the returning company. Relieved, he left the stone platform and while still under escort of the two burly guardsmen, who were used to standing around a much cooler throne room, he climbed down a set of three wide stairs to stand upon the hot hard packed sandy floor of the courtyard.

When King Ramie spotted Brother Samuel, preparing for the wounded, he immediately walked over to him and the gathering crowd of castle servants parted for him like the Red Sea in the time of Moses. Without saying anything, he approached Sam from behind and laid a gentle hand on his old friend's left shoulder. The former navy commander, turned defrocked priest and now preparing to work as Silene's chief surgeon, was kneeling in the white sand and making preparation for his first case.

"Once again, you come to the aid of my people and I Thank you," King Ramie said with gratitude.

Turning to a voice he knew all too well, Sam smiled graciously, but his smile turned to a grimace of pain, as he rose to his feet and his old knee muscles cried out. On his feet, one hand on King Ramie's shoulder to steady himself, he nodded to the two guards to ensure he meant no harm to the king, and said to his royal friend, "Your highness, excuse my poor condition, but I would also like to point out how these are my people too."

"Well said," King Ramie said with appreciation. "I will now leave you to this grisly chore, but I will be nearby until my daughter arrives and I can see for myself she is well." King Ramie started to leave but he then saw Richard and Paul preparing makeshift beds for the wounded, "Does the one called Paul know this medicine you perform miracles with? Is he as gifted as you are in saving lives?"

"Yes, Sire," Sam said to reassure him and then gestured to Richard, "Richard, our young friend from the Sudan also knows of many of my skills and how to use them."

"Even this Black Moor of the Sudan?" King Ramie said in astonishment.

"Sire, Richard spent some time in our country and both men have some knowledge and training. I know they will do everything they can to help our people."

Taking his friend at his word, King Ramie presented his best political smile to both men as they looked his way He nodded his head in acceptance and mouthed a quiet, "Thank you," before he walked toward the main gate and waited with his escort for Captain Rynarr to arrive.

Sam suddenly grabbed the hand of a senior kitchen servant, a man who had been in the castle for nearly 35-years, "Sal-Rysa, I need all the hot water you can bring me."

He then held up his pile of bandages, "I must have much more of this, all you can find, and it must be clean. Check with the midwives, Sal-Rysa and if needed, steal it from the shops in town. But I must have more clean linen. Understand?"

The servant, a middle-aged man who was missing his tongue, could only nod his response, and then he rushed off to ensure the hot water was being prepared. Sal-Rysa was an older man of mild temperament, who had lost his tongue in the dungeon several years earlier and was indentured into a life of slavery for offering a misspoken word in a foreign dignitary's presence—or so the pompous official reported. Sam had tried to defend Sal-Rysa, but King Ramie was forced by protocol to take the action dictated by law. But Sal-Rysa had never forgotten Sam's attempt to help him and was always willing to do whatever was necessary to aid him.

Shouts could be heard outside the main gate as excited townspeople announced the troop's return. From the crowds, several people were demanding death for the Egyptian prisoners and Captain Rynarr had had to use his mount to block two men from dragging an Egyptian prisoner off his horse.

While Sam waited for the hot water, he looked to the open gate and after a moment, he spotted Captain Rynarr entering on horseback and was saddened by his friend's wearisome appearance. Not only the captain, but even his proud mount, now covered in lathers of sweat, walked with his head down in sheer exhaustion.

Directly behind Captain Rynarr came two ranks of army horsemen, followed by a supply wagon and then came nine Egyptian prisoners on horse. The Egyptians hands were tied together, and a long rope connected all nine horses to the back of the supply wagon. One army soldier rode in the back of the wagon and he kept a bow ready in the event an Egyptian tried to get away. Behind the Egyptians came two more ranks of Royal Guardsmen on horseback, one of them looked as if he was about to fall off at any moment and his leg was bandaged. Princess Lonnia's royal cart then followed the guardsmen, which after three days of force marched now resembled a utility wagon that was about to fall apart as it creaked along. The second wagon was completely filled with wounded men of both friend and foe; many of them in complete agony. The last wagon carried the Egyptian prisoners who were in semi-satisfactory condition, but unable to ride a horse.

The six surviving foot soldiers and their wounded lieutenant followed behind the last wagon, keeping an eye on the prisoners, which left Princess Lonnia's second cart and the four surviving camels to bring up the rear. One of the older camels, the meanest in the bunch, had taken an Egyptian spear in the chest and died. The two herders and one of the wagon drivers had painstakingly skinned the old beast and used the fur to offer some degree of cushion for the wounded. The stench was awful, for they did not have time to clean the hide, but it was better than the hard planks of the wagon. Mushid, who was marked several times in his battle to protect the princess, had asked Princess Lonnia for the use of her sleeping furs for the wounded and as he expected—she refused. She was not at all happy, but still, Mushid had the responsibility to escort the princess across the desert and through the city. But once she was through the gate, Mushid rode to the rear of the escort to ensure everyone was accounted for.

When Paul and Richard caught sight of GW, they breathed a sigh of relief. They were also happy to see that Mushid, their new friend, had also returned without any serious looking wounds. GW, who looked completely exhausted, was in far better shape than his horse; Valiant had suffered from several minor wounds to his neck and flanks and the forced march had reopened one of the wounds on his neck. A single narrow stream of blood was running down his right front leg and it greatly worried GW.

Once the company came to a halt in front of the castle keep, soldiers in the castle guard rushed up to the horses and violently dragged the prisoners off. Off-duty soldiers also dragged the lighter wounded Egyptians from the wagon and nearly put all of them to the sword right there and then in the courtyard. If not for Captain Rynarr's quick intervention, a lot of blood would've been spilled in front of the king. Captain Rynarr had eight Royal Guardsmen on hand escort the prisoners to the dungeon with orders for them to be fed, given water and kept alive. Those Egyptian's who could ride, helped the injured ones into the dark coolness of the Castle Keep.

Seeing this and knowing where they were headed, Paul was pretty sure the old dungeon master was already shining up all his pretty toys as he awaited his new guests.

While removing the Silene wounded, the Egyptians were again tossed aside and dropped to the hot desert sand. Their cries of pain were ignored until Sam moved in and intervened. He insisted Captain Rynarr have the Egyptian wounded be treated, before they were jailed and after some heated discussion, Rynarr agreed, but only after all the men of Silene were treated.

Sam stood beside a mounted Captain Rynarr and good naturedly slapped his leg with his hand before he returned to work. He was letting Paul and Richard handle the minor wounds without his help, but he would need their services soon for one or two of the difficult surgeries. Two of the witchdoctors stood by, scoffing at his tender treatment, but were soon chased off like the pests they were when a weary Captain Rynarr came on the scene. As a young man he had watched his father being treated for wounds under their abrasive care and hoped he would never have to suffer that fate.

Within an hour, one man had died during open-air surgery and Sam suspected the man's heart gave out from the stress of pain brought on during the operation. Leaving the body to be taken away by servants, Sam went on to the next case where he had to set a broken leg on a man who was trampled by a rider less horse breaking through the line of defenders. Another guardsman had lost three fingers to his sword hand during the fight, but infection had set in from the long hike home and Sam had to remove the entire hand to save him from gangrene poisoning. A fiery rod was used to seal the ghastly wound, but the man had already feinted, and his body only jerked under restraint. Sam knew this man's biggest battle would be depression, causing his healing to take additional time, unless someone could teach him to handle his tools of warfare with his other hand. Yet, he knew it was possible, and put it on his mental calendar of things to talk about with Captain Rynarr.

Paul removed a steel arrowhead from one Egyptian's arm and then sewed the wound up while Sam looked on. The man bit down hard upon the leather strap and two of his friends held him in place. The Egyptian kept glaring at Paul, and Sam realized the man was probably wondering what sort of man was treating him. Halfway through surgery the man passed out– which made the operation actually run a whole lot easier.

By the time they were all done, nine-wounded men were treated for various injuries and only one had died during surgery. Six Egyptians were also cared for, three of them seriously and all of which survived. Three horses received stitches and bandaging, including Valiant and one camel was treated for several lacerations on its neck from what appeared to be caused by either a dagger or sword. Sam suspected the camel happened to get in the way and suffered for it.

Of an estimated fighting force of 100-Egyptian raiders, only 17-men survived to be taken prisoner and this included the six wounded men. Sam and his staff did what they could with their wounds, but Mushid wondered why all the concern. Everyone seemed to believe the Egyptians would be executed within the week, maybe sooner. After all, they had entered Libya illegally and attacked a royal caravan. So, by Mushid's way of thinking, they should begin building the gallows now, or make things easier by feeding them to the dragon and everyone could watch for amusement.

Mushid had discussed the whole sacrifice thing with Sam on many occasions in the past, always wondering why maidens and not just prisoners? Sam's only answer was the wording in the lottery, how only maidens could be sacrificed and that was to happen twice a month.

"Can we still feed it our prisoners?" Mushid asked.

Sam had frowned, "Why would you want too, my large friend? Better to execute a man in proper fashion if you must then to have him devoured by that hellish creature."

"You Christians are too soft. Why grant an enemy any lesser pain then what he deserves?"

"Yes, Mushid, we may appear soft to you, but if you were taken prisoner here in Silene would you prefer the executor's axe or to be ripped apart by the dragon?"

Mushid was never able to answer that question directly, and it was such questions that made him believe Brother Samuel was probably the smartest man in the kingdom.

Having stood by the side of the road and watched the troop arrive and having not seen his son, a frightened father requested entry onto the castle grounds to learn where his son, the herdsman was. Hearing of this man's search for his son, Captain Rynarr met with the father and explained what had happened. While the father listened, his cheeks moistened with tears of grief, he heard Captain

Rynarr speak highly of the young man's contribution to the battle and how gallantly he had acted to enter the fight freely and save the princess from being taken.

Upon hearing of this young man's death through Captain Rynarr's words, King Ramie summoned the father to him and startled the two guardsmen and those who stood nearby, by embracing the father warmly and offered his condolences. "Your son has given his life so my daughter, Princess Lonnia, might live. I can ask no greater gift for our kingdom and my family. Thank you." King Ramie finished with the Muslim hand blessing.

King Ramie would send the man five-pieces of gold, an offering of goodwill for his son's sacrifice, but he knew presenting the gold now was not in good taste. Tomorrow, he would have the senior herdsman responsible for the king's camels deliver the gold for him.

The elder herdsman was then escorted out into the waiting crowds, where friends grieved with him and others gave a shout in his son's honor. For the young herdsmen who survived, Captain Rynarr introduced them to King Ramie and requested the bravest lad, the one who left the camels and fought so well, be transferred from the herds to the army. "This is one we should have carrying a spear, Sire, not guiding our camels and sheep."

King Ramie gave the young man a close look and noticed how the boy didn't back down from his gaze. "I think you are right, Captain, but what does his father think?"

"One of my lieutenants will seek the father's permission, my Liege. If he agrees, the lad will begin training immediately. Maybe within a few years, he may even wear the blue tunic."

Upon hearing these words, the young man's eyes grew wide with excitement. To leave the herds and possibly become a Royal Guardsmen was something he couldn't believe. Truly, he missed his friend and would always remember their first and only battle together, but he would not grieve long for a young man who had given his life so bravely.

When the royal cart had pulled up in front of the castle keep's main entry, Princess Lonnia's driver dropped the reins and climbed down. He offered his sweaty hand to the princess to help her down, but she was offended by his gesture and lashed out at him with the leather quirt she carried. Seeing this, Mushid dismounted, moved the driver aside gently and offered her his hand, to which she did accept and climbed out of the cumbersome cart with visible effort. Her leg was sore, and she had detested this odorous cart from the first day and now it only reminded of her ill-fated plan. Her handmaiden was dead, she was out gold to the spy and both GW and Rynarr were still alive. She wouldn't have murdered her handmaiden if she thought the plan wouldn't have succeeded. The long ride back with so little sleep and only that vile odor of her driver to smell for three days was nearly unbearable. At night, she had to have that same unwashed man prepare her meals and she dearly hoped the memory of him would rapidly fade away.

Standing outside her cart, she looked for her father, expecting to find him waiting for her. But she saw him speaking with the illustrious Captain Rynarr and this angered her. She walked to the other side of the cart so she was more visible, but King Ramie was still ignoring her. Impatient and offended, she became infuriated when her father stopped to speak to the various wounded soldiers. Then her eyes became cold as ice when she saw her father lower himself to actually put his royal arms around that filthy camel herder. Enraged that she had been bypassed for a lowly herdsman, she stormed off and nearly stumbled in her anger on the stone steps of the platform.

Before she even entered the great doorway of the castle keep, she lashed out with her leather quirt against two innocent servants and severely cut their faces. Her third handmaiden, a young girl of 19-years, who was slightly-humpbacked and an orphan from the Tripoli slave market, stood ready with a lit torch to guide Princess Lonnia's way through the darkened passageways. Seeing the injury her mistress had inflicted on the other servants for only standing there, her trembling hands nearly dropped the torch as the princess passed her by.

When GW wearily approached the stable, leading his wounded stallion, his whole body shook with fatigue and he nearly fell-down. Tired from the long march through mile after mile of endless desert sand and the early morning attack, which was followed by a forced march back to Silene, he felt as if his legs were going to give out. He stood leaning against a stable post, half-asleep and almost didn't recognize Paul and Richard when they grasped him by the shoulders and assisted him to the nearest water troth. A stable hand, nervous to be so close to Valiant, cautiously took the warhorse's reins from GW's hand and led him off to be watered, and fed.

GW turned to watch his horse being led away, he felt as if he was losing a part of him as the distance between them grew farther apart. He tried to pull away from his friends, to follow Valiant, but they restrained him and plopped him down on his butt by the water troth.

"Don't fight us, dude, you're too worn out and need some rest," Paul said and then he nodded to Richard, who picked up a full water bucket and promptly poured the entire contents over GW's head. The shock, hitting his dry and sun burned skin almost caused him to pass out.

"Don't worry about your horse, GW...he'll be well taken care of," Richard said. He began pulling GW's damp tunic and shirt of mail over his soaked head. Paul, he dipped the bucket into the water troth and refilled it.

"You look like a half-fried rat, old buddy," Paul said and then dumped a second bucket over GW.

"So, tell us about it," Richard said. "What happened out there?"

GW shook the water droplets from his hair and used his right hand to wipe the moistness from his face. He remained silent as he accepted a drinking goblet of juice from a young servant, who was carrying a tray of clay goblets around for the returning men. After a couple of refreshing gulps of melon juice, GW looked at his two friends and once he cleared his throat, said, "It was a fire-fight...but like none I've ever experienced before." He waved his right hand over his shoulder and pointed to the south. "They came at from the south, must...must've been 100 of them on horseback. We thought at first they were Egyptian raiders, but these guys were regulars and guys, they were glorious to see."

"Glorious?" Paul asked in confusion.

"Yeah, like from some old movie...But they were real and man oh man, those guys knew how to ride like the wind." GW took another gulp of juice. "Spears waving, swords swinging and their horses...every one of them looked like a beast of Satan as they rode toward us with the bright morning sun right behind them."

"Wow!" Paul exclaimed. "100 horsemen, that's like 4 to1 odds and you survived it." He looked to Richard, "That must've been a great fight."

GW stared at him briefly before answering, "No, Paul, it was the bloodiest thing I've ever seen," GW replied. "Nothing like Nam, we had no rifles to shoot, no grenades or artillery. This was a real personal situation out there, one on one and the survivor only went on to fight again." GW glanced from Paul to Richard, "Once the alarm came, Captain Rynarr got us all lined up for what he called a scorpion move. The men-at-arms were with the wagons, while the mounted troops separated into two groups and rode out wide of the attacking force. This caused the Egyptians to separate into three units, with the largest section attacking the wagons. Then when Captain Rynarr gave the signal, our two mounted units charged in to attack the Egyptian's other two sections like a scorpion closes in with its pincers."

GW poured another goblet of water over his face before he continued; he was sweating profusely and the sand all about him was wet, "Our men-at-arms struck the main body first with three volleys of arrows, then it was down to lance and sword, battle axe and spear. Before long men were fighting with their hands. I even saw one guy blind another with handfuls of sand before he suffocated him with a second handful. Several men were trampled by rider less horses when they hit the wagons, and one or two of the Egyptians were pinned down by dying horses struck down by arrows. I watched a battle axe hurled across the battlefield with almost inhuman strength and it sent an Egyptian flying off his horse.

"Spears were flying every which way and the wounds; the blood was everywhere. Others... it was really horrible, guys."

Both Paul and Richard could see the strain GW was under from the last few days, the stress manifested in the sweat that poured off him in sheets and they grew concerned.

"You look pretty beat, big guy." Paul said.

Richard heard his name being shouted out and he looked up from GW to see Sam summoning him with an urgent hand gesture. "Looks like we're needed again, Paul."

"Look, GW you stay here and rest," Paul said. He then looked over to see Sam's frantic wave. "You've got plenty of water and we'll get someone to bring you some food. Sam's got us on first aid detail and he's got his hands full."

"You go ahead, I'm all right. I'll sit here for a while and then check on Valiant." GW replied and waved them away with a weary hand gesture of his own. As they dashed off to help Sam, he dipped his juice goblet into the water bucket again and poured the warm water over his face. He then leaned back against the wooden pole and closed his eyes to rest. The sun was hot, but the stable provided some shade and he was simply too sore to move anywhere else for the moment.

Paul then suddenly appeared at his side again, startling him, "Valiant looks pretty used up, but Sam said to tell you his wounds are very minor."

GW looked into Paul's eyes, tears welling up and the emotional weight he carried on his chest seemed to burst, "Captain Rynarr told me I killed 10-men, but I don't remember anything, Paul. Everything got really quiet and suddenly, Valiant carried me into battle. I didn't realize I'd done anything until I saw my broken lance and my hand held a scimitar drenched in blood."

"You're alive, buddy," Paul said as he stood to his feet. "That's all that matters, you're still kicking."

GW nodded his head in agreement and then looked over to where Sam was working on a patient, "You'd better get over there, Paul. See how many men you can save...They're a pretty good bunch." GW then closed his eyes again.

Once he was left alone, GW rested for a bit, but he was unable to fall asleep. He was simply too keyed up and then suddenly, he was struck with hunger pains and a deep roar emanated from his stomach. So shirtless, he used the wooden pole for support to rise up and went in search of some food. He didn't really much care whether it was dried out roast chicken, cold mutton or some three-day old slimy fish—he only needed something to fill the void and maybe then he could get some sleep.

Valiant had his wounds treated by careful hands and was then duteously groomed by GW's favorite stable hand; the one Valiant seemed to trust. A special salve Sam had concocted from a mixture of fish innards, honey and strained camel urine coated the various wounds all the warhorses sustained, which brought about a quick healing and fought infection, though it reeked enough to get Sam's eyes watering. Sam had produced it after he learned of it during a barter session with some Greek fishermen. He also traded for several bags of ground up sulfur and half-dozen rolls of new parchment on that trip.

Knowing the Chinese had already invented gunpowder in the 10th century, Sam didn't think he'd be violating any time sequence for important discoveries by producing the lethal concoction. He hoped to use the gunpowder to kill the dragon. But to do so he needed to locate the charcoal base and potassium nitrates to form the ingredients needed for the mixture. Sadly, he couldn't find or trade for those ingredients and he had no way of reaching a Chinese trade source from Libya. Silk had been obtained, but it had come to Tripoli by way of Greece and Bagdad.

Still, the sulfur worked as an antiseptic and it saved both man and animal. The odorous concoction upset those religious leaders he was always up against, but the proof was in the results and King Ramie allowed it to be used for all those who were injured or sick. Within months, word of this sulfur as a wound healer spread to Tripoli and Sam began to wonder if he had accomplished the one thing he had worked so hard not to do: violate his own rule on messing with the sequences of history's timed discoveries. He racked his mind, trying to remember when sulfur was first used in medicine and couldn't recall, then decided what's done is done, and put it behind him.

The sulfur did a lot of good after he ground it up into a fine powder and added a few special herbs he located years earlier on the shores of the Upper Nile River. Herbs he remembered reading about in some recently discovered parchments and how ancient Egyptians in Biblical times used them to effect healing. Sam felt he was safe in using these but didn't see a lot of success until the sulfur came into his hands.

While concocting his healing mixture in front of Paul one day in the study, Sam had confessed, "My biology and science instructors at the academy should see me now. They thought I spent too much time on engineering and nearly flunked me because I wasn't spending enough time in the labs." Sam pointed to the clay bottles lined up in front of him, "Now I'm a doctor, a veterinarian and a social science teacher to the royal family. My dad doubted I'd ever succeed at anything, but he was a former Marine who rarely talked to me after I sunk so low as to join the Navy.

"Now I know they are growing opium poppies in the Middle East and my sources advise me Princess Lonnia has some of this powder refined from the flower petals. She uses it for her secret experiments, which she conducts in her hidden laboratory she doesn't think I know about. But I haven't been able to purchase any myself as of yet. Opium is known to make a fine sedative and with it I could sedate my patients. Less of them would die from the shock of surgery."

"How did you learn so much about Opium, Sam?" Paul asked.

"In my freshman year at the academy I did a paper for my US History class on the building of the US railways along the western frontier. I did a lot reading about the men and women who were involved in this hazardous task and some of them were Chinese. Thousands of them were heavily involved in the track laying.

"A lot of non-Chinese workers got addicted to an opium-based liquid known as Laudanum. Some even got addicted on opium in its powder form, by smoking it. It sedated some of them to the point they simply starved to death in some of the opium dens. Countries like China and Afghanistan grew the poppy as a major source of income."

"Boy, for someone lost in the past, you sure know a lot," Paul said with admiration.

"But, my young friend, I have to be extremely careful. We all do. I'm not sure what will or can happen if we mess with the time line too much. Like your friend Richard says, maybe we are here as part of a grand-plan," Sam glanced down at Valiant's leg to inspect his bandaging, "I do believe Valiant's leg is going to heal just fine and our friend GW will ride again."

Leaving the stable, Sam, stretched out his arms and yawned. He was very tired, but he needed to check on the wounded one more time to ensure they were as comfortable as he could make them.

By his policy, once a wounded man was stabilized, they were carefully moved onto a stretcher; another of Sam's new devices, and they were carried back to their barracks and placed in their own beds. Servants would monitor them, and Sam would try to check on them once a day, more if needed. For those who had undergone major surgery Sam didn't want them moved right away and left them under the canopy.

Servants with some degree of medical training were assigned to each of these patients, while several slaves were used to fan the flies away with great palm leaves. Sam was always on call, but those who trained under him didn't like to bother him unless they absolutely had too. They all knew the old monk was wearing down and most of them feared for the day he left them for his Christian heaven.

Due to Sam's intervention, wounded Egyptian prisoners were not taken straight to the dungeon, where he knew infection was sure to kill them. Instead, he had them left under a canopy until he could treat them. Once he had learned the enemy was actually soldiers, it was Sam's intention to ask King Ramie for permission to use these prisoners in a straight prisoner exchange for Libyans held in Egypt or trade for them for various Egyptian goods Silene could use. Such ideas were some of the reasons why King Ramie held Sam in such high regards: his superior intelligence, his great compassion for the Muslim people and his keen ability to negotiate a good trade.

## ROYAL FAMILY CHAMBERS

Princess Lonnia, now in fresh change of clothes, had her traveling garments and sleeping furs burned. She wanted nothing in which would remind her of her failed scheme and the dreadful return to Silene.

Favoring her crippled leg, she now stood beside a large window and looked down upon the main courtyard. The flies were bad in her room, which was unusual due to the height of her quarters, and she ordered her handmaiden to begin fanning her with a large palm leaf. Her dark olive skin hands, the left one somewhat mangled from her accident so long ago, gripped the stone edge of the window, as she glared down upon Captain Rynarr. Dismounted, he helped with the blood splattered wounded and she watched as he spoke to the lowly families of the dead men. Her hands became tightly clenched fists, the left one causing great pain and her face flushed with anger to see him down there, the Captain of the Royal Guardsmen, treating those beneath him as actual equals. Much as her father had treated those filthy herdsmen. Captain Rynarr was an affront to her ideals of the Royal Family, as was her father and this continued to infuriate her.

She was down to two-handmaidens, one who had been with her for several years and a much-less experienced one of a very young age. She had caught the occasional look of contempt in the older girl's eyes, when she didn't think the princess was looking. But until she was able-to purchase new handmaidens in Tripoli, she would have to ignore these insults—at least for now anyway. Purchasing new handmaidens was a tiresome task, which involved her traveling across the western desert to reach the slave market of Tripoli. Only she could select the girls she found worthy of purchase and as a princess she rarely had to haggle over prices with the auctioneer. Then she had to use up valuable time to train them up properly. A task she regarded as laboring and utterly tedious. She had always felt such household slaves should be trained up properly before being put up for sale, to learn proper service techniques and how to not damage her expensive clothing. She had grown weary of her drinks being spilled by clumsy girls, tearing her fine silks when packing them away and not even remembering how she liked her food cooked. No, Princess Lonnia didn't think it was fair for the price she paid.

There were household slaves on the slave block, but these women were too attractive or too old for her desires. Twice, Princess Lonnia had used older women to supervise her handmaidens and ensure her chambers were taken care of properly. The first one was a holdover from her mother, but the woman behaved too much like an overbearing grandmother and Princess Lonnia had sold her off for a single gold piece.

The second one, purchased from a good house in Tripoli for an outlandish price, was caught attempting to sell some of Princess Lonnia's garments and she received 100-lashes. Unfortunately, the woman, who was approaching her 48th year, died with the 27th strike of the whip. Still, Princess Lonnia demanded all 100-lashes be delivered, stating it was the principle of the thing and she stayed to observe the punishment be carried out.

Since then, Princess Lonnia had taken the task upon herself to train up her handmaidens, but this was growing tiresome and she was now forced to contemplate the idea of looking for another senior female servant.

Since becoming an adult, she refused to have a man in her quarters, although of late she had thought over the possibilities concerning the acquisition of a personal bodyguard- a man with the skills she desired as a protector and a gifted assassin; one trained in all known forms of weaponry, but who was not a member of the army or the accursed Royal Guardsmen. She knew this would be extremely costly, but she had the gold. Her personal wealth of gold and silver coin from numerous countries, and her stash of precious jewels far outweighed the total accumulation of King Ramie's treasury.

Through her many schemes, acts of black mail and outright theft, she was the richest woman in Libya and possibly in all Africa. For the last five years she had partnered herself with a band of ruthless brigands in the slums of Tripoli. Men who carried out her biddings quite willingly and through her, they learned of the various trade caravans passing Silene and the routes they would be taking through Libya. Many of these attacks were blamed on

Egyptian raiders, but in fact they were the Black Princess's brigands. Initially, she thought of using them to attack the escort detail, but their numbers were too few with so many of them pursuing the many caravans moving across the desert.

As she looked scornfully down upon Captain Rynarr, who now spoke with Mushid and a third soldier, she suddenly heard a noise of someone behind her. She quickly turned around with rage in her eyes to see who would enter her domain without permission, only to find Princess Lennia standing there, "What do you want?" She growled.

Princess Lennia was taken back by her sister's greeting, "Nothing. I am happy to see you safe, my sister," Princess Lennia replied. "I feared for your life when word of the battle first came."

"You needn't worry, little sister," Princess Lonnia said mockingly. "Our men fought well, too well."

"Too well, what do you mean by that?"

Princess Lonnia locked eyes with Princess Lennia, suspicious at first but then seeing the innocence in her sister's young eyes, she only replied, "Nothing, you dolt. I am simply tired and have lost two of my trusted servants. So, go away!"

With a hurt expression, Princess Lennia replied with a barb of her own by shouting back, "Alright!" She was used to her sister's rudeness, but as she grew older, she was losing the grace she needed to have in dealing with her.

Princess Lennia left her sister's quarters and walked down the narrow stairs of the outside stairwell in search of either Sam or her father. She requested several times to assist Sam in his medical practices, but Sam refused. "As I explained earlier, this is not something a Princess of Silene should be doing or even observing, and it makes the men uneasy to have you present."

## MAIN COURTYARD

When Princess Lennia came outside the darkened passageway and into the bright afternoon sun, the heat wave that attacked her felt like someone was waving a burning torch in her face and the sand burned her sandaled feet. Jumping back up on the stone steps, she looked for her father and soon spotted him. The king was currently involved in a conversation with Captain Rynarr and a knight she knew to be called Mushid. They stood over a young officer who was apparently wounded and lying on a bed of furs. Not wanting to bother them, she gritted her teeth against the heat of the sand and quickly walked over to where Sam was up to his elbows in blood with the wounded. She decided in an instant that if she was the oldest princess, she could take it upon herself to ignore Sam's wishes when she wanted too, and this was one of those times. She also hoped he would not be too mad at her.

Several servants with large palm fans were waving them back and forth in an attempt-to keep the desert flies off the wounds, even though a slight breeze was blowing in from the north. The scene before her was shocking, but she refused to give justice to Sam's concerns and looked away when she began to feel the bile building in her stomach.

Princess Lennia also saw two of the newcomers; the one she knew to be called Paul and the Sudanese known as Richard. She couldn't remember if she had mentioned it to Brother Samuel, but she thought Richard to be a very unusual name for a Sudanese. Richard was bandaging an arm wound of a soldier, who was biting upon a strap of leather to keep from crying out. The man named Paul, a name she heard many times when Brother Samuel told her of his Christian stories, was covered in dried blood. Paul was using a bucket of water and a wad of linen to bathe down a man she knew to be a knight. By the looks of the man and the amount of stitches his upper body displayed, Princess Lennia knew Brother Samuel had spent quite some time working on him.

Princess Lennia had learned GW went along with the escort, at Princess Lonnia's suggestion, but she didn't see him standing about or lying with the wounded. This caused a sudden tightness of her chest, for she feared he might be dead. Looking about wildly, ignoring the strange looks of others as she did so, her eyes finally dropped on the shirtless backside of a medium tanned white man sitting back against a watering troth. She knew this had to be GW, as outside of Brother Samuel there were only two other white men in Silene. There were Berbers of course, but not inside the castle's courtyard or running around shirtless.

As she drew closer she saw that the man, whose unusual green pants were soaked, was casually consuming slices of fruit and pieces of meat. His backside was sweaty, and she grinned as she watched him bat away several pester-some flies.

A sense of relief led to a sudden release of tears, surprising her and she looked away, so GW wouldn't see her display of emotion if he turned around. But her tears didn't escape Sam's observation and he nearly dropped a stitch in a man's forearm.

What Sam feared most seemed to be transpiring and GW, who was looking the other way, didn't even know the instrument of his death was right then standing behind him. Sam could even imagine a tall black-robed character with an ax in his arm preparing to swing for GW's unwary head.

"Daughter, are you alright?" King Ramie asked as he approached his youngest daughter with concern.

Startled, she quickly looked up into her father's face, wiped her eyes with a silk scarf, once she ensured her veil remained in place, and replied, "Yes, my father and though I am very happy my oldest sister is alive, the sacrifice of our brave soldiers saddens me and so I weep for them. Please forgive my display in public."

"No, it is good for the soldiers to see your emotion, your display of sadness for the loss of life and pains of the wounded. Yes, it is sad, but Captain Rynarr has told me of the great valor shared by many of our men here." With a wide wave of his hand, he gestured to all the wounded, "In truth, we did lose many a good man to the Egyptians but having faced far greater numbers they have returned victorious."

Taking her father by the arm, she purposely guided him away from where GW sat unaware and walked over to where Captain Rynarr now stood. By now all of the horses were turned over to stable hands and prisoners incarcerated. The wounded were still being treated and Captain Rynarr, seeing the king and princess approach, now wanted to discuss his thoughts over how and why their small party was mysteriously located in the vast Sahara Desert. He would use the argument that they were not a stationary target such as a farm or an outpost, and nor were they a sizeable caravan that might stir up the sand and could be seen for miles away. At least these could be explained as a target for such a sizable Egyptian mounted force.

He was about to speak when a guard atop the battlement facing to the southeast shouted out word of a good-sized party approaching Silene on the road from Tripoli.

Within moments, word reached King Ramie by a winded army runner, "Sire, the lead rider carries the banner for the Great Imam of the Royal Court of Tripoli."

King Ramie did not like to be surprised by visitors, especially by such dignitaries as the High Cleric himself. He glanced from Princess Lennia to Brother Samuel and then to Captain Rynarr as he thought over his next actions. He knew protocol required certain things of him and this entailed him to show proper respect for the highest ranking religious leader in Libya.

He said to Captain Rynarr, "Prepare your Royal Guardsmen, Captain, we are about to have guests...but keep the show at a minimum, I don't want them to stay too long." King Ramie then guided his youngest daughter into the castle keep, his escort followed, while Captain Rynarr began shouting orders to everyone within earshot.

Without feeling too obliging, Sam cautiously had the remaining wounded gently moved inside the barracks. Servants were needed to escort the wounded to continue with their fanning of the flies. Additional slaves with rakes swept over the bloody sand, so the Great Imam would not see the blood-soaked ground. Meanwhile, all the townspeople were ushered out of the courtyard to make room for the Great Imam's extensive escort detail.

The kitchen was warned, and the staff was frantic to ready platters of juice, water, fresh fruit and meats for an estimated party of 20-horsemen and 80-foot soldiers. It was also reported the grand coach carrying the Great Imam was leading a line of 20-camels bearing supplies, and the animals would need forage.

King Ramie, who didn't even like the Great Imam, thought it absurd for the Holy Man to travel with such a large party and especially to such a poor kingdom as Silene. As to why the Cleric was coming, King Ramie could only hazard a guess. But he would not meet the man on the steps to his castle keep; that would be a display of respect he reserved for his friends. No, the Great Imam would have to follow protocol himself and be presented properly before the king in the royal court.

"We maybe a small kingdom, my dear," King Ramie said to Princess Lennia as they traveled the upper passageways, "but I am king and the Great Imam, no matter how powerful he believes he is, is not."

## THE ROYAL GUARDSMEN BARRACKS

Sam, who had finished stitching up a minor sword wound to the left arm of a semi-conscious Royal Guardsman, ordered Paul and Richard to complete their tasks and then return to their quarters. "Stay there until you hear from me and that is an order. I will explain later."

Then Sam remembered GW, "Paul, leave now and find GW, get him out of the courtyard before the Great Imam comes through the gate. I do not want him, or you seen right now."

"Why, what's the problem?" Paul asked as he finished wrapping a leg wound with clean linen and used thin steel pins to hold it. Tape was not something they had yet in ancient Libya and Sam had remembered his grandmother's sewing basket and used handmade narrow-gauge pins to hold his bandages in place.

"This is the Great Imam coming, the highest Muslim Cleric in Libya," Sam said. "He can order your execution on the spot and the King wouldn't even hear of it until it was too late, and your heads lay on the sand."

"Got it!" Paul said loudly and went off at the run to locate GW. He found him in the same place, sitting beside the watering troth and snoring loudly.

# 10 – THE GREAT IMAM

CASTLE OF SILENE
MAIN COURTYARD

The Great Imam, Supreme High Cleric to his majesty, the Caliph of Libya, and religious leader for over 1,000,000 Libyan Muslims, was reported to be of some 87-years of age and a true fanatic when it came to his faith. He was much too old to ride a horse or even sit comfortably in a camel chair, and the man was quite arrogant enough to actually demand of the Caliph of Libya to provide him with one of his fine coaches. In this case it was an ornate two-axle coach of finest cedar and pulled by four-Black Arabian thoroughbreds. The coach was a gift to the Caliph on his 70th birthday from his cousin, the Caliph of Bagdad. Its outer doors displayed dozens of intricate hand-carvings inlaid with a bright gold, which reflected the desert sun. The hand rails and even the spokes of the wheels were covered in gold leaf; a demonstration of wealth from one cousin to another.

Inside were two extremely overly stuffed couches lined in multi-colored and highly decorative fine silk and these were covered in soft furs, scented with fine perfume for the passenger's comfort. The curtains, dark enough to repel the bright sunlight, were of thick tightly woven lamb's wool. The coach also came to Libya with a highly experienced driver and a second coachman, who handled the coach's baggage and saw to the comfort of the passengers. A footman, belonging to the Caliph of Tripoli would normally accompany the coach, but he was not along for this trip. The footman, along with the driver and coachman all had reputations for absolute silence: but in fact, they have all had their tongues cut out upon entering into the service of the Caliph of Libya.

The high cleric himself was known by his enemies to be a man filled with his own self-importance, to the point of extreme pompousness and believed to have his own political ambitions. As proof of these accusations, the high cleric had appeared before the

Caliph and felt this fine coach and a 100-man escort was truly needed for his journey to Silene. Though the trek across the northern desert was relatively safe between Tripoli and Silene, he explained to the Caliph his position in Libya warranted it. True, there was the dragon of Silene, but the Caliph had pointed out the road between the two kingdoms remained a safe distance from the accursed dragon's watery lair.

Still, the Caliph decided it was a small price to pay to have this pesters-some holy man away from his court for a few days and out of his hair. He knew it would also provide the company of mounted troops and two-companies of infantry he would send along as a chance for them to get out of the barracks. He also knew Captain Rynarr would take this opportunity to pass on some words of wisdom to a couple of the Caliph's new officers, both of whom were promoted solely because of family ties to the Libyan throne.

The Caliph highly respected Captain Rynarr's intelligence and capabilities, as he had his father before him and on more than one occasion had presented a serious offer to Rynarr to leave Silene and join his army in Tripoli. But Captain Rynarr ever so politely refused the Caliph, for not only his love for King Ramie and his family which held him here, but also his blood quest to see the cursed dragon slain, and the death of his father and sister avenged.

When the more experienced scout riders first entered the castle courtyard to ensure no danger awaited the Great Imam, they rode with their scimitar drawn, but quickly relaxed when they found an alert Captain Rynarr on horseback waiting for them. They also observed the captain's honor guard; ten-Royal Guardsmen on foot, each armed with shield and spear in position of salute, with extremely shiny shields held in left arm at chest level and their spears held tightly under their right arm, point outward at an upward angle-but not threatening. They stood with backs straight and eyes straight ahead as they waited, preparing to give the Great Imam an escort of honor from his coach to the castle's main entrance.

Ignoring the guardsmen for the moment, they pranced around in tight circles to spot any possible threat, as this was their assigned task and Captain Rynarr understood this as he waited patiently for the grand coach to enter the courtyard. Upon seeing the coach's lead pair of horses entering through the gateway, he gave a hand signal to a soldier standing upon the northwest battlement tower. The soldier, wearing the brown uniform of a man-at-arms, carried an antelope horn in his hands and he raised it to sound the Great Imam's arrival with a single long blast.

Almost immediately following the blast of the horn, another soldier from the northeast battlement echoed this with a long blast of his horn. Such was standard protocol for dignitaries in such high status as the Great Imam. Only the arrival of the Caliph himself would call for the blasts of all four horns from surrounding battlements and his visits were extremely rare.

Captain Rynarr felt the highly decorative coach was a bit gaudy for a high cleric, but he had come to know the Great Imam was very unlike other Muslim holy man. From bitter experience, Captain Rynarr had learned the Great Imam valued his high prestige and wealth right up there with his faith and this made Captain Rynarr quite uncomfortable with the vile man. Though he remained respectful of the office the high cleric held, he felt no respect for the man.

Captain Rynarr remained mounted and his back straight, as the great coach pulled through the main gate and the driver reined in his four beautiful horses to a gradual stop in front of the huge stone platform. The man had done his job well, lining up the coach's door directly in front of the stone steps, which led up to the great platform and main entrance to King Ramie's keep.

With a loud commanding voice, Captain Rynarr ordered the honor guard into position and only then did he dismount his warhorse and hand off his reins to a waiting stable hand. Captain Rynarr straightened his tunic, made sure his short sword and dagger were in proper place along the silver-studded leather belt he wore, and only then did he approach the coach door. There he waited, while the coachman jumped down from beside the driver and rush around the coach to open the coach door with much pomp and ceremony, as he was trained.

Having known the Great Imam since he was a young lad, Captain Rynarr had no fear of the old gray bearded man who had allowed himself to become too overweight to move around without assistance. Looking at the man now, Captain Rynarr thought the Great Imam now resembled more like a fat Zeus of Greek mythology than a holy man of Libya. Still, out of respect for the office he held and his love for King Ramie, he bowed his head, with the blade of his scimitar resting on his right shoulder, as the man clumsily dismounted the coach.

The Great Imam, huffing from withdrawing himself from the soft cushions, had a bit of a hard time compressing himself through the narrow coach doorway. He had to be pushed by one of his assistant clerics from inside the coach.

The Holy Man was dressed in his standard long flowing black robes, with long sleeves that covered over his fatty hands. He wore a tight fitting black turban, which was adorned with a miniature golden symbol of the Caliph's coat of arms; a proud lion standing on its back legs, front paws in a position of challenge and crossed scimitars in the background behind the lion's head. The coat of arms was extremely similar-to many of the Arabian families and it was believed the Caliph of Libya was a descendant of the kings of ancient Persia.

While Captain Rynarr waited with head bowed, the Great Imam was helped to the ground. Seeing Captain Rynarr, he held out his hand for official greeting and Captain Rynarr touched his forehead to it to symbolize obedience and respect. The coachman then helped the Great Imam over to the first stone step, where he waited impatiently for his assistant clerics, of which there were three and all dressed in white robes, to dismount the coach and assist him.

Captain Rynarr also noticed the Great Imam was wearing black slippers instead of sandals, with a double-wide thread of gold in the shape of a desert flower sewn into the toes. He also wore several lengths of gold chain about his neck, which Captain Rynarr thought to be overly garish for a holy man. He could feed a thousand people for what those chains are worth.

The Great Imam was born in Tripoli to the name of Aazad, son of Mohammad—a simple rug seller. He had grown into a strapping young man who enjoyed sports and as a young adult felt a calling to the faith to become a cleric. From an unknown source, but suspected to be a wealthy widow, who admired Aazad's physical attributes, he obtained the necessary funds for travel to Damascus and Baghdad for religious studies. He did not return to Libya until the age of 41-years old and through a strong will and an eye for intimidation, by the age of 60, he was one of 9-senior clerics in the Caliph's court. At 77-years of age, he became the high cleric to the Caliph and all came to know he preferred to be called the Great Imam.

With age, too little exercise and excessive fine foods, his once muscular body turned to one of extreme obesity and he now needed assistance when even having to kneel and rise from his prayer rug.

If Captain Rynarr was to hazard a guess, he would put the man's weight at an excess to 350 lbs., and he only stood to Rynarr's chin.

Though Captain Rynarr had never known a senior cleric to dress in such finery, the Great Imam's plump fingers were laden with expensive jeweled rings and his fingernails painted and manicured by one gifted in the art. His heavily wrinkled face was mostly hidden by a great gray beard and as he rose from his bow, Captain Rynarr studied the man's hawkish nose, now quite reddish in color and his still intelligent eyes; piercing, cold and dark brown. He was always looking about and Rynarr suspected he was hoping to catch someone unaware and find where an opponent was vulnerable. Those eyes radiated with an inner vigor his outward body no longer displayed, but Rynarr suspected this glare of his displayed more allegiance to evil then of servant-hood to Allah. For all but the Caliph feared this man and the power he wielded over the people; all except King Ramie, Captain Rynarr and Brother Samuel that is.

Although there were three other clerics riding in the coach, Captain Rynarr only waited for the Great Imam's feet to touch the warm sand before he welcomed him to Silene.

The Great Imam, Chief Protector of the Faith, exchanged a brief word of pleasantry with Captain Rynarr, holding his voice to only a whisper and then he looked about the courtyard to inspect the castle's defenses. He was also wondering where King Ramie was and why he wasn't here to meet him. Not seeing the king, he frowned, shook his head in frustration and began to make his way across the stone platform.

He held on to an assistant cleric's hand for support, as to not trip over the ancient stones. While he slowly ambled along, he began to glance about for the king's daughters and if not them, possibly his arch-nemesis, Brother Samuel. He had hoped the infidel might dare to show his face. For truly he carried the powers as Protector of the Faith, which gave him the authority to execute Brother Samuel on the spot, but he was not sure Captain Rynarr would let him. But the idea of making the attempt out here in the open did intrigue him. Then not seeing anyone he could berate or challenge, he shrugged his beefy shoulders once again and made his way up the three-ancient wide-stone steps leading into the main entrance. Here he was met by a nervous slave, who would serve as the Great Imam's torch bearer.

Captain Rynarr had thought of briefing the Great Imam on the recent desert attack, but decided it was better for the king to do so. So, he handed off the Great Imam to one of his minor-clerics and went to release the honor guard. Afterward, he walked over to meet with the senior officers in the escort detail, several of whom he recognized and knew well. They would need quarters for the 100-man detail, corral space for their animals and food for both; which Silene could ill afford.

Though under constant observation from the battlements, the coach was of such value it would be placed beside the guardsmen's stable and kept under constant guard by a four-man detail around the clock. If anything was to happen to the coach, it would not only bring great embarrassment to the king, but also a slow death to those guards on duty.

Sam, who was perturbed to be rushed off by Captain Rynarr at the very last moment, remained busy with several of the wounded men in their barracks. He shook his head in wonder, as he looked out a window to view the Great Imam's grand entourage. He stood inside the barracks and watched the grand coach be driven off to the stables. His look of admiration for how well Captain Rynarr carried off the welcoming ceremony soon turned to one of dismay, for he knew from sad experience that anytime the Great Imam came to Silene it could only mean bad news for King Ramie and himself.

For nearly four decades, Sam and the clerics of Tripoli had squared off and the Great Imam had become the worst of the lot. Whenever he visited Silene, the two of them exchanged icy stares, scornful glares and heated words; the Great Imam's voice laced heavily with religious barbs, while Sam attacked the man's abusive manners for one sitting at the king's table. Only King Ramie's protection kept Sam, the infidel, from being executed, imprisoned in the dungeon or sent out into the desert without water to die a horrid death under an unforgiving sun.

During the last visit, the Great Imam went so far as to order King Ramie to have Sam punished unto death for refusing once again to accept the Muslim faith. But King Ramie, weary of the high cleric's demands, stood his ground and refused to comply. Sending the cleric into a fit of temper, dire threats and causing his assistants to spring from their chairs and almost forcefully lead him away before their high cleric could suffer a seizure. It had happened before, but not in Silene.

What then concerned the King and Brother Samuel was what would happen if King Ramie's dear friend and sire, the Caliph of Libya, ever ordered such punishment be carried out?

And, true to form, a very embittered holy man returned home from that trip and took the matter of Brother Samuel, the infidel, to the Caliph. But the matter was almost immediately passed down to King Ramie to decide upon, which left the high cleric disgruntled and very dangerous. What the Great Imam didn't know was how the Caliph used this situation between the old cleric and King Ramie as a way of controlling the holy man; a way to put him in his place and remember who the true Caliph of Libya was.

The Caliph, though a devout Muslim, had known for quite some time how devious the Great Imam was and how he secretly wished to seize control of Libya, and place the desert country under a Muslim theocracy for the entire world to see. An event the Caliph did not want to see come about and in the event of his assassination, a plan was in place to prevent the Great Imam from succeeding him. A very expensive contract was drawn up with a well-known guild of assassin's in Damascus to carry out the deed. Afterward, the Caliph had one of his minions purposely leak word of this contract to the Great Imam for added security. So far it had worked, for the Caliph was still very much alive and the high cleric continued to become more embittered with each passing day.

With little fondness for the high cleric himself, King Ramie would often invite Sam to sit at the court's immense dining table, which the king had set up in the throne room, so more people could attend when the various state dinners were held.

Lavished with rich foods the King could ill-afford, the table was covered in the finest dinner ware. He knew the Great Imam was visibly uncomfortable to be sitting among so many who were of such low status and he often seated him between a couple of overly talkative dignitaries from Damascus. But King Ramie also knew having to listen to Brother Samuel join in the various dinner conversations was a major affront and this usually forced the Great Imam into a rage and he'd storm out of the room, red-faced with disgust. This was why the king placed Brother Samuel to his immediate right and nearly right across from the Great Imam.

For those who remained at the table after the high cleric stomped off, people long since used to having Sam in their midst, they would then relax and enjoy their evening in comfort.

At those few times the old man didn't leave, and they were very few, the high cleric turned the evening into an unsettling one of heated religious debate; shouting at Sam in hostile words taken from the Koran and decreeing how this Jesus Christ of Sam's was only a mere prophet of Allah and not the Son of God as Christians believed.

Captain Rynarr would often be absent from these state dinners, for he would be playing host to the visiting the escort's senior officers in Silene's officer's dining room. Here the soldiers could relax, without concern of offending mere civilians with their highly detailed stories of bloody battles, heroic feats or court intrigue from Tripoli. Though there would be no alcoholic beverages passed about, tempers could still flare as stories were shared and manhood questioned, which could lead to challenge and a match of swordplay a top the various dining tables. It was up to Captain Rynarr as host to ensure not too much blood was spilled, for it upset the cooking staff and servants stuck with clean up.

He also had to be on the alert for those locked into long standing family blood feuds between families of Tripoli and Silene. Rynarr had regaled Brother Samuel with one such night in his youth where three brothers from Tripoli attended one state dinner here in Silene and went after a young man, whose oldest brother had been criminal enough to dishonor their older sister. Though the brother was executed for this heinous act, they felt the young brother should also die. Thankfully, Rynarr's father had been able to separate them and sent the boy out on a very long patrol into the Sahara.

Brother Samuel also recalled one dinner when the argument between the Great Imam, only one of 9-senior clerics back then, and himself, became so heated, the senior cleric violated protocol by drawing a golden dagger from under his outer robe, springing up from his chair in a burst of anger and rushing at Sam with intent to kill him. He was in late 60's and a bit thinner in those days and only the timely interference of a Royal Guardsmen lieutenant, who moved in at the right moment to accidentally interfere with the senior cleric, which saved Sam from possibly being stabbed.

The soon-to-be Great Imam stood there holding the dagger in his aged trembling hand and frustrated to the point of spitting out his angry words in Sam's face, he glared at the young lieutenant with ice in his eyes.

The room was utterly silent, which caused King Ramie to slowly rise from his chair and match hard glares with the senior cleric.

Sam also rose. He was fearful the enraged man might push the young officer aside and make a plunge for his heart. Court protocol was one thing and basic survival another.

As tension mounted, suddenly a minor cleric appeared at his superior's side, whispered a few words in his ear and cautiously, but respectfully, led the older holy man away from the table for a time to cool off. Had he gone through with injuring or killing Sam at the king's table, violating protocol and basic good manners, the Great Imam might not have risen to his current post and Sam was sure, this was what the minor cleric had whispered into the older man's ear that night.

For Sam, it was a point of victory. Whenever he was able to cause the man who would become the Great Imam to lose his temper in a debate over religion, Sam came off the better in the eyes of the king. But he did remember to thank the young lieutenant for his intervention later in the evening and out of the cleric's earshot.

Sam never wanted such a heated issue to come about after that night, for he did not wish to embarrass King Ramie. So, he did his best not to bring insult to the high cleric or one of his many assistants. Heated debate was still allowed, for King Ramie respected Sam's views on religion and the handling of government issues, but he also expected Sam to know when to back off and let the high cleric save face in front of so many other court officers of lesser status.

Another matter, which always surfaced at the grand table, was the subject of King Ramie's two oldest daughters. The Great Imam always wanted to know how the king was dealing with his two oldest daughter's blasphemous conduct; Princess Lonnia's practice of witchcraft and suspected murder, and Princess Lannia's behaving like a man; a warrior, taking up arms, wearing men's clothing and armor, and rumors of loving another woman?

Whenever these questions were presented to the king, a hush would fall over the table, guests and servants alike would freeze in mid-sentence, and King Ramie would produce his finest kingly-glare and slowly place a bite of food into his mouth. This hopefully would signal to the Great Imam that these questions would not be answered at this time, in front of so many people and he should move on to another subject or risk the king's displeasure. Not that the high cleric was fearful of King Ramie, but he was also smart enough to know he was a long way from Tripoli. His troops, even though numbering 100, were still greatly outnumbered if it came to a battle and he doubted the majority of them would actually defend him in a battle against fellow Libyans. He was not on the best of terms with the Libyan military.

Both King Ramie and the high cleric knew the old tales of how the great Sahara had a way of hiding the bodies of all those who stood against the realm and those who made other mistakes the king or Caliph wanted to keep hidden. There were even those who had attempted assassinations, flirted with a princess or slandered a king resting under its white sands. Whole troops had gone missing, dignitaries had simply vanished and whole cities had been covered over by massive sand storms in the desert's long history.

The Great Imam knew in such event he went missing, the Caliph would only send out a token investigative team and then select another high cleric from the nine senior clerics and probably one who would not give him such trouble or threaten his throne. So, for this trip, the high cleric hoped he could hold his temper to ensure this didn't happen to him.

Sam knew under Muslim Law, King Ramie was dictated to execute both of his daughters for their reputed heinous acts, but he also knew the father still loved both children and had made promises before Allah to protect them with his life. This left the king torn as to which law he should follow; to honor Allah by killing the women or honor Allah by letting both live for the promises he made?

King Ramie had spoken of this problem with Sam across a chessboard on many occasions and in each case, Sam would respectfully remind the king of the love of Christ, highlighting his Savior's words of forgiveness and because of this, he could offer little in the way of help without speaking out against Muslim Law. Sam had originally promised the king when he was released from the dungeon he would not evangelize the people of Silene with his Christian message versus the Muslim religion, something he found harder to do with each passing year. He admittedly fudged a bit on this promise in his talks of Christianity with Princess Lennia, going beyond the basic outlines of Christianity. King Ramie had requested such lessons on the Christian laws to acquaint his youngest daughter with these teachings for the time these strange men would arrive upon the Silene's shores. Though they would be on their way to Jerusalem, he knew how rough the Mediterranean Sea could become and some of the ships would seek shelter here in Libya at a time when the seas rose to towering heights.

Still, the longer Sam wore these heavy robes of a priest, both by weight and responsibility to his faith, the more he felt and acted as one. Giving him a near overwhelming desire to spread the Lord's words through the town of Silene and let the headman's axe fall where it will. During lighter moments, this made him question if his name would ever come up in the Catholic Church's list of martyrs.

Sam had other things on his mind now though, he was gravely concerned with the Great Imam's unannounced arrival for fear it could lead to his friend's execution as heretics or a lesser sentence of banishment. But in either case, it meant at least GW and Paul could come to harm if the high cleric learned of their presence. Sam hoped if things did turn sour, at least Richard might be able to pass himself off as a Muslim from Sudan. A Baptist playing a Muslim to survive persecution, hopefully God would understand.

As it happened to be, the Great Imam was a descendant, supposedly from his mother's side, of the Black Moors, who once covered most of North Africa at one time.

As a result, the high cleric was rumored to have some degree of regard for the black skinned people of faith and used two or three as minor clerics back in Tripoli.

Sam knew this other matter of Princess Lennia's affection for GW couldn't come about at a worse time and there was also Captain Rynarr's suspicion of Princess Lonnia's knowledge of the Egyptian attack. As to why the Black Princess would be involved, it still gave Sam wonder. All in all, Sam didn't think he was going to get much sleep while the Great Imam was in Silene and he still had less than eight-days before the next lottery. Is that why the holy one is here, so he could witness the savagery of a maiden being devoured? No, I would not think even he could stoop that low. There's got to be something else and it might be me. That old coot would like to see me dead before he passes on, hoping to claim a few more virgins for doing away with such a dangerous infidel...I'm really getting too old for this!

## THE QUARTERS OF GW, PAUL AND RICHARD

Droopy eyed and struggling to stay awake, GW had trouble understanding his friends' apparent nervousness and why they had physically rushed him into their room. They relayed Sam's orders to stay put, but not as to why.

"It's too hot in here, guys. I want to go for a walk," GW said. A fly landed on his cheek and he smacked it, and then used a piece of his soiled tunic to wipe the dead fly away and the sweat from his forehead. GW then glanced at the tunic and announced, "Things dirty!" He tossed it to the end of his bed.

"You can wash it later," Paul said. "Right now, get some sleep."

Without windows and the door closed, air movement was non-existent in their quarters. The flies became a problem during midday and because of this, the three men usually found someplace to be where the breeze kept the flies at bay or some servant was using a large palm fan to keep the air moving.

"Paul, this place is like a sauna," GW complained as he stood to his feet. "I gotta get out of here!"

Paul pushed GW back down on to his bunk, who was simply too bone-weary to give Paul much resistance, "I told you, man, Sam's really worried about this old bigwig who just arrived out of the blue. He's some kind of big Muslim preacher, but whoever he is, he's got Sam really rattled." Paul sat back down at the foot of his bunk and used a torn scrap of bandage he had with him to clean the dried blood off his KA-BAR blade with.

Richard, who was pacing about the room like an expectant father, and keeping GW from getting out the door, pointed a thumb over his right shoulder and in a low voice whispered, "I heard one of the servants say this man is called the Great Imam. If I remember right, and remember Islam is not my best topic, that means he's the head holy man for this part of the world and at least probably all of Libya. Kind of like a Catholic cardinal I think."

Seeing Paul had GW apparently under control, Richard then plopped down on his bunk, one hand behind his head and the other fanning his face with an empty wooden bowl. He began to think about all the men he treated today. "My dad should've seen me in action today. He always wanted me to be a doctor… I think he'd be proud of what I did today." Richard then used the bowl to swat at two large flies circling high overhead.

GW sat up on his bunk, putting both Paul and Richard on guard, and glanced back and forth between his two friends for a silent moment and then he spoke, "I think you guys are really starting to feel right at home here, playing doctor and getting down with the boys," GW's voice grew more intense, "...and you're not even worried about this Great Imam or whatever he wants to call himself."

GW gestured toward the closed door, "Don't you realize this guy can put our heads on the block simply because we're not Muslim and I don't even know how Sam handles it?" GW stood up and held his hands out, "If you ask me, I think we should be on our knees asking God to save us from that axe. Man, just thinking about another stay in that rotten dungeon makes me feel sick inside...and you clowns sit here feeling all happy you got to play doctor today!"

Paul got upset, "Hey, man, I know you had it rough out there in that big bad desert and we're cutting you some slack here, but take it easy—okay?" Paul then gestured at GW with the point of his KA-BAR. "Settle down some, you're letting the heat get to you."

"And when did you get so religious all-of-a-sudden?" Richard asked. Tossing the bowl aside, he sat up on his bunk and stared at GW with a doubtful expression and then added, "Look, I grew up among holy-rollers...real Bible thumpers as we used to say. We sang, we cheered, and we prayed. Oh, how we did pray. But you know what—the thing I really miss was the sheer joy of being a Christian." He pointed to the door, "You see any joy in these people? Only singing I hear is their chanting of prayers."

"So, what are you saying here, Professor?" Paul always reverted to calling Richard Professor when his friend spouted off with philosophy.

Richard thought about it for a moment and then replied, "Maybe that's why we're here—to bring the Lord to these people and show them what we believe in. How about it, GW, do you agree?"

GW wasn't sure how to respond to that question at first, but then said in almost a whisper, "I'm not sure, Richard. Not really. Oh, I believe, but maybe not as hard as you do...But something happened to me out there and I don't think I can explain it...not yet anyway." GW reached out and swatted at a few more pester some flies, which one made the mistake of landing on his bare shoulder. He then began to walk around their small room as he recalled those bizarre moments in the desert.

With so little space, the room only gave him freedom for roughly seven-steps in either direction before being forced to turn around, GW tried to explain himself, "Look, we all saw a lot of action in Nam, maybe you were like me and didn't think God, the guy with the big 'G' in front of his name, actually cared about us little people. I mean he's got this whole universe to control." GW continued to speak in a calm voice, as he continued his pacing. Richard was now leaning his back against the wall, letting GW have the room.

"I mean that last day. You guys remember when everything hit the fan. The NVA came at us from everywhere and we took off running like they had us scared out of our wits...Well, we were pretty scared." GW admitted, and the others shook their heads in agreement. "This prayer stuff...God, He wasn't even on my mind back then. I was just freaked out and looking for a place to hide. I heard all those other guys calling out for their mom's and a few yelled to God, but I simply wanted to live." GW glanced back and forth between his two friends. "But it was different out there in the desert. I was on Valiant and well, I felt like Superman...I really felt something...maybe it was what you could call spiritual. Whatever it was, I had some kind-of presence guiding me, controlling and ...and like, protecting me.

"Only way to explain it, I mean, I wasn't even scratched. Oh, Valiant was hurt, sure, but Captain Rynarr said I beat ten men, killed them and those dudes were probably a whole lot better about this horse fighting thing than I was." He pointed at himself, "I mean look at me, I walked away without a single wound and Captain Rynarr said I even saved his life...but I don't remember it."

"Yeah, you were lucky, GW, but now you're here preaching at us, saying we should pray," Paul said in disbelief. "Man, I'm not much into that holy Joe stuff. My old lady was Roman Catholic, used to drag us off to church every Sunday and then confession once a week. I mean what's a ten-year old got to confess?" He grinned, "Guess you could say I like bad women, good booze and partying down with some good weed too much to be a Bible thumper."

"Then you are sure in the wrong place now, aren't you?" GW asked him with a touch of mockery to his voice. "You struck out on all three!"

"Hey, you gotta admit the big dude has a sense of humor," Paul said in jest.

"Keep it respectful when you talk about God, Paul," Richard warned. "I was never much into the weed scene or spending my hard-earned money on beer, but...well, it seems funny to be talking about this now. I thought I'd never bring God up with you guys unless Sam was here and joining in the conversation."

"Why Sam, Professor?" Paul asked. "You know he's not a real priest, he's only playing a Friar Tuck scene to stay alive and I don't blame him none. You gotta do what you gotta do, right?" Paul then saw the confused look on Richard's face and added, "You know, from Robin Hood...Errol Flynn...men in green tights...Friar Tuck with the fat little guy in the monk robes."

"I understand, Paul. I saw the movie," Richard replied in low voice and his right eyebrow rose to show he was not amused.

"Sam isn't playing no Friar Tuck, he is behaving like a priest...or what I think a priest acts like...and I'm not even a Catholic," GW said with a grimace. "But maybe it's his 1940's roots that helped him gain an understanding of God I don't have." GW replied.

"Back then, almost everyone in the US of A was a Bible preaching Christian and look at us now," GW added.

"Right!" Richard agreed. "He's also been standing alone in amongst an army of Muslims and that's got to stand for something."

"Look, I get where you're both coming from, but does either of you boneheads know anything about this Muslim religion?" Paul asked.

GW didn't respond right away but reached down and picked up his right boot to give it a good looking over. He'd patched up two holes in the sole with camel leather, but now the heel was nearly gone, and he wasn't sure what he could replace a hard rubber heel with? Maybe I could use a horse's hoof? When he thought of having to wear the Silene sandals, which he thought resembled Ho Chi Minh sandals back in Vietnam; a flat sole made of used tire rubber and held together by thin leather straps, he began to wonder if he could fashion a pair of soft camel-hide knee-high moccasins like the hippies back home made.

GW remembered seeing a lot of those moccasins back in Los Angeles, they had become popular. Long hair was in, thanks to the Beatles, Stones and a hundred other rock bands. Peace and love was the scene on school campuses, dope was the trip, and no one loved the military anymore.

But as he thought about Paul's last question, he had never given Muslims a thought until now. Before coming here, he would probably have said they were just another weird religion like the Buddhists, and un-American, which was to say- he knew very little about their religion and their beliefs.

"I got no answer for you, Richard. I'm blank," GW said in a weary voice.

Richard nodded his head in understanding, his friend was really worn out and he needed to bring this conversation to an end so he could rest, "Only thing I can remember from history class and my work in the museum was how a lot of the Muslim people in this time period were confused over the issue of this infidel thing...meaning us," Richard said in response. "On one side of the coin the Muslims tolerated us, befriended us even-like now, and tried to live in peace with Christians and Jewish people alike in Jerusalem.

"But on the flip-side, other Muslims believed the Koran teaches that you either accept the Muslim faith or die! These were the fanatics and a lot of people were slain in the name of Allah."

Richard butted in, "Either of you thinker dudes read anything about the crusades?" Paul asked. "I saw the movie, a black and white film made long before I was born."

"I think I saw that one too," GW said. "But I remember reading how there were several crusades, but it wasn't until the 3rd-crusade the Christian army made it to Jerusalem with King Richard. People had to travel a long way back then and a lot of the knights from northern Europe and England got seriously sea sick from the voyage. Some were lost at sea, while others died of sickness before they even made it into battle."

"Well, you know more about then I do," Paul said. He finished wiping his knife down and slid it into its sheath on his belt. He liked to have it close by incase someone came knocking with less than honorable intentions on their mind or jumped him in the dark corridors. He then used the same rag to wipe the sweat off his face and neck, before he tossed it on the foot of his bunk.

"All I can remember hearing about was how these nights killed a bunch of Arabs in the name of God. So, it seems we got us two religions killing for their God, and we're stuck here in the middle of it...any ideas, bright boys?" Paul asked.

"I think we'd better speak to Sam," GW said, and he lay back down to swat flies.

"You really think this bigwig means trouble for us?" Paul asked.

"Could be, cowboy," GW replied in his best, but not quite good enough, John Wayne voice impersonation.

"Was that supposed to be Roy Rogers or Mae West?" Paul asked with a laugh.

"Okay, so I can't do John Wayne, but don't insult me with that singing cowboy."

"Hey, Roy was cool," Paul replied. "Trigger was the smartest horse ever and Bullet, man that dog would've been a prime killer-hound in Nam."

"You can have the horse, even the dog, but Roy never made a decent cowboy flick. He couldn't even lick the Duke's boots," GW said. He was now fully awake to defend one of his heroes.

Richard looked at his two friends, who were now shooting at each other with invisible two-handed six-guns. I guess we're off the topic of God now. Sorry Lord. Forgive them for they no naught what you have given them…Richard suddenly glanced up at the stone ceiling, now where did that come from? He shook his head, lay back down and tried to recall the last time he was in a church with his dad. While all around him Roy Rogers and the John "Duke" Wayne were shooting it out with the famous everlasting-never running out of ammo Hollywood six-gun.

Richard glanced up at the ceiling and frowned, overhead, flights of B-52 sized black flies were flying sorties over their three intended targets.

"You know what I really miss?" Richard said, hoping to stop the gunplay before these spirited gunslingers tipped his bed over for cover and spilled the water bucket.

"What?" GW asked as he popped up from behind his bunk.

"Toilet paper."

"Oh, don't even start!" Paul replied and then shot Richard twice with his Roy Roger Ivory gripped nickel-plated six-shooters.

## PRINCESS LONNIA'S BEDCHAMBER

For more than an hour she had attempted a nap, having been driven from her laboratory by the stifling heat, but something was amiss, and it troubled her. So, she climbed off her bed of soft silks and wearing only a simple blue sleep gown, limped over to a nearby window in hopes the faintest sea breeze coming off the waters to the north might cool her some. But she felt only the stifling heat of a midday sun and it drove her back, for the stone ledge was hot to the touch.

Princess Lonnia loathed this time of year and wished she could have arranged a sea voyage, but the responsibility of the lottery held her here in Silene. She desired to see other parts of the world, experience other cultures and maybe even visit this Isle of Britain. She had heard of a special race of shamans had come from there and they were known to the local people as druids. She wanted to learn their magic, to add it to her own and make her more powerful in the dark arts. Until no one could challenge her, for she desired to be the greatest shaman of all and with a dragon to do her bidding, she would be unstoppable. She hoped that she could find a potion or a spell that could transform the beast into a flying dragon, to bid her will and able to leave its sea home and terrorize the world.

From the passageway outside her chambers she heard sounds of people rushing back and forth and suddenly, she wondered if the castle was under attack. But she hadn't heard the alarm sounded, so it wasn't that, but she needed to know who was making all the noise and why?

She clapped once and waited for her two handmaidens to appear and when they didn't, she clapped again. They arrived a few moments late, for having thought their mistress was asleep they were off visiting with some of the other girls on the floor. Surprisingly, she didn't grow upset and strike them when they arrived, and this was a relief, for the handmaidens were extremely frightened.

"What is happening, why is there so much activity in the upper chambers?" She asked brusquely.

"Mistress, the Great Imam has arrived. Servants take his baggage and that of his party to the guest quarters down the hall," the older of the two said. "We did not think they would've awakened you, or we would have asked the servants to be quieter."

"The Imam is here?" She asked in alarm.

"Yes, Mistress," The younger handmaiden said. Normally she would say nothing, being the 4th in line of rank. But now, for at least the present, she was ranked number two and took a chance by speaking.

Princess Lonnia barely heard her, her mind was filled with vile thoughts, as she thought of the Great Imam; a man who wanted her killed, being on the same floor with her. In fact, only two smaller rooms and three thick walls of stone were all that separate them and that is much too close for the Black Princess.

"Prepare my clothes, you dim-wits; I will see my father immediately!" She barked, and as the two handmaidens rushed to the closet, Princess Lonnia faced the direction of the Great Imam's rooms. Concentrating, she used her hands to make a series of evil signs to curse the high cleric and protect her from the cleric's own magic.

## SAM'S STUDY

It took Sam some doing, but he made it through the passageways and up the various levels to reach his home without being seen by the Great Imam or his entourage. After long hours in surgery and caring for the wounded, he was tired and in no mood to banter words with the old windbag and would rather hide for the moment.

Word was passed to Sam that his three friends were in their quarters and would stay there until they had word from him. This greatly relieved him, for he was concerned one of the men would've been caught by a member of the entourage. A white man, even a tanned one, or a Nubian, stuck out in a castle filled with brown skinned people. GW's height was enough to make him stick out, for he stood nearly a head taller than most of the Libyan people.

Opening the thick wooden door to his classroom and study, which creaked loudly, he was surprised to find the beautiful Princess Lennia sitting on a stool beside his work table, fanning herself with a small palm fan. Normally there would be a servant to do this task for her, but in accordance with Sam's wishes there were no royal servants here in Sam's rooms.

"I would've thought you'd be with your father, young lady," Sam said. With a loud plop-like sound, he dropped his heavy medicine bags down on the floor and went to a clay water pitcher sitting on the window ledge. There the sea breeze would keep it cool, but not today and oh how he missed refrigeration and a simple thing like an ice cube.

He needed to wash off for a second time, having used a horse-troth in the courtyard for the major blood stains and he now went into finer detail to clean himself. His apron was left for a servant to find another use for. It was simply too heavily stained with so many men's lifeblood to be of much use. Thankfully, he had two other aprons and would soon order up another one from the man who did the tanning of skins.

Princess Lennia answered his question, "I do not like the way the Great Imam behaves in my father's presence." Princess Lennia casually moved the fan back and forth, as she glanced down at an old parchment and read the Greek silently.

"Your father knows how to tolerate the old blowhard."

She smiled, "But I know how that old blowhard thinks of my family. He'd like to see both of my sister's heads in some dreadful straw basket."

"Please be careful, my dear. I may refer to the old blowhard as the old blowhard in my own tongue, for he will never know what I say. But you may mistakenly speak it in your tongue and we'd have hell to pay," Sam said. With warm water and a bar of goat soap he washed his hands and took a drink from a separate wooden bucket with a long hand-carved wooden dipper. He then looked to the princess and asked, "Do you want a drink or are you the reason why my pitcher is almost empty."

"It's hot," She said. She wore the face of a child, but there was clearly a hint of mischief in those lovely eyes.

"Well now you can stand up, go to the door and summon a servant to have the pitcher refilled." Sam took the drinking container from the window ledge and placed it on the table. "Maybe I should have you carry it down those several flights of stairs and refill it yourself."

"Are you mad at me?" She asked, as she rose from her stool and stood before him with an expression of concern on her face.

Sam's bushy left eyebrow rose a bit, while he thought over his answer. Both of his hands rested on his wide hips. She was too much like a daughter for him to stay mad, "No, my dear, I am not mad at you, but yes, I am gravely concerned."

Sam then gestured for the princess to return to her stool. "I have expressed my wishes for you to avoid any contact with my clansmen and yet, I have witnessed the display of compassion you showed when seeing GW by the watering troth. I only hope I was the only one to see it."

See couldn't look into his eyes and lie to him, those same eyes that have looked kindly and protectively upon her growth from child to young adult. "No, I disobeyed you and you are right, it was foolish of me. I can't help it!" She leapt to her feet and stomped the fading rug with her bare foot like she did as a young adolescent when he wouldn't let her get away with anything.

"Does this man even know who you are, I mean who your really are?" Sam asked.

"We've never spoken, not once." She walked to the window and wished for a cooling sea breeze to blow over her and refresh her.

She turned back to Brother Samuel, "Truthfully, I've watched him train, spending those long hours on horseback until he rides better than anyone...except maybe Captain Rynarr. He's so handsome, Brother Samuel, and a compassionate man like I've never seen before. The servants and stable hands all like him and it's easy to see his horse loves him. That's says a lot doesn't it."

"I agree he is a unique individual, Princess, but he is still an infidel of no standing and your attention to him would either kill or banish him from the kingdom." Sam walked to the door, opened it and summoned one of the servants who worked this part of the castle. Normally, he'd take the water pitcher and bucket down the stairs for exercise and have one of the young men help carry it back up. But he was thirsty from his labors and knew there wasn't enough water in the pitcher to last out the day.

Once the servant was gone on the errand, Sam picked up another hand fan and began cooling himself off. There wasn't a day gone by during the long days of late spring through early fall that he would gladly exchange his priestly robe for a tunic of light silk. But to survive, he must wear the costume he had made for him once they released him from the dungeon. A priest he pretended to be and a priest he would dress as, but heat stroke was always a concern of his. As it was, the only garment he wore under his robe in the summer was silken-boxers he had made for him once he designed them for the various tailors he used over the years.

It was a bit of a joke, since he believed he was the only one in Silene to wear such things as men's boxers, but Sam began to suspect there might be others in the kingdom now sporting the sporty undergarments and he wondered if he had messed with the time sequence once again. Had he brought boxers into civilization long before they were due to be discovered and how might it affect clothes fashions? Such things always troubled him but staying cool overrode the fashion world and right now he had more on his plate to worry about.

"What shall I do?" Princess Lennia pleaded in her own tongue, revealing to Sam how upset she was. She then sat on the ground, crossed her legs and sulked.

He considered his answer for a moment and then carefully knelt in front of his student, ignoring the cracking joint pains as he did so. "There is something happening here, something I do not understand, and I cannot explain it to you right now. You must trust me and for the present, please avoid these men, especially while the Great Imam is here. Later, maybe something can be done..." Sam didn't get a chance to finish before Princess Lennia interrupted.

"Do you really think something can be done? Do you think he'll like me?" Suddenly she was behaving like an excited high-spirited teenager with boys on the mind.

"When can I talk to him? Will you arrange it?"

He put his hands up to stop her, "Hold it! I didn't say anything about setting up a meeting or you even talking to him...not yet anyway." He placed his thick and wrinkled right hand on her soft cheek. "Be patient, young one. We have to wait until that old windbag leaves and only then we shall see about you meeting my clansmen."

A single tear fell from her eye, caught by her thin silken veil and she looked at her favorite person outside her father and sighed. "I do trust you, Brother Samuel, but I feel such a draw to this man...so much it hurts."

"I've heard it called first love and some refer to it as love at first sight and it usually happens to teenagers and it's almost always fatal."

"Fatal!" She said in alarm.

He broke into a big jovial smile, "Not really. You only feel like it is and sometimes, but not very often, this young love blooms into something very beautiful." Sam stood up and stared out the window, remembering his young wife and those early days in his life he was privileged to share with her before the war separated them.

"Brother Samuel, were you ever in love? I mean when you were my age?"

Sam continued looking out across the desert sand, watching a small herd of camels being brought toward town as a company of cavalry headed north passed them by on the Tripoli Road. He then turned to face Princess Lennia, "Yes, my dear, I was once in love and it was so very long ago. She was a few years older than you, quite beautiful and now, she is gone from me."

"I am sorry." Princess Lennia apologized. "We've never talked of this before…. Did she die?"

"No. I had to leave our land and she couldn't come with me." Sam then remembered his masquerade and quickly added, "I was a priest and we are not allowed to be married. But I've told you that before. Our order believes all priests should be single as St. Paul was."

"You've told me of this St. Paul, but I still do not understand why having a wife would interfere with your church duties."

"Nor do I, but that is the way of things." Sam heard a knock at the door and turned to see the servant enter and walk in with the water pitcher.

"Thank you, young man."

"You are welcome, Brother Samuel," the servant said and then he placed the pitcher on the table. He turned to bow to the princess before leaving and quickly left the room.

Sam gazed upon his student, smiled and said, "We will talk more on this later. Right now, I think you should probably be with your father. The Great Imam often gives him heart burn and you are a soothing influence."

Princess Lennia grinned in response and rose to her feet. "I must admit, I do enjoy the debates between you and the Great Imam. Maybe at dinner tonight you could engage him in another one. I like to watch his face turn red and his eyes swell with anger. He looks as if he is about to pop open like an over-filled water bag."

Sam frowned at her, "Young lady, he is still your elder and I might mention he is also your religious leader."

"Oh, you are no fun at all." She grinned again, gave him a quick hug and ran out the door. Then she stopped and turned to look back at Sam, "What is a teenager?" she asked.

"Another time, my young one," Sam said. There was a hint of a smile on his face and then he added, "I am tired, and this fat old man needs a nap."

"You are younger than you believe, but truly, a nap would prepare you for tonight and your meeting with the Great Imam," She said before leaving the study.

However, when Sam went to close his door, he glanced down the hallway and noticed Princess Lennia stop briefly in each of the passageway intersections and he wondered if she was looking for GW? But he pulled his head back in and closed the heavy door so he might have some privacy.

First, he put his medical supplies away for the next time he might need them and wrote down the items he needed to replace. He then stood at the window ledge and watched as a small bird of prey began circling a large herd of sheep. Thinking a little big, aren't you? A nap attack then captured him, and he went to his bed and slept peacefully for a whole two hours.

Two levels above him in another part of the castle the Great Imam was having a serious discussion with his assistants concerning his main reason for coming to Silene. A matter in which the high cleric was sure would cause more than a little heartburn for King Ramie and if all came off as he planned, he might see the last of his nemesis; Brother Samuel.

# 11 – WILL DARKNESS PREVAIL?

CASTLE OF SILENE
PRINCESS LONNIA'S LABORATORY

For most of the people in the castle, the late evening and early morning hours brought some relief from the sultry heat of the summer day, but Princess Lonnia's windowless laboratory remained a sweltering oven. To make matters worse, her newest concoction had produced a foul pungent odor that was beginning to overwhelm her senses.

Finally, unable to stand the vile odor any longer, she hurriedly poured the slimy contents of her mixing bowl into a dark fetid hole in the stone floor beneath her table. From her lab, the rejected ingredients of her many experiments carried downward through various levels of thick clay pipe and eventually reached the very sewer tanks Brother Samuel had built for the king.

Reeling from the odors, she swayed about the room until she was able-to open her door and then promptly fell through it, landing hard upon the outer room stone floor. As she lay there gasping for breath, a vision came upon her. With the strange blurriness beginning to clear, she saw her youngest sister, Princess Lennia, in the embrace of the infidel she knew to be called GW. They stood in what she thought to be the Royal Guardsmen stables, with a saddled grayish colored Arabian behind them. They were kissing tenderly and then the momentary vision ended as her mind began to clear. But the stink of her repulsive mixture was all too real, drifting upward through the spiraling flight of stone stairs and causing a wall mounted torch to flare up.

She didn't know how long she had lain there, but when she opened her eyes she found herself lying there on a dark brown Moroccan rug. With sudden realization, she knew just how close she had come to death from the noxious gas her experiment had produced. With her laboratory hidden, she also knew no one would find her down here, especially since the stairwell door at the top of the stairs was hidden behind the tapestry and securely locked.

But most importantly to her for the moment was the vision of her sister and the vile infidel locked in a forbidden embrace. It infuriated her to no end to see an infidel dare to touch her sister.

She struggled to control her anger but ended up throwing any item she could lay her hands on against the walls. Her angry cries went unheard due to the thick walls, but then winded, she suddenly stopped and stared at the far wall, unseeing, as her mind switched from madness to stark realization. A smirk then appeared on her scarred face and she began to thank the ancient gods she served, for she now understood this was a vision they had sent her, a tool to be used in its proper time.

This was not the first vision she'd received while working in her lab or when using her poppy concoction. Whenever something really important needed to be done in her life, the deities she worshipped provided such insight into the future as tonight's revealing vision.

In the first event, brought about in the late of night as she poured the ingredients of a new poison into a stone pestle, and read out loud from an aged Egyptian scroll of papyrus; believed to be part of the legendary Book of the Dead, which she had purchased from the estate of an Egyptian sorcerer in Thebes, her head began to reel, her vision blurred and then she found herself standing in the presence of a faceless creature. Human-like in shape, the creature was clothed in thick woven robes of great wealth and sat upon a magnificent golden throne. It gestured her forward with a silvery-gloved hand, one detailed in fine jewels, and suddenly a deep raspy voice filled her mind.

Somehow, she knew this to be an oracle of old, for she saw no mouth, yet through pictures and words strangely spoken in complete silence, the oracle foretold of Princess Lonnia's rise in power and of how she would soon become a queen of great prominence. Pictures flashed of things she must do and who she must serve for such events to come true.

Twelve deities she must serve, each the oracle named through a picture in her mind and she knew from previous research they were all ancient Egyptian gods: Re—the Sun God; Sed-spirit of power and strength; Osiris-King of Egypt; Isis-Queen of Egypt and sister to Osiris; Thoth-God of wisdom and creation; Amon-Lord of all gods; Nun-snake god; Nuntet-snake god and sister to Nun; Anubis-god of the underworld; Hathor- also known as Wasret and goddess of love; Meretsedar-serpent goddess.

For several weeks later she wondered why these twelve gods above the others? In her years of research, she had discovered more than fifty such deities and their descriptions were of part man and part-animal, or much worse—a scaly reptile. Still, she followed the oracles words and since then, she had murdered three times and attempted several other such killings. Now it appeared her sister was the next target for her prophecy to come about, but out of jealousy for her sister's beauty and relationship with their father, she cared little for the girl. What angered her so was an infidel daring to embrace a member of the royal family and for this she knew he must face a horrible fate to satisfy her.

"Little sister, you have become my next stepping-stone to greatness and a price I willingly pay for my kingdom to be born," Princess Lonnia said out loud, hoping the gods would hear her. She slowly rose to her feet but favored her bad leg and had to use a candle-stand to help her rise from the floor. Winded from her ordeal and with some effort, she limped to her laboratory door. "So, you love this infidel, this one called GW—such a stupid name for a man, even for a lowly infidel. Have you no shame, sister?" She reached up to secure the two-heavy locks to her lab door. "However, sister of mine, you two will be my newest pawns in a deadly game of power I play with our father." She said this in a thick sleazy voice and then began laughing loudly in a haunting way.

"So sad, of my sisters you were once my favorite." Princess Lonnia's mocking words dripped from her plump red lips like droplets of blood and her eyes, outlined in thick bluish hue, radiated with a glint of sheer evil.

Leaning against the stairwell wall for balance, she labored to climb the steep stone stairs to her bedchamber above. Though tired from the heat and long hours in the lab, she must prepare for the upcoming meeting between her father and the Great Imam. She also had to decide how best to use the vision the dark gods had blessed her with.

A moment or two would be required for Princess Lonnia to locate the name slip for next week's scheduled sacrifice. She had reclaimed it upon return to Silene. Vengeance was always a motivating factor behind her choices, selecting an innocent girl whose family had spurned or ridiculed her in the past. Or maybe a maiden who laughed at her disability or whispered unkind words to a friend as the princess limped by.

But remembering her vision as she entered her bedchamber to dress for court, Princess Lonnia didn't take notice of the ruffle in the rug before her and tripped. Catching herself by grabbing the back of a chair before she fell, she burst out with a string of curses to Allah for the pain surging through her bad leg, caring little for who might hear her or who might be offended.

As the pain subsided, her mind became filled with thoughts of her beloved little sister and how their father would react if his youngest and most special Lennia were the one chosen for the upcoming sacrifice. Such tragedy over the loss of his favorite daughter would cause him the utmost pain and this idea gave her much to contemplate on. Why had I not thought of this before?

## GW, RICHARD AND PAUL'S QUARTERS

By late evening Sam, weary from the long day, had little to say, as he stood inside the door of his friend's room and leaned his overweight and aged frame against the doorframe. Leaving the door open let the fresh sea air carry into the room from the outer passageway to cool off his friends and by standing there, he could make sure to close it if he saw a member of the Great Imam's company passing through the hallways.

He immediately felt the sultry heat inside the room strike him when he opened the heavy wooden door but reminded himself it was better to be hot and sweaty, even in this oven, then dead.

"I know this is almost unbearable, but you must remain here and it's for your own good. If the Great Imam or one of his party were to see you, there would be many questions and you'd all end up either dead or banished into the desert beyond."

Wiping his forehead with what was left of an old t-shirt, Richard asked, "Sam, at least have some more water brought here."

"Yeah," Paul agreed. "I stuck my head out a couple times, but no one's around to bring us water or food."

"Of course, I didn't think," Sam said in apology. "I'll have water, juice and food brought to you soon. All of the servants from this area were moved to the upper level to serve the Great Imam's people. With everything going on, I'm afraid I simply forgot." Sam pulled a large piece of soiled linen from a robe pocket and wiped his face.

"No problem." Paul said. "You've got a lot on your mind, but can you tell us just who is this guy is...this Great Imam? Sounds like some wrestler."

"Wrestler?" Sam asked, confused by Paul's question. But unable to stand any longer, partially from the heat and partially from weariness, he stepped further into the small room and dropped down on the foot of GW's bed, and released a deep sigh. Every muscle cried out and he regrettably knew he was getting far too old for days like this. He had attempted to train up a team of corpsmen, but the ones smart enough for the job were equally afraid of the castle's holy men. Just before his new friend's arrival he was ready to appeal to the king for some sort of decree to protect the men he would choose for medical training from the Muslim clerics.

Now he looked to the three men in the room and hoped he would now have the men capable of assisting him with the various tasks he needed to accomplish while in service to the king. He knew these men would have no fear of the clerics and two of them had already displayed some degree of first aid training, which had greatly assisted him today.

"I forgot...you've never seen a TV," Paul said. "In our time they have this television, we told you about that already, and early on they had certain nights where they'd show these professional wrestling matches. It was all fake, of course. But these hulking wrestler dudes had these phony names like Mister Handsome, the Diabolical Demon or Macho Man. Get it?"

"Macho Man?" Sam asked, again in confusion. "No, I don't get it, but I'll trust you." Then after a moment of thought, he looked to Paul and asked, "But some guy actually called himself Macho Man?"

"It was all theater stuff, Sam," Richard said.

Then with a shake of his head in disapproval, Sam said. "This television sounds like a complete waste of time. Does anybody work for a living anymore?"

"Sure," GW replied.

Paul then added, "They have some pretty cool shows on now...or they did when we left our time." Paul then walked over and closed the door, taking a brief moment to breathe in the cooler air of the stone passageway. "Got to be careful, never know who has big ears and this all sounds pretty weird."

Richard shook his head, "No one understands us." He then pointed to Sam, "We had lots of cool westerns and Walt Disney had a great show on Sunday nights. Hollywood put out a whole lot of cop shows during the week and the women really went wild for the soaps."

"Soaps?" Sam asked. "You said they 'went for the soaps', I thought you had these televisions in your home?" Sam asked. He tried to get more comfortable on the rope cot and set up against the wall for support.

"That's just slang, Sam," GW said. "Like your twenty-two skid-do...which meant they enjoyed it."

"I'll have you know, young men, this 'twenty-two ski-do' stuff was for the generation before me; the late 1920's and early 30's." Sam grinned, remembering his teenage years and how all his friends always tried to keep up with the current slang.

"Before I joined up, we used words like, Krispy, which I guess would line up with how you use the word, cool. We also used new phrases like feeling it—meaning we understood it—but it was more than that. It also meant an emotional understanding, rather than mental."

"Yeah, your World War II jazz enthusiasts paved the way for the beatniks, then the Beatles revolution and then came the peacenik hippies," Richard said. With a small fan he chased the flies off him.

"Hippies... Those are the long-haired people you told me about, correct?" Sam asked.

"Right," GW replied. "Mostly they hang out around San Francisco to protest the war in Vietnam. They were moving on to the college campuses when I left to join up."

"Now tell me about these 'soaps' the women went for."

Richard gestured to his two friends, signaling he'd answer Sam's question, "Soap operas were daytime half-hour and hour-long drama shows for the female viewer to watch, while her husband is off working, and the children are at school. The advertisement people used the soaps to sell their junk to the housewives...like dish soap and laundry detergent...I think that's how the soap part started, and it caught on big-time."

"Strange, I had imagined things would've changed with the war...my war," Sam said in a strained voice. With the folded cuff of his robe he again wiped his forehead. "Most of our women went to work when all the men went off to fight. I'd have thought that after the war, the women would still be working. Getting a taste of it and not wanting to go back to subservient womanhood, as my wife might say."

"C'mon, Sam, quit using those big words," Paul complained. "Anyway, a lot of the women work, sometimes it takes both a husband and their wife's paycheck to cover the bills...but I'd guess an equal number still stay home and they like to watch their soaps, while the kids either play outside or go to school. My mom said they were addictive. Especially some program about these doctors and their love life."

His face flush from the heat, Sam decided it was time to leave and get some rest, but he did enjoy these conversations. "Well, you've told me of drug addiction, how something called the Beatles brought Rock& Roll to the American teenager, of how man was heading toward the moon and women wore short skirts and their swim suits were 'skimpy two-piece jobs called bikinis'. How cars were going faster and yet, traffic was moving slower." Sam glanced between the three men and held his two hands palm up in a gesture of wonder, "Your world sounds so confusing, yet so rich in life. I am sorry I've missed it all and you've been pulled back here, where life is so dangerous, and we have little in the way of entertainment." Sam then pointed to himself, "Here, too few of the men reach the age of 50-years old and I am considered unusual for being as old as I am. Let us not forget we also have slavery and human sacrifice to contend with."

"You didn't drag us here, Sam," GW said. With a kind gesture he placed his left arm around the old man's beefy shoulders. "If it hadn't happened, we'd probably be dead now, or at least prisoners of war and I'd rather be here than in some NVA prison camp."

"Thanks," Sam said, and he patted GW's leg. "Now I'll see about getting you some food and water before you three pass-out."

"How long do you think we'll have to stay in here?" Richard asked.

"I'm not sure. I haven't yet learned why the Great Imam is here, but I expect it will involve either King Ramie or I, as the high cleric dislikes us both."

"Please keep us up to date," Richard asked. A large black fly zoomed by his head and he attempted to kill it with his fan but missed.

"If you find a deck of cards lying about...?" Paul asked with a grin.

"No cards, but you can cut up some parchment and make your own. But if I could, I'd bring you one of those televisions you speak of. But then we'd all been burned for witchcraft." Sam then stood up, swaying a bit until GW rose to steady him.

"Maybe one of us should walk you back to your room, this heat can be overwhelming," GW offered. He escorted Sam to the door.

"I appreciate your concern, but we cannot take the chance." Sam approached the door, turned to his friends and said, "I'll be all right. I've had 40 years of this heat. Thankfully the wind from the north has picked up and the castle will cool down in no time."

Paul opened the door and Sam walked through the doorway, but he then remembered to insist Paul close the door. "You must remain unseen, sorry." Paul nodded his head in agreement and closed the heavy wooden door. He then turned to his two friends, "Yeah, right now I'd settle for those stupid soaps, anything to pass the day with."

"We could catch flies, tie strings to their legs and build us a carousel," Richard suggested.

Paul pointed his finger at him, "You get the water first. I think the heat has shrunk your noggin some." Paul returned to his rope and wood cot, pulled out a pair of socks from a camel-hide bag and began darning them with a handmade needle and a length of wool thread. This was his next-to-last pair of socks and all the others had rotted from the combined desert's summer heat and humidity. His GI boots were in similar disrepair, having used camel-hide to patch the soles and very thin lengths of sheep hide to replace his broken bootlaces.

"You know, I've always hated these dang boots, but right now I'd love to have a dozen pair… and a couple pair of sneakers."

For all three men, their GI issue green pants were torn and sewed back up a number-of times. Patches of various sizes, made from multi-colored linen or canvas, gave their pants an almost clown look and in Paul's case, his pants' belt was replaced by a length of rope. Surprisingly, the material covering their flak-vests was holding up, but they seldom wore them. Besides GW, who was given his mail shirt, Paul was presented with one of Sam's very old mail shirts and Richard, who continued to instruct the soldiers in hand-to-hand fighting techniques, received his ill-fitting mail shirt as a gift of appreciation from Captain Rynarr.

All three agreed they needed to make an appointment with one of the castle's blacksmiths to have the mail shirts fitted to their sizes. The shirts were too heavy and cumbersome, but in most cases, they would stop an arrowhead, or a sword point from impaling them. The flak-vest, though it would do much the same, didn't go too well with the tunics they were now wearing as guests of the Silene Royal Guardsmen. The hardest part of the Silene uniform, besides the silly plumed half-pants they wore, was the turban.

All three men had a difficult time learning how to wrap the turban around their heads correctly and it was Paul who provided a lot of laughs for his fellow soldiers, as he came off looking like an Egyptian mummy. The wrap often fell down around his face, blocking his vision. He'd then become upset and throw the turban to the ground in frustration, while GW and Richard looked on in sympathy for their friend. But they continued to practice and before long they looked like proper soldiers-except for the dilapidated GI issue boots and the multi-colored patched-work green pants.

## ROYAL COURT OF KING RAMIE

Late evening approached, which brought some relief as cool air blew in from the Mediterranean Sea. With the window curtains pulled aside, the breeze soon filled the court and with it, came the salty smell of the ocean and the occasional whiff of rotting fish.

King Ramie, clearly in a foul mood, sat upon his throne and waited impatiently for the late arrival of the Great Imam and was startled when he heard a commotion in the corridor leading into the throne room and looked to see the high cleric bursting in. The man had broken with protocol and simply, and rudely, walked past King Ramie's men-at-arms, court advisors and the Royal Guardsmen lieutenant, to stand contemptuously and without his entourage in front of King Ramie. His minor clerics, clearly showing their nervousness by glancing around the room, approached with bowed heads and knelt to their knees, while remaining behind the Great Imam.

The high cleric, still dressed in his black robes, his eyes displaying his contempt for King Ramie, bowed slightly and presented King Ramie with the traditional Muslim hand-gesture of blessing. "May Allah give you good health and long life, Sire."

King Ramie, his eyes cold with disdain for the high cleric, remained upon his throne in silence. He glared down upon the

Great Imam, the position of his throne giving him a six-foot advantage over the head of the high cleric and did not return the blessing as a sign of his scorn for the man's rude behavior.

Princess Lonnia, who arrived in the court room right then, quietly seated herself and smiled with contempt behind her thick royal blue veil, as she witnessed the silent, but hateful exchange, between these two powerful men.

Finally, a senior, but squeamish court officer, appeared beside the Great Imam and made the unnecessary, but proper introduction, which brought him a cold look of spitefulness from the high cleric. "Had I desired your assistance, I would have requested it. Now be gone!" The Great Imam ordered, and the man returned to stand with the others.

"I remind you," King Ramie said in a loud voice, "you are in my court and in my castle...and under my guards."

King Ramie then slowly rose from his throne, his hands clenched tightly into fists and his forehead lined with deep furrows. Struggling to control his temper, he glanced around the court and only then did his eyes come to rest upon the Great Imam, "You, sir, will show me proper respect or the Caliph will hear of this breach of protocol and simple manners a man of your status, would and should display before a royal Libyan court. Our Caliph does not tolerate such misconduct in his own court or in the courts of his king's, and you...you of all people should know this."

"I am but an old man, King Ramie, and I have little time for such frivolousness." The high cleric replied in mock sheepishly.

"Age is no excuse for a man with your experience," King Ramie reminded him curtly. But then he added, "But if you are so old and decrepit, I will provide you a chair."

King Ramie snapped his fingers once and a servant, who stood off to the side, had heard his king's word and promptly obeyed his king's command. He quickly produced a high-backed chair for the Great Imam and placed it beside the high cleric and then backed away in a half-bow, facing his liege, with his eyes lowered out of respect to his king and not the high cleric.

Although not surprised by the air of hostility between the high cleric and the king, the three assistants to the Great Imam observed the wordplay with trepidation and began to sincerely hope they would leave this castle with their heads intact.

The Great Imam, showing he was amused by the king's response by showing just the hint of a smile, seated himself directly in front of the king and brushed his heavy gray beard. He seemed to be putting much thought into his beard and King Ramie, uncomfortable with the high cleric's strange behavior, was growing further impatient.

The Great Imam slowly nodded his head several times and then finally said, "I thank you, King Ramie, for your kind hospitality. This chair is most suitable, and might I also have a cup of water too to help my tired old blood move faster through these aged veins?"

King Ramie struggled to repress a smile, suddenly realizing the pompous old man was playing mind games with him. There were times he enjoyed a good battle of the wits, but the hour was late. He then snapped his fingers a second time and a second servant soon appeared at the Great Imam's side with a pitcher of water and a silver goblet in hand. He poured the water, handed the goblet to the high cleric and then stepped back a few steps in the event the Great Imam wished more water.

"You are so kind, dear king and I will assuredly advise the Caliph of such." He then held the goblet in the air as one of his minor clerics stepped up to taste the water first. This was seen as a slap in the face to the king, but his court lieutenant stepped forward and announced, "Truly it is good to be safe as there might be those who wish to do our beloved king harm and poison our water. But I would've thought the Great Imam would be protected of same by his supreme faith in our beloved Allah?"

Smiling and speaking before the Great Imam could lash out at his lieutenant, he addressed the old man, "Alright, enough of your games, why are you here?"

The high cleric looked to the ceiling and waved his right hand around in a tight circle, "Sire, might I remind you I am the Great Imam, Lord Protector of the Faith and Muslim leader for all of the people in this kingdom of yours. So, I should say your subjects are also mine, on a spiritual sense of course and being as this is so, and I think you would agree with me, I then believe, no I demand, this same respect granted to me that your subjects offer to you. In this way, I should be properly treated as a dignitary of similar ranking as you, Sire," he said at length with a voice of authority. "I have come to Silene to ensure our people are being cared for properly, their teachings of Allah's word continue to be taught in accordance to our beloved Koran and all are content, as Allah demands." He then pointed his right finger toward the king, "Yet, you show me no respect. You failed to meet my coach, to welcome me to Silene, and act as if I was a simple cleric on routine rounds."

The king's face turned rigid, his jaws clenched shut and his eye lids narrowed to hide only a slender slit of dark brown pupil. "You go too far, you ..." King Ramie stopped abruptly. He knew even in his own kingdom it was not smart politics to insult the high cleric and it would bold ill with him if the Caliph was to hear of it. He also knew why the Great Imam was behaving in such a way, to bring shame down upon him for insulting the Great Imam in front of so many people.

In a strained, but clear voice, he addressed the high cleric, "I grant, you are their religious leader, but with no more authority then what the Caliph grants you to ensure these teachings of Allah prevail over his vast and wondrous kingdom. You were met by an honor guard led by Captain Rynarr and two horns were blown to announce your arrival as protocol degrees for someone of your status. As to why I was not there to meet you, I had affairs of state to see too and one such involved the murderous attack on a royal escort," King Ramie said. He was growing weary of this exchange and wished the old man would come to the real point of his unannounced visit.

"A royal escort, Sire? Is it possible one of your daughters has met with harm?" the high cleric asked in a voice dripping with sarcasm and displaying his mock concern.

"No, Princess Lonnia is safe, but I owe her life to the bravery of my men. Though greatly outnumbered, the defeated the Egyptian cavalry and brought back several prisoners. Still, I lost a lot of good and loyal men."

The Great Imam nodded his head, took a sip from his drink, now in his hands, and then glared at Princess Lonnia over the rim of his water goblet. This look of disdain caused the king to suspect the high cleric was here to once again complain about his daughters' blasphemous misconduct.

Princess Lonnia didn't quiver under the Great Imam's stare but matched him as she whispered ancient curses under her veil for the Great Imam' demise. Strangely, all this produced was a look of triumph in the old man's eyes and this concerned her.

The high cleric then turned his gaze back upon the king and if he was reading his mind, said, "No, Sire, I am not here to demand the deaths of your two daughters, or the execution of the infidel you tenderly call Brother Samuel. For I have released them all to Allah's will for a suitable punishment and you too, Sire, for allowing them breath, as they continue to blasphemy our Lord Allah."

"I grow tired of this, cleric," King Ramie said in a heated voice. He rose from his throne. "Advise me of your purpose or leave my court and be thankful you come under the Caliph's protection, for you have outlived your welcome." This caused an uneasy silence to spread across the royal court and brought a smile to the Great Imam's face.

The Great Imam's assistants were offended by the king's shameful attitude toward their high cleric. They did not believe even a king should speak so rudely to their beloved Great Imam. It simply wasn't done.

"Please, Sire, let me speak and then I will depart...if only for the day," The Great Imam said calmly.

Princess Lonnia then took this moment to cause more difficulty by rising to her feet and shouting, "Yes, you should leave, you, disgusting old man, but not as you are. No, your rotting head shall remain on a spear, mounted over the main gate as a reminder to all of whose kingdom this truly is!"

"Daughter!" King Ramie shouted. "You've gone too far!" He was greatly embarrassed by his oldest daughter's words, that she would threaten a guest and such a prestigious one at that, in his court in such a direct way. Though admittedly, the high cleric had openly demanded her life on more than one occasion in this very room.

"Father, this vile man is contemptible!" She shouted back. She pointed an accusing finger at the high cleric and glared at him over her veil.

As if on cue, the assistant clerics pointed accusing fingers at the Black Princess in defense of the high cleric. They demanded her death and one of them was even so bold as to pull a dagger from the arm sleeve of his robe. This caused the king's bodyguards to move quickly and take up position in front of the king, their shields ready to block arrows or thrown weapons from striking King Ramie. The Royal Guardsman lieutenant also stood in to block the assistant cleric from reaching Princess Lonnia and he quickly disarmed the angry man of his dagger.

"You may leave here NOW, daughter!" King Ramie ordered in a loud voice.

"But, Father..."

"Leave here now! I said," he ordered. This time his voice was loud enough for not only all the court to hear, but possibly most of the castle and surrounding grounds. Princess Lonnia stood there silently for a moment, glaring at her father. Her whole body was rigid with hate, for both her king and the high cleric.

An uneasy silence passed between the three key characters in this heated melodrama, she began to limp away. But before leaving the court, she turned and addressed the high cleric once more in shouted words, "You will never leave here alive, you old buffoon!" She then disappeared behind a heavy curtain of spun wool before her father could respond to her unwise words.

"A pleasant girl, Sire...Truly, a most pleasant girl," the high cleric replied. He wore a smile of triumph upon his lips.

King Ramie ignored the Great Imam's expression and his words. He turned to summon his attending officer, the young lieutenant representing the Royal Guardsmen who had disarmed the minor cleric of his dagger. He was still holding the upset assistant cleric by the arm, "Let that man go, Lieutenant and clear the court of everyone. I want only my most trusted advisors, my loyal men-at-arms and the Great Imam and his party to remain here. Do this immediately."

"Yes, Sire." The lieutenant promptly obeyed and with the help of four men-at-arms in blue tunics, he cleared the room of disgruntled nobility and mildly offended court officers of lesser ranking and foreign dignitaries. Most were simply curious and wished to stay to observe the duel of wills between their king and the high cleric, but they were ushered out.

King Ramie then ordered this same lieutenant to place two Royal Guardsmen on Princess Lonnia's door, with orders she was not allowed to leave her rooms. "No matter what she threatens them with...if I see her outside her rooms before I summon her, those two men will be executed." The king began to turn away, but then remembered his closest advisor was not present, "Also, summon Brother Samuel to me."

"Yes, my liege," The lieutenant replied. He was only 24-years old, but a favorite of Captain Rynarr's, and he often served in the king's court as the attending officer. But today he was more concerned than usual for his king's welfare and after finding Brother Samuel, he would find Captain Rynarr and advise him of tonight's court affairs.

While all this was being done, the Great Imam remained sitting in silence before the king and simply sipped from his goblet. The servant refilled his glass and then departed to return a moment later with a small wooden tray of fruit, to which the Great Imam declined, but thanked the servant with a brief word of appreciation.

His assistants attempted to speak to him, but he silenced them with a curt wave and shared casual glances with King Ramie, while the courtroom was cleared. Once the court was emptied, he looked to the king and in a calm voice asked, "Is this so there would be no witnesses, my liege, for my untimely demise?"

"For one so old you speak as a child," King Ramie said. "After all, you are the Great Imam and no harm shall come to you. Especially since you went to so much effort to have the throne room filled with witnesses. But without all them in audience, I thought you might cease this childish banter and finally get to the subject of your visit."

The Great Imam leaned forward and placed his goblet on the ground beside his chair and then gazed upon the king, "I have never doubted you a wise king, Sire, but in your daughter's sacrilegious conduct against Allah, you have failed gravely as a Muslim father. But alas, they are not why I am here." The Great Imam said and then slowly rose to his feet. An assistant stepped forward and offered his arm to the Great Imam for support. He stood in silence for a moment and then glanced to his right, as a very weary-eyed Sam appeared in the courtroom and approached King Ramie to offer his respects.

The Great Imam and Sam exchanged a simple nod of the head of mutual disdain for one another, but no words and no icy stares this time. In fact, Sam thought he could see a hint of a smile on the high clerics face and this chilled him to the bone.

After Sam was allowed time to formally appear before the king, as protocol demanded it here in the throne room, the Great Imam used the arm of the one assistant for support to step forward and address the king. "Sire, I have come on bequest of our Caliph and I now humbly represent him in my poor fashion before you. As such, I did not kneel before your throne or wait for an introduction, for by proxy I am here in his stead." He cleared his throat and continued on, "I stand here in obedience, following the commands of our great Caliph's and with humility, I speak his benevolent words of wisdom through me," the Great Imam said this with authority. With a sneer, struggling not to snicker, he enjoyed the look of confusion and some small degree of fear in the king's widening eyes.

"Do you have evidence of this?" King Ramie asked, his voice showing strains of uncertainty.

The tallest of the three assistants, his head still bowed, stepped up beside the high cleric and handed to him a rolled parchment, secured by a thin golden ribbon. King Ramie knew ribbons such as this, were often used by the Caliph for his official business.

The Great Imam accepted the document without a word to his assistant and stepped forward to present it to King Ramie. "From our Caliph, Sire…You will of course recognize his seal at the bottom of the page."

King Ramie gave the high cleric a momentary glare, but he accepted the document and then slipped the ribbon off. He unrolled the thick parchment and began to read the words in silence and his eyes grew wider, for in effect, this document granted the high cleric great power to speak for the Caliph in manners of state security. And now, my oldest daughter chooses this moment to insult and threaten this man in front of dozens of witnesses. He finally has her where he has long wanted and there is little I can do to stop him from taking her.

"May I see this, Sire?" Sam asked as he approached the king's throne from the left side.

Entering the court, Sam was surprised to find Princess Lennia's throne empty. Sam thought Princess Lennia had planned to be present for this meeting and wondered where she was.

King Ramie handed the state document to Sam, which caused the Great Imam to complain, "Sire, this infidel should not lay hands upon this document." The Great Imam placed his hand under his robe and began to approach the throne like a threatening old grizzly bear stalking its prey. His actions caused the young lieutenant to react by drawing his scimitar and quickly taking a position between the throne and the Great Imam.

"Please, Great Imam, do not approach my king," The young lieutenant requested, his shiny scimitar blade reflecting the Great Imam's image.

"You…" he said in a threatening tone, as his voice grew louder, and he glared coldly upon the lieutenant, "…you simply allow this infidel to lay his filthy hands upon our Caliph's orders and then stand there to threaten me!? Are you not a follower of the true faith, boy? Who do you follow, king or Allah!?"

His voice aquiver, his weapon hand trembling, the lieutenant replied, "I serve my King, who I have sworn before Allah to do so."

"Well said," Sam replied. He glared openly down upon the Great Imam. "Do not berate this fine young officer for my sake, we both know this is simply another of your ploys to attack me."

The Great Imam slowly pulled his empty aged hand out from under his black robe as a surprising smile appeared on his grizzled face. "For an infidel, you speak wisely."

"What is your will?" King Ramie asked. "Let us not play here, speak what is to be done."

"In truth, Sire, though this document appears to grant me near limitless power, I am under verbal orders from our great and wise Caliph of how I may use it."

"Yes?"

"As much as I would like to see this infidel beheaded, his limbs pulled from his body and his remains fed to the vultures, I may not. Nor may I have your two daughters stoned to death, beheaded or fed to this accursed dragon of yours." The Great Imam hesitated briefly and then added in a sarcastic tone, "At least not on this visit."

King Ramie breathed an audible sigh of relief, but Sam knew there was something important to the high cleric's final words, At least on this visit?

"Then say what is on your mind, cleric. Speak, man!" King Ramie said in a heated voice, but then forced himself to calm down. He then asked, "How may my kingdom serve our beloved Caliph and the Great Imam?"

"Then hear me well, Sire, for these are the words of our beloved Caliph: For hundreds of years your small kingdom has been cursed by this vile watery beast in the northern lake. You have sacrificed countless maidens to it and a great many sheep. Men and women have lost their lives, ships lost, and your army defeated countless times in your fruitless attempts to kill this dragon. Egypt to the east laughs at us and Silene is now the poorest kingdom in Libya. You can ill afford to pay your taxes and even now some of the great caravans bypass you," The Great Imam said. He waved his fatty arms around for effect, as he slowly and cautiously approached the king's throne. He ignored the lieutenant but didn't come any closer than the bottom step of the massive stone stage, which held the four thrones. But a wise officer, the lieutenant remained between him and the king.

"You need not remind me, I know all this, but what are we to do? We have tried to kill it, to drive it away, but all have failed," King Ramie replied in a tone of desperation.

"Truly, the Caliph knows all this," The high cleric said in response. "Even so, the people of Tripoli have appeared before him, fearful you will seek their young maidens as the numbers of your daughters grow ever few. The wealthy, the influential, have also complained of how you have purchased a great many slave girls in the markets, reducing the number of quality female slaves needed for the fine houses of Tripoli."

"Who is this who seeks the Caliph's help?" King Ramie asked in a loud voice, as he was offended by such accusations. "Silene would never take by force the daughters of Tripoli, our Caliph would never allow this."

"Who is not important, but what is to be done, Sire, is."

"So, what does the Caliph seek of me? What must I do and speak quickly, old one, for my eyes grows heavy with the need for sleep?"

"This is his royal decree, Sire: you may not seek maidens for sacrifice outside the borders of your kingdom, except for prisoners taken from Egyptian raiders. You may not invade Egypt for such maidens and risk war with that country. You may not purchase herds of sheep from outside your kingdom, except for those herds taken from Egypt by others and sold to you. And most importantly, you have one-year from this day in which to slay this dragon or Brother Samuel shall be fed to it as a sacrifice to Allah."

"What!?" King Ramie shot to his feet. "What has Brother Samuel got to do with the dragon? The dragon was here long before Brother Samuel was taken from the sea," King Ramie said. He then pointed an accusing finger at the Great Imam, "He's invented many weapons to kill this dragon, weapons our Caliph now uses for his great army."

"I stand before you in the Caliph's absence, with his full authority in matters of state security. With that power granted to me," He pointed to the rolled-up parchment, "I take these steps to ensure the safety of Silene. I have the utmost faith Silene will truly be saved from this curse by sacrificing this infidel to the dragon. For all I know, Allah may have the beast choke on the infidel's bones.

"However, since I must return to Tripoli to receive the Caliph's signed authorization to execute this infidel, since he is under a king's protection, I may grant you a whole year to carry this action out.

"I have expressed my belief to the Caliph, words I have received from Allah, that it is this infidel's presence in Silene which prevents the dragon from being destroyed. So, unless Brother Samuel turns away from this false god he serves and truly accepts Allah, or you find some way to slay the creature, this infidel will die one year from today in the way I described."

"You did this, didn't you? You really got the Caliph to believe such nonsense?" Sam asked, forgetting his place by speaking in the court without the king's permission.

"Yes, ignorant infidel. I finally persuaded the Caliph that it was you and your presence, which keep this loathsome creature alive and with either your death or your acceptance of Allah, the creature would die." This was of course a total falsehood. For though the parchment and the authority it granted to the Great Imam was true, the high cleric only come up with the plan to execute Brother Samuel in this way since his arrival here today. He saw this as a way to avenge himself against the callous treatment he received from the king and cause great trouble for Brother Samuel. He had high hopes the infidel would flee Libya and be discovered in another Muslim country and be slain. As to the authorization for execution, he knew the Caliph would never sign such a document for he did truly value Brother Samuel's many inventions.

King Ramie promptly dismissed everyone but Brother Samuel and the Great Imam, including the assistant clerics and he ordered the young lieutenant to guard the door from the other side. Only the king's bodyguards remained, but they were sworn to silence by penalty of death.

Once everyone was out of the throne room, Sam addressed the high cleric, "Don't lie, not between us. You care little of my acceptance of the Muslim faith. You would gladly prefer to see me dead...Admit it." Sam now stood only two feet from the Great Imam, two aged men glaring at one another like two great bears preparing to lunge out with dagger-like claws for the juggler vein.

"Yes, infidel, I freely admit it. I prefer your death and in one year I will have it!" The Great Imam inched closer, but Sam didn't back away and the two men were nearly nose-to-nose and this made the two bodyguards quite nervous.

"But why wait?" Sam asked. "You apparently have the power, why not kill me now and be done with it?" Sam's angry spittle struck the high cleric and he then shook his finger in the high cleric's startled face, "You are no man of god and not even your Allah would even tolerate such a cretin as you."

King Ramie had to break this up and ordered his bodyguards to separate the two before violence erupted. Even he couldn't stop Sam's immediate execution if he was to lay a hand on the Great Imam. A lot of devout Muslims would tear the castle apart to avenge their supreme holy one.

Waving a clenched fist at Sam, as the nearest bodyguard came between them, the high cleric briefly forgot himself and blurted out, "If I could kill you, I would, infidel!"

"So, you do not have all the powers of the Caliph as you hoped to make us believe," King Ramie said.

Sam stepped back from the Great Imam and grinned, but all the excitement was wearing him down and he needed to sit down.

"It matters not," The Great Imam muttered his reply and then his voice grew loud, "For all these years you've been unable to kill this beast, do you think you can in the period of one year? No, I will see the death of this infidel and soon after, I will see the death of those two heretic princesses. Their father can no longer protect them. For heed me, Sire, you will surely lose this kingdom, even if force is needed, if this beast still lives in one year. Your kingdom is cursed and maybe, with Allah's help, I can convince the Caliph it is the king who should fall to save us all."

"Leave now!" King Ramie ordered. "Be gone by morning, or I may surely forget I am a Muslim and have your head placed on a spear as my daughter demanded." King Ramie, his face rigid with rage, then turned his back on the Great Imam and walked out of the throne room. The two bodyguards, visibly shaken by what they had observed, followed their king.

Hands clenched into tight fists, his heart racing and blood boiling, King Ramie went to his bedchamber to lie down. A year he had, only a year to come up with an answer and if not, only a year before his best friend and two daughters would surely perish. As to his own throne, he wasn't much concerned about it at the moment. But as to his belief in Allah, something was happening in his heart he couldn't explain, and he needed time to dwell upon it. Yet in his mind he envisioned this one-year grace period and how fast it would pass. Already the first day was nearly over and only 364-days remained.

Sam stood there before the four thrones, watching as the high cleric's assistants returned to physically help the old man leave the court. As with Sam, the Great Imam was physically drained and needed rest. But a part of Sam wanted to slay the man where he stood, grab a spear from off a far wall and end it for his friend, the king. Yet another part of him thought to pray for this wretched man, to ease his burdens and show him the true mercy of the Lord Jesus Christ. This inner conflict deeply troubled him, but right now he needed sleep most of all. Once the Great Imam had left the Royal Court, Sam dropped to the stone platform, desperately needing to ease his hurting back and knees.

Sam had come to realize the longer he wore the robes of a priest, even these threadbare ones, the military man inside of him; a Naval Academy graduate in fact, seemed to be shrinking away. He had actually thought his past dead, but then these soldiers appeared from the future and the naval lieutenant commander was reborn. Still, admittedly he struggled with his promise to the king not to evangelize the people of Silene and was having a growing desire to see a joyful transformation for these people; from followers of Allah to a blessed Christianity.

Sam took a few moments to rest and then rose to slowly return to his room, his shoulders heavy with stress and each step an effort to make. Once inside, his robe removed, he collapsed onto his bed in only his silken underwear and was unconscious within minutes.

Was it a dream that came that night, a wish or was it prophesies unfolding?

# 12 – AN ULTAMATUM

As the midnight hour approached, the air in their room had become stifling and just unbearable, even the flies had deserted them. The heavy wooden door was still closed tight, as Sam had ordered and the heat inside was well over the 100-degree mark and humidity near the 50 percent mark. Because it was so hot, the three men were unable to sleep. Rivulets of sweat poured from their bodies and now bouts of nausea from breathing in the stuffy atmosphere were becoming a problem.

GW decided enough was enough. He bolted from his bed, rushed over to the door and swung it open wide to let some fresh air in. But the dimly lit passageway, built in the same stone rock as the room, was still warm to the touch from the long summer day and offered little relief. When he turned around, he was surprised to find both of his friends standing in front of him.

"I couldn't take it anymore…it's worse than the jungle," GW said. He flicked his right wrist, casting off several droplets of sweat. GW knew Sam would be upset with him, but they had to get out of this room and find some relief from this insufferable heat.

"Either of you bright boys have any ideas where we can go before we melt?" GW then turned to poke his head out and look down the passageway again to ensure there was no around about.

Richard thought about it for a moment, while he wiped the moisture from his face with the palm of his right hand and then he got an idea, "Stables! Let's go down there and at least wash off in one of the troths. Preferably one recently refilled."

"Good idea, Professor," Paul added. With a quick grasp, he retrieved his soiled tunic from the foot of his bed. "I could wash this out while were down there—the thing reeks."

"We've got to be very careful, or Sam is going to have our hide," GW warned.

"Better him then that grand whatever dude. He's liable to take our heads too," Paul said in a whisper. His tunic balled up, he led the three of them out of the room. Shirtless and attired in only their tattered pants and run-down boots, they cautiously moved down the darkened corridor.

Like the young adults they were, they disobeyed Sam by sneaking out of their room like 1940's style movie gumshoes. They hugged the walls and moved stealthily through the empty passageways and then down the steep darkened stairwells. They took great pleasure in feeling even a faint cool breeze coming from off the ocean to the north, as it circulated through the castle and began to gradually lower the temperatures one degree at a time.

The number of lit torches inside the castle were drastically reduced at night, giving these three men the cover of darkness to move around in, but it also made it difficult for them to observe how some of the stones along the stairway were uneven in their placement. Twice, Paul tripped over such a stone and thankfully on the second stumble, his fall was cushioned by Richard's legs, who, in turn fell forward and collapsed against GW's backside- causing all three to hit the floor in a mangled heap.

Though highly trained stealthy soldiers used to close combat in the jungles of Vietnam, these three battle-hardened veterans behaved more like they were in a Saturday morning episode of the Three Stooges. They pushed and shoved one another about to stand up and then broke the silence of the night with such remarks as, "Get off me, man...you're breaking my leg with that lard butt of yours", and, "Get that size 18-foot out of my face, Professor...or I'm gonna put mine where the sun don't shine!"

Thankfully, the Great Imam's people were behind closed doors and settled down for the evening and Captain Rynarr's single night guard in this part of the castle had recognized these three clumsy dolts when they began coming down the stairway and did not challenge them. Of course, by their strange actions he was a bit unsure as to why these friends of Brother Samuel were behaving in such a bizarre way; sneaking about without their tunics on, without torches or even candlelight to see by. But being a close friend of Mushid and knowing how the knight felt a particular companionship for these strangers, he decided to ignore the three men and continue on his rounds. Tomorrow he would ask Mushid about his friend's strange behavior to satisfy his curiosity.

Ducking under the unlit wall-mounted torches, the three men sincerely hoped this Great Imam fellow and his party didn't hear their stumbling about. But the walls were made of thick blocks of stone and the doors of heavy wood, so chances were they wouldn't be caught by one of those people. There were still the guards, but they had gone too far to turn back now and the thought of returning to that sweltering hole of a room only made their resolve toughen up more.

It had struck GW odd how the Sahara Desert could be so blistery hot during the day and over a few hours in the evening become so comfortably cool and he whispered this to his friends. Of course, the professor was right on hand to remind him they were living on the northern coastal region of the Sahara, where the ocean breezes off the Mediterranean Sea brought some relief from the summer's high temperatures. "But further south, the temperatures do not vary so greatly and the sun-bleached bones of both men and animal strewn about the land was evidence of how dangerous the Sahara Desert could be."

"You sure must've done a lot of reading in that museum, Professor," Paul said.

Richard grinned in the darkness as he recalled his days surrounded by great volumes of books, "Our week days were pretty slow, unless a school class was taking a field trip, but the curator would let me study whatever I wanted too. His only rule was that I could not take any of the museum's material home; some of it was near priceless, you know?"

Paul put his hand on Richard's shoulder, "Ever get the urge to rip the place off, pawn some of the junk and party down?" Paul then glanced around the southeast corner of the castle to ensure they had a clear path to the north end of the Royal Guardsmen stable.

"Are you kidding?" Richard asked quietly in disbelief. "You get caught stealing that kind of stuff and you don't see daylight for years. Those wealthy judges donate a lot of money for those museums to stay open and if you were unlucky enough to appear before one of them for a crime like that...Man, you'd be history. Last sounds you'd hear would be that cell door slamming shut and some real big dude with tattoos on his arms saying, 'Hello there cutie'."

GW was stifling a laugh, or at least trying to, when Paul asked him what was so darn funny? "Out with it but keep it to a whisper before you blow this caper and we're back in lock-up."

"Oh, it's just that here we are big tough corporals and the professor here, the guy with the brains, is only a lowly PFC." GW looked at Richard, "You should've been an officer, Richard and maybe you wouldn't be in this mess."

"I had the reading and maybe the brains, but no college degree." Richard glanced to the ground, "Besides, last time I saw a bunch of young lieutenants, they were lying dead on the ground."

Both Paul and GW glanced at their feet too and then Paul spoke to break the silence, "Look, forget the past...It's clear, let's hustle over the stables. I think GW's brain is beginning to overheat..." He shook his head and blurted out, "Officers! They're a bunch of glory hunting college boys hoping to make general...and on our backs."

GW grabbed Paul by the arm and shook him, "Move it, toots!"

Paul sneered at him and then took off to hide behind a nearly full manure wagon, which was parked alongside the castle wall.

"Oh, this smells just great!" GW complained, when he joined him. "What's next, the sheep pen?"

"Reminds me of home," Paul said.

GW moved closer, so he could whisper his next remark, "Okay, smart guy, you got any ideas how we're gonna get across the courtyard? Looks like three, maybe four guards out there at the stable."

Paul glanced around, looking for alternate routes and then he smiled at GW, "If there wasn't a risk, where'd the thrill be?"

"Oh, you're one of those guys," GW said in a whisper. "Live for the thrill of it."

"Sure, what else is there?"

GW shook his head in response, "Not me, buddy. There's got to be more...I just haven't found what it is."

Sam's order was being violated, but each man agreed staying in that sauna-of-a-room would most assuredly kill him before morning. Still, they didn't like disobeying Sam, but they also knew Sam's plate was overly full from a long day of surgery and the additional stress of dealing with this Great Imam character.

Though Richard was the first to recommend the stable, GW would have recommended it soon enough because he wanted to check on Valiant. They talked about going into the lower levels for a brief moment, close to the dungeon, but Paul refused to go anywhere near that place. He still believed there were bats in the lower levels and if not bats, very big rats. "You'd have to knock me out and drag me down there and when I woke up, I'd feed you to those big hairy things!"

"Okay okay, but if I thought we could, I'd say we should saddle up and take a nice moonlit ride through the surf," GW said wishfully.

Paul shook his head, "You're not going to get me anywhere near that dinosaur-thingee out there. I've seen those teeth and I've listened to the stories of how that thing could smell any animal within 50-feet of the water. That's too creepy for this boy!"

"Like I said, we could ride to the ocean, it's not much further than the lake," GW suggested.

"Sounds great, ol' masterful one, but don't you remember we're confined to the castle grounds unless under escort," Richard said. "We'd never make it through the gate without having Mushid or Sam with us. Soon as you start to saddle up, you'd have guards all over you."

Richard then glared at GW, "And remember, dear Corporal...I don't ride."

"Okay, it was only an idea," GW replied. He was hot, sweat was pouring off of him and he was feeling a bit irritable. But he knew the guys felt much the same way and said, "Whatever we do, we'd better do it soon or I am going melt right here and it will make an ugly mess for you two to clean up."

"I'm melting...I'm melting!" Paul was doing his wicked-witch impersonation from The Wizard of Oz. But he didn't get any laughs.

"Funny," GW said without a smile.

"Lighten up," Paul said in response. He looked to Richard and then back to GW, "Okay, we'll go down to the stables and take a swim in the watering troughs. Not real clean, but it'll be refreshing."

"You can go ahead and submerge yourself, I'll use a bucket," Richard said. With a grunt, he unfolded his blue silken tunic. "I've got to wash this out too."

The blacksmiths and carpenters in the courtyard shops had finished for the day, leaving the smoldering forges to cool and any unfinished projects to wait for tomorrow. After a final check of the horses, all the stable hands; bone tired and shoulders drooping from a long day, returned to their various fires in hopes a late dinner of mutton stew. Afterward, they would slide under a threadbare blanket and lay upon a simple pallet of straw.

Outside the castle keep, the three men had several close calls with the locals. There were many servants, some carrying flaming torches and all dashing about to finish up their tasks before calling it a night. Here in Silene a servant's work day began at dawn and often ended at midnight or even later. With so little sleep, the servants and slaves often made clumsy mistakes and if observed by a superior, they were punished severely for it with the lash of a whip. Servant hood and slavery were extremely harsh on a man or woman in the 12$^{th}$ century. Sam had tried to lessen the punishments, but King Ramie told him the various headmen followed Muslim Law in the treatment of slaves and indentured servants, and those men fell under Princess Lonnia's control.

"My friend, the Princess must learn the affairs of this castle, if she is to someday become the queen of my kingdom. It is simply the way of things," King Ramie said to Brother Samuel.

There were some other servants rustling about in the outdoor kitchen, preparing the fires for tomorrow's breakfast. Feeding an extra 100- troops increased the work load and the cooking staff had to bring supplies up from the underground storage rooms. The food was kept in these wooden lockers as a way to keep the food cooled down during the summer season. They had to dig the cellars deep, nearly 30-feet down, to keep the food well below the hot sand and this was another of Brother Samuels's ideas.

Using their training, the three, former, 101st airborne troops made it to the ground level without being seen. But getting to the stable was going to be tough, for they would have to move across several yards of open ground. Unfortunately, the courtyard was well guarded because of the Great Imam's coach and they couldn't simply sneak by the four men-at-arms.

But chance seemed to be on their side; Richard recognized two of the men from one of his training classes. He turned to his friends and whispered, "Follow me and act as if you lunkheads didn't have a care in the world. I doubt if they've heard Sam's orders for us, but if they have, we might still be able to get by as long as we don't try to ride off." He then looked directly at Paul, "No wisecracks and no jokes, got it?"

"Hey, you can lighten up too, Professor," Paul said in his defense.

Richard, a brave smile on his face to hide his uncertainty, led them through the darkened courtyard until they were within hearing range of the guard. There was light there, provided by several torch-stands.

His chest tight, Richard forced himself to keep his voice calm as he began purposely talking loud enough for the guards to hear him, "I mentioned to Captain Rynarr how well the latest class was doing in training, and he was most delighted to hear of this."

"Halt!" An oafish looking guard ordered. His eight-foot long spear was pointed at the three men. The other three guards also came alert, their spears now pointed at the intruders. But it was the oafish fellow who was closest, and they let him do all the talking. He wore the brown tunic of a regular man-at-arms soldier, one who was a former slave six-years ago and sold by his owner to the army in lieu of unpaid taxes. Not that he minded. He preferred this to his laborious duty around the farm and having to drive a stinking manure cart for his former owner.

"Who are you...where you go?" The guard asked in a deep voice. His spear point was mere inches from Richard's chest.

But then one of the other guards stepped forward, "I know this man!" This guard had trained in Richard's hand-to-hand fighting class and this acknowledgment was what Richard had counted on. Stories of Richard's skill had traveled through the army and each man of the brown tunic hoped he would receive such training. Either that or they'd risk a good beating every time they had some beef with some of Richard's students.

"My friend Richard, come forward," the soldier ordered in a loud, but friendly tone. Then he addressed the other guard, "Stand aside, Azraz, this is Richard of Sudan, who could defeat ten-men if he wanted too and he does not fear your spear."

Azraz lowered his spear and bowed his head in submission, "Forgive me, Richard of Sudan, for I not know it was you."

"Blessing be upon you, Azraz and all of you," Richard said. A wide grin was now on his face in a show of friendship. "We have accompanied our friend here, so he might check on his horse, the steed called Valiant."

"His horse is known," Azraz said

GW and Paul came up behind Richard. They too were wearing big grins on their faces in hopes to convince the guards everything was on the up and up. They recognized the one man from seeing him train with Richard, but the other soldiers were unknown.

"A fair night it is, my friends," GW said. "Sad, you must have guard duty on such a warm night."

"Truly, I'd rather be in the barracks, listening to a good story or asleep dreaming of my wife," the same guard replied sadly. He had not seen his wife since he was conscripted into the army over two-years ago, because she went to live with her family in southwestern Libya. He had shared his sad story with Richard during a break in training and the young American had promised he would see what he could do about the man's situation. But Richard had forgotten all about it until this moment, and he felt a pang of guilt.

The men-at-arms, thankful for even this small break in the monotony of late night guard duty, moved aside to allow the three men entry into the massive, but quiet stables. Being friends of Captain Rynarr, Azraz knew better than to challenge them for leaving the castle keep at this late hour without proper escort. Everyone knew of the foreigners and the rules they were sworn to abide by, but on such a warm night Azraz and his fellow guards saw no problem in the three men walking to the stables to check on GW's gallant steed. Especially with them clearly unarmed and all the exterior gates closed.

Richard walked up to the man who was married, "I must admit to you, I have forgotten of your long separation from your wife and ask you forgive me." Richard then reached out and clasped his hand on the man's shoulder, "But I will speak to Captain Rynarr of this matter tomorrow, before I can forget about it again. Hopefully, he will grant you an extended leave and the loan of a mount, which will allow you time to make the long journey to your wife's home and have time with her."

The man nodded his head, "By your own words I see you as a man of honor and yes, I can understand how you might have forgotten me, Richard of the Sudan. I leave this matter in your hands and will await the captain's decision as to my need to journey home to see my wife. I only need a passing of the moon to ensure she is well, and then I will return to do my duty as Allah commands of me."

"I will see what I can do." Richard nodded his head, smiled and continued on to the stable. He glanced over at the grand coach and shook his head in bewilderment, the value of the coach could feed so many starving people in Libya and yet, it sits here, reserved for one man's use.

"The horses are strangely quiet tonight," GW said in a whisper. "In fact, everyone seems to be quiet tonight...too quiet. Feels like the proverbial calm before the storm."

"Yeah, now that you mention it," Paul agreed. "Reminds me of the night before we left for the A Shau Valley; the air was so thick and muggy... made me feel...well, real tight. You know what I mean," he said to GW.

"It's good to have these quiet nights," GW said. "So, we're ready for when the enemy is upon us and we can remember the calm and quietness."

"You know, buddy, you're starting to sound a lot like Sam," Paul said. "All these heavy thoughts...poetic license and all that and you've been reading too many of those wordy parchments...You're starting to worry me, guy."

GW shook his head, grinned, but in the darkness, Paul couldn't see it and GW left Paul's side to walk into Valiant's stall. By Valiant's response, he knew his friend was glad to see him. The horse rocked his head back and forth and stamped his front hooves against the ground and he leaned into GW touch, as the master rubbed Valiant's neck.

GW then turned to Paul, "First off, I can't read most of that stuff...Guess it's this entire Ali Baba and the Forty Thieves thing we got going on around here. Makes my head reel and the heat...oh, forget it. Let's finish up here and hit that watering troth. See how many laps we can do before sun up."

"Laps, you wanna do laps?" Paul asked. Petting Valiant's backside, he gave GW a worried look. This boy's been in the heat way too long!

Due to their higher status in the kingdom's hierarchy, the Royal Guardsmen stable had additional stable hands assigned to keep the stalls clean and the horses better cared for. As he had approached the long wooden structure, GW noticed how nearly every stall was filled with impressive looking mounts.

His thoughts were dancing back and forth between the 12th and 20th centuries. In the process of daydreaming, he failed to notice a partially filled water bucket at the back of Valiant's stall and tripped over it. With hands outstretched, he fell forward, but was able to catch a stall post hook with his right hand to keep from falling flat on his face. GW pulled himself up, shook his head and made a mental note to speak to the stable hand about making sure to put Valiant's water bucket away. He then leaned closer to Valiant and said, "A flashlight would've really helped about now...but again, they'd probably burn me for a witch for having such a thing."

GW wiped down Valiant's backside a final time and looked up and down the length of all stalls he could see. He eyes had adjusted to the dim light provided by the few torches used by the guards and what illumination came from the castle keep. There were also the torches upon the battlements, but most of the courtyard was in total darkness. In the event of necessity, dozens, if not hundreds, of torches could be lit to illuminate the entire castle grounds, but on such a peaceful night only the minimum were burning.

GW still found it strange that every stall seemed to be full, knowing there should have been at least a dozen or more horses missing for the city patrol and he commented on it to his friends, "I guess every patrol is in...but that's kind of strange."

Paul was silent, but Valiant responded with a quick nod of his head and then Paul said, "With that Great Imam fella in town and him bringing in such a large compliment of troops, Captain Rynarr probably just wanted his troops close by in the event of trouble."

"That makes sense," GW replied.

Valiant raised his handsome head high and then shook his head back and forth several times, while he pawed the sand with his right front hoof. This made GW think Valiant was trying to say he agreed with Paul's suggestion. It had him grinning, as he started to step away from his mount.

"I gotta get going, boy," GW said. He patted Valiant on the hind-end one last time and began to leave the stall, but Valiant didn't want GW to leave. He backed up and moved to the left to pin GW against the side of the stall. He then brought his head around to the left and nuzzled up against GW affectionately, bringing his forehead over to gently knock against his master's head. GW again grinned again at his friend's display of emotion and petted Valiant's long nose. "Guess I got time to check your bandages again, but then I need to take a bathe." He pushed Valiant away, which was no easy task, and moved to Valiant's right side. GW looked down to make sure the bandages were clean of blood and then gently unwound them to ensure the wounds were healing well.

"Looking good, buddy. Another couple-days and you'll be as good as new…Well, at least for an old warhorse that is."

Six stalls down, Paul, who had his wish finally granted, was rubbing down a magnificent Black Arabian; a three-year old mare nearly as tall as Valiant. He was still getting to know his mount and continued to approach her cautiously, often with a slice of fruit in his hand. The mare was supposedly a gift from Captain Rynarr for the emergency services Paul provided to his men following the attack and their return to the castle, but Paul suspected Sam had a lot to do with it.

Meanwhile, Richard, who preferred not to ever have a horse, went straight to the watering troth and immediately picked up a large water bucket, dropped it into the warm murky water and promptly poured the contents over his head. The night sea air had cooled the troth water down a few degrees, but it remained quite tepid and a bit slimy from dozens of horses drinking out of it during the day. The troth would be refilled in the morning from one of the water wagons, but for now Richard was stuck with what remained in the wooden troth. But he didn't care, he had grown used to the conditions here in Silene and released a voice of contentment, "Ahhh-h-h". He then tossed his soiled tunic into the troth for it to soak and plunged the bucket back under the water for a second dousing.

While Richard was enjoying his dip, Paul was spending several moments with his mount, grooming her and feeding her straw from his hand. Most of the straw had come from the west, piled loosely into large wagons and pulled by oxen to Silene at great expense to the king. They had tried growing their own crops here in the kingdom but were only able to harvest enough to satisfy a quarter of their needs. Sam suspected it was due to such close proximity to the ocean, but others, the more superstitious ones who mingled around the fountains to spread gossip and their varied beliefs, blamed it on the dragon and curses over the valley.

There was one such story of how the Greeks had called up their gods to curse all North Africa for the sudden death of Alexander the Great. But Sam rebuffed these so-called prophets of doom and challenged them to find where in Islam it is allowed for such curses from foreign gods to have such power over Muslims.

This pretty well shut them up. Still, there was the dragon and the talk of curses continued in the safety of whispers and fireside conversations.

Paul's mare remained fidgety with him; for he had a strange odor about him she found unlike the soldiers of Silene. Most of this strangeness came from Paul's lifetime of American foods and a modern-day man's desire to bathe frequently. Being a desert people, where water was scarce and men of Silene saw no value in bathing. Swimming in the ocean was frowned upon, for they knew there were great sharks in the water capable of devouring a man with a single bite. This then left the people of Silene with quite an odorous mixture of diet, non-bathing and the wearing of clothes that were rarely, if at all, washed. When they did bathe, it was what the Americans would refer to as a GI spit bath; once under each arm, a dribble to the groin area and a slap to the face with a handful of water.

Having lived with these people for as long as they had, the three men wondered how the people of the Middle Ages had survived. Thankfully, with Sam's creation of goat soap, some of the populace was endeavoring to keep cleaner, but the soldiers felt it was for clerics, women and children, but not warriors. They found it most strange for these friends of Brother Samuel to engage in washing their whole bodies and going so far as to use this smelly stuff Brother Samuel had created. Mushid felt men should smell like men, not like goat milk and he often voiced his opinion whenever he picked up that strange obnoxious odor on Sam. "You smell like an old goat!"

"You smell like what sheep leave behind in the field," Sam replied. Then they laughed, slapped each other on the back and continued in their day.

Petting his mare's neck, Paul looked off into space, as he again considered a name for her. But he didn't want to rush into it and tried to remember some of the names for the horses on his father's ranch. While struggling with this problem, he looked over at GW and Valiant, and knew he wanted a stand-out name like Valiant. But so far, nothing quite right had come to mind. He had wrestled with Star, Midnight and Moonlight, Diablo and even Black Beauty, but none of them seemed to fit her.

With a final caress of her neck, Paul left his horse and went to join Richard in a refreshing dousing. But GW remained with Valiant, grooming him from neck to hoof and then adding straw to his feed try.

GW was again rubbing Valiant's neck when he thought he heard a strange sound to the south, over by the castle's outer wall. With the stable area so utterly quiet, the majority of the horses asleep and the guards walking their rounds in silence, it wasn't hard to pick out a noise that didn't seem to belong. He then tensed up when he saw a shadowy figure dart between the stone stairs leading up to the southeastern battlement. There was a small door leading into a storage room inside the great wall and he thought he saw a dim light as the door closed.

He thought at first someone might be trying to steal something from the storage room, but he did not hear the room's heavy wooden door open and then, he saw the dark figure disappear briefly in the darkness. Then the figure reappeared again, only a shadow produced by the torches upon the battlement. GW began to think this someone was attempting to make a stealthy approach to the stables from the southeast side, but then GW heard a noise. The intruder, or whatever he was, had mistakenly brushed against a pile of old lumber. The figure murmured something curtly GW couldn't understand, but apparently in response to making that earlier noise. Whoever it is, they're not too hot at sneaking around in the dark. GW glanced around for a weapon, but all he could see was a thick handled stable rake and it was too far away.

The person was coming from the dark side of the castle, which was mostly the large empty space between the keep and the battlements. This was the courtyard area GW trained in with Valiant. He thought this to be unusual because it was clearly the long way around and he couldn't imagine anyone thinking they could steel a horse from this stable. Besides, the big gate was closed and the walls too well guarded. He then thought about the coach and the gaudy expense which decorated it. But one man against four armed guards, who could be that stupid?

GW looked over at the guards and noticed the person's clumsiness had not alerted them and wondered if he should call out. It could be a stable hand that didn't get a job finished and was willing to risk his life to avoid a whipping.

With the battlements, all manned for the night and the relief guard not to be posted until after dawn, GW decided whoever it was had probably come from the kitchen and had taken a large loop around the north end of the courtyard to avoid being seen. They had stayed close to the wall to avoid being detected by the guards, but in doing so risked being caught by a battlement guard or even impaled by a nervous guard's arrow. GW was unsure of what he should do and if he should call out to his friends. He knew if it was a stable hand the punishments they dished around here were tough on a man's backside.

"We'll stay quiet and see who this clown is running about like a ghost," GW whispered into Valiant's ears.

GW listened quietly as the person cautiously walked across the sandy courtyard.

He also determined from their soft footedness—This dude is definitely not a soldier.

What surprised him more was Valiant's carefree attitude, he seemed more interested in the feed in GW's hand than sensing his master's growing excitement. With a perturbed expression for his mount's laxity, GW looked back to where the intruder was approaching. Either there's no danger, or my trusty steed is more interested in chowing down then warning me something's up. Looks like Libyan warhorses make lousy sentry dogs!

As the intruder drew closer, entering the area of the courtyard dimly illuminated by torchlight, GW's eyes widened when he saw the lone figure was quite small and wore a dark hooded full-length cloak. This concealed the face and body of the intruder, which also told GW, this is not the clothing of a simple stable hand or a soldier; too expensive.

Uncertainty set in and his imagination turned to fear. Fear this might be one of the assassins he had heard stories spread about around the fireside; fabled men who were trained to kill quietly and suddenly, practiced in their skills learned from ancient from Bagdad and Damascus. They were paid quite well for their services and were rarely known to fail. He also knew the clansmen of Brother Samuel had made some enemies since their arrival here and he might do well to prepare himself for attack.

He was about to warn his buddies, but then he held off when he watched the cloaked figure dart back into the shadows. He found it strange the intruder or assassin would expose himself and then once more hide in the shadows in such a clumsy way, He's acting like he wants me to know he's there, but why? There's no way I'm going out there to meet him...but for some bizarre reason I don't feel afraid...Who is this person?

With no blade at hand, he ducked under Valiant stomach and reached for the horse's leather reins left hanging on a large metal hook. With this he might be able to defend himself against an assassin's blade. "If only I'd taught you to kick like a mule," GW whispered to Valiant. He may be afraid, but he didn't want to be stupid.

He knew he should've brought a weapon down here, even a dagger, but the long hours of heat had left him rummy and now he might die because he was not prepared. He watched from Valiant's stall as the hooded person dashed across the lighted area of the courtyard and entered into the midway entrance of the stable. Then the cloaked individual slowly moved from horse stall to horse stall, stopping a brief moment to pet the rear flank of an occasional horse, but always staying in the shadows. Then the figure suddenly stood in the center pathway, which ran the length of the stable with stalls on each side. His cloak still hiding his identity, he began to walk brazenly toward a confused GW.

With a look of bewilderment, GW watched as the intruder stopped at one horse to run a gloved hand in a gentle caress along the hips of the animal. This strange act of affection left GW wondering, just who the heck is this?

Then as the shadowy figure moved closer, a beam of bright moonlit split between to aged roof boards, illuminated the possible assassin and even through the cloak, GW saw the intruder to be a small, almost petite person with very identifiable and extremely nice feminine curves. This sudden revelation caused GW to leap up and challenge this female trespasser.

"Who are you?" GW asked in a forceful whisper. He wasn't sure why he didn't yell out, but something held him back. He also figured he could handle a woman assassin and didn't want to risk alerting the castle and bring Sam's wrath down upon him and his buddies for disobeying him. He might be posing as a fat little monk, but the guy is still an officer in the Navy. If we ever get out of here, I don't want disobedience to orders hanging over us...Man, where do these thoughts come from, I'm stuck here in the 12th century, about to face some female assassin and I'm worried about disobeying orders. Oh boy, I really could use an ice-cold beer right about now...and who is this girl?

The shadowy figure with nice curves stopped abruptly at the challenge and suddenly dropped to one knee in an act of submission.

"Identify yourself woman, or you risk a beating for your actions this night," GW ordered sternly in his best Libyan tongue. He was still worried about his mispronunciation of the Libyan words and how they might come off meaning something different, I probably just told the woman her mother was a wagon wheel and her father was an ugly old goat.

Slowly, the figure rose and brought up a very small gloved right hand, "Do not fear me, Irishman, I bring you no harm and I am not a thief," she said. Using both of her hands, she then pulled back the cloak's hood to reveal herself.

Though there was little illumination to see her by, GW knew right off this person was unlike any assassin of thief he had ever heard or read about. Even through her shimmering silver veil he knew she was a young and extremely beautiful woman with long flowing black hair and fine olive skin. Her headdress and veil were quite ornate, and he believed the jewelry she worse about her neck had to be worth a fortune. When he pulled his eyes back in, he suddenly realized, Hey. She just spoke English!

There were not many torch-stands around this part of the stable, so GW couldn't really make out all the details of her face, but he sensed there was something real special about this girl. I don't think she's very old, so she must be just a girl...but wow! What a girl to meet out here in the dark. She even speaks English! He also couldn't explain this weird feeling he was having; those butterflies in the stomach thing he'd heard about, a tingling on the back of his neck and an almost racing of the heart as he looked down upon her. Then he remembered this was the same sensation he got on the back of his neck whenever he thought someone inside the upper floors of the castle was watching him train with Valiant in the courtyard.

"Just who are you?" GW asked in a gentle whisper, hoping the girl would come closer so he could see more of her face. The whole veil thing irritated him, it didn't allow him to see much beneath her eyes, but he somehow knew she was quite beautiful. Then while he stared at her veil, he suddenly recognized the royal colors and decorative patterns, and his heart jumped once again.

"My god, you're the princess!" He blurted out, a bit louder than he intended. In response, she raised her right hand and gently placed in upon his mouth, "You must be quiet, or we will surely be discovered."

GW glanced back over to where his friends were involved in a water fight and then to the four guards, who were now involved in a heated conversation of which GW had no idea what it involved and right now he simply didn't care.

He carefully pulled her hand away and said, "Princess, you do not belong here...you risk too much...and you have no chaperon. This could bring my death if we were discovered."

She then spoke in a voice that made GW think of a gentle spring rain shower and these words were also in English. "At this moment, I am simply a servant girl and have no need of a chaperon." She then added, "I admire your great skill with this beautiful stallion. You treat him...as a friend, rather than a simple animal. I've never seen such a companionship between man and horse...it is beautiful to watch."

A bit embarrassed from her words, GW placed a hand on Valiant's left rear flank and said, "This is Valiant."

The girl nodded her head in acknowledgement and used the word "Valiant", several times to remember how GW pronounced it. Then in Libyan, she said– "Valiant, this is truly a proud name for such a fine warhorse."

In the same way, the princess conversed with Brother Samuel, she and GW switched back and forth between the two languages, as they talked in whispers, "Valiant is much more than a warhorse, he is my...like you have said, my friend." GW wanted to say buddy but didn't know how to translate that into Libyan and did not know if she would understand it in English. But then he decided to give it a try anyway, "We say buddy instead of friend...if the friend, a male friend that is, is real close to us."

Princess Lennia nodded her head, "I understand. You and he are more than mere man and horse." Then slowly and cautiously, she moved closer until GW could see her sparkling eyes over the top edge of the veil.

"You...you're beautiful," GW said in surprise. The words escaped through his lips before he remembered who he was talking to.

"Thank you," she said in modesty. But she did not lower her head and continued to gaze into GW's wide eyes.

GW had to shake his head to break away from her stare. The torchlight only emphasized her beauty and he was slightly embarrassed by his gaping expression, "But why are you in the stables at this hour? It is extremely dangerous for a young lady, especially one of your...your royalty," he was about to say ranking, "...to be wandering about in the courtyard and without a chaperon."

"Again, you bring up my need of a chaperon...should I fear you?" She asked, as she reached over to comb Valiant's tail with her hands.

GW was surprised when Valiant reacted with a simple nodding of his head and then returned to his feed. Then GW looked down into those eyes and in a faint whisper, he replied, "No, my Princess, but I fear you...or what can happen to us both if we should be caught together."

"I wish to know you, to be your friend," She said in a whisper, hoping not to be overheard by the guards. "True, I am the youngest daughter to King Ramie of Silene, but I give you permission to call me Lennia when we are alone like this."

GW shook his head in amazement, "I was warned about you." He stepped back against the side of Valiant, who seemed to be totally ignoring this moment of danger by continuing to eat.

"Warned?" She asked as she moved forward to pet Valiant on the nose, which he seemed to enjoy her touch and this unusual reaction troubled GW. He thought for sure his horse would've turned to bite her, as he did so many others.

"Strange...he so easily accepts you," GW said. "Not many people can say that and most runaway in pain from one of his bites."

"You said you were warned about me, please explain," She said in a quiet, but assertive voice.

He loved the youthful sound of her voice; it reminded him of a sunset back home on the beach and a gentle breeze. Man, what's this beach and breeze crap... I'm sounding like a jerk!

Still, her tender voice seemed to draw him closer to her, "Sam...Brother Samuel said I should avoid you under pain of death...my death to be exact."

"I like your Irish language, it is much more beautiful than ours. You have so many colorful words to describe things and so much more feeling to these words you use. I can hear a strange music to your tongue and Brother Samuel has spent many years trying to teach me this music."

Right then, Paul came close to the stable and called for GW to leave his precious horse and come cool off, "Professor's going to empty the troth if you don't hurry. I want to see those laps you promised."

GW looked in Lennia's eyes and he felt himself being drawn to her like the proverbial moth to the flame. He couldn't understand how someone this beautiful and this gentle could pose such a risk to him. But remembering Sam's warning he forced himself to turn from those exquisite eyes and turned toward his friend, "I'm going to be a minute or two longer, I have to re-do Valiant's bandage."

"Okay, but you'd better hurry or you're going to be stuck with using the sheep troth."

GW ignored Paul. All he could do was stand, frozen in place and gaze into the veiled face of this young princess. He could hear his heart thumping, loud enough to make him think it was about to break out of his chest. He was captured by her sheer beauty and he still hadn't seen her without the veil, "Princess, you shouldn't be here, and I shouldn't be here with you. If someone was to see us, I'd be executed and only the king, your father, could save you from being punished for being alone with an infidel."

A twinkle came to her eyes and he knew she was smiling under her veil, "I know, we could both die for this, but it was vital I see you."

"Why?"

"I know my sister, Princess Lonnia, plans to kill all of you. She hates Brother Samuel so much and you are his clansmen."

"I was already warned of her desire to kill us, but I thank you for your concern." GW stepped away from Valiant, allowing Princess Lennia an opportunity to step into the stall and get better acquainted with his friend. "He's very gentle for a warhorse, unless there's a battle going on and then he seems to have a mind of his own."

"Yes, I have heard of your great valor against the Egyptians."

"Valor…I don't even remember the fight." He patted Valiant's flank, "He carried me through it and I woke up when it was all over."

Off in the distance GW could hear Paul and Richard fooling around at the watering troth. He could also hear the guards talking to one another by the coach, and someone inside the castle was arguing with someone else about chores and he thought it must be some of the kitchen staff.

"Truly, I have also heard of your humility and the compassion you showed to the Egyptian wounded. Most men would kill a wounded prisoner, rather than bring them back here."

"They were prisoners of war. I no longer saw them as the enemy when they lay bleeding in the cart. Where I'm from, we treat our prisoners in a humane way" He suddenly recalled that day on the battlefield, when the NVA were slaughtering the prisoners. He shook his head rapidly from right to left to escape those grizzly pictures and then looked back upon the face of the princess.

"Humble, compassionate and wise, three valuable traits in one so young," Princess Lennia said. "But does your head hurt?"

"No, I was just thinking about something else and I didn't want to...but Princess, I'm older then you are." GW said in a loud voice.

"If you get much louder you won't have to worry about getting much older."

GW shook his head again, but less violently, and grinned. He then knelt to the ground and gestured for her to follow suit. When she did, he apologized, "I'm sorry, Princess, but it's been a very long time since I talked to a girl; especially such a beautiful one. Knowing that in having this conversation, I could end up dead only adds a degree of excitement to my boring life."

"You speak so strangely. I know your words, but your meaning seems to escape me." She felt his bare shoulder with her fingertips, "Where is your tunic?"

"Oh, wow!" GW forgot he was without a shirt, "I apologize, I completely forgot I wasn't wearing a shirt...I was uncovered...Uh, my tunic was filthy, and I planned to wash it down here in the troth."

"I am not offended. I think your...shoulders are very lovely...Did I say that right?"

GW was extremely embarrassed, "Men are handsome or simply good looking. We use lovely and beautiful for complimenting women...but thank you." GW had his arms crossed as he knelt before her. He was now feeling a bit underdressed to be out here in the dark and before a princess.

"You are very silly. Why do you hide your chest from me now, I have seen it already?"

GW was unsure where this was headed, but he knew it was his head that would fall if he didn't get a handle on this situation right away, "Princess, I really like talking to you, but this could go bad really fast. You need to go."

GW realized this was one of those moments his dad told him about, when he would begin behaving like a man instead of a mindless teenager. *Here I am in the dark with a beautiful girl, probably the most desirable woman I've ever seen and now I start acting like a man. Talk about bad timing!*

"Brother Samuel teaches me that death on this world could only be a starting point to a great journey into...into eternal life through your God." *She had to remember the eternal life part.*

"I thought Brother Samuel couldn't teach you about Christianity?"

"No, my father asked him to teach me so that I may know what to expect from the Christians who come to our land. We know they will come, just as the Romans, Greeks and Moors did. You are here now, so more will follow."

"But it sounds like he's taken your lessons a step further and where I'm from, we call it evangelizing. I'm sure your father would frown on that."

"Are you a Christian?" She stood to her feet and he did likewise, but her face was a bit too close to his chest and he felt a trembling in his body. *Is this nerves? Is it from excitement or fear?*

"I guess you could probably call me one, but I don't go to church very often. I'm not so sure God really thinks about us that much. Where..." he almost said *when*, "I'm from, a lot of young men have died in a terrible war and most of them were probably Christian."

"Are they not now in this heaven Brother Samuel teaches of?"

"I hope so." He thought it strange that he'd had a similar talk with Sam only earlier today.

"Then maybe this God of yours thinks of you a lot more than you believe and provides this heaven, so you may rest in this eternal life Brother Samuel speaks of."

"When you say it, you make it sound so simple." GW then heard another sound and placed his hand in front of her mouth, touching her veil ever so gently, "Sh-h-h."

"What is this sh-h-h?" She asked, but she didn't attempt to remove his hand.

"Be quiet," he whispered in reply and then added, "...please."

"Hey, GW, where are you?" Paul called out. "You teaching that horse how to play poker or what?"

"Stay here!" GW ordered her, his voice filed with the fear he was now feeling. Though he felt a bit strange ordering a princess around, he turned away from her and addressed his friend, "I'm finishing up grooming Valiant. Don't get all excited, I'll be right out."

"Not much water left, you'd better hurry."

GW shook his head and then looked back into her eyes, which sparkled in the moonlight beaming through the cracks of the stable's wooden ceiling. His heart seemed to miss a beat and his shoulders quivered with nervous energy. He then whispered to her, "I must go before we're discovered. This is far too dangerous for you...and me."

"Brother Samuel says I am a worrier, now I think you are one too."

GW closed his eyes and sighed, "I can see you are very young and have no idea how dangerous this is." He just then noticed the cloak she wore over her gown, which seemed to be made of fine shimmery material. "Aren't you hot in that get-up?"

"Get up? What is a get up?"

GW had to think for a moment before he replied, "It is an Irish word for the style of clothes you wear. You are wearing a lot of clothes for such a hot night." He reached out and felt her robe and was surprised to find how lightweight the wool was. He realized that in the darkness her cloak looked heavy, but the spun sheep wool was quite light in the way the castle tailors had made the princesses' outer wear. Even the dark shimmery gown was constructed of a fine light silken material.

"True it is very warm, but I needed something dark in color for this night."

"Well, you had me fooled. But now you had better return to the castle and pray you are not discovered." GW gently laid a hand on her left shoulder and attempted to guide her out of the stall in hopes she would leave.

But Princess Lennia held her stand and looked up into his eyes to ask, "Will you see me again?" Her veil was now hanging loosely, and this allowed GW to see a bit more of her face and a smile of appreciation for her beauty came to his face.

"A princess should never ask a man to see her, not a beautiful one at least. It should be the man who pleads with his princess to have one more moment of her time...to bask in her presence." Where'd this bask stuff come from? I've never talked like this before...must be the summer air and this fairy tale atmosphere getting to me.

"You speak as one who has some experience with women."

"Not a whole lot," GW confessed, but his grin straightened out to an expression of seriousness. "But yes, I will risk death to see you again." There I go again, there's got to be someone up there pulling my strings. Either that or I've really lost it.

She turned to leave, "Tomorrow night then?"

GW hesitated for a moment, but then replied, "But you risk too much, Princess...maybe we should wait," he continued to admire her from the toes of her leather slippers to the top of her head. He had never seen such a beautiful woman before and having to travel back to the 12$^{th}$ century to find her only added to the mystery of this strange encounter.

"No." She said, in a very matter-a-fact tone. "I do not know how I know, but I feel deep within my heart there is something special between us. I felt a...a shaking inside me the first time I saw you and I feel it even greater now as you stand before me."

"I know, I feel it too," GW agreed. "But you must leave now." He glanced over his shoulder to make sure his friends were still busy and that the guards remained with the coach. He then grasped Princess Lennia by both shoulders, "Meet me here tomorrow night, when the moon raises two hands above the south battlement." He pointed to the battlement he meant and then demonstrated what he meant by the two hands. He knew they used hourglasses in Silene, but few people had access to one and trying to explain the workings of a wristwatch could blow the whole shooting match up in their faces.

She nodded her understanding and then said, "Then for now, I will say good night." She began to turn away, but then surprised him by facing him, pulling her veil aside a couple inches and giving him a very quick kiss on the cheek. Then she was gone into the shadows, vanishing like an apparition and leaving him in a state of bewilderment.

"Wow!" GW stood there, unmoving as he stared off into the darkness and only then did he move, when he finally heard the door to the kitchen open and close. Once he knew she was safe, he turned and patted Valiant on the neck, "Man-o-man, I'm sure playing with fire here, buddy, but I don't know what else to do. I'm already in love and I've only seen most of her face... and only one kiss on the cheek. Now what do I tell the guys? They'll never believe this...never-never-never!" He shook his head to clear his thoughts, "I'm not sure I believe it."

## THE ROYAL FAMILY CHAMBERS

Besides Sam, Princess Lonnia had been attentive to Princess Lennia's absence from the Royal Court and upon recalling her vision she took it upon herself to stand vigil over the stables for a couple of hours. Though painful to her crippled body, it paid off.

From the royal family chambers, which the main visitation room faced the Royal Guardsmen stables, Princess Lonnia was able-to sit upon a large soft pillow on a window ledge and look down upon the stalls. The large pillow provided some relief for her bad leg and the darkened room kept any onlookers below from seeing her.

She had watched the moon rise slowly and sail across the night sky. The part she actually enjoyed about the moon was observing the weird-shaped shadows it cast upon the desert floor and the great walls of the castle. Ghost-like figures seemed to dance about on the sand and stone, helping her to imagine the night was alive with desert demons playing about and she, the Black Princess, was in command of the symphony.

Princess Lonnia was about to give up for the night when she spotted the three strangers leave the keep and were almost immediately challenged by the soldiers who guarded the Great Imam's coach. But she was then confused when these guards simply released them, for she knew the standing orders were for them not to be on their own. She was now most curious and decided to continue watching the three men as they walked to the stables. Though the area was dimly lit by the few torches left burning around the stables, she was able to see that only two of three men went inside and before long, one of the figures left the stables to rejoin the other man. Even in the darkness, she knew the one who remained by the water troth was the Nubian and friend to Brother Samuel. His clown-like actions were quite visible by the bright torchlight in the area-of the watering troth and its closeness to the grand coach. She had frowned when the Nubian, this Richard of the Sudan, behaved so childishly with a bucket of water and decided these people of the Sudan were certainly stupid louts.

But she couldn't tell who had left the stables to join this Richard, for the two clansmen looked much alike and especially from a distance. However, she knew this left one man still in the stables and her heart rate picked up, for she couldn't help but wonder if this third man might be GW? She had seen him often during their long journey together but had never conversed and now she wished they had. Still, his strange Irish name confused her. GW sounded like a noise someone might make when uttering a curse and it made her wonder if it carried some dark power with it. Could he be a druid?

A few moments later, she heard a door close beneath her and for only a second or two she observed a single dark figure leave the castle keep in haste and quickly disappear into the darkness by the north wall and then make a dash for the guardsmen stables. She wasn't sure, and the darkness prevented her from making a positive identification, but the figure was small, much like a young girl or boy, and she wondered if quite possibly this was her darling little sister en route to a rendezvous with her lover?

She nearly fell of the window ledge when she tried to get down, for her crippled leg had gone to sleep on her. Cursing, she righted herself and in pain, she limped back into the room. She went to a small round table, where an unlit lamp stand stood. Here she removed a smoldering torch from its wall perch and lit a single candle. Beside the foot-long candle was an aged golden framed 12-inch hourglass and she turned it over. She watched as the first grains of sand began to fall from the upper to lower glass bowls. She wanted to see how much time passed for the one stranger and her darling sister to remain un-chaperoned in the stables.

She left the lit candle beside the hour-glass and returned to the window ledge. She only had to wait a few moments before she soon spotted the dark figure coming out of the stables and move quickly through a dimly lit area of courtyard before then darting back into the darkness. She heard the downstairs door creak as it was opened and then closed again. Princess Lonnia knew then that some degree of intrigue was occurring below and after receiving her vision, had wished she had had the foresight to put a couple of her spies inside the stables to observe the activities transpiring below her.

She grew excited, her dark powers telling her this cloaked person was her beloved Lennia. She gave great thought into wondering if her darling little sister was simply observing this GW or was she stupid enough to actually make contact with this infidel? Were they whispering their secret thoughts to one another, lifting her veil and...touching her innocent lips with...his foul infidel mouth! She grew angry and slid off her perch to land hard upon the stone floor. Pulling herself up, relieved no one was around to observe her clumsiness, she limped around the room, ignoring the pain and thought over her options. The two of them were meeting, so all she had to do was catch them in the act and both her sister and her lover would pay dearly. By tomorrow night or the next, she would be ready to catch them in the act. Tomorrow! Yes, I know they can't stay apart for too long...not true love. Her headdress and veil on her bed, she spat to the floor, while her eyes turned cold and an evil sneer appeared on her scarred face.

Several servants in the upper levels of the keep could hear Princess Lonnia's cackle; a laugh like no other in the castle and it sent shivers through them. For those who were long-term servants, they knew this eerie laugh usually preceded someone's misfortune or even their demise, and they prayed it was not theirs.

"Have you gone crazy, dude?" Paul asked.

"You're playing with fire, GW and Sam's not gonna be happy." Richard frowned and dropped to the bottom of the troth with a loud splash.

GW had reluctantly told them of his meeting with the princess, and they had both responded as he thought they would.

Paul and GW were sitting in the sand beside the wooden water troth, while the moon slowly passed overhead. Richard, depressed by the news, simply lay soaking inside the troth with mournful expression on his face. That is until he heard the rest of what GW had planned for tomorrow night and he leaned over the side of the troth to echo Paul's question with, "Are you nuts!?" He followed this up with by splashing a handful of water on GW and exclaiming, "Not only you, but you're gonna get us all killed! And I'm not talking about no electric chair or a firing squad here. I'm talking a slow and painful dismemberment and they'll probably use your own horse...or worse...the dragon."

"Look, guys, this doesn't involve either of you. I'm only asking that you don't tell Sam about this."

"First-of-all, we can't even tell Sam about us being out here," Richard said. With a grunt, he carefully pushed and pried himself out of the troth. Then he was struck with an idea; he picked up a full water bucket and dropped its murky contents all over GW.

GW, water cascading down his upper body, wiped his face and frowned at Richard and then glanced down into the nearly empty troth, "Does anything about this bother you at all? I mean, we're bathing in this crap and then washing out our clothes...My old man would be shocked to know I've sunken this low."

"Hey, if they'd let us go to the ocean or the stream...even the fountain, I'd handle my bathing needs there. But this is all we got, brother," Richard said. Then he turned around and began washing out his tunic, using the side of the troth like a washboard. He had a small piece of goat milk soap from the bar Sam had given them and Richard realized it was not going to go too far in removing his sweaty stains.

"I think your washing can wait," Paul said. Then he non-too gently pushed Richard back into the troth head-first.

He then turned to face GW, "Look, man, Sam will never trust us again," Paul reminded GW. "He might forgive us for leaving that inferno, but you making-it with her royal highness...we're vulture bait. The way he cares about that girl, he'll probably pound the first spike in your heart. I mean that girl is like a daughter to him."

"I didn't make it with her highness. We just talked."

"Okay, I can dig it... conversation's a good thing," Paul said with a nod of his head and a wink. "But Sam won't buy it. He's from a whole different world, where they didn't even kiss until the 10th date."

Richard, struggling with Paul to get out of the troth, the two of them playing like school kids, gave Paul a quick wrist throw which landed Paul right into the other end of the troth. Richard then stepped out and began shaking the water off-of him.

"Hey, mellow out before we wake up the whole castle," GW said. Reaching down with his right hand, he pulled an upset Paul out of the water troth.

"I forgot all about Judo Joe over there," Paul said, while pointing an accusing finger at Richard.

"Look, GW, we're fellow Americans and all that, but Sam's only known us for a few weeks," Richard said, ignoring Paul's comment. "He's known the princess since she was born."

Paul pointed the same accusing finger at GW's chest, "You've really screwed the pooch here, buddy." Paul then shook his head a second time. "Man, that's some pretty crummy water. I'll probably get typhoid."

"Horses are still healthy," Richard said. "Maybe you could just ignore her and forget all about tomorrow night."

GW shook his head, "Could I ignore my heart?"

"Don't start sounding like some valentine card," Paul said in frustration. He had water in his right ear and it didn't want to come out. "We'll think of something."

"This isn't about you two, this is my business and I shouldn't involve you."

"Look, my man, we've been in this together ever since we ran into that stupid cave," Paul said. He stood beside Richard and pointed at GW. "He sure don't look like a fish, but he sure do smell like one."

Richard took the hint, stepped in and grabbed GW by the arm, with Paul on the other. Between the two of them they plopped GW into the bottom of the troth, where the water was less than six inches deep now.

"Oh, man, get me out of here!" GW ordered.

Richard of the Sudan ignored his complaints and looked at GW, "You might remind our friend here of how we didn't actually run into the cave...we all fell into it." Richard then turned to walk away, his wet tunic over his bare shoulder, but decided he wasn't finished with Paul. He turned to face him, "Just to let you know, we were bathing tonight in fresh water–not sea water. So, it is illogical to say he smells like a fish. Fresh water fish only stink after they begin to rotten. It's the salt that makes ocean fish stink. It's also doubtful you'll catch typhoid as I've seen no cases of it since we arrived."

"Get the professor here," Paul gestured to Richard with a right thumb over his shoulder and then added, "Okay, GW smells like the backend of a goose-feathered three-legged hippo. Better?"

"You're impossible." Richard gave Paul a friendly punch in the arm.

"I'd punch you back, but you'd probably throw me back in the troth."

"I would too," Richard replied and then began walking toward the castle keep entryway. Paul slowly followed, but GW remained standing beside the troth, unsure of what he should do next? He still had the tunic to wash out and he needed to give this princess thing a whole lot more thought.

"Sleep on it tonight, man," Paul suggested from several yards away. "Right now, we have to sneak back in and spend the rest of night in that hot box."

"Yeah, I'll be right behind you." With a heavy heart, GW dragged his tunic through the filthy water several times, rung it out and then headed for the entry. He stopped to say goodnight to the guards at the coach and then entered the castle keep.

The three Americans didn't know it at the time, but their playful antics at the water troth had greatly entertained the four guards and the story of their bizarre behavior would quickly spread through the ranks. Not only had GW displayed great courage in battle, but he had demonstrated himself to be just one of the guys in his rough housing with his two friends. These were only two of the many attributes to come that began GW's rise in the respect of the common soldier and would eventually aid him greatly in the birth of a legend.

## SAM'S STUDY

Following a night of restless sleep and too many trips to the water closet to relieve his aged bladder, Sam wasn't feeling his best and came off a bit grumpy when GW appeared in his door.

"I thought I told you to stay in your room!" Sam growled when he opened the heavy wooden door and looked upon his new friend.

"Sam, its 200 degrees in there and even the flies have melted," GW replied. Without waiting for an invitation, he walked into the room and made sure to close the door behind him, before he took a cool drink from out of Sam's pitcher. "At least you got windows."

"Right, I forgot," Sam replied. He wore a look of guilt upon his face. "Must be my age, I should've had you three moved long ago."

Sam stashed some drawing he'd done into a make shift cabinet drawer and shook his right index finger in GW's face, "But you still took a big chance in coming here."

"I'd rather die from an executioner's axe, then from heat stroke." GW took another drink and then poured a ladle of water over his head.

"Paul is looking pretty bad and Richard's upchucking morning chow. It's just too damn hot in there. You have to do something before we schedule a jailbreak." GW poured another dipper of water over his face and smiled as he relished in the moment.

"I'll do it now," Sam said. "You'll move down here, I have a somewhat empty room next door and it does have windows. But you'll have to move your cots and we must be extremely careful. I do not want the Great Imam seeing you."

"Thanks, Sam." GW walked across the room and then turned to face his friend, "How'd it go with the Imam, did you find out what he wants?" GW was relieved to know they'd be moving, even if it was into quarter's right next to Sam. It would make it more difficult to sneak out tonight to see the princess, but he would have to work it out.

Whenever he thought of her, he remembered her kiss and how she had touched his cheek. He couldn't ever recall being so gone over a girl before, especially one he just meant. Maybe it's the danger? The thrill of possibly being caught and dismembered and again, maybe I shouldn't even think about that part? He glanced out Sam's window and remembered his mom and what she would've said. She'd say I was smitten...what a corny word. Man, I miss her.

"The Great Imam, an enemy of mine for nearly four decades, has the king over a barrel," Sam said. He walked around the table where he'd been working to stand before GW.

"We have 364-days left to kill that infernal dragon. We've been given a royal decree from the Caliph himself."

"Why exactly 364-days?"

"We were given one-year and we've already used up one day, quarreling with that religious windbag."

"What happens if you can't kill it?" GW asked. "I mean you've tried and so far, nothing's worked."

Sam placed his aging and scarred right hand on GW's shoulder, "Then, my young friend, I'll be dismembered as a heretic and an infidel, or devoured by the dragon. In any case, I'll be assuredly dead, and I am sure you three would soon follow." Sam dropped his hand and walked over to the window to feel the sea breeze blowing in. He loved the smell of the ocean at this time of day and it seemed to revitalize him. "Won't be so hot today, we're getting some relief from the north. But I sure wouldn't want to be out there on the lower Sahara. I imagine the temperatures will be hitting 130 or better out there." Sam then remembered GW's question and answered, "Oh, in addition he's also given me a choice of turning from my Lord Jesus Christ and accepting Allah as my god, but he knows I would never do that. He also knows we have little if no chance of destroying that foul beast out there. I know. I've tried many times, at the cost of so many lives and failed."

"Maybe we can come up with something, a better weapon or a better mousetrap."

"Mousetrap?" Sam asked. But then he understood the remark and smiled. "Maybe so, but right now we should get your friends moved before they fall deathly ill and I would be to blame for my forgetfulness."

"Sam, we don't blame you," GW said as he approached the old man and patted his back gently. "You've saved our lives and brought us into a new world, rich with mystery and beauty."

"Thank you," Sam replied, a bit puzzled by GW's words, but then he noticed the far-off gaze in GW's eyes. He wondered what could be on this young man's mind. When he was his age, that look usually involved some female and as far as he knew, these three friends of his hadn't discovered any ladies. They knew the castle slaves and servants were off limits, so who could GW be thinking about? Maybe a young lady from his past, a girl he left behind when he went to war? But he's beginning to sound a lot like Richard.

Had Sam known about Princess Lennia arrangement to meet with him tonight, GW suspected Sam would probably have had his bogus clansman hanging from the upper levels of the prayer tower; to bake in the sun for all eternity or shipped off to Tripoli as a slave on the first caravan heading deep into the Sahara Desert.

It took some effort and the use of four of Sam's most trusted servant-friends, but they were able-to get the three Americans moved into the upper level without being seen by anyone outside of a young female servant. She was carrying trays down to the kitchen and Paul grinned at her when she batted her eyes at him. She was one of Sam's friends and he wasn't worried about her. "She won't say anything," Sam said to his friends. "Last year she lost a younger sister to the lottery and ever since then, she refuses to speak to any of the royal family or members of the court. Most think she's mute, but this is simply her way of rebellion against this foul practice."

"Why doesn't she hate you then?" Paul asked.

"I appealed to the court on her sister's behalf, even got the king so mad I nearly ended up in the dungeon myself," Sam replied. "And the people know how hard I've worked to slay the creature."

"Sam, this dinosaur is aquatic, it cannot move too far away from its watery home. So, why doesn't the king simply keep everyone away from the lake?" Richard asked. "I mean, I doubt if this creature could ever reach the castle walls." He was feeling quite a bit better having left that oven below and his spirit picked up as he walked through the cooler passageways, vented via numerous windows.

"Remember, Richard, these are extremely superstitious people and in their minds this dragon has come straight from the very fires of Hell. Whether it has fins or feet, or slithers on its belly, they'll think it has the power of Satan and you can't tell them otherwise."

"But it's just a dinosaur, has a smaller brain than a horse..." Richard was interrupted when Sam held up his hand.

"I know it, you know it, but you'll never convince them of it." He pointed toward the lake, "Out there is a fiend of Hell—a curse upon this land and the only way to save these people is to kill it. Then pray there isn't another one to replace it."

"You think there's more than one?" GW asked.

"No, not now," Sam replied. "But according to ancient writings there were many at one time. So, what happened to them and why is this one still here, I do not know."

"Well, once we get our cots set up in our new room, you can show us what you've used so far to combat that thing. Maybe then we can come up with something better?" GW said. Then he carried one end of his cot into the new room, with a servant on the other end for help.

"Like a better mousetrap?" Sam asked.

"Right on, Brother Samuel," Paul said, flashing Sam the two-finger peace sign of the 60's. "Peace, brother."

Sam studied Paul for a moment and then shook his head in wonder, "Youth, it's wasted on the young."

Several wooden trunks were now piled on top of each other at one end of the room, giving them enough space for the three cots and some walking space in between. Sam showed them where the water closet was first off and then one of his first inventions after leaving the dungeon- a toilet and an attached toilet seat. He told them how he never came up with suitable version of toilet paper. All his attempts had proved fruitless and eventually, he accepted the local tradition of using water to clean himself. A tradition the three newcomers still had great difficulty with, even though it was still practiced in most 20th century Asian countries.

"I've got the only private water closet, as I call it, in the castle. Just make sure you lock the door, or you might end up with company. Several of the servants sneak up here, they like their privacy too and my toilet seat entertains them."

"Too bad you don't have any comic books. I like to read when I'm doing my business," Paul said. This comment warranted another look of wonder from Sam.

GW struggled with himself, he wanted to come clean with Sam and tell him of his meeting with Princess Lennia, but he was too scared. Not so much for himself, but for her getting into trouble. But she was right, there was something drawing them together, a feeling stronger then he'd ever felt before and one he couldn't understand. That's what he wanted to talk to Sam about. Not Sam the navy commander, but Sam the Christian monk. But now wasn't the time.

GW knew Sam, who was much older than GW's father, was deep in thought over surviving this next year. Sam wanted to rescue these people of Silene, to slay the foul beast and in the process bring them all to Christianity. GW could see it in Sam's face, he had truly become the priest he had masqueraded as for so long and GW found this strangely enlightening.

Later that afternoon, GW walked through the doorway separating the study and their new room, to find Sam laboring over a drawing; another invention, a weapon, one that would require many weeks to build. Upon seeing GW, Sam stepped aside to show his complex diagram to him. "More power on the block and tackle, a larger pulley at the base and a larger arrow shaft-roughly ten-feet long...like a short telephone pole.

"I plan to have blacksmith design me a two-foot long arrowhead, one with six-heavy barbs and the sharpest point he can give me to penetrate that thick hide."

"Looks deadly, but how much pull will it give you?" GW asked. He studied the drawing for a moment, recalling how he had seen similar weapons in a book of drawings of medieval weaponry.

"It will require nearly three-times as much pull as my earlier attempts."

"What happened last time use shot that dragon?" GW preferred calling it a dragon, it sounded better to him than dinosaur and it got a rise out of Richard when he did.

"One arrow imbedded itself, but it soon fell off and another simply bounced off the creature's thick hide. I'm hoping with more power and a stronger point, we can kill it.

But even a severe wound would allow us to move in and finish it off with lances and spears. Once the creature is down, the people's fear will give way to their desire to see it dead."

"How long will it take you to have it made?" GW asked as he pointed to the drawing.

"I think it will probably take the carpenters a good month, maybe five-weeks to build the frame. The blacksmith, with help, could have the two-shafts I want ready before that. The hard part is cutting the wood thick and strong enough and threading the ropes to handle the strength of the pull I need. Normal rope will tear apart as we strengthen the pull...I've already had that happen. The rope I need now will be four times as thick and that'll take at least three weeks for the weavers to make and maybe even longer. But, the king has given me his highest priority, so I am estimating we can make an attempt in probably six-weeks if it all comes together or at least eight-weeks if we hit a snag."

"That means two... maybe three girls will die before we can try," GW said with sadness in his eyes.

"Yes, unfortunately, you are quite right." Sam turned to remove his dipper from the water pitcher and sip from it. He then offered it to GW, but he wasn't thirsty and declined.

"Sam, were you much of a Christian when you came here?"

Sam smiled in response. He'd been expecting this question for some time. "I knew God, but my walk with the Lord Jesus was a stumbling one. I was one of those who often said you couldn't find an atheist on the front lines, but I was wrong. People, those so hard in their hearts they simply wouldn't allow the Lord in, they died that way." Sam gestured to a hand-built set of chairs, "Let us sit, my legs are tired."

Sam built the chairs out of old ship wood, some of it he believed to be teak from Asian boats. Strong enough to handle his weight, the heavy wood gave him great difficulty in producing suitable chairs for comfortable sitting. But with an old carpenter for help, they produced high backed chairs from lengths of the hardened wood. He used various kinds of furs to provide a thin soft cushion for his old weary body. He also built a stool, which wasn't much more than the base of a large palm covered with the hide of a camel.

"My devotion to the Lord increased as I watched these people live out their lives. I saw little joy under their faith. Far too much discipline and the women are nothing more than second-class prisoners to their husbands or owners. So, even without a Bible to study, I began to remember my old Bible lessons from Sunday school and this helped me through those unbearable times in the dungeon.

"The guy you had down there is nothing like my dungeon master. Oh, I agree he is uglier and smells a whole lot worse, but my guy had a certain joy in making me beg for mercy. Those devices down there are real, GW, they're not simply there for effect. I was a victim to each one and only God kept me alive, much to my torturer's embarrassment."

"I had no idea, I thought you were only held there and probably starved a lot."

Sam stood up very carefully and lifted his robe. Outside his silken underwear, his body was covered in ugly scars from various cuts and burns. "My arms have several too, but I imagine you've seen enough."

GW was revolted by what he saw. He could not imagine anyone surviving such wounds. "I'm sorry, Sam, I didn't know." GW eyes were now teary.

"Do not worry, my friend." Sam dropped his robe and returned to his chair, letting out a sigh as he fell back into it, "It is only a bad memory now and the occasional nightmare, but I have learned what my people go through in a more personal way.

"Remember, I slugged the captain of the Royal Guardsmen and by all rights, I should've been slain on the spot. Except, I was a curiosity and they were concerned I was a spy for an upcoming invasion and they wanted to know my secrets. When I had nothing to tell them and the weeks turned to months, they realized I wasn't a spy. They knew no one could've stood up to that kind of torture and not reveal something.

"If I hadn't learned their language and came up with a new plumbing design for the castle, I wouldn't be here now talking to you. So, God had a design in this. I believe it and so should you."

"I believe, or I think I believe, Sam. But I don't understand how a compassionate Lord could allow so many good men to die? I watched as my friends were killed and I killed a fair share of the enemy myself. I was even awarded a Bronze Star, but I had to kill several men to win it. Vietnamese, American, all a bunch of young men spilling their blood and where was God?"

"We've had this conversation before and my answer is the same—I also asked how God could allow so many to die when Pearl Harbor happened and over 2,000-men and women died needlessly. I didn't want to see a war, GW, but we are a sinful people. From Adam right down to modern day man from your time, man has sinned. We are not perfect, only our Lord Jesus was perfection and as a result we fight with one another. Think about all the men who perished in our Civil War and they were all Americans."

"So why doesn't God intercede. He could stop all this stupid killing."

Sam grinned and looked down at his hands, he studied the burns and scars from having his fingernails ripped out and for a moment he tried to remember when they had gotten so old looking? Then he looked up at GW, who patiently waited for an answer.

"GW, God's greatest gift to us was free choice—choice to choose Him or to choose other ways, or other gods. Satan wanted to take this free choice from us. He wanted us to be mindless servants, but God said no and kicked Satan and his followers out of Heaven. They became the demons that plague us today.

"This free choice allows us the freedom to make war and kill or make peace and live happily. But again, we are a sinful people and down through history we have chosen war. One day a final war will be fought, the largest and most deadly in man's history and afterward, we will live happily with our Lord Jesus Christ as King."

"You're talking about the Book of Revelations?"

"Yes. The Battle of Armageddon, the last war for mankind."

GW studied this old man, whose gray beard covered his massive stomach, but whose kind eyes were not filled with the pain and hate from those long months of torture, but with the joy of serving his Lord. He looked at Sam's hand, really looked and for the first time, he noticed Sam didn't have any fingernails and it sent a cold shudder up his spine.

"You really believe this and will risk your life to stand for this belief?" GW asked in a sense of awe and great respect for the old man.

"I have stood in my belief for nearly 50-years and the Lord Jesus Christ hasn't left me. He won't leave you either, GW. He will always be there. You only have to ask him into your life."

"I did once, but I was only 11-years old and it was at Vacation Bible School. Since then I've lived a real ungodly life."

"What happened to you out there on the battlefield with the Egyptians?"

"That's the funny part. I don't remember much of anything. Valiant charged forward when Captain Rynarr gave the signal and I felt this quietness all around me. Then it was over, and they told me I had killed 10-Egyptians and saved Captain Rynarr's life. I don't understand it, Sam. What happened to me and how did I survive the battle?"

"It sounds to me as if the Lord was with you...pretty simple deduction."

"I'm so mixed up here, Sam. I wish I knew why I'm here? I feel this strange closeness to Valiant, as if we can speak to each other and there's still that shaman dude who spoke with me before I left camp."

Sam smiled broadly at GW's use of the word dude. For a brief moment, GW thought Sam looked like Santa Claus and then Sam said, "I strongly believe God has His hand on you, my young friend. You have something very important ahead of you and our Lord is protecting you. But remember this, He gives us free choice and if we choose to walk away or simply step aside from God's Will, He will choose another for the task ahead. So be alert and do not give in to temptation."

"So, what else should I do?"

"Remember the day you gave your life to Him, think of that young boy you once were. Then repent and ask forgiveness for the ungodly life you've led since then. It's easy, takes only a moment. If you're truly serious, you've just hit a homerun!"

"Thanks, Sam."

"I'm hungry, what about you?"

"You bet," GW replied. "Knowing those two, they're probably chewing camel leather by now. I asked them to give us a private moment, but I think I can hear Paul's stomach growling from here."

"I'll go to the kitchen, have some food and drink sent up. One of the cooks is a dear friend of mine." Sam pointed to his stomach. "I owe this to him... He knows you're in hiding and he'll take good care of you.

"Actually, it's kind of surprising to see how many people in the castle dislike the Great Imam. Riding around in the rich coach with such a large escort has a lot of Muslims angry. There's too many people hungry for their church leader to be behaving in such a pompous way."

"Have you thought of asking the king to release you from your promise to share the gospel?" GW asked.

Sam looked to the ceiling as he thought over his answer, "Let us say I have some thoughts swirling about and we will keep it there for the moment. I'm hungry."

# 13 – THE WILL OF ALLAH

Black thunderheads lay far off to the north of the Libyan coast, forming a threatening wall 5,000 feet high between southern Europe's coastline of Italy and Greece, and the hard-baked sandy shorelines of North Africa. But even with the threat of a summer storm looming off in the distance, nary had a summer breeze appeared this day to relieve the tortured people of Silene.

With the rising of the sun to the west, the bright rays of morning began to slowly transform the night's cool air into a sweltering furnace. Even the few remaining shady spots behind the castle's great wall were quickly heating up and by noon, the temperatures in Silene would rise into the high nineties, or even worse. To add to the near unbearable heat wave was the presence of an ever-increasing high percentage of humidity, and together, these two elements would make life miserable for anyone who must work outside. An adding a bit of cruelty into the mix, the heat only increased the stench of the stables, manure carts and the open-air refuse trenches; used primarily by the soldiers and the poorer class.

Summer in North Africa was not a pleasant time for man or beast, tasking both of strength and will, as life's essence simply dried up. Yet, there was one task that had to be done this warm morning and it involved twenty men-at-arms and an officer on horseback, who were given the dangerous task of escorting three fearful sheep herdsmen and their small flock forward toward the accursed lake to the north of the castle's Great Wall.

The herdsmen used repeated blows from their staffs to drive the sheep on and these men, who had spent their lives with these herds, they could sense the fear in their animals. Some of the herdsmen often wondered how these dumb animals could know the fate that awaited them. Brother Samuel had watched this spectacle for over 40-years and knowing something of animal husbandry, he knew it simply came down to the animals sensing the apprehension and fears in their masters. These sheepherders and soldiers alike trembled with each approaching step they made toward that infamous body of water and Sam knew it was no wonder why the sheep acted so strangely.

Once leaving the safety of the Great Wall, the detail looked out upon the deep blue-green waters of the lake and saw how strangely calm the waters of the ill-favored lake were this morning. Yet, they knew all too well how any sense of tranquility in this lake was far misleading.

Each man felt the beat of their hearts race. Fear gripped their chests and made each cautious step a challenge to their courage. But to turn and flee meant death from the archers upon the Great Wall, for Captain Rynarr hated cowardice above all in his military. But a sudden unexplained sound or a man stumbling could cause the wary eyes of each man to dart back and forth excitedly, searching for any sign of the dreaded beast. The soldiers silently griped their weapons tightly, while herdsmen hurriedly moved their sheep along. Though each man had spent time in morning prayers, they still continued to offer up whispered prayers to Allah, hoping for yet one more day of life upon this sun-bleached desert land.

Thirty-head of sheep were being herded to the lakeside; an offering to the dragon. Sheep were sacrificed one week and a fair maiden the next and three herdsmen on foot were the number needed to keep the sheep grouped together, or the timid and frightened animals were known to break away in times past. Herdsmen and foot soldiers had lost control of the small herd and on a few occasions frightened men had come dashing back to the Great Wall in fear the dragon had surfaced, with the racket being made by the sheep. Before things were straightened out, several men and sheep had fallen to a flight of arrows from the Great Wall. Now an additional force of ten mounted soldiers were on stand-by at the Great Wall in the event they were needed to stop a stampede of 30-sheep going off in all directions.

When the men arrived at the lake, all eyes were busily scanning the waters for any sign of the beast, while the sheep were rushed into a small 12-foot by 12-foot wooden pen. This structure would be routinely rebuilt that very afternoon. Court advisors, including Brother Samuel, believed a well-fed dragon would be content with its meal of mutton and leave a small work party alone. Only once in recorded history did the dragon rise up from its watery home to attack a work party and the beast seemed contented with two slow carpenters and a slow older horse, which had pulled the wood cart, before returning to its watery lair. It was following that episode the royal court issued a decree to increase the amount of sheep from twenty to its current number of 30 sheep, in hopes it would satisfy the beast's hunger.

Castle carpenters cast aside the bloody wood debris and built one barely strong enough to keep the sheep from running off when the dragon appeared. At five-foot high, it was rare an ewe or ram could jump free and this chore was usually done in under an hour, and sometimes in much less time. A jittery five-man escort detail quickly lent a hand in the building process, while a single blacksmith hustled over to the sacrificial rock to repair or replace the needed manacles.

Once the sheep were secured in the pen this morning, the herdsmen didn't hang around a second longer then needed and quickly fled to the south. They had hopes of reaching the Great Wall before the dragon reared its gruesome head; a sight known to freeze some good men in their tracks.

Their army escort, having had to carry their long spears and hefty battle shields, were much slower, but were also equally enthusiastic about reaching the protection of the Great Wall. For the first 100-yards it resembled a foot race between the soldiers, while their mounted officer rode out in front of them. But after that first mad dash and having no sign of the dragon, the officer reined up and turned to wait on his men and order them into a loose formation for a quick march south to the Castle.

Seeing the men were will clear of the lake, a soldier standing upon the Great Wall lifted a large antelope horn to his dry lips and summoned the dragon forth with several long blasts. Sam often thought the shrieking like sound was reminiscent to a large goose releasing a startled and fearful honk.

There were some people in Silene who didn't believe the horn actually summoned forth the loathsome beast, but suspected the dragon remained alert for movement along the lakeshore and cautiously moved in to collect its prize; be it two or four legged.

Then off in the distance; some 100-yards or so from shore and less than a quarter-mile down the beach and east of the sheep pen, a couple of large air bubbles broke the surface. This quickly gave way to a multitude of bubbles, which quickly produced a frothy white foam and spread out in a circle-like pattern for dozens of yards. This was easily visible from where the men stood upon the Great Wall and word spread quickly enough, "The dragon is coming."

The waters of the lake swirled violently, as a large elongated and bluish head, behaving in an almost cautious nature, barely broke the surface. This allowed the beast's two large, cold and glassy black eyes to gaze upon the south shoreline. Then, when it spotted the sheep, the creature gradually lifted its head higher, until it had raised high above the waters. Looking up and down the shorelines, it cautiously moved toward the beach and used its massive seal-like fins to propel itself forward through the shallow waters and then onto the beach. Still, it continued to remain ever watchful, for off in the distance it could see the soldiers who stood poised upon the Great North Wall.

Upon reaching the beach, the dragon rose to its full height of nearly 50-feet and lumbered clumsily forward, sending small waves rushing forth to break upon the beach and its waves to smash up against several rock outcroppings. Its head, larger than a 16-hand warhorse and its eyes almost lifeless in nature, glared down upon the pen filled with terrified and noisy sheep. Some of the animals stood paralyzed, while others trampled over one another in an attempt to flee. But they couldn't escape; the wooden pen held them in place. But the sheep were not alone in their fears, several of the soldiers who lined the Great Wall stood frozen, sickened as they watched the creature began to devour the sheep, while others trembled, frightened from hearing the animals' mournful cries.

One and then two sheep tried to jump out of the pen, using the other animals as steps to clear the top boards. But they were the first to die. The dragon swooped down with its long neck and scooped them up in its gaping mouth of sword-like teeth. Seeing for the first time so long ago, Sam had thought the beast's actions resembled a large white swan scooping small fish out of a lake.

While seasoned men-at-arms watched in mixed awe and revulsion, newer troops recoiled in horror from the grisly scene. The dragon's head dropped down into the pen over and over, until all the sheep were gone.

The winded foot soldiers and weary herdsmen, now safe behind the wall, didn't have the energy to climb to the top of the Great Wall to observe the scene. Several of the men, though life-long Muslim, spoke in whispers as they wondered why Allah, their benevolent god, would continue to allow such a vile creature to plague their kingdom? They had individually voiced their concerns to their clerics, but none had received a satisfactory answer. Not even the clerics themselves could answer that question amongst themselves, but they never mentioned this to the faithful masses.

For the three herdsmen, two of them of an older adult age, had felt an emotional loss for their sheep. These were innocent animals they had raised from birth. They had sheered them, cared for them and sang songs to them in the fields. Now it was time for them to be sacrificed and the herdsmen watched as their herds were slowly depleted.

The Kingdom of Silene had once been known for its massive herds of sheep and goats. At one time they had covered the valley, moved about the land for forage and now, the herds were down to less than ten percent of what they had once been. For every lamb being born, five older sheep were being fed to the dragon. It only took Brother Samuel a short time to figure out the king's sheep herds would be all gone in four-years. Some toying with the old decrees were being made with the substitution of older goats in the place of sheep. But the goat herds were already down to less than 2,000-goats and the king was gravely concerned with his people going hungry within a couple of years. With the curse hanging over the kingdom, fewer people were willing to trade with Silene and the great caravans from the east were routing their travels to the south. Now, the people of Silene were being forced to travel to Tripoli for their trade goods and there, they were often treated poorly by the locals

But thankfully, as allowed by the lottery decree, the herdsmen were only required to sacrifice the older ewes, the ones that no longer gave birth and their wool was not of the best quality. They also offered up the occasional old ram. Sam had pointed out to Captain Rynarr on several occasions on how the sheep sacrifice had far different guidelines to go by then the human sacrifice did. "We send to death the best of our maidens, but then we send out the worst of our sheep." In response to this, Captain Rynarr would simply shrug his shoulders and shake his head. During one such exchange, Rynarr asked if Sam thought it better to sacrifice older women instead and send out their finest sheep. Then it was Sam's turn to shrug his shoulders, thinking of the old ladies manacled to the bloody rock and he'd walkway in dismay.

Brother Samuel, in his role as senior advisor to the king, had attempted poisoning the sheep in hopes of killing the dragon, but the beast declined to consume the dead sheep in the pen. Sam knew there were some reptiles, which avoided dead animals and wondered if this was an instinct passed down from their dinosaur ancestors.

So, he tried a milder poison to keep the sheep alive, but if anything, he only gave the dragon a stomachache and over the years his many other experiments to slay the beast also failed. His various weapons had indeed left several nasty scars upon the dragon's hide and once, a hidden net of ropes was brought up to encase the beast, which allowed a brief moment of time for some brave knights to rush in and use their lances against the creature. But the dragon's great strength and sharp teeth shredded the netting and a dozen good men and their mounts had died.

Now Sam had a new weapon and he sincerely hoped and prayed this new device would work. His design, if followed correctly by the carpenters and weavers, would be far stronger and deadlier than any device he'd made before. But it would take time to build and at least two maidens would lose their lives before the weapon was ready and this saddened him. The use of several pulleys for maximum effect had at first confused the carpenters, but they soon understood and went about carving out the devices needed for the weapon. The blacksmith would have to melt down several older weapons to produce the point Sam needed for the heavy spear shaft and was working nearly around the clock to forge a sturdy point. So far, nothing the blacksmith had created was capable of piercing the beat's thick hide and Sam hoped this new spear would do so, or it was all in vain. He also hoped the Blacksmith was capable of producing two or possibly three shafts in the event the first one didn't hit the target. Sam knew the animal's most vital spot was at the base of his neck and directly over where Sam thought his heat to be. He knew the beast's ribs protected his heart, much like a human, but at the base of his neck would be the animal's main artery to it brain. If he was capable- of severing that artery, the beast would assuredly die.

## SAM'S STUDY

Though quite hot and not even noon yet, the boys were out training in the courtyard. This allowed Sam some classroom time with his one and only student; Princess Lennia. Today was a grueling session involving early Christianity and Sam, whose memory was beginning to leak out his ears from age, struggled to remember some of the more important teachings of the Apostle Paul.

"Brother Samuel, you speak of this man Paul, who you say was once a tax collector, and hated by his own people. You say this man was mysteriously blinded by your Lord and then in a miracle, healed three-days later. You also say this man was a despicable man who was responsible for sending many of his fellow Jews to prison and he persecuted...I believe this is the right word...persecuted, am I right?"

Sam nodded his agreement, while wiping his forehead of sweat with a length of cloth, as she continued, "He persecuted these followers of your Lord...to even death...Am I correct in this?" She asked with a troubled look upon her young face.

She had painstakingly made her statement and asked her questions in the Irish Sam taught her and was even now, not all that sure of all her words.

"True," Sam replied in Arabic, which was the second language of the Libyans. He was attempting to find a sufficient position for his great backside upon his stool but couldn't get comfortable. Lately, he'd been having more and more trouble with his back and knew this was being caused by arthritis. So, disgusted with his physical handicaps, he painfully stood to his feet, which were also quite sore, and released a mighty sigh as he stretched his back. While on the other side of his study table, the princess rested comfortably in one of Sam's chairs and looked upon her teacher with sympathy.

"You should burn that stool!" She strongly advised in Libyan.

"Then where would I sit when I need to work?" Sam replied in English and then pointed to the chairs he made, "Those sit too low to the ground."

"Then you should lower the table or build a stool wide enough and strong enough to hold your," She hesitated, "...your largeness," she said in English. She hoped that was the right word for she didn't want to offend her dear friend and mentor.

"Largeness, is it? Where did you learn that word?" Sam asked.

"From you, old man, who else teaches me?" She asked in Arabic.

Sam threw his arms up in surrender, "Okay, from now on we speak in one language and right now we will use your Libyan dialect. All this bantering back in forth in three languages is giving me quite a headache."

Princess Lennia smiled at him and nodded her head in agreement.

"Then let us return to our lesson, young lady and we were discussing the Apostle Paul."

"Why did your lord blind him and heal him three days later? Why not simply slay him for the harm he caused these people?"

Sam leaned against his table, his arms folded as he replied. "My Lord Jesus Christ wanted to use Paul, who at the time was known as Saul and also known later as Saint Paul. Our Lord needed to demonstrate his immense power to a hard-hearted man. By blinding him and then healing him three days later, Paul was convinced Jesus was in fact the Son of God and he served Him unto his death."

"He was Saul, then Paul, then St. Paul and he never collected taxes again?"

"No, he didn't."

"Did not the king he served come after him for not doing his job?"

Sam grinned, "Not right away. Paul was also a Roman citizen, which gave him certain rights the other apostles didn't have. But in the end, he gave his life for his belief in Jesus Christ, as did all the original twelve disciples."

Princess Lennia stood to her feet and began to walk about the room, "I listen, Brother Samuel, but I find this Christianity very confusing. You say your Lord is a god of love, of grace and mercy, yet your knights come into the land of the Muslims and slay our women and children. They kill the innocent," She said. "Why is that? Are not your knights Christian too?"

Sam studied her face, unsure how to quite answer her question and knowing how his answer would be extremely important for her continued lessons. He put his hand up, a gesture showing he needed a pause and he walked over to the nearest window. There he looked down and watched Richard workout with 20-men in a simple, but effective martial arts drill.

GW was riding Valiant around the courtyard, using his training lance against his opponent; Mushid, in a joust. They were riding at half-speed to allow GW practice in aiming his lance at Mushid's heart.

Having thought about his answer for a moment, he returned to the table where Princess Lennia was cutting up a ripe melon for both of-them.

"You have been brought up in this castle, spent your entire life around Muslims and have seen for yourself the differences in the men who serve your father. There are those who have integrity, those who are honest and value life...Men such as Captain Rynarr and my friend Mushid of the Royal Guardsmen. But you have also seen those Muslims who show varying degrees of disrespect for the Koran by drinking of fermented fruit, abusing women and even slaying of the innocent. You have even witnessed the Great Imam's shameless disrespect for your father in this court his demand for the brutal death of your sisters."

"What are saying, teacher?" She was about to put a piece of melon in her mouth but stopped, for the words of her friend confused her.

"I am saying, we, as humans, are far from perfect. We make a lot of mistakes and we all have opinions. These opinions often or not demonstrate these mistakes," Sam said. "Only one man was perfect, and He was our Lord Jesus Christ. He never sinned, and He provided a gateway for us to have eternal life."

"Does not your Lord offer you 70-virgins as a reward for dying in battle?" She asked. She reached out with another slice of melon for her dear friend.

"No." Sam replied. Struggling to stifle a smile and in dear hopes he was not blushing, he accepted the melon slice and said, "When we get to heaven, a splendid place I might add and where the streets are paved in gold, men and women are treated alike and together we will worship our Lord for all eternity."

Princess Lennia simply nodded her head, as she chewed her melon and then cut off another slice of the moist melon and offered it to Sam. After finishing her slice, she walked over to the same window so she could observe GW train.

This made Sam uncomfortable, for he couldn't help but notice the look of affection in her eyes and the half-smile to her lips, as she looked down upon the courtyard. He knew she was watching GW and was in a quandary for what to do about it.

When she turned from the window, but remained leaning against the stone ledge, she asked another difficult question "You have explained why your people fight for this Jerusalem and why my people fight to hold it, so who will win do you think? Whose god is more powerful?"

Sam studied the girl who was rapidly becoming a woman, "I believe many men, women and children will perish before the fighting is over, and it will go on for many years. I also believe there will be conflict between our two faiths for quite a long time, probably for centuries. But as to who is more powerful, I have to believe my God, for if I didn't, I would've accepted Allah as my master long ago."

A young servant girl then appeared at the door to summon Princess Lennia to her father. She dismissed the girl and turned to Sam, "I must go, Brother Samuel, but you have given me much to consider."

"Good," Sam replied in English. "Next we will study math."

"You are a terrible old man," Princess Lennia said in mock accusation. "This math is a curse upon my mind and I see no use for it."

"It's nice to know when your kingdom's treasury is being squandered by a thief who acts as an advisor or stolen by a relative. You also need know the area of your kingdom, the numbers of animals you own and the goods you purchase compared to the goods you sold or have on hand." He looked upon her kindly, "You, not some treasurer with sticky fingers and little conscience, should be able to add these figures up yourself."

She bowed her head in submission and said, "Truly you are wise, old man." She then looked up, smiled and added in haste, "But you are still a terrible old man!" She then dashed out the door, leaving Sam standing by the window with a satisfied expression on his face. But the expression vanished when he turned to look out the window and watched as GW and Mushid slammed shields against each other in an attempt to force one another to fall from their horses. But neither did. They both swayed back and forth in their saddles as they rode away from each other.

Then to Sam's surprise, GW stood Valiant up on his rear haunches, reined him hard back around to the right and leapt forward to chase Mushid down at full-speed.

Mushid, who was half-expecting such a move, and knowing he couldn't turn his mount in time, simply dropped his training lance to the sand and quickly dismounted his horse with a great leap. Then pulling his training scimitar, he planted his feet in the hot sand and with his shield held at the ready, waited as GW approached on the run.

In mere seconds, GW was upon Mushid and struck the knight's shield with the blunted point of his lance and it broke, while knocking the bigger man to the ground.

Sam heard the sound-of the snapping lance and knew with the amount of force used, GW's arm was going to be very sore tonight.

With adrenaline covering the pain in his shoulder, GW dropped his broken lance and with a Libyan battle yell, slid off Valiant's back and landed on his feet. He then drew his wooden scimitar and rushed forward to meet Mushid in mock combat. With his shield held defensively at shoulder height, he waited for Mushid to rise and then seeing his trainer was ready, he swung his blade first and began walloping Mushid's shield repeatedly until the large knight had had enough.

With the strength of three men, Mushid slammed his scimitar against GW's shield and knocked the younger man back several feet and nearly over on his backside, but GW was able-to maintain his balance.

When GW shook off the knight's tremendous blow, thankful this was only a training exercise. He quickly readied himself for another exchange. But he was then surprised to see Mushid standing there, laughing at him and his youthful eagerness to keep at it.

Hearing his friend laugh so freely and quite loudly, GW simply responded by lowering his blade and shaking his head. "You are too big, too strong and too much a friend for me to stand out here fighting in this heat," GW said. With his scimitar pointed to the ground, he walked to his friend, exchanged a display of comradeship by a casual striking of the shields and then accompanied Mushid over into shady area by the stables.

One of the stable boys, the one who Valiant tolerated, rushed out into the courtyard to grab Valiant's reins, while a second, but older boy, retrieved Mushid's mount.

"Walk them around the courtyard three times to cool them down and then give them water," Mushid ordered. "Afterward, take them to their stalls and brush them. They've worked hard today, and it is too hot to continue."

"Yes, Sir!" The older boy replied.

Mushid stood by a stable watering troth, his shield by his feet and accepted a wooden dipper of water from GW, who was keeping his eyes on Valiant. When the horse was walked off, GW relaxed and poured a dipper of lukewarm water over his head to cool down. Then he gulped down a second full dipper and released an audible sigh. "Your summers are too hot!" GW said in Libyan. He then switched to English and blurted out, "I'd give anything for some decent air conditioning!"

"What did you expect to find in the Sudan?" Mushid asked. "It's much hotter down there and no sea breeze to cool you down in the evening."

GW had forgotten their cover story, about being paid mercenaries en route to the Sudan, "Just not what I expected. I am used to the cooler weather of Ireland."

"Your skin is too fare for our desert, but you ride like the wind is driving you and as a fighter, I saw what you did to those Egyptians. The people of Sudan would value your sword arm, if you didn't perish from their heat first," Mushid said with a hint of humor to his tone. He handed his shield and wooden scimitar over to a middle-aged servant, one of several who maintained the training weapons.

"That is truly a compliment, my friend and I owe it to your teachings."

"Maybe, but I sense there is more at work here," Mushid said. His deep voice then took on a more serious note. "You ride too well for someone who says he had little experience, though I do not doubt your word, and you carry a lance like one born to it. Then there is this strange bond you have with your horse, a once cursed animal you have given a name that speaks of great courage. No, I have never seen such a relationship between man and horse before...and your skill with a scimitar improves daily."

"Truly, my friend, I cannot explain it," GW said in honesty. Then he pointed to the courtyard, to where Valiant was being cooled down by a slow walk. "But when I am on Valiant...I feel unstoppable. I feel his strength and his wisdom surging through me."

"Truly, the Egyptians could not stop you and paid for it dearly with their lives."

Before GW could respond, Richard and Paul walked up to visit with their friends. Richard was sweating profusely and promptly dunked a bucket of water over his head.

Paul, who was feeling his usual humorous self, had a large melon in his hands and he tossed it high into the air toward Mushid and shouted, "Catch, big guy!"

The huge knight spotted the incoming fruit, pulled his dagger from his sash and while in the air, sliced the melon in two with a downward slash.

Before their amazed eyes, both pieces fell to the sand, where GW reached down and picked them up. After carefully washing them off in the troth, he presented one piece to Mushid and kept one for himself.

"I wish I could do so well," Paul said in amazement.

"Practice, my friend and you might," Mushid replied and then bit into the melon slice.

"Right!" Paul exclaimed in frustration. "Brother Samuel's got me checking and re-checking his diagrams for the new weapon. I have to make sure the carpenters and blacksmiths are following his instructions to the letter, not to mention the weavers." He then turned to GW, "Have you seen the size of the rope he wants? It's wider than Mushid's fist."

"You should be honored to have such a task, my friend. To serve Brother Samuel is an honor. Remember, if not for him, you could still be in the dungeon or worse." To make a point, Mushid slowly pulled his huge index finger across the width of his throat and finished by giving Paul a cold glare. This caused Paul to feel much like a wilting flower.

"Hey, I know I'm honored, don't get me wrong," Paul said in English. Forgetting Mushid could only speak or understand a few words of their tongue.

Seeing the look of confusion on Mushid's face, Richard stepped in and quickly said to the Libyan knight, "Paul is greatly honored to serve Brother Samuel, he simply wishes he could train to be a knight again."

Mushid nodded to Richard and then momentarily, he gave Paul a sympathetic look. This made Paul even more uncomfortable, until Mushid walked over to the stables and pulled a training shield and a wooden scimitar off a hook. He returned to where the Americans stood and tossed the training weapons at Paul's feet, "Now show me what you desire to become."

Paul gazed down upon the training weapons and then looked at his two friends, before he locked eyes with Mushid. "Let's do it, big man!"

GW and Richard, both weary from training all morning under a hot sun, ambled over to the stables and plopped down on a small pile of straw. "This should be fun," GW said wearily. The jousting and then the battle with Mushid had worn him out, but he knew Paul would need some enthusiastic fans, as he hadn't been feeling much like a soldier since Sam dragged him away in disgrace.

But Richard, who responded by nodding his head in agreement, preferred a nice afternoon nap then to watching grown men beat each other over the head with wooden swords. He rolled over to his side and closed his eyes, "Wake me up if someone dies."

Paul lifted the filthy training shield to his left arm and slid his bare arm through the sweaty leather straps before he grasped the heavy wooden scimitar with his right hand. "This beats a desk job out anytime," Paul said in English, which no one bothered to translate for Mushid.

"Remember his arm length and his strength," GW warned Paul in Libyan.

"This is like David and Goliath," Paul said. With shield held high, he began to move away from the watering troth and out into an open area. He wanted to be ready in the event Mushid rushed him to catch him off guard.

Several of the stable hands stepped away from their chores to observe the uneven match-up. Though roughly the same height, Mushid outweighed Paul by quite a bit and it was all muscle. The knight's great arms were larger around then Paul's thighs and Mushid's shoulders were mountainous compared to Paul's rolling hills.

"Who is this David and Goliath you speak of?" Mushid asked. He waited for the servant to bring him his training weapons and proceeded out to where Paul waited.

"Christian Bible heroes from long ago," GW replied. Then he looked to Paul and added, "I don't think Mushid is nearly tall enough to be considered a Goliath."

"He looks big enough to me," Paul said with widening eyes. He watched closely as Mushid hefted his weapons and swung them about to stretch his massive and sweaty brown arms.

"Hey, I fight with him every day and you used too," GW complained.

"Guess I've been clerking too long for the man," Paul said in English. But then he signaled Mushid he was ready by striking the front of his shield with the training scimitar.

Mushid nodded his head once and began his approach, holding his shield in his left arm at shoulder level and raising his scimitar for an impending blow.

Paul didn't wait, deciding to go on the offense. He quickly stepped in and struck Mushid's shield was a hard, slashing move that Mushid barely felt, or at least he didn't react too.

Mushid then responded by using his shield as an offensive weapon and he swung his shield arm out wide, catching Paul flatfooted and knocked him to the ground. However, Mushid then backed off rather than continue the assault. This act, whether of compassion or a feeling this Irishman was not worth his time, got Paul upset, which was precisely what the young man needed.

Paul jumped to his feet and moved in fast with one slashing blow after another in an attempt to get under Mushid's guard.

His ferocity surprised Mushid, who was forced to back up a couple steps as the blows became stronger. He could've knocked Paul to the ground with a downward strike, but he continued to allow Paul to show his growing prowess in swordplay.

Then seeing his opening, Paul ducked under one of Mushid's defensive actions and placed his right leg behind Mushid's left ankle. Then in the same instant, he used the elbow of his sword arm in a hard blow to Mushid's shield, forcing it against his chest and tripping him over onto his back. Paul, not wanting to lose his advantage, moved in quickly and knocked Mushid's shield aside and place the point of his wooden scimitar at the base of Mushid's throat. He had his kill.

Stunned at first by the move, Mushid slowly nodded his head in submission to Paul's win. He dropped his own sword to the sand and accepted Paul's hand of friendship to help him to his feet.

"You did well!" Mushid said, slapping Paul on the back with a blow that could cripple some men.

"Thank you, Mushid," Paul said as GW moved in to congratulate him.

"Why did you not display such skill before?" the knight asked.

"I guess it was because you were laughing at me today, made me angry. I've never taken that from anyone," Paul replied with a look of seriousness to his eyes.

"I do not think anyone will laugh at you again, my young friend. To trick me in such a way is no simple task for I have fought in many engagements and have never lost."

"But we only fought with play swords and I know you were not really trying to hurt me."

"Do not strip yourself of this. True, I could have disarmed you earlier or if in a real battle, I would have killed you. But you still used great skill in a clever move to drive me to the ground, one I did not expect and was unprepared to counter. You also displayed an aggressiveness you have not demonstrated before and you kept your focus on the battle. This is what makes a knight."

GW slapped Paul on the shoulder and spoke to him in English, "I'll speak to Sam, get you back down here in the training yard. With Mushid's coaching, you'll master the art of the scimitar in no time."

Seeing the look of confusion on Mushid's sweaty face, Richard, who had suddenly appeared at GW's side, translated for him. Mushid then nodded his understanding in return and voiced his agreement, "With Allah's blessing, you will become a Royal Guardsman and will one day serve our king."

"How long does it take to become a knight?" Richard asked.

Mushid thought over his answer for a moment, considering their level of skill and then replied, "For you two," he pointed at Richard and Paul, "...four years." He then pointed to GW. "For him, he need only accept Allah as his master and the king would award him his knighthood now."

"Is that because of the battle he fought against the Egyptians?" Richard asked.

"Yes, but also for the way he rides. He is truly a master horseman."

Richard, not wanting Mushid to hear him, switched to English and asked GW, "What do you think about becoming a Muslim, GW?"

GW could only grin in response at first, but then realized Richard was serious in his question. "First off, I think Sam would sincerely dislike that idea and secondly, if we ever got home, my old man's cuss words would light up the neighborhood. He was never too happy about the way I avoided church, but to accept Islam, I'd never be able to walk into our house again. For that matter, just hanging out with a Baptist could bring on me a world of hurt."

"Hey, that hurt," Richard said.

"But you know we'll never get home again," Paul reminded him.

Mushid, realizing they were conversing in their foreign tongue so he wouldn't understand, grunted once to display his displeasure at their rudeness and walked over to sit in the shade of the stable.

"I think we offended him," Richard said.

"He knows there will be times we will talk in our own language, but I'll tell him we mean no offense by it." GW then returned to the question of knighthood. "I can never accept Islam, so becoming a knight is a moot point. Not going to happen."

"No knighthood, no princess," Paul reminded him.

"Hey, shut-up will yuh!" GW said in anger.

"Who's going to understand us?" Paul asked him.

"I don't care," GW growled at his two friends. Then he spun around to go have words with Mushid.

"Touchy, isn't he?" Paul said to Richard.

"Girl problems!" Richard blurted out. "You go back nearly a thousand years in time and guys still have girl problems. You'd think we would've learned something by the 1960's," Richard said. With a look of disgust on his face, he walked over to the watering troth and picked up a half-full bucket of water and promptly poured it over Paul's sweaty head.

"I really wish you'd quit doing that," Paul said as he shook the water from his hair.

"You needed cooling off."

"And you need a bath." Paul quickly brought up both of his hands and struck Richard on the chest with a hard shove, propelling him backwards into the watering troth.

For two of the people standing nearby, they saw no humor in the playful activities of two grown men. They were the servants responsible for keeping the watering troths by the stables full. With all the water splashed out, they would now have another grueling couple of hours, hand carrying heavy buckets of water from the courtyard storage tank to refill the troth. No, they were not laughing one bit as they picked up their buckets and began their burdensome task.

## GW, RICHARD AND PAUL'S QUARTERS

He had wanted to speak to Sam, but such a dire feeling of foreboding prevented him from addressing the serious subject of his previous late-night meeting with Princess Lennia. His mind raced with the various outcomes if Sam found out GW and the young Princess was planning a second meeting tonight. His latest scenario had Sam hog tying GW to his bed, then having Mushid guarding him throughout the night. Probably followed by a rough trip to the infamous sacrificial rock, where he'd become an impromptu tidbit for the dragon.

Still, he didn't feel right about going behind Sam's back and yet, remembering those beautiful brown eyes and the faint odor of jasmine in her hair was enough incentive to curtail any desire to come clean with Brother Samuel.

Richard surprised GW when he threatened to go to Sam, but it was because he was afraid for GW and Paul's sake. Paul, on the other hand was a bit more up front, he simply threatened to knock GW's block off if he tried to leave their room tonight. But after explaining how he felt, how a herd of wild horses couldn't keep them separated or the threat of an executioner's axe hinder his path to romantic bliss, both Paul and Richard gave up.

"What do we tell Sam if he comes in?" Richard asked.

"Simple. I'm down with Valiant. He knows I'm always in the stables."

"Except we're not supposed to be out by ourselves...did you think of that?" Paul asked and then added a second question before GW could answer the first, "Just how long are you going to be down there groovin' out with your dang horse?"

"What a question to ask. Affairs of the heart between a man and his horse know no bounds of time, realty becomes..." GW was stumped he couldn't come up with a witty saying to wrap things up.

Richard answered it for him, "Reality becomes like that vortex thing that sucked us here in the first place."

Paul then added in, "Remember that when you're holding your...horse."

"You're both just jealous I've found a girl and you two only have each other."

"Darn right!" Paul exclaimed. "I'd settle for one of her handmaidens and you'd better see if you can get me a date."

"I'll try, but you might end up sharing a meal with that dinosaur out there...Remember, infidels are not too welcome around here."

"Go with God, young man," Richard said. He made the sign of the cross with a wave of his hand.

"You're Baptist, not Catholic," Paul said.

"Yeah and I think I'm the first Baptist in Libya too."

"First Baptist in Libya... sounds like the title of a movie," GW said in jest.

"Laugh now, for tomorrow you may be dragon food," Richard said and there was no humor in his tone.

"You guys are all laughs." GW stood up from his cot and grabbed his wool robe. It was dark and had a hood, much like Sam's priestly garments. Sam had the local weavers pay off some favors by weaving the three men robes and he presented them as welcome wagon gifts.

"I'll be back before it's too late and she might not even show."

"Man, don't take any chances." Paul walked to the study's door and gave the passageway a good perusal and then signaled for GW to come, "Looks clear. Good luck."

"Thanks!"

## ROYAL GUARDSMEN STABLES

The moon had not risen yet, so the castle courtyard was mostly pitch dark; the exception being a few torch-stands by the castle keep, to help a few late-night servants move about, as they prepared equipment and retrieved storage items for the morning staff.

The stable area, just over 50-yards yards from the keep's kitchen area, was amerced in a sea of shadows. Even after allowing time for his eyes to adjust to such limited light, mostly provided from the area surrounding the Imam's coach, GW managed to injure himself twice when he stumbled over an empty water bucket and then slammed his knee into an open stall gate.

"For my next act, I'll trip over my own feet and fall into a pool of blood thirsty sharks," GW whispered in disgust, while rubbing his sore knee.

He was beginning to realize that with it so dark, he'd probably never see the Princess coming and even if she did, they'd never be able to find one another until the moon showed itself. Yet not wanting to give up, he wandered the length of stalls until he reached Valiant and began to groom his partner with a coarse horse brush.

"I bet you know how to handle your women?" GW asked his horse. "Take no guff, right? Show 'em whose boss and..." GW was soon interrupted when he heard the kitchen door open and close, the same one he suspected Princess Lennia had used the night before. He glanced over his shoulder and saw that the moon was up by an estimated two hands.

"You behave, understand?" He told Valiant. "This is really important to me and I don't want to botch this."

Excited, he failed to notice Valiant's lack of a response and while counting off the seconds before she should appear, he took in a deep breath and held it in hopes to hear her footsteps upon the sand. He didn't hear her though and finally exhaled, as he leaned against Valiant's side.

After several moments, he did hear someone approaching or maybe he felt it, in any case, he knew she was near for he smelled her jasmine and his heart began to race. He brushed his hair back with a quick sweep of his right hand and then nervously asked in a low whisper, "Is that you?"

"Yes, it is I." She replied softly, "...but, where are you? I can't see anything."

"With Valiant, same stall. Keep coming toward the sound of my voice."

"Then keep talking, or I'll end up in the straw bin or worse."

GW grinned, knowing she meant a manure pile. He stood beside his horse, brushing his mount's mane. He was so excited he was not even curious why his friend was so quiet tonight. His mind was only on the Princess, nothing else mattered and within seconds they would be together to watch the moon rise up high above the desert. Then, they could look into each other's eyes and possibly see their future together.

"I wasn't sure you'd come tonight," GW said.

"I desired to see you and only here are we alone," Princess Lennia replied. She came into Valiant's stall and stood before GW.

Unsure of what to say or do at that moment, GW dropped his horse brush and put his hands out to touch hers, but as he did so, the sharp blade of a knife rose from out of the darkness and pressed against his throat. He tensed up and in a blink of an eye, a dozen thoughts raced through his mind; Do I fight and if I do, what will happen to her? What will Sam say? How did this guy sneak up on me and why didn't Valiant warn me? The list went on and then his conscious thought was interrupted by a deep raspy voice in his right ear, "Resist me, infidel, my knife wishes to taste your blood."

A single torch was ignited in the adjacent stall and GW saw a middle-aged army officer standing beside a torchbearer and two younger soldiers armed with spears. Princess Lennia, too frightened to move, looked from GW to the officer and then to the knife at her lover's neck.

"In the service of my King, I arrest you!" The officer yelled and on cue, two other soldiers suddenly rushed into the stall to restrain GW. He hadn't planned to move anyway, not with a blade at his throat and he still hadn't seen the face of his attacker.

An order was given from outside the stable and a dozen torches suddenly ignited, illuminating the stable area. Only then did GW discover the horse he was brushing was not Valiant, but one that closely resembled him in size and length of mane and tail. With it so dark and all of the butterflies in his stomach for the upcoming encounter, he never noticed his horse had been traded for another.

Five soldiers suddenly appeared and though not restraining her, they surrounded Princess Lennia as prearranged. Horrorstricken, she first ordered and then pleaded for GW's release. But her orders and pleas fell on deaf ears. Gently, she was edged out of the stall and she soon found herself standing outside the stable, while two hefty dudes with ropes began tying GW up like a parcel. They didn't stop until they'd used nearly 30-feet of rope and every knot they used he knew was probably in Boy Scout handbook. He couldn't move an inch, even if he wanted to and not too surprisingly, his nose was beginning to itch.

Then from out of the darkness came the one who orchestrated this evening's entertainment. Wearing a black hooded cloak, Princes Lonnia limped into the light and made her appearance with an air of superiority. After having spent some time with her in the desert, GW knew Princess Lonnia presence meant nothing good was about to come of this.

The officer who made the arrest promptly stepped forward and spoke to the Black Princess, "Highness, we have him bound tightly and there is no danger."

Princess Lonnia ignored the officer and stepped closer to GW, grabbing a torch so she could see his face clearly, "Did this infidel touch her with his vile hands?" She asked. Her tone quite ugly and threatening and now GW knew he was in real serious trouble.

"We waited as you ordered, but Azir stepped in before the infidel could lay a hand upon her highness."

"You acted foolishly, Azir." Princess Lonnia said as evil poured off her tongue.

Azir backed away, knowing his fate had been cast. He knew before sunrise his body would be buried in the desert sands, for this was the way of the Dark Princess. And to prove his suspicions, two men moved in and stripped him of his weapons.

"Truly, he is handsome for an infidel. Such eyes, a woman could find herself lost in them. I can see now how he used his bewitching ways to entrap my sister." She raked the long fingernails of her right hand across GW's cheeks and drew blood.

"Sister, why do you do this?" Princess Lennia asked, her voice quivering as tears cascaded down her cheeks. "Please, release him and I will never speak to him again."

"So, touching, my dear," Princess Lonnia said in mock sincerity. "You, a princess of Silene, begging for the life of your infidel lover...You should be shamed!" Princess Lonnia began to laugh, but it was far from joyful and began to border on insanity while her soldiers stood by uncomfortably, and one or two men were becoming frightened. These soldiers obeyed her, some took her bribes, but all of them were terrified of her to some degree.

"Why are you doing this?" Princess Lennia screamed. "What harm have I caused you?" She lashed out at Princess Lonnia, but her hand was blocked by the shoulder of one of the guards.

Princess Lonnia's laugh faded and she shook her head in contempt for her younger sister. She then ordered the officer to have the princess escorted to her chambers.

"Place armed guards at her door, I want her protected from the other infidels. No one shall enter, and she may not leave without my permission. If she escapes or is harmed, the guards will be put to a slow death."

She then starred back at GW, "Then, you are to send a detachment of your best soldiers to Brother Samuel's quarters, imprison the infidel priest and his two friends..." She then reconsidered, "No, do not take them to the dungeon, not yet, but hold them there in the priest's quarters. No one goes in or out without my permission. Is that understood, Lieutenant?"

"Yes, your highness," The officer replied. He then began selecting the men he wanted to use for guard duty.

The rich jewels of Princess Lonnia's veil sparkled under torchlight, as she returned her gaze upon her prisoner, "You planned to corrupt my sister, to poison her mind with the heretic ways of your Christian world and I have stopped you. Now the king, my father, must take notice of what Brother Samuel has done to our kingdom.

"You, who thought he could equal a royal princess, will find painful retribution for your heinous acts against my family. I shall watch from the rooftop as the dragon consumes you and I pray the vile-some creature takes its time."

"Wow! I can see why you're known as the Black Princess," GW said. But for his brave reply he received a nasty slap across his face. He tasted blood now from the princess's many rings, but his main concern was Princess Lennia and what might happen to her.

"Take this creature to the dungeon, but I want him alive! No torture," She ordered. She then limped off to fade away into the darkness.

Due to the rope job, GW was unable to walk, so several soldiers stepped in and manhandled GW into a part-carry and part-drag routine across the courtyard and down through the inner workings of the castle keep. They would keep him alive, but these soldiers didn't care if he got a few bumps along the way.

By the time he reached the dungeon, he was able-to notice through one banged up eye that his favorite dungeon master was on hand to welcome him. Great! Old home week, GW was bruised over most of his body from wall slams and sudden drops down stone steps. His hair was matted with blood and his left eye blackened by someone's knee and they left him tied when he was rudely thrown into his former cell. Even the house rats scurried away when they saw the rough condition GW was in.

Two days later GW discovered the soldiers involved in his arrest and mistreatment were all regular men-at-arms in brown tunics. Not one of his friends in the Royal Guardsmen knew off the ambush, or he at least hoped he would've been warned. But as word spread of his grievous insult to the family, even the royal guardsmen were upset. But no ones' anger could compare to Sam's and poor Richard and Paul were stuck in the room with him.

# 14 – AN UNHAPPY PRIEST

**W**hile GW laid suffering in the stinking dungeon, squirming in his ropes to keep a six-pound, one-eyed rat at bay, Sam, his face grim, his eyes filled with anger, was pacing the floor of his study. He walked back and forth between from bedchamber and study, ignoring the fact part of this area had been turned into his clansmen's quarters. Where Paul and Richard remained silent, lounging uncomfortably on their cots, while Sam used those great lungs of his to berate GW. Then he would turn and lash out at both Richard and Paul for allowing their friend to commit such an utter blunder.

"I can't believe it!" He roared with his arms lifted high above his head and loud enough for even the king to hear him. "How could you all be so totally brainless to think you could get away with this?

"I warned you!" Sam shouted at them. "We talked about this numerous times...Weren't you even listening to me?" His face was past the point of glowing red, now those little veins on his nose looked as if they were beginning to burst and his eyes bulged outward to the size of small lemons. He continued to wave his arms about in a demonstration of his rage and as Paul had become so used to conversing in the Libyan language as of late, Paul suddenly realized Sam was yelling in English and hadn't uttered a single profane word. Paul never knew it was possible to lose one's cool and still keep a civil, yet extremely loud, tongue.

"That young idiot's damaged everything I've done here!" Sam again roared out so all in the castle could hear him and then followed up by kicking the nearest target; one of his all-too sturdy chairs. A cry of pain burst from his lips and he limped across the room to plop his ancient bones upon his heavily constructed bed.

While the boys watched with concern on their faces, Sam massaged his injured foot, but he still continued-to exclaim his ill-feelings for what GW had done.

"They'll probably cut his head off at a minimum, but maybe they'll castrate him first and then cut his head off. Maybe they'll feed him alive or toss his remains to the dragon." He then glared at Richard, "You know they could bury him up to his neck in the low tidal areas and watch as the tide comes in...These people are very creative in their torture techniques. Some of the things they learned from both the Romans and the Greeks." He looked across the room to where Paul was standing up from his cot. The young man now wore a startled expression on his face, as he imagined such a horrific fate befalling his friend.

"Remember, they've had centuries to learn how to torture people and I'm only scratching the surface of what GW could face for his act of utter stupidity. And there is little I can do to stop them!"

A moment of silence followed and then Paul asked a question, "Can we break him out?"

"Can you break him out?" Sam asked in disbelief. "This isn't some Texas hoosegow, boy." Sam wagged his finger at him, "No, this is a 12th Century dungeon he's imprisoned in and that's two-levels below ground in a castle guarded by over a 100-men on duty. Add to that, you're Christians deep in ten thousand miles of Muslim country. So, where would you go, bright boy?"

"Sam, back it off a bit," Paul said with a bite to his tone. He was beginning to grow weary of this old man's outbursts at GW and belittling of him and Richard. "I respect you, okay. I'm even real fond of you, but what's done is done as my old man used to say. All this shouting ain't going to get us anywhere. We need a plan."

Sam glared at him, but soon, with some effort, his aged eyes softened, and he nodded his head in agreement, "Okay, I'll attempt to calm down and hope my skyrocketing blood pressure doesn't lead to my next heart attack."

Richard walked over to Sam's water pitcher and retrieved a dipper of water for their friend, who nodded his thanks and then poured the contents over his face to quill the fire. "Another, please...Richard of the Sudan."

"Sure." Richard replied in a friendly tone.

Paul walked closer to Sam and seeing the rough shape the old man was in, he wet down one of Sam's old linen undershirts and laid it over the back of Sam's neck. "This should help. We carry a towel in the field to keep our necks wet and wipe the sweat off our faces. The jungles in Vietnam are a lot like your dungeon; too hot, too much stink and too much humidity."

"That feels good. Thanks." Sam said as he used the wet ends of his undershirt, to wipe his face. He had used his cast-off undershirts as bandages, but only after he boiled them and cut them into long strips. The shirts were made for him after he'd given the design to a local tailor and were very comfortable to wear under his priestly robes. He even had two shirts made of lightweight silk but saved those for special occasions; lengthy court banquets and for when he used to go on long trips.

Sam looked up at Paul, "Listen, Paul, I can understand your desire to free your friend, but right now it's totally impossible. They've taken all of our weapons away and have armed guards at our doors, with others patrolling the passageways in the event we were able to break out of here. We have no rope to make an attempt of scaling down the outside wall, which would probably earn us an arrow in the back from one of those highly skilled archers on the battlements. I'm also sure the dungeon is well-guarded and even if we were able to defeat 100-armed men and free GW, where would we go?"

"Maybe we could make it to the ocean, find a way to meet up with some those Berbers you talk about," Paul suggested.

"Now you want to become a pirate?" Richard asked his friend in disbelief.

Paul glared at his buddy, "No, I don't want to be a pirate, but I also don't want to just sit here and lose GW to some freaky dinosaur."

"Maybe we could get Mushid and some of the others to help us escape?" Richard asked Sam, but the old man shook his head in response.

"You are fighting against the wind, Richard. This is a cultural and religious barrier your friend dynamited with his blunder.

"Sure, I understand he thinks he's in love, but I warned you about how these people think about their monarchy. Not to mention the whole Muslim-infidel thing. Mushid loves his princess a whole lot more then he likes any of you." Sam stood up and slowly ambled over to the window ledge and remained silent for a moment before he turned to face his friends, "Think of how you might feel if some degenerate from a poor neighborhood tried to run off with your favorite sister, only more so."

"So, Captain Rynarr probably won't help us either then?" Paul asked.

"I sincerely doubt it," Sam said. "I can probably say the good captain will be the one in charge of the execution detail." He then took the linen off his neck and set back down on one of his heavy chairs to wrap the moist cloth around his sore foot in hopes it might stop the throbbing. He was actually concerned he may have broken something when he went off like a crazed idiot and kicked this chair.

"No jailbreak then," Paul conceded. "Any ideas on what we can do then?"

Sam shook his head and then said, "For now we wait. I imagine the king will summon me in the morning and then maybe, I'll know something of GW's predicament and what options are left open to us."

"Do you think he's still alive?" Richard asked, his expression was one of graved concern

"I'd know if he was dead. One of my friends would've gotten word to me," Sam said.

"Then I guess all we can do is try to get some sleep," Richard said. Paul was reluctant to agree, but a moment later he nodded his agreement.

First, they made sure Sam was comfortable, using another dampened length of linen to wrap his foot and then they returned to their own beds. Lying upon their rope cots, struggling to get comfortable, they listened to the men-at-arms march up and down the passageway. Paul noted there was a lazy one on duty who was dragging the end of his spear along the stone floor. Every so often, one of the guards at the door would slam the passageway door to Sam's quarters with either the back of his foot or a fist. GW's mistake had cost Sam several of his friends and this only added to Paul's discomfort.

When they blew out their candles and a single oil lamp, the room suddenly filled with the moon's light streaming in from Sam's windows. Nearly a full quarter, the luminescent moon could be seen over the hillsides to the east, along with a million stars on display. The eerie dim light of their room produced a series of strange shadows, which made Richard feel uneasy. Unable to sleep, he began to remember those long terrifying hours trapped in the cave. But he received a reprieve from his nightmarish memories when Paul suddenly broke the silence with a question in a low voice, "You asleep?" Paul lay there with his hands behind his head and gazing up at the ceiling.

"No. I was thinking back to our experiences in the cave."

"Didn't think on it," Paul cautioned him. "I'm just going over ideas on how we could best help GW. Wanted to go over them with Sam, but he needs his rest. He'll need to be on his game tomorrow."

"Yeah, you heard him when he mentioned another heart attack. We're lucky he didn't have one tonight, he turned so red I was sure his head was about to explode." Richard batted at a flight of flies, nailing one and was wishing he had gone ahead and constructed a fly swatter out of layered fish net and a wooden frame. Not usually a procrastinator, he just seemed to be busy with his martial art drills or working with Sam and hadn't gotten around to building the thing. Now, confined to their room, he wished he had.

"You think he can do a Perry Mason for us tomorrow," Paul asked. "Get the idiot off with a year in the joint, maybe six-months off for good behavior?"

Richard swung his legs around to sit up on his cot and face Paul, wiping some sweat off his shoulders with a piece of cloth. "I think it's more serious than that, but I don't know how much more...so, where does that leave us."

"Well, I'm not gonna just stand there and watch 'em feed him to no dragon...excuse me, Professor, that dinosaur...Or, any other torture," Paul said with conviction. "They'll have a fight on their hands, maybe a short fight, but one they won't forget."

"I'm with you there...We'll give it our best shot."

The two friends then fell silent, each of them wondering how GW was doing in the dungeon below and both wishing they had done something to prevent this from ever happening. Paul eventually fell asleep with the thought of how he should've had Richard break one of GW's arms to keep him from meeting with the princess. Anything was better than this.

Richard's thoughts were filled with several, I told you so! He believed if they had informed Sam earlier, they might have curtailed these events. Still, within moments, Richard's snores filled the room and the old man was back up on his feet pacing his study with a slight limp as he contemplated tomorrow's actions.

## PRINCESS LONNIA'S LABORATORY

Princess Lonnia was feeling quite happy with how the events had played out, which led to the imprisonment of GW and confinement of Brother Samuel. She knew her father would not even be notified of their imprisonment until morning and after leaving orders for her guards, she returned to her laboratory for some alone time. She wanted to be prepared for her upcoming meeting with her father.

Her secret room was unusually cool this night. She lit several of her candles and draped her secondhand sorcerers' cloak over her shoulders. The thick blocks of her stonewalls, first constructed by the Greek and then rebuilt by the Romans, and added on to by the Moors, were almost icy to her touch. Beyond the pungent odor of her concoctions and the sweet smell of several tall candles, she could actually smell the essence of pure evil filling her room and relished in it. She preferred using the taller candles over the more modern oil lamps, knowing the old shamans had once used similar candles when they performed their incantations. The precise positioning of her candles and other items of occultism provided her with the proper setting she required for her dark gods to be appeased.

To assist her for the sure-to-be significant encounter in court, she sat at her table and carefully opened her heavy and ancient Book of the Dead. Once she selected the right page; one filled with incantations in a long dead language, she began to read out loud a spell for empowering her with great wisdom. Some of words she didn't completely understand, but as she spoke a tone of authority came upon her voice. Her twisted mind, filled with years of hatred and the practicing of black arts, took upon another personality, but she thought this to be the channeling of evil spirits through her and not her own growing mental illness. In her delusions for gaining power, she was not aware or did not care how close insanity came to demonic possession recorded in the Bible, or how these demons targeted such tormented people as she for their uses.

As it were, she read her evil words while the burning candles produced various shadows that she took to be demonic in nature. They began to form on the walls around the room and she began to sway with music only her mind could hear. These apparitions, first still, now dancing to this silent tune, lead Princess Lonnia's into a frenzy, until she pushed herself back from the table and began to dance with her spirit guests. She waved her arms about and a new deeper raspy voice escaped from her lips.

She began to laugh insanely, exhibiting the same cackle she had displayed in the stables. Amongst the eerie laughter, she shouted out the Egyptian names of her dark masters one by one, followed by yet another darker name, of which had not been heard for eons. Not since the building of the great pyramids and the deaths of so many slaves.

She knew this was her moment. Her time to strike deep into the heart of her father's oppressive reign and this time, Brother Samuel could do little to stop her.

## THE BED CHAMBER OF PRINCES LENNIA

Her eyes were red and her cheeks flush from the shedding of so many tears and an endless night of grief. For here in her darkened bedchamber, Princess Lennia lay on her bed in fear. Not for herself, but for GW, a man she had come to love with only a few words spoken between them. Her heart was breaking, and her stomach ached, as she imagined the sentence her father would lay upon him. She saw her lover torn limb from limb by the cursed dragon, dismembered by horses or beheaded by the kingdom's executioner, and there was nothing she could do for him.

She had tried to see her father, begging on her knees to the guards to summon the officer of the court, but the lieutenant refused to meet with her. He knew what had happened and felt contempt for her actions and had a strong desire to slay the infidel.

In the moments after GW's arrest, Princess Lennia had attempted to send word to her father through a high-ranking soldier; but the man had been bought years before with the Black Princess's bribes and promises of promotion for when she as queen would sit upon the throne.

So, she could only lay there upon her bed and pray to Allah, hoping for divine intervention to save her love and when she wasn't satisfied Allah was even listening to her dire pleas, she began something new. With some hesitation and fear, she began speaking out loud to this mysterious God of the Christians. First, with only a spoken word or two she attempted to converse with Brother Samuel's God, but then in desperation she suddenly cried out to this Lord Jesus Christ and begged Him for a miracle. She went so far as to crawl off the bed and kneel on the floor, her arms raised in hopes her prayers might be heard. Yet, she still heard nothing in return. Just as it was when she prayed to Allah, and she began to wonder if anyone at all was listening?

Frustrated, she used the silken sleeve of her tunic to wipe the tears from her eyes and as frustration grew, she stood to her feet, approached a nearby table and picked up a clay vase. In her anger, she threw it against the far wall and watched it break into a hundred pieces. This caused her handmaidens to rush in to see if she was all right.

"Be gone!" She yelled. "I told you to stay away."

Startled by her unusual outburst, the handmaidens stood stunned, but then quickly retreated to their room. This left the grieving princess alone with her doubts—does Allah or this Jesus Christ truly exist?

Princess Lennia stood there in her room, staring at the walls and an idea began to grow in her mind, both-of these gods, like the ones of the Egyptians, of the Greeks and so many other gods of the great civilizations before them were simply fabrications to enslave the people.

It would be another hour before a weak young lady fell asleep and one brave handmaiden dared to enter the room to clean up the mess and ensure her princess was all right.

## KING RAMIE'S CHAMBER

Princess Lonnia was wrong about her father not being notified until morning of Brother Samuel's arrest and confinement. A loyal soldier sent word and an older servant awakened King Ramie to explain what had transpired within an hour of the incident.

King Ramie was enraged. He was also angry Princess Lonnia had acted without his permission to arrest his senior advisor. As a father he was embittered for this GW's contemptuous actions against one of the royal family and to have behaved in such manner after being befriended by the Royal Court of Silene. Yet, he knew the hurt his youngest daughter must be feeling right now and it saddened him. He had heard of how she had gone to meet this GW, so he knew she cared for him deeply. But she had behaved stupidly.

So as both King of Silene and a father, he stood wearily in his bedchamber, wrestling with his thoughts and the actions he must take. Meanwhile, his loyal Royal Guardsmen stood their posts outside his door. With the sun rising, his eyes were bloodshot from lack of sleep and his feet sore from pacing most of the night. He had earlier settled in for a long-needed night of uninterrupted sleep when the army officer brought the news to the loyal servant. Since then, he'd been awake, balancing between bouts of rage and a father's deep concern for his favorite daughter's poor choice of actions in choosing this young infidel to love.

He wanted to summon Brother Samuel, but his daughter had placed him and the other two newcomers under confinement and this left him in a quandary. He had favored Brother Samuel over his oldest daughter numerous times, embarrassing her in court many times and to summon Brother Samuel so soon after his daughter's order was given, could only cause further friction between them.

There were times, and he never admitted this to anyone else, not even Brother Samuel, but he actually feared her dark powers. He suspected her of murder on two different occasions and knowing not what to do, he had failed to act. He had contemplated her execution several times for her misconduct in court and blasphemous statements against Allah, but each time he recalled his promises to her mother to protect her and surrendered to a father's responsibility for his child over a king's accountability to his kingdom. Sadly, his weakness before his god had left him in a gloomy mood and his sessions with Brother Samuel over a chess board only led to increased confusion. A part of him wanted to hear more about this God of Abraham and His son, this Lord Jesus Christ. But at the same time, he was king and by decree he was required to ensure the teachings of Islam and no other religious practices, were taught in his kingdom.

After several long hours of deep thought, he decided to wait until morning and then have Brother Samuel summoned to his private chamber under guard before the court met. He hoped his waiting until morning to act would satisfy his oldest daughter, but he doubted it. As to his youngest girl, he decided she would remain confined in her quarters until his rage lessoned to a manageable point and he could address her illicit behavior without wanting to bite her head off.

He understood love. He'd been in love, but with an infidel? No, she had crossed the line of proper court etiquette and there would be Hell to pay. If the Caliph was to hear of this, he shuddered to think of what might occur. He only hoped the Great Imam was ignorant to his daughters' behavior, or there would indeed be hell to pay. If it became known, he might not be able to stop the old windbag from carrying out the execution of both of his daughters, possibly all three, and the four infidels.

Had he known what dire plot his oldest daughter was planning, he would have arrested her this night and without remorse, turned her over to the Great Imam's Council of Law Giver's. This council was made up of five-senior clerics of the Islam faith; hand-picked men who reported directly to the Great Imam and they performed his religious trials. They were feared for the power they carried and from this council the Caliph would select the next Great Imam. Sadly, many falsely accused men and women were executed on their say so, only out of their desire to seek notice from the Caliph of Libya.

The Council of Law Giver's had already tried and sentenced Princess Lonnia to death, as well the Princess Lannia. But the Great Caliph had stepped in and prevented the Great Imam from using force to seize the two princesses, if only to keep the Great Imam in line and remind him who truly weld the power in Libya.

King Ramie released a deep sigh, troubled over his kingdom's plight with witchery and an accursed beast from Hell. Not to mention the random attack by Egyptian raiders and seagoing Berber pirates. His massive sheep and goat herds, which had once numbered in the tens of thousands, had been reduced in lesser numbers, and his once proud herds of Arabic horses, camels and oxen now numbered only in the hundreds. He knew this was partially due to the animal sacrifices but was also due to acts of thievery by his army officers. Flocks of sheep and goats mysteriously vanished at night and the king received word they were reportedly sold in Tripoli by men paying well and welling to keep the providers as anonymous. The King never suspected his loyal Royal Guardsmen of such a crime. But added to his depression and soured stomach was his growing economic problems; unrest amongst his people; his tax problems in Tripoli and then there were the Egyptian raids to the south, which kept his small fighting force hard pressed to deal with.

Silene was one of the few areas in North Africa where great herds of sheep and goats existed, for here the shoreline temperatures matched in similarity to the lands of Greece. The sheep had first been herded over land to support Alexander the Great and his fierce armies in his conquering of the known world. It was believed the goats had been brought up from Central Africa. Later, when it was proven the great flocks of both animals prospered in Silene's massive valley, especially with the fresh waters running down from the nearby low mountains. This made irrigation possible and farmlands were established.

Now the Great Imam had brought forth the Caliph's order preventing King Ramie from buying slave girls in Tripoli. King Ramie was building his treasury to send his senior court officers to Tripoli and even further west for the purchase of female slaves. He had hoped to use them for this horrific sacrifice, but the Caliph had made this impossible and he wasn't sure what he was going to do as the numbers of suitable maidens was quickly dwindling. He was also now prevented from entering Egypt, even though he had proof now the Egyptian Army was entering Libya. This would force him to order additional raids into regions to the far south of Libya and this was a long trek for his soldiers to make and across an unbearable and unforgiving desert. Captain Rynarr had reportedly detained several families who had attempted to send their daughters to Tripoli, or worse, to Egypt, to escape the lottery. But by Captain Rynarr's request, no action was taken against the families. They were simply returned to their homes and patrols were ordered to be vigilant for further attempts.

Sadly, there had been one case where a father had actually slain his two daughters to keep them from having to endure such a horrid fate at the sacrificial rock by the lake. The man was taken before the king's court and sentenced to death for his actions, though several fathers in Silene were sympathetic to the man's desire to save his daughters from the dragon.

King Ramie was contemplating on sending his second daughter into the Sudan to the south. He knew people of course valued their children highly and complaints would quickly reach the ears of the Sudanese King and war could develop.

King Ramie would have to seek the advice of his loyal Captain Rynarr and other advisors of the court he trusted. He knew Brother Samuel was working on a weapon, but King Ramie wondered if he would continue to work on it once this infidel was executed for his outlandish actions against the royal family. And what to do with the other two infidels, men who were helping train his troops? This left the king in a quandary, one which brought on a stress caused headache and rendered further thought useless. King Ramie returned to his bed of soft furs, but unable to sleep he lay there tossing and turning while two muscular slaves with large palms casually fanned him to keep the flies of summer away.

Meanwhile, deep within the castle his oldest daughter was planning his death and the take over of the kingdom. She knew that not only must she remove her father, but her plans for a military coup could only win out with the deaths of Captain Rynarr, his loyal lieutenants and if at-all possible—the Great Imam. She was no longer concerned with Brother Samuel, for she sincerely believed her actions this night removed him from any concern.

Her other problem was the beast and she was seeking a way that she might learn to control it. Her books had shed little insight and she had received no words of knowledge from her dark gods in how to force such a creature to bid her will. Still, she truly believed she would be unstoppable with the hellish creature doing her bidding and not a single navy could halt her progress as she swept the coastal countries.

Among her papers she had a plan to excavate a large canal between the lake and the deep blue waters of the great Mediterranean Sea. The plan was drawn up for her some time ago by a Greek harbor builder, who she had brought to Silene in secret. The man had planned the canal in eight stages and designed it to be started from the north, using the great tidal waters of the ocean to help in the construction. Shortly after presenting his ideas to the Black Princess, he departed Silene with a bag of gold and then mysteriously disappeared on the road to Tripoli. She had used her brigands to ensure his silence.

Princess Lonnia's desire to use the dragon as a weapon far outweighed the needs of the kingdom to remove the curse. She did not want to allow the beast to escape out into the ocean waters until such time she knew how to control it. Only then would she begin construction of the canal and to gain the support of the people she would stop the sacrifices. Once the beast could feed in the ocean, she saw no reason why it would need to be fed by members of the kingdom. There would be plenty of food to find as the enemy's ships were sunk by the animal and the sailors vanished beneath the waves, adding further to her power and spreading fear for those who stood against her.

# 15 - WHAT, NO TRIAL?

The hot sweltering North African sun broke over the eastern horizon several hours earlier, causing a worrisome Sam to wonder why he hadn't called before the king. Knowing of how the king usually liked to handle distasteful state affairs right off, often before his breakfast, he was beginning to wonder if he and his two friends were going to have to spend another long blistering day in confinement. Black flies, some the size of a peanut, were beginning to return, which caused Sam to pick up a small palm fan and use it to keep them at bay. It was at times like this he really wished the winter months could come sooner and relieve the kingdom of these flying pests. He had weathered locusts, sand fleas and even the occasional scorpion, but it was the huge black African flies that bothered him the most. Added with the infernal heat, he often thought of having a large boat built and setting out for the new world– long before Columbus was credited with the find. But he knew he must not violate the time paradox, which could greatly affect his own history and that of his family back in the future. That and the trouble of finding a boat crew brave enough to sail out into the great void and beyond. Here in the 12th century the consensus in this part of the world was the world was flat and great demons, such as the Silene dragon, were out there in the great beyond to devour foolish boat crews. But even Sam, schooled in the 1930-1940 era, wasn't aware how modern-day archeologists had turned up proof of how the Norsemen and other explorers had visited America long before Columbus. Not that he would care at the moment. He was feeling miserable and he didn't know what was happening to GW, not to mention these blasted flies buzzing his head.

Libyan's summer months were tough on local crops and the people. Many of the fresh water streams dried up until the fall rains blew in from the north. Dozens of sheep and goats perished from the occasional drought, along with some of the older camels and horses. For the people, it was the elderly and sick that would never see another winter, making Sam wonder how many more of these hot summers remained in his future.

With each hour passing, Sam sweated off another ounce or two of fat and his anxiety grew for worry over GW's future. A middle-aged servant with a minor limp had brought breakfast for the three of them, but he had no word of court activity. There were several court advisors and lesser officers milling about the large courtroom, along with numerous attendees who waited in the entryway for an opportunity to speak before the king to settle some dispute or ask yet another month of mercy from paying overdue taxes.

Being a poor kingdom, many of the nobles and merchants were far behind in their taxes owed to both this tiny kingdom and the Caliph in Tripoli. King Ramie gave them as much time as he could get away with, but after several months of leniency, he was forced to confiscate their land and property. On more than one occasion he was required to send the offender to Tripoli for judgment before the Caliph and most of these people never returned. Their entire holdings were turned over to the Caliph, who then ordered King Ramie to use his dwindling funds to maintain the land and stock, which only added to the king's stress. However, this morning while King Ramie remained in seclusion, with orders for his armed guards to permit no one into his chambers, Sam, who refused to eat, continued to pace the floor like an expectant father in the maternity ward. His breakfast tray remained untouched on top his study table, except for a swarm of flies beginning to crawl about on the fruit and meat.

However, the water pitcher needed refilling and Sam took it upon himself to hail a guard outside his door. Of course, as expected, the guard passed the task down to a lowly servant.

"Why are we waiting so long?" Paul asked from his cot, where he set observing Sam pace the room. He then spotted some sort of unidentifiable bug scurrying across the floor and promptly threw one of his dilapidated boots at it– but he missed.

Sam only glared back at Paul and shook his head in response. He didn't want to answer right away but walked across the room to stand by a window in hopes of catching some relief from the rising heat. There he stood until suddenly a refreshing mild sea breeze blew in from the northeast to slightly cool him off. With a sigh of relief, he thought about GW's predicament, while he gazed off over a great distance of shifting desert sand and the low rolling hills which eventually led to the Egyptian border. A large flock of sheep was being herded to the north in hopes of finding some wild grass closer to the coast and a caravan of camels, walking in a long single file, was making its way to Tripoli.

Sam then turned his head to acknowledge a silent Paul and Richard, "I can only imagine this was an extremely long and torturous night for our king. Not only must he decide the fate of a man he recognizes as my clansman and very possibly our fate too, he must also put his fatherhood aside and make a kingly decision over his daughter's fate."

"What do you think he'll do about the princess?" Richard asked. He picked up a piece of fruit and put it in his mouth, but Paul had left his tray untouched.

"Twice he has refused the Great Imam and his Council of Law Giver's judgment and spared his two older daughters from execution...to save a third might bring forth a harsh judgment from the Caliph. He'll have to consider this and I know it has to weigh heavily upon his mind. I know He'll summon me when he is ready, until then I suggest we pray."

"Pray?" Paul asked. With a waving hand, he set up to attack a buzzing fly.

They were then interrupted by a hard knock at the door and Richard walked across the room to open the heavy wooden door. The same servant who had brought their breakfast now stood there with two full clay pitchers of water. Rather than let the servant in, Richard simply took the pitchers off his hands, nodded his thanks and with some effort used his right foot to kick the heavy door closed.

"Yes, Paul, I said pray," Sam said. "Right now, GW and even the three of us could use some spiritual intervention to save our lives."

"Maybe you're right, Sam, but I saw a lot of frightened guys praying in Nam and they still got zapped. The wounded prayed too and a lot of them still died. Their parents and girlfriends prayed too, and they only received body bags for their efforts. So, you can imagine how I feel about prayer at a time like this."

"You only fool yourself, Paul. I've seen your eyes when we've discussed the Lord and you truly believe, but you're afraid to voice it. Has being a Christian in your time of war become one of shame then?"

"No!" Richard answered in a heated tone, before Paul could reply. "But there are those who look down upon soldiers, believing Christians to be weaklings when we pray or read from the Bible. Sadly, this has caused a lot of men to be less then forthcoming with their beliefs.

"Back in our time, there is also some sort of eastern spiritualism being spread through the country. Some of this comes out through our modern rock music and our rock star's lifestyles. Then there are the movies. It's confusing the youth of today...I mean of the 1960's. There are those who believe the communists are behind the propaganda campaign to drive us away from God and it has caused a major effect on how the people think about our war in Vietnam.

"In your war, the people were behind their soldiers... and sailors, but in the late 1960's, the college kids and even high schooler's, are holding anti-war rallies and spitting on returning war vets."

Sam was shocked by this, saddened to hear how the returning veterans were being treated and he slowly nodded his head in agreement, "I remember reading how the Russians didn't believe in God. Word had come out of Europe how the Russian soldiers were ordered to burn the churches, but it was being kept from the people...the civilians, since the Russians were our allies."

Sitting on his cot, Paul shoved his breakfast tray away and stood up. Richard decided he had had enough food and gulped down a mouthful of tepid water. He then looked over at Paul and then to Sam, "A lot of us believed we were fighting Russian weapons, Russian advisors and even Russian pilots in Vietnam. Supposedly the CIA has a high bounty for the first Russian soldier caught in South Vietnam." Richard's statement about the bounty surprised Paul, for he hadn't heard of this.

Sam dragged his stool from the study table and into his friend's bed chamber, "So, tell me...what is the main belief of these Vietnamese people you speak of?"

"Mostly, they're Buddhists," Paul replied. "Like most of the orient, but I have seen some Catholics too."

"I know nothing about these Buddhists, but I've come to know quite a lot about Islam and the confusion it has caused. Some of these people read the Koran and from it they behave warlike toward the infidel, while others take an opposite approach and only seek to walk a road of peace and knowledge." Sam then stood up, sighed again as his back rejected his movements and pain shot up through his lower back. He then crossed the room to where Richard had set the pitchers down on the big table. He used the long wooden dipper to sip a drink. For his friends, they found the water warm and murky, having been used to clear cool waters of the modern world. But to Sam, he had grown used to these foul-looking waters and found those water casks stored underground in the dark lower levels to be quite refreshing on a hot summer day.

"Have you ever seen or received any answers to your prayers, Sam," Richard asked.

"I'm still alive aren't I? Sam asked. "And I've been the only Christian here among thousands of Muslims before you arrived. I am also an old fat man, yet I can still walk, and I've become Chief Advisor to a Muslim king. A man I hold as a true friend." Sam took a second drink, "But, I really miss iced tea or a nice cold beer." Then he left the dipper in the pitcher and returned to the window to soak up the morning breeze before the afternoon's desert heat turned the winds into a blast furnace.

"Will, maybe you should lead us in prayer then, but I gotta tell you I'm not too hot in the whole kneeling bit," Paul said.

"All you need to do is simply agree with me, for the scriptures say '...if any two of you shall meet in my name, I shall be there with you.' I used to remember what book and verse that was, but the old memory is weak and growing worse with each passing year."

"It's in one of the four gospels, Sam," Richard said. "But I'm at a loss too as to which one."

Sam walked over to where Richard and Paul were standing and placed a hand on each of their shoulders, "Then let us pray..."

## THE DUNGEON

Hog-tied and unable to sleep, GW's night had been long, painful and hot, as he fought to ward off an aggressive rat and his buddies. He also needed to keep a wary eye on his jailer. He'd been bitten twice in the leg by the rat and was terrified of rabies, but the critters finally scurried off under a lump of filthy straw. The vile creatures retreated after GW was able to get one good kick in. His legs were still tied together, so it was a double leg kick that sent the rats, which were nearly the size of small cats, bouncing off the grimy bars.

Unfortunately, this racket also got the attention of the dungeon master, the same freakish individual who had last supervised their earlier imprisonment. Behaving as if GW had personally insulted him, the man stormed into the cell and began to kick GW in the ribs and stomach until a weakened and bruised GW finally gave out with a cry in pain.

Satisfied, the dungeon master snarled at his prisoner and returned to other duties, which left GW to lie in a pile of soiled straw covered in old fecal matter and dried blood. He was now bleeding from the nose and mouth and was concerned with internal injuries from the ugly dude's assault. The cell, which hadn't been cleaned since his last visit, reeked with the foul odor of previous prisoners and now he could only wonder how long he would remain tied up and imprisoned here this time? You sure stepped into this time, old buddy. Acting out before thinking it through, same old problem!

There were other prisoners in the dungeon, but they were held in other cells and after the dungeon master informed the others of what the infidel had done with the beautiful princess, adding fiction to fact, they turned on him with eyes filled with hate and a desire to ring his infidel neck.

The dungeon master thought about putting a few prisoners in with GW, but reconsidered it when he remembered his strict orders concerning the Irishman. He was to soon appear before the king and a badly injured prisoner could lead to his own imprisonment or a stretch of a diet of bread and water for 30 to 90 days.

GW needed a drink, his throat was parched, but he was afraid to ask and then receive another beating. But at this point he had little more to lose, so he decided to give it a chance.

"I need water!" He yelled out in Libyan, needing to be heard over the mournful cries of several torturous souls who suffered severe burns and other such nasty wounds at the hands of this deranged Lord of the Dungeon. If anything, GW thought the jail guard appeared to be even uglier then before, but he was growing weaker with each passing hour and shouted out his request a second time. Finally, the jail guard looked his way and released a guttural snarl in response.

"Look, idiot, I need water and you're supposed to keep me alive-remember?" GW shouted out in English, hurting his throat and only to gain a look of confusion from his nemesis. "I need water to survive!" He then yelled again, but this time in a dry raspy Libyan dialect.

The man turned away from GW, but within a few moments, he appeared at GW's cell door with a water bucket in hand. But instead of getting a dipper of water, the jail guard opened the door, stood over the top of GW and poured the contents out on GW's head.

Seeing it coming, GW opened his mouth to drink in whatever he could, but admittedly, he was refreshed by the waterfall and grinned back at the guard in response. This wasn't the reaction the guard expected and enraged, he promptly kicked GW in the side three times and was about to use the bucket as a club when the dungeon door suddenly creaked opened. The guard quickly turned, startled to find Captain Rynarr and several Royal Guardsmen standing there.

Captain Rynarr stepped forward and glanced down at GW. When he saw his condition; bruised and battered, he glared at the guard with a look that shook the man to his bones. Even if GW had touched the princess, for Rynarr had learned their actual contact was at the most minimal, Captain Rynarr still owed his life to this man and it sickened him to see GW in this way.

"You were ordered to keep this man alive, you, vile misshapen son of a hump-less camel, not to mistreat him," Captain Rynarr said in a threatening voice. He was not a profane man and often compared those louts he encountered to beasts of burden. He then added injury to insult by backhanding the guard across the face and knocking him to the ground. "This is an evil place, you foul secretion of a worm and not even Allah would accept your mistreatment of prisoners as justified behavior."

Captain Rynarr turned to his nearest guard, "Lock this vermin up in his own cell, I'll have someone down here within the day to take over his duties."

The dungeon master begged, he pleaded and crawled forward on hands and knees to go so far as to kiss Captain Rynarr's feet, until Captain kicked him away and watched as two guards towed his despicable body into the cell where GW still lay.

"Take the infidel out and have him washed and his wounds treated. He will appear before the king shortly and I do not want his appearance to frighten our liege."

As GW was carried out of the cell he felt a strange wave of sympathy for the dungeon master who now replaced him and then he locked his one open eye with Captain Rynarr, as his ropes were cut away. For a-brief moment, they shared a mutual expression of friendship, but then Captain Rynarr dropped his eyes, shook his head in dismay and then quickly walked out to escape the stench of the dungeon.

Once free of restraints, GW cautiously stretched out his arms and carefully began to stumble about, as feeling slowly returned to his legs. He then inspected his rat bites while his former friends stood by, giving him a moment of relief before they took him elsewhere to clean up. They had liked and respected GW, but he had brought shame to their ranks by his misconduct with their princess. Their own reactions to this situation greatly troubled them. On one side they battled with a sheer desire to kill him on the spot and say he had fallen down the stairs while trying to escape, but yet they held an appreciation for him as a fellow fighting man- one who had distinguished himself against the Egyptians and saved their captain.

GW lightly touched his injured face and the swelling of his closed eye, Score one for the ugly guy with the big feet. I won't be seeing anything out of this eye for a week. Ribs really hurt, wonder if any of them are busted. These guys got their licks in before ugly dude used me for football practice...they sure know how to kick a guy when he's down and I'm betting these are the dudes ol' Richard trained. I'll have to have a word with him about this.

Once GW was able-to walk by himself, they left the dungeon and GW would always remember the mournful cries of his former jail guard, when the heavy wooden door was closed, and the Lord of the Dungeon was left alone in his rat-infested cell. The vile man was whimpering like a child, giving some of his fellow prisoners a good laugh. GW knew another man would replace him and over time, the evilness of the place would grasp the man's soul and turn him into the beast he had just left behind.

The guards had to assist GW up the stone stairs since no one had seen fit to install handrails. He then soon found himself in a soldier's washroom area and here, with painful difficulty he pulled off his filthy clothes and scrubbed himself down with a stiff heavy brush. He asked for a bar of Brother Samuel's goat soap and after several minutes of argument between the guards, as to whether, or not they should honor his request, he received a half-used bar of the strange smelling goat milk soap. He knew he was probably going to be sentenced to death, but he didn't want to smell like the dungeon when he appeared before the royal court.

Once he was clean, a Royal Guardsmen handed him a simple but clean brown tunic and the accompanying plumed pants to wear. His own GI pants were too bloody, and he had to finally throw them away and as he put his new clothes on, GW wished they were royal blue in color. He knew he'd never wear the revered Royal Guardsmen tunic ever again and it saddened him. The new brown uniform didn't fit too well, but he knew better than to complain. He already had his new moccasin boots taken from him by a foul-mouthed guard, who thought these boots would look good on him. So, GW was forced to walk barefoot, and each step was a painful one from the abuse he had suffered.

He was then taken to the kitchen where he was fed a simple meal of bread, goat cheese, a single chicken leg. He was also given a wooden mug of melon juice. GW thought it was the best tasting meal he'd ever had, and he thanked the kitchen workers. But they only looked upon him with scorn, for everyone in the castle knew by now what he'd done, and his vile act was unforgivable. Had it been with Princess Lonnia, they would've cared little for the Dark Princess was feared and hated. But Princess Lennia was greatly loved and respected.

Once fed, the guards then escorted him to a small chamber room, where he was told he would wait until summoned before the king. With no windows and no means of escape, they left him alone there and two Royal Guardsmen were posted outside the locked door.

Left in a room the size of a walk-in closet and only the floor to sit on, GW began to pace the darkened room. The heat was stifling, and he had only a single candle to provide illumination. There was no decoration of any type on the walls and the furniture consisted of a small three-legged wooden table, which held the candle. He heard a buzzing sound and looked up to see a single black fly circling above him, "You're a prisoner too, huh?"

He then ignored his fellow prisoner and continued to pace off the room in hopes to limber up his hurting muscles. He discovered the room to be seven small steps wide and eight small steps long. So, he decided to do his thoughtful pacing in a circular route to take advantage of the most room possible, but the walking was causing him a lot of pain and he had to stop.

He surprised himself by entering in a one-sided conversation with God. He was not asking much for himself, but he wanted God to intercede for his lovely princess. He knew she was in serious hot water, probably not to the extent he was, but he had come to know a little of Muslim Law and the princess could receive quite a harsh punishment for her transgression with an infidel. If not a princess, she would most likely be put to death by stoning but being the king's daughter, her life might be spared.

GW had hoped he might hear an audible word from God about why the Lord had brought him and his friends to 12th century Silene. He really needed to know what God had planned, what was their part of the grand scheme they needed to fulfill and how he could do it now with a death sentence hanging over his head? He then felt a heavy weight upon his heart and suddenly dropped to his knees to pray, asking for God's help to keep the princess, Sam and his friends safe.

"Lord, if I am to die today, give me the strength to die well," GW said in a whisper. "I've outlived so many of my friends who were killed in combat...If my time is now, I pray you give peace to my dad back home...who has totally no idea what has happened to me...to us, and this strange adventure you've brought us on.

"And, Lord, protect my dear princess, keep her from harm and...let your Will be done." A single tear flowed down his cheek, below his one good eye, and he sat back against the wall to watch the fly's continuous circling above and it reminded him of a Huey helicopter on scout. "I think I got it bad, you've only got about 24-hours to live your entire lifetime...got any girlfriends yet?"

## KING RAMIE'S PRIVATE CHAMBER

A somewhat apprehensive Sam stood before King Ramie in silence. His hands were locked together and resting on his great stomach, as he waited for his monarch to offer up the first word. He'd been summoned before the king late in the afternoon and when he arrived under armed escort, King Ramie was already sitting in his high-backed chamber chair. He gave Sam a hard glare, as the First Advisor to the Royal Court of Silene made his way forward.

With a wave of his hands, King Ramie dismissed his personal bodyguards and servants, leaving the two men alone. King Ramie's angry glare softened and gradually turned to one of great concern. He was the first to break the strange, tense-filled silence between them by asking, "What do we do now, my old friend?"

Sam released a deep sigh, relieved to know the friendship he had developed with this man over forty-some years still existed and his guidance was once again requested. Before answering, he gestured with his right hand to the chair he normally set in when they had these quiet moments together and upon a single nod of King Ramie's head, he seated himself and released a great sigh of relief to be off his feet. "My Liege, we are indeed stuck between the proverbially rock and the hard place."

"Rock and the hard place?" King Ramie asked. "I recall you using this strange statement before...many times."

"Simply a quote from my land, your highness," Sam said. "It means the same as...the problem has us up to our neck in camel fecal matter, but the soldiers use another word for fecal matter."

King Ramie nodded his head, but he did not smile. "This I understand and yes, you are quite right. We are in a dilemma and I seek your assistance. What should I do with this clansman of yours and not lose your friendship? And what of my daughter, how shall I respond to her flagrant misconduct with an infidel? So many of our men witnessed this, I cannot simply say it didn't happen."

"Sire, as to your first concern; truthfully I am greatly concerned with my clansman and grievous over his misconduct toward the royal family. But as to your other concern, I am also equally distressed with the princess's conduct and what you might have to do where she is involved."

"Spoken like a true friend," King Ramie said. With a look about the room, he rose up from his chair and laid his hand down upon Sam's shoulder in a gesture of friendship. "Let us go to the window, the heat in this room can be stifling at this time of year. Maybe there is still some breeze from the north to lift our sorrows."

"Have you spoken with the princess, Sire?"

"Not yet, I am not sure what to say to her. Do I speak as a king or a father? Am I to be harsher because she is my daughter or grant some grace because she is simply one of my subjects and a stupid young girl?"

"I must be honest with you, Sire," Sam said as he looked the king in the eye, "I have seen this growing and should have come to you before this ever happened."

"I do not understand."

Sam turned from the king and walked a couple steps away from the window, before he released a deep sigh and turned to address his friend, "I saw the look in her eyes while she watched this young man train in the courtyards below and I saw her thoughts escape her lips when she spoke out to him in whispers from high up above. But he never heard her words and I am also sure she would have never spoken such deep intimate words had he been able to. Young women look at love so differently than a man does. They add in their dreams, their deepest wishes and a fantasy we are unable to grasp.

"I repeatedly spoke to her about this growing curiosity for these three strangers, but it fell upon deaf ears and I could easily see it was becoming an unquenchable thirst; especially for this one I know as GW. I also spoke to my men, over and over, about our customs and culture, and ordered them to avoid any conduct with all of your female subjects. When I saw some degree of fondness growing between Princess Lennia and GW, I cautioned him again at what he risked."

"Then he knew and still..." King Ramie stopped himself, he could feel his blood pressure soaring.

Sam lowered his gaze briefly and then returned to look deeply into his king's eyes, as he wrestled with his words in hopes he would say the right thing, "Yes, Sire. He knew and understood the danger, but what can one say when young love is involved?

"There is an attraction, maybe it is a true love between them. If so, for them this breaks down any barrier of religion, rank or custom. It crosses all culture foundations and if I know GW, he spent this night not worried for his own life, but for that of your daughter."

"Yes, yes, and I have been informed by my senior servant how my daughter spent the night crying and her main concern seemed to be only for this GW fellow," King Ramie said. Then he walked away from Sam but turned his head to glance back over his shoulder, "If the whole castle did not know of this I could handle things differently, but now I must act as king, as my subjects expect this of me. You understand, my friend, I also must contend now with the Great Imam too. He, the fool, will never let this pass and word of whatever I do will be carried swiftly to the Caliph."

"Yes, Sire, I know this all weighs heavily upon you as father and as king." Sam thought to say more, but something in his spirit held him back and he stood silent.

"I will speak with my daughter. While I do so, you may visit this GW, but be warned it may be the last time."

Before he left, King Ramie gestured for him to wait, "This name—GW, what kind of name is this?"

It surprised Sam that with all that was going on in the king's life he was bothered by a simple name. "Sire, in Ireland our sons are often named after men; a relative who has fallen, a close friend or a maybe a hero. In this way we bless our sons with a strong name. Much the same as you do here in Libya."

"Yes, I understand how a name is passed down, but what is this GW and what does it stand for. Do you have a historic figure with this name in your family?"

Sam knew this was not the time to smile and he had to force back a grin, "Sire, we occasionally take a person's name and use only his first initials. In my case I could have used a simple S in my name instead of Samuel. Such as GW might have a name of Gregory or Gary, and possibly George. But GW prefers to use the initials. As to the W, this stands for his middle name and usually this comes from a family name on the father's or mother's side of the family. This could be Washington, Wordsmith or something similar. Again, GW prefers to use initials for both his first and middle name and this is quite common. I have several old friends from…Ireland, who use these methods to be identified."

King Ramie shook his head, "This may be normal for your people, but it sounds a stupid way. If parents name a child, the child should respect his parents to go by that name." The king shrugged his shoulders and then dismissed Sam, "You may go."

"Thank you, Sire." Sam bowed before the king and turned to leave the chamber, but quickly found he was still under guard.

## GW'S NEW QUARTERS

"You're an idiot!" Sam said as he stepped through the door and found GW sitting on the stone floor with his head braced in his hands, elbows on his knees and his eyes closed. Deep in thought, he had not even heard the door open to let Sam in.

GW slowly and painfully rose to stand and then he spoke, "I agree with you, okay, but is the princess all right?"

Sam waited until the door was closed behind him before continuing, "I believe she is okay, but she spent a restless night worried about you. You are both in trouble and not only that, you've created a mess for the king. He must take action because the Great Buffoon is here and whatever action King Ramie takes, word will be sent to the Caliph."

GW slammed a fist against the stone wall and winced from the pain, "What will the king do about her? It's all my fault! He's got to realize that. She's young... an innocent and I misled her. You could say I corrupted her. You've got to convince the king of that, Sam."

Sam could see the tears welling up in GW's eyes, even the closed one and his concern for the princess was deeply carved into his face, "Well, that speaks highly of your chivalry, but a little late, my young friend." Sam walked to the far side of the room, all of a few steps and leaned his back against the wall, "Why didn't you tell me, maybe I could've done something before it got this far."

"I wanted to. I almost did, but I thought you'd keep us apart and probably send me off into desert to save me from the executioner's axe."

Sam nodded his head in agreement, "I might've, but you didn't give me a chance."

"I'm sorry, Sam, I should've trusted you."

"That's behind us now," Sam said, and his eyes softened. For some reason, he had such a hard time remaining mad at GW and always wondered why. Maybe it was because he saw much of himself in this young soldier from the future or maybe it was because he thought GW was a representation of his son; the boy he never saw grow up?

"Now tell me about what happened, how you two came together and how did Princess Lonnia learn of your relationship."

GW stretched his arms out wide, palms up in a gesture to show his lack of understanding. "We only kissed once, or I should say she kissed me and that's all there is to tell. I've got no idea how her older sister learned of us."

"That one kiss is enough to get you both killed under Muslim Law."

"I know it sounds strange, yet somehow I know I love her, Sam."

"You've talked to her twice and only briefly, what do you know about love?"

"I didn't think you'd understand."

"Why do you say that?"

"Well, you're old enough to my grandfather and people back in your day looked at romance as something proper. Holding hands on the fourth date was probably looked down upon as carrying things too far."

Sam laughed out loud, surprising GW, "What do you think I am, some sort of 1880's Quaker preacher? I'll have you know I was holding hands with my wife on our first date and I kissed her good night too! Much to the dislike of her father, who was watching us through the living room window and kept flicking the porch light on and off."

GW laughed, which was his first laugh in the last 30-hours and it hurt his ribs to do so. "So, did you love her right then?"

"Yes. Right from the very beginning and I still do and always will," Sam admitted. Then he smiled wisely, as he remembered her face that first night. He could still feel her soft lips and then recalled the reddened expression and cold beady eyes of his future father-in-law.

"Then maybe you do understand," GW said in a voice just above a whisper.

"Maybe I do, young man, maybe I do."

"So, what happens now? Do I get dismembered, the executioner's axe or given over to the dungeon master for torture?"

"You may get all three. But first you'll be summoned before the king and he will render a verdict before the court."

"What, no trial?"

"That is all the trial you'll get," Sam said. "This is a Muslim country; young man and you've been found guilty already when you were arrested for such a vile crime. Infidels have no right to trial, unless the Council of Law Givers calls for one. But usually they do not act in such a case like this. They simply kill us and forget about us."

"What is this Council of Law Givers?"

Sam walked over to the far wall, bracing himself against it with his back as he slowly lowered himself to sit upon the floor. The act was a painful one but after a moment, he relaxed a bit. "This might be a bad idea, but my legs hurt." Then Sam answered GW's question. "They like to consider themselves as scholarly Mullah's, men of simple faith, but they are far from that. No, these men are ruthless, hand-picked for their enforcement of the faith and loyalty to the Great Imam."

"Will I get a chance to speak today?"

"Probably not, but maybe I will on your behalf."

"What will you say?"

"I am going to press for banishment and maybe from my years of work for the king he will sentence you to this fate."

"What of Paul and Richard? They didn't do anything."

"They will most likely be given your fate also, guilty by association you might say. Infidels have little sway here, but you might survive this way." Sam braced his one hand against the wall and allowed GW to help him to his feet, with some effort on GW's part.

Sam then placed both hands on GW's shoulders, "Let us pray now for God's wisdom and mercy."

"I've been praying since they put me in here."

"Good," Sam said. With a bowed head and eyes closed, he began to pray as GW bowed his head and agreed. Overhead, the fly had suddenly disappeared and from out of nowhere a whisper of a cool breeze blew into the room from the tower far above the room.

## THE ROYAL COURT OF SILENE

The wooden door creaked open and before GW could rise to his feet, three guards rushed in to grab him and drag him from his cell. He was punched three times to the side of his head, bringing on a semi-conscious state, as they dragged him up stones stairs and down long passageways. GW was then jerked to his feet and with one guard on each side, pinning his arms back, which he guessed had apparently been tied at his wrists while he was dopey from his roughing up. The guards, having to force onlookers away, shoved GW through the angry crowd and into the royal court.

GW was shaken by the looks he received from people he had once called friends. He saw the look of utter scorn on the enraged face of a man he had saved in the battle in the desert. So easily they forget. Another man, one he had given first aide to after the battle, tried to kick him, but Mushid suddenly appeared and he stood in the man's way while GW was escorted by. But GW would always remember the way these people stared at him and shouted out threats to his life. These same people he had only yesterday had called him a friend.

GW was marched forward and forcefully shoved to the stone floor, placed on his knees 15-feet in front of the four thrones. He glanced up to observe King Ramie sitting upon his ornate chair, talking with Brother Samuel, who stood behind the throne. GW saw that Princess Lennia and Princess Lannia's two chairs were empty, and he grew concerned for Princess Lennia's safety.

Princess Lonnia was present and he couldn't help but notice her icy glare, it made him feel dirty all over and he sneered back at her.

Princess Lonnia did not appreciate his expression and she gestured to one of the two guards, both in brown tunics and pointed at GW. The guard quickly nodded in response to the princess and stepped forward to strike GW across the face with the back of his hand. This caused GW to be knocked backwards and onto his left side. Lying there, unable to rub his jaw, he looked back over his shoulder and gave the guard a hard glare.

"You're pretty good at hitting a man with his hands tied behind him. But how good are you facing me man to man?" GW asked. In response, the guard moved up and kicked GW twice in the side before Captain Rynarr could order him to stop.

"The prisoner will keep silent and not raise his eyes above the floor unless the king grants you, permission," Captain Rynarr said in a curt tone. He then ordered the two guards to pick GW up and place him back where he was without delay.

By now, everyone in Silene knew about GW's arrest and his appearance today before the king. There were crowds at the gate, with the expected loud mouths shouting out demands for his head or to have him fed to the dragon. Yet no one said anything about the princess, as she was deeply loved.

A senior court officer, an elderly man with as long white beard and a long wooden staff in hand, who was attired in a floor length blue and gold robe, stepped forward from the side of the large room to quiet the court. He then addressed GW, formally advising him of his crimes against Allah and the Kingdom of Silene. This got the crowd in the court stirred up again with their demands for a harsh punishment, bringing a smile to the Black Princess. But strangely enough, she remained silent during this part of the procedure.

GW remained on his knees. His face battered and blood droplets coming from the sides of his mouth and nose, he was unable to move without facing more abuse and forced to admire the fine stone work of the floor. Nervously, he awaited a chance to speak his piece.

Finally, the court officer finished the lengthy reciting of the charges and stepped back into the crowd of fellow advisors and lesser officers of the court. The crowd of onlookers then waited in silence for the King to render his punishment. Some hoped the infidel would be fed to the dragon, others, the more blood thirsty of the crowd, wished for slow torture and there were a few who strongly desired the executioner's axe for the infidel.

Struggling with a stressful headache and too little sleep, King Ramie felt uneasy as he gazed out over the mass of people jostling for position in the rear of the court. From reports, he knew there to be at least a couple hundred or more of his subjects at the gates to the castle, all of them awaiting word of the infidel's sentence.

King Ramie leaned forward from his plush throne to study this GW and then glanced to his left at the empty throne of his youngest daughter. His heart saddened, he then studied his oldest child and recognized all too well the icy expression of sheer loathing and he wondered if it was for this lowly infidel or her king?

King Ramie then turned and gestured a casual hand toward Sam. "Brother Samuel, stand here beside me as I issue forth my decision," King Ramie ordered. Sam moved up closer to stand to the right of the throne and within the king's vision.

There was a small disturbance in the crowd and King Ramie looked up to see Captain Rynarr enter the court. He was having returned with an escort of five Royal Guardsmen, each armed with spear and shield. At Brother Samuel's request, Captain Rynarr had brought Paul and Richard to court so they may observe the sentencing of GW. King Ramie, who normally didn't like interruptions in his court, waited impatiently until the other two Americans had knelt beside GW, one on each side of their friend and their heads lowered. Though Richard and Paul shared whispered greetings with GW, but then stopped talking when a very authoritative Mushid stepped up and ordered them to be silent and struck both-of them on the feet with the blunt end of his spear.

King Ramie then stepped from the throne and surprised everyone by approaching the three kneeling men. He stood before GW and reached down with his right hand to lift GW's face up by the chin. He desired to know what his youngest daughter had seen in this young man. True, he found the young man to be a very strong and handsome man and yes, he had proved himself upon the battlefield, but there was something else about this young man that seemed to trouble him. He saw in this man's eyes both intelligence and integrity, yet he was willing to risk all for some brief moments of time in his daughter's presence. You're not an idiot, nor a fool, so you may truly love my daughter...but still, you have offended the laws of my court...what must I do with you? I have Brother Samuel to consider in this too, for I do not wish to lose the friendship of my closest advisor.

Having already released his rage during the early morning hours, while pacing his chambers, he was now able to look upon GW as a king and not simply a father. Here and now he saw a life spark of something very special in GW's eyes and as he gazed upon him, King Ramie began to feel a lightheartedness that he had not felt in a very long time.

King Ramie released GW's chin, gazed at the other two men for a moment and then turned to retrace his steps back to his throne. Before sitting back down, he gave Brother Samuel a hard look and Sam knew from the king's worrisome expression his long-time friend was warring inside himself over the decision he was about to pass down.

The court remained totally silent. All waited for the king to speak, but they were beginning to grow restless for the king had never displayed such a hesitation for a doomed prisoner before. Some began to speculate amongst themselves in low whispers, until the officer of the court silenced them with the display of his scimitar.

King Ramie remained on his feet and continued to behave unusually, for he again approached GW for a second closer look. By his strange actions, two of the guards escorted the king this time, scimitars at the ready to defend their liege.

Then in a whisper only GW could hear, King Ramie spoke to GW and this brought a surprised Princess Lonnia quickly to her feet. But she still couldn't hear the words her father spoke. "I've been told you love my daughter, is this true?"

"Yes, Sire," GW replied. His one open eye now gazed upward upon the king, but because his head was no longer bowed a murmur of anger spread through the people.

"You are willing to die for Princess Lennia?" King Ramie asked, again in a feint whisper.

"I love her, Sire. If I am to die, I see no better reason than to sacrifice myself for her."

"You are a foolish young man...even for an infidel."

"Yes, Sire. Brother Samuel has informed me of this many times and I ask you not blame him or my friends for my recent conduct."

"You need not be concerned with Brother Samuel, for I value his friendship and his invaluable service to my kingdom. But as to your friends, they will face your fate for being true friends they should've stopped you. They at least should have informed Brother Samuel of your intensions and for this they have violated the bond they have with my kingdom."

"Please, Sire…" GW attempted to say, bur the king placed his hand over GW's mouth in an unusual display of familiarity and it caused an audible expression of surprise from the people of the court.

"Be silent now. Do not speak a word or what I plan will not come to pass and the three of you will surely perish this night."

This reply greatly confused GW, but he obeyed and maintained his silence while the king slowly returned to his throne.

"Well, father, have you satisfied your curiosity with this infidel?" Princess Lonnia asked. She had returned to her seat and glared at her father. She felt he had belittled himself by touching the infidel with his hand and as a result, made herself look poorly before those in attendance.

"Yes, I am ready to announce their sentence," King Ramie replied.

"What about Brother Samuel?" Princess Lonnia asked. "I find him up here when he should be down there kneeling with the other infidels."

"Brother Samuel is where he belongs, at my side. His confinement period is over, and we will not debate this. Now be silent or leave this room immediately!" King Ramie gestured to Captain Rynarr and within seconds, Princess Lonnia found herself guarded by two Royal Guardsmen.

Enraged, Princess Lonnia turned to glare at Brother Samuel and he could almost feel the daggers striking his chest. But his response was a simple grin, which further infuriated her, and she actually snarled back at him. Her actions caused one of the guards to step back, tightening his grasp upon his spear.

She turned to look back at GW, pointed at him and shouted, "I want him to die for touching my sister!"

"Be silent, daughter!" King Ramie shouted back in a booming authoritative voice that seemed to have the force of a strong wind that blew through the startled crowd.

"You saw that I have touched him. Do you wish my death also?"

"You are weak, my father," Princess Lonnia replied. She refused to humble herself before him and the crowd of onlookers. "You need to vacate this throne, now, father and let me take over reign. I'll set this kingdom right by killing these infidels and the pious holy men who plagues us. I'll bring back the old ways and the old religions that were here long before this false Christ and this Allah you kneel before like a frightened child." She was on her feet now, pointing her finger at her father and raising her voice with each proclamation.

"You have mishandled this kingdom! Made it the poorest in Libya…You've allowed this foul beast to cripple are trade when you should have killed it long ago!" She bellowed, and spittle showered from her lips.

"Be silent!" King Ramie ordered again. He then ordered the guards to take custody of the princess. "Escort my daughter to her quarters. She is ill and see that she is not disturbed…by anyone."

"Yes, Sire," the closest guard answered. He then grasped the princess by the arm with his free hand and with the help of his fellow guardsman, forcefully removed her from the court. A third guardsman was needed, in order they didn't actually hurt the princess by bodily removing the hysterical woman. She was shouting out threats, kicking and screaming and then broke free for a moment. She lifted her arms up and gestured to the crowd wildly and then shouted, "Rally to me, my people and slay this false king. I promise you great riches if you follow me…" Princess Lonnia was stopped abruptly. Captain Rynarr's men had secured her again and wrapped a silken scarf around her face to silence her. She fought much like a man would with the strength of two and this surprised the three guardsmen. Mushid moved up to assist, accompanied by two other Royal Guardsmen and they finally had her secured between them. She was then carried out of the court, one man holding either a leg or an arm, while Mushid kept the silken scarf wrapped around her face to silence her ravings.

Everyone in the court watched on in stunned silence during the whole disturbance, for this was the first time Princess Lonnia had ordered her father's death during one of her outlandish demonstrations. Then as Princess Lonnia was bodily carried out of the throne room and down the hallway, they heard an eerie raspy cackle escape her lips and it sent a cold shudder through the crowd.

All knew she was a witch, but now she seemed to be exhibiting even more power and they whispered of her curses until the guardsmen in the room once again silenced them.

King Ramie waited for his daughter to be removed and then addressed the prisoners and his crowd of subjects. "I have made my decision and it will stand. By my royal decree, these three men will be banished from our kingdom. They are never to return here upon threat of death. They may have rations for three days, but no weapons and no horses. Anyone who assists them will be put to death. That is all, I have spoken."

Brother Samuel breathed a sigh of relief. The banishment will be hard on the three men, but it was far better than a horrid death. "Thank you, Sire," Sam whispered to the king.

# 16 – NO PIRATES?

For three tiring days, the men cautiously proceeded east on foot, trudging through wet sand and climbing over piles of coastal rocks. They stayed on the shoreline and the high tides erased their footprints in the sand. They didn't want to lead an enemy to them, either an avenging soldier from Silene or local raiders that frequented the shores. But it seemed only the occasional gull showed any interest in them.

GW remained fearful the Black Princess might send some of her paid lackeys after them to avenge her sister's disgrace and use their deaths to strike back at Brother Samuel. Richard tried to convince him that Princess Lonnia's contemptuous conduct at court would assuredly keep her locked up for a time, but GW was not so sure.

"She's still the king's daughter...and remember, that witch has let her mouth run away in the past and she's still alive," GW said.

"Why worry about something we can't do anything about?" Paul asked. He kicked a rock out of his path and looking up he saw a small sail in the distance traveling to the west and wondered if it was a merchant or a fisherman.

GW shrugged his shoulders, reached down and picked up a small rock and tossed it against an outcropping of dark colored stone. He then looked back over his shoulder, shook his head and replied, "You know I have no idea, but she's also a king's daughter. I'm hoping she gets her hand lightly slapped... maybe some confinement and the matter will be dropped. I figure if it was going to be anything worse than that, I'd be hiking back there to free her."

Paul pointed to the boat, "Do you think they're pirates?"

The three Americans were warned to be watchful for Egyptian and Berber pirates, who could either enslave them for sale in another country or simply slice their throats for the weapons and supplies they carried.

"If they are, we've got plenty of time to hide. It'll take them at least a half-hour to bring their boat to shore and I doubt they've even spotted us. We've got all this," GW gestured to the landscape all behind them, "...and their sail sticks up because of an empty horizon. I doubt we have anything to worry about, at least with that boat."

For the first night, the men were exposed to several hours of heavy rainfall. The blackened clouds moved in from the north and made it hard for them to see any farther then 20-feet. Powerful gusts of wind and blowing sand nearly blinded them and they wrapped cloth around their faces to protect themselves.

Unable to find any cover with the storm moving ashore, it took only a blink of an eye before they were completely soaked to the skin and foul tempered from the experience. Seeking shelter behind a low rolling sand dune, they sat in their wetness with backs together in an attempt-to maintain some body warmth between them. No fire could withstand the weather, so they remained cold and shivered throughout the night. Two of them would attempt to sleep, while a third, with his scimitar in his lap, kept watch. By morning, when they were able-to see, all three were running further inland when the incoming tide brought great windswept waves further into shore and pounded the beach with deep thundering explosions.

Wet, weary and mad, and suffering from too little sleep, they plopped down with packs in hand behind another sand dune and dug into the bottom of their packs for their helmets, which they used to scoop out a shallow hole to sit in and then cover their faces. Normally they would've hung their helmets from the sides of the rucksack, but in not believing they would need them, they had packed them down deep in the bottom of their bags to protect their meager supply of melon. For some reason, their knives had been returned, but not their shovels. They were not aware the shovels were turned over to the senior blacksmith, who was attempting to make copies for the Silene troops.

Paul also dug out another tunic top, a brown one with silvery trim, which was made for him by one of Sam's older servants. Paul had kept an army guard from beating the servant after a heavy tray of dirty dishes fell from his gasp in the passageway outside Sam's quarters and some of the debris fell upon the soldier's boots. He used the tunic to drape over the three of them as a make-shift canopy. It wasn't much, but it was all they had on hand.

All day and night the storm raged, which reminded the men of the monsoon storms they had weathered in Vietnam. Shortly after midnight, the storm's strength finally began to lesson and there were growing periods of time without rain. Still, the stars remained hidden and the men wondered if the storm was truly over. But with the coming of dawn on the second day, the storm had abated itself and a new sun was breaking through the dark clouds. With no wind to chill them, this allowed the drenched men to strip down to the raw to dry out. They made their way back to the shore and draped their wet clothes out on the rocks. They then spread their packs and extra clothes and equipment over the large beach rocks to dry out. Once the sand had turned hot, they then picked up the clothes off the rocks and stretched them out upon it.

By early afternoon they were back in dry clothes and once again proceeding east along the shoreline. Before early evening, they came upon a fresh water stream, narrow enough that a man could jump across as it fed into the ocean. Here they refilled their water bags and what few canteens they still had with them. They also used this time to consume their evening meal. As a precaution, they decided not to build a fire, concerned the smoke could be seen in the distance. They would wait until darkness before they dug a pit deep enough to hide their flames and night would hide the smoke. Still without suitable cover, they began again and proceeded on until the sun set and the coming darkness brought them to a halt. Along the way they had picked up two arms-full of semi-dry beach wood and with some effort were able to get a small fire going. They had dug a two-foot deep pit and were grateful for the warmth it provided, as the desert night cooled.

Since leaving Mushid at the border, they had found no sign of any coastal settlement or in fact any evidence of man. This left each man wondering what might lie ahead and if when they came upon the local inhabitants, would they be friendly? Over the fire they discussed what they might say to anyone they encountered, but after much friendly debate that could not come up with a satisfactory answer to their dilemma.

Then on the late morning hours of the third day, they came upon a wide stream bed feeding into the ocean and found a large flock of sheep watering there. Off in the distance they could see some herders. Crossing the stream and moving through the sheep cautiously, keeping their scimitars strapped to their rucksacks, they met an Egyptian family of herders. Being fare skinned, Paul and GW frightened the Egyptians, thinking them to be Berbers; meaning there were most likely pirates nearby. But Richard, who resembled a Black Moor or a Sudanese, was able-to quiet their fears and speak to them in his recently acquired Arabic tongue. He explained how they were peaceful travelers and newly departed from Libya and on their way to Damascus. But he didn't get into the true reason why they were forced to leave because this would lead to a lot of questions they couldn't answer.

Though timid somewhat, the herders were still uneasy by these three strangers who suddenly appeared in their midst. The oldest of the Egyptian herders stepped forward and identified himself with a one-word name, "I am Makeen." He invited the strangers for evening meal and they followed him to his small encampment, which was over several rolling sand dunes to the east.

During the mealtime, Richard told his tale of how he and these fair skinned men accompanying him had come to the shores of North Africa following a shipwreck. A bold face lie, the three of them had used in Silene and once more hoped to explain their presence and possibly prevent them from being killed.

For Richard, he was the easiest to explain for his disguise was of a Black Moor; a Nubian from the Upper Sudan region. He had journeyed north to Ireland, an enemy of the Britain's, to find well-trained mercenaries to better prepare the Sudanese armies to fight the expected onslaught of Christians journeying to the Holy Land.

"My sultan had heard of these legendary fighters through other travelers, but upon our return to North Africa the boat was sunk in a fierce storm and only the three of us survived.

"We washed up on the shores of Libya and were briefly imprisoned in the Dungeon of Silene-a very unhappy place, but Allah preserved us. Upon learning of our journey, King Ramie, a fellow Muslim, blessed be the name of Allah, took mercy on us and had us escorted to the Libyan border under heavy guard and banished us from ever returning." Richard felt uneasy using Islam as a-way to protect himself and he sincerely hoped the good Lord would understand.

GW was impressed with how easy the Arabic lingo poured out of his mouth, but then Richard hesitated when a herdsman then spoke up in a tone of skepticism, "Yet, this king who allowed you to live also left you with weapons?"

"I am a minor advisor to a great sultan. This king of such a small kingdom did not want to risk hostilities with Upper Sudan. He provided us with food and water, and these new weapons, since ours were lost to the sea. But sadly, he had no horses to spare for Silene is a very poor kingdom."

Makeen nodded his head in understanding and gave his youngest son a raised eyebrow for embarrassing him and then asked, "Yes, I have heard of this Silene you speak of...does not a dragon live there? Do they not offer sacrifices to this great beast to keep the kingdom safe?" The elder then wiped mutton grease from his mouth and tossed a leg-bone into the fire.

They had roasted a young lamb in honor of their guests, but one crippled from a previous attack by wild dogs two-nights earlier. This was the first the three Americans had learned of wild dogs and GW wondered if these might be wolves?

The Americans had grown weary of mutton and between them they had shared wishes they could come across a herd of cattle but knew that were pretty-unlikely. But they accepted what was offered with a smile and listened as Richard spun his yarn.

Paul continued to have trouble with the Arabic and GW had to interpret for him. In doing so, Richard was forced to explain to the herders how this strange sounding language was the tongue of the Irish.

"Yes, we heard much of this, but we never saw the dreadful beast," Richard replied. He then placed a well chewed upon rib-bone on to a wooden platter. "But, I did notice the sadness in the people's faces, as if Allah, blessed be his name, no longer looked upon their kingdom with kindness."

The elderly herdsman Makeen, his aged robe threadbare and soiled, used a weathered staff and a younger boy's strong shoulder to rise to his feet. He used his staff to gesture toward a medium size brown canvas tent, "You are our guests this night and may use this tent and may our blessed Allah fill your dreams with joy."

Right then a stiff ocean breeze suddenly hit the camp, bringing a sharp chill to stranger and herdsmen alike. Another storm was coming ashore, and supplies were quickly packed to keep them from being blown away and the fire was extinguished; a safety precaution to keep the flames from reaching the tents.

Once the chores were done, the small company of herdsmen and three Americans sought shelter in their tents.

"They're nice people," Paul said. He then promptly collapsed down upon a thin pile of blankets of soft wool. Though in disrepair, there were also three medium-sized multi-colored rugs to cover the sand and to be used as their beds.

"Yeah, they seem like good people," GW agreed. "But right now, I'm missing my cot. I've gotten too soft in the wrong places for all this ground sleeping."

"Well, at least we have a tent over our head and these nice wool blankets to keep us warm," Richard said. He pulled an old threadbare blanket up over his legs and chest and used his pack for a pillow.

"You think one of us should stay awake, make sure we don't get our throats slit during the night from these nice people?" Paul asked.

"Good idea," Richard agreed. "I didn't like the tone from that one guy and he kept eyeing my scimitar. I volunteer for first watch." Richard held up his right hand.

"Okay, wake me up when you can't keep your eyes open any longer," Paul said. Which meant GW got stuck with the early morning watch. He really didn't mind all that much, as he was still carrying the burden of blame for their banishment and it weighed heavily upon his spirit.

While he lay on his side with a single thin blanket over him, GW listened to the wind blow and thought about his beautiful princess. He wondered what she might be enduring back in Silene and if he would ever see her again? Before he dropped off to a restless sleep, he remembered to ask God for her protection and Sam's.

In the early morning hours of the fourth day, the men thanked the herders for their kindness, finished off a small breakfast of fresh fish cooked in fish oil and continued-on their trek. They continued to remain close to the dark blue waters of the Mediterranean Sea and took short breaks every hour or so. When the sun approached the noon hour, they stumbled upon the ruins of a small settlement and it wasn't hard to discern from the blackened wood the destruction was caused by fire.

"I think about fifty, maybe sixty people once lived here," Richard said as he sifted through some of the debris with his new staff; a piece drift wood he had found and whittled on to shape it.

"Guess we might as well see if there's anything we can use," Paul suggested. He then began to pick up pieces of blackened wood, see if they were of any future use as firewood and tossed the useless ones aside and possible burnable ones into a pile.

GW gave Paul a single raised eyebrow expression, "You really like digging through other people's trash, don't you? I bet you were probably the company scrounger, weren't you?"

Paul grinned, "Only the number two man. Our main guy could get anything you wanted, but at a price. But I used to find my share of good bargains, even some good booze now and then. But my specialty was weapons and uniforms. I had a source in supply to get my squad better rifles and that's how I got my KA-BAR."

"Maybe it worked back in Nam, but I don't think you'll find any great bargains here...and I can guarantee you won't find any beer here," GW said with a laugh.

Paul nodded his head in agreement and shoved some heavily burned debris aside with his foot to look underneath them. They soon discovered the blackened remains of three small boats and while searching further, GW discovered a human skull. "I've found one of the locals, but only his or her skull."

Then GW discovered several more skulls and as he used his foot to move them aside, he began to feel queasy, "I think I just found the rest of 'em."

"Just skulls?" Paul asked.

"Yeah, only skulls and some of them are pretty small." GW felt sick.

"I wonder what happened to the rest of them? Their bodies I mean," Richard asked.

"Probably carried off by those wild dogs that herder talked about," Paul said.

"Yeah, some of the skulls have teeth marks on them...or at least what I think is teeth marks." GW then closely examined one of the larger skulls and wondered what the person might have looked like and how he or she was killed?

"They look pretty clean, not like all those bodies we found in that Vietnamese village," Paul said.

"I think these are pretty old...the crabs probably got to them and cleaned them off," GW said. He remembered seeing all those crabs along the shoreline. They had even dined on a few of them with the herdsmen and now he wished he hadn't. His stomach recoiled a bit.

"How many do you count?" Paul asked. He stared down at the skulls and his mind flashed back to that small Vietnamese village. He shook his head, trying to shake that old memory out of his mind.

"Looks like fourteen, but two of them are a bit small and must've been babies."

"So close to the shore, I'm betting their town was attacked by pirates." Richard picked up a broken arrow and displayed it to the others. "This looks real old, but I don't recognize the art work on the shaft. Maybe pirate, but could be Moor or even some African tribesmen from the south. I should have studied more while I worked at the museum."

"Doesn't matter, Richard, they're all dead and it looks like it was long ago." GW dug a shallow grave nearby with Paul's help and they placed all the skulls inside. "Probably some archeologist will dig this up in 800-years and never know we found it first."

"Hey, I got an idea...put your corporal stripes inside one of the skulls. That'll drive those eggheads, crazy," Paul suggested. But Richard responded with a shake of his head, "We can't mess with the historic timeline, anything could have an effect on our own future and we must tread lightly."

"Hey, I'm only talking about his corporal stripes. That's not going to cause a big uproar."

"Remember what Sam said," Richard said, giving Paul a hard glare. "We have to be extremely careful, especially with what we say and what we leave behind."

"Okay, professor," Paul replied. But there still some degree of mischief in him, but he'd keep it in check at least for now.

"Besides, our stripes haven't changed since world War II. Someone in the 1940's could come across this site and cry out a war crime on some innocent American unit."

"You're right," Paul agreed. "I hadn't thought of that."

"Let's find some shelter, guys, those storm clouds to the north look menacing and I'd rather not get soaked again," Richard said as he pointed out over the ocean.

"Well, none of this burned wood is much any good so let's get a move on," Paul replied.

GW studied the grave for a moment of silence and wondered if this was how the three of them would end up? Would some academic in the future come across their bodies and wonder who they were and where we came from? He then looked to the Heavens and offered up a prayer for continued safety as they continued-on their trek.

For nearly two hours they tread through the beach sand, searching for some beach wood and hopefully, a shelter to keep them dry. But the rain began to fall, and it was beginning to look like another wet night.

"Hey, lookee there!" Paul shouted, hoping to be heard over the rain. He pointed to a large set of rocks, where an old dilapidated hut set. It had a patchy roof of dried palms and looked as if had already weathered several storms and might remain standing for them.

"Our castle awaits us!" Richard hollered back as he sprinted for the hut to get out of the downpour.

The rain was warm and with the wind picking up, the growing waves crashing on the beach reminded GW of the booming sounds created by an F-4 Phantom fighter jet on take-off.

Once under the palms, which they adjusted for best cover, the men began to look around for something to burn. But there was nothing, not unless they tore the hut itself apart. They weren't about to do that.

"Looks like another wet and cold night, boys," GW said. Before he plopped down in the sand, he took his wet shirt off to ring the rainwater from it.

Paul kept his shirt on but was sifting through his pack for something to eat, "I thought the desert was always hot and dry."

"Normally is," Richard said. "But we're here on the coast and I've read how the rain storms of the Mediterranean Sea can be quite frightful. Records show how quite a few boats were sunk by storms when Crusaders sailed toward the Middle East."

"Professor, you are just filled with useless information," Paul said mockingly, but then he added a grin for his friend. "Don't take offense, I'm just jealous. You've got brains and I'm a little short in that area."

"Paul, what you may think you lack in intelligence, you make up for with integrity and courage." Richard moved the roof palms around again to keep the rain off them. As long-as the rain kept coming straight down they'd be all right, but if a breeze or worse a high wind came up they were exposed to a torrent, they might lose the palms. Only the weight of the huge palms and surrounding rocks had kept the shack from blowing away, but they knew a hurricane force-like wind would make quick work of this place.

"You two are a lot of fun," GW said and then he added, "A straight man and his comic." GW shook his head and smiled. "The USO could use you two...if we had one."

"Okay, bright guy, I guess that makes you the hero in our little play, right?" Paul asked without looking at GW.

"Not me," GW replied as he pointed at his chest. "When the lieutenant in Boot Camp asked for heroic types for Airborne, I thought he was saying he needed a volunteer for chapel guide. Next thing I know some sergeant is shoving my terrified butt out a perfectly good airplane and I was risking my life on something a silk worm threw up."

"So, how'd you get picked for rear guard action?" Richard asked. He was adjusting his helmet in the event the palms fell in on them.

"Like you. I was just minding my own business and dodging bullets when some glory-seeking lieutenant spotted the bulls-eye on my back and thought I'd do just fine."

"Well let's stop all this palaver before I start to ball my eyes out, it's time for dinner." Paul looked at what he had left in his pack and began to sulk: three pieces of smashed and slimy mutton chunks and something that resembled crushed fish sticks mixed in with a handful of dates.

"Doesn't anyone think of beef over here?" Paul complained-again.

The slept through the night, taking turns on guard duty and the next morning they headed eastward. For another week, the men continued-on, but they didn't come across any more settlements or find any sight of another human being. Several times they did spot sailing ships off to the north, but fearing pirates, they didn't attempt to signal them. Fresh water wasn't a problem. They came across fresh water streams about every day to refill. However, their food supply was now extinguished. So, they looked for fish, but the various streams they encountered were empty of life and an endeavor to dig for clams also proved unproductive and there wasn't a crab in sight.

"There's got to be some crabs around here!" Paul yelled. He was jumping up and down in frustration like a child who wasn't getting his way might behave.

Richard ignored him and stood there staring off toward the ocean, "No tidal pools or rocks...only long miles of empty beach. You'd find most crabs there in the pools, because there's nothing for them to eat here except sand."

GW dropped his pack beside a low dune, plopped down on his butt and untied his boots. He then used his bootlaces to tie his bayonet on to a thick wooden branch he'd found along the beach the previous day and whittled it down to a six-foot walking staff. He entered the waves with his homemade spear in an attempt-to impale the fish with it and nearly drowned a moment later, when a large wave caught him unprepared and bounced him off the sand like a runaway dodge ball.

Seeing his friend was having trouble, Paul entered the water and used a life guard's technique of a right arm under GW's jaw and dragged him back to the beach. Both Paul and Richard were extremely happy to find their friend was still breathing and he hadn't lost his spear.

"Good thing you're breathing. I'm not sure I'd be able to give mouth-to-mouth to a guy...all that lip-to-lip thing," Paul complained.

"My friend, you are one class act," Richard said. But he then patted his buddy on the shoulder while GW coughed up what he thought to be several quarts of seawater.

Once GW was able-to walk, they continued-on for approximately another mile before all three were ready to collapse from weariness. Here they found several large boulders that offered some small defense from the wind, or if an enemy showed itself. But once again they found no wood for a fire and went to sleep hungry and cold.

Two days later, the men hungry, they spotted a small boat overturned on the beach and while checking the boat out, they spotted a lone fisherman. He man knelt behind a small sand dune for a windbreak. Richard told his friends the man was probably mending his net from the movements he was making.

Not wanting to startle him, Richard called out a friendly greeting in Arabic and waved his right arm to show he held no weapon in it. Likewise, both Paul and GW kept their hands away from their weapons and smiled in an attempt-to show they were not going to harm the older man.

Realizing these men stood between him and his boat, the elderly gentleman stood to his feet and dropped his knife to the sand. He then offered the ritual greeting between Muslims to which Richard replied in the same fashion.

His name was Abdul-Bashir, an olive-skinned fisherman of some 73-years of age, who wore a soiled tan turban to cover his balding head and draped down his back. He would use this long drape of cloth to cover his face when the winds were up. He had a long, heavy coarse beard of gray-black colors that covered most of his chest and his simple tan colored tunic was covered in dark bloody stains. They were to learn later most of the stains came with the hazardous job of fishing; wrestling with his fish, occasionally impaling himself with his hooks and then the cleaning of the fish and repairing of his nets.

Shorter then the three men and of small slender build, Abdul-Bashir's arms were old, but strong for his age and his hands were large, calloused and deeply lined. His face, on which he possessed a large hawk-beak like nose, and intelligent, but heavily bloodshot dark brown eyes, was deeply lined and weather-beaten. Abdul-Bashir remained silent and stood very still as the three men approached him, his aged eyes darting back and forth between the three strangers. But he was also looking for a path of escape if one was needed.

As planned, Richard was first to speak, identifying himself and then the others. He stuck pretty much to the old story and explained why they were walking along the shore without horse or camel. Once the story was told, he advised the old man of how hungry they were and asked if he might share some fish with them?

Old Abdul-Bashir eyes displayed a wary look as he studied the three men for a moment. He nearly startled the Americans when he suddenly broke into a big grin, spread his arms wide and exclaimed, "Praise be to Allah, of course I will share what I have with three weary travelers. But first I must mend my net before the sun goes down."

"Can we help?" GW asked in Arabic.

"Do you know of nets?" Abdul-Bashir asked with a skeptical eye.

"No," GW replied. "But you can teach us."

Abdul-Bashir broke out into laughter, "Truly, you speak honestly. Blessed Allah has brought you to me as my eyes grow weary and the mending of my nets grows harder to do with my aging hands."

Over the next hour, Abdul-Bashir gave the men a fast course in the mending of nets and then stood back as the three men began the task. It didn't take long for the net to be repaired as it wasn't as damaged as Abdul-Bashir first suspected. Soon they were done, and they then helped al-Bashir roll the net up and place it upon the sand near the boat.

"Do we need to turn the boat over?" Paul asked.

"Not now," Abdul-Bashir replied. "We leave it overnight this way in case the rains come again. Tomorrow, then we will turn the boat over."

"What of the net? Are you not afraid of thieves?" Richard asked as he pulled his nearly empty rucksack over his shoulders.

"No thieves here. Pirates will not come ashore for a simple old boat of no value to them," Abdul-Bashir said. He then looked to the south and for the first time the men spotted a black smoke plume rising-up from a fire some several hundred yards away.

"Come, we will go to my camp and you will meet my sons."

"Sons? Why were they not here helping you?" Richard asked.

"They fish!" Abdul-Bashir replied simply and in a loud voice, as if that was all the answer he needed to provide.

Walking through deeper sand and avoiding a large outcropping of rock, it was a short time before Abdul-Bashir and his guests arrived in his small encampment. There was a small stream running near the encampment and making its way down to the sea. Here they found three tan colored tents in various sizes and a circular fire pit between them. What the men next saw though were a dozen large fish, impaled on long shafts of steel, being roasted over hot coals. Such a sight caused the three guests to salivate, for each of the silvery fish was better than 12-inches in length and thick with meat.

Seeing that their father was not alone, the men of the camp quickly rose-up from around the fire pit and each instantly produced a large homemade knife. Upon their faces, they wore expressions of grave concern for their father and GW knew these were the old man's sons.

"Easy, my sons, Abdul-Bashir said. "Allah, blessed be his name, has brought us guests." But his three sons remained on guard as the Americans entered the encampment.

Once they grew closer to the fire pit, Abdul-Bashir began his introductions in hopes to put his sons at ease, "This big brute to my left is my first born. His name is Ammaree, an ancient name of honor from his mother's tribe to the far south. My second son, the one with the wary look and his heavy hand still resting upon his knife's hilt, is Hassan. Thankfully, he takes much of his looks from his blessed mother for I'd wish this nose on no child of mine." Abdul-Bashir pointed to his nose and grinned as he walked closer to his youngest son, "And this handsome boy is my third son, who is called Mohammed after our Blessed Prophet and is the best fisherman of the lot."

Richard was first to speak, "Greetings to you sons of Abdul-Bashir and may the bounty in your nets increase 10-fold for the kindness you have shown us this day." Richard then pointed to his two friends, "This tall one is known only as GW, an Irish name from the island of Britain, and my friend here is called Paul, also of Ireland." Richard then gestured to himself, giving the Muslim blessing with his right hand and identified himself quite elegantly, "I am Richard," pronouncing it with a French slant as "Rou'shard...I am a Moor from my sultan's court in the Upper Sudan. I was sent to the Island of Ireland by my sultan to recruit men to help train our soldiers for battles against our enemies. Once there, I was to learn the Britons were once again preparing for a crusade against Jerusalem. I was nearly killed for my faith but was saved by an old man who greatly hated the Britons and I came to learn he was Irish and from this Ireland."

Abdul-Bashir rubbed his chin and then spoke, "I have heard of this Britain you speak of, but I do not know this Ireland."

"Ireland lies to the west of Britain. Only a small body of waters separates them. But the Irish and the Britons have been at war for a long time and will not join in this crusade against the Muslim people." Richard hoped he was keeping his history straight.

Hassan pointed at GW and challenged, "Are you not an infidel?"

Richard, knowing something about protocol for one invited into a camp, stood in front of GW, "You are Muslim, yet you slay your brother in Libya. He is a Christian, who slays his brother in

Britain, who is also your enemy. There is an old saying where I am from, 'The enemy of my enemy is my friend'. He is also a guest in your camp."

Abdul-Bashir frowned at his son, "I like your saying and will remember it. Now please continue-on with your story, for I enjoy a good story with my meal."

Richard wondered if he had somehow started the saying which he believed had come from ancient China. But he continued-on with his story as everyone seated them-selves around the fire pit, "We were shipwrecked on the shores of Libya and soon after, imprisoned for a short time and then banished from their lands because the king, whose kingdom is quite small, did not want to risk angering my sultan by killing us."

"This Ireland you speak of, why do the people dislike these Christians of Britain? Why would your lord send you such a distance for only two men?" Abdul-Bashir asked.

"As I said, there were others with us, but except for us three, all drowned in a terrible storm. Why Great Allah blessed us three only, I am only his simple servant and do not attempt to know the ways of his great plans." Richard gestured with his right hand to Paul and GW, "We live and now must return to my home.

"But while in Ireland I saw how the barbaric Britons treated the Irish people. The women were mistreated, and the children enslaved. Men who were unable to work were killed and their farm lands confiscated by a greedy British monarch. The Irish fought bravely in small armies, but they are greatly outnumbered, and I fear they will lose their war."

"You say these two of the fare skin are soldiers?" Mohammed asked in a tone of disbelief.

"In their land, these two men are considered equals to the hated knights of Britain. They are to teach our horsemen the work of the lance and sword, but also a skill we call wrestling," Richard said.

"I have heard of this wrestling from the dreaded Turks," Ammaree said and then he spit-upon the sand in disgust.

Abdul-Bashir frowned at his son and then turned to Richard, "I do not know much of such things, we are simple fishermen who Allah has blessed today for my son's nets were full and tonight we eat well. Come, share in our food and we will tell more stories." Abdul-Bashir gestured with a wave of his hand for the three guests to seize a blackened and nearly-cooked fish from the fire.

Their stomachs were crying out, but the three men waited until Abdul-Bashir took his first choice and began to eat. Only then did the others grab up a steel shaft, which GW, Paul and Richard soon learned was extremely hot to the touch. Then they noticed how the fishermen were using parts of their robes to hold the steel shafts.

Due to their severe hunger, they completely forgot about how the steel shafts would maintain the heat of the hot coals and now they had lightly burned fingers for their mistake.

Soft leather bags filled with fresh water were also provided, along with several bags of date juice, which GW and the others shied away from. No matter how they tried, they just couldn't get over the weird taste of the date juice.

Over the next couple of hours Abdul-Bashir entertained them all with stories of his youth, most of which his sons had heard all too often. He spoke of his family's history and their leaving the banks of the Northern Nile to pursue saltwater fishing.

"The fish are large here, there are no crocodile to pull us from our boats, but the work is harder, and we had fewer storms on the Upper Nile. Still, there are few of us here and our nets come back filled with Allah's bounty, blessed be his name."

When Abdul-Bashir became quiet and Richard waited a polite amount of time, he broke the silence and told lies about his youth in Sudan; a country he knew nothing about and of Ireland; a country he had never visited and only knew a thing or two from Sam's imagination and limited knowledge of the place.

But the four fishermen listened in awe for Richard had become a gifted storyteller and they enjoyed hearing of the land of green for they had known only desert. Though he occasionally tossed in a word of English now and then when he did not know the Arabic translation, he hoped Abdul-Bashir and his sons wouldn't take notice or pass it off thinking Richard was speaking in his Sudanese tongue.

Richard had learned through Sam that much of the Arabic language had several slants from the different regions it was spoken. There was the basic Arabic, which almost everyone spoke from the Middle East through much of Africa. But there was also local dialect such as Egyptian-Arabic or Sudanese-Arabic and Libyan-Arabic.

Richard's story telling was followed by a time of questions, as Abdul-Bashir's sons were curious of both this Sudan and of this strange far off Ireland. Richard and the others did their best to answer them with bold lies and the occasional spot of truth.

GW struggled to remember his geography and historic time lines in the battles between Ireland and England, so as he wouldn't share in anything that hadn't happened yet. But he was sure he got Scotland and Ireland mixed up a few times, not that it mattered as he doubted these men would ever go to the British Isles.

Now Paul, who got caught up in the story telling, began to speak of the Irish Republican Army (IRA) exploits and GW had to give him an elbow in the ribs to get him to stop.

"The IRA hasn't happened yet and won't for probably another 600 to 700 years," GW whispered to his friend in English.

"Oh, sorry," Paul said. "I thought something like the IRA was always there."

Seeing how their father was growing tired, for the old man had dropped off a couple of times during Richard's storytelling, the sons thanked GW and the others for helping their father and announced it was time to sleep. Mohammed looked to GW and quickly pointed to his father, and whispered, "He needs much rest, but will not leave before his guests are ready."

"I understand." Richard stood to his feet and stretched out his arms, presenting his best fake yawn. "It has been a long day and a good meal, but I think it is time for me to say good night and offer up my prayers to Allah for pleasant dreams for us all this night."

"Truly, blessed be the name of Allah, for this has been a night of pleasure. I am thankful you were brought to us and that we might share our food with you," Abdul-Bashir said as Mohammed carefully helped him to his feet.

"You have rescued us, Abdul-Bashir, for we were hungry, and you fed us, and I pray Allah will reward your kindness," Richard replied as he bowed before the old man.

"I only wish we were home, where I could shower you with fine foods and you might meet my daughters," Abdul-Bashir said in a weakened voice.

"How many daughters do you have?" Paul asked in a tone of excitement that didn't escape either Richard or GW.

Abdul-Bashir waved his arm to the heavens and said, "Allah has blessed me with seven daughters, but alas, there are few men in our land. Almost every able-bodied man is selected for service in the army." He lowered his head and his voice turned sad, "Our Egypt prepares for a war against these Christian invaders, called into battle for this Jerusalem; a place I have never seen and some of my sons might yet still die there. Only fishermen, herdsmen and farmers may stay home, but I fear in time they too will be called upon soon and my beloved sons will leave me."

"I didn't know Egypt was sending an army to the Holy Land?" GW said.

"Truly, the great kings and sultans of all the Muslim lands have come together to defend Islam and one great warrior king will be selected to lead an army of over 100,000 men."

GW suddenly remembered the history of the crusades and how the Holy Land would be covered in an ocean of blood before an uneasy peace might be restored and he looked to Abdul-Bashir's three sons and wished they could avoid such a slaughter.

Abdul-Bashir then turned to speak to his sons briefly in a whisper, before he turned to address his guests in a louder voice, "Tonight you will sleep in Ammaree's tent. He will sleep with his brothers and ignore Hasan's great camel-like snores."

Displaying a grateful expression, Richard once again bowed to Abdul-Bashir, "You sincerely bless us, Abdul-Bashir." Richard then turned to thank Ammaree also.

Leaning against his younger son for support and drawing on the boy's strength, Abdul-Bashir said to his guests, "Tomorrow we break camp and move eastward, for we must take our catch home before the fish rot. You are welcome to join us if you wish." Abdul-Bashir said.

Richard looked to GW and Paul, and the three of them huddled together to discuss this offer. Paul and Richard were agreeable, but there was something in GW's spirit, a nudge of sorts that was telling him otherwise, "Let's sleep on it, guys."

Paul and Richard hesitated, but then nodded their heads in agreement. Richard then turned to speak, "We will tell you in the morning of our plans."

"Yes, it is good to sleep before making some decisions. Only a fool would rush in when caution could be observed. For we are new friends and from different lands," Abdul-Bashir said. He then said his good night and entered his tent. He left the camp chores to his sons and was snoring quite loudly before GW, Paul and Richard even entered their tent.

"What's your hold-up, man? These are cool people," Paul said. He dropped his pack to the ground and plopped down upon a pallet of smelly furs. "Man, these things smell like fish."

"What did you expect, they're fishermen," GW said. Shaking his head, he painfully lowered himself to a recently made bed of camel hair rugs, old netting material and warm sand. His back had been bothering him some since he was bounced around by that wave and walking across the North Africa was not helping any.

"You seem out of sorts, Corporal," Richard said. There was a look of concern on his face as he studied GW body language.

"I'm just sore from that wave...but you're right, something is gnawing at me and I'm not sure what it is," GW replied. "But I agree with you about Abdul-Bashir and his sons as a possible remedy to our situation. Still, I've got this feeling that something is really-wrong and I'm not sure if we should move on with these men. For all we know our presence might endanger these people."

"You know, we could be caught up in this Egyptian draft," Paul added.

Richard shook his head, "Me maybe, but you two still look like Berbers, or worse...foreigners from either Europe or Britain. They'll think you're infidel's first, kill you quickly and then ask questions over your bodies."

Sitting there in the tent, GW studied the sands at his feet and ignored the fish smells of the furs he sat upon, while he thought over what they should do. Then, struck with a deep thought, he looked to his two friends and made a-suggestion, "We could split up. I could stay and you two could travel with Abdul-Bashir."

"No way!" Paul exclaimed. Without even taking time to consider it he pointed his right index finger at GW's chest. "We came here together, and we will stay together. Right, Professor?" Paul asked Richard, hoping for support.

"Hey, remember I'm only a Private First Class, low man on the totem pole. I go where I'm ordered," Richard replied.

"It doesn't work that way anymore, Professor," Paul said before GW could respond.

"You make up your mind on what you feel is right, we're not in the army anymore...just three friends trapped in an episode of Twilight Zone."

"Richard, if you feel you want to go with these people, it's okay with me. You have the best chance of surviving here," GW said as he looked-into the eyes of his friend.

"You speak the language better than either Paul or I, and at least here you have the right skin color. Here, we're foreigners...and maybe this is your chance."

"Forget it!" Richard said in a loud outburst of English. His voice filled with attitude. "We came here together, and I owe my life to you two. I wouldn't know what to do without you guys around."

"Okay, we stay together, and I think for now we should hold up here. Maybe we can talk Abdul-Bashir out of some supplies," GW said.

"Maybe we can scrounge a boat off him?" Paul suggested.

"Don't hold your breath," GW replied.

The three men settled down for the night, but as a precaution one of them remained on guard. They liked Abdul-Bashir and his sons, but they were still strangers and they didn't want to have their throats slit during the night because of stupidity. GW took the first watch, Paul the second and that left Richard with the early morning hours.

The night past slowly and Richard was getting groggy when it was time to wake the other two, thankful the sun was making its appearance from the east. He wasn't sure he would've lasted another hour and decided it was due to too much fish on a weakened stomach.

While consuming a small breakfast of fruit and dried fish, which Paul thought had the texture of leather, Richard advised Abdul-Bashir of their decision to stay behind. This saddened the old man and GW thought this was because Abdul-Bashir was probably looking at the Richard as a prospective son-in-law and future fisherman.

GW thought of how strange it was how here in the Muslim world of the Middle East and North Africa of how it was the white race held in suspicion and bigotry. He knew this was mainly due to the offensive actions of the crusading and arrogant Britons and pirating Berbers. Brown skinned Arabian and Black Moors often got along, sharing the Muslim faith, unless tribal or countrywide warfare was going on between them.

"We will return to this area in nine-days, for the fishing here is good. If you are still here, you are welcome to share in our meals and we will talk more. I like your stories," Abdul-Bashir said. He then looked down at the men's packs and new they were in dire need of food if they were to survive.

"I will leave you with some food and one small net. You may use it to fish from the shore in the lagoon to the east of us. If Allah blesses you, you'll catch enough fish to keep you alive." He pointed to the east, "There is plenty of water in the nearby streams but be wary of wild animals and avoid the Berbers for they sail by this point of land often. This is why we drag our boats ashore, that and to drain the rain water from them."

"We are very thankful for your friendship, Abdul-Bashir and we pray Allah will bless your trip home and that you will find your wife and daughters safe," Richard said.

All three men bowed before Abdul-Bashir, which was then followed up with the hand gesture of the Muslim blessing.

With the American's help, the boats were pushed into the tidewaters and loaded down with fish and supplies. GW hadn't realized it, but Abdul-Bashir and his sons kept their catch in a large man-made tide pool to keep the fish from rotting, but this would only last so long. It was now time to head home with what GW estimated to be several hundred pounds of a fish he didn't recognize, but thought they resembled a mackerel-like looking fish.

Final goodbyes were made, and the three men stood upon the shore as their Egyptian friends began rowing east and slowly vanished off in the distance.

It didn't escape GW of how not so long ago he'd spent a whole afternoon killing Egyptians raiders and now he had befriended several Egyptian fishermen and sheep herdsmen. It made him wonder what God had in store for him next.

"You ever wonder how God thinks about us pretending to be Muslim...doing this whole Allah blessing stuff?" GW asked Richard, while they examined the net left for them.

"Yes, but I've had to decide that the good Lord brought us here for a reason He only knows and for us to survive, we have-to assume these fictitious roles," Richard replied. He then stretched a piece of netting out.

"Right," GW said.

"GW, you have to quit making it so difficult. We're playing a part in some grand scheme and if it makes you feel any better, ask the Lord to forgive you for the lies you've had to tell to survive. It works for me."

"You mean repent...right?" GW asked.

"You got it," Richard replied. "Simple as ...Man, I think I spent way too much time around Sam. I'm sounding like some chapel-guide in boot camp."

While in Boot- Camp each company had one man assigned as chapel-guide to ensure the troops were in tune with all the church services, assisted the chaplain in various tasks and even marched the men to church. This was often easy duty and got the man out of a lot of laborious work.

Over the next two days, the men took their turns at flinging the fish net out over the gentle waters of a nearby lagoon. So far, they had caught five small fish in nearly nine hours of hard labor, but GW refused to give up and continued to fish after the others had given up and returned to their small camp to clean the fish and cook them up.

Almost at the point of giving up, GW was finally rewarded when he found himself in the fight of his life. A huge monster of a fish had entered the lagoon and became entrapped in GW's net.

"Help!" GW shouted out in alarm. He was being dragged into the water. "I need some help over here!" He could've let go, but then they'd lose the net and he wasn't about to allow that.

Hearing GW's shout for help, Paul and Richard came running over the dune to find GW being dragged deeper into the water by something very dark colored and huge enough to dwarf their friend. They also saw how GW refused to let go of the net, though he appeared to be losing the battle.

Charging forward, both Paul and Richard grabbed a piece of the net and it was right then that Richard recognized the back fin of the beast and shouted out, "Shark! You've caught a shark."

"I know...I know! Now pull before I become its lunch!" GW yelled. "I don't want to lose the net or the shark either."

It took them nearly an hour of fierce struggling and lashing out with their knives to land the shark and even on shore the beast was trying to strike out at them with its tail fin or roll close enough for a bite. They had forgotten to bring their scimitars with them and Paul rushed back to the camp to retrieve them. While he was gone, leaving Richard and GW to deal with a ten-foot long shark with their pitiful knives, that fish was now fighting for its life out of the water. Several times one of them was jumping out of the way to avoid being attacked as the frantic shark, starving for its watery oxygen, fought to return-back to its home by wildly thrashing about on the sand.

Once Paul returned with two scimitars, the battle ended when he and GW delivered strong blows to the shark's head and cut deep into its brain. But in the process, they also sliced up the net, though the shark had done severe damage to it already.

The three of them were sitting on the sand, exhausted from their battle and admiring their prize. It was GW who finally broke the silence, "Either of you had shark before?"

"It's a fish, right?" Paul asked. He was on all fours, his scimitar lying in the sand.

"I've heard it's quite good," Richard said. "...but we need to cut it up quickly and repair the net. With no way to refrigerate the meat, all we can do is leave the bulk of it to soak in the same tide pool Abdul-Bashir and his sons built."

That evening they ate a fine meal of roasted shark and GW decided it was the best fish he'd ever tasted and remembered to thank God for their bounty. He had already decided to make shark tooth necklaces for the three of them, once the jawbone had dried out. The number and rows of shark teeth surprised him and the length of the ones in the front row made him glad the beast never grabbed hold of his legs during the fight. He estimated several of the teeth to be two-inches at a minimum and maybe three-inches in length.

Later that night and once the shark was stretched out, the three of them agreed it was nearly 10-feet in length. But they couldn't decide what kind of shark it was.

"I think it's a Great White, but I'm not sure," Richard said.

"Like I said, it's a fish and it tastes pretty-darn good," Paul said as he used a piece of bone to pick his teeth.

Abdul-Bashir had left them with the partial remains of a tent canopy and some wooden poles, which allowed them to construct a small tent with barely enough room for them to lay side-by-side in. They used the same fire pit Abdul-Bashir and his sons had used and continued to keep one man on guard at all-times. When the rains came ashore, they got soaked, but the clouds moved along with a stiff breeze and the sun returned to dry them out. Afterward, they went to work on mending the net, but when they finished, it was somewhat smaller than before.

With what supplies Abdul-Bashir had left and the shark meat, they stayed fed for the next four days, but after that the shark was no longer eatable and they began using it as bait. This provided them with enough fish to live on, but they were growing quite weary of the sea's bounty and were talking of moving on again.

It was during their simple noonday meal of fish soup cooked in GW's helmet they began to hear strange sounds from off to the west. Fearing Egyptian soldiers or even worse, pirates; GW and Paul quickly dropped their tent down and tossed sand over it for camouflage, while Richard attempted to bury the fire pit by kicking sand over it.

They'd forgotten all about smoke from their fire and kicked themselves for becoming lax in their security, not that it mattered now as someone had apparently seen their smoke and was drawing near.

Hiding behind a small dune, their scimitars and homemade spear-staffs ready for any attackers, the noises drew closer and GW began to identify the sounds as coming from a creaky wagon wheel. He remembered the noise well from the two wagons he helped escort into the desert with Captain Rynarr's detail.

GW popped his head up for a better look and spotted a single-axle wagon, pulled by one large brown horse and one heavy-set man driving it along. He also saw a large mounted man riding beside the wagon, appearing to be in conversation with the driver. Then GW observed the wagon was also pulling along another two horses in the back and he thought he recognized one of them.

As the wagon drew closer, GW suddenly jumped to his feet, which surprised both Paul and Richard, and began waving his arms about and shouting, "We're over here! We're over here!"

"What are you doing?" Richard asked in bewilderment, as he attempted to pull GW back down behind the dune.

GW slapped Richard's hand away and began running toward the wagon. Only then did Richard and Paul recognize the driver and the horsemen. "Sam!" Richard shouted out, while at the same time Paul was yelling, "Mushid! Mushid!"

Sam, his aged back aching from the long ride from Silene, smiled and with all the enthusiasm he could muster, waved back as his three friends approached. He then brought the ugly little wagon to a halt with a pull of the reins, grateful their long journey was half-over. But they still had to return. He looked over to his mounted escort and sighed.

Mushid, who was also weary from the long ride, but happy to see his friends were safe, began to dismount, as his three companions ran up with big smiles and arms waving in greeting.

"Sam, what are you doing here?" GW asked as he grasped his friend's hand and helped him climb down from the wagon wooden seat. GW also noticed the pile of furs on the seat to cushion the long ride.

"We'll speak of it in a minute. You'd better greet your other friend too for it has been a long ride for both of us and across a forbidden border."

GW hugged Sam quickly and then turned to Mushid, who was receiving a royal greeting with hugs and back slaps from Paul and Richard. In the midst of hugs, Mushid looked at GW and gestured to the back of the wagon with a shake of his head.

Not knowing of what Mushid meant, GW rushed to the back of the wagon and his face lit up. A grin from ear to ear broke out and his eyes welled up when he found his beautiful Valiant standing there, shaking his head up and down. Valiant's large black eyes were glistening with happiness to see his master and his hooves began stomping the desert sand.

Unable to speak, heart-filled emotion clinching his chest, GW stepped forward and began stroking Valiant's neck and pressed his head against Valiant's right cheek.

"I've missed you, my dear friend," he was finally able to say.

Then GW heard Paul shout out, "I don't believe it!" For the horse beside Valiant was Paul's Black Arabian, who also appeared happy to be see his master standing there with a silly, but joyful look upon his face.

"I don't understand, why are you here and how'd you get our horses away from the castle?" GW asked.

"Give me a moment, young gentlemen, to stretch out my old bones," Sam said. "Boy, I'm too old to be driving this dreadful thing across the desert, but it was better than walking and there was no way I was going to ride a horse or one of those dreadful camels...Now, do you have a camp for me to rest my old weary bones?"

"Yes, sir," GW replied. "Over this dune, but we buried it all thinking you were soldiers or pirates."

"We're a sorry lot of pirates," Sam said.

"We'll go dig it back up," Paul said. "I am hungry. Do you have any food in that wagon? I'm really tired of fish."

"Some mutton, but ol' Goliath over there has eaten all the chicken," Sam advised them. He then pointed to a large covered basket in the back of the wagon. "While we eat I'll explain why we're here looking for you."

"Has something happened? Is Princess Lennia in danger?" GW asked in his excitement. "What's happened?"

"You never were a patient lad," Sam replied. "Yes, something has happened and it's all bad news. So, let us eat now and then we'll talk."

"Sam?" GW stood before the old man, but Sam's steady glare told GW he wasn't going to get any information until Sam had eaten and rested his pained backside. "Okay, we'll eat."

GW untied Valiant and led him in the direction of their camp, while Paul did the same with his Black Arabian. Richard climbed up on the wagon seat and directed the wagon's horse on as Sam walked beside GW at a slow pace through the sand.

Mushid rode ahead, wanting to check out the area to ensure their safety. He would let Brother Samuel explain their purpose for being here and then wait for GW's response. He was pretty sure what his trainee would say, but he was gravely concerned with what might happen and they only had five days to return to Silene to keep Princess Lennia from being sacrificed to the dragon.

# 17 - PROPHECY OR LEGEND— MAYBE BOTH?

A hastily built fire was burning in a shallow pit and a shank of mutton was hanging over it on a blackened spit, which Paul would slowly turn every minute or so to keep it from burning. While doing so, he hummed a Beatle classic. The others waited impatiently, while sitting or lying about the fire pit. They had all washed their hands in GW's tepid canteen water and were now prepared for their meal. They made Sam as comfortable as possible by using their rucksacks and some wool blankets to brace Sam up. Sam had brought the blankets with him. GW, Paul and Richard were anxious to hear Sam's story in why they had come and once the old man was content with his positioning, the three of them remained quiet and waited. Not Mushid, he knew why they were here and he only wanted to eat and wished the meat would cook faster.

The mutton shank was an offering from Mushid and Sam, who had encountered Makeen the herdsman while in their search for GW and the others. At first wary of the two strangers, one of them he knew to be a warrior, Makeen eventually learned Sam and Mushid to be peaceful travelers. A bit of trading was done over a noon-day meal and both parties went away content in thinking they'd gotten the better of the deal.

"All right, Sam, you're as comfortable as I can make you and dinner...Well, it's going to be awhile." GW pointed to the blackened mutton and then said in English, "So, can you please tell us what's going on and why you're here? Understand I am happy to see the both of you. But you have our curiosity up big time."

Mushid, who had removed his turban, a dark brown wrapping he often wore when not in his blue uniform and poured some water over his sweaty head to cool him down. Always the warrior, he continued to stand on guard while the others sat. He heard GW's foreign words and waved his wet right hand at GW in protest, "Though this is your camp, my young friend, it is not polite to speak in your foreign tongue. If we are indeed friends, for we have been in battle together and with great courage we have slain our hated enemy, then all should understand what is being said here between us."

GW looked up at Mushid for a moment with a blank expression, as he struggled briefly over a few of the words Mushid had used and then replied in Libyan, "Yes, you are right, my friend and I do apologize." GW finished with a smile upon his lips.

Sam looked up at his large friend and waved his hand around the fire pit at his friends, "My clansmen have worked hard to learn our words, but sometimes they slip back into the language of our home and for this, you must not be offended for no offense was meant. Truly, you are their friend and mine and," Sam raised his voice a bit, returning to his usual and all too recognizable growl, "I wish for you to sit down now, my friend."

Sam was uneasy enough being here in Egypt and Mushid wasn't helping with his constant vigilance, yet he knew Mushid was probably right in maintaining a watchful eye on the surrounding desert. But he also knew his old friend, though still a great warrior, was growing old and needed to rest when possible.

"I am used to your growls, old man, but I must remain wary for we are in Egypt and not all are like those friendly herdsmen we traded with."

"I know we are in Egypt!" Sam growled again in a louder voice. "If you want play guard, go ahead, but do it sitting down as you're making me nervous with your pacing about."

Mushid shook his head in frustration, "You sit here, old man and tell your tale. I'll check the horses and walk the perimeter to ensure you are not disturbed with an Egyptian arrow in that large Irish stomach of yours." With scimitar in hand, Mushid walked toward the horses while GW continued to grow impatient for he wanted to hear news about his princess and suspected she must have something to do with Sam's taking such a dangerous and painstaking journey to find them.

Paul, who had seriously grown weary of fish, had most of his attention devoted to the roasting mutton shank and for the moment, he continued to slowly turn the spit and rotate the meat over the burning coals. He had tried to keep the meat from turning so black, but he lost the battle and now fought to keep the meat from becoming too well-done to enjoy. The trick was to get the inner parts of the meat cooked. Too many times he'd bitten into a shank only to find the inner parts raw and distasteful. He truly missed a good old-fashioned hamburger with all the trimmings

"Sam, I'm about to throw you in that lagoon over there if you don't tell me why you've found us," GW said in a tense voice. His hands were now clenched into tight fists and it was his worry for his princess that was making him this way.

"All right, lad, I was simply trying to figure out how best to tell you all that's happened since you three left Silene," Sam said. He kept moving his hands around nervously while sitting there in hopes of thinking up the best way to begin. He was also struggling to find a better position for his large rump. The wagon ride had been rough on his old physique and he was not looking forward to the long ride back. He seriously missed automobiles, a train ride, a decent hamburger and especially his wife's tender smile and a long kiss when he came home from a hard day at the base.

"I really must go on a diet," Sam said as he patted his huge stomach.

"Sam!" Richard exclaimed. His outburst surprised Paul.

"You too, huh?" Sam replied, with a shake of his head and a grin.

"I'm sorry, sir," Richard said. He bowed his head shamefully.

"Please, just start at the beginning," GW suggested.

Sam released a deep audible sigh, looked up to the heavens briefly and then gazed upon GW for a moment before he began his tale of woe. Then he began his dark tale and spoke of how the guards learned too late the Black Princess had had a secret passageway down into the lower levels of the castle keep. Once free of the guards, she made her way to the castle's mosque and sought asylum from the king's mullah. Being a very old, but faithful man, who, we came to know later, was also fearful of Princess Lonnia's dark powers. He allowed her to stay there and sent word to the king of her presence and how he had granted her safety under the Great Prophet's laws. The mullah also allowed her the use of his servants to summon a few of the army officers loyal to her from the bribes she had paid them in the past.

"She wanted revenge against her father, and, also against me," Sam said. "She quickly made her plans with those same army officers and I hope they all rot in Hell for their disloyalty to their king."

Richard was surprised by Sam's statement, for it was not one of a forgiving nature and they all knew Sam had pretty much become the monk he pretended to be, and Richard had to ask, "Was there a coup, Sam? Did the army rise up to seize the kingdom?"

"No, that didn't happen—at least not yet anyway. Too many of the soldiers are either fearful of the Royal Guardsmen or they distrust the Black Princess. She found her assistance limited, which left her a prisoner inside the mosque and there was no way for her to safely leave the castle. Every guard was poised to arrest her had she attempted to leave the grounds.

"So, she came up with another idea, one I suspect she was already planning and put it into action with the help of her few key officers. I might also add these officers were all from the army ranks and not one traitor from the Royal Guardsmen.

"Anyway, by now King Ramie and I knew Princess Lonnia was in the mosque, but the king would not violate the laws of the prophet and forcefully remove her."

Paul looked over his shoulder at Sam and interrupted, "I thought it was the Catholics who did this church asylum bit?"

"You're right, Catholics have used asylum, or I should say sanctuary for centuries and so do the Muslims I've recently learned. This means she is safe there and the Mullah will ensure her well-being while she remains there."

"Maybe I should've run into the mosque when all this went down," GW suggested mockingly.

"Wouldn't have worked for you, lad," Sam said. "You're not Muslim and they'd have killed you for violating their holy ground."

"Okay, so what happened then?" GW asked.

Sam studied the simmering mutton shank for a moment, sighed once more as his stomach growled and then continued. He advised the three of them of how Princess Lonnia set her nefarious plan into play by having her officers spread word through the castle and township of how Princess Lennia had been chosen as the next sacrifice offering. But King Ramie was keeping it hidden until another girl could be chosen.

"What?" GW became enraged and jumped to his feet, and while doing so he accidently kicked some sand into the fire pit and spread hot ash over Paul's feet.

"Hey, cool it, man!" Paul yelled as he brushed the ash off him.

Sam gestured to GW, "Calm down, lad. There is much more to speak of and you must not lose your rationality, or all is truly lost."

GW glared at Sam, "Truly-truly-truly! You truly this and truly that, don't you get tired of this truly crap? Even when you speak English, you sound like an Arab."

Sam fought down his own anger and his desire to put GW in his place, but he remembered there was much at stake here and remained quiet as he waited for GW to finish his tirade.

After a period of vocal anguish with GW venting over all that's happened to them since leaving the firebase, he finally collapsed and placed his head and his hands and became still.

"Now that you've finished with that, I will remind you of how many years I have lived here—twice the amount of time I lived as an American. So, if I sound Arabic, or Libyan, or even Irish, you'll simply have to live with it as I have. Now may I continue?"

GW looked up with a blank expression on his face, that slowly turned into an expression of heavyheartedness weighing down upon him, "I'm sorry, Sam. None of this is your fault and you've done so much for us. I just lost it. Sorry."

"I accept your apology, lad," Sam said. He then continued, telling them of how the townspeople rose-up in their anger and demonstrated at the castle gate, where they demanded the king turn Princess Lennia over for sacrifice. Even his soldiers and some of the castle servants believed Princess Lonnia's tale, causing King Ramie to worry he was losing his control over his kingdom.

"Captain Rynarr and his Royal Guardsmen moved in to keep the soldiers and townspeople in line, but the false tale of the king's deception and corruption quickly worked its way through the ranks like blazing forest fire.

"I kept Princess Lennia in my quarters. She used your room and Captain Rynarr's most loyal guards stood outside our doors. Mushid stayed with me as a personal bodyguard in the event Princess Lonnia attempted my assassination, and the king's protection detail was doubled for the same reason.

"Court had to be temporarily closed because most of the daily petitioners only appeared to demand the king turn over his daughter. As loved as she was, too many of the townspeople had also lost their daughters, granddaughters and nieces to the lottery. They now felt it was time for the king to join with them in their grief of losing a child to Silene's curse.

"King Ramie, saddened by the whole affair, appeared at the castle gate to address the demonstrators. He offered to them a king's ransom in gold to release his daughter from this duty. This was all the money he owned, without going into the town's coffers, but the people wouldn't listen to him. Some of them actually began assaulting the gate with stones and axes. They had to be driven off by mounted men.

"Captain Rynarr pulled the king back and was eventually forced to have his bowmen fire into the crowd to finally disperse them. Five of the townspeople fell with arrows in them and I was the one who worked feverishly to save them after the crowd fled. Three out of the five died, but with the Lord's help I was able to save the other two."

"Sounds like one of our race riots back home," Richard said as he recalled the 1960's Watts Riots of Southern California and how many people were struck down by their own neighbors.

"When I returned to my quarters to rest, I found Princess Lennia waiting for me. She wanted to see her father and as I suspected, she insisted her father put a stop to all this by offering up herself."

"No!" GW shouted, and he leapt to his feet and began to stomp off toward his Valiant.

Sam stretched his arms out, "Wait, I'm not finished."

GW shook his head in frustration, returned to the fire pit and told Sam to go on. But he remained standing, with his hands on his hips.

"King Ramie denied her request at first, but as the disturbances grew into riots and several people were killed and buildings, including a stable were set on fire, he finally relinquished and appeared before the townspeople once more.

"Standing on a battlement and with a deep sadness over him, he spoke on how Princess Lennia herself requested to fulfill her duty and become the next offering to the dragon.

"But, I had spoken with him briefly before his announcement and talked him into giving me ten days to come up with a plan to destroy the creature. Now you must understand this went past the time allotted for the sacrifice, but the townspeople didn't seem to care once the king announced his decision." Sam then looked to his three comrades and said, "An additional count of 30-sheep is to be offered up on the prescribed day."

"But why the ten-days, Sam?" Paul asked. He'd stopped turning the spit as all his attention had gone into Sam's story and the mutton was beginning to burn on the side facing the hot coals.

"Turn the meat, Paul, or we'll end up eating charcoaled mutton," Sam said.

Mushid had returned at this point. Looked to Sam and said, "Have you told him?"

Sam looked at his friend with an expression of one perturbed, "No, I haven't gotten to it yet."

"Time is valuable, we must leave soon, or all is lost," Mushid said in an unusually testy voice. He then continued walking guard by circling the encampment and keeping a wary eye on the surrounding desert and outward over the dark waters to the north.

"That's the fourth or fifth time I've heard this 'all is lost' bit. What's lost?" GW asked.

"We must destroy the dragon or Princess Lennia dies. If she dies, King Ramie will die heartbroken and Princess Lonnia will then seize the throne. With her in power, darkness will cover the kingdom...at least until the Caliph sends an army to seize the castle and execute her. But I have heard through one of my sources of how that witch, for that is what she is, is trying to gain some form of access to the dragon...to use it as her weapon to secure the Caliph's throne and then probably all of North Africa. She sees herself as another Cleopatra.

"What will happen once old Cleopatra is taken down by the Caliph?" Richard asked.

"I imagine the Great Imam will have his way and the kingdom of Silene would be divided up into smaller parcels, picked up by greedy land barons and the kingdom, as we know it, is no more. All is lost...as I have said," Sam said.

"Wow!" Paul exclaimed. "And you think that's going to happen?" Paul reached across with his hand to test the meat by pulling off a sliver of lamb to taste.

"It will, if we don't kill the dragon and this is where GW comes in," Sam said. He watched as Paul savored the meat and grinned.

"Me?" GW asked.

"You!" Sam replied, and he pointed his right index finger at GW's chest. "My weapon will not be ready for some time, too late to kill the beast and save Princess Lennia."

Sam then gave GW another hard look, "No, my lad, it is you who must do battle with the dragon and, this is why we must return in haste." Sam, smelling the cooked meat, looked at the mutton and said, "I'll take mine now if you don't mind." He then slowly stood to his feet to stretch his backside and grimaced as his beefy legs creaked loudly, followed by a quiet cracking of his lower back. He then rotated his neck gently and listened to a gentle popping sound. Lord, I sure get weary of getting old.

Accepting a good-sized slab of meat, he smiled his thanks and then said, "I do not look forward to the ride back, but we must leave soon."

"Sam, I'm missing something here. You expect me to fight it out with some 50-foot tall dragon...and win?"

"I thought you loved her, lad? Of how you would give your life for her...Have you changed your mind?" Sam asked.

"No...I do, I would, or I will. But a dragon...I mean a dinosaur?" GW said in English. He locked eyes with Sam. "How am I supposed to defeat that monster? Sure, give me an automatic rifle, some grenades and I've got half a chance. But all I've got is this scimitar and I'm a bit small for close combat with a critter that's got a good 30-foot reach with its neck."

Sam smiled again, surprising GW and the others. He then walked up to GW, stood before him and put his one free hand on his shoulder. With the way his stomach was growling he wasn't about to part with his dinner. "Listen, lad, you will fight this foul beastie and you will vanquish it to the Hell that spawned it. After which, you will marry the princess, bring salvation to this kingdom and live happily ever after...a real fairy tale come to life."

"Sam, this isn't some fairy tale and I'm not some prince with a magical sword to slay the dragon. For that you've got to look to Walt Disney."

"No, it's not a fairy tale...but a legend you've walked right into. You have a gallant steed and the courage for the task at hand, and yes you have a magical weapon of a sort." Sam patted GW on the shoulder with his large hand and turned to walk over to his wagon. While he walked he was chewing on his meat. He was not one to let a good piece of mutton go to waste.

"Boy, you can say I'm really confused now," GW said. Both of his comrades nodded their heads in agreement as they watched Sam approach the wagon.

Mushid then returned and spotted Sam over at the wagon going through his pack of belongings. He knew what the priest was looking for and quietly nodded his head in approval, until he saw a troubled GW standing by the fire pit and realized Brother Samuel hadn't finished breaking all the news to him.

Paul, glancing between Sam and GW, returned to cutting up the meat. He was struggling to figure out what was going on here. But he'd been a bit off kilter since leaving the cave months ago and wished Dorothy would tap her red shoes together and they'd all go home. Meanwhile, Richard, the thinker of the three, studied the sands at his feet and tried to make some sense of what Sam had just told them.

Worried about the time they were using up and with a look of determination on his face, Mushid walked right up to GW and slapped him on the shoulder with his gloved hand, "Watching you defeat the Egyptians with ease, I was still unsure if you were the one spoken of in prophecy. I did not want to hope, but I trained you hard to prepare you for what lie ahead. But your faith continued to concern me, for I believed the chosen one to be a Muslim knight of great strength." Mushid then pointed to Valiant, "But I am only a man and must accept the will of Allah and his mysterious ways, for I have seen this strange bonding between you and your horse, a thing I have never seen before. Truly an infidel is the chosen one of our ancient prophecy."

"Chosen one?" GW asked in Arabic and then switched back to English, "What's this chosen one bit, Sam? C'mon, give me something, anything, but you guys are driving me crazy here."

Mushid seemed to ignore the impoliteness of GW's foreign tongue and stood nearby, as Sam returned from the wagon carrying a small canvas satchel. Again, he stood before a very anxious and confused young man.

Gulping down the bite in his mouth, he let out a loud burp and then began, "Excuse me, that was rather impolite of me by our western standards...Now, you must listen, lad. We have only minutes and then you will need to make all haste in returning to Silene in time to save your lovely princess."

"You've got all my attention, Sam…though I am really confused."

"God save us!" Sam said in aspiration. "Okay now, Mushid and I were in my study looking over my various weapon designs, hoping to find something I might be able to assemble with the parts already completed for the new spear launcher. I came across this," Sam opened his satchel and pulled out the flint piece the Montegnard holy man had presented to GW.

"Yeah, I remember you wanted to study it and I never got it back from you."

"Right," Sam said. "But what I hadn't noticed before is your handwritten note you kept wrapped up with it and when I read the word out loud, our big friend here got really excited and he repeated the word right back to me, 'Ascalon'." Sam then handed the flint piece to GW.

"Yeah, I wrote it down because I knew I'd forget it otherwise. The old holy man said the word belonged to this, but even he didn't understand what the word meant."

"Some very old prophets believed the word or name came from an ancient Middle East town called 'Ashkelon'," Sam said.

"How'd you know that?" Richard asked.

"Mushid told me. It was part of the ancient prophecy," Sam replied. He then looked back at GW, "It seems there is a prophecy told around here from very long ago, back when Silene was a growing Christian kingdom and Islam hadn't blazed across North Africa. The prophecy spoke of how a stranger would appear one day, a brave knight, who rode upon a proud steed like no other. This knight would rid the kingdom of this cursed dragon. But more importantly, he would carry a shield bearing the cross of the one true God and a lance he called, 'Ascalon'.

"So, after some preparation and a private meeting with King Ramie and Captain Rynarr, Mushid and I secretly left Silene and followed the coastline in hopes of catching you before someone either killed you off or enslaved you."

GW was speechless, but not Paul, "So just the two of you rode into enemy territory to find us?"

"Only from the border," Sam said. "We have a company of Royal Guardsmen waiting for us at the border to escort us into

Silene and prevent the princess's army from interfering with what GW must do to fulfill prophecy and establish the legend."

GW was walking in small circles, looking at his feet with the flint piece lying across both of his hands. This whole prophecy thing was overwhelming and now he was again recalling the weird little holy man back at the firebase and of course the events that soon followed. But this legend thing was now clouding his mind and he stopped abruptly to face off with Sam.

"Okay, old man. You know I'd give my life for her and with what's happened so far, I can almost buy into this prophecy bit because I'm staring right down at this chunk of rock. I've learned to live with this whole time-travel bit...time bubbles or whatever, but now you're talking about some legend and I just don't understand what you're rattling on about? That's a dinosaur back there and I've got this rock here."

Sam face broke out into a grin and then widened it into a smile, "You're an extremely humble man, George. Lord always uses humble men for the harder tasks to be carried out."

GW glared at him and stammered out, "How'd you know my name was George? And I really hate that name, so let's not use it again, okay?"

"George?" Paul said. "Well the G had to stand for something, but I thought it might be Greg or Gary. What's the middle initial stand for, George?" Paul asked with that look of mischief in his eyes he was known for.

"Whitney!" George growled. "George Whitney Sanders! I was named after my mother's grandfather. But do me a favor and never use it again, I've always preferred GW."

Sam shook his head, "Sorry, George, but in the legend, you do not go by GW, you go as George."

"That dang legend again!" George exclaimed as he dropped the flint piece on the sand and shot both hands up over his head. His hands were balled into fists and he was ready to burst a seam.

That's when a look of surprise and realization exploded all over Richard's face, "I've got it! I've got it!" Richard yelled as he jumped about and patted both Mushid and Paul on their backs before he raced up to George and grabbed him around the shoulders and hugged him.

"What have you got?" Paul asked as he looked at Richard with a look of alarm on his face. Mushid, he already knew the truth and simply stood there with an expression of satisfaction. He knew this young Christian was here to fulfill the prophecy and free his kingdom of this curse.

"About time." Sam growled, but his sneer soon broke out into another big smile as he saw the confused expression on the hero's face.

"Okay, Professor, you've got it. So, explain it to me and remember I'm a bit dimwitted so use real small words," George said in a threatening tone, as he glared at Richard and pushed him away.

"Don't you get it, Corporal?" Richard said. His voice was filled with enthusiasm as he shouted, "You're George!"

"Right, I'm George and I've always been George."

"You don't understand," Richard said as he knelt-down and picked up the flint piece, careful not to touch the edges for they were extremely sharp.

"Then explain it to me!" George shouted.

"Easy, George," Sam said in a calming voice. "Let me explain it, Richard."

"Sure, Sam," Richard said a bit more calmly, but he was still excited.

Sam looked over at Mushid, "My good friend, I'm going to explain this to him in our home language as he still struggles with some of the Arabic words and we have so little time."

Mushid nodded his head in agreement, but remained standing close by, for he remained fearful for enemy attack and the fire pit had released a lot of black smoke.

"George, do you remember your children's fables, maybe some mythology from high school where a knight by the name of St. George killed a dragon and saved a princess?"

"Sure, everyone knows about St. George and the..." George stopped abruptly, and his eyes grew wide. "You've got to be kidding me! That's supposed to be me?"

"Looks like it, buddy," Paul said as he took the rest of the mutton off the fire and complained, "I don't think there's enough to go around, guys."

Sam laughed, "Don't worry, Paul. We'll have more for the trip back. But give the remainder to George and Mushid, for they will need the strength for their ride ahead."

"I can't believe it's taken us this long to figure it out," Richard added. "I kept looking at the dinosaur as a fantastic discovery, not as a dragon from some fairy tale."

"Makes me think of King Kong, you know that old 1933 flick where the giant ape breaks through a huge wall to steal the princess, they go to New York and at the end some heroic dude rescues her." Paul then assumed the figure of an ape and scratched the sides of his chest and made ape-like facial expressions.

"You left out the part where the Air Force zapped Kong with machineguns." George reminded him.

"Don't kick yourself, Richard," Sam said. He then tried to get the image of King Kong out of his mind and frowned at Paul.

"Lads, I didn't come to realize this until Mushid shared with me the ancient prophecy. Since then I've tried to remember the legend, but I can only recall how George here will win and something very big is going to happen to Silene when he does." Sam then turned to find George collapsed to the sand. He was lying on his back, his eyes tightly shut as he struggled with the breaking news that he, George Whitney Sanders, was to become the legendary figure of St. George and the Dragon fame. And Dad thought I'd probably make a good tradesman, boy if he only knew!

"Now listen, George, I know this is a lot to take in. Mushid has gone over the prophecy with me several times and as I've said, I've tried to recall the catholic legend for which you would someday become a saint..." Sam was interrupted by George. "A saint—me?"

"Yes, a saint. Remember, you'll be known as St. George."

"But I'm not catholic!" George exclaimed.

Sam's responded with the shaking of his head, "That means little in these times, George. It will be a while before the protestant faith comes about."

"Whatever," George said in surrender. Then he added a bit of sarcasm and said, "What else do I have to do besides kill a 50-foot dragon? You got any giant apes around, maybe a one-eyed giant or two...or how about a giant squid?"

"Easy, kid," Sam said. Ignoring his own discomfort, he reached down and offered a large aged hand to his young friend. "I know you're scared, but we already know the outcome of this duel and you win."

"What happens if I lose?" George asked. He grasped Sam's hand and stood to his feet.

"Then you're not the right George, the princess dies and Silene has to wait for the real guy to come along."

George shook his head, "Thanks, Sam. That helped a lot."

"You asked," Sam said. "But we'll go on believing you're the right guy, okay?"

"Well, what have I got to do?"

"Knowing the prophecy and the legend to follow, I spent all day and most of the night preparing your armor. You'll carry a reinforced lance with a special fitting for that piece of flint. I believe and so does Mushid, this flint will pierce the creature's hide where no other lance would, and you'll carry a special shield." Sam left George's side and returned to the wagon. He soon walked back with a large shield in his hands. It was painted white and on it was a large red cross painted in Celtic style.

"I saw an old Cecil B. DeMille movie before the war, it was called The Crusades," Sam said. "All the knights carried shields, but their cross was red on a white surface. Of course, the cross stands for our Lord Jesus Christ and there is something in the legend about the shield too."

"How do you plan to fit the flint piece into the lance?" Richard asked. He grasped the shield, liked the feel of it on his left arm and smiled as he thought of Sam using an Irish style cross to go with the tale of their background. He also noticed the blue paint of the cross was identical to the color used by the Royal Guardsmen.

"That's the easiest part. We'll put it together with a groove and heavy reinforced strapping. Much like the Indians used for the arrows in the Old West with their flint arrowheads and similar–to what the army here uses for their arrows," Sam replied.

"I'll get started on that right now, because you, Mushid and Paul have to start as soon as I've completed it. Richard and I will follow with the wagon as fast as we can, but time is of the essence."

George studied the shield bearing the cross of Christ, looked to the heavens and whispered a brief prayer of, "Are you sure about this, Lord?"

## CASTLE OF SILENE
## INSIDE THE MOSQUE

The mullah, who sincerely wished he could be elsewhere for the moment, stayed away from the Black Princess as much as possible. He only provided one servant to care for her needs. Whenever one of the army officers entered the mosque to speak with Princess Lonnia, the Mullah looked down upon the man for his traitorous and blasphemous conduct for serving such an evil personage. Twice he had attempted to send messages to the Great Imam, hoping to advise him of the current happenings, but the messengers were intercepted, and the carrier slain by those soldiers loyal to Princess Lonnia.

Believing her plan for revenge and eventual seizure of the throne was working, Princess Lonnia laughed loudly when she gazed upon the bare walls of her small empty room and relished in the thought of how this citadel to the Muslim faith was protecting her from her father's soldiers. In less than a week, a creature, one spawned from the very Hell she worshipped, would devour her baby-sister.

Afterward, her father would become heartsick and guilt-stricken, unable to continue-on as king. Then she, with the support of her loyal officers and 300-soldiers, would quickly move in to seize the throne before Captain Rynarr could bring enough of his Royal Guardsmen in to stop her. Most of them were patrolling in the outer areas of the kingdom and only those assigned to the castle and one company of horsemen remained here. What she couldn't decide on was whether to leave her father rotting in the dungeon for a lifetime of torture, or entertain the locals with a public execution to show who was now in charge? There was also the question of the Caliph and the Great Imam, would they seek to remove her? She knew a war would mean an expensive campaign and there was always the loss of life. Would the Caliph think it was worth it? In any event she would need an escape plan, one that would take her to Alexandria. There, she knew of several secret sects who still worshipped the dark gods of old Egypt and she would find a welcome there.

## CASTLE KEEP
## PRINCESS LENNIA'S PRIVATE CHAMBERS

Two loyal Royal Guardsmen guarded the princess's door against intruders, while another two heavily armed guards patrolled the passageway. Inside the room, a grief stricken young lady lay on her bed while her handmaidens attempted to comfort her with soothing words. She knew her days were numbered, and sleep only meant nightmares with images of the dragon tearing her body apart.

"You must rest, Princess," a handmaiden suggested repeatedly.

She was too weak from crying to even respond. She had spent long hours praying to Allah but felt no satisfaction as she waited for some answer.

Captain Rynarr had appeared and she sent her handmaidens away. He came to advise her of Brother Samuel's venture into Egypt, attempting to locate the three who were banished. Before he left her room, he approached her and whispered into her ear, "If it happens, my princess, I will not leave you alive to face this horrendous fate."

"What are you saying, Captain?"

"I've done it before and for you I will do it again." He pulled out his dagger, "It will be over quickly, and you will feel little pain."

"But you risk much," she said and rested her hand on his arm.

"No, I risk little for after you die the kingdom will crumble. Your father, he will never be the same and your sister will seize the throne. Since I have confronted her many times in the past, I will be the first to be executed. So, you see I risk little by my act of mercy."

Princess Lennia looked in Captain Rynarr's eyes, "Do you think Brother Samuel and...my love will have any chance at all against the dragon?"

He backed away from her, remained silent and left her to her returning handmaidens, for he wasn't sure how to answer her question and wasn't one to give false hope.

She watched him go through the door and was unsure of why he wouldn't answer her. She then walked over to the window to look out over the courtyard and recall those timeless hours of watching her lover train with his beautiful stallion.

She thought it strange how she referred to him as her lover, for they had only shared a single kiss to the cheek, but lover was how she felt. Now depressed, she contemplated jumping, but after several long moments she knew this wasn't the answer.

"I must give Brother Samuel and my young knight an opportunity to come up with some plan to save our kingdom— even if it proves futile," She whispered to herself.

Right then, an alarm was sounded from the direction of the Great Wall. Several antelope horns were blown to announce the dragon's approach.

She looked to the south but was unable to see much of the barrier wall to the north. Though she did see a company of army horsemen leave the stables at a fast trot and others on foot making a dash for another section of stables to prepare their mounts.

From this activity, she knew the creature was drawing dangerously close to the wall, having devoured the small herd of sheep and the entire reserve force was being called up. This would mean huge catapults and though they proved ineffective in the past, these huge contraptions were being pushed into line behind the wall. Canvas bails, well-oiled, would be lit and then launched against the creature, attempting to drive the dragon back to the lake. Spear launchers with single shafts four-feet in length, smaller versions of the weapon Sam had planned recently, were also being prepped to defend the city if the dragon got past the wall.

Standing there at the window, unable to do anything or go anywhere, she knew the townspeople would be rushing about in fear. Those given the duty to support the army would be running to their posts, while frightened civilians with nothing to do but panic, would be seeking shelter in the town's mosque. Only if the creature broke past the Great Wall would the civilians be allowed to enter the castle grounds, but this had never happened for as long as anyone could remember.

But then after several long moments, another single horn was blasted, giving notice, the creature was returning to its watery home and everyone in Silene breathed a great sigh of relief. Everyone except for Princess Lennia, for she knew this close encounter would probably cause the townspeople to demand for her day of sacrifice to be moved up.

For today should've been the day of sacrifice and she knew the dragon had come looking for her. How it knew this was the day she couldn't fathom, but it had made its appearance and now the townspeople were frightened. Especially those few guards who stood guard along the Great Wall and came very close to having an extremely dangerous encounter with a hungry dragon. Why or how, she couldn't understand how this foul beast could know the difference between 30-sheep and a single small young lady.  But by the actions the vile animal was demonstrating it was clearly was not happy in finding only the sheep this time. This made her wonder what the beast would do if no sacrifice, be it a virgin or a lamb, was made to it and what would happen to Silene?

# 18 – THE RETURN

Wearing the non-stretchable long-sleeved shirt of heavy mail Mushid had provided him, George now felt as if he was lugging around an extra 50-pounds of dead weight. With his body already covered in thick layers of sweat, the armor slid over his shoulders with only a little effort. George noticed the chain links of his mail shirt were heavily tarnished and damaged in several places, particularly in the heart region, but decided not to comment on it since it was a gift from a friend. Mushid then added the deep blue tunic of the Silene Royal Guardsmen, which dropped to George's knees, but the young man couldn't help but feel a wave of pride flow through him as Mushid inspected him and made a few adjustments here and there. Mushid also added the thick leather belt to hold George's scimitar and dagger. But George continued to wear his threadbare Army green fatigue pants, which by now were covered with various patches of a brown canvas material and grease stains of all shapes and sizes. He used the hand cut leather laces to secure his badly beaten up GI jungle boots and last of all, Mushid placed upon George's head his own guardsman's turban. Mushid polished the silvery metal top and added one last buff before leaving it on George's head.

A very nervous George walked about to let his friends look him over, "So, what do you think—dragon bait or heroic figure?"

"Quite dashing, really," Richard replied in English. "But if you've seen one 12th century desert knight, you've seen them all," he added mockingly. But Mushid didn't understand the words and he frowned at Richard.

"Sorry, big guy," Richard said hastily in English and then switched to Libyan. "I said he looked real good."

"Me, I'd go with dragon bait," Paul said. "Add some ketchup..." He then growled in his best Grizzly Bear imitation, followed-up with a grunt, then a grin. "Nah, you look good, GW. Only wish I was going with you to watch your back."

Sam stepped up with another shirt of mail and another blue tunic, "Oh you are, lad, didn't I mention it."

Paul turned and stared at Sam for a moment and pointed at the grinning hero, "I thought this was his bit. No one said old St. George had a sidekick and we all know what happens to the comic sidekick; he the one that gets killed first!"

"Not too worry, Paul, you'll only ride with him as far as the Great North Wall. You're there to help prevent Princess Lonnia's men from interfering with our plans." Sam handed the armor over to a not-so-inclined young corporal.

Paul looked down at the armor and tunic for a moment and then glanced over his shoulder at his Black Arabian, "Guess that's why you brought my horse, huh?"

"I knew you'd want to be with George. To 'cover his back' as you just said." Sam, struggling not to smile, then turned to Richard. "Unfortunately, my Sudanese friend, you're stuck with this fat old man." He pointed to the wagon, "Knowing your adversity to horseback riding, you'll have to ride in that horrid wagon with me."

Richard looked at his two friends, sighed and then upon returning his eyes to Sam, he said with a graceful bow, "It is my pleasure and my honor to accompany you, Sir."

"Thank you, Richard. Now we'd better get moving and get his lance ready and if you're nice, I'll let you drive."

Both George and Paul resembled turtles with their oval shields strapped on to their backs for the long ride back to Silene. White oval shields with a red Celtic cross painted on both and two inner leather straps to hold the shield securely with their left forearm.

"Man, I really feel like a knight now," Paul said. "But I sure hope I'm still around for the victory party."

"You're too ornery to die, Paul," Richard said in English.

"Maybe, but I'd feel better with an M-60 in my hands. You guys know I was never any good with a lance."

Mushid asked Sam for a translation and upon hearing of Paul's concern he nodded his head in agreement and walked back over to the wagon. There he lifted a pile of blankets in the back and pulled out a weapon he was saving for himself. He approached

Paul and presented the weapon to him, "Use this, we'll leave the lance in the wagon."

Paul was impressed with the pure savagery of the heavy mace in his hands and began waving it about to get the feel of it. The wooden handle, a bit thicker than a broom handle, was wrapped in camel skin for a good grasp and slightly over two-feet in length. From its end, three separate heavy chains sprouted out; each one made of 12-metal links and at the end they each carried a heavy metal spike ball about the size of a tennis ball.

"Wow, I can do a lot of head banging with this thing," Paul said and then turned to thank Mushid.

"Make sure you don't hit your horse in the process," Richard said. But he smiled and shook his head in wonder at his friend's boyish attitude concerning highly lethal weaponry.

George, the name he decided to go by now, walked over to the wagon and pulled his special lance out. He marveled at the work Sam had done to reinforce the lengthy shaft, knowing he must have spent quite a bit of time on it. Unlike any other lance, the heavy wood was wrapped in metal armor to keep it from shattering. Sam had also grooved the end of the lance to slide the flint piece into it and then while George was suiting up, he had strapped it into place with long lengths of wet camel hide. As the hide dried, it would tighten until the flint piece was secure and its point could handle the piercing of the dragon's thick hide. With the lance heavier than usual, Mushid created a boot for the hand piece to slide into and allow George to carry it easily until he needed it. After seeing how well it worked, Mushid decided he would construct one for himself and Captain Rynarr when he returned to Silene.

When he saw that the men were saddled up and ready to leave, Sam approached the three horsemen and said a prayer over George and Paul as they knelt before him. For these two, he blessed them in English, but he surprised them when he followed it up with a prayer in Arabic for Mushid's benefit. Sam believed the Lord would understand for it made his friend content with what lay ahead and Mushid put his gloved hand upon Sam's shoulder and nodding his head in thanks.

Richard walked over to pet Valiant's neck while he spoke with George, "You'll never be able to pierce the creature's chest; its bones are too heavy for that. For a quick kill, you will need to drive your lance in at the base of its neck, in the front, right above the chest plate." Richard pointed at the bottom of his own throat, "Drive it in as hard as you can. This should either pierce the heart or at least severe its main artery."

"Any other advice for me, Professor?" George asked. He then reached down to shake hands with his friend.

"Yeah, be wary of its front fins. It will swing them to knock you away or off your horse. Remember, this creature has been fighting highly skilled knights for a very long time and I suspect you'll have only one shot to get in under its neck and make the kill. With its neck reach, you won't get a second chance and if you get thrown from your horse, run like the flames of Hell were coming at you...because they are!"

"Thanks," George replied. "Gee, I'm beginning to wish you could be there, too."

"I know you're joking, but I really hate to miss this," Richard said. With a concerned look, he then glanced back over at Sam, "But I'd better stay with Sam...He isn't looking too good."

"Yeah, I noticed- he's a bit pale. The ride out here took a lot out of him." George looked over at Sam again and waved cheerfully. "Thanks, Old Man for everything. If this works out, I'll name my first son after you."

"You do that," Sam said in a weary voice.

"We ride now," Mushid said. He mounted his horse and then waved quickly to Sam and Richard for them to follow. He put his spurs to his horse and rode westward. Mushid planned to ride all night, which they could do as long as they kept the shoreline to their right. This way they wouldn't get lost in the vast and featureless Egyptian desert.

Riding hard, George was pleasantly surprised to see how much ground they covered on horseback and it felt good to be on the back of Valiant once more. He talked with his horse as they rode, behaving much like two teammates preparing for the big game.

During the early morning hours, before sun-up, they surprised a night herdsman when they came over a sand dune and suddenly came upon Makeen's heard of sheep. George shouted a greeting, but now wearing his tunic and mounted upon Valiant, the frightened herdsman didn't recognize him and only responded with a loud curse, before he turned and fled toward Makeen's encampment.

Not having the time to visit Makeen, they rode on and nearly two hours later they rode by the burned ruins of the small community where they buried the skulls. As the sun reached its zenith, George realized they had crossed into Libya. Here, they came upon the Royal Guardsmen camp and found the company of men sitting about, some eating or gambling with handmade wooden dice, while others were simply taking the time for a noonday nap after prayers.

Mushid rode right into camp, startling the men, who jumped to their feet and rushed for their weapons until they recognized the angry face of their leader. It wasn't until then that George realized Mushid had been promoted to a rank equal to that of a US Army captain. He was in-charge of this company.

Mushid was upset to find only two guards posted and neither of them had spotted the three horsemen before Mushid had entered the encampment. They had too large of a fire burning during the day, which let off a large black smoke plume to mark their position. Clearly upset, Mushid dismounted his sweating horse and stormed over to the man he had left in command. Without a word, he knocked him to the ground with a backhanded slap and only then did he voice his displeasure for the man's lack of attention to security.

"Remind me to never let Mushid catch me sleeping on post," Paul said to George. They both studied the man's bloody face and how he was now missing front tooth.

"You'd never sleep on post," George said. "Then again, you might goof off if your princess was about. So, get a good look at that guy's new dental work. He won't be eating anything solid for a week or two."

George soon learned how all the remaining Royal Guardsmen officers had remained in Silene to assist Captain Rynarr in the protection of King Ramie and Princess Lennia. With a large force of Royal Guardsmen riding the desert country to the south, accompanying Princess Lannia, and out of contact, the number of guardsman inside the castle were extremely few. Too few to stand-off the regular army and townspeople. If the army had decided to stage a coup, there would be little the guardsmen could do but escort King Ramie and the princess to safety through underground passages few people knew about.

"Break camp, we ride now for Silene immediately!" Mushid ordered in a loud grumpy voice.

Knowing it would take several moments for the men to saddle up; George and Paul took this opportunity to water and feed their weary horses. They also had a few minutes to feed themselves with what little food was available and stretch out their legs and aching backs. But it was made apparent some of the guardsmen had spent some of their leisure time fishing, because there were several large fish roasting over one of the fire-pits.

When they first rode in the men didn't recognize George, but once he dropped his veil to show his damp face, they walked up to him. Fearful at first, they might want to exact vengeance for his reported misconduct with the princess, he was greatly relieved for friendly black slaps and greetings of friendship. George was told they had heard from Mushid of what actually happened and how he reminded them of the ancient prophecy of the lone knight saving Silene. He also added in how the princess felt about this man. Once more they welcomed him into their ranks and it moistened George's deeply tanned cheeks with tears.

Some of them didn't believe in the prophecy, but they knew better than to confront Mushid. But they liked this man and were busy showing their fondness for George by knocking him to the ground with their joyous vigor. Still, upon seeing George mounted upon Valiant as he rode in, carrying his special lance with the strange point, it brought a sense of hope and this feeling spread quickly through the ranks of horsemen. A few of them had also fought alongside George during the battle with the Egyptian raiders and while waiting for Mushid to return from Egypt, they had told the rest of how George had slain ten of the raiders and saved Captain Rynarr's life. So even before confronting the dragon, George had become a warrior legend to the Royal Guardsmen.

Once camp was broken up, the fires put out and the men mounted, the company rode westward in a column of twos. Mushid led, with George and Paul following behind him. Two guardsmen followed a safe distance behind as rear guard, a single horseman stayed several hundred yards out in front as point and another horseman rode out wide to the left flank. With the ocean to their right they needed no one to ride that flank. Mushid knew by the countryside's natural markings that they had returned to Libyan soil, but he had no trust for what the Egyptians or some Berber pirate captain might do, and ambush was always on his mind. These guards would protect the main body from surprise attack, possibly sacrificing themselves to warn the others. If Berber pirates were to sweep in, Mushid would hopefully see their sales from a long way off. His only concern with pirates was if they had seen them ride toward Egypt earlier and had come ashore to plan a surprise attack for the returning horsemen. The horses the men rode, were extremely valuable, along with the weapons and any wealth they carried.

Both Paul and George were already sore from the constant bruising of their backsides from the long ride and it was rapidly turning into sheer torture. George was beginning to wonder if he'd be in any condition to do battle with a 20-ton Dino?

"Mushid, we've got to stop soon. I'll be in no shape to fight a dragon, not after a ride like this," George pleaded.

"No time!" Mushid shouted to him. "We must reach Silene to see what is happening. Then you may rest." He followed it up with a whisper of doubt that he didn't think George would hear, "We might already be too late."

But George did hear him, and he shouted out, "No! We're not too late. If I am the knight in the prophecy, we will arrive in time. If not...it does not matter."

"You got some special sixth sense, buddy?" Paul asked through clenched teeth. His hands, back, butt and feet were beginning to compete to see who was sorer the most.

"I know she's all right."

"Hope you're right, buddy. I sure don't want to be going through this for nothing."

"I thought you were a cowboy?" George said in English.

Paul sneered at him, "Even cowboys take coffee breaks! You know, sit around a campfire, play a harmonica and swap lies."

Mushid ignored their English and continued to push them. They rode on for several more hours. By this time, Paul was leaning forward on his horse, trying to keep from feeling the collision of his butt against his proud Arabian's back. He was already feeling sick and was now concerned he might commit the unmentionable act of actually falling off his mount, something a cowboy only did while drunk, asleep or dying. Even the sleepy ones were noted to tie themselves to the saddle and Paul had done it himself once or twice and was thinking about doing it again now. But these saddles didn't have saddle horns and he wasn't sure what he could tie himself to.

Finally, as darkness approached from the east, George began to recognize the countryside and then he spotted the first of the castle's towers way off in the distance. He then recalled how the hillsides beyond the castle held the cave they climbed out of and this fairy tale began.

"We stop here!" Mushid ordered, bringing his company to an abrupt halt. Further orders were given to make a cold camp by the shoreline, so they would not give their position away with a plume of smoke or the flare of a fire. He then posted four guards in each direction and allowed others to walk their mounts and those of the guards, through the cool shallow waters of the Mediterranean Sea.

Satisfied with the activity, Mushid dismounted and began to walk his horse through a small breaking wave. Once he believed his mare to be cooled down, the sweat washed away by the salt water, he brought her back to camp and allowed her to drink and consume two handfuls of grain.

George and Paul were doing the same, but both were limping badly, as they carefully and cautiously led their horses through the waves. The long ride had cost them greatly and every step was painful until they unlimbered some. George, his inner thighs chapped from sweat and abuse, doubted he was in any shape for a duel with the dragon. Paul, he handed his reins to George and walked out to where there four-foot waves crested and fell face first into one.

George thought about it, but with the metal shirt on and his last experience with the waves, he decided against it and simply reached down and rinsed his face and hair off with the cool salt water. He had left his turban on his saddle and his scimitar and dagger belt strapped to it as well, not wanting the salt water to touch his fine blades. His special lance was left in the camp, protected by two men who took over the duty without asking. They both knew this weapon to be part of the prophecy and felt it an honor to guard it.

Mushid tied his horse's reins to his lance and used the lengthy weapon as an anchor when he shoved the pointed end in to the sand to keep the horse from wandering off. He knew from experience how the sand wouldn't hurt the sharpness of his lance point. He then stretched his back from side to side and while extending his arms out wide and rotating his neck from side to side, he loosened up his joints. He also cringed with each cracking sound, as his upper spine seemed to grind in its movement. Satisfied everything was popped back into place, he approached George and Paul. Both of whom showed all appearances of being in far worse shape than any of his other men.

Giving Paul a hard glare, he pointed his finger at him and warned, "Your mail will rust! You must now clean it in fresh water, then dry quickly." He then addressed George, "We will rest here. I will send my best man to the castle to make contact with Captain Rynarr. When he returns, we will know what must be done."

"Good thing we stopped, I haven't hurt this bad since Airborne training," George said in a mixture of Libyan and English. He continued to stretch, in hopes he could get all the kinks out before the appointed time.

"Airborne?" Mushid asked, he did not recognize the word, even though George had spoken most of his statement in the Libyan tongue.

George shook his head at Paul and then translated the word to mean a warrior's school in Ireland.

"Remember, old buddy, a slip of the tongue can sink a ship," Paul said in English.

"I think you mean, 'Loose lips sinks ships', a World War II slogan," George replied.

"Sorry, I'm just too tired to remember the history of the world," Paul said. With a wearied expression on his face, he leaned up against his horse and began to amble off toward a fresh water spring located on the east side of camp.

Mushid watched him walk away and then addressed George, "You must eat now, my young friend. You will need great strength for what lies ahead. Sleep if you can, we have at least a couple of hours before my rider returns with news."

"Right," George agreed. "But I'll walk Valiant a bit more while the men prepare our meal, then I will sleep."

Mushid watched George lead his mount toward the waters again and studied this brave young man and again wondered about this ancient prophecy. Was George's Christian God the one true god and Allah only a religion spread by the Moorish oppressors of long ago? Such a thought spoken out loud would have led to his death, but now his mind began to fill with doubts.

When Paul returned, his mail shirt draped over the back of his mount, he spotted George coming from the Mediterranean. "Can you believe this?" Paul asked. "If anyone had told me this could happen to us, I'd have told him he was either drunk or droppin' too much acid. Yet here we are in the 12th century, dressed up like knights, and you're about to fight some fishy dinosaur. I can't believe it. I keep expecting to wake up in some prisoner of war camp, with the Viet Cong shoving bamboo slivers up my toes."

"Hey, this whole legend bit has me shook up too, or maybe it was the last 30-hours on horseback. But I'm no hero, Paul. Oh, I'll do anything to save Princess Lennia, but going up against a dragon by myself...Man, it's time for the 7th Cavalry to come riding over the hill to save the day and I'd kiss ol' General Custer on both cheeks."

"Bad example, dude...Remember they got wiped out at the Little Big Horn."

"Thanks, I'd forgotten that for a whole 30-seconds."

George remained quiet and Paul had become too weary-eyed to say anything witty. He left his friend to his silence. But after a few moments, George took on a serious tone and approached his friend, "Do you think I can do this, Paul? Do you really think I can kill a real-live dinosaur with a ten-foot toothpick?"

Paul considered his answer. He didn't want to come off flippant when he knew his buddy wanted a serious response. After a few more steps through the sand, Paul replied, "George, the way I see it, you've got this whole legend and prophecy thing going for you and don't forget, that Montegnard holy man showed up with your lance point back in our 20th century. He also gave you its name, which is foretold in the prophecy, right?"

George nodded his head in agreement and trudged along through the sand, while he patted Valiant on the shoulder and remained silent.

"Well then, it's going to happen. You've also got Valiant there, probably the strongest and smartest horse in the land, which you have this strange-like psychic bond with. Add in the fact we're here, I'd say God was behind the whole thing." Paul pointed toward the castle, "So go kick butt, marry the princess and make lots and lots of babies."

"Thanks, buddy, you make it sound pretty easy. But what about you and Richard, what's your future and why were you brought here if my coming was an act of God?"

"What do you mean?" Paul looked back at George with a confused expression on his face.

"Well, if, and I stress the if part here, manage to kill this dragon, what are you two going to do while I'm making all these babies?"

"Oh, well I've been thinking on that, but haven't had time to talk it over with Richard yet." Paul pulled the rein on his Arabian and turned his horse around to walk in the opposite direction. George did the same and they were now heading back toward camp.

"I've been tossing the idea around about going to the Holy Land. I want to see this Jerusalem I've heard so much about. Richard knows the lingo pretty good and maybe we can help. You know, the mess those crusaders made. Sam had his story down, how he helped the women and children. Maybe we can actually do it?" Paul looked toward the heavens and then added, "I've got a lot of bad I did in Nam that I need to pay for and maybe that's why I'm here. For Richard, maybe we just needed the professor here to keep us alive."

With both horses now watered and fed, they left them tied up to a strong rope stretched across the sand. George and Paul then shared with the others a small meal of dried fish; battlefield rations, which reminded George of fish-flavored sawdust.

Sitting on the shoreline's warm sand, stripped down to bare chest as sweat poured under the hot sun, George turned to his friend, "You know, Paul, I really believe you will go to the crusades. According to Sam, the legend says it was the crusaders who take the story of St. George and the Dragon back to Europe." He pointed at Paul with a fishy finger and grinned, "You and Richard are going to be my story tellers."

"Man, this is just too weird. God must have lost a marble or two when he thought this up and chose me for the job. I nearly flunked history and geography was never my strong point either."

"I think you're the right man for the job."

"Don't go all mushy on me now, Corporal. You'd better get some sleep. I'll wake you when we get some news."

"Sounds good," George replied. He then rinsed off his hands from his water bag and rolled over on his side to catch a few winks. Sleeping in the heat of the day would be hard, but after the long ride he was snoring lightly within minutes.

Paul was worn out too, but he felt he should stay awake and watch over George, but within a moment, he too was fast asleep and entertaining the others nearby with his whistle-like snores.

Mushid looked over the two sleeping men, amazed how they and the one called Richard had affected his life in such a strong way and in such a short time. He'd come to value their friendship, but more than that, he'd come to respect them as warriors. He also felt there was something bigger here than mere mortals could understand and remembered how the ancient prophecy had come from a time when Silene was a brand-new Muslim kingdom. Only a few of the old ones even dared speak of it, but like any good tale it existed through the ages. Once again, his mind filled with doubt about his faith in Allah and as he lay back on the side of a low sand dune, he stared up at the heavens with a thoughtful look to his weary eyes.

The Koran spoke of this Jesus Christ, but Mohammad simply called him a prophet. Why would this Christ even be mentioned unless this one true God wanted it so? He had too many questions for a tired mind and decided they could wait until after prophetic word was played out. If George was indeed this Chosen One, then Mushid knew he would have some serious decisions to make about his future as a Muslim.

## KINGDON OF SILENE
## CASTLE KEEP
## THE KING'S COURT

Unhappily sitting upon his ornate throne, King Ramie looked out over an empty court room and sighed heavily, for he'd asked his blessed Allah for answers to his grave concerns and none had come. Only moments ago, the castle's aged Mullah had left him saddened and troubled by current events. The holy man was unable to provide much in the way of spiritual insight and lacked the ability to bring comfort to his liege.

Things had turned from bad to worse with his eldest daughter's ill-fated words of the king's trickery spreading through the kingdom like a ravenous disease. It was all lies of course, of how King Ramie had attempted to corrupt the lottery in order to save his youngest daughter. Of how Princess Lonnia, in charge of the royal lottery, was forced to seek sanctuary in the castle's mosque to escape her father's punishment for not adhering to his commands to choose another maiden for sacrifice.

In the process of spreading these dastardly lies, Princess Lonnia's lackeys presented her to the local townspeople as a heroine. They spoke of how her enemies had spread libelous tales about her occult practices and blasphemous ways to prevent her from fulfilling her duties as eldest daughter and advisor to the king. Sadly, people began to believe it. The curse over the land and the many years of sacrificing their daughters had weakened the people's resolve and belief in their king. Many of the people had even stopped their prayers to Allah and some no longer believed in anything but their own misfortune. The Kingdom of Silene had reached its lowest point and was ripe for takeover by the Dark Princess.

A senior army officer, who was paid quite well with stolen gold from the kingdom's treasury, appeared at the main fountain and spoke out to the masses, "Though Princess Lennia is her younger sister and greatly adored by many, Princess Lonnia's first and primary duty is to the great people of Silene. Her association with the occult is a lie and spread by those vermin loyal to her enemies in the court. The King himself assigned her to oversee the lottery and though greatly grieved by the lottery's choice of her beloved sister, she dared to cross her liege, her father, and take a hard stand to obey the laws of the royal lottery decree, even to the point of sacrificing her darling sibling. This is indeed a woman of integrity. One you should all follow and ensure this sacrifice is completed, which our long standing royal decree orders it so.

King Ramie heard of this and other such disloyal statements, shouted by various high-ranking soldiers in his army and a few impudent court advisors. Such men were no longer allowed to enter the castle keep, blocked by the Royal Guardsmen who controlled the main entryway, castle passages and two of the four corner battlements.

Hearing the sound of footsteps coming down the stone corridor, King Ramie looked up to see his personal guard stand aside to allow Captain Rynarr and another guardsman into the empty court.

"My liege, may we approach?" Captain Rynarr asked with his head bowed.

"Certainly," King Ramie replied. He was anxious to hear any news that might bring a ray of light into this darkest of days.

Captain Rynarr and his one guardsman moved through the empty court until they stood within ten feet of the throne, "Sire, my men have closed off the castle, preventing Princess Lonnia from speaking with her traitorous scum or escaping. I only pray Allah will strike these men down for their disloyal conduct."

"Yes, yes, what else?" King Ramie wasn't so sure Allah was even concerned with the current goings on, for his prayers had gone unanswered for quite some time and right now he was more concerned with the current strategy to defend his throne.

"With exception of one small company, under the command of your faithful Mushid, all your Royal Guardsmen now control the keep. But sire, the army, which as you know outnumbers our forces at better than seven to one, now controls the castle grounds and patrols the city streets." He locked eyes with the king and said, "Sire, we are in a state of siege, but this may change when Princess Lennia is taken to the lake."

"How can I allow that, Captain? You and I both know this lottery was circumvented by my eldest daughter for revenge and provides an opportunity for her to seize my throne. May Allah slay her where she stands for her blasphemous ways and disloyal conduct toward me." Yet, even his curse upon his daughter lacked the strength of conviction, for she was still his daughter and he had tried so hard to love her.

"Yes, Sire." Captain Rynarr agreed. "But we have a plan and with Allah blessing our timing, we will once again have the townspeople behind us and most of the soldiers."

"You have found this GW person?"

"Yes, Sire," Captain Rynarr said. He then pointed to the guardsman who stood beside him. "This is Salaam, son of Abdul-Mutazz, who also once served you until he fell before the Egyptians."

"You are most welcome to my court, Salaam, son of Abdul-Mutazz."

"Sire, you honor me greatly," Salaam said. He then bowed at the waist before his king, followed by dropping to one knee to show his submission to his king.

"Rise up, Salaam," King Ramie said and then he addressed Captain Rynarr, "You have news?"

"Yes, Sire," Captain Rynarr replied. "Mushid and Brother Samuel did enter Egypt and located the three who were banished. While the one called Richard remains with Brother Samuel for the journey home by wagon, the ones called GW and Paul have ridden with Mushid to join with a small detachment of Guardsmen across our border."

Captain Rynarr then gestured for Salaam to speak and the young man said, "Sire, we broke camp and rode through the night to arrive here and our camp is well hidden off to the west."

Captain Rynarr then gestured for Salaam to step back so he might speak now, "Sire, you know of the old prophecy, which has come down through the centuries and many believe this GW to indeed be this Chosen One," Captain Rynarr said with enthusiasm. He then waited for a response from the king. But King Ramie, whose saddened face showed the strain he was under only remained silent.

"My king, I also know he carries the lance Ascalon, as prophecy foretold, and he returns to save the life of his princess."

King Ramie's eye opened wide when he heard the name of the lance and he nodded his head in understanding. He too had heard the prophecy from his childhood and upon hearing the name of Ascalon, he quickly rose to his feet and asked, "What will the army do when this chosen one enters the city?"

"I am not sure, Sire, but he will be accompanied by the one called Paul and escorted by a loyal company of Royal Guardsmen. I've also ensured words of this prophecy are spread throughout the castle grounds and town."

King Ramie nodded his head in agreement for Captain Rynarr's actions and then glanced to his left at his youngest daughter's empty throne, "What of my daughter, Princess Lennia?"

"As ordered, she is under confinement until such time you summon her. I have two guardsmen at her door and four-more in the passageway. I've also ordered her handmaidens to keep her away from the windows and to call out to the guards if they have any problems with the princess attempting to escape."

"Yes, in her current mind-set she'd probably march right up to army posted outside the castle and insist she be sacrificed immediately to save my throne."

"Yes, Sire, she would," Captain Rynarr said.

King Ramie tapped a finger against his right cheek, "Has she been informed of this young man's return?"

"No, Sire," Captain Rynarr replied. "I thought it best this way, unless you tell me otherwise."

"You are right as usual, Captain," King Ramie said. "Do you have any advice?"

"May I approach closer, Sire. I would not like what I have to say to be overheard by someone with large ears and we both know these stonewalls allow voices to carry very far."

King Ramie Summoned Captain Rynarr forward with the gesture of his raised finger and then listened, as his chief Royal Guardsman laid out his plans for tomorrow. If they were able to maintain control of the castle throughout the night, the sacrifice would be carried out during mid-morning hours, when most of the townspeople were awake to observe the event. They would then witness this Chosen One's appearance, when he rode in to save the princess and hopefully, slay the accursed creature. The townspeople's presence might also ensure there was no foul play by Princess Lonnia's soldiers.

Nodding his head in agreement, as he listened to Captain Rynarr's plans, King Ramie began to feel some of his heavy burden slide off his shoulders. He looked up into the eyes of Salaam, the guardsman who accompanied Captain Rynarr and saw a young man who, by the youthful expression on his face and steadfast look in his eyes, was ready to give all for his king and Princess Lennia. He wondered in times like this, where such young men came from? Silene was not a kingdom able to pay well for its soldiers, but here a loyal man stood to do honor to his king and kingdom with his life and it caused King Ramie to swell up with heartfelt pride.

Without hesitation, King Ramie removed a jeweled dagger and golden sheath from his waist band and hand it to Salaam, "Take this gift with my blessings and may Allah reward your loyalty."

Startled by the gift and the blessing, Salaam was speechless and unable to move. Captain Rynarr had to physically move him forward to accept the ornate gift from the king's hand.

## ROYAL GUARDSMEN HIDDEN ENCAMPMENT

Having once more donned a soldier's brown tunic to get past the lines imposed by Princess Lonnia's officers, the Salaam lowered his veil he used to hide his face and was once more mounted and en route to Mushid and the others. He'd only ridden for a short distance from the town's outskirts when he encountered two of his friends; both guardsmen now on foot and well hidden. They were using the desert camouflage techniques Richard and Paul had taught them to conceal themselves.

The two guardsmen sprang up, catching Salaam by complete surprise, to accost the young rider and wrestle him off his mount. He was thrown hard to the ground, with a sharp dagger at his neck, before the guardsmen realized they'd only caught their comrade, Salaam.

"You blundering sons of a serpent!" Salaam yelled. He painfully stood to his feet and wiped sand off his face and reattached his veil.

"Your own fault, you should have changed tunics before now. For all we knew, you were an army scout about to discover our camp," One of them said.

The other guardsman slapped Salaam's left shoulder and said, "You have no idea how close you came to having your throat cut. If it hadn't been for Mushid's order not to kill our own soldiers, you would've died here tonight and joined your ancestors."

Angry, Salaam pushed his comrade away, "I'll remember to thank Mushid, but I still owe both of you a good beating."

Both guardsmen laughed and the larger of the two said, "Salaam, you boast big, but you'd need Mushid's help to honor such a threat. He only sent you to the castle because you're a thinker and not a fighter. He knew you'd find a way to sneak in undetected and you did." The man pointed to the brown tunic and then added, "But anytime you feel like a rooster, I'll be ready to give you a lesson in any weapon you choose."

"Oh, be quiet and give me my horse. I have messages to carry to Mushid."

Salaam was handed his reins by one, while the second guard wiped some sand off Salaam's back and suggested, "Change your tunic before you go further, or someone in camp may put an arrow through this one. Not everyone thinks so kindly of the army as we do and will feel only wounding you in the arm or leg would satisfy Mushid's order not to kill."

Looking at his fellow guardsmen in disbelief, Salaam began to nod his head in agreement. A veteran of a few scrapes himself while defending the honor of his elite force he knew all to will of the bitter rivalry between Royal Guardsmen and regular Army troops.

He walked over to a canvas bag, which hung from the side of his saddle, and retrieved his blue tunic that was carefully rolled up. He first thought was to toss the brown tunic to the sand, but he changed his mind. Mushid might send him back to the castle and he would need the tunic to allow him entry into the castle's ground. Only upon being recognized by his fellow guardsmen at the kitchen outer door was he allowed to enter the keep.

Once mounted and wearing his tunic of royal blue, Salaam turned to the larger of the two guards and said, "When we do battle, it will be with wits and you will be unarmed." He then used his spurs to the sides of his horse, a brown mare they had taken from the army's herd only an hour before he left for Silene and dashed off. Salaam would be glad to have his own horse back, but the mare had allowed him to complete his disguise, since only the guardsmen were allowed to ride the black Arabians.

Salaam ignored the contemptible taunts of his comrades and quickly rode off toward Mushid's camp. As he vanished over a sand dune, the two men shook their heads in amusement and returned to their hidden positions.

It was a short ride and Salaam arrived within moments. Once dismounted, he handed the reins of his warhorse over to the guardsman in charge of the horses and went in search of Mushid. Salaam found him at the water's edge, speaking with the Chosen One and his friend Paul. Upon seeing his scout return safely, Mushid turned away from George and greeted Salaam.

"Salaam, I expected you sooner and was beginning to wonder if you might have been caught and imprisoned," Mushid said. He grinned and slapped Salaam hard on his nearest shoulder. Salaam's knees nearly buckled under the hard slap of comradeship, but he maintained his stance and told Mushid of his orders, "Captain Rynarr sends his greetings and thanks you for your speed in returning." Salaam glanced at all three men and then turned around to see if any enemy might be close enough to listen in, which caused Mushid to smile at the young man's untrusting nature. "You are in my camp, Salaam. There are no spies here, but it is always good to be alert." Mushid then gave Salaam a serious look, "You may continue your report."

Salaam nodded his head in understanding and then said, "Our comrades control all of the keep and Princess Lonnia remains confined to the Mosque- though I suspect the Mullah would prefer her elsewhere."

"What of Princess Lennia?" George asked anxiously, for he was greatly concerned with her safety.

Salaam first looked to Mushid, who nodded his permission and then said, "You may advise the Chosen One of our Princess."

Salaam then addressed George, but it was apparent by his hesitation that Salaam had identified George as this Chosen One and now held him in some reverence. All of which made George quite uncomfortable. Still, he wanted any news of his princess.

"Chosen One," the name made Paul chuckle, but he stopped abruptly when he saw the stern looks on both George and Mushid's faces.

Salaam continued, "She is also well guarded by our comrades. Captain Rynarr believes she would turn herself over to the army before we could put his plan into play. He knows how worried she is for her father and because of this, she does not know of your return."

"Very good, Salaam, but now tell us of our Captain's plan," Mushid said.

Before he replied, Salaam again looked up and down the shoreline and then over his shoulder, remaining fearful an enemy might be close enough to hear his words. But once satisfied they were indeed alone, he began, "We are to remain here for the night. Tomorrow, with the rising of the sun, we are to ride toward the Great Wall and avoid any contact with the army. Five of our men in the castle will go to the stables and prepare mounts for twenty-guardsmen, plus Captain Rynarr and Princess Lennia. The army will be advised the sacrifice will be carried out as decree states and under an escort of Royal Guardsmen. The detail will accompany the Captain and Princess Lennia to the sacrificial stone. At their approach to the stone, we are to ride and join at the Great Wall with our comrades in the detail.

"Captain Rynarr will remain with the princess, while the remaining guardsmen will join with us. Once the horn is sounded, summoning the dragon, the Chosen One," Salaam pointed to George, "...will ride to save her. If in the event this man falls, Captain Rynarr will ensure our beloved princess does not suffer."

George was startled, "What do you mean by she will not suffer?"

Mushid gave George a hard look and slowly shook his head from side to side just before he wiped a finger across his throat, "Quick death and no suffering."

"You must not fail us," Salaam said to George, a look of sincerity upon his face.

"But, what of the King?" Mushid asked of Salaam.

"Our remaining comrades will guard the upper levels of the castle and protect the king from assassination. Captain Rynarr suspects that once he is out of the castle, Princess Lonnia will make her move against the king and our men will be ready."

"And what of the prophecy, what do the people say?" Mushid asked.

Salaam smiled for the first time in several days, "As we speak, word of the prophecy is being spread through the army and the townspeople. Captain Rynarr suspects there will be some initial trouble, being how the Chosen One carries with him a Shield of Silene painted over with the cross of the Christian God. This is why we are to be ready to prevent anyone from interfering with the Chosen One's duty."

"Swell, not only do I have to worry about fighting a dragon, I've got to watch my back for an arrow from the very people I'm trying to save."

"Hey, George, if it was so easy I'd volunteer," Paul said in jest to break the tension.

George gave him a harsh glare, "If I could, I'd hand this duty over to you in a flash! Then sneak into the castle to free my princess and we'd be back across the border to Egypt before anyone missed us. Remember, Abdul—Bashir gave us a job offer and I'd hold him to it."

"You'd leave me alone here to fight this monster?" Paul asked mockingly in English.

"You bet!" George exclaimed in English also. "And I can't understand why you're still here, especially after that torturous Baja 500-ride we took to get here."

"Prophesy, buddy," Paul reminded him. "Have to see the fight so I get all the bloody details right. Remember, most legends began with fact as Sam repeatedly told me. I've got to do history right. Besides, I was always a sucker for rooting for the little guy and in this case, you really are the little guy."

"A joker! I've got me a real joker in my corner."

"Think of it this way, old buddy, I'm president and club chairman for the first St. George fan club. Think of the money I'll make off the buttons alone."

Mushid cleared his throat, which sounded more like a deep growl and was his friendly way of saying they were rude for speaking in their Irish tongue and their words were thoroughly confusing poor Salaam.

"I apologize, Mushid, for our rudeness," George said and then addressed Salaam, "When arguing with one another, we often fall back to our native language."

Salaam, his face expressionless, slowly nodded his head in understanding.

"You need rest now," Mushid said to Salaam and led the three men back to camp.

Unable to have a fire, most of the men had fallen asleep quickly to the gentle sounds of a calm ocean. But when darkness began to blanket the desert, guards were once again rotated. This changing of the guard was again accomplished once more during the night with only George, Salaam and Paul relieved of this tiresome duty. When a new dawn appeared, the entire camp was awakened, and preparations were made to ride.

The Royal Guardsmen were excited, each man either giving George a respectful eye, a smile and a nod of the head, or many enthusiastic back slaps, which left the Chosen One's shoulders quite sore.

# 19 – THE WORD CARRIES

With Mushid handling things outside the castle, Captain Rynarr prepared for today's series of events. Events that could possibly change Silene forever and he wasn't all that sure this was a good thing to happen or not? True, he accepted Islam at an early age as was expected of him and he lived the life of a proper Muslim, with the exception of missing a time of prayer now and then due to his duties. But for several years, his duties involved the sacrifice of the many maidens and he was beginning to doubt this god of Islam and his supposed love for the Libyan people.

He'd had many serious talks with Brother Samuel about his Christian God throughout their years of friendship and honoring his promise to the king, never once did his Sam try to sway Rynarr into changing religions. He simply answered questions about this Jesus Christ, a prophet in the Koran, and offered up, when asked, what Christians generally believed in.

But now, knowing ancient prophecy was unfolding this very day, or at least he thought these prophetic words were transpiring today, he began to have doubts of his belief in Allah. He had lost his father and sister to this accursed monster and Allah never answered his prayers to protect them or the young maidens to follow. There was also the recent battle with the Egyptian raiders, where a young Christian had saved his life; a man, reportedly new to the lance and sword, a man who killed ten Egyptians and was barely scraped during the combat.

Captain Rynarr also thought of the Black Princess; a woman who dealt in the black arts and how Allah had never struck her down. Now, here was this blasphemous woman sheltered in a mosque and protected by the very religion she scoffed. Yet, she still lived.

All these thoughts were on his mind, while he walked through the torch lit shadowy passageways, inspecting his men on guard and making his way to Princess Lennia's chambers.

## MAIN CASTLE KEEP POINT OF ENTRY

More than a dozen sweating men in heavy shirts of mail, covered by the blue tunics of the Royal Guardsmen and carrying spears or scimitars ready for battle, rudely shoved their way through a line 30-brown tunic soldiers. They stood by, while 5 of their party made their way from the keep to the stables. Captain Rynarr ordered his men to avoid a fight if at all possible and thankfully, they found only one or two of the soldiers prepared to do battle. Word of the prophecy had done its work and the soldier in charge of the detail ordered his men to step back and keep their swords lowered to prevent any misunderstandings. He had no love for this Black Princess and was only going to obey his senior officers to a point. He did not believe he was a traitor to the king and he didn't believe his men were either, but he desired more time to think of what actions he was prepared to carry out in the event Princess Lonnia staged her coup. Like so many others, he too wondered where Princess Lannia was with her troop of guardsmen. At any moment, they could sweep in to support Captain Rynarr, in the event of a coup attempt.

"Allow them through, we were only ordered to guard the castle. Not to do battle with our fellow men-at-arms," the senior man said in a loud voice.

The way was clear and when the Royal Guardsmen arrived at their company stables, they were happily surprised to find all the remaining mounts saddled and ready. The stable hands and courtyard servants had joined together to form a small army of 90-men, armed with hoes, pitchforks and a few old spears, in the event the army had attacked the guardsmen.

"You honor us with your courage and may Allah bless you...thank you," Ishmael said. He was a senior-guardsman, placed in charge of this detail by Captain Rynarr. Ismaael was a stout, 42-year old man, with a heavily scarred face from his many battles. He had massive shoulders and muscular arms, and his aged hands were large enough to grasp the oldest stable-hand by the shoulder and nearly drive him to his knees as he saluted this servant's bravery. Though a slave for many years and then a servant to the king, this middle-aged man who was named Fataah, was very humble and became teary-eyed as the knight embraced him as a fellow warrior.

"But, my old friend, you must know that as a servant to raise your weapons against a soldier of Silene means your death?" Ishmael said with true concern in his voice.

Fattah shook his head in response. He had no voice to reply because his tongue had been cut out long ago when he was taken captive. Once a soldier himself from the lands to the far south, Fataah, a light-skinned Black Moor, was a good twenty-five years older than Ismaael, but he'd been treated well as a servant and had come to respect these Royal Guardsmen.

A fellow stable hand approached and addressed Ishmael, "Sire, he ...and us, serve the king and in some way, we have come to know you men of the blue tunic as our masters, but yet, our friends. We all feel this way."

"I had no idea," Ishmael replied. "After today, there will be some changes made, but for now I ask you to stay here and protect our mounts. If you see us in battle, then join in for our Kingdom needs such men as all of you."

Fataah stepped back and lowered his head in respect, as Ishmael walked to his warhorse, inspected his saddle and mounted up. He then took the reins to Captain Rynarr's horse and led his men back to the main entryway. Each horseman carried the leather reins to four other saddled horses. They would wait for their captain and Princess Lennia to appear at the front entrance.

## THE CHAMBERS OF PRINCESS LENNIA

"Are you ready, your highness?" Captain Rynarr asked. With sad eyes, he looked upon the frightened young lady.

"I will do my father proud today, Captain. But if I stumble, please let me rise up on my own for the people must know I am prepared to die for them, as those maidens who went before me." She wore only a simple long, over the knee tunic in royal blue color, covered by an open floor length robe of a silvery fabric that once belonged to her mother. Her head was covered by a matching head scarf and on her feet, she wore a pair of open-toe camelhair slippers, given to her by her father on her 12th birthday. The slippers still fit and were covered in ornate designs of silver and gold beads. Her veil was of purple, leaving only her tear-filled eyes visible to an onlooker and her hair was tied tightly into a bun by a length of silvery cord.

"I will be with you all the way my Princess and I will ensure you will not suffer."

Princess Lennia struggled to keep the tears back, her eyes reddened from a night of crying. Not so much for herself, but for her gallant knight she knew she would never see again. Before leaving the room, she looked to her handmaidens, each one was weeping openly, and said in a whisper of a voice, "You have served me well and I have valued your friendship. I have left a gift for each of you with my father. Please know each gift came from my heart." She wanted the gift to be a surprise, for she had granted them their freedom and a share of her clothes and personal belongings her father would not want. In this way, she knew they would have some small riches to begin their new lives with.

Unable to reply to their mistress, the teary-eyed handmaidens fled the room. They did not want to make a scene in front of the captain and embarrass their princess.

Princess Lennia approached the captain and briefly bit her lip to maintain her composure, "In the event my father is unable...unable to carry out my wishes, I have left letters in his private chamber. These letters show my desire to free my four handmaidens from slavery. There are a few other wishes and I pray you are able to carry them out. Will you ensure this happens...in case my father is...?"

"If I am alive, my princess, your wishes will be carried out," Captain Rynarr said. He then bowed his head and gestured her toward the door, "We must go now, your highness, for time is extremely important today if destiny is to be fulfilled."

Princess Lennia looked at him sadly and asked, "Destiny?"

"This will be a day of strange events; Princess and I sincerely hope you will still be here with us when the sun sets. But, for our plan to be carried out, you must behave as if you are headed for death. This is extremely important."

"I am confused, Captain, is there treachery at play here?"

Captain Rynarr shook his head, "No, not from I or the men of the Royal Guard, and maybe I have said too much."

"I do not understand?"

Captain Rynarr reached up and stroked his beard as he thought over his response, "Princess, I can say no more, but today you must play the actress or your father's kingdom may be lost and all three of us killed. So, please listen to my words, follow my instructions and be prepared for anything. Your sister will not be satisfied until she sits upon your father's throne and she is capable of anything."

"Yes, two of my handmaidens believe she also controls the dragon with her black magic."

He nodded his head, "Today I believe anything is possible." He pointed to the door, "We must leave now."

## ON THE EASTERN OUTSKIRTS OF SILENE

With the lance named Ascalon encased in armor and quite heavy, George was grateful for the boot Mushid had fabricated for him. Riding westward, he balanced the lance upright with his gloved right hand and glanced over his shoulder to see the men riding behind him. He felt extremely proud to have such brave men riding with him toward possible death. Some of these men had lost fathers, uncles and older brothers and sisters to this dragon and now, today, they escorted the one who prophecy said was the Chosen One. George could also sense most if not all of them felt proud to be in his company and their blood surged with excitement, as they drew closer to the Great Wall.

Here, today, on this very desert, they expected to witness an ancient prophecy come about and the curse lifted from their kingdom, and they would be here to be participant. Some of the guardsmen were not quite sure what was going to happen to Silene once the dragon was dead? Some of them also feared the Black Princess's demonic arts, but not enough to commit treason against their king. Still, the prophecy also said the kingdom would once more return to the faith of Christianity and for the hard-line Muslims they could not see this as possibly happening.

Had it not been for the prophecy and the death of this hellish creature, a good share of these Muslim knights would turn on this Chosen One and slay him as the infidel he was to protect their faith. But each one of them felt a strange vibrant sensation, and their blood was beginning to burn, for the cry of forthcoming battle was in the air. Every horseman rode with uncertainty weighing down upon them and they clasped their lances tightly to fight against the nervous jitters.

Mushid rode proudly, his lance held straight up, with the base of his hand-guard resting in its new leather boot. He knew today was probably the most important day in his life and as he glanced over his shoulder to gaze upon the Chosen One, his chest grew tight with pride. He was riding in the lead of the vanguard escorting the Chosen One and he knew this would be a day no one would ever forget. For generations, people would be told this story of valor and just maybe, his lowly name would be mentioned too?

Paul, he wasn't sure exactly what he was feeling except his backside was screaming obscenities at him for putting him through another horseback ride. With all this prophecy thing being bantered about, the whole fight the dragon legend was simply too big for him to take in completely. Still, he'd go along with it for George's sake. Partly to honor his friendship to George and a nagging feeling he really didn't want to anger the Big Guy upstairs, if in truth this was His prophetic Word. He also thought that if he tried to run now, he'd probably end up with a dozen arrows in his back, which on its own merit was a good incentive to remain in the ranks.

As the company of guardsmen closed in on the Great North Wall, the guardsmen were shocked to see the sheer number of townspeople and soldiers waiting for them. Nearly the entire town and those from surrounding farms had come out to see events transpire. Most of the townspeople had walked to the Great North Wall to observe the prophecy play out, while others rode theirs wagons or pulled carts with family members aboard for the ride. There seemed to be a strange sense of well-being in the air and hardly anyone seemed to fear the dragon, at least for the moment. They seemed to be only in fear of missing out on the grand battle between monster and this Chosen One.

"Great, I've got an audience!" George exclaimed. He rode up beside Mushid and then spotted Captain Rynarr, who was escorting the Princess to the Great North Wall. They were accompanied by another company of some twenty guardsmen.

"Looks like the army is siding with us for the moment and I bet Princess Lonnia's none too happy about it," Paul said. With mace in hand he pointed toward the Great North Wall.

## THE CASTLE MOSQUE

Hundreds of voices outside the castle grew to a steady roar and Princess Lonnia soon realized the words were not calling for her baby sister's sacrifice, but were in fact, yelling out their support in unison for someone they called the Chosen One.

Angry, she summoned the Mullah with her shouts, but he refused to come. He had locked himself into the top level of the prayer tower, having the best seat in the house to observe the festivities. If events went against this Chosen One, he could say he was praying and never heard her calls.

Princess Lonnia sent her one frightened servant to locate one of her senior army officers, but no one came and even the servant went missing. She also knew to leave the mosque meant arrest, but she couldn't remain here and not know what was going on outside the castle walls. So, making a mad dash or as fast as her bad leg would allow, she ran from the mosque and fled down the empty passageways of the darkened keep. This also surprised her, for the castle servants were also missing and she soon realized everyone was outside the castle. She didn't know why, and this infuriated her to the point where she began to shout out curses to everyone she could think of who lived in the castle.

Her guards had left her too, now taking up position in the upper levels to protect the king. As a result, she had no problem in reaching her secret tunnel, which led to her private chambers. From there she went in to her laboratory, picked up her shaman's cloak of dark magic, two of her more important books of ancient spells and a single ancient relic of a dagger. It was said this dagger had once belonged to Queen Cleopatra and she had paid a small fortune of her father's gold for it.

She left her lab, entered her bedchambers and used surprise to stab a lone guardsman in the chest. The man was walking the passageway to bring refreshments to the men upstairs and his hands were full when Princess Lonnia leapt out from the shadows and killed him. She then remained in the morning shadows and climbed a little used stone stairwell to the roof. The steps were narrow, and she nearly dropped her books, as she climbed up to a crumbling bowman's tower atop a battlement no longer in use.

From here she was able to see the masses, both townspeople and soldiers, either at the Great North Wall to the north or making their way to it. She was so confused, never before had people willingly left the safety of the town to view the sacrifice from the Great North Wall. Not by choice anyway. Then she spotted the two separate companies of Royal Guardsmen, one by the Great North Wall, where she saw Captain Rynarr and her dear sister, and a second company approaching the Great Wall from east. Those men were too far away, and she couldn't make out who was in charge, but it seemed whoever it was had the attention of crowds.

"Chosen One! Chosen One!" was soon shouted out over and over and people were pointing in the direction of the second company of guardsmen. People and soldiers were then moving in that direction, but Captain Rynarr's men headed them off and blocked them with a line of lances.

Princess Lonnia saw Captain Rynarr speaking to them, but she was unable to hear his words. She also didn't see any of those army officers she had paid so well to ensure their loyalty and wondered what had happened to them, but most of them had fled toward Tripoli. They were frightened off as the words of prophecy spread through the town. Others were in hiding, waiting to see what transpired. If the Chosen One was slain, then the prophecy was unfounded, and the young princess would be sacrificed. After that, they could return to their positions and serve their new queen.

Princess Lonnia's frown turned to a smile, knowing her sister was out there and within a few minutes she would be led toward the sacrificial stone. At first, she thought her sibling was the one being identified by the crowds as the Chosen One, but it wasn't adding up. Why would all these people expose themselves to danger to simply see another sacrifice?

"Are you surprised, daughter?"

Startled, Princess Lonnia dropped her books and jerked her head around to see her father standing there on the battlement. He was well guarded by six very-large guardsmen with scimitars at the ready.

"How'd you know I would be here, dear father?" Princess Lonnia asked. She kept her knife hidden, as she hoped the dark gods she worshipped would allow her a moment to carry out her vengeance. She knew one of the guards would kill her, but she would still have the satisfaction of ending her father's reign and right at this moment, that was all she wanted.

"I know you too well, daughter," King Ramie said. "You had to see the sacrifice of your sister and you knew I'd be up above the keep, as I always am. But today is different. I am not here to observe your treacherous plan be carried out and your sister devoured as you had hoped. No, dear daughter, I am here to watch prophecy unfold."

"Prophecy? What prophecy do you speak of?" She was troubled, for she knew nothing of this prophecy he spoke of.

King Ramie, keeping his distance for he knew how tricky his daughter could be, told her the details of the prophecy and watched the expression on her face change from confusion to a look of pure villainous evil.

"If you had spent as much time reading the history of our kingdom as you do with those books of evil, you would have known of this. But then, maybe the God of this Chosen One put blinders on your eyes so you would not learn of this. Otherwise, I am sure you would've killed this man long ago. Instead you entrapped your sister and hoped to sacrifice her as a way to gain my throne. But you have failed, daughter."

"No!" She shouted. "These words are lies...and be warned, old man, I now control this dragon through those same gods I worship." She waved her hands over her head, the dagger concealed in her robe's inner pocket. "My gods are more powerful than Allah and this false god you call Jesus." Suddenly, as she spoke out the Name of the Lord, her books of evil suddenly burst into flame and this startled everyone on the battlement.

King Ramie then smiled and said, "Maybe your dark gods are not so powerful, daughter. I also doubt you control that beast, for it came from Hell and that is where it will return."

"Killed by this Chosen One? How can a single man stand up against the powers of darkness, father?"

"Yes, daughter, truly he is a single man. A man you once tried to kill and failed. A man empowered with the strength of his God to rid Silene of this monster...and a man who loves your sister enough to risk his life against such a foul creature."

"Who?" She was suddenly confused and could not remember the stranger her father was speaking of.

"By the look in your eyes I sense your mind has become clouded. But you knew him as GW, your sister's suitor and now about to become the hero of Silene. He has returned as prophecy foretold, for he is the Chosen One and he carries with him a lance called Ascalon, as was foretold in the ancient words."

Princess Lonnia glared at her father with all the hate she could muster, then as her mind began to clear, she slowly withdrew her dagger from her cloak and once ready, she sprang at him with the uplifted knife.

The king stepped back, his right arm up in defense, but the guardsmen were ready, and the nearest man moved in and quickly wrestled the knife out of her hand. Princess Lonnia cried out in pain as she fought against the first guardsmen and kicked out against two others who stepped in to assist. Three strong men were too much for the enraged princess and she withered under their strong grasp. She was shoved to the stone floor of the battlement, where she knocked her head hard on the side. Her lame leg collapsed beneath her and she now lay there, cursing her father to the point of tears and threatening the men who had dared to touch her.

"Leave two men with her, but be vigilant for she remains dangerous," King Ramie ordered. "Right now, I want to watch and the best place to see the battle is from    right over there." He pointed to the bowman's tower Princess Lonnia was standing only moments before and walked in that direction.

"You will die, father!" Princess Lonnia screamed. "You will all die, and I will reign!"

King Ramie never turned around, only shook his head in grief and stepped up to the bowman's perch. From here he could observe the battle about to come. But he was troubled, who would he pray too? Would Allah bless this Chosen One since the prophecy was said to reclaim Silene for Christianity? Or could he, a Muslim, pray to this Jesus Christ and have his humble prayers honored.

He shook his head in dismay and looked to the north and watched as the company of guardsmen from the east move ever closer to the Great Wall. He knew that whatever was going to happen, was about to happen very soon and he feared for his youngest daughter.

# 20 – A LEGEND BORN

KINGDOM OF SILENE, LIBYA, NORTH AFRICA
THE GREAT WALL

With the rising of the sun, a sweltering heat wave descended upon the Kingdom of Silene and with a cloudless sky overhead, there didn't appear to be any break in the miserable weather forthcoming. With rising temperatures, the stench of Silene's open sewage pits, slaughterhouses and cast aside animal remains rose too, bringing scores of buzzing black flies to the town and castle. But only a few were concerned with the smell or the flies, both were simply a fact of life. No, this morning was going to be a very unusual one in the lives of the town's people and they had emptied their shops, tents and homes to travel out into the desert. They had walked and ran, rode camels or horseback, while some came in single axle hand-pulled carts and a few, the ones who could afford it, by overly crowded wagons, to reach the Great Wall. Everyone wanted to be in time, to find the best position to witness an ancient prophecy unfold before them. And hopefully, to have their prayers answered with the death of this accursed dragon.

There were many who never heard of the prophecy and others, who had heard of the Chosen One but not the part of how Silene would return to a Christian kingdom if a brave knight from the east would slay the dragon to save his princess. But while waiting, most of the people, who numbered over a thousand, continued to raise the name of Allah. Some shouted out their prayers to the heavens for their kingdom's salvation and though no one knew for sure this Chosen One could actually slay this vile beast, there seemed to be a sense of celebration amongst the people. But on one section of the Great Wall stood the minor clerics, who disbelieved this ancient prophecy and prayed for Allah to strike this knight down or simply allow the dragon to devour him in order to save this Muslim kingdom of theirs from Christianity.

Abdul-Badrudeen was one such Muslim, who doubted the prophecy, but being a curious fellow, he was sitting astride his largest camel. An unfriendly beast, the camel would often spit in his handler's face or kick one of Abdul-Badrudeen's many loaders.

He rode to the Great Wall in haste, desiring to find a good spot a top the wall to observe the battle. A spice seller from Tripoli, he had only recently arrived in Silene and was rudely awakened this morning by his chief servant. Though kicked twice and cursed down to his fifth child, the middle-aged servant quickly briefed his master on this morning's ceremonial event. He'd known that if he hadn't awakened his master with words of this bizarre occurrence, the lashings he would receive would've been far worse than the simple beating about the head and shoulders he normally received.

A trader like his father and his father before him, Abdul-Badrudeen was a cynical old man, who had seen many strange things in his caravanning across the great deserts.

Though he too cared little of this so-called prophecy spreading through the crowds, he didn't want to miss a chance to see the actual Dragon of Silene devour this stupid infidel and a royal princess. It was well worth waking up early for.

He slapped his servant one more time to the side of his head and sent him away to heat up some tea, while he dressed. He made sure to secure his pouch of gold inside his leather vest and armed himself with not one, but two long daggers. He then left his tent and walked to the fire pit to order his senior handler to prepare his camel.

With only a little tea to warm his stomach, Abdul-Badrudeen, a tall stringy middle-aged man of mixed blood; Greek, Arabian and Libyan, whose beard was long and white and his heart black, made his way through the crowds to where his camels were temporarily stabled. He met up with his handler, who was still busy saddling his master's tallest camel. The animal was giving the handler some problem, trying to bite him, until Abdul-Badrudeen grabbed the camel by right ear and dragged it down to go eye-to-eye with the beast and struck the animal on his front knee caps with a wooden riding stick.

"Do not tempt me, you filthy brute, or I will turn you into stew and use your stomach for a water bag and your flea ridden hide for a new saddle," he shouted into the camel's face and then released him. He then waited for his servant to kneel, so he could use the old man as a step-stool to mount the camel. While most people had the camel kneel-down, Abdul-Badrudeen got better satisfaction of abusing his servants in this demeaning way.

Now, as he rode through the town streets with little care for those on foot, he made his way to the Great Wall at a rapid pace. At the outskirts of town, he stopped briefly and watched and then cursed violently, as the masses were being brought to an abrupt halt by the Royal Guardsmen under Captain Rynarr's command. He recognized these men of the blue tunic as the same soldiers who had stopped his caravans on many occasions to search his goods for contraband. He had lost a lot of gold to such conscientious men and seeing them only made his old stomach gurgle with remembered stressful fears over previous encounters.

With his riding stick he encouraged the animal forward in hopes of finding a suitable location for a man of his wealth to observe the forthcoming activity. He didn't even notice the two young girls in front of him and nearly rode over them, except one of the two girls was quick enough to pull the other one out of the way.

Hearing a local's warning cry from behind, Afrah, the older sister, glanced over her shoulder just in time to see the huge camel coming at her. With youthful reaction time, she grabbed her younger sister, Areej, up by the scruff of her neck and jerked her out of the way.

These were the only two daughters of Haani the pot maker and they had come very close to being crippled or killed by a very large camel. Afrah saw how the man atop the beast didn't even bother to slow the camel down or give either Areej or Afrah any notice at all, as he rode away. But the older daughter, already wise in the way of street slang, showered this man's impoliteness with gutter curses, while she pushed her little sister along.

"Stupid girl, you almost got yourself killed and who would clean our father's feet if you were dead?"

"Why, you would," Areej replied, with a smirk on her face. She then jumped to the side to miss being knocked over by a sudden rush of several people hurrying to reach the Great North Wall.

"Yes, I would, and I've done it before and won't do it again," Afrah said. Then    she turned her head and shot daggers at three young soldiers who were giving the two sisters a leering eye. "Now come, we have to hurry, or we will miss everything…and do not encourage those soldiers with the batting of your eyes."

"But why? She asked. "They're cute and I like soldiers." She then tugged on her sister's arm and said, "There will be too many people at the wall and we will never see anything. I am too small, and you are not strong enough or big enough to put me on your shoulders."

"Stupid, girl!" She exclaimed, not caring who might be listening. "We are girls and that is enough for these filthy soldiers. They care little about our age and when we reach the wall, we will find someone to help us and then we will watch the battle."

"Our father will whip us for leaving the shop unattended," Areej said.

"Maybe, but there is no one left in town to shop and it will be worth a beating to see the dragon die. Then you and I will never have to fear being chosen for sacrifice."

"I'm not old enough for sacrifice," Areej said, as she was literally being pulled along by her older sister.

"No, but I will be in three months, so I want to see this dragon die!" Afrah then yanked on her sister's arm once more to pull her along through the crowds.

"Stop it!" Areej yelled. "You're hurting me."

"Be quiet!" Afrah ordered. She then slapped her younger sister on top her head, a bit harder than she had planned. "Keep up or I will leave you behind for all those soldiers to toy with and then you'll understand my warnings."

Areej grabbed her head and with tearful eyes, threatened her older sister, "Father will whip you if you leave me alone."

"Then keep up!" Afrah exclaimed and continued to drag her little sister through the crowds.

Excited onlookers: townspeople and soldiers alike, stood elbow to elbow along the battlements and walkways of the Great Wall. The entire length was packed with people shoving each other about for a better spot, until the crowd was standing in nearly three rowdy roles. People jostled one another and here and there a fist fight broke out as tempers flared. One guy attacked another over a misspoken word and the two of them wrestled until they rolled down a flight of stone steps, where they were separated by perturbed soldiers. With all the excitement and foul tempers mixed in, several of the bystanders came all too close to being driven over the front of the wall and were saved by alert guards.

Soldiers had tried to keep the townspeople off the battlements, but an officer saw such an endeavor would prove fruitless and any scuffles resulting could cost lives. He issued orders for the men to desist any further confrontations and stand aside as the townspeople climbed the ladders and stone steps to reach the top of battlements. Only the guard towers remained off limits and these were quickly filled up with arriving off-duty soldiers, now pressed into duty for crowd control in the event the dragon was the victor this day and a-thousand frightened people began rushing for the town.

Looking out over the crowds, Captain Rynarr wasn't too sure his single company of guardsmen could keep the townspeople back from the front of the wall and he feared their presence on the northeast side of the Great Wall could possibly keep the dragon from either making an appearance. That or the beast attacking the crowds before George could act.

If everything went as he planned, Captain Rynarr would escort Princess Lennia to the sacrificial stone on horseback and he would remain with her while George attacked and killed the monster. If George happened to fall before the beast, then he would attempt to save his king's throne by executing the princess as he did with the courageous young lady before. In this way, the townspeople would be satisfied the sacrifice was carried out and the king would know his daughter was dead before the dragon touched her.

Spotting an army officer, a young lieutenant he knew very well and was being considered for a move into the Royal Guardsmen, Captain Rynarr summoned him with a shout and ordered him to call up his company of soldiers. "You are to reinforce my guardsmen by keeping the crowds back behind the Great Wall. No one is to enter the field of battle."

It took some doing, but the lieutenant was able to pull together 38-men-at-arms, each one carrying a seven-foot long spear and positioned them in front of the mounted guardsmen. With their spears pointed at the townspeople, this joint action seemed to do the trick as the crowds began to settle down.

"Are you ready, Princess?" Captain Rynarr asked. With reins in hand, he rode up beside her. He'd left two of his men at her side and now relieved them to join up with their company at the Great Wall.

Teary eyed, she choked back a sob and looked in the kind face of her Captain, "Ride with me, Sir and I will rely on your strength to carry this through."

Captain Rynarr's face lit up with respect for this young lady, "All is not lost, Princess, for a surprise awaits you."

"You continue to speak to me in riddles, Captain."

"Let us be on our way, Princess."

Princess Lennia looked to the Great North Wall and was shocked by the number of people who seemed to be literally hanging off it or pushing and shoving to get to the front of the wall's northern ledge. In her grief, she really hadn't taken notice earlier of how many people were massing to see her sacrifice. "I didn't know so many of my subjects hated me so."

"Princess, they do not hate you, for you are beloved by all, but they have come here to see a great prophecy unfold." Captain Rynarr said. He then put spurs to his mount and shot forward at a slow trot, with the princess's reins in his right hand to lead her out.

Grumpy from a long sleepless night and far too many hours in the saddle, Mushid saw the trouble Captain Rynarr's men were having with the crowds at the Great North Wall. In response, he sent all his guardsmen, but Salaam and Paul, to assist them.

Mushid, Paul and Salaam were to remain ready to protect George from any attempted assassination. They were much too far for a bowman's arrow now, but there still could be a rush of mounted soldiers from the northwestern end of the Great North Wall.

"Captain Rynarr wanted to split his force, hoping to cover both ends of the Great North Wall, but he knew this wouldn't work," Mushid said. He then gave both Paul and Salaam a hard-glaring eye, "You two, watch for treachery. If anyone comes from the wall and you do not recognize them as friends, it will be the enemy in the service of the Black Princess."

"I have my bow," Salaam said with pride. He was one of the few guardsmen who actually continued to practice daily with the bow and could out shoot most of the army bowmen. This was why Mushid had kept him with them, that and he was smarter than most of the others in the company. Mushid knew Salaam was headed to become an officer if he didn't get killed first.

Sitting upon his mount, Mushid raised his left hand and pointed toward the Great Wall, "Captain Rynarr will order the horn to be blown with a wave of his arm. A soldier on the Great North Wall then summons forth the vile beast with this horn and then we wait."

George shook his head and said, "You will wait, my friend, but I must ride to my princess so she will know I am here to defend her." George struggled to keep Valiant reined in as he spoke. His horse could feel the growing excitement in the air and knew a battle was forthcoming. This standing around only caused his blood to boil and his legs to stiffen from nervous energy.

"Valiant, be still!" George ordered, and his mount quieted down. He patted his neck, now covered in royal blue trappings. "Wait, my brother, the time is not yet right. Soon, very soon we will fight, and I pray you and I are ready for what lies ahead."

Sitting on his mount, Mushid looked away from the wall to study George for a moment. As he did so, he attempted to recall the details of the prophecy. Then he remembered, there was mention of the knight offering his services to the princess and she refused, hoping to keep the strange knight from harm. But the knight remained steadfast and attacked the dragon.

"Yes, you know what is best," Mushid agreed. "We will stay here to prevent any interruptions and my friend, ride to your princess and may your God bless you this day."

This strange blessing surprised both George and Paul, but George didn't have time to think about it now. He still had several hundred yards of deep sand to ride through until he reached the hard-packed surface of the lakeside shoreline.

"Goodbye, my brothers!" He shouted out and Valiant shot out at the charge, and like a single identity, they dashed toward their shared destiny.

When they reached the blood stained sacrificial stone, Captain Rynarr dismounted and then walked over to help Princess Lennia off her horse. When he turned to the Great North Wall, the number of people atop the battlements and standing in the desert to each side astonished him. Captain Rynarr also saw how another lieutenant had taken the initiative to gather up another good-sized force of foot soldiers to keep the crowd back at the other end of the Great North Wall. If he had not done this, Captain Rynarr feared the people would have been stupid enough to endanger themselves by coming too close to where the fight would occur or might cause the dragon to stay away. With so many years of observing the creature, he knew the beast was not stupid and a large force might cause it to be wary and stay in the deeper waters.

"Captain, if they haven't come to see me die, what else is going on here?"

"My princess..." Captain Rynarr stopped abruptly when he spotted a single knight approaching from the east.

Princess Lennia turned to where Rynarr was looking and asked, "Who is this coming?"

The good Captain grinned under his veil and turned to slap the princess's mount on its rear flank to send it running off toward Silene, though he kept his own faithful mount by his side. He maintained a tight grasp of his reins and said, "That, my Princess is your young hero."

"My hero?" She asked in puzzlement. She didn't recognize the knight. He was veiled and wearing the blue uniform of the Royal Guardsmen. But she did see he was carrying a strange lance and a shield painted in white, with a large red cross painted on the center of it. Then as the knight grew closer, she recognized the horse for there was no other steed like Valiant in North Africa.

Charging forward through deep sand, George found it cumbersome to keep a firm grip on the lance. But it took surprisingly little time with Valiant's long strides to reach the hard-packed surface of lakeside and only a moment later he was before the disgraceful sacrificial stone.

George reined in his sweaty mount and held on tight to his lance. With his knees pressed in hard against Valiant's shoulders, the horse actually slid several feet on his hindquarters and came to an abrupt stop in front of the princess and Captain Rynarr.

With adrenaline surging through his blood, George sat there proudly upon his gallant steed. His back was rigid, and his right-gloved hand held a narrowing section of the Ascalon lance, while his new shield covered his left-arm. His scimitar was strapped to his side by his waist wrap and he also wore his knives. Seeing her again, his heart began to race, and he smiled with great enthusiasm from behind his veil. He then bowed his head to show his respect for her and Captain Rynarr.

"I am at your service, my lady."

"GW?" she asked in a hesitant voice. She had recognized Valiant, though the blue trappings were new, but she was confused by the guardsman tunic and strange shield George carried. "Is this really you?"

"Yes, my Princess, but you should know me as George now, for it is my proper name and Brother Samuel said I should use it now," he said in a calm voice. Though he really wanted to jump down and take her in his arms and kiss her, he held fast upon his mount. He looked to his left and was startled to see the crowds at the Great Wall, Talk about a lot of people! I sure better not blow this one, be pretty embarrassing for the Christians...Dragon-1, Christians -0...What am I saying! I gotta get my mind back in the game or I'm liable to become a tasty treat for the giant lizard out there.

He turned to look in Captain Rynarr's watchful eyes and nodded his head once before he then again gazed deeply into her beautiful eyes and finally said, "I am here to offer you my services, Princess."

She first looked at George with a blank expression and then switched her confusing look to Captain Rynarr, before then gazing out over the calm lake waters. Then her reddened eyes grew wide with fear, not so much for herself but for her heroic knight.

"No, you mustn't," she whispered. Then her voice grew louder, "You'll die, my darling. Then I will die and both of us will surely be dead. No, you must flee here now and live."

George stuck his shield out and in proud words said, "I'm so glad you said that, Princess, for it was as said in the prophecy you would first deny my services. Now I ride this day for you, but I also ride for my Lord Jesus Christ and the people of Silene."

Captain Rynarr stepped forward to get her attention, "Princess, there is an ancient prophecy from a time long ago when Silene was a Christian kingdom and North Africa was coming under the sword of Islam. The prophecy spoke of how a strange knight will come into our lands and kill the dragon to save a princess."

He then waved toward the Great Wall with his left hand extended out. "All have heard of this and have risked great danger of risking the dragon's wrath to watch this prophecy unfold."

"I thought my sister had covered their eyes and ears with her black magic," She said. Princess Lennia turned to wave to her subjects and in return a loud shout rose up from the Great North Wall.

"No, my princess, your people truly love you. But yes, words and lies of your sister have hardened their hearts…until now." He waved his hand a second time toward the Great Wall, "They come to see their kingdom rescued and their favorite princess saved."

Thinking Captain Rynarr was signaling for the ceremonial horn to blow and summon forth the dragon, the soldier assigned the duty filled his chest and brought the antelope horn to his lips. With eyes closed tightly, he blew hard into the horn and listened as its shrill and mournful sound carried out over the lake.

Startled by the blowing of the horn, Captain Rynarr looked back toward the wall and angrily waved his arm from side to side repeatedly, but still the horn blew. For the soldier, seeing the Captain's signal repeated made him think the Captain wanted the ceremonial summoning to continue. But Captain Rynarr wasn't ready. He hadn't even secured the princess to the stone yet. If George was to fall before the dragon, he knew she would surely panic and make a run for it. Any sensible person would, and this would force him to give chase and everyone upon the Great Wall and in the surrounding desert would watch him catch her and drag her back to the rock. He would have no time to escape then, for he knew by then the dragon would be upon them. Angrily biting his lower lip to keep from shouting out curses in front of his princess, Captain Rynarr knew it was his own fault. He'd been the one to arrange the signal and in his sharing of the tender moment when George and the Princess came together, he forgot all about the arranged signal. The young soldier, one of a very few capable of using the ceremonial horn with the needed skill, was only obeying his orders.

"You have so little time, George. You must prepare yourself," Captain Rynarr hurriedly warned him.

"I am ready," George replied. With a slight jerk of Valiant's rein, he turned his horse to face the lake. This was as close as George had ever come to the lake's shoreline and was saddened to see all the shipwrecks scattered about. Here, ghostly remains of once proud vessels rested in the shallow waters or on the beach; a sad reminder of the dragon's strength and aggressiveness. He knew many a brave man had come to their death in such ships in their futile attempts to kill the dragon. Some of the wrecks were quite old and he wondered if these ancient hulls were from the times of the Greek or Roman civilizations that once controlled Libya?

"We will stay here and wait for our hero to return," Captain Rynarr said. With a new rope in hand to secure her to the chains, he stepped forward to be close to Princess Lennia.

"Will you do me a favor, Captain?" George asked as he leaned down to whisper his request to Captain Rynarr.

Captain Rynarr stepped up to stand beside Valiant, "Anything in my power, my friend."

"If I should fail, grant my lady a quick and merciful death."

"You need not ask, for I will do my duty to her highness," Captain Rynarr answered in a whisper. Then sensing a change in the air, an ominous feeling that heightened his senses, he quickly looked to the lake and then brought up his left hand to point. "Ready yourself, sir knight, for the dragon comes."

Captain Rynarr then gently pulled a frightened Princess Lennia back to the sacrificial rock and carefully secured her in the manacles and ropes, "I am sorry, my princess, but I must do this in the event our hero fails. I must ensure you do not attempt to run, but I will remain here with you until the last."

"But, Captain, you will not have enough time to escape."

Captain Rynarr looked in her eyes, blinked once with his left eye in an unusual show of affection and shrugged his shoulders. He then released his mount and slapped her on the rear to encourage her to run. Sensing the dragon's approach in the air, the horse needed little encouragement and charged off toward the Great North Wall.

"At least one of us was intelligent," Captain Rynarr said. With trepidation, he turned to the lake and looked to watch the rise of the creature.

George felt the restlessness in Valiant first, but then he jerked his head around at Captain Rynarr's warning to see the lake waters swirling about several hundred yards from shore. Then the warning shouts and yells from the people at the Great North Wall could be heard, telling the three of them of the dragon's approach.

With a glance to his princess and then a look to Captain Rynarr, George looked back to the water and could see from the disturbance there was something massive underneath the waters and coming his way. Even in this heat he felt a cold shudder down his backside. A trail of white froth began to form, pointing toward the shore, as the creature came near the shallows. Then everything suddenly stopped, the waters once more became calm and an eerie hush fell over the crowds. Not one of them spoke. They all searched out the waters with their eyes for some sign of the dragon.

"This has never happened before," Captain Rynarr said thoughtfully. "It's as if the creature knows you await it."

Captain Rynarr left the princess and stepped out in front of Valiant. He was drawn to the lake and continued to gaze out over the still waters for some sign of the monster. Then without looking over his shoulder at George or the princess, he said quietly so only George might hear him, "Maybe there is some truth to the rumor our Black Princess now controls this beast and has warned it of your intent to slay it."

"No matter," George replied. "Her ways of black magic may control this dragon, though I doubt it, but she has no power over my Lord." George then felt a strange inner strength grow outward from deep inside him, a rush like he'd never felt before and he lifted his shield up high to aim the Cross of Christ toward the bright morning sun.

Suddenly, bright golden rays shot downward from the heavens and struck the shield, bounced off it and painted the waters directly in front of them with its glory. Seeing this happen, Captain Rynarr dropped to his knees and was speechless. Then he heard George shout out in Libyan, "In the name of my Lord Jesus Christ, I summon you dragon to rise up and face me!"

Captain Rynarr was simply struck dumb by such a display of faith and he trembled as George moved Valiant further forward by a few steps. George was concerned Valiant might trample the dear Captain when the dragon appeared, and he wanted some distance from the princess for the fight to come. Valiant became over-excited and began to get restless, pawing at the sand with his hooves and jerking his head around.

Almost immediately, the waters near the shore began to boil up and a large blanket of white froth appeared. This was exactly the same spot where the rays of the sun bounced off the shield and struck the lake. This sign and George's yell to invite the beast did not escape notice from the crowds at the Great Wall.

"Rise up beast and do battle!" George shouted again. He knew he was sounding like some B rated movie actor, but he couldn't help himself as the words flowed over his lips. Valiant, all 17-hands of Arabian blood, also felt a strange energy surging through him too, causing him to suddenly rise and stand on its two strong back legs and taunt the creature, as George struggled to hold on.

"Easy boy!" George shouted. He tugged on Valiant's reins. "It doesn't look good for the hero to fall off the horse before the battle even begins."

For the spectators at the Great Wall and even King Ramie, who watched from the roof of the castle, George presented quite a spiritual sight when a strange holy radiance began to glow from him. Startled by this, Captain Rynarr backed away and stood by a very astonished Princess Lennia.

George didn't know about any glowing, but he knew he was ready. He now felt ready, as if all his senses, every bone and nerve in his body was ready for battle. He'd said his prayers earlier in the morning and again now. He offered all up to God and was prepared to face off with this devilish creature now making its grave appearance.

First the slimy head rose, shining off the sunlight and letting all to see its hellish ink-spot eyes. Then, the gaping mouth, with the lake's waters cascading through its sword-like teeth and becoming a frightening sight for all to behold. George zoomed in on its four frontal fangs, estimating each of them to be nearly the length of a guardsman's spear. He was reminded of a photograph of an alligator he saw at school, and then suddenly recalled the black dragon in Walt Disney's cartoon Sleeping Beauty. He now almost expected the creature before him to spew out bellows of fire and black smoke.

"Yeah, Prince Charming did it with only a sword. Here I've got a 50-foot tall dinosaur and only this lance...Should be a piece of cake," George whispered in English so only his horse could hear him.

But Valiant wanted to spring into action, which caused George to shout, "Steady, boy, this is just beginning." George reined him in again and then added, "There's still a lot of water out there, boy, and we need that thing on land if we're to win this day."

Only ten feet above the water, the dragon slowly moved its head to the left, as its shark-like lifeless eyes studied the stone barrier where stood a great number of its prey and they were making strange noises. It found their behavior unusual. Then its attention returned to the prey in front of him, one who resembled so many of those who had tried to hurt him in the past. It then looked to the stone. Its meal was waiting for him, but again he was confused by seeing another of these creatures nearby.

As it had grown conditioned like any domesticated animal, when the strange sound carried over the water, there was always a prey waiting for it to consume. But today, it was puzzled. There was a meal at the rock, but now there was three nearby and one was with a tasty four-legged morsel. Then it returned its predator's gaze upon the one close to the shore and began to move forward in that strange rocking fashion it used ashore. As the dragon came, its elongated neck stretched upward until the creature stood at least 50-feet in height. It stopped briefly and released a deep and all-too threatening roar that sent a frightened gasp through the crowd.

Dozens of people on the wall suddenly began to flee, no longer so eager to observe the event of a lifetime. Hysterical, they began to knock others off the Great Wall, causing their victims to fall to their deaths from such a great height. Within minutes there was a general panic. Terrified people climbed down, some dropped from perilous heights to escape, while others simply fell from the battlements. This left a pile of wounded and dead bodies strewn out along the base of both sides of the wall and woeful cries could be heard from dozens of now mangled bodies. Those people who made it to the ground or were running from the open desert, fled across the hot sand toward their homes. Those irrational ones sought safety in the castle and would soon find the gate held closed and guarded by heavily armed soldiers.

A few people dropped to their knees in the roadways, lifted their arms to the heavens and cried out to Allah to save them from the creature, only to be trampled upon by others whose only desire was to look out for themselves.

Abdul-Badrudeen, who indeed had found a choice spot on the Great North Wall, found great excitement in seeing the dragon rise from the waters, but upon hearing its great roar had now taken flight with so many others. Upon seeing that one lone knight on the lakeside, he decided his position was not so advantageous and rushed down a narrow flight of stone stairs. He nearly lost his footing on the stairs but was able to push off the shoulder of an elderly man, which sent the man to his doom. But all Abdul-Badrudeen could care about was his own safety and was soon mounted upon his camel. With a whip, he violently lashed out against the animal to drive it on through the crowds and more than a couple people were trampled beneath his camel in Abdul-

Badrudeen's haste to escape the Great North Wall. Then, only 50-yards from the wall, Abdul-Badrudeen's camel collided with another camel, its rider equally terrified and this resulted in Abdul-Badrudeen losing control of his frightened animal. The terrified camel bounced between a fleeing wagon and an unoccupied hand-cart. Abdul-Badrudeen lost his perch and suddenly tumbled from his saddle to land hard upon the sand. There, his own frightened animal, scared by the fear it sensed in the crowd, first dashed ahead and then was driven back by the masses and returned to trample Abdul-Badrudeen to death. But not before Abdul-Badrudeen looked up from the sand and into the wide terrified eyes of Areej, who, shielded by her older sister, stood cowering, while hundreds rushed by in their escapes.

Others, either more courageous or curious than the ones who had fled, remained on the wall or close by, mesmerized by the scene playing out before them: one single knight brave enough to stand alone against a fearsome dragon. Prophecy may have foretold it, but seeing it happen left these few hundred people, spellbound.

Mushid, Salaam and Paul shared glances with each other as they fought with their desire to rush forward to fight alongside George, but they knew this was George's battle to wage alone.

Captain Rynarr's loyal troops pleaded with their officers to leave their posting and save their captain, but Captain Rynarr had prepared his lieutenants for this and they kept their men from breaking ranks with their sheer force of well and a ready scimitar.

Captain Rynarr did not want to lose any of his good men if this prophecy proved to be simply another fable, but he also didn't want any witnesses if he needed to take the Princess Lennia's life with his own blade.

As ordered whenever the dragon showed itself, the catapults at the wall were loaded with oiled bushels of straw and soldiers stood by each of them with a lit torch in hand in the event the dragon attempted to breach the Great North Wall. Spear launchers were also prepared, though they had been proved ineffective against the thick hide of the dragon. One army officer, still loyal to his king, had prepared a mounted force of 57-men to support the Royal Guardsmen, in the event their knight failed to slay the dragon. This same lieutenant had also affected the arrest of three senior officers and was holding them under guard for the charge of treason.

George directed Captain Rynarr to take the princess behind the sacrificial stone, "I may need a lot of room to maneuver and I don't want to have to worry about the two of you getting in the way."

Captain Rynarr now back on his feet, but somewhat befuddled from George's spiritual display, simply nodded his head in agreement and gently released the frightened princess and tugged at her to follow him. She began to offer some resistance, until George glanced back over his shoulder at her and ordered her to go with him. "Go, now

She reluctantly obeyed, but her cheeks were wet with new tears and she shouted, "May your Lord bless you this day, my love!"

Valiant moved side-to-side, stepping forward and then retreating. George knew his proud friend wanted at the creature, but they had to wait. "Steady, Valiant!" George said over and over to calm him down.

"Only a few more minutes," George whispered into his friends perked up ears, "Then we will charge straight at him. But when he drops his head down to take a greedy bite, you'll stop as we've trained and jerk hard over to the right. But as he lifts his head back up before taking another try, we will then spring back around, and I'll skewer him like a large fish at the base of his neck."

Valiant nodded his head up and down, seeming to understand George's words. But George didn't think otherwise, he knew his horse-brother was mysteriously linked to him and this only added to his belief God was truly behind him.

**ATOP THE CASTLE KEEP**

Two of King Ramie's loyal guardsmen, caught up in the action below, were no longer keeping a close eye on Princess Lonnia. As with everyone else, their eyes were glued on George and the Dragon. This allowed Princess Lonnia an opportunity to sneak out of the crumbled bowman's tower and slither away on her belly for a short distance to reclaim her dagger, which lay on the roof. Her first thought was to stab both of her guards, but that would avail her nothing. Her true target remained to be her father. One of her guards was sure to call out in pain and she would surely be struck down by one of the other four guardsmen close by.

She observed her target through hateful eyes and muttered a prayer to her dark gods. With his four other guards beside him, King Ramie stood openly upon the upper most battlement and watched excitedly as the dragon left the lake waters and slowly approached the Chosen One.

"Why does he simply sit there?" The King asked in an angry tone. He pointed at George with a wiggling right index finger.

One of the guards closest to the king replied, "Sire, your knight is choosing his ground. He's making the dragon come to him and getting it as far from the water as he can."

A second guardsman then added, "He doesn't want a wounded dragon returning to the lake to lick its wounds as it has in the past."

King Ramie nodded his head in understanding, "Of course, you're both right." He then braced himself against the walls of the battlement, filled with nervous energy, while he gripped the sides of the huge stone ramparts.

Princess Lonnia knew she would have only one chance to slay her father, to take his guards by surprise and drive her dagger deep into the middle of her father's back. She decided the right moment would be when this cursed infidel entered in battle with her god's creature and all attention would be on the fight. She would wait in hiding behind the bowman's tower and spend these last moments praying this infidel, her sister and the good Captain Rynarr would be slowly and painfully devoured by the beast. She wanted vengeance and saw this as the moment when all she wanted would come to her.

**THE LAKE**

George left the base of his heavy lance in the leather boot, knowing how hard it would be to carry the weapon in his own hand until he was ready to use it. A regular lance weighed about 28-pounds, but Ascalon, with its armor weighed closer to 90-pounds and a lengthy period of wielding it about would sap his strength and leave him vulnerable.

He wasn't thinking about legends or prophecy at the moment. He was only concerned with killing this thing before it could kill him and then eat his lovely princess. A part of him wanted to ask for help, to have all the Royal Guardsmen charge in to assault the dragon from all sides, but he also knew this was his job alone and fought to quell his fears and stop his sweaty hands from shaking.

George reached up with his left hand to wipe the sweat from his eyes and then looked to the heavens. He then spotted a single white seagull flying directly overhead in circles. He suddenly remembered a Bible scripture having to do with rising up like an eagle and figured a seagull was more appropriate for the shores of North Africa, "You and me, God. But I have to still wonder why you chose me for this?" George then whispered a short prayer, "Strengthen me, oh Lord, for I ride into the Valley of Death. Give me wisdom in knowing when and where to strike and protect Valiant and I from harm…in the name of Jesus Christ, Amen."

As the huge dragon slid its bulk upon dry land, moving itself forward on its huge stomach with the help of its massive frontal fins and great strength, dozens of seagulls suddenly appeared from the north to fly tight circles about its alligator-like head. George reached up with his left hand and pulled his veil away and shouted out to the creature, "Time for you to see who you're facing, you, ugly bastard!"

He straightened his shoulders, adjusted his shield's placement, grasped his reins tightly and gave Valiant his head, "Now charge, Valiant and let's kill this thing!"

Like a tight spring cut loose, Valiant shot forward at the charge. But still George had not freed his Ascalon from its boot. He rode with his head down low, shield facing the dragon, while Valiant brought him closer and closer to the creature.

He kept a close and wary eye on the dragon, waiting for it to drop his head, knowing the creature was making its play to seize his attacker with its huge teeth. When it happened, George reined Valiant to the right and spurred him on with a not-to-gentle tapping to his lower flanks.

"Now…move it!" George yelled in a trembling voice. Adrenalin surged through every part of his body and he suddenly noticed the fear was gone.

Valiant jerked hard to the right, digging deep in the sand like a professional baseball short-stop going for the double-play and nearly unseating his rider in the process. But they stayed together long enough to escape the dragon's deadly teeth. The beast's mouth closed on empty air and it clearly angered the animal.

The crowds went wild, shouting out their support when the dragon missed it prey and George had escaped without harm. The beast reared up and roared out its displeasure, the sound sending a cold shiver down Mushid's backside and he had to fight to keep his mount under control. Paul's black steed charged forward a few feet before he could rein his mount in and turn him around to return to Mushid's side. But Salaam had the worst time of all. His frightened horse rose on its hind legs and unprepared, Salaam toppled from his saddle to hit the ground with a soft thud-like sound. Thankfully the deep sand dune cushioned his fall, but the horse had taken flight. Mushid had to ride hard to catch the frightened horse and return it to a very embarrassed Salaam, all while the battle ensued.

"Rein up!" George shouted. This was his call for yanking on Valiant's reins and putting his horse into that slide butt-to-sand maneuver they had practiced so many times.

Valiant immediately complied and reared back, sliding across the sand on his hind legs and prepared to jerk around to the left. George yanked Ascalon out of its boot and grabbed its reinforced handgrip tightly in his right hand. The weight of Ascalon was almost too much for George to maneuver with, but he managed to get the lance point over the top of Valiant's ears. As the horse came around, he leveled the lance beside Valiant's left eye, to the right of George's shield.

Then George suddenly realized, though this was the standard positioning for a lance while jousting or in battle, it wasn't going to work for this dragon. He wasn't striking a shield or impaling an enemy knight as he rode by. No, he was about to impale a creature the width of a two-car garage and there would be no riding by. He had to go right at him, like a locomotive running down the track and into a brick building.

Within only a dozen feet from the dragon, George was forced to rein-up a second time and flee from the creature's great mouth of sword-like teeth. He had to prepare himself for a new plan and a second try. In the process, the weight of the lance became too much for him to handle and as Valiant jerked around on his hindquarters, George was suddenly thrown from his saddle. He flew like a man shot out of cannon for the 11-feet and thankfully, he didn't drop the lance when he bounced off the hard-packed sand.

Immediately he was up on his feet and running for his life with a very angry dragon coming right after him. Had the beast had legs, George would have been done for, but having to slide on its stomach slowed it down some and this gave George a very narrow chance to escape. But the gallant Valiant hadn't deserted him. The steed ducked under the dragon's attempt to crush him with its left frontal fin and with a bolt of speed charged forward to give George a chance to grab his reins and be dragged clear. He didn't have time to mount, not; and, also, hold on to the lance.

The crowd on the Great Wall raved in support when Valiant rescued George, which caught the attention of some of those who had tried to escape. Suddenly, men and women were returning to the Great Wall, but the stoic Mushid simply nodded his head in approval. He knew the dragon couldn't hold a candle to an Arabian stallion like this Valiant.

Paul was a bit more enthusiastic. He waved his scimitar from side to side and shouted out George and Valiant's name over and over. But poor Salaam, extremely embarrassed for losing his horse, remained quiet. Though he did have a grin on his face and his eyes lighted up when he saw the rescue of the Chosen One.

His feet braced wide apart, he watched Valiant run toward him and ignoring the pains from his fall, George grasped Ascalon tightly in his right hand and with his shield still in place around his left arm, he started to jog away from the dragon. Within seconds, Valiant was slowing down beside him and he was able to catch hold of his friend's reins in his left gloved hand and allow himself to be literally dragged off across the sand.

George looked back to see the dragon coming toward them and he was surprised he wasn't afraid, he only knew he had to get away to make another try. He looked to Valiant's ears and shouted, "Run, boy! Get us clear!"

When Valiant felt they were far enough away, he came to a slow halt and this allowed time for his master to remount.

However, they needn't worry any longer about pursuit. The dragon had switched its attention from George to Princess Lennia and Captain Rynarr. With the sacrificial stone only a mere hundred yards off, the dragon turned around its great hulk and began to slither toward them like a snake. George figured the dragon decided two easy prey on foot were more appetizing then a mounted knight too fast to catch.

"Let's go, Valiant. Mr. Dinosaur is neglecting us, and we need it to refocus its attention." Oh, Lord, why couldn't it have been a Minotaur…maybe a huge lion or even a three-headed dog guarding the gates of Hell? Why'd it have to be a dragon? They seem to come in one-size only- damn big!

Seeing the dragon coming their way and George being dragged away by Valiant's reins, Captain Rynarr grabbed the princess by the shoulder and turned her around to look at him and then pulled out his dagger. "Forgive me, princess," he said to her face. He then spun her around and grasped her about the upper chest to hold her in place with his left arm and was about to cut her throat. Afterward, he'd slice his own, not wanting to be alive when the dragon reached for them. But George was remounted and clearing his minds of stupid thoughts, he was making a mad dash to reengage the beast. From over 200 hundred-feet away and closing in from the south, George was able to see what the Captain intended and hollered at the top of his lungs, "Wait! I'm not done yet!"

Princess Lennia grasped the hand that held the knife at her throat and with her other hand pointed to her knight. She then gently and cautiously pushed the blade away from her throat and in a strained voice he yelled, "Let's give him another try, Captain...okay?"

Captain Rynarr was speechless. He looked out to see George returning to do battle and he slowly nodded his head in agreement and lowered his dagger. They both waved George on as he charged the creature once more.

The time-stuck dinosaur, possibly the last of its kind upon 12th century earth, sensed movement to its left and turned its horrific head to see its prey returning. Slowly, it used it frontal fins to twist itself to the left and now face this strange behaving animal head on. It had fought these creatures many times and often it had felt pain, but in every encounter, it had survived to relish in the taste of its prey. It knew nothing of defeat, only a life of swimming and consuming the wealth of meat it was provided by these strange creatures. Whenever it heard the strange sounds coming from the southern shores of its lake home, there was always meat waiting for it. Though it had once preferred the taste of fish, preferring dolphin above all, it had long ago eaten all the fish in the lake and was now on a diet of maidens, sheep, and the occasional foolish knight and his horse.

Once again it felt the pains of hunger and here came two creatures to satisfy its natural urges to prey upon the weaker and then return to its watery home. It had no fear and operated completely on instinct. It knew nothing of sacrifices or what these creatures were, it faced. They only provided needed succulence to survive.

With Ascalon ready, George and Valiant drove in to attack the dragon. This time he had Ascalon pointed over Valiant's right ear, but the weight of the lance was tiring, and the point wobbled, with the space between man and dragon drawing closer. Several times he ended up striking Valiant's head with the side of the lance and George sensed his friend was growing tired of it.

"I'm sorry, boy," George apologized. "Just a moment longer and we'll be done."

## ATOP THE CASTLE KEEP

Knowing this was her chance, with every eye was on the battle below, Princess Lonnia removed her shaman's cloak and slid through the narrow opening provided for the bowman to shoot their arrows through. She didn't look down and inching her way, she cautiously stepped around the outside of the bowman's tower. If she had lost her footing, she would have fallen over 150-feet, but she had a good handhold on the old stones and made her way safely until she now had a straight shot at her father. She only had to cover 20-feet and everyone, including her father, had their back to her as they leaned out over the battlement stones to watch George' s next attack.

Clutching her ritual knife tightly in her right hand and feeling a sense of power in her grasp, she whispered a prayer to her dead Egyptian gods and sprang off her good leg to dash forward. Her limp was not even noticeable as she ran across the rooftop with her dagger raised high and a vengeful cry shouting from her lips. She was about to bring the knife down to impale her father in the back, when she suddenly began screaming out in like a banshee and tumbled forward to land flat on her back and in withering pain.

## AT THE LAKE

"Okay, buddy, this time we're going straight in," George warned his mount. "It's got to rise up before it drops its head and that's when we spear it. Just like frog gigging in the canals back home. Only this critter is one huge frog!"

Valiant seemed to understand every word and his speed began to pick up until both knight and steed were coming at the dragon like that locomotive barreling down the track.

From off in the distance, Mushid watched in bewilderment. He had never before seen a horse display such speed, especially one carrying a knight in armor. Valiant actually appeared to be flying over the sand, his legs were moving so fast they became a blur, while the distance between George and the Dragon closed rapidly.

George locked his lance arm in against his side, clutching Ascalon tightly in his grasp. He knew the impending collision was going to hurt a whole lot. He tried not to think of what will happen to Valiant and he, focusing his mind only on driving Ascalon deep into the lower throat of this over-aged dinosaur. He slid his shield forward, wanting the dragon to see the Cross of Christ before it died, sensing this truly was a battle between good and evil.

Weary, but still game, he aimed the tip of the lance to where hopefully, Richard was right, its heart should be. Then as George hoped, the dragon's head rose up, preparing to lunge downward for a tasty morsel.

A loud roar came from its gaping mouth as first it looked upward, and Paul thought it looked like the beast was cursing God. Its eyes seemed to widen and glare with a burning rage. Paul didn't think it possible, but for a split second he thought the dragon's whole face seemed to display a sinister-like expression in the micro-seconds before George collided with it. It's only a dinosaur...right? He wanted to ask Mushid if he had seen the same thing, but then the ugly sounds of collision came, and he stared off in the distance to see his friend flying through the air.

Total silence filled the air in the area of battle seconds before knight merged with dragon. Those on the Great Wall and those standing in the desert remained frozen, their mouths agape in astonishment as their Chosen One struck the dragon.

From the east, Mushid watched in utter horror as his brave friend drove toward his target in one final desperate attack. He listened to a sickening dull-thud like sound carry across the desert and at nearly the same time, a snapping of a narrow tree, when Ascalon broke into two pieces. These were sounds the people of Silene would never forget.

With all his strength, he braced himself for the collision. He had his old dilapidated GI boots rigid in the stirrups and his knees pressed in to guide Valiant, while he now used both of his hands to hold Ascalon steady. He tried to drop his head down below the edge of the shield. He felt no fear at this moment in time, a sense of calm had cascaded over him, as he sped toward the creature. He wanted to have one final glance at his princess, but there was no time. Everything mattered on this one last lunge with Ascalon—the life of his princess, Captain Rynarr and the Kingdom of Silene reverting to Christianity in a country shrouded in Islam. He sincerely hoped the prophecy was right.

Then came impact and George saw only blackness and for a brief moment, more pain than he ever thought possible. Then there was nothing.

Ascalon; a strange stone point, hand-crafted by a 20th Century Montegnard holy man in Vietnam, carried a great distance through an enemy-held jungle and delivered to battle-scarred American youth. It sliced deeply into the tough thick hide of the beast and impaled the dragon's heart.

Valiant never looked up, he kept his head down and ran for all he was worth. He collided headfirst with the slimy upper belly of the dragon and it was almost like hitting a brick wall at nearly 50-miles per hour. His neck broken in several places, skull fractured, and shoulder bones driven deep into his chest, Valiant died instantly and was knocked aside by the collision to land some 15-feet away.

Captain Rynarr watched in horror, while Valiant was thrown backwards and bounced several times off the hot sand before coming to a rest with all four legs misshapen and clearly broken. Valiant lay still, not breathing and everyone knew this unusual gallant steed was assuredly dead.

Shadowing Valiant's body with its great mass, the curse of Silene withered in agony and raised its head to release a desperate mournful cry. Several times it tried to pull the lance from its throat, but all in vain for the dragon was unable to reach the shaft with its teeth and was now dying.

George didn't fair too well either in the collision. As his armored Ascalon snapped in two only inches from his handgrip and the larger section sticking deeply into the beast, George was lifted up like a high school pole-vaulter and he somersaulted in mid-air over Valiant's head. He was thrown right into the beast's throat only a few feet above the lance shaft, striking the monster with his back, upside down and then bounced skyward. In doing so, he barely missed the creature's sharp fangs when the creature dropped its head attempting to pull the weapon free. He was thrown to the right, where he impacted again with the dragon's left frontal fin and he slid off the beast to land hard on the hot sand. He was nearly 40-feet from where Valiant lay and he too was unmoving. His chest no longer rose with life's breath.

Yet Ascalon had done the trick for all to see. The once-fearsome dragon rose up and lifted its head to cry out in agony in a piercing shrill-like sound no one had ever heard before. The broken lance stuck out of its lower neck for all to see and the dragon's lifeblood spurted out of the wound like an Oklahoma gusher.

Ignoring the motionless knight and horse, the dragon struggled to return to the sea, but its fins no longer worked and as the crowds watched in stunned silence, the dragon slowly dropped its neck to the sand and rolled half-way over on its left side. One final gasp escaped the beast and then it died. The Dragon of Silene was finally dead.

At that same precise moment of impact between knight and dragon, as Ascalon pierced the dragon's heart, Princess Lonnia, who was about to drive her dagger into her father, released a banshee-like wailing and fell to the ground clutching her chest. Her sudden appearance and cry of vengeance had startled the king and his guards, and they were caught unaware. They would probably have been too late to save their lord and to make matters worse King Ramie had even turned around to expose his chest to his daughter's blade.

Without fully realizing it a bond of sheer evil had formed between the Dark Princess and the dragon and now she laid there on the rooftop, unable to move and her eyes growing wide as intense pain gripped her. With all watching, her assassin's knife slid from her grasp and King Ramie jumped back, as bright red blood suddenly vomited outward from her mouth. They all watched, unable to help her if they wanted to, when she died at her father's feet. Her facial expressions were forever locked in the agony she felt in those last moments of her tragic life. Her last gasp was timed perfectly with the dragon's last breath, which left the king and his guards wondering what strange and demonic connection the Dark Princess had with the Dragon of Silene.

Knowing his own daughter was about to kill him, a girl he thought he no longer felt love for and indeed saddened by the promise he had once made to his wife, King Ramie looked upon her pain-stricken face and was surprised by the wave of grief he felt.

He turned to his senior guardsman and ordered, "Please, carefully remove her and have her handmaidens prepare her for a royal burial."

"Yes, Sire."

King Ramie then looked back over the battlement to ensure himself the dragon was really dead and was relieved to see it lying in the sand, unmoving, as a massive spillage of blood pooled around it. Glancing over his shoulder at his daughter's body, he suspected then his eldest daughter's dabbling in the dark arts of an ancient magic had indeed linked her with this beast and she had paid the price for it.

He then spotted his youngest daughter and Captain Rynarr running across the sand toward what he knew to be George's body. A guardsman pointed to the east, "Sire, three horsemen are riding toward them."

King Ramie believed this to be Mushid and the one called Paul. Knowing Richard was with his friend, Brother Samuel, he suspected this third man to be another guardsman.

From the castle keep rooftop they could hear the shouts of celebration begin, which built into a roar, with crowds of townspeople pushing past celebrating soldiers and guardsman to run toward the battle scene.

King Ramie turned to another guardsman, a man new to his personal guard detail, "Get down there quickly," he ordered. "Keep everyone away from the dragon and our brave dead knight. We will honor this George as a hero of Silene, and the beast, it will be burned this day and the ashes scattered across the lake waters."

"Yes, Sire." The man replied and hustled off to carry out the royal command.

Seeing no life in her hero and grieving her loss, Princess Lennia knelt-down beside George's body. With tears cascading down her cheeks, she gently caressed his blood-splattered left cheek. His eye was closed, and his legs deformed; broken from his collision with the dragon. His sacred shield, stained with the blood of the dragon and George's own lifeblood from his many wounds, remained in the tight grasp of his left arm. The face of the shield lay in the sand and Princess Lennia reached over to grab it and cover her love. With the masses coming to view the dragon and the knight, she didn't want them to see her love.

Captain Rynarr remained standing, his scimitar out and ready in the event the dragon stirred. He glanced down at his dead friend and slowly shook his head, for he couldn't believe George was actually dead. He recalled the prophecy, and this wasn't how it was supposed to end. "The knight would vanquish the beast and live to marry the princess as the kingdom celebrated its return to a Christian land". He knew this to be one of the last lines.

Mushid, Paul and Salaam rode up and quickly dismounted, rushing forward to see if they could assist George. But Captain Rynarr shook his head and said, "He is dead, but not a braver knight has ever lived, and he will long be remembered."

Then Princess Lennia felt a slight vibration from the shield, while she slid it over him. The Cross of Christ was again on display and suddenly, a beam of light only four feet in diameter shot down from the heavens and radiated the shield with intense brightness. The brightness covered all of George's body and all of those nearby had to step back and shield their eyes until the light faded.

"What the heck was that!" Paul exclaimed in English and Mushid was too stunned to berate him for speaking in that foreign tongue of his and especially in the presence of the princess.

Then Princess Lennia gasped when she felt movement in her love's left leg, which was immediately followed by his right foot. She jerked back and blurted out, "He's still alive!" They all watched as his legs were mysteriously straightened out by some invisible force and then his back straightened, and George was heard to then whisper in English, "Oh man, I sure had one heck of a dream."

"What did he say?" Captain Rynarr asked with insistence.

"He said he was dreaming," Paul said with a smile. Then Paul was laughing, as he knelt-down to slap his friend on the shoulder. "You had us scared, buddy. I thought we'd lost you," he said again in English and switched back to Arabic, "I think he's going to be very sore for a while."

"Valiant? Where's Valiant?" George asked. Slowly, with Princess Lennia's assistance, he slowly rolled over on his side and blinked his eyes against the bright sun. His turban was gone, and it was sometime before anyone located it. For a moment, he couldn't remember the fight and suddenly recoiled in fear when he saw the head of the dragon lying only a few yards from him.

Captain Rynarr stepped forward and said in a mournful tone, "Valiant is dead, my friend. I am very sorry, for he was indeed a fantastic horse."

George shook his head and he began to remember everything. He looked to the princess and then replied to Captain Rynarr in a calm voice, "No, Captain, he's not dead." George then ordered in a raspy voice, using both Arabic and English, "C'mon help me up! I'm a bit stiff."

Both Mushid and Paul looked at each other and then moved in to carefully lift George to his feet. By now the first of the crowds were arriving and they began to encircle the hero and his friends. Captain Rynarr quickly ordered up his arriving guardsmen to keep the enthusiastic crowds back. The last thing he needed was having the Hero of Silene trampled or smothered by well-wishing townspeople.

"Funny, I don't really hurt," George said. "Only, I feel..." George stopped when he saw his friend, Valiant.

George leaned on Paul's strong shoulder as they made their way to where Valiant lay in the sand. The crowd split to allow him passage and they watched in grief as black flies already attacked the horse. But Mushid and Salaam rushed up to quickly wave them away.

When he reached his lifeless friend, he asked for his shield, which Captain Rynarr now carried. Once in hand, George gently laid the shield on his horse's exposed shoulder. He then knelt-down on one knee and began to pray to the Lord Jesus in Arabic, for all to hear. He was not sure why he was doing this, only that he had heard a voice in his head to do so and he was being obedient.

By now more than three hundred people or more had arrived, but the mounted guardsmen kept most of them back with their lances. Soldiers, who were also both excited and wanting to praise their hero, were ordered to keep the crowds back from the carcass of the dragon. There was much celebration, but grudgingly the crowds of onlookers obeyed the soldiers and guardsmen and some resemblance to order was maintained.

Within moments, groups had formed two circles –one for the hero and one for the dragon. The larger group wanting to praise their hero slowly turned silent, wanting to listen to George's prayer over his dead horse. Most of them recognized the Cross of Christ on the shield and for those who didn't another bystander quickly informed them of the significance of it.

Then all were stunned when the miraculous again began to occur; a strange glow covered the horse and Valiant's broken legs slowly straightened out. Then his shoulders and neck reformed to their proper positions. But stunned silence quickly turned to gasps of wonder when Valiant's chest began to rise with fresh breath and his eyes opened. George petted the neck of his mount and then stood him up with Paul's help. Everyone watched when Valiant slowly rolled over and then stood to his feet. With a frenzied shake of his long mane and the whip of his tail, he walked up to George and nuzzled him with his forehead.

Onlookers began to shout, "It's a miracle!" and then came first one voice, followed by others which hollered our, "Christ is truly the one true God!" Still, there were some who hollered back, "Praise be to Allah!" Only to be frowned upon by one of the others, who was now praising Jesus Christ and yelling, "Only a true God could perform such miracles."

George reached up and petted Valiant's nose and in response the warrior-horse again nuzzled up against George's cheek like a newborn colt would its mother.

Paul retrieved the shield, studied it for a moment and then fastened it on to Valiant's saddle. He didn't want anyone walking off with it as a souvenir. He then petted Valiant's neck, "Glad to have you back, Valiant."

Princess Lennia moved up between Mushid and Captain Rynarr and looked in her lover's eyes, "What now, my love?"

George, ignoring the shouts of praise from the crowds, studied her for a moment as he held Valiant's reins, "Next, I will appear before your father with two requests."

"Two?" Princess Lennia asked.

"Yes, my Princess. For prophecy states the knight will ask of the king two things and I must follow these ancient words."

"Then we will go to my father."

"Not yet, Princess, I must wait for Brother Samuel and Richard to arrive. They come by wagon and it will probably be tomorrow before they show themselves. I also need a day to rest my body." He looked to his horse, "Valiant may be fine, but I probably have a lot of bruises to tend to."

"Well for someone dead and both legs and your back broken, you look pretty darn good!" Paul said.

Doubting his friend's report of his injuries, George looked in both Captain Rynarr's eyes and those of his love with a questionable expression.

"Your friend speaks the truth," Captain Rynarr said. "Both of your legs were broken; your back was contorted, and no breath came from you."

"Funny, I only remember aiming the lance and then waking up here," George said. But then he added, "I do remember a strange dream-like sequence...I was walking down this beautiful hallway, everything was a light bluish color and I started to hear this strange commanding voice. But then I woke up here."

"Your God has truly healed you, and in his love for you he has also healed your horse," Mushid said.

"Seems so," George replied. He looked down at his legs and then shrugged his shoulders, before leading Valiant over to where the dragon lay. "I want the rest of the lance, Mushid. Could you see to it?"

"Of course, my friend," Mushid answered. "It will be done."

George and Paul were both weary-eyed from a noisy night of celebration. First in the town and then the castle, which Captain Rynarr kept things quite lively into the early morning hours with recounting George's heroic deed. George was growing weary of hearing how he had been bashed to ribbons and decided he needed to retire for the evening.

Ordered by the king, the dragon's carcass was burned, and it took the men most of the night for the carcass to be consumed by flame. The ashes were then to be bagged up and later scattered across the length of the lake. Mushid ensured the lance was cut out of the body, which took some doing since the tip of Ascalon cut through the beast's uppermost rib, pierced the heart and severed the main artery.

In the days to follow, dozens of laborers were assigned to strip anything usable off the shipwrecks and burn the remaining hulls. King Ramie wanted no lasting memory of the Curse of Silene.

Brother Samuel, constantly complaining of his aches and pains, while he drove the rickety wagon back to Silene, was quite relieved to drive through the main gate of the castle. Riding in the uncomfortable wooden bench seat beside him, Richard was overjoyed to see the trip was finally at an end. After such a trip, nearly his entire backside was one big bruise and he hoped to never ride in such a contraption again.

Notified by a friendly servant of their arrival, George and Paul made their way to the main entry and stood there ready to welcome their friends. Having already been notified several dozen times of the great battle by excited townspeople, both Richard and Sam only shook their heads in delight and sighed with relief to see George alive.

"I am so sorry to have missed your conquest, Corporal," Richard said. "I also wish I could've seen that dinosaur up close."

"You wouldn't have enjoyed the stench, Professor. Two days in this hot sun and he would've been ripe," Paul advised him.

"Well, you can tell us all about the battle after we get washed up and I can rest my weary backside in some soft cushions," Sam said.

Off by themselves, Richard shared with Paul his promise to never take another long ride with Sam ever again, "That old man never shut up."

"You're here now and as they say, that's what matters," Paul said in English. He then laid his hand upon Richard's shoulder, "Professor, you'll never believe what has happened. Miracles, Professor and I was right there to see them happen. Both George and his Valiant came back from the dead and I ain't lying. Oh, I'm a believer, Professor, like never before. I saw the healing power of the Lord Jesus Christ and the empowering the Lord gave George to slay that dragon...oh, sorry, a dinosaur."

"Man, let us rest first." Richard playfully pushed Paul aside. "I'm hungry and thirsty and I want to sit on something really soft," Richard said as he walked through the entryway with Paul close behind.

## KING RAMIE'S COURT

At the king's direction, Princess Lonnia's throne was removed from the court and burned with the dragon. She was buried that same night, but the king didn't appear and only the mullah and his servants were on hand to perform the Muslim rituals.

Sam, using a wooden cane to help him move around, was allowed by the king to sit in a simple high back wooden chair, now positioned behind and to the right of the king's throne. In this way, King Ramie could look over his right shoulder and confer with his chief advisor.

Sam was sitting there when Captain Rynarr approached the throne and bowed, but he didn't perform the standard Muslim blessing. "Sire, I wish to present before you...George." He hesitated briefly for George had no real title.

"Bring the Chosen One before me, Captain," King Ramie ordered. He then looked to his left and saw that his youngest daughter was sitting in her throne and smiling. He knew she was in love, it radiated off her and this made him happy. Though, his grief for the loss of his oldest daughter remained and he still wondered where his second daughter was? But right now, he had this matter of George to deal with.

George, dressed in the blue tunic of the Royal Guardsmen, but without weapons or turban, walked through the opening made by the happy crowd of well-wishers and approached the throne. He stood beside Captain Rynarr and bowed at the waist.

"You concern me greatly, George," King Ramie said.

George looked up and replied, "Sire, what have I done to upset you?"

King Ramie leaned forward and pointed his right finger at George, "Young man, you've turned my kingdom upside down. Here I banished you, an infidel who had the gall to make love to my youngest daughter and then you come back to not only save my daughter but relieve my kingdom of a curse that's haunted us for hundreds of years."

"Sire, your daughter and I..." George was interrupted.

"Be quiet, I am not finished yet," King Ramie ordered and then continued, "Now these strange miracles you performed, bringing both you and your horse back from the dead. I have heard this was witnessed not only by my daughter and my captain, but by hundreds of both townspeople and my loyal soldiers." King Ramie pointed over George's head, "And only moments ago, I am told of stranger happening in the very spot the dragon fell, and its blood poured out. We had the dragon burned, but the blood-soaked sand remained. From here a spring has strangely gurgled up from this very sand, which they say has miraculous healing powers."

"Sire, I know not what you speak of?" George looked to Princess Lennia, who nodded her head with enthusiasm.

"I said, young man, it seems a fresh water spring has bubbled up and some say it has healing powers. One of my advisors has a withered hand. He's had it since birth and when he went to taste the waters, his hand was healed. Dozens of miracles are happening as we speak. People are being healed by this miraculous spring and do you know what this means?"

"I'm not sure, Sire," George replied nervously. He was mystified by King Ramie's question and glanced over at Princess Lennia again, who was still smiling.

"It means, young man, people will come to Silene from all over the land to sample these waters. They will bring commerce to my dying town and our fair community will blossom. Silene will never be the same."

"This is good, right?" George asked. Puzzled by what was going on.

"Of course, this is good, but I still banished you!"

George looked troubled and then he said, "Sire, I will return to Egypt if it will help."

"Don't be absurd," King Ramie said. Then he sat back in his throne and studied this infidel in front of him. He had to bite his lip to keep from smiling, for he was having fun with this young man who had saved his kingdom and delighted his daughter so much.

"Now I was told by my chief advisor that you have two requests. Well, what are they? I don't have all day here to deal with once banished infidels."

George looked to Sam and then to Princess, he was feeling really uncomfortable by the king's attitude. This wasn't what he expected at all. He had killed the dragon and he thought that should amount to something than the tongue lashing he was receiving.

"Sire, as you know I come from a distant land and only recently have I come to really believe in my Lord Jesus Christ. I know this is a land where Islam is taught, but I ask two things. The first, I ask to be baptized as a Christian in these same waters you speak of and to have Brother Samuel perform the ritual. Secondly, though I am only a mere soldier, I ask for the hand of your daughter, Princess Lennia."

King Ramie shot to his feet, "You dare to ask for my daughter's hand?"

George wouldn't back down, "Yes, Sire."

King Ramie looked to Captain Rynarr and in a booming voice, ordered, "My sword, Captain!"

George didn't know if he should flee or fight, but then that same warn calm feeling he had felt in the desert and while fighting the dragon, came over him. He looked in Princess Lennia's beautiful eyes and seeing no fear in her, he stood fast.

"Kneel, young man," King Ramie ordered, when Captain Rynarr presented his sword to him.

Captain Rynarr then stood beside George, as King Ramie brought the king's ceremonial scimitar, passed down from ten generations, down to touch George on his shoulders, "I, King Ramie, Lord and Protector of the Kingdom of Silene, grant you, George, a knighthood and lieutenant's commission in the Royal Guardsmen. Until such time you marry the Princess Lennia and from then on you will be known as Prince George, Hero of Silene. You may now rise, Lieutenant George."

With a big grin on his face, George stood to his feet and bowed to his king. "Sire, thank you for such an honor and may I serve you loyally." Sure hope I said that right. Watching all those old Arabian Nights' movies sure comes in handy.

"Now as to your other request...I suspect there will be many others who will wish to join in your baptism. Already, most of my kingdom now seems to be worshipping Jesus Christ as their new Lord. As our ancient prophecy foretold, the Kingdom of Silene is once more returning to a Christian kingdom."

"Sire, what of the Caliph?" Captain Rynarr asked.

"Captain, we will face that battle when it comes. But I would truly like to be in Tripoli and see the Great Imam's face when he hears of this. I know our former Mullah is already on the road for Tripoli with news of this. But as I said, that is for a later time. Tonight, we continue our celebration and prepare for a royal wedding.

## BROTHER SAMUEL'S QUARTERS

George, now dressed as a full lieutenant in the Royal Guard, stood before Sam's study table in silence, while the old man wrote down a few notes in English. This was the first time since the leaving Sam at the border, has George had a moment alone to talk with his friend.

After a few minutes, George broke the silence with a question, "So, what do you think of all this?"

Sam looked up from his notes, "Like the Word of God says, Our Lord moves in some mysterious ways, with signs and wonders for all to see."

"But why me?"

Sam smiled, and he combed his beard with his right hand, "How can I answer you when I have had to ask the same question of myself over and over until I'd bitten off all my fingernails.

"We...you and I, are simply here, George. We've witnessed God's power in a way no one outside our little world would believe and we've watched His plans unfold to give birth to a legend. Oh, there will be some who will want to question everything that's happened here, and those who will want to say this tale was only metaphorical—a good versus evil fairytale. But the legend of St. George and the Dragon will stand for centuries to come and of this we, from the future, already know. There will be great statues of you throughout Europe, mounted upon Valiant and carrying Ascalon to slay the dragon.

"But what really concerns me right now is the Caliph, I do not believe he will accept a Christian kingdom in Libya and a war could be facing us."

"Who knows, Sam, maybe God will protect us," George said. He was lazily studying Sam's makeshift globe.

"Maybe you are right, but I am an old man, lad, and I've seen more than I ever thought possible. For this I thank you for your courage and your faith."

George was quiet for a moment, embarrassed by Sam's compliment and then he asked, "Have you been to the new springs?"

"Yes. It is true. The waters are clear as I've ever seen, and people are being healed, but I can't help wondering how long the waters will continue to spew forth from the sand. It is an underground spring and I can't find where it might be fed from. Already we have a detail of guards there to keep the people from hurting one another to reach the waters. Stretchers bring the crippled and maimed, and I admit it is a pleasant sight watching them praise Our Lord.

"Strange, so many years have passed by and now I can actually behave as a Catholic priest; bless babies, perform marriages and convert lost souls."

George grinned as he saw the sparkle in Sam's eyes, "I heard that weird thing about Princess Lonnia's death...that was pretty strange."

Sam's sparkle left, and he replied, "She sold her soul to the devil and he collected."

George nodded his head in agreement and walked over to the window, where he leaned out to look down upon the courtyard and watched, while Paul worked with his Black Arabian around the training yard.

"What's going to happen with Paul and Richard?"

"King Ramie has offered them both positions in the Royal Guards and both have talked with me about it. We agree, for the legend to reach others, the story must be carried as legend foretold it would."

"You mean they're off to see the crusades?" George asked in wonder.

"Yes, they will carry your tale through the Holy Land and on into Europe. One day, probably not in your lifetime, some Pope will grant you sainthood," Sam said and then looked at George and added, "Pretty strange, huh?"

George shook his head and sighed, "I wish my Dad could know about this, it would really blow his mind..." He thumped his own chest and added, "Me, his son, a real saint who made history killing a dinosaur."

"He'll know when he gets to heaven and you and your children and grandchildren, and on down the line are waiting for him."

"This whole time-thing drives me crazy, Sam. Is my dad one of my descendants, who will then give him birth?" George had a puzzled expression on his face.

"Don't even start," Sam warned him. "It could drive you batty trying to figure it all out. I know! I took a whole month working on that subject and all I got to show for it was a massive headache and no fingernails...chewed them down to...so just forget it."

George laughed, "Sam, will you perform our marriage ceremony?"

"Of course, lad, right after you are both baptized. Besides, who else could? I haven't trained up anyone to fill my shoes yet, but it looks like I'm going to have several volunteers now. Thankfully, the king has released me from my vow and now our discussions over chess have changed to his conversion and when. He will move slowly. He always has, but I imagine soon he will be a new convert."

George gave Sam a friendly smile, "Thanks, Sam, without you none of this would've ever happened. We'd still be in that dungeon or dead."

"Right back at you, lad. You done killed the beastie and brought Christianity back to an entire kingdom of Muslims. I think that's enough for anyone's lifetime.

Sir George and the Princess Lennia were baptized two days later in the healing waters by the lake. Nearly the entire population of Silene was present for the event. Paul followed, having a desire to cleanse himself from his war memories and be reborn as a restored man of faith. Afterward, Brother Samuel spent the rest of week baptizing some 884 townspeople and military.

Mushid waited for the third day, he spent the time off by himself and in deep thought before coming to his decision to give his life to Christ. More than two dozen of the guardsmen followed right behind him and on the fourth afternoon of dunking souls in the waters by the lake, Captain Rynarr stepped in and when he rose from the waters he had a big smile on his face and received a brotherly embrace from Brother Samuel.

The wedding ceremony was a lavish affair and had to be held in the castle's training yard for all to attend. Though no one attended from Tripoli, there were guests from all parts of the kingdom. Invitations were sent by courier to outlying-areas, which included Egypt. But the Egyptians thought it might be a trick and none attended. Still, word of Silene's miracles and the conversion to Christianity would later reach the shore of Europe and even Britain.

But for the wedding, it was mostly a Silene affair and everyone was decked out in the finest clothing. Paul, Richard and Mushid stood together as George's Best Men. He couldn't decide on which one to pick, so he picked all three. Saleem, choked up by the honor, was chosen as Officer of the Court and he stood guard over the king during the ceremony.

Princess Lannia, with her company of Royal Guardsman, was finally located deep in the southern desert and they arrived barely in time to participate in the ceremony. The King's second daughter was shocked and surprised to hear of the tale. She also announced that though she saw no advantage in becoming a Christian or remaining a Muslim, she would stay nearby in the event the Caliph or Great Imam put up a fuss.

It was a beautiful affair, the king wept and even Brother Samuel was teary-eyed as he repeated the vows as he remembered them. Afterwards, the couple mounted their horses, ornately decorated for the event and they rode off to secluded section off the coast for their time alone together.

Two-months later, Paul, who was mounted upon his Black Arabian and Richard, driving his well-reinforced single horse wagon with a bench seat cushioned with furs and loaded with weapons and supplies, said their final goodbyes and headed eastward for the Holy Land. Saying so long was tough on everyone, but Richard and Paul both were looking forward to their journey. They both wondered what was over that next rise in their lives.

Prince George, now dressed in richly robes to fit his new station, stood alone upon the uppermost rooftop battlement and watched his two best friends, escorted by an escort of Captain Rynarr's finest mounted troops, disappeared in the distance. With a weighty heart, he turned to find his beautiful wife waiting for him. As he approached, she lifted both hands for his and as they joined, she looked deeply into his sad eyes. Then with a sparkle of whimsicalness in her own, she asked, "Now, Dear Husband, tell me of this United States and what you were doing in 1968?"

# AUTHOR'S NOTES

I really enjoyed researching the St. George and the Dragon Legend and was greatly surprised to find it had supposedly occurred in Libya. With all the statues scattered about in Europe, I had thought it was a European legend. My only difficulty has always been the size of the dragons depicted in the statues of St. George. Most of them looked as if he was combating a large serpent, yet, most of the paintings, showed the dragon to be winged and of some monstrous size. So, in my tale I made him an aquatic dinosaur of some ghastly size. The Plesiosaurus is believed by some to be the ancestor of the porpoise or dolphin and maybe neither. It was believed to run in packs like other fish but measured in the 15 to 25-foot size, or even smaller. However, there were some believed to have reached monstrous size as the depicted in my story. But, this is a work of fiction and not a science study book.

In my research, I found some mention of the destruction of the legendary Kingdom of Silene by a massive tsunami, believed to be generated by a late 13th Century earthquake. By then, the Legend of St. George had spread widely across Europe.

# ABOUT THE AUTHOR

 William Casselman was raised in Southern California and he enlisted in the U.S. Air Force in 1971 to become a Law Enforcement Specialist/Military Working Dog Handler. He served the next ten years in the military and met his lovely wife, Mona Sue, at Eielson AFB, Alaska.

A Vietnam veteran, he left the service to become a police officer in Dillingham, Alaska and spent the next twenty years in Alaskan police work. From patrolman to investigator, he has worked with four police departments and became Public Safety Director for the City of Whittier during the tragic Exxon Oil Spill of Prince William Sound in 1989.

William, a 36-year Christian, retired as Senior Investigator for the State of Alaska gaming program. With 40 years in Alaska, six children and 22 grandchildren, and two great-grandchildren, William and Mona Sue now live in rural Alaska.

## Other Titles from
## ALASKA DREAMS PUBLISHING

### By William Casselman

Apache Snow
In Search of Honor
A Coming Storm
Arizona Rangers Series – Blake's War

### Titles by other authors from ADP

My Life In The Wilderness
All Over The Road
Ghost Cave Mountain
Inside the Circle
The Silver Horn of Robin Hood
Alaskan Troll Eggs
Through My Eyes
The Professional Ghost Investigator
The Adventures of Jason and Bo

Please visit www.alaskadp.com and sign up for the ADP mailing list to be notified of future titles by Alaska Dreams Publishing.